THE BIG BOOK OF
GREAT SHORT STORIES

It was with Henry and Henry alone that Fletcher dared his nightly stunt.

[*See p. 567*

THE BIG BOOK OF
GREAT SHORT STORIES

Edited by
H. DOUGLAS THOMSON
and C. CLARK RAMSAY

ODHAMS PRESS LTD.
LONG ACRE, LONDON, W.C. 2

Copyright, 1935

Printed in Great Britain

INTRODUCTION

ALLOW us to unfold the map before you take the high-road to Romance; for to plan beforehand, and to pause to survey the delights and adventures in store for one, may well serve to whet the appetite and heighten one's appreciation. Whether, as you turn these pages, you keep to the route that has been marked out for you or let your fancy dictate the order of your going, there is much to anticipate.

It has been our purpose to give you Life and Love and Laughter as the necessary ingredients of happy, exhilarating reading, and you will find the stories grouped into *Tales of Wit and Humour*, *Tales of Love and Romance*, and *Tales of High Adventure*. Of change of scene there is no end—from the wharves of London's dockland with W. W. Jacobs to the glamorous South Seas with Stevenson and Stacpoole. New friends there are in plenty to greet you as well as old acquaintances. P. G. Wodehouse's inimitable Jeeves; Edgar Wallace's pawky Steward; Wee MacGreegor, J. J. Bell's immortal urchin; Michael Arlen's bright people of Mayfair; Barry Pain's Eliza; and even a talking horse! You will read of undying romance—exquisite stories of love in this and every age by authors whose names alone spell charm—Jeffery Farnol, Warwick Deeping, Temple Thurston and Guy de Maupassant. And there is adventure everywhere—H. G. Wells finds it in the tap-room of a village inn, Phyllis Bottome in the tiger cage of a menagerie, and Walter de la Mare in one of those strange haunted places of his imagination.

To other anthologists let us leave the reading that " Maketh a Full Man ". To us the Reading that Maketh a Happy Man. If there is something to be learnt by the way in light-hearted reading, let us by all means take it in our stride, but, above all, let us be entertained, choosing our tales for enjoyment and recreation not in the lamplight of the study, but out in the sunshine of literature where it is good to be alive !

H. D. T. *and* C. C. R.

CONTENTS

TALES OF WIT AND HUMOUR

TALES OF LOVE AND ROMANCE

TALES OF HIGH ADVENTURE

ILLUSTRATIONS

18

ACKNOWLEDGMENTS

The Editors wish to express their thanks for permission to include in this volume, stories by the following authors :

A. J. ALAN, *My Adventure in Norfolk* : to Charles Lavell, Esq.

ALPHA OF THE PLOUGH, *On a Map of the Oberland* (from *Leaves in the Wind*) : to the Author and Messrs. J. M. Dent & Sons, Ltd.

F. ANSTEY, *The Talking Horse* : to Messrs. John Murray.

MICHAEL ARLEN, *Major Cypress goes off the Deep End* (from *These Charming People*) : to the Author and Messrs. Doubleday, Doran & Company, Inc.

BARTIMEUS, *The Greater Love* (from *Naval Occasions*) : to the Author.

J. J. BELL, *An Experiment* (from *Wee MacGreegor*) : to the Author.

ARNOLD BENNETT, *The Dog* (from *Tales of the Five Towns*) : to Messrs. Chatto & Windus.

J. D. BERESFORD, *Reparation* : to the Author.

PHYLLIS BOTTOME, *Henry* (from *Strange Fruit*) : to the Author.

G. K. CHESTERTON, *The Tremendous Adventures of Major Brown* (from *The Club of Queer Trades*) : to the Author and Messrs. Harper and Bros.

AGATHA CHRISTIE, *The Sign in the Sky* (from *The Mysterious Mr. Quin*) : to the Author.

WARWICK DEEPING, *The Girl on the Mountain* (from *Countess Glika*) : to the Author and to Messrs. Cassell & Co., Ltd.

WALTER DE LA MARE, *All Hallows* (from *The Connoisseur*) : to the Author.

GUY DE MAUPASSANT, *Happiness* (from *Boule de Suif*, translated by Marjorie Laurie) : to Messrs. T. Werner Laurie, Ltd.

ELEANOR FARJEON, *Anthony in Blue Alsatia* (from *Kaleidoscope*) : to the Author.

JEFFERY FARNOL, *Fortune's Fool* (from *The Shadow*) : to the Author and Messrs. Sampson, Low, Marston & Co., Ltd.

J. S. FLETCHER, *The Convict and the Clerics* (from *The Malachite Jar*) : to the Author.

GILBERT FRANKAU, *One Week at the Ritz* (from *Men, Maids and Mustard Pots*): to the Author, Messrs. Hutchinson & Co., Ltd., and Messrs. Harper and Bros.

IAN HAY, *Natural Causes* (from *The Lucky Number*) : to the Author and Messrs. Hodder & Stoughton, Ltd.

W. W. JACOBS, *The Lady of the Barge* : to the Author.

HERBERT JENKINS, *The Bindles at the Zoo* : to Messrs. Herbert Jenkins, Ltd.

STEPHEN LEACOCK, *Soaked in Seaweed* (from *Nonsense Novels*) : to the Author and Messrs. John Lane the Bodley Head, Ltd.

W. J. LOCKE, *The Adventure of the Kind Mr. Smith* (from *The Joyous Adventures of Aristide Pujol*) : to the Author and to Messrs. John Lane the Bodley Head, Ltd.

A. A. MILNE, *More Cricket* (from *The Day's Play*) : to the Author and Messrs. Methuen & Co., Ltd.

BARRY PAIN, *The Horse that Did No Wrong* : to the Author's Executors.

EDEN PHILLPOTTS, *Madonna of the Fireflies* (from *Peacock House*) : to the Author and Messrs. Hutchinson & Co., Ltd.

" Q," *Pipes in Arcady* (from *News from the Duchy*) : to the Author and Messrs. J. W. Arrowsmith (London), Ltd.

RAFAEL SABATINI, *The King's Messenger* (from *Chronicles of Captain Blood*) : to the Author, Messrs. Hutchinson & Co., Ltd., and Messrs. McClelland & Stewart, Inc.

SAKI, *A Holiday Task* (from *Beasts and Super Beasts*) : to the Author and Messrs. John Lane the Bodley Head, Ltd.

SHEILA KAYE SMITH, *Mockbeggar* (from *Joanna Godden Married*) : to the Author and Messrs. Cassell & Co., Ltd.

H. DE VERE STACPOOLE, *Maru* : to the Author.

R. L. STEVENSON, *The Bottle Imp* : to Lloyd Osbourne, Esq., and Messrs. Charles Scribners' Sons.

E. TEMPLE THURSTON, *Some One Else's Romance* : to the Author's Executors.

EDGAR WALLACE, *Solo and the Lady* (from *The Steward*) : to Messrs. Edgar Wallace, Ltd.

H. G. WELLS, *The Man who could Work Miracles* : to the Author.

P. G. WODEHOUSE, *Jeeves in Springtime* : to the Author and Messrs. Herbert Jenkins, Ltd.

P. C. WREN, *Buried Treasure* (from *Good Gestes*) : to the Author and Messrs. John Murray.

TALES OF WIT
AND HUMOUR

" *Gimme my scarlet tie,*"
     Says I.
" *Gimme my brownest boots and hat,*
Gimme a vest with a pattern fancy,
Gimme a gel with some style, like Nancy,
And then—well, it's gimes as I'll be at,
Seein' as it's bangkolidye,"
     Says I.

          BARRY PAIN. *Bangkolidye.*

F. ANSTEY (1856–1934), *whose real name was Thomas Anstey Guthrie, relinquished a career at the Bar for that of a social satirist and humorous novelist. His best work was written during the eighties, in the years immediately after the sensational publication of " Vice Versa," which still remains one of the funniest books of our time. Indeed, his fantastic style of humour still remains almost without parallel.*

THE TALKING HORSE

IT was on the way to Sandown Park that I met him first, on that horribly wet July afternoon when Bendigo won the Eclipse Stakes. He sat opposite to me in the train going down, and my attention was first attracted to him by the marked contrast between his appearance and his attire : he had not thought fit to adopt the regulation costume for such occasions, and I think I never saw a man who had made himself more aggressively horsey. The mark of the beast was sprinkled over his linen : he wore snaffle sleeve-links, a hard hunting-hat, a Newmarket coat, and extremely tight trousers. And with all this he fell as far short of the genuine sportsman as any stage super who ever wore his spurs upside down in a hunting chorus. His expression was mild and inoffensive, and his watery pale eyes and receding chin gave one the idea that he was hardly to be trusted astride anything more spirited than a gold-headed cane. And yet, somehow, he aroused compassion rather than any sense of the ludicrous : he had the look of shrinking self-effacement which comes of a recent humiliation, and, in spite of all extravagances, he was obviously a gentleman ; while something in his manner indicated that his natural tendency would, once at all events, have been to avoid any kind of extremes.

He puzzled and interested me so much that I did my best to enter into conversation with him, only to be baffled by the jerky embarrassment with which he met all advances, and when we got out at Esher, curiosity led me to keep him still in view.

Evidently he had not come with any intention of making money. He avoided the grand stand, with the bookmakers huddling in couples, like hoarse lovebirds ; he kept away from the members' inclosure, where the Guards' band was endeavouring to defy the elements which emptied their vials into the brazen instruments ; he drifted listlessly about the course till the clearing-bell rang and it seemed as if he was searching for some one whom he only wished to discover in order to avoid.

Sandown, it must be admitted, was not as gay as usual that day, with its " deluged park " and " unsummer'd sky," its waterproofed toilettes and massed umbrellas, whose sides gleamed livid as they caught the light—but there was a general determination to ignore the unseasonable dampness as far as possible, and an excitement over the main event of the day which no downpour could quench.

The Ten Thousand was run : ladies with marvellously confected bonnets lowered their umbrellas without a murmur, and smart men on drags shook hands effusively as, amidst a frantic roar of delight, Bendigo strode past the post. The moment after, I looked round for my incongruous stranger, and saw him engaged in a well-meant attempt to press a currant bun upon a carriage-horse tethered to one of the trees —a feat of abstraction which, at such a time, was only surpassed by that of Archimedes at the sack of Syracuse.

After that I could no longer control my curiosity—I felt I must speak to him again, and I made an opportunity later, as we stood alone on a stand which commanded the finish of one of the shorter courses, by suggesting that he should share my umbrella.

Before accepting he glanced suspiciously at me through the rills that streamed from his unprotected hat-brim. " I'm afraid," I said, " it is rather like shutting the stable-door after the steed is stolen."

He started. " He *was* stolen, then," he cried ; " so you have heard ? "

I explained that I had only used an old proverb which I thought might appeal to him, and he sighed heavily.

" I was misled for the moment," he said : " you have guessed, then, that I have been accustomed to horses ? "

" You have hardly made any great secret of it."

" The fact is," he said, instantly understanding this allusion to his costume, " I—I put on these things so as not to lose the habit of riding altogether—I have not been on horseback lately. At one time I used to ride constantly—

constantly. I was a regular attendant in Rotten Row—until something occurred which shook my nerve, and I am only waiting now for the shock to subside."

I did not like to ask any questions, and we walked back to the station, and travelled up to Waterloo in company, without any further reference to the subject.

As we were parting, however, he said, " I wonder if you would care to hear my full story some day ? I cannot help thinking it would interest you, and it would be a relief to me."

I was ready enough to hear whatever he chose to tell me ; and persuaded him to dine with me at my rooms that evening, and unbosom himself afterwards, which he did to an extent for which I confess I was unprepared.

That he himself implicitly believed in his own story, I could not doubt ; and he told it throughout with the oddest mixture of vanity and modesty, and an obvious struggle between a dim perception of his own absurdity and the determination to spare himself in no single particular, which, though it did not overcome my scepticism, could not fail to enlist sympathy. But for all that, by the time he entered upon the more sensational part of his case, I was driven to form conclusions respecting it which, as they will probably force themselves upon the reader's own mind, I need not anticipate here.

I give the story, as far as possible, in the words of its author ; and have only to add that it would never have been published here without his full consent and approval.

My name (said he), is Gustavus Pulvertoft. I have no occupation, and six hundred a year. I lived a quiet and contented bachelor until I was twenty-eight, and then I met Diana Chetwynd for the first time. We were spending Christmas at the same country-house, and it did not take me long to become the most devoted of her many adorers. She was one of the most variously accomplished girls I had ever met. She was a skilled musician, a brilliant amateur actress ; she could give most men thirty out of a hundred at billiards, and her judgment and daring across the most difficult country had won her the warm admiration of all hunting-men. And she was neither fast nor horsey, seeming to find but little pleasure in the society of mere sportsmen, to whose conversation she infinitely preferred that of persons who, like myself, were rather agreeable than athletic. I was not at that time, whatever I may be now, without my share of good looks, and for some reason it pleased Miss Chetwynd to show me a degree of favour which she accorded to no other member of the house-party.

It was annoying to feel that my unfamiliarity with the open-air sports in which she delighted debarred me from her company to so great an extent ; for it often happened that I scarcely saw her until the evening, when I sometimes had the bliss of sitting next to her at dinner ; but on these occasions I could not help seeing that she found some pleasure in my society.

I don't think I have mentioned that, besides being exquisitely lovely, Diana was an heiress, and it was not without a sense of my own presumption that I allowed myself to entertain the hope of winning her at some future day. Still, I was not absolutely penniless, and she was her own mistress, and I had some cause, as I have said, for believing that she was, at least, not ill-disposed towards me. It seemed a favourable sign, for instance, when she asked me one day why it was I never rode. I replied that I had not ridden for years—though I did not add that the exact number of those years was twenty-eight.

" Oh, but you must take it up again ! " she said, with the prettiest air of imperiousness. " You ought to ride in the Row next season."

" If I did," I said, " would you let me ride with you sometimes ? "

" We should meet, of course," she said ; " and it is such a pity not to keep up your riding—you lose so much by not doing so."

Was I wrong in taking this as an intimation that, by following her advice, I should not lose my reward ? If you had seen her face as she spoke, you would have thought as I did then—as I do now.

And so, with this incentive, I overcame any private misgivings, and soon after my return to town attended a fashionable riding-school near Hyde Park, with the fixed determination to acquire the whole art and mystery of horsemanship.

That I found learning a pleasure I cannot conscientiously declare. I have passed happier hours than those I spent in cantering round four bare whitewashed walls on a snorting horse, with my interdicted stirrups crossed upon the saddle. The riding-master informed me from time to time that I was getting on, and I knew instinctively when I was coming off ; but I must have made some progress, for my instructor became more encouraging. " Why, when you come here first, Mr. Pulvertoft, sir, you were like a pair o' tongs on a wall, as they say ; whereas now—well, you can tell yourself how you are," he would say ; though, even then, I occasionally had reason to regret that I was *not* on a wall. However, I persevered, inspired by the thought that each fresh horse I crossed (and some were very fresh indeed) represented one more barrier surmounted between myself and Diana, and encouraged by the discovery, after repeated experiments, that tan was rather soothing to fall upon than otherwise.

When I walked in the Row, where a few horsemen were performing as harbingers of spring, I criticised their riding, which I thought indifferent, as they neglected nearly all the rules. I began to anticipate a day when I should exhibit a purer and more classic style of equestrianism. And one morning I saw Diana, who pulled up her dancing mare to ask me if I had remembered her advice, and I felt proudly able to reply that I should certainly make my appearance in the Row before very long.

From that day I was perpetually questioning my riding-master as to when he considered I should be ripe enough for Rotten Row. He was dubious, but not actually dissuasive. " It's like this, you see, sir," he explained, " if you get hold of a quiet, steady horse—why, you won't come to no harm ; but if you go out on an animal that will take advantage of you, Mr. Pulvertoft, why, you'll be all no-how on him, sir."

They would have mounted me at the school ; but I knew most of the stud there, and none of them quite came up to my ideal of a " quiet, steady horse " ; so I went to a neighbouring job-master, from whom I had occasionally hired a brougham, and asked to be shown an animal he could recommend to one who had not had much practice lately. He admitted candidly enough that most of his horses " took a deal of riding," but added that it so happened that he had one just then which would suit me " down to the ground "—a phrase which grated unpleasantly on my nerves, though I consented to see the horse. His aspect impressed me most favourably. He was a chestnut of noble proportions, with a hogged mane ; but what reassured me was the expression of his eye, indicating as it did a self-respect and sagacity which one would hardly expect for seven and sixpence an hour.

"You won't get a showier Park 'ack than what he is, not to be so quiet," said the owner. "He's what you may call a kind 'oss, and as gentle—you could ride him on a packthread."

I considered reins safer, but I was powerfully drawn towards the horse ; he seemed to me sensible that he had a character to lose, and to possess too high an intelligence wilfully to forfeit his testimonials. With hardly a second thought, I engaged him for the following afternoon.

I mounted at the stables, with just a passing qualm, perhaps, while my stirrup-leathers were being adjusted, and a little awkwardness in taking up my reins, which were more twisted than I could have wished ; however, at length, I found myself embarked on the stream of traffic on the back of the chestnut—whose name, by the way, was Brutus.

Shall I ever forget the pride and ecstasy of finding that I had my steed under perfect control, that we threaded the maze of carriages with absolute security ? I turned him into the Park, and clucked my tongue : he broke into a canter, and how shall I describe my delight at the discovery that it was not uncomfortable ? I said, "Woa," and he stopped, so gradually that my equilibrium was not seriously disturbed ; he trotted, and still I accommodated myself to his movements without any positive inconvenience. I could have embraced him for gratitude : never before had I been upon a beast whose paces were so easy, whose behaviour was so considerate. I could ride at last ! or, which amounted to the same thing, I could ride the horse I was on, and I would "use no other." I was about to meet Diana Chetwynd, and need not fear even to encounter her critical eyes.

We had crossed the Serpentine Bridge, and were just turning in upon the Ride, when—and here I am only too conscious that what I am about to say may strike you as almost incredible—when I heard an unfamiliar voice addressing me with, "I say—you ! " and the moment afterwards realised that it proceeded from my own horse !

I am not ashamed to own that I was as nearly off as possible ; for a more practised rider than I could pretend to be might have a difficulty in preserving his equanimity in this all but unparalleled situation. I was too much engaged in feeling for my left stirrup to make any reply, and presently the horse spoke once more. "I say," he inquired, and I failed to discern the slightest trace of respect in his tone—" do you think you can ride ? " You can judge for yourself how disconcerting the inquiry must have been from such lips. I felt rooted to the saddle—a sensation which, with me, was sufficiently rare. I looked round in helpless bewilderment, at the shimmering Serpentine, and the white houses in Park Lane gleaming out of a lilac haze, at the cocoa-coloured Row, and the flash of distant carriage-wheels in the sunlight : all looked as usual—and yet, there was I on the back of a horse which had just inquired " whether I thought I could ride " !

" I have had two dozen lessons at a riding-school," I said at last, with rather a flabby dignity.

" I should hardly have suspected it," was his brutal retort. " You are evidently one of the hopeless cases."

I was deeply hurt, the more so because I could not deny that he had some claim to be a judge. " I—I thought we were getting on so nicely together," I faltered, and all he said in reply to that was, " *Did* you ? "

" Do you know," I began, striving to be conversational, " I never was on a horse that talked before."

" You are enough to make any horse talk," he answered ; " but I suppose I *am* an exception."

" I think you must be," said I. " The only horses I ever heard of as possessing the gift of speech were the Houyhnhnms."

" How do you know I am not one of them ? " he replied.

" If you are, you will understand that I took the liberty of mounting you under a very pardonable mistake ; and if you will have the goodness to stand still, I will no longer detain you."

" Not so fast," said he : " I want to know something more about you first. I should say now you were a man with plenty of oats."

" I am—well off," I said. How I wished I was !

" I have long been looking out for a proprietor who would not overwork me : now, of course, I don't know, but you scarcely strike me as a *hard* rider."

" I do not think I could be fairly accused of that," I answered, with all the consciousness of innocence.

" Just so—then buy me."

" No," I gasped : " after the extremely candid opinion you were good enough to express of my riding, I'm surprised that you should even suggest such a thing."

"Oh, I will put up with that—you will suit me well enough, I dare say."

"You must excuse me. I prefer to keep my spare cash for worthier objects; and, with your permission, I will spend the remainder of the afternoon on foot."

"You will do nothing of the sort," said he.

"If you won't stop, and let me get off properly," I said, with firmness, "I shall *roll* off." There were some promenaders within easy hail; but how was I to word a call for help, how explain such a dilemma as mine?

"You will only reduce me to the painful necessity of rolling on you," he replied. "You must see that you are to a certain extent in my power. Suppose it occurred to me to leap those rails and take you into the Serpentine, or to run away and upset a mounted policeman with you—do you think you could offer much opposition?"

I could not honestly assert that I did. "You were introduced to me," I said reproachfully, "as a *kind* horse!"

"And so I am—apart from matters of business. Come, will you buy, or be bolted with? I hate indecision!"

"Buy!" I said, with commercial promptness. "If you will take me back, I will arrange about it at once."

It is needless to say that my own idea was to get safely off his back: after which, neither honour nor law could require me to execute a contract extorted from me by threats. But, as we were going down the mews, he said reflectively, "I've been thinking—it will be better for all parties, if you make your offer to my proprietor *before* you dismount." I was too vexed to speak: this animal's infernal intelligence had foreseen my manœuvre—he meant to foil it, if he could.

And then we clattered in under the glass-roofed yard of the livery stables; and the job-master, who was alone there, cast his eyes up at the sickly-faced clock, as if he were comparing its pallor with my own. "Why, you *are* home early, sir," he said. "You didn't find the 'orse too much for you, did you?" He said this without any suspicion of the real truth; and, indeed, I may say, once for all, that this weird horse—Houyhnhnm, or whatever else he might be—admitted no one but myself into the secret of his marvellous gifts, and in all his conversations with me, managed (though how, I cannot pretend to say) to avoid being overheard.

"Oh, dear no," I protested, "he carried me admirably—admirably!" and I made an attempt to slip off.

No such thing : Brutus instantly jogged my memory, and me, by the slightest suggestion of a " buck."

" He's a grand 'orse, sir, isn't he ? " said the job-master complacently.

" M—magnificent ! " I agreed, with a jerk. " Will you go to his head, please ? "

But the horse backed into the centre of the yard, where he plunged with a quiet obstinacy. " I like him so much," I called out, as I clung to the saddle, " that I want to know if you're at all inclined to part with him ? "   Here Brutus became calm and attentive.

" Would you be inclined to make me a orfer for him, sir ? "

" Yes," I said faintly.   " About how much would he be ? "

" You step into my orfice here, sir," said he, " and we'll talk it over."

I should have been only too willing, for there was no room there for the horse, but the suspicious animal would not hear of it : he began to revolve immediately.

" Let us settle it now—here," I said, " I can't wait."

The job-master stroked away a grin. No doubt there *was* something unbusinesslike and unpractical in such pre-cipitation, especially as combined with my appearance at the time.

" Well, you *'ave* took a violent fancy to the 'orse and no mistake, sir," he remarked.

" I never crossed a handsomer creature," I said ; which was hardly a prudent remark for an intending purchaser, but then, there was the animal himself to be conciliated.

" I don't know, really, as I can do without him just at this time of year," said the man.   " I'm under'orsed as it is for the work I've got to do."

A sweet relief stole over me : I had done all that could be expected of me.   " I'm very sorry to hear that," I said, pre-paring to dismount.   " That *is* a disappointment ; but if you can't, there's an end of it."

" Don't you be afraid," said Brutus, " *he'll* sell me readily enough : make him an offer, quick ! "

" I'll give you thirty guineas for him, come ! " I said, knowing well enough that he would not take twice the money.

" I thought a gentleman like you would have had more insight into the value of a 'orse," he said : " why, his action alone is worth that, sir."

"You couldn't let me have the action without the horse, I suppose?" I said, and I must have intended some joke.

It is unnecessary to prolong a painful scene. Brutus ran me up steadily from sum to sum, until his owner said at last: "Well, we won't 'aggle, sir, call it a hundred."

I had to call it a hundred, and what is more, it *was* a hundred. I took him without a warranty, without even a veterinary opinion. I could have been induced to take my purchase away then and there, as if I had been buying a canary, so unaccustomed was I to transactions of this kind, and I am afraid the job-master considered me little better than a fool.

So I found myself the involuntary possessor of a Houyhnhnm, or something even worse, and I walked back to my rooms in Park Street in a state of stupor. What was I to do with him? To ride an animal so brutally plainspoken would be a continual penance; and yet, I should have to keep him, for I knew he was cunning enough to outwit any attempt to dispose of him. And to this, Love and Ambition had led me! I could not, after all I had said, approach Diana with any confidence as a mere pedestrian: the fact that I was in possession of a healthy horse which I never rode, would be sure to leak out in time, and how was I to account for it? I could see no way, and I groaned under an embarrassment which I dared not confide to the friendliest ear. I hated the monster that had saddled himself upon me, and looked in vain for any mode of escape.

I had to provide Brutus with stabling in another part of the town, for he proved exceedingly difficult to please: he found fault with everything, and I only wonder he did not demand that his stable should be fitted up with blue china and mezzo-tints. In his new quarters I left him for some days to his own devices: a course which I was glad to find, on visiting him again, had considerably reduced his arrogance. He wanted to go in the Row and see the other horses, and it did not at all meet his views to be exercised there by a stableman at unfashionable hours. So he proposed a compromise. If I would only consent to mount him, he engaged to treat me with forbearance, and pointed out that he could give me, as he expressed it, various "tips" which would improve my seat. I was not blind to the advantages of such an arrangement. It is not everyone who secures a riding-master in the person of his own horse; the horse is essentially a generous animal, and I felt that I might trust to Brutus's honour. And to do him justice, he observed the compact with strict good faith. Some of his " tips," it is true, very nearly tipped me off, but their result was to bring us closer together ; our relations were less strained ; it seemed to me that I gained more mastery over him every day, and was less stiff afterwards.

But I was not allowed to enjoy this illusion long. One day when I innocently asked him if he found my hands improving, he turned upon me his off sardonic eye. " You'll *never* improve, old sack-of-beans" (for he had come to address me with a freedom I burned to resent) ; " hands ! why, you're sawing my mouth off all the time. And your feet ' home,' and tickling me under my shoulders at every stride— why, I'm half ashamed to be seen about with you."

I was deeply hurt. " I will spare you for the future," I said coldly ; " this is my last appearance."

" Nonsense," he said, " you needn't show temper over it. Surely, if I can put up with it, *you* can ! But we will make a new compact." (I never knew such a beast as he was for bargains !) " You only worry me by interfering with the reins. Let 'em out, and leave everything to me. Just mention from time to time where you want to go, and I'll attend to it,— if I've nothing better to do."

I felt that such an understanding was destructive of all dignity, subverting, as it did, the natural relations between horse and rider ; but I had hardly any self-respect left, and I consented, since I saw no way of refusing. And on the whole, I cannot say, even now, that I had any grave reason for finding fault with the use Brutus made of my concessions ; he showed more tact than I could have expected in disguising the merely nominal nature of my authority.

I had only one serious complaint against him, which was that he had a habit of breaking suddenly away, with a merely formal apology, to exchange equine civilities with some cob or mare, to whose owner I was a perfect stranger, thus driving me to invent the most desperate excuses to cover my seeming intrusion : but I managed to account for it in various ways, and even made a few acquaintances in this irregular and involuntary manner. I could have wished he had been a less susceptible animal, for, though his flirtations were merely Platonic, it is rather humiliating to have to play " gooseberry " to one's own horse—a part which I was constantly being called upon to perform !

As it happened, Diana was away in Paris that Easter, and

we had not met since my appearance in the Row ; but I knew she would be in town again shortly, and with consummate diplomacy I began to excite Brutus's curiosity by sundry careless, half-slighting allusions to Miss Chetwynd's little mare, Wild Rose. "She's too frisky for my taste," I said, "but she's been a good deal admired, though I dare say you wouldn't be particularly struck by her."

So that, on the first afternoon of Diana's return to the Row, I found it easy, under cover of giving Brutus an opportunity of forming an opinion, to prevail on him to carry me to her side. Diana, who was with a certain Lady Verney, her chaperon, welcomed me with a charming smile.

"I had no idea you could ride so well," she said, "you manage that beautiful horse of yours so very easily—with such light hands, too."

This was not irony, for I could now give my whole mind to my seat ; and, as I never interfered at all with the steering apparatus, my hands must have seemed the perfection of lightness.

"He wants delicate handling," I answered carelessly, "but he goes very well with *me*."

"I wish you would let me try his paces some morning, Pulvertoft," struck in a Colonel Cockshott, who was riding with them, and whom I knew slightly : "I've a notion he would go better on the curb."

"I shall be very happy," I began, when, just in time, I noticed a warning depression in Brutus's ears. The Colonel rode about sixteen stone, and with spurs ! "I mean," I added hastily, "I should have been—only, to tell you the truth, I couldn't conscientiously trust anyone on him but myself."

"My dear fellow !" said the Colonel, who I could see was offended, "I've not met many horses in my time that I couldn't get upon terms with."

"I think Mr. Pulvertoft is *quite* right," said Diana. "When a horse gets accustomed to one he does so resent a strange hand ; it spoils his temper for days. I never will lend Wild Rose to anybody for that very reason ! "

The Colonel fell back in the rear in a decided sulk. "Poor dear Colonel Cockshott ! " said Diana, "he is so proud of his riding, but *I* think he dragoons a horse. I don't call that *riding*, do you ? "

"Well—hardly," I agreed, with easy disparagement. "I never believe in ruling a horse by fear."

" I suppose you are very fond of yours ? " she said.

" Fond is not the word ! " I exclaimed—and it certainly was not.

" I am not sure that what I said about lending Wild Rose would apply to *you*," she said. " I think you would be gentle with her."

I was certain that I should treat her with all consideration ; but as I doubted whether she would wholly reciprocate it, I said with much presence of mind, that I should regard riding her as akin to profanation.

As Brutus and I were going home, he observed that it was a good thing I had not agreed to lend him to the Colonel.

" Yes," I said, determined to improve the occasion, " you might not have found him as considerate as—well, as some people ! "

" I meant it was a good thing for *you* ! " he hinted darkly, and I did not care to ask for an explanation. " What did you mean," he resumed, " by saying that I should not admire Wild Rose ? Why, she is charming—charming ! "

" In that case," I said, " I don't mind riding with her mistress occasionally—to oblige you."

" You don't mind ! " he said ; " you will *have* to, my boy,— and every afternoon ! "

I suppressed a chuckle : after all, man *is* the nobler animal. I could manage a horse—in my own way. My little *ruse* had succeeded : I should have no more forced introductions to mystified strangers.

And now for some weeks my life passed in a happy dream. I only lived for those hours in the Row, where Brutus turned as naturally to Wild Rose as the sunflower to the sun, and Diana and I grew more intimate every day. Happiness and security made me almost witty. I was merciless in my raillery of the eccentric exhibitions of horsemanship which were to be met with, and Diana was provoked by my comments to the sweetest silvery laughter. As for Colonel Cockshott, whom I had once suspected of a desire to be my rival, he had long become a " negligible quantity " ; and if I delayed in asking Diana to trust me with her sweet self, it was only because I found an epicurean pleasure in prolonging a suspense that was so little uncertain.

And then, without warning, my riding was interrupted for a while. Brutus was discovered, much to his annoyance, to have a saddle-raw, and was even so unjust as to lay the blame on me, though, for my own part, I thought it a mark of apt, though tardy, retribution. I was not disposed to tempt Fortune upon any other mount, but I could not keep away from the Row, nevertheless, and appeared there on foot. I saw Diana riding with the Colonel, who seemed to think his opportunity had come at last; but whenever she passed the railings on which I leaned, she would raise her eyebrows and draw her mouth down into a little curve of resigned boredom, which completely reassured me. Still, I was very glad when Brutus was well again, and we were cantering down the Row once more, both in the highest spirits.

"I never heard the horses here *whinny* so much as they do this season," I said, by way of making conversation. "Can you account for it at all?" For he sometimes gave me pieces of information which enabled me to impress Diana afterwards by my intimate knowledge of horses.

"Whinnying?" he said. "They're *laughing*, that's what they're doing—and no wonder!"

"Oh!" said I, "and what's the joke?"

"Why, *you* are!" he replied. "You don't suppose you take *them* in, do you? They know all about you, bless your heart!"

"Oh, do they?" I said blankly. This brute took a positive pleasure, I believe, in reducing my self-esteem.

"I dare say it has got about through Wild Rose," he continued. "She was immensely tickled when I told her. I'm afraid she must have been feeling rather dull all these days, by the by."

I felt an unworthy impulse to take his conceit down as he had lowered mine.

"Not so very, I think," I said. "She seemed to me to find that brown hunter of Colonel Cockshott's a very agreeable substitute."

Late as it is for reparation, I must acknowledge with shame that in uttering this insinuation, I did that poor little mare (for whom I entertained the highest respect) a shameful injustice; and I should like to state here, in the most solemn and emphatic manner, my sincere belief that, from first to last, she conducted herself in a manner that should have shielded her from all calumny.

It was only a mean desire to retaliate, a petty and ignoble spite, that prompted me thus to poison Brutus's confidence, and I regretted the words as soon as I had uttered them.

" That beast ! " he said, starting as if I had touched him with a whip—a thing I never used—" why, he hasn't two ideas in his great fiddle-head. The only sort of officer *he* ought to carry is a Salvationist ! "

" I grant he has not your personal advantages and charm of manner," I said. " No doubt I was wrong to say anything about it."

" No," he said, " you—you have done me a service," and he relapsed into a sombre silence.

I was riding with Diana as usual, and was about to express my delight at being able to resume our companionship, when her mare drew slightly ahead and lashed out suddenly, catching me on the left leg, and causing intense agony for the moment.

Diana showed the sweetest concern, imploring me to go home in a cab at once, while her groom took charge of Brutus. I declined the cab ; but, as my leg was really painful, and Brutus was showing an impatience I dared not disregard, I had to leave her side.

On our way home, Brutus said moodily, " It is all over between us—you saw that ? "

" I felt it ! " I replied. " She nearly broke my leg."

" It was intended for me," he said. " It was her way of signifying that we had better be strangers for the future. I taxed her with her faithlessness ; she denied it, of course— every mare does ; we had an explanation, and everything is at an end ! "

I did not ride him again for some days, and when I did, I found him steeped in Byronic gloom. He even wanted at first to keep entirely on the Bayswater side of the Park, though I succeeded in arguing him out of such weakness. " Be a horse ! " I said. " Show her you don't care. You only flatter her by betraying your feelings."

This was a subtlety that had evidently not occurred to him, but he was intelligent enough to feel the force of what I said. " You are right," he admitted ; " you are not quite a fool in some respects. She shall see how little I care ! "

Naturally, after this, I expected to accompany Diana as usual, and it was a bitter disappointment to me to find that Brutus would not hear of doing so. He had an old acquaintance in the Park, a dapple-grey, who, probably from some early disappointment, was a confirmed cynic, and whose society he thought would be congenial just then. The grey was ridden regularly by a certain Miss Gittens, whose appearance as she titupped laboriously up and down had often furnished Diana and myself with amusement.

And now, in spite of all my efforts, Brutus made straight to the grey. I was not in such difficulties as might have been expected, for I happened to know Miss Gittens slightly, as a lady no longer in the bloom of youth, who still retained a wiry form of girlishness. Though rather disliking her than not, I found it necessary just then to throw some slight effusion into my greetings. She, not unnaturally, perhaps, was flattered by my preference, and begged me to give her a little instruction in riding, which—Heaven forgive me for it!—I took upon myself to do.

Even now I scarcely see how I could have acted otherwise : I could not leave her side until Brutus had exhausted the pleasures of cynicism with his grey friend, and the time had to be filled up somehow. But, oh, the torture of seeing Diana at a distance, and knowing that only a miserable misunderstanding between our respective steeds kept us apart, feeling constrained even to avoid looking in her direction, lest she should summon me to her side !

One day, as I was riding with Miss Gittens, she glanced coyly at me over her sharp right shoulder, and said, " Do you know, only such a little while ago, I never even dreamed that we should ever become as intimate as we are now ; it seems almost incredible, does it not ? "

" You must not say so," I replied. " Surely there is nothing singular in my helping you a little with your riding ? " Though it struck me that it would have been very singular if I had.

" Perhaps not singular," she murmured, looking modestly down her nose ; " but will you think me very unmaidenly if I confess that, to me, those lessons have developed a dawning danger ? "

" You are perfectly safe on the grey," I said.

" I—I was not thinking of the grey," she returned. " Dear Mr. Pulvertoft, I must speak frankly—a girl has so many things to consider, and I am afraid you have made me forget how wrongly and thoughtlessly I have been behaving of late. I cannot help suspecting that you must have some motive in seeking my society in so—so marked a manner."

" Miss Gittens," said I, " I can disguise nothing : I have."

" And you have not been merely amusing yourself all this time ? "

"Before Heaven," I cried with fervour, "I have *not* ! "

"You are not one of those false men who give their bridle-reins a shake, and ride off with 'Adieu for evermore ! '—tell me you are not ? "

I might shake *my* bridle-reins till I was tired and nothing would come of it unless Brutus was in the humour to depart ; so that I was able to assure her with truth that I was not at all that kind of person.

"Then why not let your heart speak ? "

"There is such a thing," I said gloomily, " as a heart that is gagged."

"Can no word, no hint of mine loosen the gag ? " she wished to know. "What, you are silent still ? Then, Mr. Pulvertoft, though I may seem harsh and cruel in saying it, our pleasant intercourse must end—we must ride together no more ! "

No more ? What would Brutus say to that ? I was horrified. "Miss Gittens," I said in great agitation, " I entreat you to unsay those words. I—I am afraid I could not undertake to accept such a dismissal. Surely, after that, you will not insist ! "

She sighed. "I am a weak, foolish girl," she said ; " you are only too able to overcome my judgment. Then, Mr. Pulvertoft, look happy again—I relent. You may stay if you will ! "

You must believe that I felt thoroughly ashamed of myself, for I could not be blind to the encouragement which, though I sought to confine my words to strict truth, I was innocently affording. But, with a horse like mine, what was a man to do ? What would you have done yourself ? As soon as was prudent, I hinted to Brutus that his confidences had lasted long enough ; and as he trotted away with me, he remarked, " I thought you were never going." Was he weary of the grey already ? My heart leaped. "Brutus," I said thickly, " are you strong enough to bear a great joy ? "

"Speak out," he said, " and do try to keep those heels out of my ribs."

"I cannot see you suffer," I told him, with a sense of my own hypocrisy all the time. "I must tell you—circumstances have come to my knowledge which lead me to believe that we have both judged Wild Rose too hastily. I am sure that her heart is yours still. She is only longing to tell you that she has never really swerved from her allegiance."

"It is too late now," he said, and the back of his head looked inflexibly obstinate; "we have kept apart too long."

"No," I said, "listen. I take more interest in you than you are, perhaps, aware of, and I have thought of a little plan for bringing you together again. What if I find an opportunity to see the lady she belongs to—we have not met lately, as you know, and I do not pretend that I desire a renewal of our intimacy——"

"You like the one on the grey best; I saw that long ago," he said; and I left him in his error.

"In any case, for your sake, I will sacrifice myself," I said magnanimously. "I will begin to-morrow. Come, you will not let your lives be wrecked by a foolish lovers' quarrel?"

He made a little half-hearted opposition, but finally, as I knew he would, consented. I had gained my point: I was free from Miss Gittens at last!

That evening I met Diana in the hall of a house in Eaton Square. She was going downstairs as I was making my way to the ball-room, and greeted me with a rather cool little nod.

"You have quite deserted me lately," she said, smiling, but I could read the reproach in her eyes, "you never ride with us now."

My throat was swelling with passionate eloquence—and I could not get any of it out.

"No, I never do," was all my stupid tongue could find to say.

"You have discovered a more congenial companion," said cruel Diana.

"Miss Chetwynd," I said eagerly, "you don't know how I have been wishing——! Will you let me ride with you to-morrow, as—as you used to do?"

"You are quite sure you won't be afraid of my naughty Wild Rose?" she said. "I have given her such a scolding, that I think she is thoroughly ashamed of herself."

"You thought it was *that* that kept me!" I cried. "Oh, if I could tell you!"

She smiled: she was my dear, friendly Diana again.

"You shall tell me all about it to-morrow," she said. "You will not have another opportunity, because we are going to Aix on Friday. And now, good-night. I am stopping the way, and the linkman is getting quite excited over it."

She passed on, and the carriage rolled away with her, and I was too happy to mind very much—had she not forgiven me ? Should we not meet to-morrow ? I should have two whole hours to declare myself in, and this time I would dally with Fortune no longer.

How excited I was the following day : how fearful, when the morning broke grey and lowering : how grateful, when the benignant sun shone out later, and promised a brilliant afternoon : how careful I dressed, and what a price I paid for the flower for my buttonhole !

So we cantered on to the Row, as goodly a couple (if I may be pardoned this retrospective vanity) as any there ; and by and by, I saw, with the quick eye of a lover, Diana's willowy form in the distance. She was not alone, but I knew that the Colonel would soon have to yield his place to me.

As soon as she saw me, she urged her mare to a trot, and came towards me with the loveliest faint blush and dawning smile of welcome, when, all at once, Brutus came to a dead stop, which nearly threw me on his neck, and stood quivering in every limb.

" Do you see that ? " he said hoarsely. " And I was about to forgive her ! "

I saw : my insinuation, baseless enough at the beginning, was now but too well justified. Colonel Cockshott was on his raw-boned brown hunter, and even my brief acquaintance with horses enabled me to see that Wild Rose no longer regarded him with her former indifference.

Diana and the Colonel had reigned up and seemed waiting for me—would Brutus never move ? " Show your pride," I said in an agonised whisper. " Treat her with the contempt she deserves ! "

" I will," he said between his bit and clenched teeth.

And then Miss Gittens came bumping by on the grey, and, before I could interfere, my Houyhnhnm was off like a shot in pursuit. I saw Diana's sweet, surprised face : I heard the Colonel's jarring laugh as I passed, and I—I could only bow in mortified appeal, and long for a gulf to leap into like Curtius !

I don't know what I said to Miss Gittens. I believe I made myself recklessly amiable, and I remember she lingered over parting in a horrible emotional manner. I was too miserable to mind : all the time I was seeing Diana's astonished eyes, hearing Colonel Cockshott's heartless laugh. Brutus made a kind of explanation on our way home : " You meant well," he said, " but you see you were wrong. Your proposed sacrifice, for which I am just as grateful to you as if it had been effected, was useless. All I could do in return was to take you where your true inclination lay. I, too, can be unselfish."

I was too dejected to curse his unselfishness. I did not even trouble myself to explain what it had probably cost me. I only felt drearily that I had had my last ride, I had had enough horsemanship for ever !

That evening I went to the theatre, I wanted to deaden thought for the moment ; and during one of the intervals I saw Lady Verney in the stalls, and went up to speak to her. " Your niece is not with you ? " I said ; " I thought I should have had a chance of—of saying goodbye to her before she left for the continent."

I had a lingering hope that she might ask me to lunch, that I might have one more opportunity of explaining.

" Oh," said Lady Verney, " but that is all changed ; we are not going—at least, not yet."

" Not going ! " I cried, incredulous for very joy.

" No, it is all very sudden ; but—well, you are almost like an old friend, and you are sure to hear it sooner or later. I only knew myself this afternoon, when she came in from her ride. Colonel Cockshott has proposed and she has accepted him. We're *so* pleased about it. Wasn't dear Mrs. —— delightful in that last act ? I positively saw real tears on her face ! "

If I had waited much longer she would have seen a similar display of realism on mine. But I went back and sat the interval out, and listened critically to the classical selection of chamber-music from the orchestra, and saw the rest of the play, though I have no notion how it ended.

All that night my heart was slowly consumed by a dull rage that grew with every sleepless hour ; but the object of my resentment was not Diana. She had only done what as a woman she was amply justified in doing after the pointed slight I had apparently inflicted upon her. Her punishment was sufficient already, for, of course, I guessed that she had only accepted the Colonel under the first intolerable sting of desertion. No : I reserved all my wrath for Brutus, who had betrayed me at the moment of triumph. I planned revenge. Cost what it might I would ride him once more. In the eyes of the law I was his master. I would exercise my legal rights to the full.

The afternoon came at last. I was in a white heat of anger,

though as I ascended to the saddle there were bystanders who put a more uncharitable construction upon my complexion.

Brutus cast an uneasy eye at my heels as we started : " What are those things you've got on ? " he inquired.

" Spurs," I replied curtly.

" You shouldn't wear them till you have learnt to turn your toes in," he said. " And a whip, too ! May I ask what that is for ? "

" We will discuss that presently," I said very coldly ; for I did not want to have a scene with my horse in the street.

When we came round by the statue of Achilles and on to the Ride, I shortened my reins, and got a better hold of the whip, while I found that, from some cause I cannot explain, the roof of my mouth grew uncomfortably dry.

" I shall be glad of a little quiet talk with you, if you've no objection," I began.

" I am quite at your disposal," he said, champing his bit with a touch of irony.

" First, let me tell you," I said, " that I have lost my only love for ever."

" Well," he retorted flippantly, " you won't die of it. So have I. We must endeavour to console one another ! "

I still maintained a deadly calm. " You seem unaware that you are the sole cause of my calamity," I said. " Had you only consented to face Wild Rose yesterday, I should have been a happy man by this time ! "

" How was I to know that, when you let me think all your affections were given to the elderly thing who is trotted out by my friend the grey ? "

" We won't argue, please," I said hastily. " It is enough that your infernal egotism and self-will have ruined my happiness. I have allowed you to usurp the rule, to reverse our natural positions. I shall do so no more. I intend to teach you a lesson you will never forget."

For a horse, he certainly had a keen sense of humour. I thought the girths would have snapped.

" And when do you intend to begin ? " he asked, as soon as he could speak.

I looked in front of me : there were Diana and her accepted lover riding towards us ; and so natural is dissimulation, even to the sweetest and best women, that no one would have suspected from her radiant face that her gaiety covered an aching heart.

"I intend to begin *now*," I said. "Monster, demon, whatever you are that have held me in thrall so long, I have broken my chains! I have been a coward long enough. You may kill me if you like. I rather hope you will; but first I mean to pay you back some of the humiliation with which you have loaded me. I intend to thrash you as long as I remain in the saddle."

I have been told by eye-witnesses that the chastisement was of brief duration, but while it lasted, I flatter myself, it was severe. I laid into him with a stout whip, of whose effectiveness I had assured myself by experiments upon my own legs. I dug my borrowed spurs into his flanks. I jerked his mouth. I dare say he was almost as much surprised as pained. But he *was* pained!

I was about to continue my practical rebuke, when my victim suddenly evaded my grasp; and for one vivid second I seemed to be gazing upon a bird's-eye view of his back; and then there was a crash, and I lay, buzzing like a bee, in an iridescent fog, and each colour meant a different pain, and they faded at last into darkness, and I remember no more.

"It was weeks," concluded Mr. Pulvertoft, "before the darkness lifted and revealed me to myself as a strapped and bandaged invalid. But—and this is perhaps the most curious part of my narrative—almost the first sounds that reached my ears were those of wedding bells; and I knew, without requiring to be told, that they were ringing for Diana's marriage with the Colonel. *That* showed there wasn't much the matter with me, didn't it? Why, I can hear them everywhere now. I don't think she ought to have had them rung at Sandown though: it was just a little ostentatious, so long after the ceremony; don't you think so?"

"Yes—yes," I said; "but you never told me what became of the horse."

"Ah! the horse—yes. I am looking for him. I'm not so angry with him as I was, and I don't like to ask too many questions at the stables, for fear they may tell me one day that they had to shoot him while I was so ill. You knew I was ill, I dare say?" he broke off: "there were bulletins about me in the papers. Look here."

He handed me a cutting on which I read:

"THE RECENT ACCIDENT IN ROTTEN ROW.—There is no change as yet in Mr. Pulvertoft's condition. The unfortunate gentleman is still lying unconscious at his rooms in Park Street;

and his medical attendants fear that, even if he recovers his physical strength, the brain will be permanently injured."

" But that was all nonsense ! " said Mr. Pulvertoft, with a little nervous laugh, " it wasn't injured a bit, or how could I remember everything so clearly as I do, you know ? "

And this was an argument that was, of course, unanswerable.

J. J. BELL (1871—) *was born and bred in Glasgow and almost all his work— which includes novels, stories and plays— reflects the individual character of Clydeside life. In his immortal character sketches of the pawky "Wee Macgreegor" he has depicted the everyday life of a small boy with a deep understanding of youth and an exact reproduction of the humorous aspects of the Glasgow accent*

AN EXPERIMENT

" An' a' ye've got to dae," said Lizzie, laying the *Fireside Companion* in her lap and beginning another spell of knitting, " is jist to licht the wee stove, an' the eggs hatches theirsel's. Maist extraornar', is't no', John ? "

" Dod, ay," returned John. " Whit did ye say they ca'ed it, wumman ? Cremation o' chickens ? Eh ? "

" Incubation, John," his wife replied, after a glance at the page. " It's the het that gars [1] the chickens come oot."

" Whit wey dae the tewkies [2] no' come oot when ye bile the eggs, Paw ? " inquired Macgregor, quitting the square blocks of wood with which he had been building " wee hooses " on the kitchen floor, and advancing to his father's knee.

" Speir [3] at yer Maw, Macgreegor," said John, laughing. " Ye're the lad fur questions ! "

" Maw, whit wey—— "

" I'm thinkin' it's aboot time ye wis in yer bed, dearie," his mother observed.

" But whit wey dae the tewkies no' come oot ? "

" Aweel, ye see, if they wis comin' oot then they wud shin be droondit," she said hastily. " Gi'e yer Paw a kiss noo, an'—— "

" Ay, but whit wey—— "

" Bilin' watter wud be ower muckle [4] het fur the puir wee tewkies," she added, seeing that the boy was persistent. " Ye've got to gar the wee tewkies think the auld hen's settin' on them, dearie."

" If I wis to pit an egg on the hob, wud a wee tewky come oot, Maw ? "

[1] Compels.　　　[2] Chickens.　　　[3] Inquire.　　　[4] Much.

" Na, na ! That wud shin roast it. Ye've got to keep it nice an' cosy, but no' ower warm ; jist like yersel' when ye're in yer bed. D'ye see ? "

" Ay, Maw. . . . But I'm no' wearit yet."

" Let him bide [1] a wee, Lizzie," said the indulgent John. " Did ye ever hear tell," he went on, with a twinkle in his eye, " o' the hen that fun' an aix an' sat on it fur a fortnicht, trying fur to hatchet ? "

" Hoots ! " murmured his wife, smiling to please him.

" Did the hen no' cut itsel', Paw ? " asked his son gravely.

" Dod, I never thocht o' that, Macgreegor," his father answered, grinning.

" It wis a daft kin' o' hen onywey," said the boy scornfully.

" Aw, it jist done it fur a bawr," [2] said John, by way of apology.

" Noo, Macgreegor, yer time's up," his mother remarked, with a shake of her head.

" I'm no wearit, Maw."

" Are ye no' ? An whit wey wis ye yawnin' the noo, ma mannie ? "

" I wisna yawnin'."

" Whit wis ye daein' then ? "

" I—I wis jist openin' ma mooth, Maw."

" Och, awa' wi' ye, laddie ! Jist openin' yer mooth, wis ye ? Deed, yer een's [3] jist like twa beads wi' sleep ! I seen ye rubbin' them fur the last hauf-'oor. Ay, fine ye ken it's Wee Wullie Winkie, ma dearie."

" Aw, Lizzie, the wean's [4] fine," put in John, as he cut himself a fresh fill of tobacco. " Come here, Macgreegor, an' get a wee cuddle afore ye gang to yer bed."

" Na," said Lizzie firmly. " He'll gang to sleep on yer knee, an' then I'll ha'e a nice job gettin' him to his bed. Here, Macgreegor, till I tak' aff yer collar. . . . Noo, see if ye can louse yer buits. . . . Mercy me ! if that's no' anither hole in yer stockin'. Luk at his heel, John ! Ye're jist a pair, the twa o' ye ! Ye're baith that sair on yer stockin's. If it's no' the heels it's the taes, an' if it's no' the taes it's the soles, an' if it's no' the soles it's—— Aweel, I've darned them afore, an' I daursay I'll darn them again," she concluded, with a philosophic smile, and stooped to assist Macgregor, who was struggling with a complicated knot in the lace of his second boot.

. . . . . .

[1] Remain.   [2] Lark.   [3] Eyes.   [4] Child.

" John," said Lizzie two mornings later—it happened to be Sunday—" I canna get Macgreegor to rise. He's sayin' he's no' weel."

" Eh ! " exclaimed her husband, laying down his razor. " No' weel ? I maun see——"

" No' the noo, John. I think he's sleepin' again. But—but wis ye gi'ein' him ony sweeties when ye tuk him ootbye yesterday efternune ? "

" Naw, Lizzie. Ye seen a' he got yersel'. Jist thon wee bit taiblet. Is he feelin' seeck ? "

" He said he wisna seeck, but jist no' weel. He's no' ill-like, but I'm no' easy in ma mind aboot him."

" I—I gi'ed him a penny yesterday," said her husband after an awkward pause.

" Aw, John ! "

" But he said he wudna spend it on sweeties—an' I'm shair he didna."

" Maybe he bocht pastry. Whit fur did ye gi'e him the penny ? "

" He askit fur it. Maybe he's jist a wee thing wearit, Lizzie."

Mrs. Robinson shook her head, and opened a cupboard door.

" Are ye gaun to gi'e him ile ? " asked John.

" Ay, when he's wauken. Oh, John, John, ye sud be mair discreet, an' no' gi'e Macgreegor a' he asks fur. But get yer shavin' dune, an' come to yer breakfast. Ye didna see wee Jeannie's flannen petticoat, did ye ? Her rid yin, ye ken ? I canna lay ma haun' on it, an' I'm shair it was aside her ither claes when we gaed to wur beds."

" Naw, I didna see it," John replied dully, and sadly resumed his shaving.

" It's maist aggravatin'," murmured Lizzie. " I doot I'm lossin' ma mem'ry. . . . Did ma doo no' get on her braw new flannen petticoat ? " she inquired of her daughter, who, however, appeared quite happy in her old garment, sitting on a hassock and piping on a horn spoon which had a whistle in its handle. " Wee Jeannie's breid an' mulk's near ready noo," she added, whereupon wee Jeannie piped with more zest than ever.

After breakfast Lizzie interviewed her son, who was again awake.

" Are ye feelin' better noo, dearie ? "

" Naw."

" Whit's like the maitter ? "

" I dinna ken. I dinna want to rise, Maw."

Lizzie refrained from referring to the penny that had done the harm. " I doot ye're needin' a taste o' ile," [1] she said.

Macgregor kept a meek silence.

" I'll gi'e ye a wee taste, an' then ye'll maybe try an' tak' yer breakfast."

" I'll try, Maw."

He took the dose like a hero, and afterwards made a meal the heartiness of which rather puzzled his mother. Then he said he was going to have another sleep.

" John," said Lizzie, " I canna think whit's wrang wi' Macgreegor. He's baith hungry an' sleepy. I wisht I kent whit he bocht wi' yer penny. I'm feart it wis some kin' o' pooshonous [2] thing. I think I'll gang ower to Mrs. Thomson an speir if Wullie's a' richt. Wullie an' Macgreegor wis oot thegither last nicht."

" Ay," said John. " Maybe he got somethin' to eat frae Wullie."

" Mabye, John. . . . If Macgregor's wauken when I'm awa', ye micht get him to tell ye whit he done wi' the penny. D'ye see ? "

" Ay. . . . I'm rale vexed aboot the penny, wumman."

" Weel, dearie, ye maun try an' be mair discreet. Ye canna expec' a wean to be fu' o' wisdom, as Solyman says."

Left to himself—Lizzie had taken wee Jeannie with her— John went over to the bed and gazed anxiously upon his son. Presently the boy opened his eyes.

" Weel, ma wee man," said John, with an effort to speak cheerfully, " are ye fur risin' noo ? "

" Naw."

" Are ye no' ony better ? "

Macgregor languidly signified that he was not.

John cleared his throat. " Whit did ye dae wi' the penny I gi'ed ye ? " he asked gently.

" I spent it."

" Ay. But whit did ye spend it on ? Pastry ? "

" Naw."

John felt somewhat relieved. " Aweel, tell me whit ye bocht."

" I—I'll tell ye anither time, Paw," said Macgregor, after considerable hesitation.

[1] Oil.   [2] Poisonous.

" Did ye git ony sweeties efter yer taiblet yesterday ? "

" Naw. . . . Can I get a wee tate [1] taiblet noo, Paw ? "

" Deed, I doot ye canna. Ye're no' weel."

" Ah, but I'm no' that kin' o' no' weel, Paw."

John shook his head sadly, and there ensued a long silence.

" Paw," said Macgregor at last, " hoo lang dae wee tewkies tak' to come oot their eggs ? "

" Eh ? "

The youngster's face was flushed as he repeated the question.

" I'm no' jist shair, Macgreegor," said John ; " but I think the paper yer Maw wis readin' said it wis twa-three weeks."

" Oh ! " cried Macgregor in such a tone of dismay that his father was startled.

" Whit's wrang, Macgreegor ? "

" I think I'll rise noo, Paw," the boy remarked soberly.

" Are ye feelin' better ? "

" Ay, I'm better."

" Whit's vexin' ye, ma wee man ? " cried John suddenly, and with great tenderness.

Macgregor gave a small snuff and a big swallow as his father's arm went round him. " I—I thocht the—the wee tewky wud come oot shin," he murmured brokenly.

" The wee tewky ? "

" Ay. But I—I canna bide in ma b—b—bed twa-three weeks." And then from under the clothes Macgregor cautiously drew a tiny red flannel garment, which he unrolled and laid bare a hen's egg. " I gi'ed ma penny fur it, Paw. The grocer tell't me there wis nae tewky in it, but—but I thocht there wis, an' I wis wantin' to—to keep it cosy, an'—an'——"

" Aw, wee Macgreegor ! " exclaimed John, realizing it all, but not even smiling.

　　·　　　　·　　　　·　　　　·

When Lizzie returned and heard the tale she was sympathetic, but not sentimental.

" I'll jist bile the egg fur yer tea, dearie," she said.

" I wud like it fried, Maw."

[1] A small portion.

G. K. CHESTERTON (1874-   ) *essayist, poet, historian, novelist, journalist, is one of the wittiest of our contemporary men of letters. His love of paradox, his faculty of presenting startling truths by the seemingly simple process of turning conventional ideas upside-down, find expression not only in his essays, but in his short stories such as " The Club of Queen Trades," from which the amusing tale below is taken.*

THE TREMENDOUS ADVENTURES
OF MAJOR BROWN

RABELAIS, or his wild illustrator, Gustave Doré, must have had something to do with the designing of the things called flats in England and America. There is something entirely Gargantuan in the idea of economising space by piling houses on top of each other, front doors and all. And in the chaos and complexity of those perpendicular streets anything might dwell or happen, and it is in one of them, I believe, that the inquirer may find the offices of the Club of Queer Trades. It may be thought at the first glance that the name would attract and startle the passer-by, but nothing attracts or startles in these dim immense hives. The passer-by is only looking for his own melancholy destination, the Montenegro Shipping Agency or the London office of the *Rutland Sentinel*, and passes through the twilight passages as one passes through the twilight corridors of a dream. If the Thugs set up a Strangers' Assassination Company in one of the great buildings in Norfolk Street, and sent in a mild man in spectacles to answer inquiries, no inquiries would be made. And the Club of Queer Trades reigns in a great edifice hidden like a fossil in a mighty cliff of fossils.

The nature of this society, such as we afterwards discovered it to be, is soon and simply told. It is an eccentric and Bohemian Club, of which the absolute condition of membership lies in this, that the candidate must have invented the method by which he earns his living. It must be an entirely new trade. The exact definition of this requirement is given in the two principal rules. First, it must not be a mere application or variation of an existing trade. Thus, for instance, the Club would not admit an insurance agent simply

51

because instead of insuring men's furniture against being
burnt in a fire, he insured, let us say, their trousers against
being torn by a mad dog. The principle (as Sir Bradcock
Burnaby-Bradcock, in the extraordinarily eloquent and soaring speech to the Club on the occasion of the question being
raised in the Stormby Smith affair, said wittily and keenly)
is the same. Secondly, the trade must be a genuine commercial source of income, the support of its inventor. Thus
the Club would not receive a man simply because he chose
to pass his days collecting broken sardine tins, unless he could
drive a roaring trade in them. Professor Chick made that
quite clear. And when one remembers what Professor Chick's
own new trade was, one doesn't know whether to laugh or cry.

The discovery of this strange society was a curiously
refreshing thing ; to realise that there were ten new trades
in the world was like looking at the first ship or the first
plough. It made a man feel what he should feel, that he
was still in the childhood of the world. That I should have
come at last upon so singular a body was, I may say without
vanity, not altogether singular, for I have a mania for belonging
to as many societies as possible : I may be said to collect clubs,
and I have accumulated a vast and fantastic variety of specimens ever since, in my audacious youth, I collected the
Athenæum. At some future day, perhaps, I may tell tales,
of some of the other bodies to which I have belonged. I will
recount the doings of the Dead Man's Shoes Society (that
superficially immoral, but darkly justifiable communion) ; I
will explain the curious origin of the Cat and Christian, the
name of which has been so shamefully misinterpreted ; and
the world shall know at least why the Institute of Typewriters
coalesced with the Red Tulip League. Of the Ten Teacups,
of course I dare not say a word. The first of my revelations,
at any rate, shall be concerned with the Club of Queer Trades,
which, as I have said, was one of this class, one which I was
almost bound to come across sooner or later, because of my
singular hobby. The wild youth of the metropolis call me
facetiously " The King of Clubs." They also call me " The
Cherub," in allusion to the roseate and youthful appearance
I have presented in my declining years. I only hope the spirits
in the better world have as good dinners as I have.
But the finding of the Club of Queer Trades has one very
curious thing about it. The most curious thing about it is
that it was not discovered by me : it was discovered by my

friend Basil Grant, a star-gazer, a mystic, and a man who scarcely stirred out of his attic.

Very few people knew anything about Basil ; not because he was in the least unsociable, for if a man out of the street had walked into his rooms he would have kept him talking till morning. Few people knew him, because, like all poets, he could do without them ; he welcomed a human face as he might welcome a sudden blend of colour in a sunset ; but he no more felt the need of going out to parties than he felt the need of altering the sunset clouds. He lived in a queer and comfortable garret in the roofs of Lambeth. He was surrounded by a chaos of things that were in odd contrast to the slums around him : old fantastic books, swords, armour —the whole dust-hole of romanticism. But his face, amid all these quixotic relics, appeared curiously keen and modern— a powerful, legal face. And no one but I knew who he was.

Long ago as it is, every one remembers the terrible and grotesque scene that occurred in ——, when one of the most acute and forcible of the English judges suddenly went mad on the bench. I had my own view of that occurrence ; but about the facts themselves there is no question at all. For some months, indeed for some years, people had detected something curious in the judge's conduct. He seemed to have lost interest in the law, in which he had been beyond expression brilliant and terrible as a K.C., and to be occupied in giving personal and moral advice to the people concerned. He talked more like a priest or a doctor, and a very outspoken one at that. The first thrill was probably given when he said to a man who had attempted a crime of passion : " I sentence you to three years' imprisonment, under the firm, and solemn, and God-given conviction, that what you require is three months at the seaside." He accused criminals from the bench, not so much of their obvious legal crimes, but of things that had never been heard of in a court of justice, monstrous egoism, lack of humour, and morbidity deliberately encouraged. Things came to a head in that celebrated diamond case in which the Prime Minister himself, that brilliant patrician, had to come forward, gracefully and reluctantly, to give evidence against his valet. After the detailed life of the household had been thoroughly exhibited, the judge requested the Premier again to step forward, which he did with quiet dignity. The judge then said, in a sudden, grating voice : " Get a new soul. That thing's not fit for a dog. Get a new soul." All

this, of course, in the eyes of the sagacious, was premonitory of that melancholy and farcical day when his wits actually
deserted him in open court. It was a libel case between two
very eminent and powerful financiers, against both of whom
charges of considerable defalcation were brought. The
case was long and complex ; the advocates were long and
eloquent ; but at last, after weeks of work and rhetoric, the
time came for the great judge to give a summing-up ; and one
of his celebrated masterpieces of lucidity and pulverising logic
was eagerly looked for. He had spoken very little during
the prolonged affair, and he looked sad and lowering at the end
of it. He was silent for a few moments, and then burst into
a stentorian song. His remarks (as reported) were as
follows :—

> " O Rowty-owty tiddly-owty
> Tiddly-owty tiddly-owty
> Highty ighty tiddly-ighty
> Tiddly-ighty ow."

He then retired from public life and took the garret in
Lambeth.

I was sitting there one evening, about six o'clock, over a
glass of that gorgeous Burgundy which he kept behind a pile of
black-letter folios ; he was striding about the room, fingering,
after a habit of his, one of the great swords in his collection ;
the red glare of the strong fire struck his square features and
his fierce grey hair ; his blue eyes were even unusually full of
dreams, and he had opened his mouth to speak dreamily,
when the door was flung open, and a pale, fiery man, with red
hair and a huge furred overcoat, swung himself panting into
the room.

" Sorry to bother you, Basil," he gasped. " I took a
liberty—made an appointment here with a man—a client—in
five minutes—I beg your pardon, sir," and he gave me a
bow of apology.

Basil smiled at me. " You didn't know," he said, " that
I had a practical brother. This is Rupert Grant, Esquire,
who can and does all there is to be done. Just as I was a
failure at one thing, he is a success at everything. I remember
him as a journalist, a house-agent, a naturalist, an inventor,
a publisher, a schoolmaster, a—what are you now, Rupert ? "

" I am and have been for some time," said Rupert, with
some dignity, " a private detective, and there's my client."

A loud rap at the door had cut him short, and, on permission being given, the door was thrown sharply open and a
stout, dapper man walked swiftly into the room, set his silk
hat with a clap on the table, and said, " Good-evening, gentle-
men," with a stress on the last syllable that somehow marked
him out as a martinet, military, literary and social. He had
a large head streaked with black and grey, and an abrupt
black moustache, which gave him a look of fierceness which
was contradicted by his sad sea-blue eyes.

Basil immediately said to me, " Let us come into the next
room, Gully," and was moving towards the door, but the
stranger said :—

" Not at all. Friends remain. Assistance possibly."

The moment I heard him speak I remembered who he
was, a certain Major Brown I had met years before in Basil's
society. I had forgotten altogether the black dandified figure
and the large solemn head, but I remembered the peculiar
speech, which consisted of only saying about a quarter of
each sentence, and that sharply, like the crack of a gun. I
do not know, it may have come from giving orders to troops.

Major Brown was a V.C., and an able and distinguished
soldier, but he was anything but a warlike person. Like
many among the iron men who recovered British India, he
was a man with the natural belief and tastes of an old maid.
In his dress he was dapper and yet demure ; in his habits he
was precise to the point of the exact adjustment of a tea-cup.
One enthusiasm he had, which was of the nature of a religion
—the cultivation of pansies. And when he talked about his
collection, his blue eyes glittered like a child's at a new toy,
the eyes that had remained untroubled when the troops were
roaring victory round Roberts at Candahar.

" Well, Major," said Rupert Grant, with a lordly heartiness, flinging himself into a chair, " what is the matter with
you ? "

" Yellow pansies. Coal cellar. P. G. Northover," said
the Major, with righteous indignation.

We glanced at each other with inquisitiveness. Basil, who
had his eyes shut in his abstracted way, said simply :—

" I beg your pardon."

" Fact is. Street, you know, man, pansies. On wall.
Death to me. Something. Preposterous."

We shook our heads gently. Bit by bit, and mainly by
the seemingly sleepy assistance of Basil Grant, we pieced

together the Major's fragmentary, but excited narration. It would be infamous to submit the reader to what we endured ; therefore I will tell the story of Major Brown in my own words. But the reader must imagine the scene. The eyes of Basil closed as in a trance, after his habit, and the eyes of Rupert and myself getting rounder and rounder as we listened to one of the most astounding stories in the world, from the lips of the little man in black, sitting bolt upright in his chair and talking like a telegram.

Major Brown was, I have said, a successful soldier, but by no means an enthusiastic one. So far from regretting his retirement on half-pay, it was with delight that he took a small neat villa, very like a doll's house, and devoted the rest of his life to pansies and weak tea. The thought that battles were over when he had once hung up his sword in the little front hall (along with two patent stew-pots and a bad water-colour), and betaken himself instead to wielding the rake in his little sunlit garden, was to him like having come into a harbour in heaven. He was Dutch-like and precise in his taste in gardening, and had, perhaps, some tendency to drill his flowers like soldiers. He was one of those men who are capable of putting four umbrellas in the stand rather than three, so that two may lean one way and two another ; he saw life like a pattern in a freehand drawing-book. And assuredly he would not have believed, or even understood, any one who had told him that within a few yards of his brick paradise he was destined to be caught in a whirlpool of in-credible adventures, such as he had never seen or dreamed of in the horrible jungle, or the heat of battle.

One certain bright and windy afternoon, the Major, attired in his usual faultless manner, had set out for his usual consititutional. In crossing from one great residential thoroughfare to another, he happened to pass along one of those aimless looking lanes which lie along the back-garden walls of a row of mansions, and which in their empty and discoloured appearance give one an odd sensation as of being behind the scenes of a theatre. But mean and sulky as the scene might be in the eyes of most of us, it was not altogether so in the Major's, for along the coarse gravel footway was coming a thing which was to him what the passing of a relig-ious procession is to a devout person. A large, heavy man, with fish blue eyes and a ring of irradiating red beard, was pushing before him a barrow, which was ablaze with incom--

parable flowers. There were splendid specimens of almost every order, but the Major's own favourite pansies predominated. The Major stopped and fell into conversation, and then into bargaining. He treated the man after the manner of collectors and other mad men, that is to say, he carefully and with a sort of anguish selected the best roots from the less excellent, praised some, disparaged others, made a subtle scale ranging from a thrilling worth and rarity to a degraded insignificance, and then bought them all. The man was just pushing off his barrow when he stopped and came close to the Major.

" I'll tell you what, sir," he said. " If you're interested in them things, you just get on to that wall."

" On the wall ! " cried the scandalised Major, whose conventional soul quailed within him at the thought of such fantastic trespass.

" Finest show of yellow pansies in England in that there garden, sir," hissed the tempter. " I'll help you up, sir."

How it happened no one will ever know, but that positive enthusiasm of the Major's life triumphed over all its negative traditions, and with an easy leap and swing that showed that he was in no need of physical assistance, he stood on the wall at the end of the strange garden. The second after, the flapping of the frock-coat at his knees made him feel inexpressibly a fool. But the next instant all such trifling sentiments were swallowed up by the most appalling shock of surprise the old soldier had ever felt in all his bold and wandering existence. His eyes fell upon the garden, and there across a large bed in the centre of the lawn was a vast pattern of pansies ; they were splendid flowers, but for once it was not their horticultural aspects that Major Brown beheld, for the pansies were arranged in gigantic capital letters so as to form the sentence—

" DEATH TO MAJOR BROWN "

A kindly looking old man, with white whiskers, was watering them.

Brown looked sharply back at the road behind him ; the man with the barrow had suddenly vanished. Then he looked again at the lawn with its incredible inscription. Another man might have thought he had gone mad, but Brown did not. When romantic ladies gushed over his V.C. and his military exploits, he sometimes felt himself to be a painfully prosaic person, but by the same token he knew he was incurably sane. Another man, again, might have thought himself a victim of a passing practical joke, but Brown could not easily believe this. He knew from his own quaint learning that the garden arrangement was an elaborate and expensive one ; he thought it extravagantly improbable that any one would pour out money like water for a joke against him. Having no explanation whatever to offer, he admitted the fact to himself, like a clear-headed man, and waited as he would have done in the presence of a man with six legs.

At this moment the stout old man with white whiskers looked up, and the watering-can fell from his hand, shooting a swirl of water down the gravel path.

" Who on earth are you ? " he gasped, trembling violently.

" I am Major Brown," said that individual, who was always cool in the hour of action.

The old man gaped helplessly like some monstrous fish. At last he stammered wildly, " Come down—come down here ! "

" At your service," said the Major, and alighted at a bound on the grass beside him, without disarranging his silk hat.

The old man turned his broad back and set off at a sort of waddling run towards the house, followed with swift steps by the Major. His guide led him through the back passages of a gloomy, but gorgeously appointed house, until they reached the door of the front room. Then the old man turned with a face of apoplectic terror dimly showing in the twilight.

" For heaven's sake," he said, " don't mention jackals."

Then he threw open the door, releasing a burst of red lamplight, and ran downstairs with a clatter.

The Major stepped into a rich, glowing room, full of red copper, and peacock and purple hangings, hat in hand. He had the finest manners in the world, and though mystified, was not in the least embarrassed to see that the only occupant was a lady, sitting by the window, looking out.

" Madam," he said, bowing simply, " I am Major Brown."

" Sit down," said the lady ; but she did not turn her head.

She was a graceful, green-clad figure, with fiery red hair and a flavour of Bedford Park. " You have come, I suppose," she said mournfully, " to tax me about the hateful title-deeds."

" I have come, madam," he said, " to know what is the

matter. To know why my name is written across your garden. Not amicably either."

He spoke grimly, for the thing had hit him. It is impossible to describe the effect produced on the mind by that quiet and sunny garden scene, the frame for a stunning and brutal personality. The evening air was still, and the grass was golden in the place where the little flowers he studied cried to heaven for his blood.

" You know I must not turn round," said the lady ; " every afternoon till the stroke of six I must keep my face turned to the street."

Some queer and unusual inspiration made the prosaic soldier resolute to accept these outrageous riddles without surprise.

" It is almost six," he said ; and even as he spoke the barbaric copper clock upon the wall clanged the first stroke of the hour. At the sixth the lady sprung up and turned on the Major one of the queerest and yet most attractive faces he had ever seen in his life ; open, and yet tantalising, the face of an elf.

" That makes the third year I have waited," she cried. " This is an anniversary. The waiting almost makes one wish the frightful thing would happen once and for all."

And even as she spoke, a sudden rending cry broke the stillness. From low down on the pavement of the dim street (it was already twilight) a voice cried out with a raucous and merciless distinctness :—

" Major Brown, Major Brown, where does the jackal dwell ? "

Brown was decisive and silent in action. He strode to the front door and looked out. There was no sign of life in the blue gloaming of the street, where one or two lamps were beginning to light their lemon sparks. On returning, he found the lady in green trembling.

" It is the end," she cried, with shaking lips ; " it may be death for both of us. Whenever——"

But even as she spoke her speech was cloven by another hoarse proclamation from the dark street, again horribly articulate.

" Major Brown, Major Brown, how did the jackal die ? "

Brown dashed out of the door and down the steps, but again he was frustrated ; there was no figure in sight, and the street was far too long and empty for the shouter to have

run away. Even the rational Major was a little shaken as he
returned at a certain time to the drawing-room. Scarcely
had he done so than the terrific voice came :—

"Major Brown, Major Brown, where did——"

Brown was in the street almost at a bound, and he was
in time—in time to see something which at first glance froze
the blood. The cries appeared to come from a decapitated
head resting on the pavement.

The next moment the pale Major understood. It was
the head of a man thrust through the coal-hole in the street.
The next moment, again, it had vanished, and Major Brown
turned to the lady. "Where's your coal cellar?" he said,
and stepped out into the passage.

She looked at him with wild grey eyes. "You will not
go down," she cried, "alone, into the dark hole, with that
beast?"

"Is this the way?" replied Brown, and descended the
kitchen stairs three at a time. He flung open the door of a
black cavity and stepped in, feeling in his pocket for matches.
As his right hand was thus occupied, a pair of great slimy hands
came out of the darkness, hands clearly belonging to a man
of gigantic stature, and seized him by the back of the head.
They forced him down, down in the suffocating darkness, a
brutal image of destiny. But the Major's head, though upside
down, was perfectly clear and intellectual. He gave quietly
under the pressure until he had slid down almost to his hands
and knees. Then finding the knees of the invisible monster
within a foot of him, he simply put out one of his long, bony,
and skilful hands, and gripping the leg by a muscle pulled
it off the ground, and laid the huge living man, with a crash
along the floor. He strove to rise, but Brown was on top
like a cat. They rolled over and over. Big as the man was,
he had evidently now no desire but to escape ; he made
sprawls hither and thither to get past the Major to the door,
but that tenacious person had him hard by the coat collar
and hung with the other hand to a beam. At length there
came a strain in holding back this human bull, a strain under
which Brown expected his hand to rend and part from the
arm. But something else rent and parted ; and the dim fat
figure of the giant vanished out of the cellar, leaving the torn
coat in the Major's hand ; the only fruit of his adventure
and the only clue to the mystery. For when he went up and
out at the front door, the lady, the rich hangings, and the

It was the head of a man thrust through the coal-hole in the street.

whole equipment of the house had disappeared. It had only bare boards and whitewashed walls.

" The lady was in the conspiracy, of course," said Rupert, nodding. Major Brown turned brick red. " I beg your pardon," he said, " I think not."

Rupert raised his eyebrows and looked at him for a moment, but said nothing. When next he spoke he asked :—

" Was there anything in the pockets of the coat ? "

" There was sevenpence halfpenny in coppers and a three-penny-bit," said the Major, carefully ; " there was a cigarette-holder, a piece of string, and this letter," and he laid it on the table. It ran as follows :—

" DEAR MR. PLOVER,—I am annoyed to hear that some delay has occurred in the arrangements *re* Major Brown. Please see that he is attacked as per arrangement to-morrow. The coal-cellar, of course.
" Yours faithfully,
" P. G. NORTHOVER."

Rupert Grant was leaning forward listening with hawk-like eyes. He cut in :—

" Is it dated from anywhere ? "

" No—oh, yes ! " replied Brown, glancing upon the paper ; " 14 Tanner's Court, North——"

Rupert sprang up and struck his hands together.

" Then why are we hanging here ? Let's get along. Basil, lend me your revolver."

Basil was staring into the embers like a man in a trance ; and it was some time before he answered :—

" I don't think you'll need it."

" Perhaps not," said Rupert, getting into his fur coat. " One never knows. But going down a dark court to see criminals——"

" Do you think they are criminals ? " asked his brother.

Rupert laughed stoutly. " Giving orders to a subor-dinate to strangle a harmless stranger in a coal-cellar may strike you as a very blameless experiment, but——"

" Do you think they wanted to strangle the Major ? " asked Basil, in the same distant and monotonous voice.

" My dear fellow, you've been asleep. Look at the letter."

" I am looking at the letter," said the mad judge calmly ; though, as a matter of fact, he was looking at the fire. " I don't think it's the sort of letter one criminal would write to another."

"My dear boy, you are glorious," cried Rupert, turning round, with laughter in his bright blue eyes. Your methods amaze me. Why, there *is* the letter. It *is* written, and it does give orders for a crime. You might as well say that the Nelson Column was not at all the sort of thing that was likely to be set up in Trafalgar Square."

Basil Grant shook all over with a sort of silent laughter, but did not otherwise move.

"That's rather good," he said ; "but, of course, logic like that's not what is really wanted. It's a question of spiritual atmosphere. It's not a criminal letter."

"It is. It's a matter of fact," cried the other in an agony of reasonableness.

"Facts," murmured Basil, like one mentioning some strange, far-off animals, "how facts obscure the truth. I may be silly—in fact, I'm off my head—but I never could believe in that man—what's his name, in those capital stories ?— Sherlock Holmes. Every detail points to something, certainly ; but generally to the wrong thing. Facts point in all directions, it seems to me, like the thousands of twigs on a tree. It's only the life of the tree that has unity and goes up —only the green blood that springs, like a fountain, at the stars."

"But what the deuce else can the letter be but criminal ? "

"We have eternity to stretch our legs in," replied the mystic. "It can be an infinity of things. I haven't seen any of them—I've only seen the letter. I look at that, and say it's not criminal."

"Then what's the origin of it ? "

"I haven't the vaguest idea."

"Then why don't you accept the ordinary explanation ? "

Basil continued for a little to glare at the coals, and seemed collecting his thoughts in a humble and even painful way. Then he said :—

"Suppose you went out into the moonlight. Suppose you passed through silent, silvery streets and squares until you came into an open and deserted space, set with a few monuments, and you beheld one dressed as a bailet girl dancing in the argent glimmer. And suppose you looked, and saw it was a man disguised. And suppose you looked again, and saw it was Lord Kitchener. What would you think ? "

He paused a moment, and went on :—

" You could not adopt the ordinary explanation. The ordinary explanation of putting on singular clothes is that you look nice in them ; you would not think that Lord Kitchener dressed up like a ballet girl out of ordinary personal vanity. You would think it much more likely that he inherited a dancing madness from a great grandmother ; or had been hypnotised at a séance ; or threatened by a secret society with death if he refused the ordeal. With Baden-Powell, say, it might be a bet—but not with Kitchener. I should know all that, because in my public days I knew him quite well. So I know that letter quite well, and criminals quite well. It's not a criminal's letter. It's all atmospheres." And he closed his eyes and passed his hand over his forehead.

Rupert and the Major were regarding him with a mixture of respect and pity. The former said :—

" Well, I'm going, anyhow, and shall continue to think —until your spiritual mystery turns up—that a man who sends a note recommending a crime, that is, actually a crime that is actually carried out, at least tentatively, is, all in probability, a little casual in his moral tastes. Can I have that revolver ? "

" Certainly," said Basil, getting up. " But I am coming with you." And he flung an old cape or cloak round him, and took a sword-stick from the corner.

" You ! " said Rupert, with some surprise, " you scarcely ever leave your hole to look at anything on the face of the earth."

Basil fitted on a formidable old white hat.

" I scarcely ever," he said, with an unconscious and colossal arrogance, " hear of anything on the face of the earth that I do not understand at once, without going to see it."

And he led the way out into the purple night.

We four swung along the flaring Lambeth streets, across Westminster Bridge, and along the Embankment in the direction of that part of Fleet Street which contained Tanner's Court. The erect, black figure of Major Brown, seen from behind, was a quaint contrast to the hound-like stoop and flapping mantle of young Rupert Grant, who adopted, with childlike delight, all the dramatic poses of the detective of fiction. The finest among his many fine qualities was his boyish appetite for the colour and poetry of London. Basil,

C

who walked behind, with his face turned blindly to the stars, had the look of a somnambulist.

Rupert paused at the corner of Tanner's Court, with a quiver of delight at danger, and gripped Basil's revolver in his greatcoat pocket.

" Shall we go in now ? " he asked.

" Not get police ? " asked Major Brown, glancing sharply up and down the street.

" I am not sure," answered Rupert, knitting his brows. " Of course, it's quite clear, the thing's all crooked. But there are three of us, and——"

" I shouldn't get the police," said Basil in a queer voice. Rupert glanced at him and stared hard.

" Basil," he cried, " you're trembling. What's the matter —are you afraid ? "

" Cold, perhaps," said the Major, eyeing him. There was no doubt that he was shaking.

At last, after a few moments' scrutiny, Rupert broke into a curse.

" You're laughing," he cried. " I know that confounded, silent, shaky laugh of yours. What the deuce is the amusement, Basil ? Here we are, all three of us, within a yard of a den of ruffians——"

" But I shouldn't call the police," said Basil. " We four heroes are quite equal to a host," and he continued to quake with his mysterious mirth.

Rupert turned with impatience and strode swiftly down the court, the rest of us following. When he reached the door of No. 14 he turned abruptly, the revolver glittering in his hand.

" Stand close," he said in the voice of a commander. " The scoundrel may be attempting an escape at this moment. We must fling open the door and rush in."

The four of us cowered instantly under the archway, rigid, except for the old judge and his convulsion of merriment.

" Now," hissed Rupert Grant, turning his pale face and burning eyes suddenly over his shoulder, " when I say ' Four,' follow me with a rush. If I say ' Hold him,' pin the fellows down, whoever they are. If I say ' Stop,' stop. I shall say that if there are more than three. If they attack us I shall empty my revolver on them. Basil, have your sword-stick ready. Now—one, two, three, four ! "

With the sound of the word the door burst open, and we fell into the room like an invasion, only to stop dead.

The room, which was an ordinary and neatly-appointed office, appeared, at the first glance, to be empty. But on a second and more careful glance, we saw seated behind a very large desk with pigeon-holes and drawers of bewildering multiplicity, a small man with a black waxed moustache, and the air of a very average clerk, writing hard. He looked up as we came to a standstill.

" Did you knock ? " he asked pleasantly. " I am sorry if I did not hear. What can I do for you ? "

There was a doubtful pause, and then, by general consent, the Major himself, the victim of the outrage, stepped forward. The letter was in his hand, and he looked unusually grim.

" Is your name P. G. Northover ? " he asked.

" That is my name," replied the other, smiling.

" I think," said Major Brown, with an increase in the dark glow of his face, " that this letter was written by you." And with a loud clap he struck open the letter on the desk with his clenched fist. The man called Northover looked at it with unaffected interest, and merely nodded.

" Well, sir," said the Major, breathing hard, " what about that ? "

" What about it, precisely," said the man with the moustache.

" I am Major Brown," said that gentleman sternly.

Northover bowed. " Pleased to meet you, sir. What have you to say to me ? "

" Say ! " cried the Major, loosing a sudden tempest ; " why, I want this confounded thing settled. I want—— "

" Certainly, sir," said Northover, jumping up with a slight elevation of the eyebrows. " Will you take a chair for a moment." And he pressed an electric bell just above him, which thrilled and tinkled in a room beyond. The Major put his hat on the back of the chair offered him, but stood chafing and beating the floor with his polished boot.

The next moment an inner glass door was opened, and a fair, weedy, young man, in a frock-coat, entered from within.

" Mr. Hopson," said Northover, " this is Major Brown. Will you please finish that thing for him I gave you this morning and bring it in ? "

" Yes, sir," said Mr. Hopson, and vanished like lightning.

"You will excuse me, gentlemen," said the egregious
Northover, with his radiant smile, "if I continue to work
until Mr. Hopson is ready. I have some books that must
be cleared up before I get away on my holiday to-morrow.
And we all like a whiff of the country, don't we? Ha! ha!"

The criminal took up his pen with a child-like laugh, and
a silence ensued; a placid and busy silence on the part of
Mr. P G. Northover; a raging silence on the part of everybody else.

At length the scratching of Northover's pen in the stillness was mingled with a knock at the door, almost simul-
taneous with the turning of the handle, and Mr. Hopson came
in again with the same silent rapidity, placed a paper before
his principal, and disappeared again.

The man at the desk pulled and twisted his spiky moustache for a few moments as he ran his eye up and down the
paper presented to him. He took up his pen, with a slight,
instantaneous frown, and altered something, muttering—
"Careless." Then he read it again with the same impenetrable reflectiveness, and finally handed it to the frantic Brown,
whose hand was beating the devil's tattoo on the back of the
chair.

"I think you will find that all right, Major," he said
briefly.

The Major looked at it; whether he found it all right or
not will appear later, but he found it like this:

Major Brown to P. G. Northover.

	£	s.	d.
January 1, to account rendered . .	5	6	0
May 9, to potting and embedding of 200 pansies	2	0	0
To cost of trolley with flowers . .	0	15	0
To hiring of man with trolley . . .	0	5	0
To hire of house and garden for one day .	1	0	0
To furnishing of room in peacock curtains, copper ornaments, &c. . . .	3	0	0
To salary of Miss Jameson . . .	1	0	0
To salary of Mr. Plover	1	0	0
Total .	£14	6	0

A remittance will oblige.

" What," said Brown, after a dead pause, and with eyes that seemed slowly rising out of his head. " What in heaven's name is this ? "

" What is it ? " repeated Northover, cocking his eyebrow with amusement. " It's your account, of course."

" My account ! " The Major's ideas appeared to be in a vague stampede. " My account. And what have I got to do with it ? "

" Well," said Northover, laughing outright, " naturally I prefer you to pay it."

The Major's hand was still resting on the back of the chair as the words came. He scarcely stirred otherwise, but he lifted the chair bodily into the air with one hand and hurled it at Northover's head.

The legs crashed against the desk, so that Northover only got a blow on the elbow as he sprang up with clenched fists, only be to seized by the united rush of the rest of us. The chair had fallen clattering on the empty floor.

" Let me go, you scamps," he shouted. " Let me——"

" Stand still," cried Rupert authoritatively. " Major Brown's action is excusable. The abominable crime you have attempted——"

" A customer has a perfect right," said Northover hotly, " to question an alleged overcharge, but confound it all, not to throw furniture."

" What, in God's name, do you mean by your customers and overcharges ? " shrieked Major Brown, whose keen feminine nature, steady in pain or danger, became almost hysterical in the presence of a long and exasperating mystery. " Who are you ? I've never seen you or your insolent tom-fool bills. I know one of your cursed brutes tried to choke me——"

" Mad," said Northover, gazing blankly round, " all of them mad. I didn't know they travelled in quartettes."

" Enough of this prevarication," said Rupert ; " your crimes are discovered. A policeman is stationed at the corner of the court. Though only a private detective myself, I will take the responsibility of telling you that anything you say——"

" Mad," repeated Northover, with a weary air.

And at this moment, for the first time, there struck in among them the strange, sleepy voice of Basil Grant.

" Major Brown," he said, " may I ask you a question ? "

The Major turned his head with an increased bewilderment.

" You ? " he cried ; " certainly, Mr. Grant."

" Can you tell me," said the mystic, with sunken head and lowering brow, as he traced a pattern in the. dust with his sword-stick, " can you tell me what was the name of the man who lived in your house before you ? "

The unhappy Major was only faintly more disturbed by this last and futile irrelevancy, and he answered vaguely :

" Yes, I think so ; a man named Gurney something—a name with a hyphen—Gurney-Brown ; that was it."

" And when did the house change hands ? " said Basil, looking up sharply. His strange eyes were burning brilliantly.

" I came in last month," said the Major.

And at the mere word the criminal Northover suddenly fell into his great office chair and shouted with a volleying laughter.

" Oh ! it's too perfect—it's too exquisite," he gasped, beating the arms with his fists. He was laughing deafeningly ; Basil Brant was laughing voicelessly : and the rest of us only felt that our heads were like weathercocks in a whirlwind.

" Confound it, Basil," cried Rupert, stamping. " If you don't want me to go mad and blow your metaphysical brains out, tell me what all this means ? "

Northover rose.

" Permit me, sir, to explain," he said. " And, first of all, permit me to apologise to you, Major Brown, for a most abominable and unpardonable blunder, which has caused you menace and inconvenience, in which, if you will allow me to say so, you have behaved with astonishing courage and dignity. Of course you need not trouble about the bill. We will stand the loss." And, tearing the paper across, he flung the halves into the waste-paper basket and bowed.

Poor Brown's face was still a picture of distraction. " But I don't even begin to understand," he cried. " What bill ? what blunder ? what loss ? "

Mr. P. G. Northover advanced in the centre of the room, thoughtfully, and with a great deal of unconscious dignity. On closer consideration, there were apparent about him other things beside a screwed moustache, especially a lean, sallow face, hawk-like, and not without a care-worn intelligence. Then he looked up abruptly.

" Do you know where you are, Major ? " he said.

" God knows I don't," said the warrior, with fervour.

" You are standing," replied Northover, " in the office of the Adventure and Romance Agency, Limited."

" And what's that ? " blankly inquired Brown.

The man of business leaned over the back of the chair, and fixed his dark eyes on the other's face.

" Major," said he, " did you ever, as you walked along the empty street upon some idle afternoon, feel the utter hunger for something to happen—something, in the splendid words of Walt Whitman : ' Something pernicious and dread ; something far removed from a puny and pious life ; something unproved ; something in a trance ; something loosed from its anchorage, and driving free.' Did you ever feel that ? "

" Certainly not," said the Major shortly.

" Then I must explain with more elaboration," said Mr. Northover, with a sigh. " The Adventure and Romance Agency has been started to meet a great modern desire. On every side, in conversation and in literature, we hear of the desire for a larger theatre of events—for something to waylay us and lead us splendidly astray. Now the man who feels this desire for a varied life pays a yearly or a quarterly sum to the Adventure and Romance Agency ; in return, the Adventure and Romance Agency undertakes to surround him with startling and weird events. As a man is leaving his front door, an excited sweep approaches him and assures him of a plot against his life ; he gets into a cab, and is driven to an opium den ; he receives a mysterious telegram or a dramatic visit, and is immediately in a vortex of incidents. A very picturesque and moving story is first written by one of the staff of distinguished novelists who are at present hard at work in the adjoining room. Yours, Major Brown (designed by our Mr. Grigsby), I consider peculiarly forcible and pointed ; it is almost a pity you did not see the end of it. I need scarcely explain further the monstrous mistake. Your predecessor in your present house, Mr. Gurney-Brown, was a subscriber to our agency, and our foolish clerks, ignoring alike the dignity of the hyphen and the glory of military rank, positively imagined that Major Brown and Mr. Gurney-Brown were the same person. Thus you were suddenly hurled into the middle of another man's story."

" How on earth does the thing work ? " asked Rupert Grant, with bright and fascinated eyes.

" We believe that we are doing a noble work," said Northover warmly. " It has continually struck us that there is no
element in modern life that is more lamentable than the fact
that the modern man has to seek all artistic existence in a
sedentary state. If he wishes to float into fairyland, he reads
a book ; if he wishes to dash into the thick of battle, he reads
a book ; if he wishes to soar into heaven, he reads a book ; if
he wishes to slide down the banisters, he reads a book. We
give him these visions, but we give him exercise at the same
time, the necessity of leaping from wall to wall, of fighting
strange gentlemen, of running down long streets from pursuers—all healthy and pleasant exercises. We give him a
glimpse of that great morning world of Robin Hood or the
Knights Errant, when one great game was played under the
splendid sky. We give him back his childhood, that godlike
time when we can act stories, be our own heroes, and at the
same instant dance and dream."

Basil gazed at him curiously. The most singular psychological discovery had been reserved to the end, for as the
little business man ceased speaking he had the blazing eyes
of a fanatic.

Major Brown received the explanation with complete
simplicity and good humour.

" Of course ; awfully dense sir," he said. " No doubt
at all, the scheme excellent. But I don't think——" He
paused a moment, and looked dreamily out of the window.
" I don't think you will find me in it. Somehow, when
one's seen—seen the thing itself, you know—blood and
men screaming, one feels about having a little house and
a little hobby ; in the Bible, you know, ' There remaineth
a rest.' "

Northover bowed. Then after a pause, he said :

" Gentlemen, may I offer you my card. If any of the
rest of you desire, at any time, to communicate with me,
despite Major Brown's view of the matter——"

" I should be obliged for your card, sir," said the Major,
in his abrupt but courteous voice. " Pay for chair."

The agent of Romance and Adventure handed his card,
laughing.

It ran, " P. G. Northover, B.A., C.Q.T., Adventure and
Romance Agency, 14 Tanner's Court, Fleet Street."

" What on earth is ' C.Q.T. ' ? " asked Rupert Grant,
looking over the Major's shoulder.

" Don't you know ? " returned Northover. " Haven't you ever heard of the Club of Queer Trades ? "

" There seems to be a confounded lot of funny things we haven't heard of," said the little Major, reflectively. " What's this one ? "

" The Club of Queer Trades is a society consisting exclusively of people who have invented some new and curious way of making money. I was one of the earliest members."

" You deserve to be," said Basil, taking up his great white hat, with a smile, and speaking for the last time that evening.

When they had passed out the Adventure and Romance agent wore a queer smile, as he trod down the fire and locked his desk up. " A fine chap, that Major ; when one hasn't a touch of the poet one stands some chance of being a poem. But to think of such a clockwork little creature of all people getting into the nets of one of Grigsby's tales," and he laughed out aloud in the silence.

Just as the laugh echoed away, there came a sharp knock at the door. An owlish head, with dark moustaches, was thrust in, with deprecating and somewhat absurd inquiry.

" What ! back again, Major ? " cried Northover in surprise. " What can I do for you ? "

The Major shuffled feverishly into the room.

" It's horribly absurd," he said. " Something must have got started in me that I never knew before. But upon my soul I feel the most desperate desire to know the end of it all."

" The end of it all ? "

" Yes," said the Major, " ' Jackals,' and the title-deeds, and ' death to Major Brown.' "

The agent's face grew grave, but his eyes were amused.

" I am terribly sorry, Major," said he, " but what you ask is impossible. I don't know any one I would sooner oblige than you ; but the rules of the agency are strict. The Adventures are confidential ; you are an outsider ; I am not allowed to let you know an inch more than I can help. I do hope you understand——"

" There is no one," said Brown, " who understands discipline better than I do. Thank you very much. Goodnight."

And the little man withdrew for the last time.

. . . . . .

He married Miss Jameson, the lady with the red hair and the green garments. She was an actress, employed (with

many others) by the Romance Agency ; and her marriage
with the prim old veteran caused some stir in her languid and
intellectualised set. She always replied very quietly that she
had met scores of men who acted splendidly in the charades
provided for them by Northover, but that she had only met one
man who went down into a coal-cellar when he really thought
it contained a murderer.

The Major and she are living as happily as birds, in an
absurd villa, and the former has taken to smoking. Otherwise he is unchanged—except, perhaps, there are moments
when, alert and full of feminine unselfishness as the Major
is by nature, he falls into a trance of abstraction. Then his
wife recognises with a concealed smile, by the blind look in
his blue eyes, that he is wondering what were the title-deeds,
and why he was not allowed to mention jackals. But, like
so many old soldiers, Brown is religious, and believes that he
will realise the rest of those purple adventures in a better
world.

CHARLES DICKENS (1812-1870). *Born in " Queer Street " himself, Dickens was always sympathetic towards people in like circumstances ; and the deep pathos and humour of most of his works betray the profoundness of his feelings. This championship of the poor and oppressed, coloured by his emotional genius, won him universal affection. " Boots at the Holly Tree " represents the master in lighter vein.*

BOOTS AT THE HOLLY TREE

WHERE had he been in his time ? he repeated, when I asked him the question. Lord, he had been everywhere ! And what had he been ? Bless you, he had been everything you could mention a'most !

Seen a good deal ? Why, of course he had. I should say so, he could assure me, if I only knew about a twentieth part of what had come in *his* way. Why, it would be easier for him, he expected, to tell what he hadn't seen than what he had. Ah ! A deal, it would.

What was the curiousest thing he had seen ? Well ! He didn't know. He couldn't momently name what was the curiousest thing he had seen,—unless it was a Unicorn,—and he see *him* once at a Fair. But supposing a young gentleman not eight year old was to run away with a fine young woman of seven, might I think *that* a queer start ? Certain. Then that was a start as he himself had had his blessed eyes on, and he had cleaned the shoes they run away in—and they was so little that he couldn't get his hand into 'em.

Master Harry Walmers's father, you see, he lived at the Elmses, down away by Shooter's Hill there, six or seven miles from Lunnon. He was a gentleman of spirit, and good-looking, and held his head up when he walked, and had what you may call Fire about him. He wrote poetry, and he rode, and he ran, and he cricketed, and he danced, and he acted, and he done it all equally beautiful. He was uncommon proud of Master Harry as was his only child ; but he didn't spoil him neither. He was a gentleman that had a will of his own and a eye of his own, and that would be minded. Consequently, though he made quite a companion of the fine

75

bright boy, and was delighted to see him so fond of reading his fairy books, and was never tired of hearing him say my name is Norval, or hearing him sing his songs about Young May Moons is beaming love, and When he as adores thee has left but the name, and that ; still he kept the command over the child, and the child *was* a child, and it's to be wished more of 'em was !

How did Boots happen to know all this ? Why, through being under-gardener. Of course he couldn't be under-gardener, and be always about, in the summer-time, near the windows on the lawn, a mowing, and sweeping, and weeding, and pruning, and this and that, without getting acquainted with the ways of the family. Even supposing Master Harry hadn't come to him one morning early, and said, " Cobbs, how should you spell Norah, if you was asked ? " and then began cutting it in print all over the fence.

He couldn't say he had taken particular notice of children before that ; but really it was pretty to see them two mites a going about the place together, deep in love. And the courage of the boy ! Bless your soul, he'd have throwed off his little hat, and tucked up his little sleeves, and gone in at a Lion, he would, if they had happened to meet one, and she had been frightened of him. One day he stops, along with her, where Boots was hoeing weeds in the gravel, and says, speaking up, " Cobbs," he says, " I like *you*." " Do you, sir ? I'm proud to hear it." " Yes, I do, Cobbs. Why do I like you, do you think, Cobbs ? " " Don't know, Master Harry, I am sure." " Because Norah likes you, Cobbs." " Indeed — sir ? That's very gratifying." " Gratifying, Cobbs ? It's better than millions of the brightest diamonds to be liked by Norah." " Certainly, sir." " You're going away, ain't you, Cobbs ? " " Yes, sir." " Would you like another situation, Cobbs ? " " Well, sir, I shouldn't object, if it was a good 'un." " Then, Cobbs," says he, " you shall be our Head Gardener when we are married. And he tucks her, in her little sky-blue mantle, under his arm, and walks away.

Boots could assure me that it was better than a picter, and equal to a play, to see them babies, with their long, bright, curling hair, their sparkling eyes, and their beautiful light tread, a rambling about the garden, deep in love. Boots was of opinion that the birds believed they was birds, and kept up with 'em, singing to please 'em. Sometimes they would creep under the Tulip-tree, and would sit there with their arms round one another's necks, and their soft cheeks touching, a reading about the Prince and the Dragon, and the good and bad enchanters, and the king's fair daughter. Sometimes he would hear them planning about having a house in a forest, keeping bees and a cow, and living entirely on milk and honey. Once he came upon them by the pond, and heard Master Harry say, " Adorable Norah, kiss me, and say you love me to distraction, or I'll jump in head-foremost." And Boots made no question he would have done it if she hadn't complied. On the whole, Boots said it had a tendency to make him feel as if he was in love himself—only he didn't exactly know who with.

" Cobbs,' said Master Harry, one evening, when Cobbs was watering the flowers, " I am going on a visit, this present Midsummer, to my grandmamma's at York."

" Are you indeed, sir ?   I hope you'll have a pleasant time. I am going into Yorkshire, myself, when I leave here."

" Are you going to your grandmamma's, Cobbs ? "

" No, sir.   I haven't got such a thing."

" Not as a grandmamma, Cobbs ? "

" No, sir."

The boy looked on at the watering of the flowers for a little while, and then said, " I shall be very glad indeed to go, Cobbs, —Norah's going."

" You'll be all right then, sir," says Cobbs, " with your beautiful sweetheart by your side."

" Cobbs," returned the boy, flushing, " I never let anybody joke about it, when I can prevent them."

" It wasn't a joke, sir," says Cobbs, with humility,—" wasn't so meant."

" I am glad of that, Cobbs, because I like you, you know, and you're going to live with us.—Cobbs ! "

" Sir."

" What do you think my grandmamma gives me when I go down there ? "

" I couldn't so much as make a guess, sir."

" A Bank of England five-pound note, Cobbs."

" Whew ! " says Cobbs, " that's a spanking sum of money, Master Harry."

" A person could do a good deal with such a sum of money as that,—couldn't a person, Cobbs ? "

" I believe you, sir ! "

" Cobbs," said the boy, " I'll tell you a secret. At Norah's house, they have been joking her about me, and pretending to laugh at our being engaged,—pretending to make game of it, Cobbs ! "

" Such, sir," says Cobbs, " is the depravity of human natur."

The boy, looking exactly like his father, stood for a few minutes with his glowing face towards the sunset, and then departed with, " Good-night, Cobbs. I'm going in."

If I was to ask Boots how it happened that he was a going to leave that place just at that present time, well, he couldn't rightly answer me. He did suppose he might have stayed there till now if he had been anyways inclined. But, you see, he was younger then, and he wanted change. That's what he wanted,—change. Mr. Walmers, he said to him when he gave him notice of his intentions to leave, " Cobbs," he says, " have you anythink to complain of ? I make the inquiry because if I find that any of my people really has anythink to complain of, I wish to make it right if I can." " No, sir," says Cobbs ; " thanking you, sir, I find myself as well sitiwated here as I could hope to be anywheres. The truth is, sir, that I'm a going to seek my fortun'." " Oh, indeed, Cobbs ! " he says ; " I hope you may find it." And Boots could assure me—which he did, touching his hair with his boot-jack, as a salute in the way of his present calling—that he hadn't found it yet.

Well, sir ! Boots left the Elmses when his time was up, and Master Harry, he went down to the old lady's at York, which old lady would have given that child the teeth out of her head (if she had had any), she was so wrapped up in him. What does that Infant do,—for Infant you may call him and be within the mark,—but cut away from that old lady's with his Norah, on a expedition to go to Gretna Green and be married !

Sir, Boots was at this identical Holly-Tree Inn (having left it several times since to better himself, but always come back through one thing or another), when, one summer after-noon, the coach drives up, and out of the coach gets them two children. The Guard says to our Governor, " I don't quite make out these little passengers, but the young gentleman's words was, that they was to be brought here." The young gentleman gets out ; hands his lady out ; gives the Guard something for himself ; says to our Governor, " We're to stop here to-night, please. Sitting-room and two bedrooms will be required. Chops and cherry-pudding for two!" and tucks her, in her little sky-blue mantle, under his arm, and walks into the house much bolder than Brass.

Boots leaves me to judge what the amazement of that establishment was, when these two tiny creatures all alone by themselves was marched into the Angel,—much more so, when he, who had seen them without their seeing him, give the Governor his views of the expedition they was upon. "Cobbs," says the Governor, "if this is so, I must set off myself to York, and quiet their friends' minds. In which case you must keep your eye upon 'em, till I come back. But before I take these measures, Cobbs, I should wish you to find from themselves whether your opinion is correct." "Sir, to you," says Cobbs, "that shall be done directly."

So Boots goes upstairs to the Angel, and there he finds Master Harry on a e-normous sofa,—immense at any time, but looking like the Great Bed of Ware, compared with him,— a drying the eyes of Miss Norah with his pocket-hankecher. Their little legs was entirely off the ground, of course, and it really is not possible for Boots to express to me how small them children looked.

"It's Cobbs! It's Cobbs!" cried Master Harry, and comes running to him, and catching hold of his hand. Miss Norah comes running to him on t'other side and catching hold of his t'other hand, and they both jump for joy.

"I see you a getting out, sir," says Cobbs. "I thought it was you. I thought I couldn't be mistaken in your height and figure. What's the object of your journey, sir?— Matrimonial?"

"We are going to be married, Cobbs, at Gretna Green," returned the boy. "We have run away on purpose. Norah has been in rather low spirits, Cobbs; but she'll be happy, now we have found you to be our friend."

"Thank you, sir, and thank you, miss," says Cobbs, "for your good opinion. Did you bring any luggage with you, sir?"

If I will believe Boots when he gives me his word and honour upon it, the lady had got a parasol, a smelling-bottle, a round and a half of cold buttered toast, eight peppermint drops, and a hair-brush,—seemingly a doll's. The gentleman had got about half a dozen yards of string, a knife, three or four sheets of writing-paper folded up surprising small, a orange, and a Chaney mug with his name upon it.

" What may be the exact natur of your plans, sir ? " says
Cobbs.

" To go on," replied the boy,—which the courage of that
boy was something wonderful !—" in the morning, and be
married to-morrow."

" Just so, sir," says Cobbs.   " Would it meet your views,
sir, if I was to accompany you ? "

When Cobbs said this, they both jumped for joy again,
and cried out, " Oh, yes, yes, Cobbs ! Yes ! "

" Well, sir," says Cobbs.   " If you will excuse my having
the freedom to give an opinion, what I should recommend
would be this.   I'm acquainted with a pony, sir, which, put
in a pheayton that I could borrow, would take you and Mrs.
Harry Walmers, Junior (myself driving, if you approved),
to the end of your journey in a very short space of time.   I
am not altogether sure, sir, that this pony will be at liberty
to-morrow, but even if you had to wait over to-morrow for
him, it might be worth your while.   As to the small account
here, sir, in case you was to find yourself running at all short,
that don't signify ; because I'm a part proprietor of this inn,
and it could stand over."

Boots assures me that when they clapped their hands, and
jumped for joy again, and called him " Good Cobbs ! " and
" Dear Cobbs ! " and bent across him to kiss one another in
the delight of their confiding hearts, he felt himself the meanest
rascal for deceiving 'em that ever was born.

" Is there anything you want just at present, sir ? " says
Cobbs, mortally ashamed of himself.

" We should like some cakes after dinner," answered
Master Harry, folding his arms, putting out one leg, and
looking straight at him, " and two apples,—and jam.   With
dinner we should like to have toast-and-water.   But Norah
has always been accustomed to half a glass of currant wine at
dessert.   And so have I."

" It shall be ordered at the bar, sir," says Cobbs ; and
away he went.

Boots has the feeling as fresh upon him at this minute of
speaking as he had then, that he would far rather have had it
out in half-a-dozen rounds with the Governor than have
combined with him ; and that he wished with all his heart
there was any impossible place where those two babies could
make an impossible marriage, and live impossibly happy ever
afterwards.   However, as it couldn't be, he went into the

Governor's plans, and the Governor set off for York in half
an hour.

The way in which the women of that house—without
exception—every one of 'em—married *and* single—took to
that boy when they heard the story, Boots considers surprising.
It was as much as he could do to keep 'em from dashing into
the room and kissing him. They climbed up all sorts of
places, at the risk of their lives, to look at him through a pane
of glass. They was seven deep at the keyhole. They was
out of their minds about him and his bold spirit.

In the evening, Boots went into the room to see how the
runaway couple was getting on. The gentleman was on the
window-seat, supporting the lady in his arms. She had tears
upon her face, and was lying, very tired and half asleep, with
her head upon his shoulder.

" Mrs. Harry Walmers, Junior, fatigued, sir ? " says Cobbs.

" Yes, she is tired, Cobbs ; but she is not used to be away
from home, and she has been in low spirits again. Cobbs, do
you think you could bring a biffin, please ? "

" I ask your pardon, sir," says Cobbs. " What was it
you—— ? "

" I think a Norfolk biffin would rouse her, Cobbs. She is
very fond of them."

Boots withdrew in search of the required restorative, and,
when he brought it in, the gentleman handed it to the lady,
and fed her with a spoon, and took a little himself ; the lady
being heavy with sleep, and rather cross. " What should you
think, sir," says Cobbs, " of a chamber candlestick ? " The
gentleman approved ; the chambermaid went first, up the
great staircase ; the lady, in her sky-blue mantle, followed,
gallantly escorted by the gentleman ; the gentleman embraced
her at her door, and retired to his own apartment, where Boots
softly locked him up.

Boots couldn't but feel with increased acuteness what a
base deceiver he was, when they consulted him at breakfast
(they had ordered sweet milk-and-water, and toast and currant
jelly overnight) about the pony. It really was as much as he
could do, he don't mind confessing to me, to look them two
young things in the face, and think what a wicked old father
of lies he had grown up to be. Howsomever, he went on a
lying like a Trojan about the pony. He told 'em that it did
so unfort'nately happen that the pony was half clipped, you
see, and that he couldn't be taken out in that state, for fear it

should strike to his inside. But that he'd be finished clipping in the course of the day, and that to-morrow morning at eight o'clock the pheayton would be ready. Boots's view of the whole case, looking back on it in my room, is, that Mrs. Harry Walmers, Junior, was beginning to give in. She hadn't had her hair curled when she went to bed, and she didn't seem quite up to brushing it herself, and its getting in her eyes put her out. But nothing put out Master Harry. He sat behind his breakfast-cup, a tearing away at the jelly, as if he had been his own father.

After breakfast, Boots is inclined to consider that they drawed soldiers,—at least, he knows that many such was found in the fireplace, all on horseback. In the course of the morning, Master Harry rang the bell,—it was surprising how that there boy did carry on,—and said, in a sprightly way, "Cobbs, is there any good walks in this neighbourhood?"

"Yes, sir," says Cobbs. "There's Love-lane."

"Get out with you, Cobbs!"—that was that there boy's expression,—"you're joking."

"Begging your pardon, sir," says Cobbs, "there really is Love-lane. And a pleasant walk it is, and proud shall I be to show it to yourself and Mrs. Harry Walmers, Junior."

"Norah, dear," said Master Harry, "this is curious. We really ought to see Love-lane. Put on your bonnet, my sweetest darling, and we will go there with Cobbs."

Boots leaves me to judge what a Beast he felt himself to be, when that young pair told him, as they all three jogged along together, that they had made up their minds to give him two thousand guineas a year as head-gardener, on accounts of his being so true a friend to 'em. Boots could have wished at the moment that the earth would have opened and swallowed him up, he felt so mean, with their beaming eyes a looking at him, and believing him. Well, sir, he turned the conversation as well as he could, and he took 'em down Love-lane to the water-meadows, and there Master Harry would have drowned himself in half a moment more, a getting out a water-lily for her,—but nothing daunted that boy. Well, sir, they was tired out. All being so new and strange to 'em, they was tired as tired could be. And they laid down on a bank of daisies, like the children in the wood, leastways meadows, and fell asleep.

Boots don't know—perhaps I do,—but never mind, it don't signify either way—why it made a man fit to make a fool of himself to see them two pretty babies a lying there in the clear still sunny day, not dreaming half so hard when they was asleep as they done when they was awake. But, lord! when you come to think of yourself, you know, and what a game you have been up to ever since you was in your own cradle, and what a poor sort of a chap you are, and how it's always either Yesterday with you, or else To-morrow, and never To-day, that's where it is !

Well, sir, they woke up at last, and then one thing was getting pretty clear to Boots, namely, that Mrs. Harry Walmerses, Junior's temper was on the move. When Master Harry took her round the waist, she said he " teased her so " ; and when he says, " Norah, my young May Moon, your Harry tease you ? " she tells him, " Yes ; and I want to go home ! "

A biled fowl, and baked bread-and-butter pudding, brought Mrs. Walmers up a little ; but Boots could have wished, he must privately own to me, to have seen her more sensible of the woice of love, and less abandoning of herself to currants. However, Master Harry, he kept up, and his noble heart was as fond as ever. Mrs. Walmers turned very sleepy about dusk, and began to cry. Therefore, Mrs. Walmers went off to bed as per yesterday ; and Master Harry ditto repeated.

About eleven or twelve at night comes back the Governor in a chaise, along with Mr. Walmers and a elderly lady. Mr. Walmers looks amused and very serious, both at once, and says to our missis, " We are much indebted to you, ma'am, for your kind care of our little children, which we can never sufficiently acknowledge. Pray, ma'am, where is my boy ? " Our missis says, " Cobbs has the dear child in charge, sir. Cobbs, show Forty ! " Then he says to Cobbs, " Ah, Cobbs, I am glad to see you ! I understood you was here ! " And Cobbs says, " Yes, sir. Your most obedient, sir."

I may be surprised to hear Boots say it, perhaps ; but Boots assures me that his heart beat like a hammer, going upstairs. " I beg your pardon, sir," says he, while unlocking the door ; " I hope you are not angry with Master Harry. For Master Harry is a fine boy, sir, and will do you credit and honour." And Boots signifies to me, that, if the fine boy's father had contradicted him in the daring state of mind in which he then was, he thinks he should have " fetched him a crack," and taken the consequences.

But Mr. Walmers only says, " No, Cobbs. No, my good fellow. Thank you ! " And, the door being opened, goes in.

Boots goes in too, holding the light, and he sees Mr. Walmers go up to the bedside, bend gently down, and kiss the little sleeping face. Then he stands looking at it for a moment, looking wonderfully like it (they do say he ran away with Mrs. Walmers) ; and then he gently shakes the little shoulder.

" Harry, my dear boy ! Harry ! "

Master Harry starts up and looks at him. Looks at Cobbs too. Such is the honour of that mite, that he looks at Cobbs, to see whether he has brought him into trouble.

" I am not angry, my child. I only want you to dress yourself and come home."

" Yes, pa."

Master Harry dresses himself quickly. His breast begins to swell when he has nearly finished, and it swells more and more as he stands, at last, a looking at his father : his father standing a looking at him, the quiet image of him.

" Please may I "—the spirit of that little creatur, and the way he kept his rising tears down !—" please, dear pa—may I —kiss Norah before I go ? "

" You may, my child."

So he takes Master Harry in his hand, and Boots leads the way with the candle, and they come to that other bedroom, where the elderly lady is seated by the bed, and poor little Mrs. Harry Walmers, Junior, is fast asleep. There the father lifts the child up to the pillow, and he lays his little face down for an instant by the little warm face of poor unconscious little Mrs. Harry Walmers, Junior, and gently draws it to him,— a sight so touching to the chambermaids who are peeping through the door, that one of them calls out, " It's a shame to part 'em ! " But this chambermaid was always, as Boots informs me, a soft-hearted one. Not that there was any harm in that girl. Far from it.

Finally, Boots says, that's all about it. Mr. Walmers drove away in the chaise, having hold of Master Harry's hand. The elderly lady and Mrs. Harry Walmers, Junior, that was never to be (she married a Captain long afterwards, and died in India), went off next day. In conclusion, Boots put it to me whether I hold with him in two opinions : firstly, that there are not many couples on their way to be married who are half as innocent of guile as those two children ; secondly, that it would be a jolly good thing for a great many couples on their way to be married, if they could only be stopped in time, and brought back separately.

J. S. FLETCHER (1863–) *was born in Halifax, and was for a long time associated as a journalist with the North of England. He had already won a reputation as an authority on rural life before he made his mark as an outstanding author of cleverly constructed detective stories and tales of adventure. He has also contributed several well-documented monographs on Yorkshire history and antiquities.*

THE CONVICT AND THE CLERICS

To a man who had just succeeded in escaping from prison, Brychester, in the still hours of an autumn morning, presented possibilities and opportunities which Medhurst, who had been a shrewd citizen of the world before he became a criminal, was quick to perceive and to take advantage of. Brychester itself was unique in its arrangements. One of the smallest of English cathedral cities, it was packed into very little room ; you could walk round its enclosing walls within half an hour. It only possessed two streets ; one ran from north to south, the other from east to west ; they met at the Cross in the middle of the city, and there split it up into four quarters. There were little lanes and alleys in those four quarters ; there were, also, at the backs of the old houses and mansions, large, roomy, leafy gardens. It was in one of these, a veritable wilderness, that Medhurst hid himself about three o'clock in the morning, after breaking out of the city gaol, which stood a mile away beyond the walls.

There had been very little of actual breaking out to be done. Medhurst, recently sentenced to a considerable term of penal servitude, consigned to Brychester Gaol to await eventual delivery to Dartmoor or Portland, had kept his observant eyes wide open from the moment he exchanged his own smart apparel for the dingy, arrow-ornamented garb of the convict. He was naturally a man of resource and ingenuity, and he meant to escape the unpleasant consequences of his misdeeds. Brychester Gaol was old-fashioned ; its warders were a little slack in attending to their duties. And Medhurst watched his opportunity, and, by means of a little interference with the lock of his cell, and a watchful observation of the movements of men on night-duty, and a carefully acquired knowledge of the outer works of his prison-house, managed to get free with little difficulty. And here he was, in the earliest hours of an October day, shivering a little, but eager and ready, in the summer-house of a shady garden—wondering what to do next.

Medhurst's great immediate difficulty was that which confronts all convicts who break prison—his clothes. There was another in the lack of money, but the clothes problem was nearest and most important. If he only had clothes he could get away—he had no doubt he could get away even in a penniless condition. Of course, if he had money, he could get away all the more easily. But clothes were the prime necessity—and he reflected that they must be good. He was a man of exceptionally good presence—a tall, well set-up, rather distinguished-looking man, as many people had observed when he stood in the dock. He felt that he would be less conspicuous in really good attire—the use of which would be natural to him—than in, say, the garb of a navvy or of a labourer. One fact was certain, before daybreak he must find garments wherein to get out of Brychester. For reasons into which it is not necessary to enter, Medhurst believed that his escape would not be noticed until six o'clock in the morning. He had, therefore, three hours in which to do something. And, believing that if one has something to do, one should do it at once, he moved stealthily out of his hiding-place and began to examine his surroundings. He was able to make out that the old-fashioned garden in which he stood was one of several lying at the rear of a number of quaint-roofed houses, situate between the high walls of Brychester Cathedral—houses, in fact, tenanted by the principal ecclesiastical dignitaries. Surely, he thought, there must be some means of penetrating into one of these quiet residences, of obtaining sober and befitting raiment ? At any rate, seeing that much depended on the matter, he would have a try for it.

It was very quiet, almost painfully quiet, in these cloistered shades. Once or twice Medhurst heard an owl hoot from its retreat in some ruinous building on the outskirts of the city ; now and then he caught the screech of a railway whistle far off across the land ; every quarter of an hour the silvery chime of the cathedral clock rang above his head. But he heard nothing of the heavy tread of the patrolling policeman ; in these quiet gardens there seemed to be small fear of interference.

He climbed a wall or two, made his way through a paling or two, looked round the rearward premises of one or two houses, always careful, always watching. And suddenly, in one of the largest houses, he found an open window. It was not much open—only an inch or two—but it gave Medhurst the very chance he wanted. In another minute he had raised the sash, squeezed himself through the aperture, and dropped quietly into what appeared to be a softly carpeted passage.

Medhurst had lately spent so much time in the dark that he had learnt how to see in it. This is an accomplishment which may certainly be acquired by any one who cares to acquire it ; all you have got to do is to wait with patience until you perceive that darkness is not quite so impenetrable as you believed it to be. Objects begin to reveal themselves—especially against windows—besides, there are gradations of darkness. Medhurst, bringing his skill to work, quickly found that he was in a side passage which led into a hall ; in the hall he had come to a broad staircase. The carpeting of passage, hall and staircase was particularly thick and soft ; nevertheless, Medhurst sat down on the bottom steps of the staircase and took off his prison footgear. For he was going upstairs— which is where raiment is usually to be found.

Big man though he was, Medhurst went up the stairs with less noise than a cat would have made. He blessed the builder of the house ; here was no inferior wood to creak at the slightest pressure. He blessed the taste of the owner of the house, who evidently loved velvet-pile carpets. And he was beginning to wish that he had a light when he saw one.

It was certainly not much of a light—a mere crack that shone from a slightly opened door. Medhurst tiptoed to it through a silence as deep as that which no doubt reigned in the aisles of the adjacent cathedral. Here, again, was matter for hearty self-congratulation ; the people of the house were evidently all sound sleepers. He arrived at the door, and listened. He peered through the slight opening, and saw that the light came from an oil-stove, partially turned on. He had an idea that this might be a nursery, and he listened more carefully than before, trying to catch the sound of a child's faint breathing. But, as he heard no sound at all, he gently pushed open the door until he could introduce his head and shoulders. And he saw that this was a dressing-room. He hesitated, listened intently, and glided across the threshold.

Always an adept at sizing up a situation, Medhurst saw the splendid possibilities of this as soon as he had given it one quick, all-comprehending glance. He was in the palace of the Lord Bishop of Brychester! There, duly laid out on a dressing-bench, all ready against the morning's toilet duties, were the episcopal garments—the breeches, the apron, the gaiters, the straight-cut coat. There was spotless linen, the round collar, the episcopal stock—there was everything. It was evident that the bishop, having taken his tub of a morning, had nothing to do but walk into this comfortably warmed dressing-room and array himself in his clothes.

" Bishops, however," soliloquised Medhurst, " have doubtless several changes of raiment. At any rate, his Lordship of Brychester won't find these togs here when he next wants them."

For Medhurst saw his opportunity, his magnificent chance. He would go out of Brychester in episcopal attire ; he would masquerade as the lawful bishop. He knew the bishop by sight—his lordship had visited the gaol during Medhurst's time. In build and appearance the convict and the ecclesiastic were not unlike. Both were tall, well-made, and athletic-looking men. This would do excellently—excellently ! In the darkness of the autumn morning nobody would be able to tell the false from the true during the few minutes at the railway-station which would be necessary. It was a veritable inter-position of Providence.

Always keeping his ears cocked, Medhurst swiftly stripped off his convict garb, and got into the episcopal paraphernalia. He had a little trouble with the apron, and with the gaiters, and with the stock, but he was a handy man, quick of ideas and possessed of supple fingers, and in a very few minutes he found himself properly arrayed. There was a full-length mirror on one side of the room. He caught a glimpse of himself in the half light, and he smiled complacently. But he smiled a great deal more when, turning to a dressing-table, he saw, lying upon its spotless cover, a sovereign, a half-sovereign, and a little silver. He gathered the coins together noiselessly, and deposited them in the episcopal breeches, feeling heartily thankful that their owner had emptied his pockets when he went to bed. Here, again, Providence certainly seemed to be favouring him.

Medhurst now wanted nothing but these very essential things ; a muffler, an overcoat, and the Doctor of Divinity's hat which bishops always wear. These, he concluded, he would find in the hall, and he was about to set off in search of them when he suddenly caught sight of his convict's dress. It would never do to leave that about. Certainly it would come out in time—in a few hours really—that a convict had broken out of his gaol and into the palace, and had exchanged his clothes for the bishop's. But Medhurst desired that the knowledge should be restricted as long as possible. Here, again, he was favoured by an inspiration and an opportunity. He saw a black handbag, inconspicuous and much worn, on the side of which was painted in faded white letters the words, "The Bishop of Brychester." He lifted this on to a chair, and opened it. Inside it he found a complete Norfolk jacket-suit of dark grey cloth, together with a cap of the same material, and certain accompaniments in the way of shirts, stockings, and ties. This, in fact, was the outfit which the bishop kept in readiness for golfing expeditions. Whenever he took such jaunts there was nothing to do but pick it up, and march off with it. Medhurst saw splendid possibilities in this. Without further delay he crammed his convict garb into an empty space, closed the bag, and carried it quietly down to the hall.

Here Medhurst took a risk. After remaining for some time at the foot of the stairs he ventured on striking a match. One tiny gleam of its light showed him the coat, the hat, the muffler. He put all these things on in the darkness. No sound came from above, or from around ; the house was as quiet as ever. And so, fully equipped for his journey, Medhurst sat down on a chair close to the hall door—to wait.

Medhurst knew Brychester. In his pre-criminal days he had often visited the city ; in fact, he had spent a week there just before his arrest. And he knew that an express train to London left Brychester station at ten minutes past four every morning, arriving at Victoria a few minutes before six. By that train he proposed to travel—in the character of the Lord Bishop of the Diocese. According to his reckonings nobody would stir in the palace until six o'clock ; it would be some time after that before the theft of the bishop's garments was discovered. Before any hue and cry could be roused he, Medhurst, would be safe in town. All that was necessary now was to wait until the cathedral clock chimed four ; then he would let himself

out, walk quietly through the Close into the little station, take
his ticket, and be whirled away.

Medhurst found no difficulty in putting this theory into
practice. On the first stroke of four he quietly opened the
front door, picked up the handbag, and stole quietly away
across the Close and through the deserted streets to the
station. And there everything turned out even better than he
had dared to hope. He had pulled down the beribboned brim
of his episcopal hat ; he had swathed his face up to the tip
of his nose in the episcopal muffler ; he had turned the collar
of the episcopal overcoat up to his ears. There were few
people about in the half-lighted station, and the clerk in the
booking-office, and the obsequious porter who possessed himself of the handbag, and opened the door of a first-class compartment, had not a doubt that the gentleman whom they sped
on his journey was the Bishop of Brychester.

" And indeed I might almost begin to believe that I am he ! "
laughed Medhurst, when the train was sliding rapidly away
over the dark country. " I am he, at any rate, for two hours.
But what's going to happen then ? "

As a preliminary to further operations, he searched the
pockets of the appropriated garments. He found nothing in
them, however, but a few cards in a well-worn case. He was
not sorry to find these cards ; he foresaw that they might
come in useful later on. Then he searched the bag again.
There was nothing in it but what he had already seen—and
his own broad-arrowed attire. He thought once of throwing
that out of the window, then of hiding it under the cushions of
the carriage ; on second considerations, he closed the bag on
it and the bishop's mufti.

The possession of that mufti gave Medhurst a new idea.
He wanted to reach the house of an old friend in Kent, a friend
whom he could fully trust, and who would certainly manage to
get him secretly away to the Continent. This friend lived in
a small village near Sevenoaks, a village so small that its
inhabitants would certainly be excited if a bishop's apron and
gaiters were seen in it. But they would not take undue notice
of a gentleman in an inconspicuous Norfolk jacket and knicker-
bockers. Obviously, then, the thing to do was to make yet
another change of attire.

When the express ran into Victoria, Medhurst seized his
bag and made for a taxicab which stood almost opposite the
point where his compartment had come to a halt. The light

was of the early morning order; the chauffeur was half-asleep. He saw what he considered to be an ecclesiastical gent in leggings and a queer hat, and sprang down and opened the door.

" Go round to the hotel," said the supposed dignitary in muffled tones. The chauffeur drove round to the Grosvenor Hotel; his fare got out, took his bag, and spoke one word : " Wait ! "

The chauffeur touched his cap, and Medhurst walked into the hall, to be welcomed by an obsequious official who knew a bishop when he saw one.

" I wish," said Medhurst, " for a room in which I can change my clothes. And perhaps you can send me some coffee up to it ? I—the fact is, I am going into the country this morning to play golf, and I wish to put on more suitable attire. I shall leave my bag here, and call for it—and to change my garments again—towards evening. You will, of course, charge the room to me for the day."

Half an hour later Medhurst, much more comfortable in layman's garb, walked down to the hall, intending to re-enter his cab. But with his hand on the latch, he suddenly came to a dead halt. Through the glass panel of the door, he saw the taxicab moving off. And in it, just settling himself comfortably against the padded cushions was—a bishop !

Medhurst glanced cautiously around him. There was nobody about in the hall beyond a servant or two engaged in domestic occupations. On its stand near the window of the office reposed the register wherein guests signed their names. Medhurst went over to it, swung its heavy covers open, and found the recent entries. There, under date of the previous day, he read one line which, to him, stood out conspicuous from the rest.

" The Lord Bishop of Tuscaloosa and Mrs. Sharpe-Benham."

Medhurst closed the heavy book, and turned away chuckling quietly. He understood the situation now. And he began to thank his stars that an unusually gloomy morning, a sleepy chauffeur, and the presence at the hotel of a Colonial prelate who, no doubt, wished to get to some very early service, had made his own circumstances much easier. It was with a feeling of immense satisfaction that he walked out of the hotel, and strolled off into the unwonted liberty of the streets.

II

THE chauffeur whom Medhurst had bidden to wait outside the hotel, had given no particular attention to his fare. He was not very well acquainted with the peculiarities of clerical attire ; certainly he could not tell a dean from an archdeacon, nor an archdeacon from a bishop. All he knew was that there were clergymen who wore what he called leggings, and had the brims of their hats tied to the crowns with bits of ribbon, and that these were big pots in their walk of life.

He saw his fare go into the hotel, and he believed it was his fare who came hurriedly out of the hotel twenty minutes later, who jumped quickly into the cab, and who bade him make all haste to St. Paul's Cathedral. He had not the ghost of a notion that this was not his original fare at all, but was in reality the Bishop of Tuscaloosa, a Colonial prelate, just then in England, who was due at St. Paul's at five minutes to seven o'clock, who had slightly overslept himself, and who, rushing out of his hotel, had leapt into the first vehicle he saw.

And when he set this genuine prelate down at St. Paul's, and had a better opportunity of looking at him, he still believed him to be the man he had taken up just an hour before, when the Brychester express steamed into Victoria. The Bishop of Tuscaloosa glanced up at the clock of St. Paul's, and turned to the chauffeur.

" I think you had better wait for me," he said. " I shall not be here very long, and then I want to be driven elsewhere."

Even then nothing struck the chauffeur as being different. He merely glanced at the tall and athletic figure careering up the steps (Sharpe-Benham had been a noted man in the playing-fields in his ante-Colonial days), lighted his pipe, purchased a halfpenny morning paper from a passing itinerant, and settled himself down in his seat until the bishop had finished his business or his devotions. He was still reading the latest racing news when, forty minutes later, the bishop emerged from the cathedral in company with another clergyman. The other clergyman, as they came up to the cab, made some facetious remark about the wickedness of keeping taxicabs waiting while the meters ran on unchecked.

" I know—I know," said the bishop. " But the fact is, I am obliged to drive some distance into the East End, and this cab is so good and comfortable that I decided to keep it."

The other clergyman laughed, shook hands, and went off in the direction of the deanery, and the bishop turned to the chauffeur.

" I want you," he said, " to drive me to St. Hedwige's Church at East Ham. That's a long way, isn't it ? "

The chauffeur folded up his newspaper, and crammed it into his pocket.

" Pretty tidy way that, sir," he answered. " Whereabout is this church, sir ? "

" That we must find out when we get to East Ham," said the bishop. " But—I think I must have some breakfast before I go so far." He paused, gazing wistfully around him at the tall buildings. " I suppose there is no restaurant or anything of that sort about here ? " he asked.

" Cannon Street Station Hotel just round the corner, sir," suggested the chauffeur. " Get breakfast there, sir."

" That," replied the bishop, getting into the cab, " will do excellently. We will go there first, then."

The chauffeur drove along to Cannon Street Station, pointed out the hotel entrance to his fare, and prepared to do more waiting. The bishop, who was a man of kindly nature, looked at his driver thoughtfully.

" Perhaps you, too, would like to breakfast ? " he said. " If so, pray do. I suppose I shall be three-quarters of an hour, at any rate."

" Thank you, sir," said the chauffeur. He glanced at the clock and saw that eight was about to strike. " I'll be back here at twenty-to-nine, sir," he went on. " Ain't had no breakfast meself yet ! " he added, with a grin.

The bishop smiled, nodded, and walked into the hotel. He was shown into the coffee-room with the politeness due to his dignity. He ordered his food, he asked for the *Times*, he settled himself quietly and comfortably to his breakfast, he took his time over it. The waiter who attended to him had given him a seat near the fire ; the bishop, satisfied with his own immediate affairs, did not pay any attention to the other people in the room. And he certainly did not observe a rather large, official-faced sort of person who came quietly in, and, under cover of a general look round, contrived to eye him, the bishop, with a searching inspection.

At a quarter to nine o'clock the bishop laid aside the *Times* on one hand, and his napkin on the other, and inserted his fingers in the pocket wherein he usually carried his ready cash. To his horror he found that there was no cash there. He hastily felt for his pocket-book, in which he kept a bank-note or two in readiness for possible emergencies. But his pocket was empty—all his pockets were empty. Then he suddenly remembered that, in the hurry incident upon his belated arising that morning, he had left his loose cash, his purse, his pocket-book, all his trifles, on his dressing-table. It was awkward, but it was no great matter, after all. He summoned the head-waiter, who came forward with a respectful presentation of the bill.

" I am sorry, but I have left my purse and all my belongings at the Grosvenor Hotel where I am staying," said the bishop. " I left there very hastily this morning to keep an appointment at St. Paul's. But I have a taxi-cab waiting for me downstairs, and I will send the driver at once to fetch my purse."

The head-waiter replied that that would be quite all right, and the bishop walked out of the room, a little vexed with himself for having slept ten minutes over his time. He went downstairs, and was about to step into the station, where he saw the taxicab awaiting him, when the official-faced person who had eyed him from the door of the coffee-room, and who had exchanged a word or two with the head-waiter when the bishop walked out, came up from behind, and stopped him with a polite but frigid bow.

" May I have a word with you, sir ? " he asked.

The bishop turned in surprise. There was a note of firmness in the man's voice which converted the request into something very like a command. The bishop, a man of spirit, felt his face flush a little.

" You wish to speak to me ? " he said.

" If you please," replied the man. He indicated the door of a side-room, and bowed the bishop within. " I am sorry," he continued, in the same firm and frigid tone ; " I understand your bill is not paid ? "

The bishop's first flush changed to something more vivid.

" Really ! " he exclaimed. " This is——" But there he pulled himself up ; after all, the fault was his own. " I have just explained to your head-waiter that I am sending for my purse," he continued. " I left it on my dressing-table, being in a hurry this morning. I have a taxicab outside—the driver will fetch what I want."

The official-faced person still seemed very firm. He glanced at the episcopal apron.

" You are the Bishop of ——" he began.

" I am the Bishop of Tuscaloosa," answered the captive, with some asperity.

" Where is that ? " demanded the inquisitor, more firmly than ever.

" Really, really ! " exclaimed the bishop. " This is—my good man, do you really suggest that——"

" I suggest nothing," replied the other. " I am merely asking for information. You come here, run up a bill, leave without paying it, and—to be plain—I may as well tell you that I am a police-officer. The fact of the case is," he went on, as another formidable-looking person entered the room, " the fact of the case is, the palace of the Bishop of Brychester was broken into early this morning by an escaped convict, who is believed to have got away by the four o'clock train from Brychester in the bishop's clothes. Now you answer the description of that convict."

The bishop felt as if he were suddenly deprived of speech. Just as suddenly he laughed.

" My good sir ! " he exclaimed. " This is ridiculous ! Utterly ridiculous ! I am the Bishop of Tuscaloosa, which is in Canada. I am at present staying at the Grosvenor Hotel ; I have just come up from St. Paul's Cathedral, where I am well known to many members of the Chapter. The chauffeur who is without will tell you that he has just driven me from the Grosvenor Hotel, and——"

The first man made a sign to the second, who left the room, and instantly returned with the driver of the taxicab. The first man directed the driver's attention to the bishop.

" Where did you drive this gentleman from ? " he asked peremptorily.

The driver glanced at all three with signs of rising suspicion.

" Well, from St. Paul's last," he answered, " and before that from the Grosvenor Hotel, and before that from Victoria Station ! "

The bishop started.

" From Victoria Station ! " he exclaimed. " My good fellow, you did not drive me from Victoria Station ! You drove me——"

The driver became actively suspicious ; so far he had not

seen the colour of the bishop's money. Besides, he had
waited twenty minutes outside the Grosvenor.

"Ho, didn't I!" he exclaimed. "I suppose I didn't
drive you round from Victoria 'rival platform to the Grosvenor,
did I, where I waited twenty minutes for yer? Oh, no!" He
made a derisive face, seeing how things were going, and turned
to the two men.

"He came into Victoria by the Brychester express," he
continued. "That what gets in just afore six—course he
did!"

The detectives closed in upon the unhappy bishop. There
was no doubt in their minds that they had effected a smart, if
lucky capture. And it was only in accordance with the nature
of things that they convoyed their captive there and then to the
nearest police-station.

III

MEDHURST strolled away from the hotel towards Victoria
Street, thinking. His next move, he reflected, ought to
be towards definite liberty. Already the discovery of his
nocturnal doings at Brychester Palace would have been made.
Well—it would take some little time for the local police to communicate with London. It would be found out—nothing
more easy—that he had left Brychester by the four o'clock
train; very good, but even then he reckoned that he still had
an hour or two's start of everything. The first thing to do was
to get to his trusty friend. And he suddenly remembered that
the trusty friend had an office in London, close to the Mansion
House. Why not go there instead of running the risk of a
railway journey into Kent? The principal stations would be
watched; he had better keep away from them until he had
effected yet another change of clothes.

Medhurst accordingly made for the City. He turned into
the Underground Railway, and took a ticket for the Mansion
House. Amongst the early crowd of men going to shops and
offices he would feel himself safe; however anxious to recapture
him the police might be, they could not set patrols in every
street of London. He would stroll about the City until nine
o'clock or so, when his friend would be likely to put in an
appearance—Medhurst remembered that the friend was an
early bird, who came up by one of the first trains. He felt no
fear now—it seemed to him that all was going very well indeed.

In the Underground train Medhurst made an interesting discovery. In the breast-pocket of the Norfolk jacket he found a cigar-case. There were four uncommonly fine cigars in it—he at once lighted one, with the keen zest and enjoyment of a man who had not tasted tobacco for long, weary weeks. But, as he was examining the case, before restoring it to his pocket, he found something else. In a slip-pocket, obviously designed to carry stamps or similar small articles, he found a couple of blank cheques of the Brychester and County Bank. Their lawful owner, the bishop, was evidently a careful man, who provided for unforeseen contingencies ; he carried a blank cheque in case he should want cash ; anybody, of course, will cash a cheque for a bishop.

Medhurst laughed over this discovery. It was, however, of no particular interest to him just then, and he put the cheques back in their place, and the cigar-case in his pocket, and smoked in great contentment until he came to the Mansion House Station. There he got out and went up into the streets, which were already beginning to be busy.

It was immaterial to him where he went for the next hour or so ; accordingly he loafed around anywhere, but took good care always to be moving, as if with a purpose. He went along by the Bank, and round by the Guildhall, and into Aldersgate, and through various small streets into Smithfield ; there he turned south, and made his way into Ludgate Hill. And loafing about there he paused to gaze into the window of a bookseller's shop, and before he was aware of it he found himself staring at a book which stood with title-page and frontispiece exposed, on a shelf immediately in front of him. The title-page conveyed the information that this was a work on Athletics and Christianity, by the Lord Bishop of Brychester ; the frontispiece was a photogravure of the right reverend author. And underneath it was a facsimile of the bishop's signature.

Medhurst was a man of rapid thought, and he was temperamentally quick at seizing opportunities. He saw a fine opportunity immediately before him. In his pocket reposed two of the Bishop of Brychester's blank cheques, there before him was a very good reproduction of the bishop's autograph. A rare opportunity, indeed ; for Medhurst was an expert imitator of other people's handwriting. That, indeed, was why he had come into contact with the law. Those who had administered the law in his case had been so struck by his expertness, in fact, that they had judged it well to consign him for a good many years to regions where his ability would be stultified. And the judge who had announced his fate to him had been unkind enough to remark, in dry and laconic fashion, that within the memory of man forgers had made the acquaintance of the scaffold and the hangman.

Medhurst walked into the shop, fingering his loose change. His keen sense of humour made him smile as he bought the bishop's book with the bishop's own money. It was a small, thin, genteel book—merely a reprint of two or three lectures given to young men—and he slipped it into his outer pocket and went away. Pursuing his previous plan, he continued to stroll about the streets, up one, down another, always keeping within easy reach of the block of buildings near the Mansion House, in which his trusted friend had his office. But Medhurst had a task to perform, an adventure to undertake, before he went to his friend—he was going to make use of his criminal facility of imitating penmanship.

He turned into a teashop at last, and ordered a light breakfast. While it was being brought to him he carefully studied the facsimile of the Bishop of Brychester's signature. It was an easy signature to imitate, there was no marked peculiarities in it ; it was not the writing of a literary man, nor of a scholar, but rather of a business-like, straightforward sort, without twirls, flourishes, or elongated downstrokes. By the time Medhurst had finished his simple breakfast he knew that handwriting so well, had so photographed it on his brain, that he had no fear of being able to write out a cheque in such accurate imitation of it that the bishop himself would be puzzled in detecting the forgery.

Medhurst went straight to business. He had already thought of a well-known jeweller's shop in Cheapside where he could do what he wanted ; it had the great advantage of being practically next door to the block of buildings into which he meant to disappear as soon as his proposed transaction was safely over. He entered the jeweller's shop with all the assurance in the world, and was politely greeted by a manager who, seeing a soberly attired gentleman in a clerical collar, set his customer down as a country parson who had come to town in his rustic garb. But Medhurst quickly disabused the manager of that impression. Drawing out the well-worn card-case, he laid one of the Bishop of Brychester's cards on the glass-topped counter. The manager bowed again, more politely than before, and gave his episcopal visitor a seat.

"I have frequently seen your watches advertised," said the supposed bishop, "and, as I have a little time to spare before going into the country to play golf, I thought I would call and inspect them. The fact is, I want to make a present to my domestic chaplain, who has just been preferred to a living, and I think a good watch—gold, of course—would be the best thing I could give him. As I say, I have noticed your advertisements in the newspapers. I believe you have a very good keyless hunter-watch at about—something under forty pounds ? "

The manager hastened to lay before his customer a variety of gold watches of many prices. Medhurst examined them with interest and with care, talking pleasantly all the time. Eventually he selected an elegant and useful article which was priced at thirty-three guineas. And upon that he produced one of the blank cheques. "I will make out this cheque for fifty pounds," he remarked as the manager handed him writing materials. "Perhaps you can give me change ? "

"With pleasure, my lord," responded the manager. He had no doubt of his visitor's identity. Had he not received the bishop's card. Was there not lying there beside the bishop's gloves a copy of a book *Athletics and Christianity*, with the bishop's name upon it ? He handed over fifteen pounds and seven shillings, and thanked his supposed lordship for his custom.

Medhurst made his most dignified bow, and put on his blandest smile. He glanced at a timepiece hanging behind the counter, and began to hurry.

"Dear me ! " he exclaimed. "I have left myself little time to catch my train at Cannon Street. I must hasten."

The manager swept round the counter, and opened the door with a deep reverence.

"Just round the corner, my lord," he said. "Your lordship will do it in two minutes."

Medhurst smiled and nodded, and passed swiftly out. He certainly went round the corner which the manager indicated. Then he went round another corner, and round another. And then he plunged into a block of buildings contrived on the principle of a rabbit-warren. Within five minutes of leaving the jewellers' shop he was in the private office of the trusty friend, who had just admitted himself, and now made great haste to lock the door on both of them.

Meanwhile the jeweller's manager, having watched the supposed bishop round the corner, went back into the shop, rubbing his hands with satisfaction at having started the day so well.

Suddenly he caught sight of the book and the gloves—entirely forgotten by Medhurst—which still lay on the counter. He snatched them up, shouted a word to his assistants, and ran after the customer. He careered down Bucklersbury, he shot across Queen Victoria Street, he raced along Walbrook, he made a perilous dash over Cannon Street and into the station. He was almost breathless when he ran up to the barrier of the departure platform, staring about him.

" Have you seen a bishop pass in ? " he panted as he approached the ticket-puncher. " Tall gentleman—Bishop of Brychester ! "

The ticket-puncher gave the jeweller's manager a glance.

" There was a party what called himself Bishop of Brychester arrested here this morning ! " he growled. " Bilked the 'otel, he did. Stuffed himself, and had nothing to pay with—that's what 'e done ! D'yer want 'im ? 'Cause you'll find him round at the p'leece-station."

The jeweller's manager suddenly felt very ill. His head swam. He walked away. Then he recovered just as suddenly. The bilker could not be the same man who had just visited him—impossible ! Still, it would not be out of his way to visit the police-station. He knew some of the officials there, and he went off to them and told his story. What he wanted to know was—how did this extraordinary coincidence come about !

The police official to whom the manager told his story listened in silence—in silence he remained for some minutes.

" Happened just now ? " he suddenly asked.

" Within half an hour," answered the manager. He smiled bravely. " Of course," he said, " mine was the real bishop. But—who's your man—who's the impostor ? "

The official crooked his finger.

" Come this way ? " he said.

He led the manager to a certain stronghold, wherein the unhappy Bishop of Tuscaloosa was still expostulating with his incredulous guardians. But even as they entered it by one door, there was ushered in at another a very great ecclesiastical dignitary, as familiar in the City as St. Paul's itself, at sight of whom everybody in the room became profoundly respectful.

He advanced upon the Colonial prelate with outstretched hands.

" My dear bishop ! " he exclaimed. " What a lamentable —what a ridiculous mistake ! What an unfortunate—— "

The police official who had conducted the jeweller's manager into the room suddenly swept him out of it.

" Quick—quick ! " he said. " Come and describe that fellow you've told me about ! That's the real man ! We must be on to him sharp ! Come on ! Where did you say he was off to ? But, of course, he hasn't gone there—not he ! "

In that the police official was quite right. At the moment Medhurst, who had already effected another change of clothes, was being quietly carried away to a reasonable prospect of ultimate liberty.

IAN HAY (1876–   ) *is the pseudonym of Major John Hay Beith. The delightful story of a boy "Pip," appeared in 1907. This success was followed up with "A Knight on Wheels," in which the dominant character is an alternately recalcitrant and inspired motor-car, "The Lighter Side of School Life," and "The First Hundred Thousand." Here we may see how gracefully he treats a dramatic situation.*

NATURAL CAUSES

MISS PHYLLIS ETHERINGTON, conscious of a sudden chilliness in her toes, crossly drew those extremities into a less adventurous position and endeavoured to recompose herself to slumber. But she was aware, even in the semi-stupor in which she lay, of a certain element of disturbance in her surroundings. Her pillow felt extremely hard, and the sun appeared to be streaming through her cabin skylight with unusual ferocity. Had she overslept herself, she wondered? How about breakfast? She must have lain long. Had she been called? Certainly she was beginning to feel thoroughly restless. Something rigid and unyielding was pressing against her ribs. A book, perhaps: she was in the habit of reading late in bed and dropping off to sleep, the volume under perusal usually being retrieved somewhere in the neighbourhood of the hot-water bottle in the morning. Should she make an effort now, or—the sluggard's inevitable alternative—give herself just five minutes longer?

The question was settled for her. Her toes were once again sending up signals for help, and their appeal was backed ten seconds later by a sudden splash of water, which broke over the sleeper's feet and deluged her to the knees.

Miss Etherington sat up suddenly, to realise that she had mistaken her whereabouts. It was a dream reversed. Instead of tumbling out of fairyland to wake up in bed, she had tumbled out of bed to wake up in fairyland.

She was sitting upon a sunny shore—a concave arc of shelving yellow sand, with blue and white wavelets lazily rolling up and down the declivity. One of these broke gently over her bare feet for the third time.

Woman-like, she took a lightning inventory of her costume —and gave a little gasp of dismay. Her toilet presented the appearance of having been begun in haste and not finished at all. Her long hair, dank but luxurious, flowed down to her waist. A saxe-blue serge skirt fluttered round her bare ankles. Her most adequate article of attire was a cork life-belt, fastened round her quilted dressing-gown. She was stiff and aching in every limb.

She remembered all now. The yacht—the tropical hurricane—the grinding crash in the dead of night—the trampling of feet overhead and the hoarse shouting of men— the heeling decks and flapping ropes—a pair of hands which had hurried her along the sloping alleyways and passed her down into a heaving cockle-shell—finally, the great green wave which had swung up out of the darkness and fallen upon them all and carried her down, down, down, until she lost consciousness. And here she was, cast up and alive upon a warm sandy beach. The life-belt was responsible for that, she supposed. She had no recollection of having put it on, though. Probably the hands which hurried her on deck had attended to that. There was a number on it: *S.Y. Island Queen, R.Y.S.—State-Room No.* 3. The number of her state-room was seven, so this could not be the belt which she had noticed rolled up in a rack above her berth, lazily wondering if she would ever need it.

Then, as her senses adjusted themselves, came the inevitable inquiry: "Where were the others? Her host, that cheerful, kindly old nobleman, was he gone? What a death for a man reputed to know the Pacific as most amateurs know the Solent! And the Arthur Denholms? And Colonel Shiell? And Margaret Alderston? And "—Miss Etherington's exquisite features hardened for a moment— "Leslie Gale?"

Then her face softened again. Death closes all accounts. Leslie Gale, lying peacefully in twenty fathoms of blue water, could never again do anything to increase or diminish the sum-total of his account with her—an account opened, run up, audited, and found incorrect in every possible way within a brief but extremely stormy period of three weeks. That vendetta was at an end, anyway.

Why had she come to dislike him so intensely? she wondered. Was it because he had asked her to marry him? Apparently not; for in that case she should at this moment be cherishing the bitterest feelings towards some seventeen other gentlemen, mostly of blameless character and antecedents, who had at various periods mooted the same proposition. Was it because he had proposed to her after an acquaintance of three days ? No ; one man had done so after one ball, and she had felt rather flattered. She had disliked Leslie Gale from the moment of their first meeting. He had not treated her with the respect—that is, the servility—to which she was accustomed. She objected also to the manner in which he had treated his dismissal. True, he had not behaved violently or idiotically, like most of the others. On the contrary, he had exhibited most exasperating detachment of mind about it, and had talked—no, *chatted* to her about herself in a manner which she resented very much. He had appeared almost sorry for her.

"You are in a difficult position," he said musingly, at that point in their interview at which a right-minded lover would have departed, with drawn features, into the night. "You are a girl with brains and character—and a bit of a spoiled child into the bargain. You cannot love a man who is your mental and moral inferior, and you are too opinionated and conceited to give in to your superior. So you fall between two stools."

At this she had been unable to resist the temptation of a crushing retort.

"Are you my superior ? " she rapped out.

"Yes."

Joy ! He had fallen into the trap.

"Then "—maliciously—" why don't you subdue me ? "

On paper, there was no answer to this question ; but this bumptious young man had replied without hesitation :

"Because you won't stand your ground. You will run away."

"Why should I run away—from you ? " inquired Miss Etherington icily.

"Because," replied Mr. Gale, " you are afraid of me."

"Indeed ? "

"Yes."

"Then you think you will subdue me ? "

"No," he said frankly—" I don't. You won't give me the chance. Modern civilisation deprives man of many of his weapons. If we were shut up together on a desert island, or if we had lived in the cave-dwelling period——"

"You would have subdued me with a flint axe, I suppose," said Miss Etherington scornfully.

"No, not at all. There would have been no need. If I had wanted you I should have used the flint axe to settle the pretensions of your other suitors, and then picked you up and carried you off."

"It is possible," said Miss Etherington gently, "that I might not have come."

"Yes, you would. You would have come gladly, knowing that the best man had got you ; and that is all a woman really cares about."

"If you honestly believe that," replied Miss Etherington almost compassionately, "all I can say is that your intelligence is even more unformed than I suspected. When you have seen a little more of the world you will realise that mankind has progressed beyond the schoolboy attitude towards life. Women are now free agents."

"Yes. And I'm not sure," remarked the experienced Mr. Gale, "that there are as many happy marriages under the new system as the old. Women are notoriously bad judges of a man. I shall watch your future career with interest, Miss Etherington—interest and apprehension. In matters of the heart I mistrust your judgment."

He rose.

"Now," he said, "if you would like to have the last word you had better say it at once ; because it is getting late, and the rest of the party may be wondering what you and I are discussing under the lee of the chart-house."

At this Miss Etherington had risen from her seat and sailed silently and majestically aft.

That was a fortnight ago. Since then, in the constricted space of a yacht, friction had been inevitable. Miss Etherington at first made an attempt to avoid Mr. Gale's society, but relinquished this on being taunted with "running away." So she changed her tactics, and treated Mr. Gale with excessive sprightliness in public and cold disdain in private. Here she was more successful. Gale's flippant and philosophical detachment did not wear well. He maintained a careless and semi-humorous pose for about a week, and then one evening, under the baneful influence of a full round moon, suddenly crumpled up and descended to sentimental entreaty. Miss Etherington, perceiving that he had delivered himself into her hands, let him run on for nearly ten minutes, and then gave free rein to a rather exceptional talent for biting sarcasm. Gale's amorous expansiveness collapsed like a punctured balloon at the first stab ; and feeling hot and foolish and being a man, he lost his temper, and said things which should not be said to a lady, however provoking.

Then followed seven days of open hostility. Finally one night, when the indefatigable Mrs. Arthur Denholm organised a dance on the deck under the awning, Leslie Gale, who hated feuds, summoned his entire stock of common sense and courage, and asked Miss Etherington for a waltz.

He met with a flat refusal, for which he was fully prepared. He persisted.

"Nonsense!" he said. "Come on! Just a little turn! It will do us both good," he added meaningly.

Without further entreaty he placed an arm round Miss Etherington's slim waist, and trundled her unresisting but unresponsive form twice round the deck. Then, a little blown by the considerable exertion involved, he paused, and remarked cheerfully :

"That was splendid!"

Miss Etherington swiftly released her waist from his arm, and crossed the deck to where one Ommaney, a callow and cub-like member of the company, was lolling against a stanchion.

"Billy dear," she said, with an entrancing smile, "will you dance with me?"

Billy, much flattered, complied.

An hour later Miss Etherington, on her way to bed, found her path barred by Mr. Leslie Gale, who was standing at the foot of the companion. His face was white, and his teeth chattered gently—but not with cold or fear.

"Let me pass, please," said Miss Etherington, rather nervously.

"I only wanted to say," answered Mr. Gale in a voice which Miss Etherington had never heard before, "that I think you are the most ill-bred and detestable girl I have ever met. You may pass now."

That was last night—say twelve hours ago. And now Leslie Gale was dead, lying with the wreck of the yacht deep down beside the coral reef that had wrecked them. Dead! And so were the others, to all seeming. She gazed round— at the horse-shoe curve of the little bay ; at the palm-covered slopes behind her ; at the boiling surge outside the bar. Was she utterly alone ? She was a plucky young woman and declined to be frightened until she was sure.

She sprang resolutely to her feet and set out inland. Not far off uprose a little hill. From the summit of this she could survey her kingdom and take an inventory of its possibilities. She was not beaten yet. Her pulse beat high. Her small bare toes resolutely crimped the sand.

Meanwhile, behind an adjacent sandhill, following the movements of his beloved with breathless interest, lay Mr. Leslie Gale. He chuckled gently. His chief asset in life— some people considered it a liability—was a strong if somewhat untimely sense of humour. Not even a recent escape from a watery grave could damp his enjoyment of the situation. He sat up in his rapidly drying pyjamas, and slapped himself feebly.

"My sainted aunt !" he murmured brokenly. "I shall have to get a flint axe !"

II

MISS ETHERINGTON, white-lipped and struggling gamely with the terrors of utter loneliness, lay face downward upon a patch of coral sand. She had completed her survey of the island, which was not much larger than a couple of full-sized golf-courses ; and lo ! it was her exclusive property. There were no habitations, and no inhabitants. She lay very still, holding herself in. Once or twice her shoulders heaved.

Suddenly, like music from heaven, the sound of a discreet and thoroughly British cough fell upon her ears, and in a moment the cobweb of terror which was beginning to enshroud her senses was swept away. Hardly believing her good fortune, she sprang up, tossed back her hair from her eyes— and found herself face to face with Mr. Leslie Gale.

"Oh !" she gasped. "You ?"

"Yes—just me !" he replied. "There is nobody else."

"And are all the others—— ?" She pointed to the tumbling seas outside the bar.

"I don't know," replied Gale, interpreting the question. "Very likely most of them got away in the lifeboat. You were in the cutter, you know."

"If they escaped, wouldn't they have landed here ?" said the girl doubtfully.

"I'm not so sure. That squall which struck us was the tail-end of a cyclone. They may have been swept out to sea. In fact," he added, covertly regarding Miss Etherington's white face and troubled eyes, "I am *sure* they were. I saw them get clear away myself. Anyhow, they are not here. I have been all over the island to see."

"Are there any traces?"

"Yes, but not of human beings. Chiefly spars and gratings. I collected all I could: they may be useful for—domestic purposes."

It was not, perhaps, a very happy way of putting it. Miss Etherington flushed, and demanded:

"What do you mean?"

"I mean what I say. We may have to stay here for months. Are you an expert in household management? Can you tend the fireside, while I labour to keep the home together?"

"I *can't* live here alone with you for months," cried the girl desperately.

"I am afraid it can't be helped," said Mr. Gale. "We may get taken off by some passing vessel, but for the present you must be content to live the life of a cave-woman."

Miss Etherington caught the allusion, and her spirit responded instantaneously to the implied challenge.

"First find your cave!" she replied disdainfully.

"By the greatest luck in the world," announced Mr. Gale calmly, "I have already done so. Come and see."

He led the way along the seashore, eager to exhibit his discovery. Miss Etherington rebelliously following. Already, she reflected, primitive man was asserting himself: in a procession of two she walked in the rear.

"Presently he will expect me to fetch and carry," she said to herself. "Let him dare!"

The cave lay close to the water's edge, in a tiny cove facing south. It ran back some fifteen feet into the heart of a lofty rock, and was floored with white coral sand, warm and dry beneath the rays of the noonday sun which streamed in through the doorway.

"Somewhere to sleep, at any rate," commented Mr. Gale cheerfully. "But what chiefly concerns me at present is the discovery of something to eat. Come and find cocoanuts."

Once more the procession moved off, its order unaltered. A cocoanut palm was speedily found, and Mr. Gale embarked upon a brief gymnastic display, which presently furnished them with a supply of solid and liquid refreshment of which both our islanders stood in considerable need.

" This landscape," said Gale, as he sat contentedly sunning himself after the fashion of man when fed, " reminds me of North Berwick Links, with a few palms dotted about and no tourists. There is Point Garry." He indicated the little promontory in which their cave was situated.

" Have you climbed to the top yet, partner ? " he continued.

" No," said Miss Etherington shortly ; " I have not."

" Well, you shall," said Mr. Gale kindly. " We may see things from there which have hitherto escaped our notice. No good sitting here moping ! "

With great energy he led the way to Point Garry and scaled the heights, assisting his companion from time to time.

" We will now scan the horizon," he announced, when they reached the top. " I think that is what Robinson Crusoe would have done under the circumstances. No—nothing ! Nothing to be seen but those big rocks jutting up out of the water over there. I noticed them this morning. They look like a row of teeth, don't they ? " he inquired chattily.

" I fail to observe any resemblance," replied Miss Etherington.

" No ? Well, I was always quick at noticing things from a child," said Mr. Gale, with unimpaired *bonhomie*. " We are not all blessed with good imagin—— Hallo ! what's that ? " He seized the girl's arm in unaffected excitement, and pointed.

" You are holding my arm," said Miss Etherington coldly. " Let go, please ! "

Mr. Gale had already done so, in order to make a pair of binoculars of his hands.

" Do you see something projecting up between the two middle teeth ? " he asked. " I think—I *think*—yes, it is— the bow of a ship ! It must be the yacht. It *is* the yacht ! I can see the top of her funnel. She must have grounded there. I was right. It was a cyclone. The wind has been playing a perfect game of rounders with itself."

" Do you think there is anyone on board ? " asked Miss Etherington, suddenly hopeful. After all, a steward or a coal-trimmer would be something with which to dilute Mr. Gale. Another woman seemed too much to expect.

" I doubt it, but I will see," said Mr. Gale.

" How ? "

" I am going to swim out."

" All that way ? "

" Yes ; not more than half-a-mile, I fancy."

" Supposing there are——"

Miss Etherington paused, suddenly remembering that the man beside her was unworthy of solicitude.

" Sharks—eh ? Perhaps, but I must risk it. If I meet one I will make a noise like a company promoter, and he'll merely bow respectfully. Do you know what that old hull means to us ? Blankets, tools, food ! Perhaps they have left a boat on board."

" Can you swim half-a-mile ? " inquired Miss Etherington.

" It is just about my limit," confessed Mr. Gale frankly. " but I can try."

" Would you "—Miss Etherington wavered between common humanity and a feminine desire not to offer anything which could be construed into encouragement—" care to have my cork-jacket ? "

" If you are *quite* sure you won't catch a chill without it," replied Mr. Gale tenderly.

He proceeded to buckle on the jacket, apparently oblivious of a look which to a thinner-skinned man would have made drowning seem an easy death, and scrambled over the rocks to the water's edge. He poised himself upon a convenient taking-off place.

" Back to tea ! " he cried, and disappeared with a splash. It is not easy to dive cleanly in a cork jacket.

Presently he reappeared, and struck out boldly in the direction of Double-Tooth Islet. Miss Etherington, seated upon the summit of Point Garry, her round chin resting on her hands, followed the course of his black head as it slowly forged its way across the limpid channel. Many thoughts passed through her mind. On the one hand, she hated Mr. Leslie Gale to the fullest extent of a nature more than usually well endowed for the purpose. On the other, she knew that there were sharks in these seas—she had seen them. Even now she could descry in the wake of Mr. Gale a tiny black dot which might or might not be the dreaded triangular fin. She closed her eyes, and kept them tightly shut for more than half-an-hour.

When she opened them, a figure, silhouetted against the skyline upon the summit of Double Tooth Islet, was triumphantly semaphoring safe arrival. Miss Etherington did not reply. Instead, she rolled gently over on to her side in a dead faint.

After all, as she argued to herself when she came to, she had had a most exhausting twenty-four hours, and her sole diet had been a portion of cocoanut.

III

MR. GALE returned more expeditiously than he had set out, adequately clothed and propelling the yacht's dinghy, which was loaded to the water's edge with miscellaneous stores.

" Help me to unload these things, quickly," he called to Miss Etherington, " and carry them up to the cave. I must go out to the yacht again before she slips off."

" Will you take me with you this time ? " asked Miss Etherington.

" Why ? "

" I want some things out of my cabin," was the prim reply.

" I'm afraid you haven't got a cabin any more," said Gale. " The stern half of the ship is under water, and I'm salving all I can from the forward part. However, I will select a wardrobe for you from what is available. I always had great natural taste."

He paddled away so quickly that Miss Etherington had no time effectively to ignore this last pleasantry. When Mr. Gale returned an hour later he found her still sitting beside the heap of stores on the shore.

" The yacht is lifting with the swell," he announced. " She is just hanging on by her eyebrows now. Rolled over fifteen degrees a minute ago. Gave me a nasty turn, I can tell you, down in the lazarette grubbing for tinned sardines—for you. They are rather a favourite delicacy of yours, aren't they ? Hallo ! Why haven't you carried up some of these stores ? Tired ? "

Miss Etherington, who had been rehearsing her part for this scene for the past hour, replied icily :

" I am not accustomed to be ordered about."

Gale, who was lifting a heavy box out of the boat—the carpenter's tool-chest—laid down his burden and sat on it.

" Insubordination ? H'm — a serious matter ! " he observed. " We must hold a court-martial this evening." He rose, and continued : " As you don't appear inclined to assist me to furnish the Home, perhaps you will kindly repair to the Home itself. I will carry this case up for you, and you shall unpack it. Then you can make the place snug with a few deft feminine touches. When I have finished my day's work I shall expect to find my slippers toasting at the fender. That is always done, I believe. Do not butter them, though, or Darby will have a few words to address to Joan. You will find me a fearful domestic tyrant."

Miss Etherington, dimly wondering whether this excursion into the realms of humour masked a threat or merely indicated mental vacuity of the hollowest type, rose from her seat and departed in the direction of the cave. But she did not halt there. Instead, she climbed to the summit of Point Garry, and there sat for a full hour surveying the sunset with an expression upon her features for which a competent under-nurse would have prescribed just one remedy.

The red-hot coppery ball of the sun dropped into the sea so suddenly that one almost expected to hear it sizzle, and the warm darkness of a tropical night rushed down from the heavens. Stars sprang out upon the velvety sky.

" Partner ! " called a voice from below.

" I won't—I *won't* ! " muttered the girl to herself between her clenched teeth.

There was a pause, and then she heard the feet of Mr. Gale climbing the rocky path which led to her eyrie. Presently his head appeared above the edge.

" Shall I bring your supper up to you, or will you come down to it ? " he inquired. " I may mention that there is an extra charge for serving meals above stairs. Your food will cost you more, so to speak."

Miss Etherington was in no mood for badinage of this kind.

" I will come," she said stonily.

A bright fire was burning at the mouth of the cave, and a stew of a primitive but inviting character was bubbling in an iron pot hung over the blaze. Crates and cases had been piled into a neat rampart round their demesne. Over the cave mouth itself Mr. Gale had hung a stout curtain of sailcloth.

" Be seated, Miss Etherington," said Mr. Gale. " That is your place."

He pointed to a seat upon the sand, fashioned out of boat cushions propped against the base of the rock.

Miss Etherington obeyed.

" This is a one-course dinner," continued Mr. Gale in

deprecating tones, " but I have no doubt that when you take matters in hand you will be able to turn out something more pretentious. What will you drink ? I have a bottle of brandy, which had better be reserved for medicinal purposes, and a dozen stone ginger which I have retrieved from the wreck at great personal risk, knowing it to be a weakness of yours. We must not be reckless about it. An occasional bottle on special occasions—birthdays and Christmases. I think to-night comes under the head of special occasions. Say when ! "

Babbling in this light-hearted strain, Mr. Gale proceeded to do the honours of the feast, incidentally making a hearty meal himself. Miss Etherington ate nothing to speak of.

When he had finished, Leslie Gale punctiliously asked for permission to smoke, and lit his pipe.

" I wonder how long half-a-pound of tobacco will last me ? " he mused, puffing comfortably. " A month, perhaps, with care. How ripping the moon looks on the water ! "

Miss Etherington did not reply. Her eyes were set. Gale stood up.

" Bed-time," he announced. " You are tired. Come and see your room."

He lit a candle and screwed it into the neck of a bottle. The flame hardly flickered in the soft air.

" Please walk in," he said, holding back the sailcloth flap.

Miss Etherington obeyed, mechanically.

In one corner of the cave Gale had constructed a sleeping-place of blankets and boat-cushions. On a convenient ledge lay a tin basin ; beside it stood a bucket of fair water. Even soap was there. A deal chest served for chair and wardrobe.

Leslie Gale held the candle aloft.

" What do you think of me as an upholsterer ? " he asked with pride. " I will see about electric bells and a hot-water tap in the morning."

Miss Etherington made no reply.

Gale set down the candle on the ledge.

" Is there anything else I can do for you in here ? " he asked.

" No, thank you."

" Quite sure ? It is the last time of asking."

Struck by a curious note in his voice, the girl looked up suddenly.

" Why ? " she said.

Their eyes met. Mr. Gale's, which were usually remarkable only for a self-satisfied twinkle, were grey and steely.

"Because," he said slowly, "I do not intend to invade your privacy again. Hereafter this cave is *yours*—utterly and absolutely—to withdraw to whenever again you feel inclined, as you did to-day, to doubt my ability to behave like a gentleman. Good-night!"

He turned towards the curtained doorway.

"Where—where are you going to shelter?" inquired a low voice behind him.

"On the beach—between a couple of oyster-shells!" he replied. "Good-night!"

A childish and flippant rejoinder, the reader will admit, utterly spoiling what might have been a dignified—nay, heroic —exit from the cave. But Leslie Gale was never one to let the sun go down upon his wrath, or mistake the theatrical for the dramatic.

IV

MISS ETHERINGTON awoke next morning to find the sun beating upon the sail-cloth curtain. Half-dazed, and failing for a moment to realise her surroundings, she uttered a stifled cry.

A shadow fell upon the curtain.

"Shriek once for the Boots, twice for the chambermaid, three times for the waiter," advised a cheerful voice. "Breakfast is served."

Ten minutes later Miss Etherington found herself subdued but hungry, partaking of fresh fish fried in oatmeal.

"Any amount of nourishment to be had for the asking over there by those rocks," said the *chef*. "It's lucky. We have enough tinned stuff to last us for months; but tinned turkey and tinned plum-pudding both taste very much alike after a few weeks; so these little fellows "—he helped himself to another fish—" will serve to drive away monotony. Have some cocoa?"

"I hate cocoa," replied Miss Etherington, with a return of her old petulance. Gale's assumption that they were settled upon the island for life angered her, as usual.

"Members," gabbled the incorrigible Mr. Gale, "are requested not to chastise the club servants personally, but to enter all complaints upon the backs of their bills, which will be considered by the Committee at its next session. But I am sorry you don't like cocoa. I will try and find some coffee for you. I am going to make a final trip to the yacht after breakfast."

" Is she still there, then ? "

" Yes, I have been out already this morning. I don't think the old thing will hang on much longer, though. There is a heavy swell outside. By the way, do you know why Robinson Crusoe was not alone when he landed on his island ? Give it up ? Because he found a heavy swell on the beach and a little cove running up the sand. . . . No ? "—as Miss Etherington remained quite impervious to this outrage. " Well, perhaps not ! It might go better with a larger audience. It used to be received with rapture in the schoolroom at home. I thought perhaps—however, to resume. Is there anything else you require before the yacht goes under ? "

" Yes—hairpins," said Miss Etherington unexpectedly.

" I'm *afraid* not," said Gale. " The only cabins not under water by this time are the engineers', and engineers always wear their hair bobbed, as you know. But really "—he respectfully scrutinised his companion's tumbled mane— " it looks very nice as it is."

Miss Etherington, upon whom last night's lesson had not been wasted, smiled, for the first time since their landing ; and Mr. Gale was conscious deep down in his heart, which possibly was not so light as his tongue, of a tiny thrill of satisfaction and relief. Was this peace — or merely an armistice ?

" I must go now," he said. " After that we will formally annex our kingdom and draw up a constitution."

" If you are sure it is quite safe on the yacht ? " asked Miss Etherington rather anxiously, staring under her hand at the lazy swell beyond the rocks.

" I will take great care of myself," said Mr. Gale in soothing tones. " Don't be anxious."

" But I *am*," said Miss Etherington warmly.

" This is most gratifying," murmured Mr. Gale.

" If you were drowned," explained Miss Etherington, " I should probably starve ; and in any case I should have to do all the cooking and washing-up myself."

Apparently it was only an armistice.

Still, when Mr. Gale returned half-an-hour later with a boat-load of what he described as " comforts," he found that his companion had cleared away the breakfast and made their encampment tidy.

He made no comment, but summoned a council of two to discuss the situation. He pointed out their probable position upon the chart.

" We seem to be a long way from anywhere," said the girl dismally.

" We are," said the Job's Comforter beside her ; " and what is more, we are a long way from any steamer route. Still you never know. Luckily we have a spring of water and plenty of tinned food, not to mention fish and products of the soil. We might catch a turtle, with luck, and perhaps I shall find something to shoot. Now, supposing I do the hunting and fishing and general hew-wood-and-draw-water business, will you undertake the cooking and general housekeeping ? "

Miss Etherington nodded.

" We must build a little wooden hut," continued Gale, with all the enthusiasm of a small boy playing at Red Indians. " I can sleep in one half and keep the stores in the other. A sort of lean-to. We will regularly *organise* this island before we have done with it ! I wonder, now, about clothes. What we have on won't last for ever. It's a pity your cabin was under water, or I might have salved a regular wardrobe for you. Number Seven, wasn't it ? "

Miss Etherington nodded.

" By the way," she asked, " what was yours ? "

" Number Three. Why ? "

" Oh, nothing."

" Well, as for clothes," continued the indefatigable Mr. Gale, " if we haven't got them we must make them. Can you cut out ? " he inquired sternly, regarding his companion with the austere air of a Dorcas Society secretary.

" Don't you think," interposed Miss Etherington dryly, " that you are taking rather too much thought for the morrow —not to speak of the day after to-morrow ? May I make a suggestion ? "

" By all means," said Mr. Gale indulgently.

" Let us go and look round for passing ships," said Miss Etherington.

The organiser, a trifle dashed, rose and meekly followed practical Eve to the summit of the rock. But there were no ships.

Mr. Leslie turned severely upon his companion.

"You see?" he said. "Twenty minutes wasted! And life is so short. Let us return and make plans."

Miss Etherington calmly followed him down again.

Still, her suggestion was not without effect. A clause was inserted in the constitution of their kingdom to the effect that Gale should climb Point Garry (as they agreed to call the headland) twice daily, at dawn and sundown, and search the horizon for passing vessels, Miss Etherington performing the same duty at other times throughout the day, during her companion's absence at the chase.

The rest of that morning was occupied with what is usually known as "settling in," a process which appears to be as inevitable to castaways in the South Pacific as to semi-detached suburbanites much nearer home. At midday Miss Etherington dished up her first meal, at which, pleasantly tired, they lay side by side upon the warm sand and conversed quite amicably. Both realised simultaneously that there is something very uniting in working to retrieve a joint disaster. With a single impulse, Mr. Gale edged a little nearer to Miss Etherington, and Miss Etherington edged a little farther away from Mr. Gale.

Thus Nature, who sets the dockleaf beside the nettle, adjusts the fine balance of sex-deportment.

When they had eaten, Leslie Gale hauled the dinghy into a shady patch of sand and proceeded to invert it over a blanket.

"What are you doing?" inquired Miss Etherington, wiping a plate.

"I propose to take a siesta," said Mr. Gale. "I have been working like a coolie since four o'clock this morning. I made two trips before you were up and I am done to the world. I advise you to retire to your cave of harmony and do likewise. We must keep ourselves fit, you know, and—and—be merry and bright. I only wish," he added awkwardly, "that you could have found yourself in more congenial company."

Then he crawled hurriedly under the dinghy's protecting shade, and rolled himself up in the blanket.

Left to her own devices, Miss Etherington, in obedience to an idea which had been obtruding itself upon her for some hours, entered the cave and inspected her cork-jacket, which lay neatly rolled up upon a ledge. Upon its outer surface, as already related, was neatly stencilled the legend, *S.Y. Island Queen, R.Y.S.—State-Room No.* 3.

Very slowly and reflectively Miss Etherington rolled up the jacket and put it back upon its ledge. Then, quitting the cave, she climbed up upon Point Garry and listlessly scanned the horizon.

She returned an hour later. The expression upon her features would have been ascribed by an expert in physiognomy to the workings of a guilty but unrepentant spirit.

Presently she awoke Mr. Leslie Gale, and set before him an evening meal whose excellence she did her best to discount by a display of cold aloofness which would have blighted the appetite of a less determined optimist.

V

"My hole, I think," said Mr. Gale.

"Well," remarked Miss Etherington with asperity, "if lizards are going to lie across the line of my putt on *every* green, I don't see how you can help winning a hole occasionally."

"These things will happen on sporting courses," said Mr. Gale sympathetically. "Still, you could have taken advantage of the by-law which says that lizards may be lifted or swept aside (but not pressed down) without penalty. Now for Point Garry! You get a stroke here. All square and one to play."

They stood upon the seventeenth green of the island golf-course. Their clubs were two home-made instruments of the hockey-stick variety, their equipment being completed by a couple of solid but well-gnawed india-rubber balls, which had been employed upon the yacht to afford recreation and exercise to their hostess's terriers. It was five o'clock in the afternoon. Supply, as represented by Mr. Gale, the purveyor, having temporarily satisfied Demand, as represented by Miss Etherington, the housekeeper, with sufficient comestibles and combustibles for the next twenty-four hours, the pair were indulging in a little exercise before proceeding from labour to refreshment.

The golf-course was an abiding joy. It had been opened with much ceremony a fortnight ago, Miss Etherington driving off the first ball from the first tee, and Mr. Gale gallantly retrieving the same from the Pacific Ocean. There were eighteen holes, ranging from five to seventy yards in length, and the course abounded in natural hazards of the most diverse description. There were no caddies, but, as Mr. Gale remarked, a caddy when you possess only one club looks ostentatious.

The golf-course is a characteristic product of British occupation of alien territory. John Bull, we all know, has a weakness for descending casually upon the unappropriated spaces of the earth, the fact that they do not strictly belong to him being, in his view, fully balanced by the fact that he causes them to prosper as they have never prospered before. If you make a desert, he argues, blossom like the rose, what does it matter whose desert it was previously? His methods of procedure seldom vary, whether he be an official man-in-possession or a younger son in search of a career. Having adjusted the local constitution to his satisfaction, he sets to work to assist the slightly flustered inhabitants to make the place pay. After that he lays out a golf-course.

There being no inhabitants upon the island, and consequently no laws to adjust, our friends had been able to get to work on the golf-course at once. Their new life had altered them surprisingly little. After three months of a semi-savage existence, so far from reverting to the service of primitive Nature, they had adapted Nature to the requirements of modern society and turned the island into a very fair imitation of a fashionable health-resort. Had they been of another caste—say, the mechanical—they would have impressed their mark in another fashion none the less indelible. There would have been water-wheels, mills, and sluices. Being of the class called leisured, accustomed to extract as much enjoyment from life as possible and on no account ever to worry about anything, they had settled down, in one of Nature's most typical strongholds, to the nearest approach they could compass to the careless artificial life that they were accustomed to live. And so powerful are use and wont that these two unruffled Britons bade fair to expel Nature from her own stronghold. Cave man and cave woman they certainly were not yet. They were members of a class which has always been carelessly indifferent to outside influences, and does not easily change its habits or mode of speech. Consequently the island had not barbarised them. They were gently denaturalising the island.

Mr. Gale took the eighteenth hole in a perfect nine, Miss Etherington's ball over-running the green and taking refuge in a lie with which only a corkscrew could have coped. The victor having offered to the vanquished the insincere condolences usual upon such occasions, the pair sat down to enjoy the afternoon breeze.

" What is for dinner to-night ? " inquired Mr. Gale.

" Turtles' eggs, fried sardines, biscuits, and bananas," replied Miss Etherington.   " It's the last tin of sardines but one."

" Oh ! How are the stores in general lasting out ? "

" There seems to be plenty of most things. We were rather extravagant at first, but since you developed into such a mighty hunter——"

" And you into such a nailing housekeeper——"

" We have become almost self-supporting."

At this fulsome interchange of compliments the pair turned and smiled upon one another.

" And we seem to thrive on it," said Mr. Gale complacently. " I must have gone up a stone in weight, and I feel as skittish as a young unicorn.   You look pretty fit, too."

He turned and surveyed his companion. She was wearing the smart blue skirt in which she had landed on the island, sadly frayed and bleached, but still bearing the *imprimatur* of Hanover Square, together with a flannel cricket-shirt. Round her neck was knotted a coloured handkerchief. Her feet were bare. The hairpin difficulty had never been overcome, and Miss Etherington usually kept her rippling mane plaited into a convenient pigtail. That appendage having developed a habit at the end of a full swing of dealing its owner a severe buffet in the face, it was Miss Etherington's custom when playing golf to gather her locks into a heap upon the top of her head, and confine the same within a coloured headband, after the fashion of the stage brigand. Just now she was unfastening the knot of this contrivance.

Mr. Gale, discoursing at ease upon diet and hygiene, suddenly tripped in his speech, for without warning, a soft wavy cascade fell about the girl's shoulders. Through the glistening veil he could descry the droop of her lashes and the curve of her cheek. His tongue began to frame silent phrases about the tangles of Neæra's hair, and his heart beat foolishly. Of late he had become increasingly conscious of this weakness—nay, vice. Common decency seemed to forbid such sentiments towards an unprotected female. But——

" Thank you," said Miss Etherington frigidly, " I am glad you think I am putting on flesh ; but you need not look at me like that.   This is not Smithfield Market."

Mr. Gale's attack of sentimentality passed hastily.

" Do you know," he said, " that we have been in this island for three months ? "

"Have we?" replied Miss Etherington. "It seems longer," she added untruthfully.

"And I don't think," pursued Mr. Gale, "that we have made the most of our opportunities."

Miss Etherington scented danger, but could not forbear to inquire:

"In what way?"

"Well," replied Mr. Gale, "look at the things Robinson Crusoe did. He built a boat——"

"We have a boat already," remarked matter-of-fact Miss Etherington.

"Yes, that *is* a bit of a hardship," agreed Mr. Gale. "Then didn't he teach a parrot to talk? Couldn't we——"

"There are no parrots on this island," replied Miss Etherington gently.

"Quite true, but you haven't grasped the principle of what I am driving at. Here we are, living on a desert island, and so far we haven't done anything that two people couldn't have accomplished by going for a picnic up the Thames. I even shave. We eat food out of tins; we do a little bathing and fishing in the morning, and play golf in the afternoon, and sit about in the evening and say how jolly it must be in Town just now. It seems to me that we are out of the picture somehow. We ought to be a little more primitive—barbaric. Do you follow me?"

"No," said Miss Etherington. "In my opinion really nice people continue to behave just as nicely on a desert island as on a yacht."

"But don't you think," continued Mr. Gale perseveringly, "that we might train two goats to play bridge with us, or teach a turtle to sing, or something? Then we should feel that we were getting back to Nature—quite biblical, in fact. 'The voice of the turtle is heard in the land,' and so forth."

"If you are going to talk nonsense," said Miss Etherington, "I will go and get dinner ready."

"When we get away from here," continued the imaginative Mr. Gale, "we could take the little troupe with us, and earn an honest living on the music-hall stage. I once saw some performing seals at the Palace. I should think performing turtles would get quite as big a salary; and then when the public got tired of them we could sell them to the Lord Mayor for soup. That is what is known in commercial circles as a by-product."

He ran on, and Miss Etherington watched him stealthily through her lashes. A man and woman, however antipathetic, cannot consort together upon an uninhabited island for three months without gaining some insight into one another's characters and motives. Miss Etherington knew the meaning of this performance. Mr. Gale suspected her of low spirits, and was endeavouring to cheer her up. He was not doing it very well ; but after all, good intentions count for something, and Miss Etherington felt grateful, despite herself. She continued to watch him furtively. He was a presentable youth. He sat beside her, healthy, clean-cut, and bronzed, wearing a ragged flannel shirt and an old pair of duck trousers. His hands were clasped about his knees ; his eyes were fixed on vacancy ; and his tongue wagged unceasingly. A hare-brained and occasionally bumptious young man, but a man for all that.

Suddenly Gale inquired :

" I say, what do you think of me now ? Has your opinion of me altered at all, after three months of me neat ? "

The next moment he repented of his inquiry. He had firmly resolved never to embarrass the girl in this fashion so long as they remained on the island together. Now he had broken his word to himself. Miss Etherington's rippling mane had been a little too much for his fortitude.

But the girl did not appear offended. She replied quite simply :

" Yes, I have. I think you have behaved very courageously in the face of all our difficulties——"

" Self-preservation is the first——" began Gale awkwardly.

" ——And I have to thank you for a good deal as well," continued Miss Etherington, with slightly heightened colour. " Besides saving my life—you *did*, you know : that was your life-jacket I was wearing that morning—you have behaved very courteously and honourably to me ever since we found ourselves here ; and I am grateful."

This was well spoken. Mr. Gale was silent for a moment. Then he inquired :

" You did not expect such behaviour from me ? "

" I—I never doubted you after the first few hours," said Miss Etherington in a low voice. " I was not quite myself then. Do you forgive me ? You will, won't you ? "

Their eyes met. Mr. Gale's suddenly blazed.

" When you look at me and talk to me like that," he almost

shouted, " I could—— Ahem ! Ha ! H'm ! Quite so !
My error ! "

Miss Etherington's cheeks were crimson.

" I think I will go and see if there are any ships going past,"
he concluded lamely.

" Perhaps it would be as well," agreed Miss Etherington.
" Don't be late for dinner."

Mr. Gale turned to go, and then paused.

" You don't ask me," he remarked in a slightly injured
voice, " whether my opinion of *you* has changed at all."

" No," replied Miss Etherington.   " There is no need."

" I wonder what in thunder she meant by that," mused
the harassed Mr. Gale, as he scrambled up Point Garry.
" Heaven help a man left alone on a desert island with a girl !
And I actually thought it would make things easier ! Flint
axe, and all that ! Why don't I—— Hallo, hallo, hallo !
Steady, my boy ! Is wisions about ? "

He had reached the summit of the bluff.   There, two miles
to the northward, slipping gently over the rollers under easy
sail, he beheld a ship—a three-masted schooner.

VI

FOR a castaway, hungering for a re-entry into civilisation,
Mr. Gale's subsequent behaviour was peculiar.

He began by staring stockishly at the passing vehicle of
deliverance, evidently the prey of conflicting impulses. Beside
him lay a neatly piled heap of firewood, collected for such a
contingency as this. His eye fell thereon. He regarded it
absently, and then raised his eyes to the schooner, which went
about and began to slant towards the island.

Mr. Gale, instead of shouting or semaphoring, dropped
suddenly to his knees and crept furtively back whence he came,
until he arrived at the edge of the little plateau, to a position
which commanded their cave and encampment. Miss Etherington, from whose eyes the schooner was screened by the
intervening bulk of Point Garry, was diligently preparing
dinner. Mr. Gale gazed down upon her long and intently.
Her sleeves were rolled up for culinary duties, and her arms
looked very round and white. Snatches of a song she was
singing floated upwards to his ears. Mr. Gale's pulse quick-
ened ; his purpose hardened ; his conscience died within
him.

"I *can't* do it," he muttered—"I can't!" A box of matches dropped from his nerveless fingers. . . .

Presently he crawled upon his hands and knees—he would not even risk the exposure of his figure against the skyline now —to a position from which he could see the schooner. The breeze had freshened ; she had gone about again, and was bowling away from the island.

VII

An hour later they met for their evening meal. With characteristic fidelity to the customs of their order they invariably dressed for dinner—that is to say, Miss Etherington put on shoes and stockings and changed from her cricket-shirt to a silk jumper, while Mr. Gale attired himself in a suit of comparatively white drill which had once been the property of the chief steward of the yacht.

They were very silent that night. Mr. Gale's conscience was coming to life again. It was true that he loved Miss Etherington—far more, indeed, than that usually astute maiden could have gathered from the somewhat flippant and informal manner in which he had declared his passion—but this fact, urged his conscience, did not give him the sole right to her society. He had robbed her of her birthright that afternoon ; he had deliberately cut her off from a return to the great world and all it held for her. He had behaved like a cad, he felt, and being an honourable young man, he was filled with a desire to make confession.

"You are not very amusing to-night," remarked Miss Etherington suddenly.

For purposes of playful badinage, there was a tacit understanding between them that everything which went wrong on the island—from cyclones to a fit of the dumps—was Leslie Gale's fault ; and that long-suffering young man was growing accustomed to being treated as something between a sinful little schoolboy and a rather incompetent court jester.

"Am I to sparkle ?" he inquired meekly.

"Yes."

"I don't feel quite up to it."

"Well, flicker, anyhow !" urged Miss Etherington.

Mr. Gale reflected, and replied :

"I can't do it to-night. That moon makes me humpy. Look at it ! What a whopper !"

Both sat silently surveying the great silvery disc which hung above them, turning their little cove, with its yellow sand and green-clad rocks, into an etching in black and white. There was a long silence, broken by a tremendous sigh from Miss Etherington. Evidently the moon was beginning to exercise its usual pernicious influence.

"To-night's Great Thought—what is it?" inquired Mr. Gale encouragingly.

"I was thinking," said Miss Etherington dreamily, "what a good thing it would be if all the people who disliked one another for no reason at all could be dropped down together upon an island like this for a month or two."

Mr. Gale, knowing full well that a woman never embarks upon a general statement without intending it to have a personal application, carefully turned this sentiment over in his mind.

Then suddenly he glowed duskily.

"You mean," he said unsteadily, "that most people improve on acquaintance?"

"Yes," said Miss Etherington deliberately—"I do."

There was a pause. Then Gale continued:

"Even—people like me?"

Miss Etherington nodded.

"Even people like you," she said. "And," she added unexpectedly, "even people like me."

Mr. Gale glanced at her, then stirred in his seat and took a mighty breath of resolution.

"You could *never* be improved upon by an acquaintance, however long."

Then he heaved a great sigh of relief. An Englishman does not say these things easily—that is, when he means them.

Miss Etherington subjected her companion to a fleeting but adequate scrutiny, and saw that he was once more at her mercy. But she felt no desire to wither him up—to annihilate the flank thus rashly exposed. Three months of life in the open had entirely cured her of conceit and petty meanness. Still they had not eradicated in her the natural predilection of a woman for dallying with the fish upon the hook.

"I wonder if you mean that," she remarked in a voice which, though in form severe, in substance invited further folly on the part of Mr. Gale.

"Yes, I do mean it," he replied, without heat or passion

" But I am not going to pursue the subject, because I have no right. I have just done you a serious wrong. I want to make confession."

He turned to her, like a penitent to a shrine.

" This evening," he said, " when I climbed to Point Garry on my usual excursion, I saw a ship."

Miss Etherington started, but made no further sign.

" She was quite close," continued Gale, " and I could have caught her attention by signalling. But—I didn't ! I let her go ! There ! "

He stood motionless at her feet, awaiting sentence.

Miss Etherington raised her clear grey eyes to his.

" Why did you let the ship go ? " she asked.

" Because I love you so," said Gale simply. " I could not bear to be parted from you, as I knew I should be. It seemed too cruel to bring this life to an end, just as——"

" Just as what ? " asked the girl quickly.

" Just as you were beginning to get used to—it," concluded Leslie Gale, coward.

Miss Etherington was silent for a little time. Then she said :

" You made no attempt to signal ? "

" None."

" Concealed yourself, perhaps ? "

Gale nodded miserably, and waited.

Miss Etherington dropped her eyes again, and began to scrutinise the tips of her shoes.

" I wouldn't worry about it too much if I were you," she said.

" Why ? "

" I saw the ship too," said the girl demurely.

VIII

THEY sat on in the moonlight—and on, and on, and on. About half-past ten Mr. Gale had respectfully but firmly taken Miss Etherington's hand. Miss Etherington had made a half-hearted attempt to withdraw it. Mr. Gale had apologetically but pertinaciously held on. After that they began to talk, and although they had not been out of one another's company for the best part of three months, not one of the many topics with which they had whiled away that lengthy period intruded itself into the conversation. They seemed to have turned over a new page in the book of life together. Under their eyes it lay, fair, blank, and gleaming with blessed possibilities beneath the rays of a tropical moon. And for the moment they were well content to leave it so. Let to-morrow, with its prosaic meticulous pen and inkhorn, stand far off and wait! There would never be another hour like this.

At last Miss Etherington rose.

"I am sleepy," she said. "Let me go now."

Gale held her to him for a moment longer, caressing her loosely-knotted shimmering hair.

"Phyllis!" he murmured reverently, and raised his face skyward, as if to give thanks. From the neighbourhood of his right shoulder there arose a muffled observation. For a moment he failed to take note of it, for he was gaping dumbly over Miss Etherington's head at the moonlit waters of their bay. Miss Etherington accordingly spoke again.

"I wish," she murmured—"I wish there were a lot of people to tell."

"To tell what? That we are "—he coughed nervously —" engaged?"

"Yes. Engaged sounds queer on a desert island, doesn't it? But when a girl gets engaged she wants to tell *everybody*."

"That's strange. When *I* get engaged I feel that the secret is too precious to pass on to anybody. It's mine! mine! Ours! ours! 'Ours'—how wonderful that sounds after years of just 'mine.' But "—he brought his gaze back seaward again—" do you really want a crowd of people to tell your news to?"

"Yes, please," said Miss Etherington meekly.

"Well, shut your eyes, and don't open them until I tell you."

Miss Etherington obeyed. Mr. Gale rotated her carefully until she faced the calm, glittering ocean.

"Abracadabra! Likewise what ho! Open your eyes!" he commanded.

Miss Etherington obeyed. There before her in the moonlight, half-a-mile from the shore, like a misty sea-wraith, floated a great white yacht, drifting to an anchorage. Even as they gazed there was a luminous splash, and the cable rattled out.

IX

THEY were taken home next day on board the *Morning Star*, brought out to search for them by their host and the other survivors of the wreck.

For many years Mr. Leslie Gale never ceased to bless the three-masted schooner whose passing had been fraught with such uniting consequences. In fact he exalted that nameless vessel into a fetish, ascribing to it match-making properties bordering upon the supernatural. It was Mrs. Gale who pricked the bubble.

" I wonder, dearest," observed her husband one day, " if you would have ever found out that you really cared for me if you hadn't seen that old hooker go sailing by—what ? "

" I wonder," said Mrs. Gale patiently.

" It was lucky," continued the fatuous Leslie, " that no ship turned up earlier on, before you had acquired a taste for me, so to speak. That would have put me in the cart, wouldn't it ? "

" Would it ? "

" Yes. Supposing that it had happened sooner ? Supposing, for instance, that after we had been together for a matter of a few hours, instead of a few months, you had climbed Point Garry and seen a ship go sailing by ? What then ? "

Mrs. Gale arose, and began to put away her work.

" I did," she said briefly.

W. W. JACOBS (1863–   ), *as a humorist, has limited his field almost entirely to Wapping wharves or a certain country inn—the Cauliflower. On the wharf is a garrulous nightwatchman, outside the Cauliflower a no less garrulous ancient. There is also an additional character who makes an all too rare appearance —this is W. W. Jacobs himself. He has also written some classic stories of the supernatural.*

THE LADY OF THE BARGE

THE master of the barge *Arabella* sat in the stern of his craft with his right arm leaning on the tiller. A desultory conversation with the mate of a schooner, who was hanging over the side of his craft a few yards off, had come to a conclusion owing to a difference of opinion on the subject of religion. The skipper had argued so warmly that he almost fancied he must have inherited the tenets of the Seventh-day Baptists from his mother, while the mate had surprised himself by the warmth of his advocacy of a form of Wesleyanism which would have made the members of that sect open their eyes with horror. He had, moreover, confirmed the skipper in the error of his ways by calling him a bargee, the ranks of the Baptists receiving a defender if not a recruit from that hour.

With the influence of the religious argument still upon him, the skipper, as the long summer's day gave place to night, fell to wondering where his own mate, who was also his brother-in-law, had got to. Lights which had been struggling with the twilight now burnt bright and strong, and the skipper, moving from the shadow to where a band of light fell across the deck, took out a worn silver watch and saw that it was ten o'clock.

Almost at the same moment a dark figure appeared on the jetty above and began to descend the ladder, and a strongly built young man of twenty-two sprang nimbly to the deck.

" Ten o'clock, Ted," said the skipper slowly.

" It'll be eleven in an hour's time," said the mate calmly.

" That'll do," said the skipper, in a somewhat loud voice, as he noticed that his late adversary still occupied his favourite strained position, and a fortuitous expression of his mother's occurred to him : " Don't talk to me ; I've been arguing with a son of Belial for the last half-hour."

" Bargee," said the son of Belial, in a dispassionate voice.

" Don't take no notice of him, Ted," said the skipper pityingly.

" He wasn't talking to me," said Ted. " But never mind about him ; I want to speak to you in private."

" Fire away, my lad," said the other, in a patronising voice.

" Speak up," said the voice from the schooner encouragingly. " I'm listening."

There was no reply from the bargee. The master led the way to the cabin, and lighting a lamp, which appealed to more senses than one, took a seat on a locker, and again requested the other to fire away.

" Well, you see, it's this way," began the mate, with a preliminary wriggle ; " there's a certain young woman——"

" A certain young what ? " shouted the master of the *Arabella*.

" Woman," repeated the mate snappishly ; " you've heard of a woman afore, haven't you ? Well, there's a certain young woman I'm walking out with I——"

" Walking out ? " gasped the skipper. " Why, I never 'eard o' such a thing."

" You would ha' done if you'd been better looking, p'raps," retorted the other. " Well, I've offered this young woman to come for a trip with us."

" Oh, you have, 'ave you ! " said the skipper sharply. " And what do you think Louisa will say to it ? "

" That's your look out," said Louisa's brother cheerfully. " I'll make her up a bed for'ard, and we'll all be as happy as you please."

He started suddenly. The mate of the schooner was indulging in a series of whistles of the most amatory description.

" There she is," he said. " I told her to wait outside."

He ran upon deck, and his perturbed brother-in-law, following at his leisure, was just in time to see him descending the ladder with a young woman and a small handbag.

" This is my brother-in-law, Cap'n Gibbs," said Ted, introducing the new arrival ; " smartest man at a barge on the river."

The girl extended a neatly gloved hand, shook the skipper's affably, and looked wonderingly about her.

" It's very close to the water, Ted," she said dubiously.

The skipper coughed. " We don't take passengers as a rule," he said awkwardly : " we 'ain't got much convenience for them."

" Never mind," said the girl kindly : " I shan't expect too much."

She turned away, and following the mate down to the cabin, went into ecstasies over the space-saving contrivances she found there. The drawers fitted in the skipper's bunk were a source of particular interest, and the owner watched with strong disapprobation through the skylight her efforts to make him an apple-pie bed with the limited means at her disposal. He went down below at once as a wet blanket.

" I was just shaking your bed up a bit," said Miss Harris, reddening.

" I see you was," said the skipper briefly.

He tried to pluck up courage to tell her that he couldn't take her, but only succeeded in giving vent to an inhospitable cough.

" I'll get the supper," said the mate suddenly ; " you sit down, old man, and talk to Lucy."

In honour of the visitor he spread a small cloth, and then proceeded to produce cold beef, pickles, and accessories in a manner which reminded Miss Harris of white rabbits from a conjuror's hat. Captain Gibbs, accepting the inevitable, ate his supper in silence and left them to their glances.

" We must make you up a bed, for'ard, Lucy," said the mate, when they had finished.

Miss Harris started. " Where's that ? " she inquired.

" Other end o' the boat," replied the mate, gathering up some bedding under his arm. " You might bring a lantern, John."

The skipper, who was feeling more sociable after a couple of glasses of beer, complied, and accompanied the couple to the tiny forecastle. A smell compounded of bilge, tar, paint, and other healthy disinfectants emerged as the scuttle was pushed back. The skipper dangled the lantern down and almost smiled.

" I can't sleep there," said the girl, with decision. " I shall die o' fright."

" You'll get used to it," said Ted encouragingly, as he helped her down ; " it's quite dry and comfortable."

He put his arm round her waist and squeezed her hand, and aided by this moral support, Miss Harris not only consented to remain, but found various advantages in the forecastle over the cabin, which had escaped the notice of previous voyagers.

" I'll leave you the lantern," said the mate, making it fast, " and we shall be on deck most o' the night. We get under way at two."

He quitted the forecastle, followed by the skipper, after a polite but futile attempt to give him precedence, and made his way to the cabin for two or three hours' sleep.

" There'll be a row at the other end, Ted," said the skipper nervously, as he got into his bunk. " Louisa's sure to blame me for letting you keep company with a gal like this. We was talking about you only the other day, and she said if you was married five years from now, it 'ud be quite soon enough."

" Let Loo mind her own business," said the mate sharply ; " she's not going to nag me. She's not *my* wife, thank goodness ! "

He turned over and fell fast asleep, waking up fresh and bright three hours later, to commence what he fondly thought would be the pleasantest voyage of his life.

The *Arabella* dropped slowly down with the tide, the wind being so light that she was becalmed by every tall warehouse on the way. Off Greenwich, however, the breeze freshened somewhat, and a little later Miss Harris, looking somewhat pale as to complexion and untidy as to hair, came slowly on deck.

" Where's the looking-glass ? " she asked, as Ted hastened to greet her. " How does my hair look ? "

" All wavy," said the infatuated young man ; " all little curls and squiggles. Come down in the cabin ; there's a glass there."

Miss Harris, with a light nod to the skipper as he sat at the tiller, followed the mate below, and giving vent to a little cry of indignation as she saw herself in the glass, waved the amorous Ted on deck, and started work on her disarranged hair.

At breakfast-time a little friction was caused by what the mate bitterly termed the narrow-minded, old-fashioned ways of the skipper. He had arranged that the skipper should steer while he and Miss Harris breakfasted, but the coffee was no sooner on the table than the skipper called him, and relinquishing the helm in his favour, went below to do the honours. The mate protested.

"It's not proper," said the skipper. "Me and 'er will 'ave our meals together, and then you must have yours. She's under my care."

Miss Harris assented blithely, and talk and laughter greeted the ears of the indignant mate as he steered. He went down at last to cold coffee and lukewarm herrings, returning to the deck after a hurried meal to find the skipper narrating some of his choicest experiences to an audience which hung on his lightest word.

The disregard they showed for his feelings was maddening, and for the first time in his life he became a prey to jealousy in its worst form. It was quite clear to him that the girl had become desperately enamoured of the skipper, and he racked his brain in a wild effort to discover the reason.

With an idea of reminding his brother-in-law of his position, he alluded two or three times in a casual fashion to his wife. The skipper hardly listened to him, and patting Miss Harris's cheek in a fatherly manner, regaled her with an anecdote of the mate's boyhood which the latter had spent a goodly portion of his life in denying. He denied it again hotly, and Miss Harris, conquering for a time her laughter, reprimanded him severely for contradicting.

By the time dinner was ready he was in a state of sullen apathy, and when the meal was over and the couple came on deck again, so far forgot himself as to compliment Miss Harris upon her appetite.

"I'm ashamed of you, Ted," said the skipper, with severity.

"I'm glad you know what shame is," retorted the mate.

"If you can't be'ave yourself, you'd better keep a bit for'ard till you get in a better temper," continued the skipper.

"I'll be pleased to," said the smarting mate. "I wish the barge was longer."

"It couldn't be too long for me," said Miss Harris, tossing her head.

"Be'aving like a schoolboy," murmured the skipper.

"I know how to behave *my*-self," said the mate, as he disappeared below. His head suddenly appeared again over the companion. "If some people don't," he added, and disappeared again.

He was pleased to notice as he ate his dinner that the giddy prattle above had ceased, and with his back turned toward the couple when he appeared on deck again, he lounged slowly forward until the skipper called him back again.

"Wot was them words you said just now, Ted?" he inquired.

The mate repeated them with gusto.

"Very good," said the skipper sharply; "very good."

"Don't you ever speak to me again," said Miss Harris, with a stately air, "because I won't answer you if you do."

The mate displayed more of his schoolboy nature. "Wait till you're spoken to," he said rudely. "This is your gratefulness, I suppose?"

"Gratefulness?" said Miss Harris, with her chin in the air. "What for?"

"For bringing you for a trip," replied the mate sternly.

"*You* bringing me for a trip!" said Miss Harris scornfully. "Captain Gibbs is the master here, I suppose. He is giving me the trip. You're only the mate."

"Just so," said the mate, with a grin at his brother-in-law, which made that worthy shift uneasily. "I wonder what Loo will say when she sees you with a lady aboard?"

"She came to please you," said Captain Gibbs, with haste.

"Ho! she did, did she?" jeered the mate. "Prove it; only don't look to me to back you, that's all."

The other eyed him in consternation, and his manner changed.

"Don't play the fool, Ted," he said, not unkindly; "you know what Loo is."

"Well, I'm reckoning on that," said the mate deliberately. "I'm going for'ard; don't let me interrupt you two. So long."

He went slowly forward, and lighting his pipe, sprawled carelessly on the deck, and renounced the entire sex forthwith. At tea-time the skipper attempted to reverse the procedure at the other meals; but as Miss Harris steadfastly declined to sit at the same table as the mate, his good intentions came to naught.

He made an appeal to what he termed the mate's better nature, after Miss Harris had retired to the seclusion of her bed-chamber, but in vain.

"She's nothing to do with me," declared the mate majestically. "I wash my hands of her. She's a flirt. I'm like Louisa, I can't bear flirts."

The skipper said no more, but his face was so worn that Miss Harris, when she came on deck in the early morning and found the barge gliding gently between the grassy banks of a river, attributed it to the difficulty of navigating so large a craft on so small and winding a stream.

" We shall be alongside in 'arf an hour," said the skipper, eyeing her.

Miss Harris expressed her gratification.

" P'raps you wouldn't mind going down the fo'c'sle and staying there till we've made fast," said the other. " I'd take it as a favour. My owners don't like me to carry passengers."

Miss Harris, who understood perfectly, said, " Certainly," and with a cold stare at the mate, who was at no pains to conceal his amusement, went below at once, thoughtfully closing the scuttle after her.

" There's no call to make mischief, Ted," said the skipper, somewhat anxiously, as they swept round the last bend and came into view of Coalsham.

The mate said nothing, but stood by to take in sail as they ran swiftly toward the little quay. The pace slackened, and the *Arabella*, as though conscious of the contraband in her forecastle, crept slowly to where a stout, middle-aged woman, who bore a strong likeness to the mate, stood upon the quay.

" There's poor Loo," said the mate, with a sigh.

The skipper made no reply to this infernal insinuation. The barge ran alongside the quay and made fast.

" I thought you'd be up," said Mrs. Gibbs to her husband. " Now come along to breakfast ; Ted'll follow on."

Captain Gibbs dived down below for his coat, and slipping ashore, thankfully prepared to move off with his wife.

" Come on as soon as you can, Ted," said the latter. " Why, what on earth is he making that face for ? "

She turned in amazement as her brother, making a pretence of catching her husband's eye, screwed his face up into a note of interrogation and gave a slight jerk with his thumb.

" Come along," said Captain Gibbs, taking her arm with much affection.

" But what's Ted looking like that for ? " demanded his wife, as she easily intercepted another choice facial expression of the mate's.

" Oh, it's his fun," replied her husband, walking on.

" *Fun ?* " repeated Mrs. Gibbs sharply. " What's the matter, Ted ? "

" Nothing," replied the mate.

" Touch o' toothache," said the skipper. " Come along, Loo ; I can just do with one o' your breakfasts."

Mrs. Gibbs suffered herself to be led on, and had got at least five yards on the way home, when she turned and looked back. The mate had still got the toothache, and was at that moment in all the agonies of a phenomenal twinge.

" There's something wrong here," said Mrs. Gibbs as she retraced her steps. " Ted, what are you making that face for ? "

" It's my own face," said the mate evasively.

Mrs. Gibbs conceded the point, and added bitterly that it couldn't be helped. All the same she wanted to know what he meant by it.

" Ask John," said the vindictive mate.

Mrs. Gibbs asked. Her husband said he didn't know, and added that Ted had been like it before, but he had not told her for fear of frightening her. Then he tried to induce her to go with him to the chemist's to get something for it.

Mrs. Gibbs shook her head firmly, and boarding the barge, took a seat on the hatch and proceeded to catechise her brother as to his symptoms. He denied that there was anything the matter with him, while his eyes openly sought those of Captain Gibbs as though asking for instruction.

" You come home, Ted," she said at length.

" I can't," said the mate. " I can't leave the ship."

" Why not ? " demanded his sister.

" Ask John," said the mate again.

At this Mrs. Gibbs's temper, which had been rising, gave way altogether, and she stamped fiercely upon the deck. A stamp of the foot has been for all time a rough-and-ready means of signalling ; the fore-scuttle was drawn back, and the face of a young and pretty girl appeared framed in the opening. The mate raised his eyebrows with a helpless gesture, and as for the unfortunate skipper, any jury would have found him guilty without leaving the box. The wife of his bosom, with a flaming visage, turned and regarded him.

" You villain ! " she said, in a choking voice.

Captain Gibbs caught his breath and looked appealingly at the mate.

" It's a little surprise for you, my dear," he faltered ; " it's Ted's young lady."

" Nothing of the kind," said the mate sharply.

" It's not ? How dare you say such a thing ? " demanded Miss Harris, stepping on to the deck.

" Well, you brought her aboard, Ted ; you know you did," pleaded the unhappy skipper.

The mate did not deny it, but his face was so full of grief and surprise that the other's heart sank within him.

"All right," said the mate at last; "have it your own way."

"Hold your tongue, Ted," shouted Mrs. Gibbs; "you're trying to shield him."

"I tell you Ted brought her aboard, and they had a lovers' quarrel," said her unhappy spouse. "It's nothing to do with me at all."

"And that's why you told me Ted had got the toothache, and tried to get me off to the chemist's, I s'pose," retorted his wife, with virulence. "Do you think I'm a fool? How dare you ask a young woman on this barge? How dare you?"

"I didn't ask her," said her husband.

"I s'pose she came without being asked," sneered his wife, turning her regards to the passenger; "she looks the sort that might. You brazen-faced girl!"

"Here, go easy, Loo," interrupted the mate, flushing as he saw the girl's pale face.

"Mind your own business," said his sister violently.

"It is my business," said the repentant mate. "I brought her aboard, and then we quarrelled."

"I've no doubt," said his sister bitterly; "it's very pretty, but it won't do."

"I swear it's the truth," said the mate.

"Why did John keep it so quiet and hide her for, then?" demanded his sister.

"I came down for the trip," said Miss Harris; "that is all about it. There is nothing to make a fuss about. How much is it, Captain Gibbs?"

She produced a little purse from her pocket, but before the embarrassed skipper could reply, his infuriated wife struck it out of her hand. The mate sprang instinctively forward, but too late, and the purse fell with a splash into the water. The girl gave a faint cry and clasped her hands.

"How am I to get back?" she gasped.

"I'll see to that, Lucy," said the mate. "I'm very sorry —I've been a brute."

"You?" said the indignant girl. "I would sooner drown myself than be beholden to you."

"I'm very sorry," repeated the mate humbly.

"There's enough of this play-acting," interposed Mrs. Gibbs. "Get off this barge."

"You stay where you are," said the mate authoritatively.

"Send that girl off this barge," screamed Mrs. Gibbs to her husband.

Captain Gibbs smiled in a silly fashion and scratched his head. "Where is she to go?" he asked feebly.

"What does it matter to you where she goes?" cried his wife fiercely. "Send her off."

The girl eyed her haughtily, and repulsing the mate as he strove to detain her, stepped to the side. Then she paused as he suddenly threw off his coat, and sitting down on the hatch, hastily removed his boots. The skipper, divining his intentions, seized him by the arm.

"Don't be a fool, Ted," he gasped; "you'll get under the barge."

The mate shook him off, and went in with a splash which half drowned his adviser. Miss Harris, clasping her hands, ran to the side and gazed fearfully at the spot where he had disappeared, while his sister in a terrible voice seized the opportunity to point out to her husband the probably fatal results of his ill-doing. There was an anxious interval, and then the mate's head appeared above the water, and after a breathing-space, disappeared again. The skipper, watching uneasily, stood by with a life-belt.

"Come out, Ted," screamed his sister as he came up for breath again.

The mate disappeared once more, but coming up for the third time, hung on to the side of the barge to recover a bit. A clothed man in the water savours of disaster and looks alarming. Miss Harris began to cry.

"You'll be drowned," she whimpered.

"Come out," said Mrs. Gibbs, in a raspy voice. She knelt on the deck and twined her fingers in his hair. The mate addressed her in terms rendered brotherly by pain.

"Never mind about the purse," sobbed Miss Harris; "it doesn't matter."

"Will you make it up if I come out, then?" demanded the diver.

"No; I'll never speak to you again as long as I live," said the girl passionately.

The mate disappeared again. This time he was out of sight longer than usual, and when he came up merely tossed his arms weakly and went down again. There was a scream from the women, and a mighty splash as the skipper went

The mate shook him off and went in with a splash.

overboard with a life-belt. The mate's head, black and shining, showed for a moment ; the skipper grabbed him by the hair and towed him to the barge's side, and in the midst of a considerable hubbub both men were drawn from the water.

The skipper shook himself like a dog, but the mate lay on the deck inert in a puddle of water. Mrs. Gibbs frantically slapped his hands ; and Miss Harris, bending over him, rendered first aid by kissing him wildly.

Captain Gibbs pushed her away. "He won't come round while you're a-kissing of him," he cried roughly.

To his indignant surprise the drowned man opened one eye and winked acquiescence. The skipper dropped his arms by his side and stared at him stupidly.

"I saw his eyelid twitch," cried Mrs. Gibbs joyfully.

"He's all right," said her indignant husband ; "'e ain't born to be drowned, 'e ain't. I've spoilt a good suit of clothes for nothing."

To his wife's amazement, he actually walked away from the insensible man, and with a boat-hook reached for his hat, which was floating by. Mrs. Gibbs, still gazing in blank astonishment, caught a seraphic smile on the face of her brother as Miss Harris continued her ministrations, and in a pardonable fit of temper the overwrought woman gave him a box on the ear, which brought him round at once.

"Where am I ?" he inquired artlessly.

Mrs. Gibbs told him. She also told him her opinion of him, and without plagiarising her husband's words, came to the same conclusion as to his ultimate fate.

"You come along home with me," she said, turning in a friendly fashion to the bewildered girl. "They deserve what they've got—both of 'em. I only hope that they'll both get such awful colds that they won't find their voices for a twelve-month."

She took the girl by the arm and helped her ashore. They turned their heads once in the direction of the barge, and saw the justly incensed skipper keeping the mate's explanations and apologies at bay with a boat-hook. Then they went in to breakfast.

HERBERT JENKINS (1876–1923) *was no less successful as the founder of a publishing firm than as the creator of the human and endearing Bindle family. The first Bindle book, published in 1916, was so well received that the author was thenceforward kept busy creating fresh situations for the family until his premature death, for which overwork in the double capacity of author and publisher was largely responsible.*

THE BINDLES AT THE ZOO

I

"YOU can get your own tea on Sunday," announced Mrs. Bindle, as she banged upon the table a yellow pie-dish containing Irish stew.

"Get my own tea?" queried Bindle, looking up from the newspaper he had been surreptitiously reading, newspapers not being popular with Mrs. Bindle at meal-times. "Why should I get my own tea on Sunday, Mrs. B.?"

"Because I'm going out, that's why," she retorted. "I suppose you'd like me to give up all my pleasures as well as wait on you hand and foot."

"Where you going, Lizzie?" he enquired pacifically. He hated storms before meat—they always affected the size of Mrs. Bindle's "helpings."

"I'm going to the Zoo."

"To live?"

A moment later he cursed himself for his glib tongue. The nice meaty chop that Mrs. Bindle had in the spoon was dropped back into the dish, and a piece of unattractive scrag selected in its place.

"Mr. Hearty has invited me to go with him."

For the next few minutes Bindle occupied himself in trying to find some vulnerable spot for his knife and fork in the piece of scrag that lay on his plate.

"He's had some tickets given him. It's a private day on Sunday," announced Mrs. Bindle presently, determined to get the full flavour out of the episode.

"Better put this 'ere piece of bone in your pocket for the

lions in case they 'aven't got enough," he said gloomily, turning over the bit of scrag and examining it from the underside.

" That's right, complain about your food. Pity you haven't got something else to grumble about "—Mrs. Bindle was out for blood. " It's grumble, grumble, grumble, morning, noon, and night. Nothing ever satisfies you, and meat the price it is."

" Can't I have somethink with a bit o' meat on it, then ? " he complained, still making valiant efforts to dissect that which nature had never intended should be dissected.

" There, look at you now ! "

In his struggle, Bindle had approached too near the edge of the plate, with the result that it had suddenly tilted towards him, depositing its contents upon his knees.

" You're not fit to eat with pigs," was Mrs. Bindle's comment, as she watched Bindle scrape from his clothes and pick up from the floor what remained of his meal, using a spoon for the purpose. This done, he pushed his plate towards her ; but Mrs. Bindle ignored the hint.

" Give us a bit more, Lizzie," he pleaded.

" There isn't any more," she announced with decision.

" No more ! " he echoed in consternation. " But there's a lot in the dish."

" That's got to do for to-morrow. You seem to forget the price of things. In future you'd better take your meals in the scullery, then you can slop your food about as you like."

" But I ain't 'ad anythink to eat yet," he grumbled.

Mrs. Bindle ignored the protest, but compromised a delicate situation by dabbing on his plate two potatoes, some gravy, and a small piece of meat.

Another time the news that Mrs. Bindle and Mr. Hearty were going to the Zoo would have filled Bindle with unholy joy ; but it is a humorous head that laughs on an empty stomach. When he left No. 7 Fenton Street to return to his work, it was with a sense of grievance that somehow seemed to involve his brother-in-law, Mr. Hearty, and the Zoo itself.

All the afternoon he brooded over the wrong that had been done him, inspired to discontent by the feeling of emptiness within.

That evening, when he left work, he took a bus to Chelsea to call on his friend, Dr. Richard Little, whom he found at home. When, half an hour later, he left the surgery, it was with a lighter heart and a brighter outlook. Dr. Little had promised to obtain from a friend tickets for the Zoological Gardens which could be used on the following Sunday. Bindle's plaintive remark that " Some'ow it doesn't seem right to miss seein' Mrs. B. and 'Earty in the monkey 'ouse " had proved irresistible.

On the following Sunday the Bindles dined early. One o'clock saw Mrs. Bindle's kitchen spotless, with not a thing awry, and tea laid for one. Mrs. Bindle herself stood at the door taking a final look round to see that everything was as it should be.

" You'll find tea in the cup. Mind you hot the pot first and see the water's boiling, then let it stand for three minutes."

She was arrayed in her best alpaca and her most biscuit-coloured gloves, tight across the palms to the point of discomfort. Her bonnet of purple, " picked out with spring-leaf green," sat perpendicularly upon her head, and the purple ribbons were tied with meticulous neatness beneath her sharp chin.

From her elastic-sided boots, with patent-leather toe-caps, to the top of her rather forbidding headgear, she was conscious that there was nothing amiss. In Bindle's idiom, she felt herself to be " It."

" And mind you don't spill your tea on the cloth," she said as she turned towards the door, " and when you've finished put your cup and saucer and plate in the pan in the sink."

" You're wastin' a lot o' breath, Mrs. B.," said Bindle at length. " I ain't a-goin' to be 'ome to tea."

" Then why couldn't you say so before, and save me laying it ? "

Bindle had postponed the announcement until the last moment. He had intended telling Mrs. Bindle that he also was bound for the Zoo ; but just as the words were on his lips he realised that a more dramatic effect might be obtained by presenting himself to his wife and brother-in-law as they were indulging in their pleasures.

Five minutes later the front door banged, and Mrs. Bindle was on her way to Putney Bridge Station, to meet her brother-in-law.

II

" I THINK," remarked Mr. Hearty, with the air of one who has given the matter mature consideration, " I think, Elizabeth, that we ought to see the lions fed."

" I should like it, Mr. Hearty," said Mrs. Bindle, drawing in her chin, which, when with Mr. Hearty, was always a sign that she was pleased. " I have never seen the lions fed," she added, as one announcing that she had never tasted artichokes.

" Can you tell me what time the lions are fed ? " enquired Mr. Hearty politely, as they passed through the turnstiles.

" Four o'clock," replied the man, in the tone of one who suffers fools professionally.

" We must see the Mappin Terraces also," announced Mr. Hearty, springing open the case of his gold hunter. Mr. Hearty never lost an opportunity of acquainting himself with the time.

" I should like to," said Mrs. Bindle, utterly at sea as to what a Mappin terrace might be ; but prepared to see every animal known to Noah.

For nearly half an hour they proceeded to stroll about, aimless and uncertain, Mr. Hearty generally half a yard in front. He realised that care was necessary in a place like the Zoo. He had already determined to do all he could to head Mrs. Bindle off from the Monkey House.

Mr. Hearty was never at home in the Monkey House. There was a certain realistic freedom adopted by monkeys which he found disconcerting.

Suddenly his eye caught sight of the words " Cat House." Recalling a previous visit to the Zoo, he piloted Mrs. Bindle past the entrance.

" Phew ! What a stink ! "

As the words assailed his ears Mr. Hearty shuddered. A moment later, his head jerked forward, as a flat and hearty hand caught him full between the shoulders.

" So I caught you, 'ave I ? "

Mr. Hearty turned to find himself blinking uncertainly into the eyes of Bindle behind a large cigar with a red and gold band. In the background stood Ginger, a gloomy picture of pimpled misanthropy, emphasised by a Cambridge-blue tie. Ginger's complexion had never been schemed for delicate tints in neck-wear.

Mrs. Bindle glared at Ginger, then, as if dazzled by his tie, she transferred her eyes to Bindle.

" What are you doing here ? " she demanded.

" Jest a-toddlin' round sayin' 'ow-jer-do to the snakes," was the response. " Been to see the old toms ? " he enquired pleasantly of Mr. Hearty, who shuddered at the question.

" Blinkin' stink ! " was Ginger's comment. " I'd poison 'em," he added malevolently. " Don't 'old wiv cats ! "

" Come along, 'Earty," said Bindle, linking his arm in that of his reluctant brother-in-law. " Funny thing seein' you 'ere. Dr. Little give me two tickets, so I brought ole Ging. The Zoo always cheers 'im up, don't it, Ging ? " he threw over his shoulder, at which Ginger growled a remark about not holding with something or other.

During the short conversation Mrs. Bindle had stood with indrawn lips. She saw in Bindle's sudden appearance with the unspeakable Ginger, whom she detested, another organised attempt to humiliate her.

As Bindle led Mr. Hearty away, she had perforce to follow with Ginger, who, conversationally, was an undischarged bankrupt. This, coupled with his openly expressed hatred of women, rendered him a questionable cavalier.

" Nothin' but one stink after another," he grumbled.

Mrs. Bindle stiffened. In her own mind she was preparing things she intended to say to Bindle when a suitable occasion presented itself.

" 'Ere, Ging, come an' look at this," cried Bindle, who had pulled up in front of a cage in which sat, with embarrassing frankness and composure, a mandrill.

Mrs. Bindle suddenly became conscious that Mr. Hearty had turned and was walking hurriedly away.

" Did jer ever see anythink like it ? " demanded Bindle of Ginger. " Looks as if 'e'd——"

" Bindle ! "

Mrs. Bindle's lips had entirely disappeared. A moment later she too turned and walked swiftly away in the direction taken by Mr. Hearty. Ginger leant forward, one hand on either knee, examining with an interest that surprised Bindle the eccentrically marked mandrill.

" Wot jer think of 'im, Ging ? "

" Funny old blinker ! " muttered Ginger presently. " Fancy 'avin' to go about wiv a——"

" 'Ush, Ging ! Remember it's Sunday," and Bindle drew his reluctant friend away from the mandrill's cage.

" Fancy a-paintin' of 'im up like that," persisted Ginger. " Funny place to——"

" 'Ush, Ging ! " murmured Bindle.

" 'Oo's 'e ? " demanded Ginger, as he and Bindle proceeded to overtake Mr. Hearty, who had waited for Mrs.

Bindle. " 'E ain't 'alf got the blinkin' 'eart bowed down,"
he added.

Bindle explained the relationship.

" 'Ullo, they're going to see the elephants," he said, as Mrs.
Bindle and Mr. Hearty disappeared into the elephant shed.

Upon Mr. Hearty's features as he entered was the expression of a man who finds the atmosphere distasteful.   He
possessed an extremely delicate sense of smell.

Taking her cue from her brother-in-law, Mrs. Bindle
drew a handkerchief from her pocket and held it to her
nose.

" I likes the smell of elephants," announced Bindle, with
the air of one announcing that heliotrope or mignonette is a
delight to his nostrils.

" I don't 'old wiv elephants," grumbled Ginger, as he
gazed at the waving trunk of the elephant before which they
were standing.

" Get away, you brute ! "

Mrs. Bindle brought her umbrella down with a vigorous
smack on the side of the trunk, which the elephant, anticipating
hospitality, had thrust towards her, opening and closing the
viscid extremity invitingly.

A moment later Mrs. Bindle started back with a scream,
dropping her umbrella.   The elephant, resenting the assault,
had blown deliberately in her face, with the result that to Mrs.
Bindle's features clung much elephantine moisture.

Mr. Hearty turned and made for the door, while Ginger
laughed.

So astonished was Bindle at the sight of Ginger laughing
that he forgot Mrs. Bindle in the contemplation of what was,
so far as his experience went, a record.

" Blinkin' old 'Un, spittin' like that," said Ginger, and he
laughed again.   Ginger had spent six months in a German
prison.

A keeper strolled up and proceeded to soothe the irate
pachyderm.

With fingers that trembled with anger, Mrs. Bindle proceeded to remove her veil and then to wipe her face.   This done,
she turned upon the keeper.

" I shall report you," she announced, " for—for not putting
that brute in a cage."

" He's harmless enough, mum," was the keeper's cool
retort ;   " but he don't like being hit.   It's a wonder he didn't

lift you up and dash you against the roof," he added, drawing upon his imagination.

Mrs. Bindle retreated a pace, realising that she was still within reach of that tenuous menace.

Mr. Hearty had disappeared, and a moment later Mrs. Bindle followed, while Bindle and Ginger brought up the rear.

" I'll report that man ! " announced Mrs. Bindle to Mr. Hearty as she continued to rub her face ; it still felt contracted, due to the elephant's stickiness.

" They ought not to allow such brutes loose," said Mr. Hearty with conviction. He had already made up his mind to approach nothing that was not behind iron bars. He almost regretted his suggestion that they should see the lions fed.

" It's ten minutes to four, 'Earty," cried Bindle from behind. " We'd better go and see 'em feed the lions."

The lions did not appear to be hungry ; they accepted their joints with a callousness that disappointed both Bindle and Ginger, who had hoped for " a bit of a scrap."

Mrs. Bindle expressed her views upon the quality of the meat supplied, the arrival of which Bindle had heralded with : " Oh, lor, don't it niff ? "

The zoological interests of Mrs. Bindle and Ginger were as poles asunder. The exhibits which interested Ginger aroused in Mrs. Bindle a feeling of repulsion. Their first differences of opinion arose in regard to the kangaroos.

Ginger was not overburdened with zoological knowledge ; but one thing he did know, and that was the way in which certain marsupials, notably the kangaroo, carry their young. With Ginger, to know a thing was to impart the knowledge to others. In general he was a man upon whose lips had fallen a great silence.

From the first he had been anxious to discover the whereabouts of the kangaroos. When at last he found them, Ginger gave a little grunt of satisfaction.

" Look ! " he said, seizing Mrs. Bindle by the arm and pointing to a lady kangaroo. " See, that's where it carries—— "

For answer, Mrs. Bindle gripped her umbrella and brought its knob in sharp contact with Ginger's chin.

" 'Ere, wot the blinkin'—— ! " he shouted.

" Steady, Ginger," grinned Bindle, " this ain't a bloomin' Cabinet Meetin'. "

" Wot she want to biff me wiv 'er umbrella for ? " he demanded angrily.

" If you give me any more of your lewd talk I'll do it again,"
announced Mrs. Bindle, pale with anger.

" I only said——" began Ginger.

" Stop it ! " cried Mrs. Bindle, raising the umbrella, and
Ginger stopped it.

Mrs. Bindle walked on with Mr. Hearty. For her, kangaroos
were irretrievably and for ever banned as disgusting beasts.

Ginger stayed behind to explain to Bindle the nursery
accommodation provided by nature for juvenile kangaroos.

Another crisis arose owing to a heated discussion between
Bindle and Ginger about a zoological matter connected with a
white-bearded gnu, which both seemed satisfied to call " gee-
new." Bindle maintained that it was a lord of creation, whilst
Ginger was equally convinced that it was what he described as
" a milker."

Mr. Hearty now had the appearance of a man possessed of
some secret dread. He approached each pen or cage with
suspicion, taking a hurried glance at the inmates before he
ventured to pause for a closer inspection. Mr. Hearty was a
man upon whom delicacy had descended as a blight.

Ginger's other zoological titbit of information was concerned
with the amazing characteristics of the camels. During the
War he had served in Egypt.

" 'Ain't got no blinkin' feelin's, 'aven't camels," he announced. " Plug 'em through the innards an' they jest
'iccups. I——" Ginger stopped suddenly, noticing a certain
rigidity about Mrs. Bindle's umbrella-arm.

" Look 'ere, Joe," he grumbled a few minutes later. " If
your missis lands me wiv 'er umbrella again, I'm goin' to dot
'er one."

Mr. Hearty received one shock. Much to his interest, he
had discovered a skirt that was short even for London, and the
limbs beneath were shapely. Mr. Hearty's zoological interest
became intensified.

" I *am* surprised at you ! " cried a hoarse voice, almost in
his ear.

Dropping his umbrella, he spun round with the air of a
man discovered in some illicit act, only to face a moth-eaten
parrot of dingy reds and yellows and blues with a huge bone
beak.

By the time Mr. Hearty had retrieved his umbrella, the
skirt, and what the skirt had inadequately covered, had disappeared.

III

THROUGHOUT the afternoon Bindle had been doing his utmost to head the party in the direction of the Monkey House, but both Mrs. Bindle and Mr. Hearty seemed determined to avoid that particular spot.

Matters were at length brought to a crisis by a remark from Ginger.

" Wot about the blinkin' monkeys ? " he demanded, suddenly coming to a standstill. " We got to see them."

Mr. Hearty, who had stared violently at the adjective, looked across at Mrs. Bindle. She appeared to hesitate.

" You ain't been to the Zoo if you 'aven't seen the monkeys," said Bindle. " Come along, 'Earty, I know the way," with which he linked his arm through that of Mr. Hearty and made off in the direction of the Monkey House.

" Funny little blinkers, them monkeys," grumbled Ginger.

He had been almost genial since the elephant's attack on Mrs. Bindle.

" Didn't 'alf spit in yer eye, did 'e ? " he added, his mind still dwelling upon the delightful feeling he had experienced at seeing Mrs. Bindle blown upon by an elephant.

Mrs. Bindle lifted her chin. She disliked Ginger intensely.

" I'll thank you to keep your remarks to yourself," she said, drawing in her lips.

" Eh ? " Ginger's mouth opened vacantly. With him it was a sign that he failed to understand.

" You've got a lewd tongue," continued Mrs. Bindle.

" No, I ain't," he contradicted, " it's fur. 'Ad a thick night last night, I did," he added, by way of explanation.

" It's what ? " she demanded.

" Fur ! " said Ginger, " Look ! " and he produced from between his lips an unearthly looking thing of grey and blue and pink.

" You beast ! " and with that Mrs. Bindle hurried forward, leaving the astonished Ginger with his tongue still protruding from his lips, puzzled to account for her reception of what, to him, was a friendly act. He showed his tongue to few women.

" If you don't stop that man saying disgusting things to me, Bindle, I shall tell a keeper," cried Mrs. Bindle on catching up with the others.

" 'E's all right is ole Ging," said Bindle genially as he turned
once more to Mr. Hearty, to whom he was explaining, much
to Mr. Hearty's embarrassment, a certain incident he had seen
in the Monkey House on the occasion of his last visit to the
Zoo. The presence of Mrs. Bindle, however, robbed the story
of much of its realism.

It had been Mr. Hearty's intention carefully to avoid the
Monkey House. He recalled once having visited it with Mrs.
Hearty, and her Rabelaisian mirth had embarrassed him so
painfully that he had left the building, preferring to wait for her
outside.

As the party entered the Monkey House, Mr. Hearty had
the air of a man determined to see nothing he ought not to see.
Mrs. Bindle was clearly on the defensive. She was prepared
to retreat at the least manifestation of that from which, in her
opinion, all nice-minded people should retire.

Ginger manifested eagerness, while Bindle's attitude was
clearly that of a man who is approaching what he regards as
" the tasty bit of the 'ole show," as he had just expressed it to
his brother-in-law.

Mr. Hearty took the precaution of moving on ahead,
leaving Mrs. Bindle wedged in a stream of people, with Bindle
and Ginger in attendance.

Never had Bindle known Ginger so loquacious. He volunteered a great deal of information about monkeys, most of which
was inaccurate ; he seemed to have a considerable store of
recollections upon which to draw.

Bindle fed the stream of reminiscence by judicious enquiry.

Mr. Hearty was doing better than he had anticipated. He
decided that the Monkey House was obviously a place to visit
alone.

" Look, Joe ! " cried Ginger, his freckled face assuming an
expression of almost animation. " Look at them two up there.
Tell your missis ! " Ginger was too wise to address Mrs.
Bindle directly.

" Hi ! " Ginger called to Mr. Hearty. " See that ? " and
he pointed to a bar on which a monkey was lying luxuriously
extended, whilst a colleague was going over him as with a
toothcomb.

" 'E don't 'alf like it," cried Ginger, his eyes fixed upon
the pair. " Look, 'e's turning over." Ginger was determined
that no one should lose the most trifling detail or incident if he
could avoid it.

"If you don't stop that man, I'll hit him again," hissed Mrs. Bindle, in Bindle's ear.

"Stop, Ging!" cried Bindle incredulously. "You might jest as well 'ave tried to stop the War as ole Ging when 'e gets on monkeys. There's only two things wot really sets 'im goin'; one's bell-tents an' the other's monkeys. You been in a bell-tent, now you——"

"Look!" cried Ginger excitedly. "Look at that little blinker!" In his eagerness he failed to realise that Bindle and Mrs. Bindle had changed positions, and he nudged her where Mrs. Bindle strongly objected to being nudged.

Without a moment's hesitation she jabbed the handle of her umbrella in Ginger's direction. The ferrule, however, caught in the cage and prodded a large grey monkey, attracting its attention from behind. In a flash it seemed to swing up above the netting and, a moment later, a long mole-coloured arm darted out from between the bars.

There was a scream and Mrs. Bindle stood bonnetless, her thin sandy hair hanging in wisps about her hatchet-like head, while an ecstatic monkey, with a purple and green bonnet, was swiftly retreating to the highest and most inaccessible portion of the cage.

"Stop him!" she cried wildly, recovering from the shock. "He's got my bonnet."

For the second time that afternoon Ginger laughed, a loud raucous bark that seemed to goad Mrs. Bindle to fury.

"You brute!" she cried. "It was your fault." She made another lunge at Ginger with her umbrella, missed him and caught Bindle on the side of the nose.

With a yelp of pain he clapped his hand to his face.

"'Ere, what are you doin', Lizzie?" he yelled.

"That monkey's got my bonnet! Here, you!" she cried, as a keeper pushed his way through the crowd.

"Go in and get it!" she ordered, as the keeper came alongside.

"I can't do that, mum," said the man civilly.

"Then I'll report you," was the furious retort. "I want to see the manager."

"See the what?"

"The manager—the manager of the Zoo," she added, as if to leave no doubt as to the identity of him with whom she desired speech.

The man scratched his head through his cap.

There was a scream and Mrs. Bindle stood bonnetless, her thin,
sandy hair hanging in wisps about her hatchet-like head.

" You mean the secretary, mum," he ventured. " He isn't here on Sundays."

" I want my bonnet ! " cried Mrs. Bindle, making frantic efforts to tuck away the wayward strands of sandy hair, her eyes fixed upon the robber of her headgear.

" Tie your handkerchief over your head," suggested a little man whose face radiated friendliness.

" Hold your tongue ! " snapped Mrs. Bindle ; then, turning to the keeper, she demanded.

" Are you going to get my bonnet ? "

The keeper once more explained the impossibility of the task.

" Then I shall report you ! " she announced for the second time. " I can't go home like this. Where's Mr. Hearty ? " she demanded, looking about her. But Mr. Hearty was making no effort to push his way to the front ; on the contrary, he had allowed himself to be forced to the outer edge of the crowd.

Attracted by the unusual sight of a bonnet in the possession of their comrade, the other monkeys had made a rush in its direction. By this time a wild game of follow-my-leader was in progress.

At length the possessor of the bonnet secured a corner at the top of the cage, on which all but a frontal attack was impossible. Here it proceeded to dissect Mrs. Bindle's millinery, the other monkeys forming an eager group before him.

As it tore the bonnet bit by bit, each portion was subjected to a careful scrutiny. When apparently satisfied that there could be no difficulty about identifying that particular piece, the long grey arm handed it to one of the waiting group. Soon the bonnet which had caused Mrs. Bindle much thought and labour was being put to a decorative use by the monkeys in a way which, as she later explained to Mrs. Hearty, made her feel hot all over.

The crowd was delighted.

In escaping from Mrs. Bindle, Ginger had captured Mr. Hearty and, with a wealth of expletive, was explaining to him what had happened.

" Pinched 'er blinkin' bonnet—look ! " he cried, as one of the monkeys adorned himself grotesquely with a piece of green ribbon. " Blinkin' ole guy, ain't she ? " he muttered, leaning towards Mr. Hearty.

Mr. Hearty started back. Although a greengrocer, he disliked onions—at least, second-hand.

" I don't 'old wiv women," cried Ginger, his eyes still fixed on the gambols of the monkeys. " Streamin' well better orf wivout 'em. Got one of yer own ? " he enquired.

Mr. Hearty was relieved from the necessity of replying by Mrs. Bindle once more demanding to see the manager.

" I tell you, I'm not going home like this," she announced.

" Well, you can't stay here all night," said the keeper gravely. " We shuts at half-past six."

" Then bring the manager to see me."

" I tell you, there ain't no manager. This ain't a music-hall."

" Look 'ere, ole sport," said Bindle, drawing the keeper aside. " 'Ave you got an 'at the missis can go 'ome in ? "

The man pondered and once more scratched his head through his hat.

" I might be able to get you the loan of such a thing, mate," he responded. " You wait 'ere ; I'll go an' see wot I can find. I don't live on the place myself ; but some of us do, with their missises. She yours ? " he enquired, jerking his head in the direction of Mrs. Bindle.

Bindle nodded.

" Well, you got my sympathy, mate," he said as he moved off.

A few minutes later he returned with the suggestion that Mrs. Bindle should accompany him in search of headgear. Without a word she acquiesced, relieved at the prospect of escaping from the gaze of the crowd, which instinctively she felt was unsympathetic.

" Of all the bloomin' larks ! " cried Ginger, slapping a biscuit-coloured thigh in high good-humour. Then a moment later, he added : " Why ain't there a blinking pub in this 'ere place ? "

Ginger's thoughts gravitated towards beer as inevitably as the needle of a compass points to the magnetic pole. The more dramatic the action, the more insistent became his thirst.

Mr. Hearty was endeavouring to edge away from Ginger and his brother-in-law ; he had the appearance of a man who is trying to lose a dog that has no intention of being lost.

Ginger continued to assure Mr. Hearty of the intensity of his enjoyment of the afternoon's entertainment, and he did so amidst a stress of picturesque language that seemed almost to numb Mr. Hearty's faculties.

Ginger's description of Mrs. Bindle's appearance at length drew from Bindle a protest.

" Look 'ere, Ging ! If it 'ad been your 'at, it wouldn't have seemed so funny, would it ? "

In Ginger's eyes was a puzzled look—he was thinking.

" Oh, my Gawd ? "

The exclamation broke involuntarily from Bindle.

Coming towards them, elbowing the crowd with characteristic determination, was Mrs. Bindle. Her dress was the same, her expression of uncompromising disapproval was the same, her umbrella was the same, and the narrow-palmed, biscuit-coloured gloves were those with which she had set out upon her day's pleasures. For all that it seemed an entirely new Mrs. Bindle that approached the three men, and Bindle in his own idiom had expressed the view of all.

In place of her austerely correct bonnet, built up high in front like the bows of a modern destroyer, was a felt hat, which industry and pipe-clay had failed to restore to its original whiteness.

The brim was narrow and shaped like a saucer, while round the crown was a faded pale blue ribbon.

" Come on, Joe," whispered Ginger hoarsely, conscious of the grins of those around him. " Let's go an' see the kangaroos," and Bindle and Ginger melted away, leaving Mrs. Bindle to Mr. Hearty, in whose direction she was making.

That afternoon Mr. Hearty suffered as he had never suffered before.

It was only a sense of nakedness that seemed capable of offending Mrs. Bindle. The consciousness that on her head was a hat seemed to satisfy her. She appeared to be oblivious of the fact that as she passed heads turned automatically and arms nudged into sides.

To the hypersensitive Mr Hearty, however, this was only too apparent. Three times he suggested that they should return home, and three times Mrs Bindle told him of things she yet desired to see.

Finally, in desperation, Mr Hearty suggested tea. For one thing he wanted refreshment, and for another he felt that, sitting down, Mrs. Bindle would attract less attention.

Mrs. Bindle made quite a hearty meal. The absence of Ginger and Bindle had raised her spirits.

It was, however, on the way home in the Tube that Mr. Hearty's misery and embarrassment reached its culminating point. Seated opposite to them was a child of an enquiring turn of mind, accompanied by a particularly affectionate mother.

From the first the child's attention was attracted by Mrs. Bindle. For some time the youngster gazed at her head in speculative wonder.

Just before she had entered the carriage, the doting mother had found occasion to censure her offspring by saying that only bad people made themselves conspicuous in railway carriages.

The rebuke had gone home. After a thorough examination of Mrs. Bindle's hat and person, and choosing a moment when the train was in the station, the child turned to its mother and in a shrill voice enquired :

" Mummie, is that a bad woman ? " and the child's index finger indicated Mrs. Bindle.

CHARLES LAMB (1775-1834) *produced those whimsical, droll and penetrating essays which have given him his unique position in literature, under two disadvantages—he spent his days in a dingy East India office, and his home life was devoted to looking after a mentally deranged sister. Yet these dismal and tragic circumstances seem to have mellowed the philosophy and spiced the wit of the "gentle Elia."*

JUKE JUDKINS' COURTSHIP

I AM the only son of a considerable brazier in Birmingham, who, dying in 1803, left me successor to the business, with no other encumbrance than a sort of rent-charge, which I am enjoined to pay out of it, of ninety-three pounds sterling *per annum*, to his widow, my mother : and which the improving state of the concern, I bless God, has hitherto enabled me to discharge with punctuality. (I say, I am enjoined to pay the said sum, but not strictly obligated : that is to say, as the will is worded, I believe the law would relieve me from the payment of it ; but the wishes of a dying parent should in some sort have the effect of law.) So that, though the annual profits of my business, on an average of the last three or four years, would appear to an indifferent observer, who should inspect my shop-books, to amount to the sum of one thousand three hundred and three pounds, odd shilling, the real proceeds in that time have fallen short of that sum to the amount of the aforesaid payment of ninety-three pounds sterling annually.

I was always my father's favourite. He took a delight to the very last in recounting the little sagacious tricks and innocent artifices of my childhood. One manifestation thereof I never heard him repeat without tears of joy trickling down his cheeks. It seems, that when I quitted the parental roof (Aug. 27, 1788), being then six years and not quite a month old, to proceed to the Free School at Warwick, where my father was a sort of trustee, my mother—as mothers are usually provident on these occasions—had stuffed the pockets of the coach, which was to convey me and six more children of my own growth that were going to be entered along with me at the same seminary, with a prodigious quantity of gingerbread, which I remembered my father said was more than was needed : and so indeed it was ; for, if I had been to eat it all myself, it would have got stale and mouldy before it had been half spent. The consideration whereof set me upon my contrivances how I might secure to myself as much of the gingerbread as would keep good for the next two or three days, and yet none of the rest in manner be wasted. I had a little pair of pocket-compasses, which I usually carried about me for the purpose of making draughts and measurements, at which I was always very ingenious, of the various engines and mechanical inventions in which such a town as Birmingham abounded.

By means of these, and a small penknife which my father had given me, I cut out the one half of the cake, calculating that the remainder would reasonably serve my turn ; and subdividing it into many little slices, which were curious to see for the neatness and niceness of their proportion, I sold it out in so many pennyworths to my young companions as served us all the way to Warwick, which is a distance of some twenty miles from this town : and very merry, I assure you, we made ourselves with it, feasting all the way. By this honest stratagem I put double the prime cost of the gingerbread into my purse, and secured as much as I thought would keep good and moist for my next two or three days' eating.

When I told this to my parents on their first visit to me at Warwick, my father (good man) patted me on the cheek, and stroked my head, and seemed as if he could never make enough of me ; but my mother unaccountably burst into tears, and said, " it was a very niggardly action," or some such expression, and that " she would rather it would please God to take me " —meaning (God help me) that I should die—" than that she should live to see me grow up *a mean man*," which shows the difference of parent from parent, and how some mothers are more harsh and intolerant to their children than some fathers ; when we might expect quite the contrary.

My father, however, loaded me with presents from that time, which made me the envy of my school-fellows. As I felt this growing disposition in them, I naturally sought to avert it by all the means in my power ; and from that time I used to eat my little packages of fruit, and other nice things, in a corner, so privately that I was never found out. Once, I remember, I had a huge apple sent me, of that sort which they call *cats'-heads*. I concealed this all day under my pillow ;

and at night, but not before I had ascertained that my bed-fellow was sound asleep,—which I did by pinching him rather smartly two or three times, which he seemed to perceive no more than a dead person, though once or twice he made a motion as if he would turn, which frightened me,—I say, when I had made all sure, I fell to work upon my apple ; and, though it was as big as an ordinary man's two fists, I made shift to get through it before it was time to get up. And a more delicious feast I never made ; thinking all night what a good parent I had (I mean my father) to send me so many nice things, when the poor lad that lay by me had no parent or friend in the world to send him anything nice ; and thinking of his desolate condition, I munched and munched as silently as I could, that I might not set him a-longing if he overheard me.

And yet, for all this considerateness and attention to other people's feelings, I was never much a favourite with my school-fellows ; which I have often wondered at, seeing that I never defrauded any one of them of the value of a halfpenny, or told stories of them to their master, as some little lying boys would do, but was ready to do any of them all the services in my power, that were consistent with my own well-doing. I think nobody can be expected to go farther than that.

But I am detaining my reader too long in recording my juvenile days. It is time I should go forward to a season when it became natural that I should have some thoughts of marrying, and, as they say, settling in the world. Nevertheless, my re-flections on what I may call the boyish period of my life may have their use to some readers. It is pleasant to trace the man in the boy ; to observe shoots of generosity in those young years ; and to watch the progress of liberal sentiments, and what I may call a genteel way of thinking, which is discern-ible in some children at a very early age, and usually lays the foundation of all that is praiseworthy in the manly character afterwards.

With the warmest inclinations towards that way of life, and a serious conviction of its superior advantages over a single one, it has been the strange infelicity of my lot never to have entered into the respectable estate of matrimony.

Yet I was once very near it.

I courted a young woman in my twenty-seventh year ; for so early I began to feel symptoms of the tender passion ! She was well-to-do in the world, as they call it ; but yet not such a fortune as, all things considered, perhaps I might have pretended to. It was not my own choice altogether ; but my mother very strongly pressed me to it. She was always putting it to me, that I had " comings-in sufficient,"—that I " need not stand upon a portion " ; though the young woman, to do her justice, had considerable expectations, which yet did not quite come up to my mark, as I told you before.

My mother had this saying always in her mouth, that I had " money enough " ; that it was time I enlarged my house-keeping, and to show a spirit befitting my circumstances. In short, what with her importunities, and my own desires in part co-operating,—for, as I said, I was not yet quite twenty-seven,—a time when the youthful feelings may be pardoned if they show a little impetuosity,—I resolved, I say, upon all these considerations, to set about the business of courting in right earnest. I was a young man then ; and having a spice of romance in my character (as the reader has doubtless ob-served long ago), such as that sex is apt to be taken with, I had reason in no long time to think that my addresses were anything but disagreeable. Certainly the happiest part of a young man's life is the time when he is going a-courting. All the generous impulses are then awake, and he feels a double existence in participating his hopes and wishes with another being.

Return yet again for a brief moment, ye visionary views, transient enchantments ! ye moonlight rambles with Cleora in the Silent Walk at Vauxhall (*N.B.*—About a mile from Birmingham, and resembling the gardens of that name near London, only that the price of admission is lower), when the nightingale has suspended her notes in June to listen to our loving discourses, while the moon was overhead ! (for we generally used to take our tea at Cleora's mother's before we set out, not so much to save expenses as to avoid the publicity of a repast in the gardens,—coming in much about the time of half-price, as they call it,) ye soft intercommunions of soul, when, exchanging mutual vows, we prattled of coming felicities ! The loving disputes we have had under those trees, when this house (planning our future settlement) was rejected, because, though cheap, it was dull ; and the other house was given up, because, though agreeably situated, it was too high-rented !— one was too much in the heart of the town, another was too far from business.

These minutiae will seem impertinent to the aged and prudent. I write them only to the young. Young lovers, and passionate as being young (such were Cleora and I then), alone can understand me. After some weeks wasted, as I may now call it, in this sort of amorous colloquy, we at length fixed upon the house in the High Street, No. 203, just vacated by the death of Mr. Hutton of this town, for our future residence. I had all the time lived in lodgings (only renting a shop for business), to be near my mother,—near, I say : not in the same house : for that would have been to introduce confusion into our housekeeping, which it was desirable to keep separate. Oh, the loving wrangles, the endearing differences, I had with Cleora, before we could quite make up our minds to the house that was to receive us !—I pretending, for argument's sake, the rent was too high, and she insisting that the taxes were moderate in proportion : and love at last reconciling us in the same choice. I think at that time, moderately speaking, she might have had anything out of me for asking. I do not, nor shall ever, regret that my character at that time was marked with a tinge of prodigality. Age comes fast enough upon us, and, in its good time, will prune away all that is inconvenient in these excesses. Perhaps it is right that it should do so.

Matters, as I said, were ripening to a conclusion between us, only the house was yet not absolutely taken, some necessary arrangements, which the ardour of my youthful impetuosity could hardly brook at that time (love and youth will be precipitate),—some preliminary arrangements, I say, with the landlord, respecting fixtures,—very necessary things to be considered in a young man about to settle in the world, though not very accordant with the impatient state of my then passions, —some obstacles about the valuation of the fixtures,—had hitherto precluded (and I shall always think providentially) my final closes with his offer ; when one of those accidents, which, unimportant in themselves, often arise to give a turn to the most serious intentions of our life, intervened, and put an end at once to my projects of wiving, and of housekeeping.

I was never much given to theatrical entertainments ; that is, at no time of my life was I ever what they call a regular play-goer : but on some occasion of a benefit-night, which was expected to be very productive, and indeed turned out so, Cleora expressing a desire to be present, I could do no less than offer, as I did very willingly, to squire her and her mother to the pit. At that time it was not customary in our town for tradesfolk, except some of the very topping ones, to sit, as they now do, in the boxes.

At the time appointed I waited upon the ladies, who had brought with them a young man, a distant relation, whom, it seems, they had invited to be of the party. This a little disconcerted me, as I had about me barely silver enough to pay for our three selves at the door, and did not at first know that their relation had proposed paying for himself. However, to do the young man justice, he not only paid for himself, but for the old lady besides; leaving me only to pay for two, as it were. In our passage to the theatre the notice of Cleora was attracted to some orange wenches that stood about the doors vending their commodities. She was leaning on my arm; and I could feel her every now and then giving me a nudge, as it is called, which I afterwards discovered were hints that I should buy some oranges.

It seems, it is a custom at Birmingham, and perhaps in other places, when a gentleman treats ladies to the play,— especially when a full night is expected, and that the house will be inconveniently warm,—to provide them with this kind of fruit, oranges being esteemed for their cooling property. But how could I guess at that, never having treated ladies to a play before, and being, as I said, quite a novice at entertainments of this kind?

At last, she spoke plain out, and begged that I would buy some of " those oranges," pointing to a particular barrow. But, when I came to examine the fruit, I did not think the quality of it was answerable to the price. In this way I handled several baskets of them; but something in them all displeased me. Some had thin rinds, and some were plainly over-ripe, which is as great a fault as not being ripe enough; and I could not (what they call) make a bargain.

While I stood haggling with the woman, secretly determining to put off my purchase till I should get within the theatre, where I expected we should have better choice, the young man, the cousin (who, it seems had left us without my missing him), came running to us with his pockets stuffed out with oranges, inside and out, as they say. It seems, not liking the look of the barrow-fruit any more than myself, he had slipped away to an eminent fruiterer's, about three doors distant, which I never had the sense to think of, and had laid out a matter of two shillings in some of the best St. Michael's I think I ever tasted.

What a little hinge, as I said before, the most important affairs in life may turn upon! The mere inadvertence to the fact that there was an eminent fruiterer's within three doors of us, though we had just passed it without the thought once occurring to me, which he had taken advantage of, lost me the affection of my Cleora. From that time she visibly cooled towards me ; and her partiality was as visibly transferred to this cousin. I was long unable to account for this change in her behaviour ; when one day, accidently discoursing of oranges to my mother, alone, she let drop a sort of reproach to me, as if I had offended Cleora by my *nearness* as she called it, that evening.

Even now, when Cleora has been wedded some years to that same officious relation, as I may call him, I can hardly be persuaded that such a trifle could have been the motive for her inconstancy ; for could she suppose that I would sacrifice my dearest hopes in her to the paltry sum of two shillings, when I was going to treat her to the play, and her mother too (an expense of more than four times that amount), if the young man had not interfered to pay for the latter, as I mentioned ?

But the caprices of the sex are past finding out : and I begin to think my mother was in the right ; for doubtless women know women better than we can pretend to know them.

STEPHEN BUTLER LEACOCK (1869–) *presents, like Lewis Carroll, the startling combination of a learned man of science—he is Professor of Political Economy at McGill University, Montreal—and a brilliant humorist. "Moonbeams from the Larger Lunacy" and "Nonsense Novels" are his best known works. The latter are perfect examples of the parodies of types of fiction first popularised by Bret Harte.*

SOAKED IN SEAWEED

or,

UPSET IN THE OCEAN

(*An Old-fashioned Sea Story*)

IT was in August in 1867 that I stepped on board the deck of the *Saucy Sally*, lying in dock at Gravesend, to fill the berth of second mate.

Let me first say a word about myself.

I was a tall, handsome young fellow, squarely and powerfully built, bronzed by the sun and the moon (and even copper-coloured in spots from the effect of the stars), and with a face in which honesty, intelligence, and exceptional brain power were combined with Christianity, simplicity, and modesty.

As I stepped on the deck I could not help a slight feeling of triumph, as I caught sight of my sailor-like features reflected in a tar-barrel that stood beside the mast, while a little later I could scarcely repress a sense of gratification as I noticed them reflected again in a bucket of bilge water.

" Welcome on board, Mr. Blowhard," called out Captain Bilge, stepping out of the binnacle and shaking hands across the taffrail.

I saw before me a fine sailor-like man of from thirty to sixty, clean-shaven, except for an enormous pair of whiskers, a heavy beard, and a thick moustache, powerful in build, and carrying his beam well aft, in a pair of broad duck trousers across the back of which there would have been room to write a history of the British Navy.

Beside him were the first and third mates, both of them being quiet men of poor stature, who looked at Captain Bilge with what seemed to me an apprehensive expression in their eyes.

The vessel was on the eve of departure. Her deck presented that scene of bustle and alacrity dear to the sailor's heart. Men were busy nailing up the masts, hanging the bowsprit over the side, varnishing the lee-scuppers, and pouring hot tar down the companion-way.

Captain Bilge, with a megaphone to his lips, kept calling out to the men in his rough sailor fashion :

" Now, then, don't over-exert yourselves, gentlemen. Remember, please, that we have plenty of time. Keep out of the sun as much as you can. Step carefully in the rigging there, Jones ; I fear it's just a little high for you. Tut, tut, Williams, don't get yourself so dirty with that tar, you won't look fit to be seen."

I stood leaning over the gaff of the mainsail and thinking—yes, thinking, dear reader, of my mother. I hope that you will think none the less of me for that. Whenever things look dark, I lean up against something and think of mother. If they get positively black, I stand on one leg and think of father. After that I can face anything.

Did I think, too, of another, younger than mother and fairer than father ? Yes, I did. " Bear up, darling," I had whispered as she nestled her head beneath my oilskins and kicked out backward with one heel in the agony of her girlish grief, " in five years the voyage will be over, and after three more like it, I shall come back with money enough to buy a second-hand fishing-net and settle down on shore."

Meantime the ship's preparations were complete. The masts were all in position, the sails nailed up, and men with axes were busily chopping away the gangway.

" All ready ? " called the Captain.

" Aye, aye, sir."

" Then hoist the anchor in board and send a man down with the key to open the bar."

Opening the bar ! the last sad rite of departure. How often in my voyages have I seen it ; the little group of men soon to be exiled from their home, standing about with saddened faces, waiting to see the man with the key open the bar—held there by some strange fascination.

.   .   .   .

Next morning with a fair wind astern we had buzzed around the corner of England and were running down the Channel.

I know no finer sight, for those who have never seen it, than the English Channel. It is the highway of the world. Ships of all nations are passing up and down, Dutch, Scotch, Venezuelan, and even American.

Chinese junks rush to and fro. Warships, motor yachts, icebergs, and lumber rafts are everywhere. If I add to this fact that so thick a fog hangs over it that it is entirely hidden from sight, my readers can form some idea of the majesty of the scene.

We had now been three days at sea. My first sea-sickness was wearing off, and I thought less of father.

On the third morning Captain Bilge descended to my cabin.

" Mr. Blowhard," he said, " I must ask you to stand double watches."

" What is the matter ? " I inquired.

" The two other mates have fallen overboard," he said uneasily, and avoiding my eye.

I contented myself with saying, " Very good, sir," but I could not help thinking it a trifle odd that both the mates should have fallen overboard in the same night.

Surely there was some mystery in this.

Two mornings later the Captain appeared at the breakfast-table with the same shifting and uneasy look in his eye.

" Anything wrong, sir ? " I asked.

" Yes," he answered, trying to appear at ease and twisting a fried egg to and fro between his fingers with such nervous force as almost to break it in two—" I regret to say that we have lost the bosun."

" The bosun ! " I cried.

" Yes," said Captain Bilge more quietly, " he is overboard. I blame myself for it, partly. It was early this morning. I was holding him up in my arms to look at an iceberg, and, quite accidentally I assure you—I dropped him overboard."

" Captain Bilge," I asked, " have you taken any steps to recover him ? "

" Not as yet," he replied uneasily.

I looked at him fixedly, but said nothing.

Ten days passed.

The mystery thickened. On Thursday two men of the starboard watch were reported missing. On Friday the carpenter's assistant disappeared. On the night of Saturday a circumstance occurred which, slight as it was, gave me some clue as to what was happening.

As I stood at the wheel about midnight, I saw the Captain approach in the darkness carrying the cabin-boy by the hind leg. The lad was a bright little fellow, whose merry disposition had already endeared him to me, and I watched with some interest to see what the Captain would do to him. Arrived at the stern of the vessel, Captain Bilge looked cautiously around a moment and then dropped the boy into the sea. For a brief instant the lad's head appeared in the phosphorus of the waves. The Captain threw a boot at him, sighed deeply, and went below.

Here then was the key to the mystery ! The Captain was throwing the crew overboard. Next morning we met at breakfast as usual.

" Poor little Williams has fallen overboard," said the Captain, seizing a strip of ship's bacon and tearing at it with his teeth as if he almost meant to eat it.

" Captain," I said, greatly excited, stabbing at a ship's loaf in my agitation with such ferocity as almost to drive my knife into it—" You threw that boy overboard ! "

" I did," said Captain Bilge, grown suddenly quiet, " I threw them all over and intend to throw the rest. Listen, Blowhard, you are young, ambitious, and trustworthy. I will confide in you."

Perfectly calm now, he stepped to a locker, rummaged in it a moment, and drew out a faded piece of yellow parchment, which he spread on the table. It was a map or chart. In the centre of it was a circle. In the middle of the circle was a small dot and a letter T, while at one side of the map was a letter N, and against it on the other side a letter S.

" What is this ? " I asked.

" Can you not guess ? " queried Captain Bilge. " It is a desert island."

" Ah ! " I rejoined with a sudden flash of intuition, " and N is for North and S is for South."

" Blowhard," said the Captain, striking the table with such force as to cause a loaf of ship's bread to bounce up and down three or four times, " you've struck it. That part of it had not yet occurred to me."

" And the letter T ? " I asked.

" The treasure, the buried treasure," said the Captain, and turning the map over he read from the back of it—" The point T indicates the spot where the treasure is buried under the sand ; it consists of half a million Spanish dollars, and is buried in a brown leather dress-suit case."

"And where is the island ? " I inquired, mad with excitement.

"That I do not know," said the Captain. "I intend to sail up and down the parallels of latitude until I find it."

"And meantime ? ".

"Meantime, the first thing to do is to reduce the number of the crew so as to have fewer hands to divide among. Come, come," he added in a burst of frankness which made me love the man in spite of his shortcomings, "will you join me in this ? We'll throw them all over, keeping the cook to the last, dig up the treasure, and be rich for the rest of our lives."

Reader, do you blame me if I said yes ? I was young, ardent, ambitious, full of bright hopes and boyish enthusiasm.

"Captain Bilge," I said, putting my hand in his, "I am yours."

"Good," he said, "now go forward to the forecastle and get an idea what the men are thinking."

I went forward to the men's quarters—a plain room in the front of the ship, with only a rough carpet on the floor, a few simple arm-chairs, writing-desks, spittoons of a plain pattern, and small brass beds with blue-and-green screens. It was Sunday morning, and the men were mostly sitting about in their dressing-gowns.

They rose as I entered and curtseyed.

"Sir," said Tompkins, the bosun's mate, "I think it my duty to tell you that there is a great deal of dissatisfaction among the men."

Several of the men nodded.

"They don't like the way the men keep going overboard," he continued, his voice rising to a tone of uncontrolled passion. "It is positively absurd, sir, and if you will allow me to say so, the men are far from pleased."

"Tompkins," I said sternly, "you must understand that my position will not allow me to listen to mutinous language of this sort."

I returned to the Captain. "I think the men mean mutiny," I said.

"Good," said Captain Bilge, rubbing his hands, "that will get rid of a lot of them, and of course," he added musingly, looking out of the broad old-fashioned port-hole at the stern of the cabin, at the heaving waves of the South Atlantic, " I am expecting pirates at any time, and that will take out quite a few of them. However "—and here he pressed the bell for a cabin-boy—" kindly ask Mr. Tompkins to step this way."

" Tompkins," said the Captain as the bosun's mate entered, " be good enough to stand on the locker and stick your head through the stern port-hole, and tell me what you think of the weather."

" Aye, aye, sir," replied the tar with a simplicity which caused us to exchange a quiet smile.

Tompkins stood on the locker and put his head and shoulders out of the port.

Taking a leg each we pushed him through. We heard him plump into the sea.

" Tompkins was easy," said Captain Bilge. " Excuse me as I enter his death in the log."

" Yes," he continued presently, " it will be a great help if they mutiny. I suppose they will, sooner or later. It's customary to do so. But I shall take no step to precipitate it until we have first fallen in with pirates. I am expecting them in these latitudes at any time. Meantime, Mr. Blow-hard," he said, rising, " if you can continue to drop overboard one or two more each week, I shall feel extremely grateful."

Three days later we rounded the Cape of Good Hope and entered upon the inky waters of the Indian Ocean. Our course lay now in zigzags and, the weather being favourable, we sailed up and down at a furious rate over a sea as calm as glass.

On the fourth day a pirate ship appeared. Reader, I do not know if you have ever seen a pirate ship. The sight was one to appal the stoutest heart. The entire ship was painted black, a black flag hung at the masthead, the sails were black, and on the deck people dressed all in black walked up and down arm-in-arm. The words " Pirate Ship " were painted in white letters on the bow. At the sight of it our crew were visibly cowed. It was a spectacle that would have cowed a dog.

The two ships were brought side by side. They were then lashed tightly together with bag string and binder twine, and a gang plank laid between them. In a moment the pirates swarmed upon our deck, rolling their eyes, gnashing their teeth, and filing their nails.

Then the fight began. It lasted two hours—with fifteen minutes off for lunch. It was awful. The men grappled with one another, kicked one another from behind, slapped one another across the face, and in many cases completely lost their temper and tried to bite one another. I noticed one gigantic fellow brandishing a knotted towel, and striking right and left among our men, until Captain Bilge rushed at him and struck him flat across the mouth with a banana skin.

At the end of two hours, by mutual consent, the fight was declared a draw. The points standing at sixty-one and a half against sixty-two.

The ships were unlashed, and with three cheers from each crew, were headed on their way.

" Now, then," said the Captain to me aside, " let us see how many of the crew are sufficiently exhausted to be thrown overboard."

He went below. In a few minutes he reappeared, his face deadly pale. " Blowhard," he said, " the ship is sinking. One of the pirates (sheer accident, of course, I blame no one) has kicked a hole in the side. Let us sound the well."

We put our ear to the ship's well. It sounded like water.

The men were put to the pumps and worked with the frenzied effort which only those who have been drowned in a sinking ship can understand.

At six p.m. the well marked one half an inch of water, at nightfall three-quarters of an inch, and at daybreak, after a night of unremitting toil, seven-eighths of an inch.

By noon of the next day the water had risen to fifteen-sixteenths of an inch, and on the next night the sounding showed thirty-one thirty-seconds of an inch of water in the hold. The situation was desperate. At this rate of increase few, if any, could tell where it would rise to in a few days.

That night the Captain called me to his cabin. He had a book of mathematical tables in front of him, and great sheets of vulgar fractions littered the floor on all sides.

" The ship is bound to sink," he said, " in fact, Blowhard, she is sinking. I can prove it. It may be six months or it may take years, but if she goes on like this, sink she must. There is nothing for it but to abandon her."

That night, in the dead of darkness, while the crew were busy at the pumps, the Captain and I built a raft.

Unobserved we cut down the masts, chopped them into suitable lengths, laid them crosswise in a pile and lashed them tightly together with bootlaces.

Hastily we threw on board a couple of boxes of food and

bottles of drinking fluid, a sextant, a chronometer, a gas-meter, a bicycle pump, and a few other scientific instruments. Then taking advantage of a roll in the motion of the ship, we launched the raft, lowered ourselves upon a line, and under cover of the heavy dark of a tropical night, we paddled away from the doomed vessel.

The break of day found us a tiny speck on the Indian Ocean. We looked about as big as this (.).

In the morning, after dressing, and shaving as best we could, we opened our box of food and drink.

Then came the awful horror of our situation.

One by one the Captain took from the box the square blue tins of canned beef which it contained. We counted fifty-two in all. Anxiously and with drawn faces we watched until the last can was lifted from the box. A single thought was in our minds. When the end came the Captain stood up on the raft with wild eyes staring at the sky.

" The can-opener ! " he shrieked, " just Heaven, the can-opener." He fell prostrate.

Meantime, with trembling hands, I opened the box of bottles. It contained lager beer bottles, each with a patent tin top. One by one I took them out. There were fifty-two in all. As I withdrew the last one and saw the empty box before me, I shroke out—" The thing ! the thing ! oh, merciful Heaven ! The thing you open them with ! "

I fell prostrate upon the Captain.

We awoke to find ourselves still a mere speck upon the ocean. We felt even smaller than before.

Over us was the burnished copper sky of the tropics. The heavy, leaden sea lapped the sides of the raft. All about us was a litter of corn beef cans and lager beer bottles. Our sufferings in the ensuing days were indescribable. We beat and thumped at the cans with our fists. Even at the risk of spoiling the tins for ever we hammered them fiercely against the raft. We stamped on them, bit at them and swore at them. We pulled and clawed at the bottles with our hands, and chipped and knocked them against the cans, regardless even of breaking the glass and ruining the bottles.

It was futile.

Then day after day we sat in moody silence, gnawed with hunger, with nothing to read, nothing to smoke, and practically nothing to talk about.

On the tenth day the Captain broke silence.

"Get ready the lots, Blowhard," he said. "It's got to come to that."

"Yes," I answered drearily, "we're getting thinner every day."

Then, with the awful prospect of cannibalism before us, we drew lots.

I prepared the lots and held them to the Captain. He drew the longer one.

"Which does that mean," he asked, trembling between hope and despair. "Do I win?"

"No, Bilge," I said sadly, "you lose."

.   .   .   .

But I mustn't dwell on the days that followed—the long quiet days of lazy dreaming on the raft, during which I slowly built up my strength, which had been shattered by privation. They were days, dear reader, of deep and quiet peace, and yet I cannot recall them without shedding a tear for the brave man who made them what they were.

It was on the fifth day after that I was awakened from a sound sleep by the bumping of the raft against the shore. I had eaten perhaps overheartily, and had not observed the vicinity of land.

Before me was an island, the circular shape of which, with its low, sandy shore, recalled at once its identity.

"The treasure island," I cried, "at last I am rewarded for all my heroism."

In a fever of haste I rushed to the centre of the island. What was the sight that confronted me? A great hollow scooped in the sand, an empty dress-suit case lying beside it, and on a ship's plank driven deep into the sand, the legend, "*Saucy Sally*, October, 1867." So! the miscreants had made good the vessel, headed it for the island of whose existence they must have learned from the chart we so carelessly left upon the cabin table, and had plundered poor Bilge and me of our well-earned treasure!

Sick with the sense of human ingratitude I sank upon the sand.

The island became my home.

There I eked out a miserable existence, feeding on sand and gravel, and dressing myself in cactus plants. Years passed. Eating sand and mud slowly undermined my robust constitution. I fell ill. I died. I buried myself.

Would that others who write sea stories would do as much.

WILLIAM J. LOCKE (1863—1930) *was born in Barbados and spent his youth in Trinidad. While he was secretary to the Royal Institute of British Architects he published " The Morals of Marcus Ordeyne" and " The Beloved Vagabond," with such success that he was able to devote the rest of his life to writing. His humorous appreciation of the French is clearly revealed below.*

THE ADVENTURE OF
THE KIND MR. SMITH

ARISTIDE PUJOL started life on his own account as a *chasseur* in a Nice café—one of those luckless children tightly encased in bottle-green cloth by means of brass buttons, who earn a sketchy livelihood by enduring with cherubic smiles the continuous maledictions of the establishment. There he soothed his hours of servitude by dreams of vast ambitions. He would become the manager of a great hotel—not a contemptible hostelry where commercial travellers and seedy Germans were indifferently bedded, but one of those white palaces where milords (English) and millionaires (American) paid a thousand francs a night for a bedroom and five louis for a glass of beer. Now, in order to derive such profit from the Anglo-Saxon a knowledge of English was indispensable. He resolved to learn the language. How he did so, except by sheer effrontery, taking linguistic toll of frequenters of the café, would be a mystery to anyone unacquainted with Aristide. But to his friends his mastery of the English tongue in such circumstances is comprehensible. To Aristide the impossible was ever the one thing easy of attainment ; the possible the one thing he never could achieve. That was the paradoxical nature of the man. Before his days of hunted-little-devildom were over he had acquired sufficient knowledge of English to carry him, a few years later, through various vicissitudes in England, until, fired by new social ambitions and self-educated in a haphazard way, he found himself appointed Professor of French in an academy for young ladies.

One of these days, when I can pin my dragonfly friend down to a plain, unvarnished autobiography, I may be able to trace some chronological sequence in the kaleidoscopic changes in his career. But hitherto, in his talks with me, he flits about from any one date to any other during a couple of decades, in a manner so confusing that for the present I abandon such an attempt. All I know of the date of the episode I am about to chronicle is that it occurred immediately after the termination of his engagement at the academy just mentioned. Somehow, Aristide's history is a category of terminations.

If the headmistress of the academy had herself played dragon at his classes, all would have gone well. He would have made his pupils conjugate irregular verbs, rendered them adepts in the mysteries of the past participle and the subjunctive mood, and turned them out quite innocent of the idiomatic quaintnesses of the French tongue. But *dis aliter visum*. The gods always saw wrongheadedly otherwise in the case of Aristide. A weak-minded governess—and in a governess a sense of humour and of novelty is always a sign of a weak mind—played dragon during Aristide's lessons. She appreciated his method, which was colloquial. The colloquial Aristide was jocular. His lessons therefore were a giggling joy from beginning to end. He imparted to his pupils delicious knowledge. *En avez-vous des-z-homards? Oh, les sales bêtes, elles ont du poil aux pattes*, which, being translated is : " Have you any lobsters ? Oh, the dirty animals, they have hair on their feet "—a catch phrase which, some years ago, added greatly to the gaiety of Paris, but in which I must confess to seeing no gleam of wit—became the historic property of the school. He recited to them, till they were word-perfect, a music-hall ditty of the early 'eighties—*Sur le bi, sur le banc, sur le bi du bout du banc*, and delighted them with dissertations on Mme. Yvette Guilbert's earlier repertoire. But for him they would have gone to their lives' end without knowing that *pognon* meant money ; *rouspétance*, assaulting the police ; *thune*, a five-franc piece ; and *bouffer*, to take nourishment. He made (according to his own statement) French a living language. There was never a school in Great Britain, the Colonies, or America on which the Parisian accent was so electrically impressed. The retort, *Eh ! ta sœur*, was the purest Montmartre ; also *Fich'-moi la paix, mon petit*, and *Tu as un toupet, toi* ; and the delectable locution, *Allons étrangler un perroquet* (let us strangle a parrot), employed by Apaches when inviting each other to drink a glass of absinthe, soon became current French in the school for invitations to surreptitious cocoa-parties.

The progress that academy made in a real grip of the French language was miraculous ; but the knowledge it gained in French grammar and syntax was deplorable. A certain mid-term examination—the paper being set by a neighbouring vicar—produced awful results. The phrase, " How do you do, dear ? " which ought, by all the rules of Stratford-atte-Bowe, to be translated by *Comment vous portez-vous, ma chère ?* was rendered by most of the senior scholars *Eh, ma vieille, ça boulotte ?* One innocent and anachronistic damsel, writing on the execution of Charles I., declared that he *cracha dans le panier* in 1649, thereby mystifying the good vicar, who was unaware that " to spit into the basket " is to be guillotined. This wealth of vocabulary was discounted by abject poverty in other branches of the language. No one could give a list of the words in " *al* " that took " *s* " in the plural, no one knew anything at all about the defective verb *échoir*, and the ortho-graphy of the school would have disgraced a kindergarten. The headmistress suspected a lack of method in the teaching of M. Pujol, and one day paid his class a surprise visit.

The sight that met her eyes petrified her. The class, including the governess, bubbled and gurgled and shrieked with laughter. M. Pujol, his bright eyes agleam with merri-ment and his arms moving in frantic gestures, danced about the platform. He was telling them a story—and when Aristide told a story, he told it with the eloquence of his entire frame. He bent himself double and threw out his hands.

" *Il était saoûl comme un porc,*" he shouted.

And then came the hush of death. The rest of the artless tale about the man as drunk as a pig was never told. The headmistress, indignant majesty, strode up the room.

" M. Pujol, you have a strange way of giving French lessons."

" I believe, madame," said he, with a polite bow, " in interesting my pipils in their studies."

" Pupils have to be taught, not interested," said the head-mistress. " Will you kindly put the class through some irregular verbs."

So for the remainder of the lesson Aristide, under the freezing eyes of the headmistress, put his sorrowful class through irregular verbs, of which his own knowledge was singularly inexact, and at the end received his dismissal. In vain he argued.   Outraged Minerva was implacable.   Go he must.

We find him, then, one miserable December evening, standing on the arrival platform of Euston Station (the academy was near Manchester), an unwonted statue of dubiety.   At his feet lay his meagre valise ; in his hand was an enormous bouquet, a useful tribute of esteem from his disconsolate pupils ;   around him luggage-laden porters and passengers hurried ;   in front were drawn up the long line of cabs, their drivers' waterproofs glistening with wet ;   and in his pocket rattled the few paltry coins that, for Heaven knew how long, were to keep him from starvation.   Should he commit the extravagance of taking a cab or should he go forth, valise in hand, into the pouring rain ?   He hesitated.

"*Sacré mille cochons !   Quel chien de climat !* " he muttered.

A smart footman standing by turned quickly and touched his hat.

" Beg pardon, sir ; I'm from Mr. Smith."

" I'm glad to hear it, my friend," said Aristide.

" You're the French gentleman from Manchester ? "

" Decidedly," said Aristide.

" Then, sir, Mr. Smith has sent the carriage for you."

" That's very kind of him," said Aristide.

The footman picked up the valise and darted down the platform.   Aristide followed.   The footman held invitingly open the door of a cosy brougham.   Aristide paused for the fraction of a second.   Who was this hospitable Mr. Smith ?

" Bah ! " said he to himself, " the best way of finding out is to go and see."

He entered the carriage, sank back luxuriously on the soft cushions, and inhaled the warm smell of leather.   They started, and soon the pelting rain beat harmlessly against the windows.   Aristide looked out at the streaming streets, and, hugging himself comfortably, thanked Providence and Mr. Smith.   But who was Mr. Smith ?   *Tiens*, thought he, there were two little Miss Smiths at the academy ;   he had pitied them because they had chilblains, freckles, and perpetual colds in their heads ;   possibly this was their kind papa.   But, after all, what did it matter whose papa he was ?   He was expecting him.   He had sent the carriage for him.   Evidently a well-bred and attentive person.   And *tiens !* there was even a hot-water can on the floor of the brougham.   " He thinks

of everything, that man," said Aristide. "I feel I am going
to like him."

The carriage stopped at a house in Hampstead, standing,
as far as he could see in the darkness, in its own grounds. The
footman opened the door for him to alight and escorted him
up the front steps. A neat parlourmaid received him in a
comfortably-furnished hall and took his hat and great-coat and
magnificent bouquet.

"Mr. Smith hasn't come back yet from the City, sir ;
but Miss Christabel is in the drawing-room."

"Ah !" said Aristide. "Please give me back my bouquet."

The maid showed him into the drawing-room. A pretty
girl of three-and-twenty rose from a fender-stool and advanced
smilingly to meet him.

"Good afternoon, M. le Baron. I was wondering whether
Thomas would spot you. I'm so glad he did. You see,
neither father nor I could give him any description, for we
had never seen you."

This fitted in with his theory. But why Baron ? After
all, why not ? The English loved titles.

"He seems to be an intelligent fellow, mademoiselle."

There was a span of silence. The girl looked at the
bouquet, then at Aristide, who looked at the girl, then at the
bouquet, then at the girl again.

"Mademoiselle," said he, "will you deign to accept these
flowers as a token of my respectful homage ? "

Miss Christabel took the flowers and blushed prettily.
She had dark hair and eyes and a fascinating, upturned little
nose, and the kindest little mouth in the world.

"An Englishman would not have thought of that," she
said.

Aristide smiled in his roguish way and raised a deprecating
hand.

"Oh, yes, he would. But he would not have had—what
you call the cheek to do it."

Miss Christabel laughed merrily, invited him to a seat by
the fire, and comforted him with tea and hot muffins. The
frank charm of his girl-hostess captivated Aristide and drove
from his mind the riddle of his adventure. Besides, think of
the Arabian Nights' enchantment of the change from his lonely
and shabby bed-sitting-room in the Rusholme Road to this
fragrant place with princess and all to keep him company !
He watched the firelight dancing through her hair, the dainty

play of laughter over her face, and decided that the brougham had transported him to Bagdad instead of Hampstead.

" You have the air of a veritable princess," said he.

" I once met a princess—at a charity bazaar—and she was a most matter-of-fact, businesslike person."

" Bah ! " said Aristide. " A princess of a charity bazaar ! I was talking of the princess in a fairy-tale. They are the only real ones."

" Do you know," said Miss Christabel, " that when men pay such compliments to English girls they are apt to get laughed at ? "

" Englishmen, yes," replied Aristide, " because they think over a compliment for a week, so that by the time they pay it, it is addled, like a bad egg. But we of Provence pay tribute to beauty straight out of our hearts. It is true. It is sincere. And what comes out of the heart is not ridiculous."

Again the girl coloured and laughed. " I've always heard that a Frenchman makes love to every woman he meets."

" Naturally," said Aristide. " If they are pretty. What else are pretty women for ? Otherwise they might as well be hideous."

" Oh ! " said the girl, to whom this Provençal point of view had not occurred.

" So, if I make love to you, it is but your due."

" I wonder what my fiancé would say if he heard you ? "

" Your—— ? "

" My fiancé ! There's his photograph on the table beside you. He is six foot one, and so jealous ! " she laughed again.

" The Turk ! " cried Aristide, his swiftly-conceived romance crumbling into dust. Then he brightened up. " But when this six feet of muscle and egotism is absent, surely other poor mortals can glean a smile ? "

" You will observe that I'm not frowning," said Miss Christabel. " But you must not call my fiancé a Turk, for he's a very charming fellow whom I hope you'll like very much."

Aristide sighed. " And the name of this thrice-blessed mortal ? "

Miss Christabel told his name—one Harry Ralston—and not only his name, but, such was the peculiar, childlike charm of Aristide Pujol, also many other things about him. He was the Honourable Harry Ralston, the heir to a great brewery peerage, and very wealthy. He was a member of Parliament,

and but for Parliamentary duties would have dined there that
evening ; but he was to come in later, as soon as he could leave
the House.   He also had a house in Hampshire, full of the
most beautiful works of art.   It was through their common
hobby that her father and Harry had first made acquaintance.

"We're supposed to have a very fine collection here," she
said, with a motion of her hand.

Aristide looked round the walls and saw them hung with
pictures in gold frames.   In those days he had not acquired
an extensive culture.   Besides, who having before him the
firelight gleaming through Miss Christabel's hair could waste
his time over painted canvas ?   She noted his cursory glance.

"I thought you were a connoisseur ? "

"I am," said Aristide, his bright eyes fixed on her in frank
admiration.

She blushed again ; but this time she rose.

"I must go and dress for dinner.   Perhaps you would
like to be shown your room ? "

He hung his head on one side.

"Have I been too bold, mademoiselle ? "

"I don't know," she said.   "You see, I've never met a
Frenchman before."

"Then a world of undreamed-of homage is at your feet,"
said he.

A servant ushered him up broad, carpeted staircases into
a bedroom such as he had never seen in his life before.   It was
all curtains and hangings and rugs and soft couches and satin
quilts and dainty writing-tables and subdued lights, and a
great fire glowed red and cheerful, and before it hung a clean
shirt.   His poor little toilet apparatus was laid on the dressing-
table, and (with a tact which he did not appreciate, for he had,
sad to tell, no dress-suit) the servant had spread his precious
frock-coat and spare pair of trousers on the bed.   On the
pillow lay his night-shirt, neatly folded.

"Evidently," said Aristide, impressed by these preparations, "it is expected that I wash myself now and change my
clothes, and that I sleep here for the night.   And for all that
the ravishing Miss Christabel is engaged to her honourable
Harry, this is none the less a corner of Paradise."

So Aristide attired himself in his best, which included a
white tie and a pair of nearly new brown boots—a long task,
as he found that his valise had been spirited away and its
contents, including the white tie of ceremony (he had but one),

hidden in unexpected drawers and wardrobes—and eventually went downstairs into the drawing-room. There he found Miss Christabel and, warming himself on the hearthrug, a bald-headed, beefy-faced Briton, with little pig's eyes and a hearty manner, attired in a dinner-suit.

" My dear fellow," said this personage, with outstretched hand, " I'm delighted to have you here. I've heard so much about you ; and my little girl has been singing your praises."

" Mademoiselle is too kind," said Aristide.

" You must take us as you find us," said Mr. Smith. " We're just ordinary folk, but I can give you a good bottle of wine and a good cigar—it's only in England, you know, that you can get champagne fit to drink and cigars fit to smoke— and I can give you a glimpse of a modest English home. I believe you haven't a word for it in French."

" *Ma foi*, no," said Aristide, who had once or twice before heard this lunatic charge brought against his country. " In France the men all live in cafés, the children are all put out to nurse, and the women, saving the respect of mademoiselle— well, the less said about them the better."

" England is the only place, isn't it ? " Mr. Smith declared heartily. " I don't say that Paris hasn't its points. But after all—the Moulin Rouge and the Folies Bergères and that sort of thing soon pall, you know—soon pall."

" Yet Paris has its serious side," argued Aristide. " There is always the tomb of Napoleon."

" Papa will never take me to Paris," sighed the girl.

" You shall go there on your honeymoon," said Mr. Smith.

Dinner was announced. Aristide gave his arm to Miss Christabel, and proud not only of his partner, but also of his frock-coat, white tie, and shiny brown boots, strutted into the dining-room. The host sat at the end of the beautifully set table, his daughter on his right, Aristide on his left. The meal began gaily. The kind Mr. Smith was in the best of humours.

" And how is our dear old friend, Jules Dancourt ? " he asked.

" *Tiens !* " said Aristide to himself, " we have a dear friend Jules Dancourt. Wonderfully well," he replied at a venture, " but he suffers terribly at times from the gout."

" So do I, confound it ! " said Mr. Smith, drinking sherry.

" You and the good Jules were always sympathetic," said

Aristide. "Ah! he has spoken to me so often about you, the tears in his eyes."

"Men cry, my dear, in France," Mr. Smith explained. "They also kiss each other."

"*Ah, mais c'est un beau pays, mademoiselle !*" cried Aristide, and he began to talk of France and to draw pictures of his country which set the girl's eyes dancing. After that he told some of the funny little stories which had brought him disaster at the academy. Mr. Smith, with jovial magnanimity, declared that he was the first Frenchman he had ever met with a sense of humour.

"But I thought, Baron," said he, "that you lived all your life shut up in that old château of yours ? "

"*Tiens !*" thought Aristide. "I am still a Baron, and I have an old château."

"Tell us about the château. Has it a fosse and a draw-bridge and a Gothic chapel ? " asked Miss Christabel.

"Which one do you mean ? " inquired Aristide, airily. "For I have two."

When relating to me this Arabian Nights' adventure, he drew my special attention to his astuteness.

His host's eye quivered in a wink. "The one in Langue-doc," said he.

Languedoc ! Almost Pujol's own country ! With entire lack of morality, but with picturesque imagination, Aristide plunged into a description of that non-existent baronial hall. Fosse, drawbridge, Gothic chapel were but insignificant features. It had tourelles, emblazoned gateways, bastions, donjons, barbicans ; it had innumerable rooms ; in the *salle des chevaliers* two hundred men-at-arms had his ancestors fed at a sitting. There was the room in which François Premier had slept, and one in which Joan of Arc had almost been assassinated. What the name of himself or of his ancestors was supposed to be Aristide had no ghost of an idea. But as he proceeded with the erection of his airy palace he gradually began to believe in it. He invested the place with a living atmosphere ; conjured up a staff of family retainers, notable one Marie-Joseph Loufoque, the wizened old major-domo, with his long white whiskers and blue and silver livery. There were also Madeline Mioulles, the cook, and Bernadet the groom, and La Petite Fripette the goose girl. Ah ! they should see La Petite Fripette ! And he kept dogs and horses and cows and ducks and hens—and there was a great pond whence frogs were drawn to be fed for the consumption of the household.

Miss Christabel shivered. " I should not like to eat frogs."

" They also eat snails," said her father.

" I have a snail farm," said Aristide. " You never saw such interesting little animals. They are so intelligent. If you're kind to them they come and eat out of your hand."

" You've forgotten the pictures," said Mr. Smith.

" Ah! the pictures," cried Aristide, with a wide sweep of his arms. " Galleries full of them. Raphael, Michael Angelo, Wiertz, Reynolds——"

He paused, not in order to produce the effect of a dramatic aposiopesis, but because he could not for the moment remember other names of painters.

" It is a truly historical château," said he.

" I should love to see it," said the girl.

Aristide threw out his arms across the table. " It is yours, mademoiselle, for your honeymoon," said he.

Dinner came to an end. Miss Christabel left the gentlemen to their wine, an excellent port whose English qualities were vaunted by the host. Aristide, full of food and drink and the mellow glories of the castle in Languedoc, and smoking an enormous cigar, felt at ease with all the world. He knew he should like the kind Mr. Smith, hospitable though somewhat insular man. He could stay with him for a week—or a month—why not a year?

After coffee and liqueurs had been served Mr. Smith rose and switched on a powerful electric light at the end of the large room, showing a picture on an easel covered by a curtain. He beckoned to Aristide to join him and, drawing the curtain, disclosed the picture.

" There! " said he. " Isn't it a stunner? "

It was a picture all grey skies and grey water and grey feathery trees, and a little man in the foreground wore a red cap.

" It is beautiful, but indeed it is magnificent! " cried Aristide, always impressionable to things of beauty.

" Genuine Corot, isn't it? "

" Without doubt," said Aristide.

His host poked him in the ribs. " I thought I'd astonish you. You wouldn't believe Gottschalk could have done it. There it is—as large as life and twice as natural. If you or anyone else can tell it from a genuine Corot I'll eat my hat. And all for eight pounds."

Aristide looked at the beefy face and caught a look of cunning in the little pig's eyes.

" Now are you satisfied ? " asked Mr. Smith.

" More than satisfied," said Aristide, though what he was to be satisfied about passed, for the moment, his comprehension.

" If it was a copy of an existing picture, you know—one might have understood it—that, of course, would be dangerous —but for a man to go and get bits out of various Corots and stick them together like this is miraculous. If it hadn't been for a matter of business principle I'd have given the fellow eight guineas instead of pounds—hanged if I wouldn't ! He deserves it."

" He does indeed," said Aristide Pujol.

" And now that you've seen it with your own eyes, what do you think you might ask me for it ? I suggested something between two and three thousand—shall we say three ? You're the owner, you know." Again the process of rib-digging. " Came out of that historic château of yours. My eye ! you're a holy terror when you begin to talk. You almost persuaded me it was real."

" Tiens ! " said Aristide to himself. " I don't seem to have a château after all."

" Certainly three thousand," said he, with a grave face.

" That young man thinks he knows a lot, but he doesn't," said Mr. Smith.

" Ah ! " said Aristide, with singular laconicism.

" Not a blooming thing," continued his host. " But he'll pay three thousand, which is the principal, isn't it ? He's partner in the show, you know, Ralston, Wiggins, and Wix's Brewery "—Aristide pricked up his ears—" and when his doddering old father dies he'll be Lord Ranelagh and come into a million of money."

" Has he seen the picture ? " asked Aristide.

" Oh, yes. Regards it as a masterpiece. Didn't Brauneberger tell you of the Lancret we planted on the American ? " Mr. Smith rubbed hearty hands at the memory of the iniquity. " Same old game. Always easy. I have nothing to do with the bargaining or the sale. Just an old friend of the ruined French nobleman with the historic château and family treasures. He comes along and fixes the price. I told our friend Harry——"

"Good," thought Aristide. "This is the same Honourable Harry, M.P., who is engaged to the ravishing Miss Christabel."

"I told him," said Mr. Smith, "that it might come to three or four thousand. He jibbed a bit—so when I wrote to you I said two or three. But you might try him with three to begin with."

Aristide went back to the table and poured himself out a fresh glass of his kind host's 1865 brandy and drank it off.

"Exquisite, my dear fellow," said he. "I've none finer in my historic château."

"Don't suppose you have," grinned the host, joining him. He slapped him on the back. "Well," said he, with a shifty look in his little pig's eyes, "let us talk business. What do you think would be your fair commission? You see, all the trouble and invention have been mine. What do you say to four hundred pounds?"

"Five," said Aristide, promptly.

A sudden gleam came into the little pig's eyes.

"Done!" said Mr. Smith, who had imagined that the other would demand a thousand and was prepared to pay eight hundred. "Done!" said he again.

They shook hands to seal the bargain and drank another glass of old brandy. At that moment, a servant, entering, took the host aside.

"Please excuse me a moment," said he, and went with the servant out of the room.

Aristide, left alone, lighted another of his kind host's fat cigars and threw himself into a great leathern arm-chair by the fire, and surrendered himself deliciously to the soothing charm of the moment. Now and then he laughed, finding a certain comicality in his position. And what a charming father-in-law, this kind Mr. Smith!

His cheerful reflections were soon disturbed by the sudden irruption of his host and a grizzled, elderly, foxy-faced gentleman with a white moustache, wearing the ribbon of the Legion of Honour in the buttonhole of his overcoat.

"Here, you!" cried the kind Mr. Smith, striding up to Aristide, with a very red face. "Will you have the kindness to tell me who the devil you are?"

Aristide rose, and, putting his hands behind the tails of his frock-coat, stood smiling radiantly on the hearthrug. A wit much less alert than my irresponsible friend's would have instantly appreciated the fact that the real Simon Pure had arrived on the scene.

"I, my dear friend," said he, "am the Baron de Je ne Sais Plus."

"You're a confounded impostor," spluttered Mr. Smith.

"And this gentleman here to whom I have not had the pleasure of being introduced?" asked Aristide, blandly.

"I am M. Poiron, monsieur, the agent of Messrs. Brauneberger and Compagnie, art dealers, of the Rue Notre Dame des Petits Champs of Paris," said the new-comer, with an air of defiance.

"Ah, I thought you were the Baron," said Aristide.

"There's no blooming Baron at all about it!" screamed Mr. Smith. "Are you Poiron, or is he?"

"I would not have a name like Poiron for anything in the world," said Aristide. "My name is Aristide Pujol, soldier of fortune, at your service."

"How the blazes did you get here?"

"Your servant asked me if I was a French gentleman from Manchester. I was. He said that Mr. Smith had sent his carriage for me. I thought it hospitable of the kind Mr. Smith. I entered the carriage—*et voilà!*"

"Then clear out of here this very minute," said Mr. Smith, reaching forward his hand to the bell-push.

Aristide checked his impulsive action.

"Pardon me, dear host," said he. "It is raining dogs and cats outside. I am very comfortable in your luxurious home. I am here, and here I stay."

"I'm shot if you do," said the kind Mr. Smith, his face growing redder and uglier. "Now, will you go out, or will you be thrown out?"

Aristide, who had no desire whatever to be ejected from this snug nest into the welter of the wet and friendless world, puffed at his cigar, and looked at his host with the irresistible drollery of his eyes.

"You forget, *mon cher ami*," said he, "that neither the beautiful Miss Christabel nor her affianced, the Honourable Harry, M.P., would care to know that the talented Gottschalk got only eight pounds, not even guineas, for painting that three-thousand-pound picture."

"So it's blackmail, eh?"

"Precisely," said Aristide, "and I don't blush at it."

"You infernal little blackguard!"

" I seem to be in congenial company," said Aristide. " I don't think our friend M. Poiron has more scruples than he has right to the ribbon of the Legion of Honour which he is wearing."

" How much will you take to go out ? I have a cheque-book handy."

Mr. Smith moved a few steps from the hearthrug. Aristide sat down in the arm-chair. An engaging, fantastic impudence was one of the charms of Aristide Pujol.

" I'll take five hundred pounds," said he, " to stay in."

" Stay in ? " Mr. Smith grew apoplectic.

" Yes," said Aristide. " You can't do without me. Your daughter and your servants know me as M. le Baron—by the way, what is my name ? And where is my historic château in Languedoc ? "

" Mireilles," said M. Poiron, who was sitting grim and taciturn on one of the dining-room chairs. " And the place is the same, near Montpellier."

" I like to meet an intelligent man," said Aristide.

" I should like to wring your infernal neck," said the kind Mr. Smith. " But, by George, if we do let you in you'll have to sign me a receipt implicating yourself up to the hilt. I'm not going to be put into the cart by you, you can bet your life."

" Anything you like," said Aristide, " so long as we all swing together."

Now, when Aristide Pujol arrived at this point in his narrative, I, his chronicler, who am nothing if not an eminently respectable, law-abiding Briton, took him warmly to task for his sheer absence of moral sense. His eyes, as they sometimes did, assumed a luminous pathos.

" My dear friend," said he, " have you ever faced the world in a foreign country in December with no character, and fifteen pounds five and threepence in your pocket ? Five hundred pounds was a fortune. It is one now. And to be gained just by lending oneself to a good farce, which didn't hurt anybody. You and your British morals ! Bah ! " said he, with a fine flourish.

Aristide, after much parleying, was finally admitted into the nefarious brotherhood. He was to retain his rank as the Baron de Mireilles, and play the part of the pecuniarily inconvenienced nobleman forced to sell some of his rare collection. Mr. Smith had heard of the Corot through their dear old common friend, Jules Dancourt of Rheims, had mentioned it alluringly to the Honourable Harry, had arranged for the Baron, who was visiting England, to bring it over and dispatch it to Mr. Smith's house, and on his return from Manchester to pay a visit to Mr. Smith, so that he could meet the Honourable Harry in person. In whatever transaction ensued Mr. Smith, so far as his prospective son-in-law was concerned, was to be the purely disinterested friend. It was Aristide's wit which invented a part for the supplanted M. Poiron. He should be the eminent Parisian expert who, chancing to be in London, had been telephoned for by the kind Mr. Smith.

" It would not be wise for M. Poiron," said Aristide, chuckling inwardly with puckish glee, " to stay here for the night—or for two or three days—or a week—like myself. He must go back to his hotel when the business is concluded."

" *Mais, pardon !* " cried M. Poiron, who had been formally invited, and had arrived late solely because he had missed his train at Manchester, and come on by the next one. " I cannot go out into the wet, and I have no hotel to go to."

Aristide appealed to his host. " But he is unreasonable, *cher ami*. He must play his *rôle*. M. Poiron has been telephoned for. He can't possibly stay here. Surely five hundred pounds is worth one little night of discomfort ? And there are a legion of hotels in London."

" Five hundred pounds ! " exclaimed M. Poiron. " *Qu'est-ce que vous chantez là ?* I want more than five hundred pounds."

" Then you're jolly well not going to get it," cried Mr. Smith, in a rage. " And as for you "—he turned on Aristide— " I'll wring your infernal neck yet."

" Calm yourself, calm yourself ! " smiled Aristide, who was enjoying himself hugely.

At this moment the door opened and Miss Christabel appeared. On seeing the decorated stranger she started with a little " Oh ! " of surprise.

" I beg your pardon."

Mr. Smith's angry face wreathed itself in smiles.

" This, my darling, is M. Poiron, the eminent Paris expert, who has been good enough to come and give us his opinion on the picture."

M. Poiron bowed. Aristide advanced.

"Mademoiselle, your appearance is like a mirage in a desert."

She smiled indulgently and turned to her father. "I've been wondering what had become of you. Harry has been here for the last half-hour."

"Bring him in, dear child, bring him in!" said Mr. Smith, with all the heartiness of the fine old English gentleman. "Our good friends are dying to meet him."

The girl flickered out of the room like a sunbeam (the phrase is Aristide's), and the three precious rascals put their heads together in a hurried and earnest colloquy. Presently Miss Christabel returned, and with her came the Honourable Harry Ralston, a tall, soldierly fellow, with close-cropped fair curly hair and a fair moustache, and frank blue eyes that, even in Parliament, had seen no harm in his fellow-creatures. Aristide's magical vision caught him wincing ever so little at Mr. Smith's effusive greeting and overdone introductions. He shook Aristide warmly by the hand.

"You have a beauty there, Baron, a perfect beauty," said he, with the insane ingenuousness of youth. "I wonder how you can manage to part with it."

"*Ma foi*," said Aristide, with his back against the end of the dining-table and gazing at the masterpiece. "I have so many at the Château de Mireilles. When one begins to collect, you know—and when one's grandfather and father have had also the divine mania——"

"You were saying, M. le Baron," said M. Poiron of Paris, "that your respected grandfather bought this direct from Corot himself."

"A commission," said Aristide. "My grandfather was a patron of Corot."

"Do you like it, dear?" asked the Honourable Harry.

"Oh, yes!" replied the girl, fervently. "It is beautiful. I feel like Harry about it." She turned to Aristide. "How can you part with it? Were you really in earnest when you said you would like me to come and see your collection?"

"For me," said Aristide, "it would be a visit of enchantment."

"You must take me, then," she whispered to Harry. "The Baron has been telling us about his lovely old château."

"Will you come, monsieur?" asked Aristide.

"Since I'm going to rob you of your picture," said the young man, with smiling courtesy, "the least I can do is to pay you a visit of apology. Lovely ! " said he, going up to the Corot.

Aristide took Miss Christabel, now more bewitching than ever with the glow of young love in her eyes and a flush on her cheek, a step or two aside and whispered :

" But he is charming, your fiancé ! He almost deserves his good fortune."

" Why almost ? " she laughed, shyly.

" It is not a man, but a demi-god, that would deserve you, mademoiselle."

M. Poiron's harsh voice broke out.

" You see, it is painted in the beginning of Corot's later manner—it is 1864. There is the mystery which, when he was quite an old man, became a trick. If you were to put it up to auction at Christie's it would fetch, I am sure, five thousand pounds."

" That's more than I can afford to give," said the young man, with a laugh. " Mr. Smith mentioned something between three and four thousand pounds. I don't think I can go above three."

" I have nothing to do with it, my dear boy, nothing whatever," said Mr. Smith, rubbing his hands. " You wanted a Corot. I said I thought I could put you on to one. It's for the Baron here to mention his price. I retire now and for ever."

" Well, Baron ? " said the young man, cheerfully, " what's your idea ? "

Aristide came forward and resumed his place at the end of the table. The picture was in front of him beneath the strong electric light ; on his left stood Mr. Smith and Poiron, on his right Miss Christabel and the Honourable Harry.

" I'll not take three thousand pounds for it," said Aristide. " A picture like that ! Never ! "

" I assure you it would be a fair price," said Poiron.

" You mentioned that figure yourself only just now," said Mr. Smith, with an ugly glitter in his little pig's eyes.

" I presume, gentlemen," said Aristide, " that this picture is my own property." He turned engagingly to his host. " Is it not, *cher ami* ? "

" Of course it is. Who said it wasn't ? "

" And you, M. Poiron, acknowledge formally that it is mine," he asked, in French.

" *Sans aucun doute*."

"*Eh bien,*" said Aristide, throwing open his arms and gazing round sweetly. "I have changed my mind. I do not sell the picture at all."

"Not sell it? What the—what do you mean?" asked Mr. Smith, striving to mellow the gathering thunder on his brow.

"I do not sell," said Aristide. "Listen, my dear friends!" He was in the seventh heaven of happiness—the principal man, the star, taking the centre of the stage. "I have an announcement to make to you. I have fallen desperately in love with mademoiselle."

There was a general gasp. Mr. Smith looked at him, red-faced and open-mouthed. Miss Christabel blushed furiously and emitted a sound half between a laugh and a scream. Harry Ralston's eyes flashed.

"My dear sir——" he began.

"Pardon," said Aristide, disarming him with the merry splendour of his glance. "I do not wish to take mademoiselle from you. My love is hopeless! I know it. But it will feed me to my dying day. In return for the joy of this hopeless passion I will not sell you the picture—I give it to you as a wedding present."

He stood, with the air of a hero, both arms extended towards the amazed pair of lovers.

"I give it to you," said he. "It is mine. I have no wish but for your happiness. In my Château de Mireilles there are a hundred others."

"This is madness!" said Mr. Smith, bursting with suppressed indignation, so that his bald head grew scarlet.

"My dear fellow!" said Mr. Harry Ralston. "It is unheard-of generosity on your part. But we can't accept it."

"Then," said Aristide, advancing dramatically to the picture, "I take it under my arm, I put it in a hansom cab, and I go with it back to Languedoc."

Mr. Smith caught him by the wrist and dragged him out of the room.

"You little brute! Do you want your neck broken?"

"Do you want the marriage of your daughter with the rich and Honourable Harry broken?" asked Aristide.

"Oh, damn! Oh, damn! Oh, damn!" cried Mr. Smith, stamping about helplessly and half weeping.

Aristide entered the dining-room and beamed on the company.

" The kind Mr. Smith has consented. Mr. Honourable Harry and Miss Christabel, there is your Corot. And now, may I be permitted ? " He rang the bell. A servant appeared.

" Some champagne to drink to the health of the fiancés," he cried. " Lots of champagne."

Mr. Smith looked at him almost admiringly.

" By Jove ! " he muttered. " You *have* got a nerve."

" *Voilà !* " said Aristide, when he had finished the story.

" And did they accept the Corot ? " I asked.

" Of course. It is hanging now in the big house in Hampshire. I stayed with the kind Mr. Smith for six weeks," he added, doubling himself up in his chair and hugging himself with mirth, " and we became very good friends. And I was at the wedding."

" And what about their honeymoon visit to Languedoc ? "

" Alas ! " said Aristide. " The morning before the wedding I had a telegram—it was from my old father at Aigues-Mortes —to tell me that the historic Château de Mireilles, with my priceless collection of pictures, had been burned to the ground."

A. A. MILNE (1882–) *walked into the Editorial offices of "Punch" one day, a poor, and unknown casual contributor, and came out with a position on the staff. His initials are familiar to all "Punch" readers. His whimsical humour and graceful style are evident in whatever he writes, be it the children's poems of "When We Were Very Young," "Now We are Six" and "Winnie the Pooh," his plays or sketches.*

MORE CRICKET

A SCRATCH LOT. I. THE CHOOSING OF THE DAY

As soon as I had promised to take an eleven down to Chartleigh I knew that I was in for trouble ; but I did not realize how great it would be until I consulted Henry Barton. Henry is a first-class cricketer, and it was my idea that he should do all the batting for us, and such of the bowling as the laws allowed. I had also another idea, and this I explained to Henry.

"As you are aware," I said, "the ideal side contains five good bats, four good bowlers, a wicket-keeper, and Henry Barton."

"Quite so," agreed Henry.

"That is the principle on which one selects an eleven. Now, I intend to strike out a line of my own. My team shall consist of three authors or journalists, two solicitors, four barristers, a couple from the Stock Exchange, some civil servants, and an artist or two. How many is that ? "

"Nineteen."

"Well, that's the idea, anyhow."

"It's a rotten idea."

"No, it's a splendid idea. I wonder nobody has thought of it before. I send a solicitor and a journalist in first. The journalist uses the long handle, while the solicitor plays for keeps."

"And where does the artist come in ? "

"The artist comes in last, and plays for a draw. You are very slow to-day, Henry."

Henry, the man of leisure, thought a moment.

" Yes, that's all very well for you working men," he said at last, " but what do I go as ? Or am I one of the barristers ? "

" You go as ' with Barton.' Yes. If you're very good you shall have an ' H ' in brackets after you. ' With Barton (H).' "

The method of choosing my team being settled, the next thing was the day. " Any day in the first week in July," the Chartleigh captain had said. Now at first sight there appear to be seven days in the week, but it is not really so. For instance, Saturday. Now there's a good day ! What could one object to in a Saturday ?

But do you imagine Henry Barton would let it pass ?

" I don't think you'll get eleven people for the Saturday," he said. " People are always playing cricket on Saturday."

" Precisely," I said. " Healthy exercise for the London toiler. That's why I'm asking 'em."

" But I mean they'll have arranged to play already with their own teams. Or else they'll be going away for week-ends."

" One can spend a very pretty week-end at Chartleigh."

" H'm, let me think. Any day in the week, isn't it ? "

" Except, apparently, Saturday," I said huffily.

" Let's see now, what days are there ? "

I mentioned two or three of the better-known ones.

" Yes. Of course, some of those are impossible, though. We'd better go through the week and see which is best."

I don't know who Barton is that he should take it upon himself to make invidious distinctions between the days of the week.

" Very well, then," I said. " Sunday."

" Ass."

That seemed to settle Sunday, so we passed on to Monday.

" You won't get your stockbroker on Monday," said Henry. " It's Contanger day or something with them every Monday."

" Stocktaking, don't you mean ? "

" I dare say. Anyhow, no one in the House can get away on a Monday."

" I must have my stockbrokers. Tuesday."

Tuesday, it seemed, was hopeless. I was a fool to have thought of Tuesday. Why, everybody knew that Tuesday was an impossible day for——

I forget what spoilt Tuesday's chance. I fancy it was a busy day for civil servants. No one in the Home Civil can get away on a Tuesday. I know that sounds absurd, but Henry was being absurd just then. Or was it barristers ? Briefs get given out on a Tuesday, I was made to understand. That brought us to Wednesday. I hoped much from Wednesday.

"Yes," said Henry. "Wednesday might do. Of course most of the weeklies go to press on Wednesday. Rather an awkward day for journalists. What about Thursday?"

I began to get annoyed.

"Thursday my flannel trousers go to the press," I said—"that is to say, they come back from the wash then."

"Look here, why try to be funny?"

"Hang it, who started it? Talking about Contanger days. Contanger—it sounds like a new kind of guano."

"Well, if you don't believe it——"

"Henry, I do. Thursday be it, then."

"Yes, I suppose that's all right," said Henry doubtfully.

"Why not? Don't say it's sending-in day with artists," I implored. "Not *every* Thursday?"

"No. Only there's Friday, and——"

"Friday is *my* busy day," I pleaded—"my one ewe lamb. Do not rob me of it."

"It's a very good day, Friday. I think you'd find that most people could get off then."

"But why throw over Thursday like this? A good, honest day, Henry. Many people get born on a Thursday, Henry. And it's a marrying day, Henry. A nice, clean, sober day, and you—— "

"The fact is," said Henry, "I've suddenly remembered I'm engaged myself on Thursday."

This was too much.

"Henry," I said coldly, "you forget yourself—you forget yourself strangely, my lad. Just because I was weak enough to promise you an 'H' after your name. You seem to have forgotten that the 'H' was to be in brackets."

"Yes, but I'm afraid I really am engaged."

"Are you really? Look here—I'll leave out the 'with' and you shall be one of us. There! Baby, see the pretty gentleman!"

Henry smiled and shook his head.

"Oh, well," I said, "we must have you. So if you say Friday, Friday it is. You're quite sure Friday is all right for solicitors? Very well, then."

So the day was settled for Friday. It was rather a pity, because, as I said, in the ordinary way Friday is the day I put aside for work.

II. THE SELECTION COMMITTEE

THE committee consisted of Henry and myself. Originally it was myself alone, but as soon as I had selected Henry I proceeded to co-opt him, reserving to myself, however, the right of a casting vote in case of any difference of opinion. One arose, almost immediately, over Higgins. Henry said:

(a) That Higgins had once made ninety-seven.

(b) That he had been asked to play for his county.

(c) That he was an artist, and we had arranged to have an artist in the team.

In reply I pointed out:

(a) That ninety-seven was an extremely unlikely number for anyone to have made.

(b) That if he had been asked he evidently hadn't accepted, which showed the sort of man he was ; besides which, what was his county ?

(c) That, assuming for the moment he had made ninety-seven, was it likely he would consent to go in last and play for a draw, which was why we wanted the artist ? And that, anyhow, he was a jolly bad artist.

(d) That hadn't we better put it to the vote ?

This was accordingly done, and an exciting division ended in a tie.

Those in favour of Higgins . . . I
Those against Higgins I

The Speaker gave his casting vote against Higgins.

Prior to this, however, I had laid before the House the letter of invitation. It was as follows (and, I flatter myself, combined tact with a certain dignity) :

" DEAR——, I am taking a team into the country on Friday week to play against the village eleven. The ground and the lunch are good. Do you think you could manage to come down ? I know you are very busy just now with—

Contangers,
Briefs,
Clients,
Your Christmas Number,
Varnishing Day,
(*Strike out all but one of these*)

but a day in the country would do you good. I hear from all sides that you are in great form this season. I will give you all particulars about trains later on. Good-bye. Remember me to——. How is——? Ever yours.

"P.S.—Old Henry is playing for us. He has strained himself a little and probably won't bowl much, so I expect we shall all have a turn with the ball."

Or, "I don't think you have ever met Henry Barton, the cricketer. He is very keen on meeting you. Apparently he has seen you play somewhere. He will be turning out for us on Friday.

"P.P.S.—We might manage to have some bridge in the train."

"That," I said to Henry, "is what I call a clever letter."

"What makes you think that?"

"It is all clever," I said modestly. "But the cleverest part is a sentence at the end. 'I will give you all particulars about trains later on.' You see I have been looking them up, and we leave Victoria at seven-thirty a.m. and get back to London Bridge at eleven-forty-five p.m."

The answers began to come in the next day. One of the first was from Bolton, the solicitor, and it upset us altogether. For, after accepting the invitation, he went on : "I am afraid I don't play bridge. As you may remember, I used to play chess at Cambridge, and I still keep it up."

"Chess," said Henry. "That's where White plays and mates in two moves. And there's a Black too. He does something."

"We shall have to get a Black. This is awful."

"Perhaps Bolton would like to do problems by himself all the time."

"That would be rather bad luck on him. No, look here. Here's Carey. Glad to come, but doesn't bridge. He's the man."

Accordingly we wired to Carey : "Do you play chess? Reply at once." He answered, "No. Why?"

"Carey will have to play that game with glass balls. Solitaire. Yes. We must remember to bring a board with us."

"But what about the chess gentleman?" asked Henry.

"I must go and find one. We've had one refusal."

There is an editor I know slightly, so I called upon him at his office. I found him writing verses.

" Be brief," he said ; " I'm frightfully busy."

" I have just three questions to ask you," I replied.

" What rhymes with ' yorker ' ? "

" That wasn't one of them."

" Yorker—corker—por——"

" Better make it a full pitch," I suggested. " Step out and make it a full pitch. Then there are such lots of rhymes."

" Thanks, I will. Well ? "

" One. Do you play bridge ? '

" No."

" Two. Do you play chess ? "

" I can."

" Three. Do you play cricket ? Not that it matters."

" Yes, I do sometimes. Good-bye. Send me a proof, will you ? By the way, what paper is this for ? "

" *The Sportsman*, if you'll play. On Friday week. Do."

" Anything, if you'll go."

" May I have that in writing ? "

He handed me a rejection form.

" There you are. And I'll do anything you like on Friday."

I went back to Henry and told him the good news.

" I wonder if he'll mind being black," said Henry. " That's the chap that always gets mated so quickly."

" I expect they'll arrange it among themselves. Anyhow, we've done our best for them."

" It's an awful business, getting up a team," said Henry thoughtfully. " Well, we shall have two decent sets of bridge, anyway. But you ought to have arranged for twelve aside, and then we could have left out the chess professors and had three sets."

" It's all the fault of the rules. Some day somebody will realize that four doesn't go into eleven, and then we shall have a new rule."

" No, I don't think so," said Henry. " I don't fancy ' Wanderer ' would allow it."

III. IN THE TRAIN

IF there is one thing I cannot stand, it is ingratitude. Take the case of Carey. Carey, you may remember, professed himself unable to play either bridge or chess ; and as we had a three-hour journey before us it did not look as though he were going to have much of a time. However, Henry and I, thinking entirely of Carey's personal comfort, went to the trouble of buying him a solitaire board, with glass balls complete. The balls were all in different colours.

I laid this before Carey as soon as we settled in the train.

" Whatever's that ? "

" The new game," I said. " It's all the rage now, the man tells me. The Smart Set play it every Sunday. Young girls are inveigled into lonely country houses and robbed of incredible sums."

Carey laughed scornfully.

" So it is alleged," I added. " The inventor claims for it that in some respects it has advantages which even cricket cannot claim. As, for instance, it can be played in any weather ; nay, even upon the sick bed."

" And how exactly is it played ? "

" Thus. You take one away and all the rest jump over each other. At each jump you remove the jumpee, and the object is to clear the board. Hence the name—solitaire."

" I see. It seems a pretty rotten game."

That made me angry.

" All right. Then don't play. Have a game of marbles on the rack instead."

Meanwhile Henry was introducing Bolton and the editor to each other.

" Two such famous people," he began.

" Every one," said Bolton, with a bow, " knows the editor of——"

" Oh, yes, that's that. But I meant two such famous chess players. Bolton," he explained to the editor, " was twelfth man against Oxford some years ago. Something went wrong with his heart, or he'd have got in. On his day, and if the board was at all sticky, he used to turn a good deal from QB4."

" Do you really play ? " asked Bolton eagerly. " I have a board here."

" Does he play ! Do you mean to say you have never heard of the Trocadero Defence ? "

" The Sicilian Defence——"

" The Trocadero Defence. It's where you palm the other man's queen when he's not looking. Most effective opening."

They both seemed keen on beginning, so Henry got out the cards for the rest of us.

I drew the younger journalist, against Henry and the senior stockbroker. Out of compliment to the journalist we arranged to play half a crown a hundred, that being about the price they pay him. I dealt, and a problem arose immediately. Here it is.

" A deals and leaves it to his partner B, who goes No Trumps. Y leads a small heart. B's hand consists of king and three small diamonds, king and one other heart, king and three small clubs, and three small spades. A plays the king from Dummy, and Z puts on the ace. What should A do ? "

Answer. Ring communication cord and ask guard to remove B.

" Very well," I said to Dummy. " One thing's pretty clear. You don't bowl to-day. Long-leg both ends is about your mark. Somewhere where there's plenty of throwing to do."

Later on, when I was Dummy, I strolled over to the chess players.

" What's the ground like ? " said the editor, as he finessed a knight.

" Sporting. Distinctly sporting."

" Long grass all round, I suppose ? "

" Oh, lord, no. The cows eat up all that."

" Do you mean to say the cows are allowed on the pitch ? "

" Well, they don't put it that way, quite. The pitch is allowed on the cows' pasture land."

" I suppose if we make a hundred we shall do well ? " asked somebody.

" If we make fifty we shall declare," I said. " By Jove, Bolton, that's a pretty smart move."

I may not know all the technical terms, but I do understand the idea of chess. The editor was a pawn up and three to play, and had just advanced his queen against Bolton's king, putting on a lot of check side as it seemed to me. Of course, I expected Bolton would have to retire his king ; but not he ! He laid a stymie with his bishop, and it was the editor's queen that had to withdraw. Yet Bolton was only spare man at Cambridge !

" I am not at all sure," I said, " that chess is not a finer game even than solitaire."

" It's a finer game than cricket," said Bolton, putting his bishop back in the slips again.

" No," said the editor. " Cricket is the finest game in the world. For why ? I will tell you."

" Thanks to the glorious uncertainty of our national pastime," began the journalist, from his next Monday's article.

" No, thanks to the fact that it is a game in which one can produce the maximum of effect with the minimum of skill. Take my own case. I am not a batsman, I shall never make ten runs in an innings, yet how few people realize that ! I go in first wicket down, wearing my M.C.C. cap. Having taken guard with the help of a bail, I adopt Palairet's stance at the wicket. Then the bowler delivers ; either to the off, to leg, or straight. If it is to the off, I shoulder my bat and sneer at it. If it is to leg, I swing at it. I have a beautiful swing, which is alone worth the money. Probably I miss, but the bowler fully understands that it is because I have not yet got the pace of the wicket. Sooner or later he sends down a straight one, whereupon I proceed to glide it to leg. You will see the stroke in Beldam's book. Of course, I miss the ball, and am given out l.b.w. Then the look of astonishment that passes over my face, the bewildered inquiry of the wicket-keeper, and finally the shrug of good-humoured resignation as I walk from the crease ! Nine times out of ten square-leg asks the umpire what county I play for. That is cricket."

" Quite so," I said, when he had finished. " There's only one flaw in it. That is that quite possibly you may have to go in last to-day. You'll have to think of some other plan. Also on this wicket the ball always goes well over your head. You couldn't be l.b.w. if you tried."

" Oh, but I do try."

" Yes. Well, you'll find it difficult."

The editor sighed.

" Then I shall have to retire hurt," he said.

Bolton chuckled to himself.

" One never retires hurt at chess," he said, as he huffed the editor's king. " Though once," he added proudly, " I sprained my hand, and had to make all my moves with the left one. Check."

The editor yawned, and looked out of the window.

" Are we nearly there ? " he asked.

IV. IN THE FIELD

IT is, I consider, the duty of a captain to consult the wishes of his team now and then, particularly when he is in command of such a heterogeneous collection of the professions as I was. I was watching a match at the Oval once, and at the end of an over Lees went up to Dalmeny, and had a few words with him. Probably, I thought, he is telling him a good story that he heard at lunch ; or, maybe, he is asking for the latest gossip from the Lobby. My neighbour, however, held other views.

"There," he said, "there's ole Walter Lees asking to be took off."

"Surely not," I answered. "Dalmeny had a telegram just now, and Lees is asking if it's the three-thirty winner."

Lees then began to bowl again.

"There you are," I said triumphantly, but my neighbour wouldn't hear of it.

"Ole Lees asked to be took off, and ole Dalmeny" (I forget how he pronounced it, but I know it was one of the wrong ways)—"ole Dalmeny told him he'd have to stick on a bit."

Now that made a great impression on me, and I agreed with my friend that Dalmeny was in the wrong.

"When I am captaining a team," I said, "and one of the bowlers wants to come off, I am always ready to meet him half-way, more than half-way. Better than that, if I have resolved upon any course of action, I always let my team know beforehand ; and I listen to their objections in a fair-minded spirit."

It was in accordance with this rule of mine that I said casually, as we were changing, "If we win the toss I shall put them in."

There was a chorus of protest.

"That's right, go it," I said. "Henry objects because, as a first-class cricketer, he is afraid of what *The Sportsman* will say if we lose. The editor naturally objects—it ruins his chance of being mistaken for a county player if he has to field first. Bolton objects because heavy exercise on a hot day spoils his lunch. Thompson objects because that's the way he earns his living at the Bar. His objection is merely technical, and is reserved as a point of law for the Court of Crown Cases Reserved. Markham is a socialist and objects to authority. Also he knows he's got to field long-leg both ends. Gerald——"

"But why ? " said Henry.

"Because I want you all to see the wicket first. Then you can't say you weren't warned." Whereupon I went out and lost the toss.

As we walked into the field the editor told me a very funny story. I cannot repeat it here for various reasons. First, it

has nothing to do with cricket ; and, secondly, it is, I understand, coming out in his next number, and I should probably
get into trouble. Also it is highly technical, and depends largely
for its success upon adequate facial expression. But it amused
me a good deal. Just as he got to the exciting part, Thompson
came up.

" Do you mind if I go cover ? " he asked.

" Do," I said abstractedly. " And what did the vicar say ? "

The editor chuckled. " Well, you see, the vicar knowing,
of course, that——"

" Cover, I suppose," said Gerald, as he caught us up.

" What ? Oh yes, please. The vicar did know, did he ? "

" Oh, the vicar *knew*. That's really the whole point."

I shouted with laughter.

" Good, isn't it ? " said the editor. " Well, then——"

" Have you got a cover ? " came Markham's voice from
behind us.

I turned round.

" Oh, Markham," I said, " I shall want you cover, if you
don't mind. Sorry—I must tell these men where to go—well,
then, you were saying——"

The editor continued the story. We were interrupted
once or twice, but he finished it just as their first two men came
out. I particularly liked that bit about the——

" Jove," I said suddenly, " we haven't got a wicket-keeper.
That's always the way. Can you keep ? " I asked the editor.

" Isn't there anyone else ? "

" I'm afraid they're all fielding cover," I said, remembering
suddenly. " But, look here, it's the chance of a lifetime for
you. You can tell 'em all that——"

But he was trotting off to the pavilion.

" Can anybody lend me some gloves ? " he asked. " They
want me to keep wicket. Thing I've never done in my life.
Of course I always field cover in the ordinary way. Thanks
awfully. Sure you don't mind ? Don't suppose I shall stop a
ball though."

" Henry," I called, " you're starting that end. Arrange the
field, will you ? I'll go cover. You're sure to want one."

Their first batsman was an old weather-beaten villager
called George. We knew his name was George because the
second ball struck him in the stomach and his partner said,
" Stay there, George," which seemed to be George's idea too.
We learnt at lunch that once, in the 'eighties or so, he had gone

in first with Lord Hawke (which put him on a level with that player), and that he had taken first ball (which put him just above the Yorkshireman).

There the story ended, so far as George was concerned ; and indeed it was enough. Why seek to inquire if George took any other balls besides the first ?

In our match, however, he took the second in the place that I mentioned, the third on the back of the neck, the fourth on the elbow, and the fifth in the original place ; while the sixth, being off the wicket, was left there. Nearly every batsman had some pet stroke, and we soon saw that George's stroke was the leg-bye. His bat was the second line of defence, and was kept well in the block. If the ball escaped the earthwork in front, there was always a chance that it would be brought up by the bat. Once, indeed, a splendid ball of Henry's which came with his arm and missed George's legs, snicked the bat, and went straight into the wicket-keeper's hands. The editor, however, presented his compliments, and regretted that he was unable to accept the enclosed, which he accordingly returned with many thanks.

There was an unwritten law that George could not be l.b.w. I cannot say how it arose—possibly from a natural coyness on George's part about the exact significance of the " l." Henry, after appealing for the best part of three overs, gave it up, and bowled what he called " googlies " at him. This looked more hopeful, because a googly seems in no way to be restricted as to the number of its bounces, and at each bounce it had a chance of doing something. Unfortunately it never did George. Lunch came and the score was thirty-seven—George having compiled in two hours a masterly nineteen ; eighteen off the person, but none the less directly due to him.

" We must think of a plan of campaign at lunch," said Henry. " It's hopeless to go on like this."

" Does George drink ? " I asked anxiously. It seemed the only chance.

But George didn't. And the score was thirty-seven for five, which is a good score for the wicket.

V. AT THE WICKETS

AT lunch I said : " I have just had a wire from the Surrey committee to say that I may put myself on to bowl."

" That is good hearing," said Henry.

"Did they hear?" asked Gerald anxiously, looking over at the Chartleigh team.

"You may think you're very funny, but I'll bet you a—a— anything you like that I get George out."

"All right," said Gerald. "I'll play you for second wicket down, the loser to go in last."

"Done," I said, "and what about passing the salad now?"

After lunch the editor took me on one side and said: "I don't like it. I don't like it at all."

"Then why did you have so much?" I asked.

"I mean the wicket. It's dangerous. I am not thinking of myself so much as of——"

"As of the reading public?"

"Quite so."

"You think you—you would be missed in Fleet Street— just at first?"

"You are not putting the facts too strongly. I was about to suggest that I should be a 'did not bat.'"

"Oh! I see. Perhaps I ought to tell you that I was talking just now to the sister of their captain."

The editor looked interested.

"About the pad of the gardener?" he said.

"About you. She said—I give you her own words— 'Who is the tall, handsome man keeping wicket in a M.C.C. cap?' So I said you were a well-known county player, as she would see when you went in to bat."

The editor shook my hand impressively.

"Thank you very much," he said. "I shall not fail her. What county did you say?"

"Part of Flint. You know the little bit that's got into the wrong county by mistake? That part. She had never heard of it; but I assured her it had a little bit of yellow all to itself on the map. Have you a pretty good eleven?"

The editor swore twice—once for me and once for Flint. Then we went out into the field.

My first ball did for George. I followed the tactics of William the First at the Battle of Hastings, 1066. You remember how he ordered his archers to shoot into the air, and how one arrow fell and pierced the eye of Harold, whereupon confusion and disaster arose. So with George. I hurled one perpendicularly into the sky, and it dropped (after a long time) straight upon the batsman. George followed it with a slightly contemptuous eye. . . . all the way. . . .

George followed it with a slightly contemptuous eye . . . all the way.

All the way. Of course, I was sorry. We were all much distressed. They told us afterwards he had never been hit in the eye before. . . . One gets new experiences.

George retired hurt. Not so much hurt as piqued, I fancy. He told the umpire it wasn't bowling. Possibly. Neither was it batting. It was just superior tactics.

The innings soon closed, and we had sixty-one to win, and, what seemed more likely, fifty-nine and various other numbers to lose. Sixty-one is a very unlucky number with me—oddly enough I have never yet made sixty-one ; like W. G. Grace, who had never made ninety-three. My average this season is five, which is a respectable number. As Bolton pointed out— if we each got five to-day, and there were six extras, we should win. I suppose if one plays chess a good deal one thinks of these things.

Harold, I mean George, refused to field, so I nobly put myself in last and substituted for him. This was owing to an argument as to the exact wording of my bet with Gerald.

" You said you'd get him out," said Gerald.

" I mean ' out of the way,' ' out of the field,' ' out of——' "

" I meant ' out ' according to the laws of cricket. There are nine ways. Which was yours, I should like to know ? "

" Obstructing the ball."

" There you are."

I shifted my ground.

" I didn't say I'd get him out," I explained. " I said I'd get him. Those were my very words. ' I will get George.' Can you deny that I got him ? "

" Even if you said that, which you didn't, the common construction that one puts upon the phrase is——"

" If you are going to use long words like that," I said, " I must refer you to my solicitor Bolton."

Whereupon Bolton took counsel's opinion, and reported that he could not advise me to proceed in the matter. So Gerald took second wicket, and I fielded.

However, one advantage of fielding was that I saw the editor's innings from start to finish at the closest quarters. He came in at the end of the first over, and took guard for " left hand round the wicket."

" Would you give it me ? " he said to Bolton. " These country umpires. . . . Thanks. And what's that over the wicket ? Thanks."

He marked two places with the bail.

" How about having it from here ? " I suggested at mid-on.
" It's quite a good place and we're in a straight line with the
church."

The editor returned the bail, and held up his bat again.

- " That ' one-leg ' all right ? Thanks."

He was proceeding to look round the field when a gentle
voice from behind him said : " If you wouldn't mind moving
a bit, sir, I could bowl."

" Oh, is it over ? " said the editor airily, trying to hide his
confusion. " I beg your pardon, I beg your pardon."

Still he had certainly impressed the sister of their captain,
and it was dreadful to think of the disillusionment that might
follow at any moment. However, as it happened, he had yet
another trick up his sleeve. Bolton hit a ball to cover, and the
editor, in the words of the local paper, " most sportingly sacrificed his wicket when he saw that his partner had not time to
get back. It was a question, however, whether there was ever
a run possible."

Which shows that the reporter did not know of the existence of their captain's sister.

When I came in, the score was fifty-one for nine, and Henry
was still in. I had only one ball to play, so I feel that I should
describe it in full. I have four good scoring strokes—the cut,
the drive, the hook, and the glance. As the bowler ran up to
the crease I decided to cut the ball to the ropes. Directly,
however, it left his hand, I saw that it was a ball to hook, and
accordingly I changed my attitude to the one usually adopted
for that stroke. But the ball came up farther than I expected,
so at the last moment I drove it hard past the bowler. That at
least was the idea. Actually, it turned out to be a beautiful
glance shot to the leg boundary. Seldom, if ever, has Beldam
had such an opportunity for four action photographs on one
plate.

Henry took a sixer next ball, and so we won. And the rest
of the story of my team, is it not written in the journals of *The
Sportsman* and *The Chartleigh Watchman*, and in the hearts of
all who were privileged to compose it ? But how the editor
took two jokes I told him in the train, and put them in his
paper (as his own), and how Carey challenged the engine-driver
to an eighteen-hole solitaire match, and how . . . these things
indeed shall never be divulged.

EX NIHILO FIT MULTUM

I SHOULD like to explain just what happened to the ball. In the first place it was of an irreproachable length, and broke very sharply and cleverly from the leg. (The bowler, I am sure, will bear me out in this.) Also it rose with great suddenness . . . and, before I had time to perfect any adequate system of defence, took me on the knee and from there rolled on to the off-stump. There was a considerable amount of applause on the part of the field, due, no doubt, to the feeling that a dangerous batsman had been dismissed without scoring. I need hardly add that I did not resent this appreciation.

What I really wished to say to the wicket-keeper was (1) that it was the first fast wicket I had played on this summer ; (2) that it was my first nought this season, and, hang it, even Fry made noughts sometimes ; and (3) that personally I always felt that it didn't matter what one made oneself so long as one's side was victorious. What I actually said was shorter ; but I expect the wicket-keeper understood just as well. He seemed an intelligent fellow.

After that, I walked nine miles back to the pavilion.

The next man was brushing his hair in the dressing-room.

" What's happened ? " he asked.

" Nothing," I said truthfully.

" But you're out, aren't you ? "

" I mean that nothing has eventuated—accrued, as it were."

" Blob ? Bad luck. Is my parting straight ? "

" It curls a bit from leg up at the top, but it will do. Mind you make some. I always feel that so long as one's side is victorious——"

But he was gone. I brushed my own hair very carefully, lit a cigarette, and went outside to the others. I always think that a nought itself is nothing—the way one carries it off is everything. A disaster, not only to himself but also to his side, should not make a man indifferent to his personal appearance.

" Bad luck," said somebody. " Did it come back ? "

" Very quickly. We both did."

" He wasn't breaking much when I was in," said some tactless idiot.

" Then why did you get out ? " I retorted.

" L.b.w."

I moved quickly away from him, and sat next to a man who had yet to go in.

" Bad luck," he said. " Second ball, wasn't it ? I expect I shall do the same."

I thought for a moment.

" What makes you think you will have a second ? " I asked.

" To judge from the easy way in which those two are knocking the bowling about, I shan't even have a first," he smiled.

I moved on again.

" Hallo," said a voice. " I saw you get out. How many did you make ? "

" None," I said wearily.

" How many ? "

I went and sat down next to him.

" Guess," I said.

" Oh, I can't."

" Well, think of a number."

" Yes."

" Double it. Divide by two. Take away the number you first thought of. What does that make ? "

" A hundred."

" You must have done it wrong," I said suspiciously.

" No, I am sure I didn't. . . . No, it still comes to a hundred."

" Well, then, I must have made a hundred," I said excitedly. " Are you *sure* you haven't made a mistake ? "

" Quite."

" Then I'd better go and tell the scorer. He put me down a blob—silly ass."

" He's a bad scorer, I know."

" By the way," I said, as I got up, " what number did you think of ? "

" Well, it's like this. When you asked me to guess what you had made I instinctively thought of blob, only I didn't like to say so. Then when you began that number game I started with a hundred—it's such an easy number. Double— two hundred. Divided by two—one hundred. Take away the number you first thought of—that's blob, and you have a hundred left. Wasn't that right ? "

" You idiot," I said angrily. " Of course it wasn't."

" Well, don't get sick about it. We all make mistakes."

" Sick, I'm not sick. Only just for the moment. . . . I really thought. . . . Well, I shall never be so near a century again."

At lunch I sat next to one of their side.

" How many did you make ? " he asked.

" Not very many," I said.

" How many ? "

" Oh, hardly any. None at all, practically."

" How many actually ? "

" *And* actually," I said. (" Fool.")

After lunch a strange man happened to be talking to me.

" And why did *you* get out ? " he asked.

It was a silly question and deserved a silly answer. Besides, I was sick of it all by this time.

" Point's moustache put me off," I said.

" What was wrong with Point's moustache ? "

" It swerved the wrong way."

" I was fielding point," he said.

" I'm very sorry. But if you had recognized me, you wouldn't have asked why I got out, and if I had recognized you I shouldn't have told you. So let's forgive and forget."

I hoped that the subject was really closed this time. Of course, I knew that kind friends and relations would ask me on the morrow how many I had made, but for that day I wanted no more of it. Yet, as it happened, I reopened the subject myself.

For with five minutes to play their ninth wicket fell. Mid-off sauntered over towards me.

" Just as well we didn't stay in any longer."

" That's *just* what I thought," I said triumphantly, " all along."

BARRY PAIN (1860–1928) *started his writing career with contributions to the Cambridge University magazine, "The Granta." He was a man of many interests, but it was as a humorous writer that he made his chief appeal to the public. His series of Eliza books, which describe the amusing vicissitudes of the suburban household of a City clerk, are the most popular of his numerous and varied literary creations.*

THE HORSE
THAT DID NO WRONG

I HAD formed my own plan for the Easter Monday immediately following my promotion. I had a long talk over the matter weeks before with Mr. Percy Jennings, who teaches riding and driving, and lets out horses and vehicles.

He heard what I had got to say, and seemed respectful, but doubtful.

"Well, sir," he said, "things being as you say, if I might advise, I should think you'd better change your mind. Let me send you a nice comfortable victoria and one of my men to drive you, and then there can't be any mistake."

"I think not, Mr. Jennings," I said. "I want to drive myself and my wife in a dogcart to the Lion at Winthorpe ; it would give me no pleasure to be driven. I know that my limited experience with—er—the humbler animal does not amount to very much, but I feel that I should be all right with a safe horse. You understand, a perfectly safe horse. I mean one that has no vice of any kind under any provocation, that does not require any looking after, and, if possible, an animal that is in the habit of going to and from the Lion, and knows the road thoroughly."

Mr. Percy Jennings sucked a straw thoughtfully.

"You're asking for miracles," he said, "but as it happens I've got just that miracle. Young horse—Tommy we call him. He's worth £60 of any man's money, and he's worth £80 to me in my business. In fact, if you offered me £80 for him now, I'd tell you to put your money back in your pocket. You see, I get gents here to learn, and when the beginners are beginning I take them out with Tommy to get confidence. Say it's an oldish gent who's never seen a horse before, and has

been told to ride by his doctor—first few times I put him up
on Tommy.   Say it's a nervous lady wants to start a governess
cart, and don't know how to drive—I starts her with Tommy.
That horse has never done anything wrong, and never thought
of doing anything wrong, since the day he was foaled.   He
couldn't do wrong if you asked him, and he'll do anything
else you ask.   Why, the blooming horse would climb a tree if
he thought I expected it of him.   The very first day he was in
the shafts I drove him straight to Winthorpe—and that's a
fact. . No work comes amiss to him, nor nothing else, either.
He'll stand like a statue with his nose over a buzzing motor,
or he'll draw you twelve miles an hour without a whip.   You
can stop him with a thread, and turn him with just thinking
about it.   And he's as pretty as he's good.   But——"

Mr. Jennings stopped short and shook his head.

" Well ? " I said.

" But I don't let that horse out to every chance comer to
knock about as he pleases on the high roads on an Easter
Monday."

" Now, Mr. Jennings," I said, " do I look like a man who
would knock a horse about ? "

" No," he said, " you don't.   If I may say it without offence,
you're the ignorant, nervous sort.   And I've known them
bring the horse and cart back safe when one of the rowdy lot,
that think they know something, will get three-parts screwed,
start racing, and go to glory.   If I'd thought that you were
one of the rowdy lot, I shouldn't so much as have mentioned
him to you.   However, we can't stop here talking all day.   Set
that horse towards Winthorpe, and he'll go there and stop at
the Lion—he's used to it—if he's not interfered with.   Let
him take his own pace up hill and down ; he knows his business.
And at night he'll take you home all right if you let him alone.
You taking all responsibility up to ten fivers, I might think
about it."

Business was subsequently arranged on these terms.

.   .   .   .

Eliza has not, perhaps, what would be called a sunny
disposition.   I said in my nonchalant way that evening, as I
stirred my cocoa :

" I've arranged about the Bank Holiday, Eliza.   I'm
going to tool you over in a high dogcart to Winthorpe.   I
understand they give you a decent dinner at the Lion.
Then I shall tool you back at night—moonlight, you know.

Best horse in Jennings's stables—not let out as a general rule."

All she would say at first was that extravagance was never any pleasure to her, and she wondered what mother would say if she knew. But after a certain amount of argument on both sides, I said that of course I should expect to make up for it in other ways as far as possible, and she admitted that she might enjoy it.

" If," she added, " we ever get home alive."

" That will be all right," I said. " I shall not ask you to drive. That will be my province, and I am not entirely without experience."

During the next few days I talked over the details frequently. There is nothing like a thorough preparation for making a success. I also kept my eye open in the streets and made some useful notes with reference to—

(*a*) Getting into the dogcart ;
(*b*) Position of the hands and expression of face when driving ;
(*c*) Arrangement of the rug ;
(*d*) Getting out of the dogcart.

I also read carefully in our public reading-room an interesting and instructive article on " How Race-horses are Trained." Its bearing on the subject was somewhat indirect, but I gathered from it the meaning of several phrases which had previously been something of a difficulty to me.

.   .   .   .

I may say at once that we reached the Lion at Winthorpe without any accident. There was one little contretemps, as the French would say. We happened to meet Miss Sakers—for which, in itself, I was not sorry. She bowed, and in raising my hat I fancy the reins got caught—I never quite understood how it happened—but the horse turned round. However, I got down, and put him back in the required direction. It was merely a mistake on the horse's part, and he showed no trace of obstinacy. I also dropped my whip once or twice, but there is always some boy to pick that up for you and glad to earn a few coppers. I could not, considering the circumstances, agree with Eliza that a halfpenny would have been sufficient. However, I was quite good-tempered about it— indeed, I felt in particularly high spirits. I was wearing a straw hat for the first time that season—it was a last year's hat, but Eliza had cleaned it with salts of lemon, so that really it was quite presentable. I also wore a black diagonal frock-coat and vest that I reserved for Sundays and similar occasions, and a pair of white flannel trousers and brown boots. The trousers were new and almost unnecessarily long and roomy. However, as Eliza pointed out at the time, that, of course, allows for shrinkage in the wash. My necktie was of white satin with sprigs of flowers embroidered in the natural colours —tasteful and, I think, uncommon. Eliza wore her mackintosh —rather against my wishes, as the day was quite fine. The general appearance of our turn-out gave me great satisfaction. I cannot help thinking that we made some impression on people that we met, and I amused myself with wondering what they thought I was.

The dinner at the Lion was good, though Eliza rather kicked at the price. I drank one pint of bitter at dinner, and no more. In the light of subsequent events the necessity of mentioning this will be apparent. The place was, unfortunately, rather crowded, and not entirely with the best class of people. There were too many Bank Holiday cyclists there for my taste. One gentleman entered into conversation with me on the subject of horses. He was an elderly man, and Eliza said afterwards that she did not like his eye. Personally I found him most civil, quite ready to listen to me and to take a word of advice. He said that he had seen me drive up, and had said to the landlord : " That man knows what he's doing, anyhow." He seemed quite surprised to hear that it was not my own horse, and said he supposed I was trying it.

" Well," I said, " under certain circumstances I might buy him."

Here Eliza drew in her breath hard and long through her nose. It is an unpleasant habit. She does it whenever I say or do anything that she dislikes. Yet I had kept strictly within the limits of truth. I have no doubt that if my income had justified it, I should have bought that horse. Indeed, as things turned out, I practically—but do not let me anticipate.

There is not very much to do at Winthorpe. We obtained permission from the proprietor to walk round the garden, but that took only three or four minutes. Then Eliza found out that there was a coconut shy in the village, and insisted on going to it. It was, perhaps, a little *infra dig.* (as they say), but I was in an easy temper after dinner, and let myself be persuaded ; also, there was nowhere else to go. Eliza won four coconuts, and seemed to enjoy it. I had rather the feeling of having left all that kind of thing behind me, myself, and said so.

Eliza and I decided almost unanimously for an early tea and a pleasant drive home to a quiet evening. The elderly gentleman joined us at tea and offered me brandy and soda-water at his expense.

" Thank you," I said, " but when I am going to handle the ribbons I like to keep my head as clear as possible."

He said that he thought I was right. He really made himself most useful and obliging when we were leaving. There was a good deal of confusion through so many vehicles being drawn up outside at the same time.

The return journey was a great surprise. I had expected that the horse going home would fly like the wind, and that I should have difficulty in holding him. It was not so at all. He seemed reluctant to start, and I could never get him beyond a very slow trot ; three or four times he seemed on the point of stopping altogether. Mr. Percy Jennings had told me that I should never want the whip, but I felt constrained to make a moderate use of it, and, really, it seemed to cause no improvement at all. The farther we went the worse the horse got, till it seemed to be less trouble to let him walk, which I did. About a mile from home Eliza pointed out to me that the horse was going very much down on one side, and very much up on the other.

" Ah ! " I said, " then he's gone lame. That accounts for everything. I shall have to blow Jennings up about this. Still, as it is a valuable animal, we perhaps had better get out and lead him the rest of the way. Personally, I shall be glad to stretch my legs."

Eliza, who is, perhaps, a little inclined to grumble at every trifle, said that anything was better than some kinds of driving, and joined me in the road. We walked slowly back, and had to put up with many silly, and even personal, remarks from those who met us. Some of them whistled the " Dead March," which was not only quite inappropriate, but, in my opinion, actually blasphemous. I suppose one must not expect the best taste from these Bank Holiday crowds. I made no reply. I could have said a good deal, but, being with a lady, I wished to avoid any fracas.

Eliza left me when we reached our house. She said that I

could take the horse and cart back to the yard while she went in and helped the girl to get supper.

Mr. Percy Jennings was standing in the yard when I led the horse in.

"What's all this ? " he said.

" That's what I want to know," I replied rather sharply. " This horse that you made so much fuss about was not fit for work. He's dead lame. No fault of ours. I can assure you we——"

" Oh, shut up ! " he said offensively. Then he called " Jim ! " and some kind of ostler person appeared.

He gave Jim some orders, and I heard enough to realize what had happened. Jim was to ride off at once to the Lion at Winthorpe and bring Tommy back if he was still in the stables there. If not, he was to find out where the horse had gone and follow him up, let the police know, and not come back without him. Neither of them took the least notice of me. I did put in a question once or twice, but they went on just as if I had never spoken at all. I am not the man to put up with disrespect. I was much annoyed. As soon as Jim had gone off, I said :

" And now, perhaps, you can give me a few minutes of your attention, Mr. Jennings. It seems through some mistake on the part of the stable people at the Lion I have brought back the wrong horse. Naturally, I disclaim all responsibility for their blunder."

" Oh, go away ! " said Mr. Jennings. " I'll talk to you when you're sober."

" I am perfectly sober, and I'll thank you not to venture to dare to——"

" Then, if you're sober—and I don't say you are, but *if* you are—you must be a bigger fool than ever I took you for. You drive out my best horse, worth a hundred and twenty to me, and you bring back this dying cripple, worth what the knacker will give for him to-morrow. I tell you if I don't get my own horse back you'll have to pay that fifty. I've got your name and address, and your employer's name and address ; and that won't half make it up to me. Worst day's work I've ever done, this is. Oh, don't stand gaping there ! Get out of the yard ! Get out of my sight ! "

I have not reported this speech exactly as it was spoken. Before every noun a certain adjective—always the same—was inserted. I have omitted that adjective.

" I am extremely sorry for the error," I said with dignity.

He said that he didn't want my (same adjective) sorrow.

" But in future," I continued, " all communications between us must be through our respective solicitors."

I rather wish now that I had not said that. The horse was never recovered, and my solicitor could only get the claim down to £34 (£10 cash, and the rest in weekly instalments). I feel that I could have done as much as that myself ; and as it was I had to pay the solicitor.

But at the time my blood was up, and I did not very much care what I said—as long as it showed him that I was not to be played with.

Mr. Jennings then made a remark about our respective solicitors which cannot be further particularized.

I, personally, simply swung round on my heel and walked right out of the yard.

.   .   .   .

I am willing to admit that I had some apprehensions as to the way in which Eliza would take this. In one way she took it far better than I expected.

Let me take an instance. A few days before, being in a playful mood, I sprang out at her from behind a door in order to make her jump. She did jump—and so far I suppose the thing was a success. But she also dropped and broke a vase —a pretty little thing, representing a boot, with maidenhair fern growing over it. She quite lost her temper, and said things which I trust and believe she regretted afterwards.

But now, when the loss was far more considerable, she was much quieter. It would be idle to say that she was cheerful about it, but she never once said it was all my fault. On the contrary, she said it was all her own fault—because she had known all along I had got the wrong horse, but she said nothing about it because she knew that she knew nothing about horses.

I thought she was wrong in saying that the man who stole our horse was the elderly man who had entered into conversation with me, and made himself so pleasant, and that he had done his utmost to bustle us and confuse us when we were leaving the hotel.

But I did not argue the point. I did not feel much like arguing about anything. One of my favourite hymns points out that the roseate hues of early dawn vanish far more quickly than a beginner might suppose. So it had been with my increasing income. What with the extra expenses that we had already incurred and this serious blow, we were now in much the same position that we had been the year before.

I paid the £10 in cash to Mr. Jennings at once. The solicitor thought it would be better. Fortunately, I had some money in hand at the time. And the balance, £8 15s., I borrowed from Eliza's mother. There is one drop of sugar in the darkest cloud—I found an opportunity to sell the flannel trousers at very little under cost.

"Q" (1863–   ), otherwise Sir Arthur Quiller-Couch, is one of the most distinguished Professors of English Literature. He has not only written some of the finest short stories of our time, in which humour and fantasy are delightfully blended; he is also the author of critical works on "The Art of Writing" and "The Art of Reading," which are valuable contributions to the appreciative side of literature

PIPES IN ARCADY

I HARDLY can bring myself to part with this story, it has been such a private joy to me. Moreover, that I have lain awake in the night to laugh over it is no guarantee of your being passably amused. Yourselves, I dare say, have known what it is to awake in irrepressible mirth from a dream which next morning proved to be flat and unconvincing. Well, this my pet story has some of the qualities of a dream; being absurd, for instance, and almost incredible, and even a trifle inhuman. After all, I had better change my mind, and tell you another——

But no; I will risk it, and you shall have it, just as it befel.

.   .   .   .

I had taken an afternoon's holiday to make a pilgrimage: my goal being a small parish church that lies remote from the railway, five good miles from the tiniest of country stations; my purpose to inspect—or say, rather, to contemplate—a Norman porch, for which it ought to be widely famous. (Here let me say that I have an unlearned passion for Norman architecture—to enjoy it merely, not to write about it.)

To carry me on my first stage I had taken a crawling local train that dodged its way somehow between the regular expresses and the "excursions" that invade our Delectable Duchy from June to October. The season was high midsummer, the afternoon hot and drowsy with scents of mown hay; and between the rattle of the fast trains it seemed that we, native denizens of the Duchy, careless of observation or applause, were executing a *tour de force* in that fine indolence which had been charged as a fault against us. That we halted at every station goes without saying. Few sidings—however inconsiderable or, as it might seem, fortuitous—escaped the flattery of our prolonged sojourn. We ambled, we paused, almost we dallied with the butterflies afloat over the meadow-sweet and cow-parsley beside the line ; we exchanged gossip with stationmasters, and received the congratulations of signal-men on the extraordinary spell of fine weather. It did not matter. Three market-women, a pedlar, and a local policeman made up with me the train's complement of passengers. I gathered that their business could wait ; and as for mine—well, a Norman porch is by this time accustomed to waiting.

I will not deny that in the end I dozed at intervals in my empty smoking compartment ; but wish to make it clear that I came on the vision (as I will call it) with eyes open, and that it left me staring, wide-awake as Macbeth.

Let me describe it. To the left of the line as you travel westward there lies a long grassy meadow on a gentle acclivity, set with three or four umbrageous oaks and backed by a steep plantation of oak saplings. At the foot of the meadow, close alongside the line, runs a brook, which is met at the meadow's end by a second brook which crosses under the permanent way through a culvert. The united waters continue the course of the first brook, beside the line, and maybe for half a mile farther ; but, a few yards below their junction, are dammed by the masonry of a bridge over which a country lane crosses the railway ; and this obstacle spreads them into a pool some fifteen or twenty feet wide, overgrown with the leaves of the arrow-head, and fringed with water-flags and the flowering rush.

Now I seldom pass this spot without sparing a glance for it ; first because of the pool's still beauty, and secondly because many rabbits infest the meadow below the coppice, and among them for two or three years was a black fellow whom I took an idle delight in recognising. (He is gone now, and his place knows him no more ; yet I continue to hope for sight of a black rabbit just there.) But this afternoon I looked out with special interest because, happening to pass down the line two days before, I had noted a gang of navvies at work on the culvert ; and among them, as they stood aside to let the train pass, I had recognised my friend Joby Tucker, their ganger, and an excellent fellow to boot.

Therefore my eyes were alert as we approached the curve that opens the meadow into view, and—as I am a Christian man, living in the twentieth century—I saw this vision : I beheld beneath the shade of the midmost oak eight men sitting stark naked, whereof one blew on a flute, one played a concertina, and the rest beat their palms together, marking the time ; while before them, in couples on the sward, my gang of navvies rotated in a clumsy waltz, watched by a ring of solemn ruminant kine !

I saw it. The whole scene, barring the concertina and the navvies' clothes, might have been transformed straight from a Greek vase of the best period. Here, in this green corner of rural England, on a workaday afternoon (a Wednesday, to be precise), in full sunlight, I saw this company of the early gods sitting, naked and unabashed, and piping, while twelve British navvies danced to their music. . . . I saw it ; and a derisive whistle from the engine told me that driver and stoker saw it too. I was not dreaming then. But what on earth could it mean ? For fifteen seconds or so I stared at the vision . . . and so the train joggled past it and rapt it from my eyes.

I can understand now the ancient stories of men who, having by hap surprised the goddesses bathing, never recovered from the shock but thereafter ran wild in the woods with their memories.

At the next station I alighted. It chanced to be the station for which I had taken my ticket ; but anyhow I should have alighted there. The spell of the vision was upon me. The Norman porch might wait. It is (as I have said) used to waiting, and in fact it has waited. I have not yet made another holiday to visit it. Whether or no the market-women and the local policeman had beheld, I know not. I hope not, but now shall never know. . . . The engine-driver, leaning in converse with the stationmaster, and jerking a thumb backward, had certainly beheld. But I passed him with averted eyes, gave up my ticket, and struck straight across country for the spot.

I came to it, as my watch told me, at twenty minutes after five. The afternoon sunlight still lay broad on the meadow. The place was unchanged save for a lengthening of its oak-tree shadows. But the persons of my vision—naked gods and navvies—had vanished. Only the cattle stood, knee-deep in the pool, lazily swishing their tails in protest against the flies ; and the cattle could tell me nothing.

.   .   .   .

Just a fortnight later, as I spent at St. Blazey junction the forty odd minutes of repentance ever thoughtfully pro-

vided by our railway company for those who, living in Troy,
are foolish enough to travel, I spied at some distance below
the station a gang of men engaged in unloading rubble to
construct a new siding for the clay-traffic, and at their head
my friend Mr. Joby Tucker. The railway company was
consuming so much of my time that I felt no qualms in returning some part of the compliment, and strolled down the line
to wish Mr. Tucker good-day. "And, by the bye," I added,
" you owe me an explanation. What on earth were you doing
in Treba meadow two Wednesdays ago—you and your naked
friends ? "

Joby leaned on his measuring rod and grinned from ear
to ear.

" You see'd us ? " he asked, and, letting his eyes travel
along the line, he chuckled to himself softly and at length.
" Well, now, I'm glad o' that. 'Fact is, I've been savin' up
to tell 'ee about it, but (thinks I) when I tells Mr. Q. he won't
never believe."

" I certainly saw you," I answered ; " but as for believing——"

" Iss, iss," he interrupted, with fresh chucklings ; " a fair
knock-out, wasn' it ? . . . You see, they was blind—poor
fellas ! "

" Drunk ? "

" No, sir—blind—' pity the pore blind ' ; three-parts blind,
anyways, an' undergoin' treatment for it."

" Nice sort of treatment ! "

" Eh ? You don't understand. See'd us from the train,
did 'ee ? Which train ? "

" The 1.35 ex Millbay."

" Wish I'd a-knowed you was watching us. I'd ha'
waved my hat as you went by, or maybe blawed 'ee a kiss—
that bein' properer to the occasion, come to think."

Joby paused, drew the back of a hand across his laughter-
moistened eyes, and pulled himself together, steadying his
voice for the story.

.   .   .   .

" I'll tell 'ee what happened, from the beginnin'. A gang
of us had been sent down, two days before, to Treba meadow,
to repair the culvert there. Soon as we started to work we
found the whole masonry fairly rotten, and spent the first
afternoon (that was Monday) underpinnin', while I traced out
the extent o' the damage. The farther I went, the worse I

found it ; the main mischief bein' a leak about midway in the culvert, on the down side ; whereby the water, perc'latin' through, was unpackin' the soil, not only behind the masonry of the culvert, but right away down for twenty yards and more behind the stone-facing where the line runs alongside the pool. All this we were forced to take down, shorein' as we went, till we cut back pretty close to the rails. The job, you see, had turned out more serious than reported ; and havin' no one to consult, I kept the men at it.

" By Wednesday noon we had cut back so far as we needed, shorein' very careful as we went, and the men workin' away cheerful, with the footboards of the expresses whizzin' by close over their heads, so's it felt like havin' your hair brushed by machinery. By the time we knocked off for dinner I felt pretty easy in mind, knowin' we'd broke the back o' the job.

" Well, we touched pipe and started again. Bein' so close to the line I'd posted a fella with a flag—Bill Martin it was— to keep a look-out for the down-trains ; an' about three o'clock or a little after he whistled one comin'. I happened to be in the culvert at the time, but stepped out an' back across the brook, just to fling an eye along the embankment to see that all was clear. Clear it was, an' therefore it surprised me a bit, as the train hove in sight around the curve, to see that she had her brakes on, hard, and was slowin' down to stop. My first thought was that Bill Martin must have taken some scare an' showed her the red flag. But that was a mistake ; besides she must have started the brakes before openin' sight on Bill."

" Then why on earth was she pulling up ? " I asked. " It couldn't be signals."

" There ain't no signal within a mile of Treba meadow, up or down. She was stoppin' because—but just you let me tell it in my own way. Along she came, draggin' hard on her brakes an' whistlin'. I knew her for an excursion, and as she passed I sized it up for a big school-treat. There was five coaches, mostly packed with children, an' on one o' the coaches was a board—' Exeter to Penzance.' The four front coaches had corridors, the tail one just ord'nary compartments.

" Well, she dragged past us to dead-slow, an' came to a standstill with her tail coach about thirty yards beyond where I stood, and, as you might say, with its footboard right over-hangin' the pool. You mayn't remember it, but the line just there curves pretty sharp to the right, and when she pulled up, the tail coach pretty well hid the rest o' the train from us.

Five or six men, hearin' the brakes, had followed me out of
the culvert and stood by me, wonderin' why the stoppage was.
The rest were dotted about along the slope of th' embankment.
And then the curiousest thing happened—about the curiousest
thing I seen in all my years on the line. A door of the tail
coach opened and a man stepped out. He didn' jump out,
you understand, nor fling hisself out ; he just stepped out
into air, and with that his arms and legs cast themselves anyways an' he went down sprawlin' into the pool. It's easy to
say we ought t' have run then an' there an' rescued 'im ; but
for the moment it stuck us up starin' an'—Wait a bit. You
ha'n't heard the end.

" I hadn't fairly caught my breath, before another man
stepped out ! He put his foot down upon nothing, same as
the first, overbalanced just the same, and shot after him base-
over-top into the water.

" Close 'pon the second man's heels appeared a third. . . .
Yes, sir, I know now what a woman feels like when she's goin'
to have the scritches.[1] I'd have asked someone to pinch me
in the fleshy part o' the leg, to make sure I was alive an' awake,
but the power o' speech was taken from us. We just stuck
an' stared.

" What beat everything was the behaviour of the train, so
to say. There it stood, like as if it'd pulled up alongside the
pool for the very purpose to unload these unfortnit' men ;
an' yet takin' no notice whatever. Not a sign o' the guard—
not a head poked out anywheres in the line o' windows—only the
sun shinin', an' the steam escapin', an' out o' the rear compartment this procession droppin' out an' high-divin' one after
another.

" Eight of 'em ! Eight, as I am a truth-speakin' man—
but there ! you saw 'em with your own eyes. Eight, and the
last of the eight scarce in the water afore the engine toots her
whistle an' the train starts on again, round the curve an' out
o' sight.

" She didn' leave us no time to doubt, neither, for there
the poor fellas were, splashin' an' blowin', some of 'em bleatin'
for help, an' gurglin', an' for aught we know drownin' in three
to four feet o' water. So we pulled ourselves together an'
ran to give 'em first-aid.

" It didn' take us long to haul the whole lot out and ashore ;
and, as Providence would have it, not a bone broken in the

[1] Hysterics.

party. One or two were sufferin' from sprains, and all of 'em
from shock (but so were we, for that matter), and between 'em
they must ha' swallowed a bra' few pints o' water, an' muddy
water at that.   I can't tell ezackly when or how we discovered
they was all blind, or near-upon blind.   It may ha' been from
the unhandiness of their movements an' the way they clutched
at us an' at one another as we pulled 'em ashore.   Hows'ever,
blind they were ; an' I don't remember that it struck us as
anyways singular, after what we'd been through a'ready.   We
fished out a concertina, too, an' a silver-mounted flute that
was bobbin' among the weeds.

   " The man the concertina belonged to—a tall fresh-com-
plexioned young fella he was, an' very mild of manner—
turned out to be a sort o' leader o' the party ; an' he was the
first to talk any sense.   ' Th-thank you,' he said.   ' They told
us Penzance was the next stop.'

   " ' Hey ? ' says I.

   " ' They told us,' he says again, plaintive-like, feelin' for
his spectacles an' not finding 'em, ' that Penzance was the next
stop.'

   " ' Bound for Penzance, was you ? ' I asks.

   " ' For the Land's End,' says he, his teeth chatterin'.   I
set it down the man had a stammer, but 'twas only the shock
an' the chill of his duckin'.

   " ' Well,' says I, ' this ain't the Land's End, though I
dessay it feels like it.   Then you wasn' thrown out ? ' I says.

   " ' Th-thrown out ? ' say he.   ' N-no.   They told us
Penzance was the next stop.'

   " ' Then,' says I, ' if you got out accidental you've had
a most providential escape, an' me an' my mates don't deserve
less than to hear about it.   There's bound to be inquiries
after you when the guard finds your compartment empty an'
the door open.   May be the train'll put back ; more likely
they'll send a search party ; but anyways you're all wet through,
an' the best thing for health is to off wi' your clothes an' dry
'em this warm afternoon.'

   " ' I dessay,' says he, ' you'll have noticed that our eyesight
is affected.'

   " ' All the better if you're anyways modest,' says I.   ' You
couldn' find a retirededer place than this—not if you searched :
an' we don't mind.'

   " Well, sir, the end was we stripped 'em naked as Adam,
an' spread their clothes to dry 'pon the grass.   While we

tended on 'em the mild young man told us how it had happened. It seems they'd come by excursion from Exeter. There's a blind home at Exeter, an' likewise a cathedral choir, an' Sunday school, an' a boys' brigade, with other sundries ; an' this year the good people financin' half-a-dozen o' these shows had discovered that by clubbin' two sixpences together a shillin' could be made to go as far as eighteenpence ; and how, doin' it on the co-op' instead of an afternoon treat for each, they could manage a two days' outin' for all—Exeter to Penzance an' the Land's End, sleepin' one night at Penzance, an' back to Exeter at some ungodly hour the next. It's no use your askin' me why a man three-parts blind should want to visit the Land's End. There's an attraction about that place, an' that's all you can say. Everybody knows as 'tisn' worth seein', an' yet everybody wants to see it—so why not a blind man ?

" Well, this Happy Holiday Committee (as they called themselves) got the Company to fix them up with a special excursion ; an' our blind friends—bein' sensitive, or maybe a touch above mixin' wi' the school children an' infants—had packed themselves into this rear compartment separate from the others. One of 'em had brought his concertina, an' another his flute, and what with these an' other ways of passin' the time they got along pretty comfortable till they came to Gwinear Road : an' there for some reason they were held up an' had to show their tickets. Anyways, the staff at Gwinear Road went along the train collectin' the halves o' their return tickets. ' What's the name o' this station ? ' asks my blind friend, very mild an' polite. ' Gwinear Road,' answers the porter ; ' Penzance next stop.' Somehow this gave him the notion that they were nearly arrived, an' so, you see, when the train slowed down a few minutes later an' came to a stop, he took the porter at his word, an' stepped out. Simple, wasn't it ? But in my experience the curiousest things in life are the simplest of all, once you come to inquire into 'em."

" What I don't understand," said I, " is how the train came to stop just there."

Mr. Tucker gazed at me rather in sorrow than in anger. " I thought," said he, " 'twas agreed I should tell the story in my own way. Well, as I was sayin', we got those poor fellas there, all as naked as Adam, an' we was helpin' them all we could—some of us wringin' out their under linen an' spreading it to dry, others collectin' their hats, an' tryin' which fitted which, an' others even dredgin' the pool for their hand-

bags an' spectacles an' other small articles, an' in the middle of
it someone started to laugh. You'll scarce believe it, but up
to that moment there hadn't been so much as a smile to hand
round ; an' to this day I don't know the man's name that
started it—for all I can tell you, I did it myself. But this I do
know that it yoicked the whole gang up like a motor-engine.
There was a sort of ' click,' an' the next moment——

"Laugh ? I never heard men laugh like it in my born
days. Sort of recoil, I s'pose it must ha' been, after the shock.
Laugh ? There was men staggerin' drunk with it and there
was men rollin' on the turf with it ; an' there was men cryin'
with it, holdin' on to a stitch in their sides an' beseechin' everyone also to hold hard. The blind men took a bit longer to get
going ; but by gosh, sir ! once started they laughed to do
your heart good. O Lord, O Lord ! I wish you could ha'
seen that mild-mannered spokesman. Somebody had fished
out his spectacles for 'en, and that was all the clothing he stood
in—that, an' a grin. He fairly beamed ; an' the more he
beamed the more we rocked, callin' on 'en to take pity an'
stop it.

"Soon as I could catch a bit o' breath, ' Land's End next
stop ! ' gasped I. ' O, but this is the Land's End ! This is
what the Land's End oughter been all the time, an' never was
yet. O, for the Lord's sake,' says I, ' stop beamin', and pick
up your concertina an' pitch us a tune ! '

"Well, he did too. He played us ' Home, sweet home '
first of all—'mid pleasure an' palaces—an' the rest o' the young
men sat around 'en an' started clappin' their hands to the tune ;
an' then some fool slipped an arm round my waist. I'm only
thankful he didn't kiss me. Didn't think of it, perhaps ;
couldn't ha' been that he wasn't capable. It must ha' been
just then your train came along. An' about twenty minutes
later, when we was gettin' our friends back into their outfits,
we heard the search-engine about half a mile below, whistlin'
an' feelin' its way up very cautious towards us.

"They was sun-dried an' jolly as sandhoppers—all their
eight of 'em—as we helped 'em on board an' wished 'em ta-ta !
The search party couldn' understand at all what had happened
—in so short a time, too—to make us so cordial ; an' somehow
we didn' explain—neither we nor the blind men. I reckon
the whole business had been so loonatic we felt it kind of holy.
But the poor fellas kept wavin' back to us as they went out o'
sight around the curve, an' maybe for a mile beyond. I never

heard," Mr. Tucker wound up meditatively, " if they ever reached the Land's End . . . I wonder ? "

" But, excuse me once more," said I. " How came the train to stop as it did ? "

" To be sure. I said just now that the curiousest things in life were, gen'rally speakin', the simplest. One o' the schoolchildren in the fore part of the train—a small nipper of nine—had put his head out o' the carriage window and got his cap blown away. That's all. Bein' a nipper of some resource, he wasted no time, but touched off the communicatin' button an' fetched the whole train to a standstill. George Simmons, the guard, told me all about it last week, when I happened across him an' asked the same question you've been askin'. George was huntin' through the corridors to find out what had gone wrong ; that's how the blind men stepped out without his noticin'. He pretended to be pretty angry wi' the young tacker. ' Do 'ee know,' says George, ' it's a five pound fine if you stop a train without good reason ? ' ' But I *had* a good reason,' says the child. ' My mother gave 'levenpence for that cap, an' it's a bran' new one.' "

MARK TWAIN (1835–1910), *the pen-name of Samuel Langhorne Clemens, is a call used by Mississippi pilots when sounding, and was adopted by this great American humorist in memory of his boyhood's ambition to become a pilot. Clemens' fame rests now on his stories of Tom Sawyer and Huckleberry Finn and the satirical books "A Yankee at the Court of King Arthur" and "The Innocents Abroad."*

THE CELEBRATED JUMPING FROG OF CALAVERAS COUNTY

IN compliance with the request of a friend of mine, who wrote me from the East, I called on good-natured, garrulous old Simon Wheeler, and inquired after my friend's friend, *Leonidas W.* Smiley, as requested to do, and I hereunto append the result. I have a lurking suspicion that *Leonidas W.* Smiley is a myth; that my friend never knew such a personage; and that he only conjectured that, if I asked old Wheeler about him, it would remind him of his infamous *Jim* Smiley, and he would go to work and bore me nearly to death with some infernal reminiscence of him as long and tedious as it should be useless for me. If that was the design, it certainly succeeded.

I found Simon Wheeler dozing comfortably by the bar-room stove of the old, dilapidated tavern in the ancient mining camp of Angel's, and I noticed that he was fat and bald-headed, and had an expression of winning gentleness and simplicity upon his tranquil countenance. He roused up and gave me good-day. I told him a friend of mine had commissioned me to make some inquiries about a cherished companion of his boyhood named *Leonidas W.* Smiley—*Rev. Leonidas W.* Smiley—a young minister of the Gospel, who he had heard was at one time a resident of Angel's Camp. I added that, if Mr. Wheeler could tell me anything about this Rev. Leonidas W. Smiley, I would feel under many obligations to him.

Simon Wheeler backed me into a corner and blockaded me there with his chair, and then sat me down and reeled off the monotonous narrative which follows this paragraph. He never smiled, he never frowned, he never changed his voice from the gentle-flowing key to which he tuned the initial sentence, he never betrayed the slightest suspicion of enthusiasm ; but all through the interminable narrative there ran a vein of impressive earnestness and sincerity, which showed me plainly that, so far from his imagining that there was anything ridiculous or funny about his story, he regarded it as a really important matter, and admired its two heroes as men of transcendent genius in *finesse*. To me the spectacle of a man drifting serenely along through such a queer yarn without ever smiling was exquisitely absurd. As I said before, I asked him to tell me what he knew of Rev. Leonidas W. Smiley, and he replied as follows. I let him go on in his own way, and never interrupted him once :

There was a feller here once by the name of *Jim* Smiley, in the winter of '49—or may be it was the spring of '50—I don't recollect exactly, somehow, though what makes me think it was one or the other is because I remember the big flume wasn't finished when he first came to the camp ; but any way he was the curiosest man about, always betting on anything that turned up you ever see, if he could get anybody to bet on the other side ; and if he couldn't, he'd change sides. Any way that suited the other man would suit him—any way just so's he got a bet, *he* was satisfied. But still he was lucky, uncommon lucky ; he most always come out winner. He was always ready and laying for a chance ; there couldn't be no solitry thing mentioned but that feller'd offer to bet on it, and take any side you please, as I was just telling you. If there was a horse-race, you'd find him flush, or you'd find him busted at the end of it ; if there was a dog-fight, he'd bet on it ; if there was a cat-fight, he'd bet on it ; if there was a chicken-fight, he'd bet on it ; why, if there was two birds sitting on a fence, he would bet you which one would fly first ; or if there was a camp-meeting, he would be there reg'lar, to bet on Parson Walker, which he judged to be the best exhorter about here, and so he was, too, and a good man. If he even seen a straddle-bug start to go anywheres, he would bet you how long it would take him to get wherever he was going to, and if you took him up, he would foller that straddle-bug to Mexico but what he would find out where he was bound for and how long he was on the road. Lots of the boys here has seen that Smiley, and can tell you about him. Why, it never made no difference to *him*—he would bet on *any* thing—the dangdest feller. Parson Walker's wife laid very sick once, for a good while, and it seemed as if they warn't going to save her ;

but one morning he come in, and Smiley asked how she was, and he said she was considerable better—thank the Lord for His inf'nit mercy—and coming on so smart that, with the blessing of Prov'dence, she'd get well yet ; and Smiley, before he thought, says, " Well, I'll risk two-and-a-half that she don't, anyway."

This-yer Smiley had a mare—the boys called her the fifteen-minute nag, but that was only in fun, you know, because, of course, she was faster than that—and he used to win money on that horse, for all she was so slow and always had the asthma, or the distemper, or the consumption, or something of that kind. They used to give her two or three hundred yards' start, and then pass her under way ; but always at the fag-end of the race she'd get excited and desperate-like, and come cavorting and straddling up, and scattering her legs around limber, sometimes in the air, and sometimes out to one side amongst the fences, and kicking up m-o-r-e dust, and raising m-o-r-e racket with her coughing and sneezing and blowing her nose—and always fetch up at the stand just about a neck ahead, as near as you could cipher it down.

And he had a little small bull pup, that to look at him you'd think he wan't worth a cent, but to set around and look ornery, and lay for a chance to steal something. But as soon as the money was up on him, he was a different dog ; his under-jaw'd begin to stick out like the fo'castle of a steamboat, and his teeth would uncover, and shine savage like the furnaces. And a dog might tackle him, and bully-rag him, and bite him, and throw him over his shoulder two or three times, and Andrew Jackson—which was the name of the pup—Andrew Jackson would never let on but what *he* was satisfied, and hadn't expected nothing else—and the bets being doubled and doubled on the other side all the time, till the money was all up ; and then all of a sudden he would grab that other dog jest by the j'int of his hind leg and freeze to it—not chaw, you understand, but only jest grip and hang on till they throwed up the sponge, if it was a year. Smiley always come out winner on that pup, till he harnessed a dog once that didn't have no hind legs, because they'd been sawed off by a circular saw, and when the thing had gone along far enough, and the money was all up, and he come to make a snatch for his pet holt, he saw in a minute how he'd been imposed on, and how the other dog had him in the door, so to speak, and he 'peared surprised, and then he looked sorter discouraged-like, and didn't try no more to win the fight, and so he got shucked out bad. He give Smiley a look, as much as to say his heart was broke, and it was *his* fault, for putting up a dog that hadn't no hind legs for him to take holt of, which was his main dependence in a fight, and then he limped off a piece and laid down and died. It was a good pup, was that Andrew Jackson, and would have made a name for hisself if he'd lived, for the stuff was in him, and he had genius—I know it, because he hadn't had no opportunities to speak of, and it don't stand to reason that a dog could make such a fight as he could under them circumstances, if he hadn't no talent. It always makes me feel sorry when I think of that last fight of his'n, and the way it turned out.

Well, this-yer Smiley had rat-tarriers, and chicken cocks, and tomcats, and all them kind of things, till you couldn't rest, and you couldn't fetch nothing for him to bet on but he'd match you. He ketched a frog one day, and took him home, and said he cal'klated to edercate him ; and so he never done nothing for three months but set in his back yard and learn that frog to jump. And you bet you he *did* learn him, too. He'd give him a little punch behind, and the next minute you'd see that frog whirling in the air like a doughnut—see him turn one somerset, or may be a couple, if he got a good start, and come down flat-footed and all right, like a cat. He got him up so in the matter of catching flies, and kept him in practice so constant, that he'd nail a fly every time as far as he could see him. Smiley said all a frog wanted was education, and he could do most anything—and I believe him. Why, I've seen him set Dan'l Webster down here on this floor— Dan'l Webster was the name of the frog—and sing out, " Flies, Dan'l, flies ! " and quicker'n you could wink, he's spring straight up, and snake a fly off'n the counter there, and flop down on the floor again as solid as a gob of mud, and fall to scratching the side of his head with his hind foot as indifferent as if he hadn't no idea he'd been doin' any more'n any frog might do. You never see a frog so modest and straight for'ard as he was, for all he was so gifted. And when it come to fair and square jumping on a dead level, he could get over more ground at one straddle than any animal of his breed you ever see. Jumping on a dead level was his strong suit, you understand ; and when it come to that, Smiley would ante up money on him as long as he had a red. Smiley was monstrous proud of his frog, and well he might be, for fellers that had

travelled and been everywheres, all said he laid over any frog
that ever *they* see.

Well, Smiley kept the beast in a little lattice box, and he
used to fetch him down town sometimes and lay for a bet.
One day a feller—a stranger in the camp, he was—come across
him with his box, and says:

" What might it be that you've got in the box ? "

And Smiley says, sorter indifferent like, " It might be a
parrot, or it might be a canary, may be, but it ain't—it's only
just a frog."

And the feller took it, and looked at it careful, and turned it
round this way and that, and says, " H'm, so 'tis. Well, what's
he good for ? "

" Well," Smiley says, easy and careless, " he's good enough
for *one* thing, I should judge—he can out-jump ary frog in
Calaveras county."

The feller took the box again, and took another long, particular look, and gave it back to Smiley, and says, very deliberate,
" Well, I don't see no p'ints about that frog that's any better'n
any other frog."

" May be you don't," Smiley says. " May be you understand frogs, and may be you don't understand 'em ; may be
you've had experience, and may be you ain't, only a amature,
as it were. Any ways, I've got *my* opinion, and I'll risk forty
dollars that he can out-jump any frog in Calaveras county."

And the feller studied a minute, and then says, kinder sad
like, " Well, I'm only a stranger here, and I ain't got no frog ;
but if I had a frog, I'd bet you."

And then Smiley says, " That's all right—that's all right—
if you'll hold my box a minute, I'll go and get you a frog."
And so the feller took the box, and put up his forty dollars
along with Smiley's and set down to wait.

So he set there a good while thinking and thinking to
hisself, and then he got the frog out and prized his mouth
open and took a teaspoon and filled him full of quail shot—
filled him pretty near up to his chin—and set him on the
floor. Smiley he went to the swamp and slopped around in
the mud for a long time, and finally he ketched a frog, and
fetched him in, and give him to this feller, and says :

" Now, if you're ready, set him alongside of Dan'l, with
his forepaws just even with Dan'l, and I'll give the word."
Then he says, " One—two—three—jump ! " and him and
the feller touched up the frogs from behind, and the new frog

hopped off, but Dan'l give a heave, and hysted up his shoulders—so—like a Frenchman, but it wan't no use—he couldn't budge ; he was planted as solid as an anvil, and he couldn't no more stir than if he was anchored out. Smiley was a good deal surprised, and he was disgusted too, but he didn't have no idea what the matter was, of course.

The feller took the money and started away ; and when he was going out at the door, he sorter jerked his thumb over his shoulders—this way—at Dan'l, and says again, very deliberate, " Well, I don't see no p'ints about that frog that's any better'n any other frog."

Smiley he stood scratching his head and looking down at Dan'l a long time, and at last he says, " I do wonder what in the nation that frog throw'd off for—I wonder if there ain't something the matter with him—he 'pears to look mightly baggy, somehow." And he ketched Dan'l by the nap of the neck, and lifted him up and says, " Why, blame my cats, if he don't weigh five pound ! " and turned him upside down, and he belched out a double handful of shot. And then he see how it was, and he was the maddest man—he set the frog down and took out after that feller, but he never ketched him. And——

(Here Simon Wheeler heard his name called from the front yard, and got up to see what was wanted.) And turning to me as he moved away, he said : " Just set where you are, stranger, and rest easy—I an't going to be gone a second."

But, by your leave, I did not think that a continuation of the history of the enterprising vagabond *Jim* Smiley would be likely to afford me much information concerning the Rev. *Leonidas W.* Smiley, and so I started away.

At the door I met the sociable Wheeler returning, and he buttonholed me and recommenced :

" Well, this-yer Smiley had a yaller one-eyed cow that didn't have no tail, only just a short stump like a bannanner, and——"

" Oh, hang Smiley and his afflicted cow ! " I muttered good-naturedly, and bidding the old gentleman good-day, I departed.

HERBERT GEORGE WELLS (1866–
). *His scientific outlook and his profound
study of mankind and world economics have
made him one of the most important writers on
social problems of the day. The astonishing
versatility of his genius is also expressed in his
scientific fantasies and his stories of everyday
life. In this extravaganza the pungent social
satirist becomes the benevolent humorist.*

THE MAN WHO COULD
WORK MIRACLES

A PANTOUM IN PROSE

IT is doubtful whether the gift was innate. For my own
part, I think it came to him suddenly. Indeed, until he
was thirty he was a sceptic, and did not believe in miraculous
powers. And here, since it is the most convenient place, I
must mention that he was a little man, and had eyes of a hot
brown, very erect red hair, a moustache with ends that he
twisted up, and freckles. His name was George McWhirter
Fotheringay—not the sort of name by any means to lead to
any expectation of miracles—and he was clerk at Gomshott's.
He was greatly addicted to assertive argument. It was while
he was asserting the impossibility of miracles that he had his
first intimation of his extraordinary powers. This particular
argument was being held in the bar of the Long Dragon, and
Toddy Beamish was conducting the opposition by a monotonous but effective " So *you* say," that drove Mr. Fotheringay
to the very limit of his patience.

There were present, besides these two, a very dusty cyclist,
landlord Cox, and Miss Maybridge, the perfectly respectable
and rather portly barmaid of the Dragon. Miss Maybridge
was standing with her back to Mr. Fotheringay, washing
glasses ; the others were watching him, more or less amused
by the present ineffectiveness of the assertive method. Goaded
by the Torres Vedras tactics of Mr. Beamish, Mr. Fotheringay
determined to make an unusual rhetorical effort. " Looky
here, Mr. Beamish," said Mr. Fotheringay. " Let us
clearly understand what a miracle is. It's something contrariwise to the course of Nature done by power of Will,

something what couldn't happen without being specially willed."

" So *you* say," said Mr. Beamish, repulsing him.

Mr. Fotheringay appealed to the cyclist, who had hitherto been a silent auditor, and received his assent—given with a hesitating cough and a glance at Mr. Beamish. The landlord would express no opinion, and Mr. Fotheringay, returning to Mr. Beamish, received the unexpected concession of a qualified assent to his definition of a miracle.

" For instance," said Mr. Fotheringay, greatly encouraged, " here would be a miracle. That lamp, in the natural course of Nature, couldn't burn like that upsy-down, could it, Beamish ? "

" *You* say it couldn't," said Beamish.

" And you ? " said Fotheringay. " You don't mean to say —eh ? "

" No," said Beamish reluctantly. " No, it couldn't."

" Very well," said Mr. Fotheringay. " Then here comes some one, as it might be me, along here, and stands as it might be here, and says to that lamp, as I might do, collecting all my will—' Turn upsy-down without breaking, and go on burning steady,' and—— Hullo ! "

It was enough to make any one say " Hullo ! " The impossible, the incredible, was visible to them all. The lamp hung inverted in the air, burning quietly with its flame pointing down. It was as solid, as indisputable as ever a lamp was, the prosaic common lamp of the Long Dragon bar.

Mr. Fotheringay stood with an extended forefinger and the knitted brows of one anticipating a catastrophic smash. The cyclist, who was sitting next the lamp, ducked and jumped across the bar. Everybody jumped, more or less. Miss Maybridge turned and screamed. For nearly three seconds the lamp remained still. A faint cry of mental distress came from Mr. Fotheringay. " I can't keep it up," he said, " any longer." He staggered back, and the inverted lamp suddenly flared, fell against the corner of the bar, bounced aside, smashed upon the floor, and went out.

It was lucky it had a metal receiver, or the whole place would have been in a blaze. Mr. Cox was the first to speak, and his remark, shorn of needless excrescences, was to the effect that Fotheringay was a fool. Fotheringay was beyond disputing even so fundamental a proposition as that ! He was astonished beyond measure at the thing that had occurred. The subsequent conversation threw absolutely no light on the matter so far as Fotheringay was concerned; the general opinion not only followed Mr. Cox very closely but very vehemently. Every one accused Fotheringay of a silly trick, and presented him to himself as a foolish destroyer of comfort and security. His mind was in a tornado of perplexity, he was himself inclined to agree with them, and he made a remarkably ineffectual opposition to the proposal of his departure.

He went home flushed and heated, coat-collar crumpled, eyes smarting and ears red. He watched each of the ten street lamps nervously as he passed it. It was only when he found himself alone in his little bedroom in Church Row that he was able to grapple seriously with his memories of the occurrence, and ask, " What on earth happened ? "

He had removed his coat and boots, and was sitting on the bed with his hands in his pockets repeating the text of his defence for the seventeenth time, " *I* didn't want the confounded thing to upset," when it occurred to him that at the precise moment he had said the commanding words he had inadvertently willed the thing he said, and that when he had seen the lamp in the air he had felt that it depended on him to maintain it there without being clear how this was to be done. He had not a particularly complex mind, or he might have stuck for a time at that " inadvertently willed," embracing, as it does, the abstrusest problems of voluntary action ; but as it was, the idea came to him with a quite acceptable haziness. And from that, following, as I must admit, no clear logical path, he came to the test of experiment.

He pointed resolutely to his candle and collected his mind, though he felt he did a foolish thing. " Be raised up," he said. But in a second that feeling vanished. The candle was raised, hung in the air one giddy moment, and as Mr. Fotheringay gasped, fell with a smash on his toilet-table, leaving him in darkness save for the expiring glow of its wick.

For a time Mr. Fotheringay sat in the darkness, perfectly still. " It did happen, after all," he said. " And 'ow I'm to explain it I *don't* know." He sighed heavily, and began feeling in his pockets for a match. He could find none, and he rose and groped about the toilet-table. " I wish I had a match," he said. He resorted to his coat, and there were none there, and then it dawned upon him that miracles were possible even with matches. He extended a hand and scowled at it in the dark. " Let there be a match in that hand," he said. He felt

*The impossible, the incredible, was visible to them all.   The lamp hung
inverted in the air, burning quietly with its flame pointing down.*

some light object fall across his palm, and his fingers closed upon a match.

After several ineffectual attempts to light this, he discovered it was a safety-match. He threw it down, and then it occurred to him that he might have willed it lit. He did, and perceived it burning in the midst of his toilet-table mat. He caught it up hastily, and it went out. His perception of possibilities enlarged, and he felt for and replaced the candle in its candle-stick. " Here ! *you* be lit," said Mr. Fotheringay, and forthwith the candle was flaring, and he saw a little black hole in the toilet-cover, with a wisp of smoke rising from it. For a time he stared from this to the little flame and back, and then looked up and met his own gaze in the looking-glass. By this help he communed with himself in silence for a time.

" How about miracles now ? " said Mr. Fotheringay at last, addressing his reflection.

The subsequent meditations of Mr. Fotheringay were of a severe but confused description. So far as he could see, it was a case of pure willing with him. The nature of his first experiences disinclined him for any further experiments except of the most cautious type. But he lifted a sheet of paper, and turned a glass of water pink and then green, and he created a snail, which he miraculously annihilated, and got himself a miraculous new tooth-brush. Somewhen in the small hours he had reached the fact that his will-power must be of a particularly rare and pungent quality, a fact of which he had certainly had inklings before, but no certain assurance. The scare and perplexity of his first discovery was now qualified by pride in this evidence of singularity and by vague intimations of advantage. He became aware that the church clock was striking one, and as it did not occur to him that his daily duties at Gomshott's might be miraculously dispensed with, he resumed undressing, in order to get to bed without further delay. As he struggled to get his shirt over his head, he was struck with a brilliant idea. " Let me be in bed," he said, and found himself so. " Undressed," he stipulated ; and, finding the sheets cold, added hastily, " and in my nightshirt—no, in a nice soft woollen nightshirt. Ah ! " he said with immense enjoyment. " And now let me be comfortably asleep. . . ."

He awoke at his usual hour and was pensive all through breakfast-time, wondering whether his overnight experience might not be a particularly vivid dream. At length his mind turned again to cautious experiments. For instance, he had three eggs for breakfast ; two his landlady had supplied, good, but shoppy, and one was a delicious fresh goose-egg, laid, cooked, and served by his extraordinary will. He hurried off to Gomshott's in a state of profound but carefully concealed excitement, and only remembered the shell of the third egg when his landlady spoke of it that night. All day he could do no work because of this astonishingly new self-knowledge, but this caused him no inconvenience, because he made up for it miraculously in his last ten minutes.

As the day wore on his state of mind passed from wonder to elation, albeit the circumstances of his dismissal from the Long Dragon were still disagreeable to recall, and a garbled account of the matter that had reached his colleagues led to some badinage. It was evident he must be careful how he lifted frangible articles, but in other ways his gift promised more and more as he turned it over in his mind. He intended among other things to increase his personal property by unostentatious acts of creation. He called into existence a pair of very splendid diamond studs, and hastily annihilated them again as young Gomshott came across the counting-house to his desk. He was afraid young Gomshott might wonder how he had come by them. He saw quite clearly the gift required caution and watchfulness in its exercise, but so far as he could judge the difficulties attending its mastery would be no greater than those he had already faced in the study of cycling. It was that analogy, perhaps, quite as much as the feeling that he would be unwelcome in the Long Dragon, that drove him out after supper into the lane beyond the gas-works, to rehearse a few miracles in private.

There was possibly a certain want of originality in his attempts, for apart from his will-power Mr. Fotheringay was not a very exceptional man. The miracle of Moses' rod came to his mind, but the night was dark and unfavourable to the proper control of large miraculous snakes. Then he recollected the story of " Tannhäuser " that he had read on the back of the Philharmonic programme. That seemed to him singularly attractive and harmless. He stuck his walking-stick—a very nice Poona-Penang lawyer—into the turf that edged the foot-path, and commanded the dry wood to blossom. The air was immediately full of the scent of roses, and by means of a match he saw for himself that this beautiful miracle was indeed accomplished. His satisfaction was ended by advancing footsteps. Afraid of a premature discovery of his powers, he addressed the blossoming stick hastily : " Go back." What he meant was " Change back " ; but of course he was confused. The stick receded at a considerable velocity, and incontinently came a cry of anger and a bad word from the approaching person. " Who are you throwing brambles at, you fool ? " cried a voice. " That got me on the shin."

" I'm sorry, old chap," said Mr. Fotheringay, and then realising the awkward nature of the explanation, caught nervously at his moustache. He saw Winch, one of the three Immering constables, advancing.

" What d'yer mean by it ? " asked the constable. " Hullo ! It's you, is it ? The gent that broke the lamp at the Long Dragon ! "

" I don't mean anything by it," said Mr. Fotheringay. " Nothing at all."

" What d'yer do it for then ? "

" Oh, bother ! " said Mr. Fotheringay.

" Bother indeed ! D'yer know that stick hurt ? What d'yer do it for, eh ? "

For the moment Mr. Fotheringay could not think what he had done it for. His silence seemed to irritate Mr. Winch. " You've been assaulting the police, young man, this time. That's what *you* done."

" Look here, Mr. Winch," said Mr. Fotheringay, annoyed and confused, " I'm very sorry. The fact is——"

" Well ? "

He could think of no way but the truth. " I was working a miracle." He tried to speak in an off-hand way, but try as he would he couldn't.

" Working a—— ! 'Ere, don't you talk rot. Working a miracle, indeed ! Miracle ! Well, that's downright funny ! Why, you's the chap that don't believe in miracles. . . . Fact is, this is another of your silly conjuring tricks—that's what this is. Now, I tell you——"

But Mr. Fotheringay never heard what Mr. Winch was going to tell him. He realised he had given himself away, flung his valuable secret to all the winds of heaven. A violent gust of irritation swept him to action. He turned on the constable swiftly and fiercely. " Here," he said, " I've had enough of this, I have ! I'll show you a silly conjuring trick, I will ! Go to Hades ! Go, now ! "

He was alone !

Mr. Fotheringay performed no more miracles that night,

nor did he trouble to see what had become of his flowering
stick. He returned to the town, scared and very quiet, and
went to his bedroom. " Lord ! " he said, " it's a powerful
gift—an extremely powerful gift. I didn't hardly mean as
much as that. Not really. . . . I wonder what Hades is
like ! "

He sat on the bed taking off his boots. Struck by a happy
thought he transferred the constable to San Francisco, and
without any more interference with normal causation went
soberly to bed. In the night he dreamt of the anger of Winch.

The next day Mr. Fotheringay heard two interesting items
of news. Some one had planted a most beautiful climbing
rose against the elder Mr. Gomshott's private house in the
Lullaborough Road, and the river as far as Rawling's Mill was
to be dragged for Constable Winch.

Mr. Fotheringay was abstracted and thoughtful all that day,
and performed no miracles except certain provisions for Winch,
and the miracle of completing his day's work with punctual
perfection in spite of all the bee-swarm of thoughts that
hummed through his mind. And the extraordinary abstraction and meekness of his manner was remarked by several
people, and made a matter for jesting. For the most part he
was thinking of Winch.

On Sunday evening he went to chapel, and oddly enough,
Mr. Maydig, who took a certain interest in occult matters,
preached about " things that are not lawful." Mr. Fotheringay
was not a regular chapel-goer, but the system of assertive
scepticism, to which I have already alluded, was now very
much shaken. The tenor of the sermon threw an entirely
new light on these novel gifts, and he suddenly decided to
consult Mr. Maydig immediately after the service. So soon
as that was determined, he found himself wondering why he
had not done so before.

Mr. Maydig, a lean, excitable man with quite remarkably
long wrists and neck, was gratified at a request for a private
conversation from a young man whose carelessness in religious
matters was a subject for general remark in the town. After
a few necessary delays, he conducted him to the study of the
Manse, which was contiguous to the chapel, seated him comfortably, and, standing in front of a cheerful fire—his legs
threw a Rhodian arch of shadow on the opposite wall —
requested Mr. Fotheringay to state his business.

At first Mr. Fotheringay was a little abashed, and found

some difficulty in opening the matter. "You will scarcely believe me, Mr. Maydig, I am afraid——" and so forth for some time. He tried a question at last, and asked Mr. Maydig his opinion of miracles.

Mr. Maydig was still saying "Well" in an extremely judicial tone, when Mr. Fotheringay interrupted again : "You don't believe, I suppose, that some common sort of person— like myself, for instance—as it might be sitting here now, might have some sort of twist inside him that made him able to do things by his will."

"It's possible," said Mr. Maydig. "Something of the sort, perhaps, is possible."

"If I might make free with something here, I think I might show you by a sort of experiment," said Mr. Fotheringay. "Now, take that tobacco-jar on the table, for instance. What I want to know is whether what I am going to do with it is a miracle or not. Just half a minute, Mr. Maydig, please."

He knitted his brows, pointed to the tobacco-jar and said : "Be a bowl of vi'lets."

The tobacco-jar did as it was ordered.

Mr. Maydig started violently at the change, and stood looking from the thaumaturgist to the bowl of flowers. He said nothing. Presently, he ventured to lean over the table and smell the violets ; they were fresh-picked and very fine ones. Then he stared at Mr. Fotheringay again.

"How did you do that ?" he asked.

Mr. Fotheringay pulled his moustache. "Just told it— and there you are. Is that a miracle, or is it black art, or what is it ? And what do you think's the matter with me ? That's what I want to ask."

"It's a most extraordinary occurrence."

"And this day last week I knew no more that I could do things like that than you did. It came quite sudden. It's something odd about my will, I suppose, and that's as far as I can see."

"Is *that*—the only thing. Could you do other things besides that ?"

"Lord, yes !" said Mr. Fotheringay. "Just anything." He thought, and suddenly recalled a conjuring entertainment he had seen. "Here !" He pointed. "Change into a bowl of fish—no, not that—change into a glass bowl full of water with goldfish swimming in it. That's better ! You see that, Mr. Maydig ?"

"It's astonishing. It's incredible. You are either a most extraordinary . . . But no——"

"I could change it into anything," said Mr. Fotheringay. "Just anything. Here! be a pigeon, will you?"

In another moment a blue pigeon was fluttering round the room and making Mr. Maydig duck every time it came near him. "Stop there, will you," said Mr. Fotheringay; and the pigeon hung motionless in the air. "I could change it back to a bowl of flowers," he said, and after replacing the pigeon on the table worked that miracle. "I expect you will want your pipe in a bit," he said, and restored the tobacco-jar.

Mr. Maydig had followed all these later changes in a sort of ejaculatory silence. He stared at Mr. Fotheringay and, in a very gingerly manner, picked up the tobacco-jar, examined it, replaced it on the table. "*Well!*" was the only expression of his feelings.

"Now, after that it's easier to explain what I came about," said Mr. Fotheringay; and proceeded to a lengthy and involved narrative of his strange experiences, beginning with the affair of the lamp in the Long Dragon and complicated by persistent allusions to Winch. As he went on, the transient pride Mr. Maydig's consternation had caused passed away; he became the very ordinary Mr. Fotheringay of everyday intercourse again. Mr. Maydig listened intently, the tobacco-jar in his hand, and his bearing changed also with the course of the narrative. Presently, while Mr. Fotheringay was dealing with the miracle of the third egg, the minister interrupted with a fluttering extended hand—

"It is possible," he said. "It is credible. It is amazing, of course, but it reconciles a number of difficulties. The power to work miracles is a gift—a peculiar quality like genius or second sight—hitherto it has come very rarely and to exceptional people. But in this case . . . I have always wondered at the miracles of Mahomet, and at Yogi's miracles, and the miracles of Madame Blavatsky. But, of course! Yes, it is simply a gift! It carries out so beautifully the arguments of that great thinker"—Mr. Maydig's voice sank—"his Grace the Duke of Argyll. Here we plumb some profounder law—deeper than the ordinary laws of Nature. Yes—yes. Go on. Go on!"

Mr. Fotheringay proceeded to tell of his misadventure with Winch, and Mr. Maydig, no longer overawed or scared, began to jerk his limbs about and interject astonishment. "It's this what troubled me most," proceeded Mr. Fotheringay ; " it's this I'm most mijitly in want of advice for ; of course he's at San Francisco—wherever San Francisco may be—but of course it's awkward for both of us, as you'll see, Mr. Maydig. I don't see how he can understand what has happened, and I dare say he's scared and exasperated, something tremendous, and trying to get at me. I dare say he keeps on starting off to come here. I send him back, by a miracle, every few hours, when I think of it. And, of course, that's a thing he won't be able to understand, and it's bound to annoy him ; and, of course, if he takes a ticket every time it will cost him a lot of money. I done the best I could for him, but of course it's difficult for him to put himself in my place. I thought after-wards that his clothes might have got scorched, you know—if Hades is all it's supposed to be—before I shifted him. In that case I suppose they'd have locked him up in San Francisco. Of course I willed him a new suit of clothes on him directly I thought of it. But, you see, I'm already in a deuce of a tangle——"

Mr. Maydig looked serious. " I see you are in a tangle. Yes, it's a difficult position. How you are to end it . . ." He became diffuse and inconclusive.

" However, we'll leave Winch for a little and discuss the larger question. I don't think this is a case of the black art or anything of the sort. I don't think there is any taint of crimin-ality about it at all, Mr. Fotheringay—none whatever, unless you are suppressing material facts. No, it's miracles—pure miracles—miracles, if I may say so, of the very highest class."

He began to pace the hearthrug and gesticulate, while Mr. Fotheringay sat with his arm on the table and his head on his arm, looking worried. " I don't see how I'm to manage about Winch," he said.

" A gift of working miracles—apparently a very powerful gift," said Mr. Maydig, " will find a way about Winch—never fear. My dear Sir, you are a most important man—a man of the most astonishing possibilities. As evidence, for example ! And in other ways, the things you may do . . ."

" Yes, I've thought of a thing or two," said Mr. Fotheringay. " But—some of the things came a bit twisty. You saw that fish at first ? Wrong sort of bowl and wrong sort of fish. And I thought I'd ask some one."

" A proper course," said Mr. Maydig, " a very proper course—altogether the proper course." He stopped and looked at Mr. Fotheringay. " It's practically an unlimited gift. Let us test your powers, for instance. If they really *are* . . . If they really are all they seem to be."

And so, incredible as it may seem, in the study of the little house behind the Congregational Chapel, on the evening of Sunday, Nov. 10, 1896, Mr. Fotheringay, egged on and inspired by Mr. Maydig, began to work miracles. The reader's attention is specially and definitely called to the date. He will object, probably has already objected, that certain points in this story are improbable, that if any things of the sort already described had indeed occurred, they would have been in all the papers a year ago. The details immediately following he will find particularly hard to accept, because among other things they involve the conclusion that he or she, the reader in question, must have been killed in a violent and unprecedented manner more than a year ago. Now a miracle is nothing if not improbable, and as a matter of fact the reader *was* killed in a violent and unprecedented manner a year ago. In the subsequent course of this story that will become perfectly clear and credible, as every right-minded and reasonable reader will admit. But this is not the place for the end of the story, being but little beyond the hither side of the middle. And at first the miracles worked by Mr. Fotheringay were timid little miracles—little things with the cups and parlour fitments, as feeble as the miracles of Theosophists, and, feeble as they were, they were received with awe by his collaborator. He would have preferred to settle the Winch business out of hand, but Mr. Maydig would not let him. But after they had worked a dozen of these domestic trivialities, their sense of power grew, their imagination began to show signs of stimulation, and their ambition enlarged. Their first larger enterprise was due to hunger and the negligence of Mrs. Minchin, Mr. Maydig's housekeeper. The meal to which the minister conducted Mr. Fotheringay was certainly ill-laid and uninviting as refreshment for two industrious miracle-workers; but they were seated, and Mr. Maydig was descanting in sorrow rather than in anger upon his housekeeper's shortcomings, before it occurred to Mr. Fotheringay that an opportunity lay before him. " Don't you think, Mr. Maydig," he said, " if it isn't a liberty, I——"

" My dear Mr. Fotheringay ! Of course ! No—I didn't think."

Mr. Fotheringay waved his hand. " What shall we have ? "

he said, in a large, inclusive spirit, and, at Mr. Maydig's order, revised the supper very thoroughly. "As for me," he said, eyeing Mr. Maydig's selection, "I am always particularly fond of a tankard of stout and a nice Welsh rarebit, and I'll order that. I ain't much given to Burgundy," and forthwith stout and Welsh rarebit promptly appeared at his command. They sat long at their supper, talking like equals, as Mr. Fotheringay presently perceived with a glow of surprise and gratification. of all the miracles they would presently do. "And, by the bye, Mr. Maydig," said Mr. Fotheringay, "I might perhaps be able to help you—in a domestic way."

"Don't quite follow," said Mr. Maydig, pouring out a glass of miraculous old Burgundy.

Mr. Fotheringay helped himself to a second Welsh rarebit out of vacancy, and took a mouthful. "I was thinking," he said, "I might be able (*chum*, *chum*) to work (*chum*, *chum*) a miracle with Mrs. Minchin (*chum*, *chum*)—make her a better woman."

Mr. Maydig put down the glass and looked doubtful. "She's—— She strongly objects to interference, you know, Mr. Fotheringay. And—as a matter of fact—it's well past eleven and she's probably in bed and asleep. Do you think, on the whole——"

Mr. Fotheringay considered these objections. "I don't see that it shouldn't be done in her sleep."

For a time Mr. Maydig opposed the idea, and then he yielded. Mr. Fotheringay issued his orders, and a little less at their ease, perhaps, the two gentlemen proceeded with their repast. Mr. Maydig was enlarging on the changes he might expect in his housekeeper next day, with an optimism that seemed even to Mr. Fotheringay's supper senses a little forced and hectic, when a series of confused noises from upstairs began. Their eyes exchanged interrogations, and Mr. Maydig left the room hastily. Mr. Fotheringay heard him calling up to his housekeeper and then his footsteps going softly up to her.

In a minute or so the minister returned, his step light, his face radiant. "Wonderful!" he said, "and touching! Most touching!"

He began pacing the hearthrug. "A repentance—a most touching repentance—through the crack of the door. Poor woman! A most wonderful change! She had got up. She must have got up at once. She had got up out of her sleep to

smash a private bottle of brandy in her box. And to confess
it too ! . . . But this gives us—it opens—a most amazing vista
of possibilities. If we can work this miraculous change in
her . . ."

"The thing's unlimited seemingly," said Mr. Fotheringay.
"And about Mr. Winch——"

"Altogether unlimited." And from the hearthrug Mr.
Maydig, waving the Winch difficulty aside, unfolded a series of
wonderful proposals—proposals he invented as he went along.

Now what those proposals were does not concern the
essentials of this story. Suffice it that they were designed in a
spirit of infinite benevolence, the sort of benevolence that used
to be called post-prandial. Suffice it, too, that the problem
of Winch remained unsolved. Nor is it necessary to describe
how far that series got to its fulfilment. There were astonishing changes. The small hours found Mr. Maydig and Mr.
Fotheringay careering across the chilly market-square under
the still moon, in a sort of ecstasy of thaumaturgy, Mr. Maydig
all flap and gesture, Mr. Fotheringay short and bristling, and
no longer abashed at his greatness. They had reformed every
drunkard in the Parliamentary division, changed all the beer
and alcohol to water (Mr. Maydig had overruled Mr. Fotheringay on this point), they had, further, greatly improved the
railway communication of the place, drained Flinder's swamp,
improved the soil of One Tree Hill, and cured the Vicar's wart.
And they were going to see what could be done with the injured
pier at South Bridge. "The place," gasped Mr. Maydig,
"won't be the same place to-morrow. How surprised and
thankful every one will be ! " And just at that moment the
church clock struck three.

"I say," said Mr. Fotheringay, "that's three o'clock ! I
must be getting back. I've got to be at business by eight.
And besides, Mrs. Wimms——"

"We're only beginning," said Mr. Maydig, full of the
sweetness of unlimited power. "We're only beginning.
Think of all the good we're doing. When people wake——"

"But——" said Mr. Fotheringay.

Mr. Maydig gripped his arm suddenly. His eyes were
bright and wild. "My dear chap," he said, "there's no hurry.
Look "—he pointed to the moon at the zenith—"Joshua ! "

"Joshua ? " said Mr. Fotheringay.

"Joshua," said Mr. Maydig. "Why not ? Stop it."

Mr. Fotheringay looked at the moon.

" That's a bit tall," he said after a pause.

" Why not ? " said Mr. Maydig. " Of course it doesn't stop. You stop the rotation of the earth, you know. Time stops. It isn't as if we were doing harm."

" H'm ! " said Mr. Fotheringay. " Well." He sighed. " I'll try. Here——"

He buttoned up his jacket and addressed himself to the habitable globe, with as good an assumption of confidence as lay in his power. " Jest stop rotating, will you," said Mr. Fotheringay.

Incontinently he was flying head over heels through the air at the rate of dozens of miles a minute. In spite of the innumerable circles he was describing per second, he thought ; for thought is wonderful—sometimes as sluggish as flowing pitch, sometimes as instantaneous as light. He thought in a second, and willed. " Let me come down safe and sound. Whatever else happens, let me down safe and sound."

He willed it only just in time, for his clothes, heated by his rapid flight through the air, were already beginning to singe. He came down with a forcible, but by no means injurious bump in what appeared to be a mound of fresh-turned earth. A large mass of metal and masonry, extraordinarily like the clock-tower in the middle of the market-square, hit the earth near him, ricochetted over him, and flew into stonework, bricks, and masonry, like a bursting bomb. A hurtling cow hit one of the large blocks and smashed like an egg. There was a crash that made all the most violent crashes of his past life seem like the sound of falling dust, and this was followed by a descending series of lesser crashes. A vast wind roared throughout earth and heaven, so that he could scarcely lift his head to look. For a while he was too breathless and astonished even to see where he was or what had happened. And his first movement was to feel his head and reassure himself that his streaming hair was still his own.

" Lord ! " gasped Mr. Fotheringay, scarce able to speak for the gale, " I've had a squeak ! What's gone wrong ? Storms and thunder. And only a minute ago a fine night. It's Maydig set me on to this sort of thing. *What* a wind ! If I go on fooling in this way I'm bound to have a thundering accident ! . . .

" Where's Maydig ?

" What a confounded mess everything's in ! "

He looked about him so far as his flapping jacket would

permit. The appearance of things was really extremely strange. " The sky's all right anyhow," said Mr. Fotheringay. " And that's about all that is all right. And even there it looks like a terrific gale coming up. But there's the moon overhead. Just as it was just now. Bright as midday. But as for the rest—— Where's the village ? Where's—where's anything ? And what on earth set this wind a-blowing ? *I* didn't order no wind."

Mr. Fotheringay struggled to get to his feet in vain, and after one failure, remained on all-fours, holding on. He surveyed the moonlit world to leeward, with the tails of his jacket streaming over his head. " There's something seriously wrong," said Mr. Fotheringay. " And what it is—goodness knows."

Far and wide nothing was visible in the white glare through the haze of dust that drove before a screaming gale but tumbled masses of earth and heaps of inchoate ruins, no trees, no houses, no familiar shapes, only a wilderness of disorder vanishing at last into the darkness beneath the whirling columns and streamers, the lightnings and thunderings of a swiftly rising storm. Near him in the livid glare was something that might once have been an elm-tree, a smashed mass of splinters, shivered from boughs to base, and further a twisted mass of iron girders—only too evidently the viaduct—rose out of the piled confusion.

You see, when Mr. Fotheringay had arrested the rotation of the solid globe, he had made no stipulation concerning the trifling movables upon its surface. And the earth spins so fast that the surface at its equator is travelling at rather more than a thousand miles an hour, and in these latitudes at more than half that pace. So that the village, and Mr. Maydig, and Mr. Fotheringay, and everybody and everything had been jerked violently forward at about nine miles per second—that is to say, much more violently than if they had been fired out of a cannon. And every human being, every living creature, every house, and every tree—all the world as we know it—had been so jerked and smashed and utterly destroyed. That was all.

These things Mr. Fotheringay did not, of course, fully appreciate. But he perceived that his miracle had miscarried, and with that a great disgust of miracles came upon him. He was in darkness now, for the clouds had swept together and blotted out his momentary glimpse of the moon, and the air was full of fitful struggling tortured wraiths of hail. A great roaring of wind and waters filled earth and sky, and, peering under his hand through the dust and sleet to windward, he saw by the play of the lightnings a vast wall of water pouring towards him.

"Maydig!" screamed Mr. Fotheringay's feeble voice amid the elemental uproar. "Here!—Maydig!"

"Stop!" cried Mr. Fotheringay to the advancing water. "Oh, for goodness' sake, stop!"

"Just a moment," said Mr. Fotheringay to the lightnings and thunder. "Stop jest a moment while I collect my thoughts. . . . And now what shall I do?" he said. "What *shall* I do? Lord! I wish Maydig was about."

"I know," said Mr. Fotheringay. "And for goodness' sake let's have it right *this* time."

He remained on all-fours, leaning against the wind, very intent to have everything right.

"Ah!" he said. "Let nothing what I'm going to order happen until I say 'Off!' . . . Lord! I wish I'd thought of that before!"

He lifted his little voice against the whirlwind, shouting louder and louder in the vain desire to hear himself speak. "Now then!—here goes! Mind about that what I said just now. In the first place, when all I've got to say is done, let me lose my miraculous power, let my will become just like anybody else's will, and all these dangerous miracles be stopped. I don't like them. I'd rather I didn't work 'em. Ever so much. That's the first thing. And the second is—let me be back just before the miracles begin ; let everything be just as it was before that blessed lamp turned up. It's a big job, but it's the last. Have you got it ? No more miracles, everything as it was—me back in the Long Dragon just before I drank my half-pint. That's it ! Yes."

He dug his fingers into the mould, closed his eyes, and said " Off ! "

Everything became perfectly still. He perceived that he was standing erect.

"So *you* say," said a voice.

He opened his eyes. He was in the bar of the Long Dragon, arguing about miracles with Toddy Beamish. He had a vague sense of some great thing forgotten that instantaneously passed. You see, except for the loss of his miraculous powers, everything was back as it had been ; his mind and memory therefore were now just as they had been at the time when this story began. So that he knew absolutely nothing of all that is told here, knows nothing of all that is told here to this day. And among other things, of course, he still did not believe in miracles.

" I tell you that miracles, properly speaking, can't possibly happen," he said, " whatever you like to hold. And I'm prepared to prove it up to the hilt."

" That's what *you* think," said Toddy Beamish, and " Prove it if you can."

" Looky here, Mr. Beamish," said Mr. Fotheringay. " Let us clearly understand what a miracle is. It's something contrariwise to the course of Nature done by power of Will. . . ."

P. G. WODEHOUSE (1881—   ) *started his literary career by writing stories of school life. Fame came to him when he turned to humour and created characters, such as Jeeves, Psmith and Ukridge. In not a few of his novels he has chosen to set down the hustling American in the midst of English tradition. "A Damsel in Distress" and "The Coming of Jeeves" are among his most successful novels.*

JEEVES IN SPRINGTIME

"Jeeves," I said, coming away from the window.

"Sir?" said Jeeves. He had been clearing the breakfast things, but at the sound of the young master's voice he cheesed it courteously.

"It's a topping morning, Jeeves."

"Decidedly, sir."

"Spring and all that."

"Yes, sir."

"In the spring, Jeeves, a livelier iris gleams upon the burnished dove."

"So I have been informed, sir."

"Right-o! Then bring me my whangee, my yellowest shoes, and the old green Homburg. I'm going into the park to do pastoral dances."

"Very good, sir."

I don't know if you know that sort of feeling you get on these days round about the end of April and the beginning of May, when the sky's a light blue with cotton-wool clouds and there's a bit of a breeze blowing from the west? Kind of uplifted feeling. Romantic, if you know what I mean. I'm not much of a ladies' man, but on this particular morning it seemed to me that what I really wanted was some charming girl to buzz up and ask me to save her from assassins or something. So that it was a bit of an anti-climax when I merely ran into young Bingo Little, looking perfectly foul in a crimson satin tie decorated with horseshoes.

"Hallo, Bertie," said Bingo.

" My God, man ! " I gargled. " The cravat ! The gent's neckwear ! Why ? For what reason ? "

" Oh, the tie ? " He blushed. " I—er—I was given it."

He seemed embarrassed, so I dropped the subject. Always the gentleman. We toddled along a bit, and sat down on a couple of chairs by the Serpentine. Conversation languished. Bingo was staring straight ahead of him in a glassy sort of manner.

" I say, Bertie," he said, after a pause of about an hour and a quarter.

" Hallo ! "

" Do you like the name Mabel ? "

" No."

" No ? "

" No."

" You don't think there's a kind of music in the word, like the wind rustling gently through the tree-tops ? "

" No."

He seemed disappointed for a moment ; then cheered up.

" Of course, you wouldn't. You always were a fat-headed worm without any soul, weren't you ? "

" Just as you say. Who is she ? Tell me all."

For I realised now that poor old Bingo was going through it once again. Ever since I have known him—and we were at school together—he has been perpetually falling in love with someone, generally in the spring, which seems to act on him like magic. At school he had the finest collection of actresses' photographs of anyone of his time ; and at Oxford his romantic nature was a byword.

" You'd better come along and meet her at lunch," he said, looking at his watch.

" A ripe suggestion," I said. " Where are you meeting her ? At the Ritz ? "

" Near the Ritz."

He was geographically accurate. About fifty yards east of the Ritz there is one of those blighted tea-and-bun shops you see dotted about all over London, and into this, if you'll believe me, young Bingo dived like a homing rabbit ; and before I had time to say a word we were wedged in at a table, on the brink of a silent pool of coffee left there by an early luncher.

I'm bound to say I couldn't quite follow the development of the scenario. Bingo, while not absolutely rolling in the stuff, has always had a fairish amount of the ready. Apart from what he got from his uncle—old Mortimer Little; you've probably heard of Little's Liniment (It Limbers Up The Legs) : he ran that till he turned it into a company and retired with a pile—I say, apart from what he got from the above, who gave him a pretty decent allowance, Bingo being his only relative and presumably his heir, I knew that Bingo had finished up the jumping season well on the right side of the ledger, having collected a parcel over the Lincolnshire. Why, then, was he lunching the girl at this Godforsaken eatery ? It couldn't be because he was hard up.

Just then the waitress arrived. Rather a pretty girl.

"Aren't we going to wait—— ? " I started to say to Bingo, thinking it somewhat thick that, in addition to asking a girl to lunch with him in a place like this, he should fling himself on the foodstuffs before she turned up, when I caught sight of his face, and stopped.

The man was goggling. His entire map was suffused with a rich blush. He looked like the Soul's Awakening done in pink.

"Hallo, Mabel ! " he said, with a sort of gulp.

"Hallo ! " said the girl.

"Mabel," said Bingo, "this is Bertie Booster, a pal of mine."

"Pleased to meet you," she said. "Nice morning."

"Fine," I said.

"You see I'm wearing the tie," said Bingo.

"It suits you beautiful," said the girl.

Personally, if anyone had told me that a tie like that suited me, I should have risen and struck them on the mazzard, regardless of their age and sex ; but poor old Bingo simply got all flustered with gratification, and smirked in the most gruesome manner.

"Well, what's it going to be to-day ? " asked the girl, introducing the business touch into the conversation.

Bingo studied the menu devoutly.

"I'll have a cup of cocoa, cold veal and ham pie, slice of fruit cake, and a macaroon. Same for you, Bertie ? "

I gazed at the man, revolted. That he could have been a pal of mine all these years and think me capable of insulting the old tum with this sort of stuff cut me to the quick.

"Or how about a bit of hot steak-pudding, with a sparkling limado to wash it down ? " said Bingo.

You know the way love can change a fellow is really frightful to contemplate. This bird before me, who spoke in this absolutely careless way of macaroons and limado, was the man I had seen in happier days telling the head-waiter at Claridge's exactly how he wanted the *chef* to prepare the *sole frit au gourmet aux champignons*, and saying he would jolly well sling it back if it wasn't just right. Ghastly! Ghastly!

A roll and butter and a small coffee seemed the only things on the list that hadn't been specially prepared by the nastier-minded members of the Borgia family for people they had a particular grudge against, so I chose them, and Mabel hopped it.

"Well?" said Bingo, rapturously.

I took it that he wanted my opinion of the female poisoner who had just left us.

"Very nice," I said.

He seemed dissatisfied.

"You don't think she's the most wonderful girl you ever saw?" he said, wistfully.

"Oh, absolutely!" I said, to appease the blighter. "Where did you meet her?"

"At a Subscription dance at Camberwell."

"What on earth were you doing at a Subscription dance at Camberwell?"

"Your man Jeeves asked me if I would buy a couple of tickets. It was in aid of some charity or other."

"Jeeves? I didn't know he went in for that sort of thing."

"Well, I suppose he has to relax a bit every now and then. Anyway, he was there, swinging a dashed efficient shoe. I hadn't meant to go at first, but I turned up for a lark. Oh, Bertie, think what I might have missed!"

"What might you have missed?" I asked, the old lemon being slightly clouded.

"Mabel, you chump. If I hadn't gone I shouldn't have met Mabel."

"Oh, ah!"

At this point Bingo fell into a species of trance, and only came out of it to wrap himself round the pie and macaroon.

"Bertie," he said, "I want your advice."

"Carry on."

"At least, not your advice, because that wouldn't be much good to anybody. I mean, you're a pretty consummate old ass, aren't you ?   Not that I want to hurt your feelings, of course."

" No, no, I see that."

" What I wish you would do is to put the whole thing to that fellow Jeeves of yours, and see what he suggests.   You've often told me that he has helped other pals of yours out of messes.   From what you tell me, he's by way of being the brains of the family."

" He's never let me down yet."

" Then put my case to him."

" What case ? "

" My problem."

" What problem ? "

" Why, you poor fish, my uncle, of course.   What do you think my uncle's going to say to all this ?   If I sprang it on him cold, he'd tie himself in knots on the hearth-rug."

" One of these emotional johnnies, eh ? "

" Somehow or other his mind has got to be prepared to receive the news.   But how ? "

" Ah ! "

" That's a lot of help, that ' ah ' !   You see, I'm pretty well dependent on the old boy.   If he cut off my allowance, I should be very much in the soup.   So you put the whole binge up to Jeeves and see if he can't scare up a happy ending somehow.   Tell him my future is in his hands, and that, if the wedding bells ring out, he can rely on me, even unto half my kingdom.   Well, call it ten quid.   Jeeves would exert himself with ten quid on the horizon, what ? "

" Undoubtedly," I said.

I wasn't in the least surprised at Bingo wanting to lug Jeeves into his private affairs like this.   It was the first thing I would have thought of doing myself if I had been in any hole of any description.   Most fellows, no doubt, are all for having their valets confine their activities to creasing trousers and what not without trying to run the home ; but it's different with Jeeves.   Right from the first day he came to me, I have looked on him as a sort of guide, philosopher, and friend.   He is a bird of the ripest intellect, full of bright ideas.   If anybody could fix things for poor old Bingo, he could.

I stated the case to him that night after dinner.

" Jeeves."

" Sir ? "

" Are you busy just now ? "

" No, sir."

" I mean, not doing anything in particular ? "

" No, sir. It is my practice at this hour to read some improving book : but, if you desire my services, this can easily be postponed, or indeed, abandoned altogether."

" Well, I want your advice. It's about Mr. Little."

" Young Mr. Little, sir, or the elder Mr. Little, his uncle, who lives in Pounceby Gardens ? "

Jeeves seems to know everything. Most amazing thing. I'd been pally with Bingo practically all my life, and yet I didn't remember ever having heard that his uncle lived anywhere in particular.

" How did you know he lived in Pounceby Gardens ? " I said.

" I am on terms of some intimacy with the elder Mr. Little's cook, sir. In fact, there is an understanding."

I'm bound to say that this gave me a bit of a start. Somehow I'd never thought of Jeeves going in for that sort of thing.

" Do you mean you're engaged ? "

" It may be said to amount to that, sir."

" Well, well ! "

" She is a remarkably excellent cook, sir," said Jeeves, as though he felt called on to give some explanation. " What was it you wished to ask me about Mr. Little ? "

I sprang the details on him.

" And that's how the matter stands, Jeeves," I said. " I think we ought to rally round a trifle and help poor old Bingo put the thing through. Tell me about old Mr. Little. What sort of a chap is he ? "

" A somewhat curious character, sir. Since retiring from business he has become a great recluse, and now devotes himself almost entirely to the pleasures of the table."

" Greedy hog, you mean ? "

" I would not, perhaps, take the liberty of describing him in precisely those terms, sir. He is what is usually called a gourmet. Very particular about what he eats, and for that reason sets a high value on Miss Watson's services."

" The cook ? "

" Yes, sir."

" Well, it looks to me as though our best plan would be to shoot young Bingo on to him after dinner one night. Melting mood, I mean to say, and all that."

" The difficulty is, sir, that at the moment Mr. Little is on a diet, owing to an attack of gout."

" Things begin to look wobbly."

" No, sir, I fancy that the elder Mr. Little's misfortune may be turned to the younger Mr. Little's advantage. I was speaking only the other day to Mr. Little's valet, and he was telling me that it has become his principal duty to read to Mr. Little in the evenings. If I were in your place, sir, I should send young Mr. Little to read to his uncle."

" Nephew's devotion, you mean ? Old man touched by kindly action, what ? "

" Partly that, sir. But I would rely more on young Mr. Little's choice of literature."

" That's no good. Jolly old Bingo has a kind face, but when it comes to literature he stops at the *Sporting Times*."

" That difficulty may be overcome. I would be happy to select books for Mr. Little to read. Perhaps I might explain my idea further ? "

" I can't say I quite grasp it yet."

" The method which I advocate is what, I believe, the advertisers call Direct Suggestion, sir, consisting as it does of driving an idea home by constant repetition. You may have had experience of the system ? "

" You mean they keep on telling you that some soap or other is the best, and after a bit you come under the influence and charge round the corner and buy a cake ? "

" Exactly, sir. The same method was the basis of all the most valuable propaganda during the world war. I see no reason why it should not be adopted to bring about the desired result with regard to the subject's views on class distinctions. If young Mr. Little were to read day after day to his uncle a series of narratives in which marriage with young persons of an inferior social status was held up as both feasible and admirable, I fancy it would prepare the elder Mr. Little's mind for the reception of the information that his nephew wishes to marry a waitress in a tea-shop."

" *Are* there any books of that sort nowadays ? The only ones I ever see mentioned in the papers are about married couples who find life grey, and can't stick each other at any price."

" Yes, sir, there are a great many, neglected by the reviewers but widely read. You have never encountered *All for Love*, by Rosie M. Banks ? "

" No."

" Nor *A Red, Red Summer Rose*, by the same author ? "

" No."

" I have an aunt, sir, who owns an almost complete set of Rosie M. Banks. I could easily borrow as many volumes as young Mr. Little might require. They make very light, attractive reading."

" Well, it's worth trying."

" I should certainly recommend the scheme, sir."

" All right, then. Toddle round to your aunt's to-morrow and grab a couple of the fruitiest. We can but have a dash at it."

" Precisely, sir."

Bingo reported three days later that Rosie M. Banks was the goods and beyond a question the stuff to give the troops. Old Little had jibbed somewhat at first at the proposed change of literary diet, he not being much of a lad for fiction and having stuck hitherto exclusively to the heavier monthly reviews ; but Bingo had got chapter one of *All for Love* past his guard before he knew what was happening, and after that there was nothing to it. Since then they had finished *A Red, Red Summer Rose*, *Madcap Myrtle*, and *Only a Factory Girl* and were halfway through *The Courtship of Lord Strathmorlick*.

Bingo told me all this in a husky voice over an egg beaten up in sherry. The only blot on the thing from his point of view was that it wasn't doing a bit of good to the old vocal chords, which were beginning to show signs of cracking under the strain. He had been looking his symptoms up in a medical dictionary, and he thought he had got " clergyman's throat." But against this you had to set the fact that he was making an undoubted hit in the right quarter, and also that after the evening's reading he always stayed on to dinner ; and, from what he told me, the dinners turned out by old Little's cook had to be tasted to be believed. There were tears in the old blighter's eyes as he got on the subject of the clear soup. I suppose to a fellow who for weeks had been tackling macaroons and limado it must have been like Heaven.

Old Little wasn't able to give any practical assistance at these banquets, but Bingo said that he came to the table and had his whack of arrowroot, and sniffed the dishes, and told stories of *entrées* he had had in the past, and sketched out scenarios of what he was going to do to the bill of fare in the future, when the doctor put him in shape ; so I suppose he enjoyed himself, too, in a way. Anyhow, things seemed to be buzzing along quite satisfactorily, and Bingo said he had got an idea which, he thought, was going to clinch the thing. He wouldn't tell me what it was, but he said it was a pippin.

" We make progress, Jeeves," I said.

" That is very satisfactory, sir."

" Mr. Little tells me that when he came to the big scene in *Only a Factory Girl*, his uncle gulped like a stricken bull-pup."

" Indeed, sir ? '

" Where Lord Claude takes the girl in his arms, you know, and says——"

" I am familiar with the passage, sir. It is distinctly moving. It was a great favourite of my aunt's."

" I think we're on the right track."

" It would seem so, sir."

" In fact, this looks like being another of your successes. I've always said, and I always shall say, that for sheer brain, Jeeves, you stand alone. All the other great thinkers of the age are simply in the crowd, watching you go by."

" Thank you very much, sir. I endeavour to give satisfaction."

About a week after this, Bingo blew in with the news that his uncle's gout had ceased to trouble him, and that on the morrow he would be back at the old stand working away with knife and fork as before.

" And, by the way," said Bingo, " he wants you to lunch with him to-morrow "

" Me ? Why me ? He doesn't know I exist."

" Oh, yes, he does. I've told him about you."

" What have you told him ? "

" Oh, various things. Anyhow, he wants to meet you. And take my tip, laddie—you go ! I should think to-morrow would be something special."

I don't know why it was, but even then it struck me that there was something dashed odd—almost sinister, if you know what I mean—about young Bingo's manner. The old egg had the air of one who has something up his sleeve.

" There is more in this than meets the eye," I said. " Why should your uncle ask a fellow to lunch whom he's never seen ? "

"My dear old fathead, haven't I just said that I've been telling him all about you—that you're my best pal—at school together, and all that sort of thing?"

"But even then—and another thing. Why are you so dashed keen on my going?"

Bingo hesitated for a moment.

"Well, I told you I'd got an idea. This is it. I want you to spring the news on him. I haven't the nerve myself."

"What! I'm hanged if I do!"

"And you call yourself a pal of mine!"

"Yes, I know; but there are limits."

"Bertie," said Bingo, reproachfully, "I saved your life once."

"When?"

"Didn't I? It must have been some other fellow, then. Well, anyway, we were boys together and all that. You can't let me down."

"Oh, all right," I said. "But, when you say you haven't nerve enough for any dashed thing in the world, you misjudge yourself. A fellow who——"

"Bung-oh!" said young Bingo. "One-thirty to-morrow. Don't be late."

I'm bound to say that the more I contemplated the binge, the less I liked it. It was all very well for Bingo to say that I was slated for a magnificent lunch; but what good is the best possible lunch to a fellow if he is slung out into the street on his ear during the soup course? However, the word of a Wooster is his bond and all that sort of rot, so at one-thirty next day I tottered up the steps of No. 16 Pounceby Gardens, and punched the bell. And half a minute later I was up in the drawing-room, shaking hands with the fattest man I have ever seen in my life.

The motto of the Little family was evidently "variety." Young Bingo is long and thin and hasn't had a superfluous ounce on him since we first met; but the uncle restored the average and a bit over. The hand which grasped mine wrapped it round and enfolded it till I began to wonder if I'd ever get it out without excavating machinery.

"Mr. Wooster, I am gratified—I am proud—I am honoured."

It seemed to me that young Bingo must have boosted me to some purpose.

" Oh, ah ! " I said.

He stepped back a bit, still hanging on to the good right hand.

" You are very young to have accomplished so much ! "

I couldn't follow the train of thought. The family, especially my Aunt Agatha, who has savaged me incessantly from childhood up, have always rather made a point of the fact that mine is a wasted life, and that, since I won a prize at my first school for the best collection of wild flowers made during the summer holidays, I haven't done a dam thing to land me on the nation's scroll of fame. I was wondering if he couldn't have got me mixed up with someone else, when the telephone-bell rang outside in the hall, and the maid came in to say that I was wanted. I buzzed down, and found it was young Bingo.

" Hallo ! " said young Bingo. " So you've got there ? Good man ! I knew I could rely on you. I say, did my uncle seem pleased to see you ? "

" Absolutely all over me. I can't make it out."

" Oh, that's all right. I just rang up to explain. The fact is, old man, I know you won't mind, but I told him that you were the author of those books I've been reading to him."

" What ? "

" Yes, I said that ' Rosie M. Banks ' was your pen-name, and you didn't want it generally known, because you were a modest, retiring sort of chap. He'll listen to you now. Absolutely hang on your words. A brightish idea, what ? I doubt if Jeeves in person could have thought up a better one than that. Well, pitch it strong, old lad, and keep steadily before you the fact that I must have my allowance raised. I can't possibly marry on what I've got now. If this film is to end with the slow fade-out on the embrace, at least double is indicated. Well, that's that. Cheerio ! "

And he rang off. At that moment the gong sounded, and the genial host came tumbling downstairs like the delivery of a ton of coals.

I always look back to that lunch with a sort of aching regret. It was the lunch of a lifetime, and I wasn't in a fit state to appreciate it. Subconsciously, if you know what I mean, I could see it was pretty special, but I had got the wind up to such a frightful extent over the ghastly situation in which young Bingo had landed me that its deeper meaning never really penetrated.   Most of the time I might have been eating sawdust for all the good it did me.

Old Little struck the literary note right from the start.

" My nephew has probably told you that I have been making a close study of your books of late ? " he began.

" Yes.   He did mention it.   How—er—how did you like the bally things ? "

He gazed reverently at me.

" Mr. Wooster, I am not ashamed to say that the tears came into my eyes as I listened to them.   It amazes me that a man as young as you can have been able to plumb human nature so surely to its depths ; to play with so unerring a hand on the quivering heartstrings of your reader ; to write novels so true, so human, so moving, so vital ! "

" Oh, it's just a knack," I said.

The good old persp. was bedewing my forehead by this time in a pretty lavish manner.   I don't know when I've been so rattled.

" Do you find the room a trifle warm ? "

" Oh no, no, rather not.   Just right."

" Then it's the pepper.   If my cook has a fault—which I am not prepared to admit—it is that she is inclined to stress the pepper a trifle in her made dishes.   By the way, do you like her cooking ? "

I was so relieved that we had got off the subject of my literary output that I shouted approval in a ringing baritone.

" I am delighted to hear it, Mr. Wooster.   I may be prejudiced, but to my mind that woman is a genius."

" Absolutely ! " I said.

" She has been with me many years, and in all that time I have not known her guilty of a single lapse from the highest standard.   Except once, in the winter of 1917, when a purist might have condemned a certain mayonnaise of hers as lacking in creaminess.   But one must make allowances.   There had been several air-raids about that time, and no doubt the poor woman was shaken.   But nothing is perfect in this world, Mr. Wooster, and I have had my cross to bear.   All these years I have lived in constant apprehension lest some evilly-disposed person might lure her from my employment.   To my certain knowledge she has received offers, lucrative offers, to accept service elsewhere.   You may judge of my dismay, Mr. Wooster, when only this morning the bolt fell.   She gave notice ! "

" Good Lord ! "

" Your consternation does credit, if I may say so, to the heart of the author of *A Red, Red Summer Rose*. But I am thankful to say the worst has not happened. The matter has been adjusted. Jane is not leaving me."

" Good egg ! "

" Good egg, indeed—though the expression is not familiar to me. I do not remember having come across it in your books. And, speaking of your books, may I say that what has impressed me about them even more than the moving poignancy of the actual narrative is your philosophy of life. If there were more like you, Mr. Wooster, London would be a better place."

This was dead opposite to my Aunt Agatha's philosophy of life, she having always rather given me to understand that it is the presence in it of fellows like me that makes London more or less of a plague-spot ; but I let it go.

" Let me tell you, Mr. Wooster, that I appreciate your splendid defiance of the outworn fetishes of a purblind social system. I appreciate it ! *You* are big enough to see that rank is but the guinea stamp and that, in the magnificent words of Lord Bletchmore in *Only a Factory Girl*, ' Be her origin ne'er so humble, a good woman is the equal of the finest lady on earth ! ' "

I sat up.

" I say ! Do you think that ? "

" I do, Mr. Wooster. I am ashamed to say that there was a time when I was, like other men, a slave to the idiotic convention which we call Class Distinction. But, since I read your books——"

I might have known it. Jeeves had done it again.

" You think it's all right for a bloke in what you might call a certain social position to marry a girl of what you might describe as the lower classes ? "

" Most assuredly I do, Mr. Wooster."

I took a deep breath, and slipped him the good news.

" Young Bingo—your nephew, you know—wants to marry a waitress," I said.

" I honour him for it."

" You don't object ? "

" On the contrary."

I took another deep breath, and shifted to the sordid side of the business.

"I hope you won't think I'm butting in, don't you know," I said, "but—er—well, how about it?"

"I fear I do not quite follow you."

"Well, I mean to say, his allowance and all that. The money you're good enough to give him. He was rather hoping that you might see your way to jerking up the total a bit."

Old Little shook his head regretfully.

"I fear that can hardly be managed. You see, a man in my position is compelled to save every penny. I will gladly continue my nephew's existing allowance, but beyond that I cannot go. It would not be fair to my wife."

"What! But you're not married?"

"Not yet. But I propose to enter upon that holy state almost immediately. The lady who for years has cooked so well for me honoured me by accepting my hand this very morning." A cold gleam of triumph came into his eye. "Now let 'em try to get her away from me!" he muttered, defiantly.

"Young Mr. Little has been trying frequently during the afternoon to reach you on the telephone, sir," said Jeeves that night, when I got home.

"I'll bet he has," I said. I had sent poor old Bingo an outline of the situation by messenger-boy shortly after lunch.

"He seemed a trifle agitated."

"I don't wonder. Jeeves," I said, "brace up and bite the bullet. I'm afraid I've bad news for you."

"Sir?"

"That scheme of yours—reading those books to old Mr. Little and all that—has blown out a fuse."

"They did not soften him?"

"They did. That's the whole bally trouble. Jeeves, I'm sorry to say that *fiancée* of yours—Miss Watson, you know—the cook, you know—well, the long and the short of it is that she's chosen riches instead of honest worth, if you know what I mean."

"Sir?"

"She's handed you the mitten and gone and got engaged to old Mr. Little!"

"Indeed, sir?"

"You don't seem much upset?"

"The fact is, sir, I had anticipated some such outcome."

I stared at him. " Then what on earth did you suggest the scheme for ? "

" To tell you the truth, sir, I was not wholly averse from a severance of my relations with Miss Watson. In fact, I greatly desired it. I respect Miss Watson exceedingly, but I have seen for a long time that we were not suited. Now the other young person with whom I have an understanding——"

" Great Scot, Jeeves ! There isn't another ? "

" Yes, sir."

" How long has this been going on ? "

" For some weeks, sir. I was greatly attracted by her when I first met her at a Subscription dance at Camberwell."

" My sainted aunt ! Not——"

Jeeves inclined his head gravely.

" Yes, sir. By an odd coincidence it is the same young person that young Mr. Little—I have placed the cigarettes on the small table. Good night, sir."

TALES OF LOVE
AND ROMANCE

I will make you brooches and toys for your delight
Of bird-song at morning and star-shine at night.
I will make a palace fit for you and me,
Of green days in forests and blue days at sea.

ROBERT LOUIS STEVENSON. *Romance.*

MICHAEL ARLEN (1895–) *is an Armenian by birth and parentage, but became a naturalised British subject in* 1922. *He suddenly found himself one of the most talked-of novelists in the country through the publication of "The Green Hat," one of the "best sellers" of a generation. In this and his other novels he brilliantly satirises the manner and morals of Society. This story is taken from "These Charming People."*

MAJOR CYPRESS GOES OFF
THE DEEP END

THIS story has no point. No story that has anything to do with Hugo Cypress could have a point, for Hugo is an utterly pointless man. Dear Hugo. . . .

I have known him since he was so high, and as I was also so high, I know him well. I could tell you of many little happenings, just to show you the sort of man he was, but one in particular, a martial one, vividly occurs to me. It was in the third year of the war, and I had been shoved into the War Office, because of a personal application of that great scientific truth to the effect that two things cannot be in the same place at once, particularly if one of them happens to be a German shell ; and, one day, Hugo called. His arm was in a sling and a light was in his eye. Dear Hugo. . . .

" Show me," said Hugo, " a man who will give me a job of work."

I showed him old Tornado Toby—officially known as Major-General Sir Tobias Blast, K.C.M.G., D.S.O., M.V.O., O.U.D.S., etc. I stood in a far corner, and was very silent.

" What d'you want ? " said Sir Toby.

" Job of work, sir."

" Where ? "

" Commission going to Iraq, sir."

" Why ? "

" Don't know, sir. But it's going."

" Idiot. Why d'you want the job ? "

" Chap must have a job of work, sir."

Tornado Toby looked him over contemptuously, and his

eye roved from the crown on Hugo's shoulder-strap to the bits of ribbon on Hugo's sleeve and the light in Hugo's eye.

" What's the matter with you as you are ? "

" Fired out, sir.   Sick."

Sir Toby's eye at last came to rest on Hugo's disabled arm. He drew a blank form towards him. I played about with a cigarette-case.

" You can smoke," he snarled.   " What are they ? "

" Virginian, sir."

" Pah ! You can't smoke."

He looked at Hugo.

" Sit down, Major."

" Thank you, sir."

Sir Toby poised pencil over paper.

" Education ? "

" None, sir."

" Where were you educated ? "

" Nowhere, sir."

" Idiot. Where were you at school ? "

" Eton, sir."

" Shake," said Sir Toby.

They shook.

" What qualifications for this job in Iraq ? Think before you answer."

" Thank you, sir."

Hugo thought.

" Can't think of any, sir," he said at last.

" Languages ? French ? "

" Very guarded, sir."

" Can you live on your pay ? "

" Live on anything, sir."

" Hum ! Any private means ? "

" Very private, sir. Never seen them."

" How d'you live in London, then ? "

" Pretty well, sir."

Hugo got that job, and in 1919 he came back to England, very bronzed and lean and gay. But the gaiety did not last very long.

Now Hugo, in the days of his first youth, had been consumed by an ambition to be regarded as the kind of man to whom no chaste woman should be allowed to speak. But nothing ever came of that, he never even succeeded in persuading a chaste woman to cut him ; wherefore in the course of time he came to think of himself as a poor harmless idiot who was liked by every one and loved by none. " Dear Hugo," people said. That was all right in its way, said Hugo, but he was not so young as he had been, and it got, he said, on his nerves a bit. . . .

Soon after he had returned from the Near East, and when the gaiety had worn off, he discovered a pressing desire to Settle Down. And he cast a keen eye round and about the fair land of Britain, and behold ! he saw Miss Shirley St. George—and, still worse, got it into his head that she had seen him. Immediately, he fell in love with Miss Shirley St. George. He had, of course, no money : she had no money. He proposed to her : she refused him. He begged : she laughed. " Dear Hugo," she said.

II

Now Miss Shirley St. George was little sister to George Tarlyon, whom I think I've told you about.

One morning Hugo arose from his bed in the chambers, which he could not afford, and directed the valet, whom he could not afford, to send this telephone message : " Major Cypress desires to see Lord Tarlyon at his club at once."

" Lord Tarlyon," came the answer, " will see Major Cypress at Lord Tarlyon's club at Lord Tarlyon's convenience, and desires Major Cypress to stand at attention when speaking to him."

There are many clubs in Saint James's Street, but there is one in particular, towards the northern part, much referred to by biographers of persons of *ton* of more elegant times. Thither, that morning at a reasonable hour, went Major Cypress, very thoughtfully. Tarlyon was there. Tarlyon was always there, at a reasonable hour.

" Bronx or Martini, Hugo ? "

" Sherry, thanks."

" Nice morning, Hugo. Up late last night ? "

" No," said Major Cypress. " No. I was not up late last night, George. And if you really want to know, I think it is a very classy morning."

" Well," said Tarlyon, " you can't say fairer than that, old man."

Silence. . . .

" Sir," said Major Cypress, " have I your permission to

pay my addresses to your little sister with a view to a matrimonial entanglement ? "

" Ho ! " said Tarlyon.

" What the devil do you mean by saying ' Ho ! ' when I ask you if I can pay my——"

" You can pay her what you like," said Tarlyon sulkily.

" I thank you," said Hugo.

" But," said Tarlyon, " can you pay her anything at all ? Major Cypress, are you in a position to support a wife ? "

" Well, I never ! " gasped Hugo. " I'm on half-pay, man ! "

" Ho ! " said Tarlyon. " I withdraw my consent. I hate to be unkind to majors, but I'm afraid I must. How are you going to live, man ? "

" Can't worry about cheques in Paradise, George."

" Good for you, old Hugo ! Very pretty. Bronx or Martini ? "

" Sherry, thanks. George, you don't know what love is. . . ."

" Keep nothing from me, Hugo. What is love ? Ah, what is love ? I insist on being told. . . ."

" Love," said Hugo, " is proposing to Shirley five times in five months and being rejected five times in five months . . . O God ! "

" What did the girl say ? "

" Say ! She laughed at me, George   Five times running ! ' Dear Hugo . . .' That's what she said ! "

" Poor old Hugo ! "

" She said, George, that she could never, never marry me. . . ."

" Well, damn it, man, you didn't take that lying down, did you ! And you a Major ! "

" I took it lightly, George. I smiled. I distinctly remember smiling. O God ! "

" I *am* so sorry, Hugo ! I really am, you know. Honestly, old man, I'd sooner have you for a brother-in-law than any man alive—except, perhaps a Rockefeller."

" Money, George, isn't everything."

" You're right there, old man. Your money is completely nothing, anyhow. What's your next step ? Orchids ? "

" I am no good at those Dago tricks, George."

" Shirley's very partial to carnations, old man."

"No, George. Not even carnations. She'd laugh at me. She'd say ' dear Hugo ' . . ."

"Well, old man, you might go further and hear worse. It's purple carnations she's especially fond of, by the way."

"George, I'm going to try just once again—without carnations. Just once more, old man. And I thought I'd get your backing."

"Full and square, Hugo, it's with you. The cheek of that girl ! Shall I ring her up and . . ."

"For God's sake don't ! But you're a good fellow, George . . . I say, if she refuses me again I don't know what I'll do."

"Have a drink, old man. Bronx, sherry, or Martini ? "

"No more, thanks."

"Well, best of luck, old man ! "

"Thank you, George. Good-bye."

"See you this evening ? "

"Look here, old man, I don't want to be dramatic and all that, but you may never see me again." And Hugo was stone-cold serious. He was probably the most serious man in England at that moment. "Good-bye, old man. Thanks so much."

"Just a moment." And George Tarlyon went to the writing-table, rapidly wrote a short note, and put the envelope into Hugo's hand.

"Give that to Shirley," said he. But Hugo looked suspicious.

"It's about the theatre to-night," explained Tarlyon. " I'm taking her to *Loyalties*, to improve her mind."

"Ah," said Hugo. "*Loyalties !* Ah ! Jew play. Very improving." Hugo thought weightily.

"Look here," said Hugo, " you know about these things— you were born to be a co-respondent, George. Got any tips to give a chap ? "

"There's only one, old Hugo—take 'em young and treat 'em rough. Hairy, primitive man business, you know. ' Come here, woman, and I'll learn you ' stuff. But it works better with some than with others, and it's rather risky. You might try giving her a thick ear, though—only in fun, of course. Cat playing with mouse *motif*. Tender brutality's your line, Hugo. Many a good woman's been won by a little tender brutality tastefully applied. Just put it to her gently that you'll give her a thick ear unless she accepts you. You can always lead the conversation to ears, somehow. . . . Well, good-bye. Luck, Hugo. Hey, don't forget your hat ! "

III

Miss Shirley St. George lived with her aunt in Audley Square, Tarlyon saying that he was no fit person for a young girl to live with, and the aunt agreeing. They adored each other, George and Shirley.

Towards Audley Square walked Major Cypress, very thoughtfully. Piccadilly had to be crossed, from the new Wolsey building to Mr. Solomon's, the florist. Piccadilly was crossed, miraculously, for the traffic was thick, though genial. A newsboy yelled "Execution of Erskine Childers" into his ear.

" Boy," said Major Cypress, " you must not do that. You must not gloat on death like that, and before perfect strangers, too. And, besides, though you may not have shared Mr. Childers's political opinions, you must admit that he did not die meanly. Here's a shilling for you, and don't let me hear you talking so much about executions in future."

Major Cypress then walked away a pace or two, and stood before the flower-laden windows of Mr. Solomon. The boy watched him.

" Balmy," said the boy.

" Mysterious disappearance of Child ! " yelled the boy.

" Damn it," thought Major Cypress. " I am in love. Oh, damn it ! "

And he stared into the flower-laden windows of Mr. Solomon. Orchids there were therein, yellow and mauve and speckled. Roses, little, tight autumn roses. Pink and white anemones, hyacinths and jonquils, white Dutch lilacs and fat chrysanthemums in white and bronze. And there were carnations—right in the middle of that pageant was a splash of purple carnations.

" Carnations," thought Major Cypress. " And, in particular, purple carnations. But that is not a proper way for an Englishman to win a wife. A little tender brutality is the way. But how to be tenderly brutal ? Hell, I wish I was a Frenchman ! A gardenia, on the other hand, may not come amiss. I will wear a gardenia. It will give me an air of high-minded depravity, which, they say, is attractive to young women."

Major Cypress entered within, and in due course was served with a gardenia.

" For your button-hole, sir ? "

" I suppose so," said Major Cypress. " But not so much vegetable matter with it, please. I want a gardenia, not a garden. Thank you."

" Thank you, sir. Nice morning, sir."

" I doubt it," said Major Cypress.

He wandered westwards, past the Berkeley. The commissionaire at the restaurant doors saluted him. Hugo liked that, and always rather sought it. Tarlyon was of opinion that the commissionaire probably mistook him for some one who had once tipped him, but Hugo said that that was not the point, while to be saluted by commissionaires on Piccadilly was a thing that happened only to very few people.

IV

AT last, very thoughtfully, he came to the house in Audley Square. As he rang, a clock struck one and gave him an idea.

" I will ask her to luncheon at Claridge's," he thought. " It will be a good opening."

Major Cypress waited in the drawing-room for quite a long time. He paced about. The floor was of parquet, mostly uncovered, and so his feet made a noise. He sat down.

" You again ! " cried Shirley.

" How are you, Shirley ? "

" I refuse to tell you, Hugo. I am tired of telling you. Don't I look well ? "

" Hum," said Hugo. He could never answer questions like that.

Shirley came near. She was in a sort of bronze dress of *crêpe marocain*, and her throat glowed very white. Her face Major Cypress did not actually look at, it tempted him so exceedingly. Shirley smiled.

" I will tell you," she smiled, " what you have come to do, Hugo. You have come to take me out to lunch."

" I do wish," said Hugo, " that you would get out of that nasty habit of calling ' luncheon ' lunch. Lunch sounds like a glass of milk and a digestive biscuit."

" Dear Hugo ! "

" Look here, Shirley, don't ever say that again ! "

Shirley was very near, and her white hands were somehow like white flowers. But at her face he did not look.

" Dea——"

" Don't ! " he roared.

Now Shirley was twenty and tall and straight and fair, and when she laughed you saw why servants were polite to her on sight. And oh, she was such a pretty girl ! "

" Hugo," she said, " you are going to propose to me again."

" Oh, am I ! "

" Yes," she said, " you are. And if you say you are not, then you are a liar, and I don't like liars."

Then something happened to Hugo Cypress ; and, after all, he was thirty-four, and she only twenty. He glared down at Shirley St. George, and from his mouth issued reasonable and critical noises, as befitted a man of thirty-four who has offered his hand five times running to a slip of a girl of twenty.

" Shirley," he said, " listen to me. You are a very pretty young lady. I have so far been so shy with you that I have not been able to tell you how beautiful I think you are——"

" Thank you, Hugo," she said very softly. And she tempted him exceedingly, but he continued on his manly way, glaring at a point half-way between her right ear and her left shoulder.

" Nor have I been able to tell you, Shirley, how I love you. That was because I was shy—but I have now finished with being shy. I adore you so frightfully, my dear, that I have made myself a carpet for you to walk on. And you have taken advantage of me, that's what you've done. Carpets get frayed. You have treated me, Shirley, exactly as a heartless, meretricious woman of thirty might treat an infatuated soap-manufacturer. That is, perhaps, because you are used to men being in love with you, and know that they will love you all the more the worse you treat them. Perhaps you are right, Shirley. But I can't bear it any more, and so I am now going to leave this building and your life. . . ." And Hugo went towards the door with a firm step.

" You're not going, Hugo ! " It was a cry.

" I am indeed, Shirley. Good-bye. And God bless you."

" Oh, dear, every man says ' God bless you ! ' " cried Shirley. " It is the most final and most bitter thing they can say, for they say it with a prayer to the devil in their hearts. Go away, Hugo Cypress. I hate you."

" Hugo," she said, " you are going to propose to me again."

" That's why I am saying good-bye, Shirley."

" But surely you can't go without proposing to me for the sixth and last time ! " And that was a cry.

Hugo opened the door ; and he smiled, in a sort of way.

" I thought I couldn't, Shirley—but I find I can."

" But you can't, you simply can't ! " she cried. " Why, I came down to see you on the distinct understanding that you were going to propose to me for the sixth and last time and only *then* going away for ever ! Hugo, you can't do one without the other—it's not fair ! "

" Don't worry, little Shirley. The day is yet young, and some one else is sure to propose to you in the course of it. You will observe, my dear, that I am being cynical, after the manner of all rejected young men."

" But, Hugo, I want *you* to—for the sixth and last time, dear, just to see what I'll say ! " And she tempted him exceedingly with her sunlit face.

" That's just it, Shirley. I know what you'll say. Good-bye."

" Oh, oh ! " cried Shirley. " How awful men are ! And how d'you know what I'll say, Hugo ? You are a clever chap, aren't you ? Are you a psycho-analyst, Hugo ? Can you tell what is passing in a woman's mind by looking at her instep ? And for heaven's sake don't go on standing in that doorway looking like a draught ! "

" Sorry, Shirley." And Hugo faded away round the angle of the door and was closing it behind him.

" Hugo, how dare you go like that ! " And that was the most frantic cry of all ; and Hugo's face reappeared round the angle of the door, and it was a rather bewildered face

" Well, damn it, my dear, I must go somehow ! "

" Yes, but you know very well you can't live without me—don't you, Hugo ? Now answer truthfully, Hugo."

" Well, you know, since you came in this morning, I've been thinking it over——"

" But how awful you are to admit that you can think of anything when you're with Shirley ! "

" There you go ! " he cried harshly. " Making a fool of me ! "

" But, my darling, I must make someth——"

" What was that you said ? " he snapped.

" Have you gone mad ? Didn't you hear me ? "

" Child, did you or did you not call me ' darling ' ? "

" Why, so I did !   I'm so sorry, Hugo. . . ."

Hugo Cypress advanced across the room and towered above Shirley St. George.

" Are you playing the fool, Shirley ?

" I   am   playing   for   time,   my   darling — lunch-time. Luncheon-time, I mean."

She giggled.

Now Shirley was not given to giggling. . . .

No one had ever seen Shirley carrying an umbrella, and no one had ever heard Shirley giggling.

" Ho ! " muttered Major Cypress.

" Don't gargle in my aunt's drawing-room, Hugo ! "

" I'm thinking, Shirley."

" Don't think ! " she cried sharply.

" Well," he began, and stopped.

" Wipe your forehead, dear ; you're rather hot."

Hugo wiped his forehead.

" Look here, Shirley, supposing—just supposing—that I so far forget myself as to prop——"

" Oh, Hugo ! "   And she clapped her hand—little Shirley ! " You must !   For the sixth and last time . . . just to make it even numbers ! "

Hugo's face was as white as his gardenia.

" For the sixth and last time, Shirley, will you marry me ? "

As she stood, with the palms of her hands pressed down on the table and her little face thrown back, she was like a dove, still and absorbed.   She was absorbed in something that was Hugo, yet in something that was much more than Hugo.   And then her lips trembled a little ; they whispered :

" Oh, Hugo, I have been such a beast !   But you are so sweet that I simply couldn't help it ! "

He didn't understand.

But he understood when suddenly she crooked an arm around his neck and brought his face down to hers, and he saw that her eyes were wet. . . .

" My God ! " he said, and kissed her bravely.

" Of course," she whispered.   " Of course. . . .

" No, not like that," she whispered.   " Not as though I were your sister.   I beg you to observe that I am not your sister.   Yes, properly, dear.   Oh, I do like you frightfully Hugo. . . ."

Then quite a lot of things happened at the same time ; and then he cried :

" But why didn't you tell me before ? "

" Because I didn't realise, my darling. I didn't know I loved you—and how can a girl know a thing like that ? Oh, Hugo, you are so sweet ! What fun to have you for keeps ! And it will be nice to chew bits of you now and then—Oh, what fun we'll have ! Dear Hugo. . . ."

" And you said, Shirley, that you would never, never marry me ! "

" I didn't know myself, dear—nor you ! Until, after the fifth time, when you went away saying that you would never come back. And then I was very sorry, Hugo."

" Oh, by the way," he said, " here's a note from George—about taking you to *Loyalties* to-night." .

She read the note.

" Oh ! " she said.

" What does he say ? " he asked.

She tore up the note.

" Only that he's got a box for *Loyalties*, and that I may ask whom I like——"

" Thanks so much, Shirley. I'd love to come. It will improve my mind."

Now this was the note from George Tarlyon to his little sister, Shirley St. George :

" Shirley, how dare you go about London refusing to marry such of my friends, if any, who ask you ? ' Never, never,' indeed ! Remember, Shirley, that there's only one bigger lie than ' never, never,' and that is ' always, always.' "

" Oh ! " thought Shirley. " Fat lot he knows about it ! " But all the same, she never said " always, always " ; she just thought it.

The rest of this story is quite uninteresting, for Hugo and Shirley were happy ever after ; which is, unfortunately, more than most people are, what with first one thing and then another. . . .

ARNOLD BENNETT (1867–1931), *who will always be remembered as the chronicler of the Five Towns, was a man of great ambition, which he lived to see amply satisfied. He had a boundless relish for life. Like Balzac, Bennett, who had known what poverty meant, showed a proclivity in his novels and tales to dwell on the splendour and glitter of wealth in such books as " Imperial Palace," and " The Grand Babylon Hotel." etc.*

THE DOG

THIS is a scandalous story. It scandalized the best people in Bursley ; some of them would wish it forgotten. But since I have begun to tell it I may as well finish. Moreover, like most tales whispered behind fans and across club-tables, it carries a high and valuable moral. The moral—I will let you have it at once—is that those who love in glass houses should pull down the blinds.

I

HE had got his collar on safely ; it bore his name—Ellis Carter. Strange name for a dog, perhaps ; and perhaps it was even more strange that his collar should be white. But such dogs are not common dogs. He tied his necktie exquisitely ; caressed his hair again with two brushes ; curved his young moustache, and then assumed his waistcoat and his coat ; the trousers had naturally preceded the collar. He beheld the suit in the glass, and saw that it was good. And it was not built in London, either. There are tailors in Bursley. And in particular there is the dog's tailor. Ask the dog's tailor, as the dog once did, whether he can really do as well as London, and he will smile on you with gentle pity ; he will not stoop to utter the obvious Yes. He may casually inform you that, if he is not in London himself, the explanation is that he has reasons for preferring Bursley. He is the social equal of all his clients. He belongs to the dogs' club. He knows, and everybody knows, that he is a first-class tailor with a first-class connection, and no dog would dare to condescend to him. He is a great creative artist ; the dogs who

288

wear his clothes may be said to interpret his creations. Now, Ellis was a great interpretative artist, and the tailor recognized the fact. When the tailor met Ellis on Duck Bank greatly wearing a new suit, the scene was impressive. It was as though Elgar had stopped to hear Paderewski play *Pomp and Circumstance* on the piano.

Ellis descended from his bedroom into the hall, took his straw hat, chose a stick, and went out into the portico of the new large house on the Hawkins, near Oldcastle. In the neighbourhood of the Five Towns no road is more august, more correct, more detached, more umbrageous, than the Hawkins. M.P.'s live there. It is the link between the aristocratic and antique aloofness of Oldcastle and the solid commercial prosperity of the Five Towns. Ellis adorned the portico. Young (a bare twenty-two), fair, handsome, smiling, graceful, well-built, perfectly groomed, he was an admirable and a characteristic specimen of the race of dogs which, with the modern growth of luxury and the Luxurious Spirit, has become so marked a phenomenon in the social development of the once barbarous Five Towns.

When old Jack Carter (reputed to be the best turner that Bursley ever produced) started a little potbank near St Peter's Church in 1861—he was then forty, and had saved two hundred pounds—he little dreamt that the supreme and final result after forty years would be the dog. But so it was. Old Jack Carter had a son John Carter, who married at twenty-five and lived at first on twenty-five shillings a week, and enthusiastically continued the erection of the fortune which old Jack had begun. At thirty-three, after old Jack's death, John became a Town Councillor. At thirty-six he became Mayor and the father of Ellis, and the recipient of a silver cradle. Ellis was his wife's maiden name. At forty-two he built the finest earthenware manufactory in Bursley, down by the canal-side at Shawport. At fifty-two he had been everything that a man can be in the Five Towns—from County Councillor to President of the Society for the Prosecution of Felons. Then Ellis left school and came to the works to carry on the tradition, and his father suddenly discovered him. The truth was that John Carter had been so laudably busy with the affairs of his town and county that he had nearly forgotten his family. Ellis, in the process of achieving doghood, soon taught his father a thing or two. And John learnt. John could manage a public meeting, but he could not manage Ellis. Besides, there was plenty of money ; and Ellis was so ingratiating, and had curly hair that somehow won sympathy. And, after all, Ellis was not such a duffer as all that at the works. John knew other people's sons who were worse. And Ellis could keep order in the paintresses' " shops " as order had never been kept there before.

John sometimes wondered what old Jack would have said about Ellis and his friends, those handsome dogs, those fine dandies, who taught to the Five Towns the virtue of grace and of style and of dash, who went up to London—some of them even went to Paris—and brought back civilization to the Five Towns, who removed from the Five Towns the reproach of being uncouth and behind the times. Was the outcome of two generations of unremitting toil merely Ellis ? (Ellis had several pretty sisters, but they did not count.) John could only guess at what old Jack's attitude might have been towards Ellis—Ellis, who had his shirts made to measure. He knew exactly what was Ellis's attitude towards the ideals of old Jack, old Jack the class-leader, who wore clogs till he was thirty, and dined in his shirt-sleeves at one o'clock to the end of his life.

Ellis quitted the portico, ran down the winding garden-path, and jumped neatly and fearlessly on to an electric tram-car as it passed at the rate of fifteen miles an hour. The car was going to Hanbridge, and it was crowded with the joy of life ; Ellis had to stand on the step. This was the Saturday before the first Monday in August, and therefore the formal opening of Kynpe Wakes, the most carnivalesque of all the carnivals which enliven the four seasons in the Five Towns. It is still called Knype Wakes, because once Knype over-shadowed Hanbridge in importance ; but its headquarters are now quite properly at Hanbridge, the hub, the centre, the Paris of the Five Towns—Hanbridge, the county borough of sixty odd thousand inhabitants. It is the festival of the masses that old Jack sprang from, and every genteel person who can leaves the Five Towns for the seaside at the end of July. Nevertheless, the district is never more crammed than at Knype Wakes. And, of course, genteel persons, whom circumstances have forced to remain in the Five Towns, sally out in the evening to " do " the Wakes in a spirit of tolerant condescension. Ellis was in this case. His parents and sisters were at Llandudno, and he had been left in charge of the works and of the new house. He was always free ; he could always pity the bondage of his sisters ; but now he was more free than ever—he was absolutely free. Imagine the delicious feeling that surged in his heart as he prepared to plunge himself doggishly into the wild ocean of the Wakes. By the way, in that heart was the image of a girl.

II

HE stepped off the car on the outskirts of Hanbridge, and strolled gently and spectacularly into the joyous town. The streets became more and more crowded and noisy as he approached the market-place, and in Crown Square tramcars from the four quarters of the earth discharged tramloads of humanity at the rate of two a minute, and then glided off again empty in search of more humanity. The lower portion of Crown Square was devoted to tramlines ; in the upper portion the Wakes began, and spread into the market-place, and thence by many tentacles into all manner of streets.

No Wakes is better than Knype Wakes ; that is to say, no Wakes is more ear-splitting, more terrific, more dizzying, or more impassable. When you go to Knype Wakes you get stuck in the midst of an enormous crowd, and you see round-abouts, swings, switchbacks, myrioramas, atrocity booths, quack dentists, shooting-galleries, cocoanut-shies, and bazaars, all around you. Every establishment is jewelled, gilded, and electrically lighted ; every establishment has an orchestra, most often played by steam and conducted by a stoker ; every establishment has a steam-whistle, which shrieks at the be-ginning and at the end of each round or performance. You stand fixed in the multitude listening to a thousand orchestras and whistles, with the roar of machinery and the merry din of car-bells, and the popping of rifles for a background of noise. Your eyes are charmed by the whirling of a million lights and the mad whirling of millions of beautiful girls and happy youths under the lights. For the roundabouts rule the scene ; the roundabouts take the money. The supreme desire of the revellers is to describe circles, either on horseback or in yachts, either simple circles or complex circles, either up and down or straight along, but always circles. And it is as though in-ventors had sat up at nights puzzling their brains how best to make revellers seasick while keeping them equidistant from a steam-orchestra. . . . Then the crowd solidly lurches, and you find yourself up against a dentist, or a firm of wrestlers, or a roundabout, or an ice-cream refectory, and you take what comes. You have begun to " do " the Wakes. The splendid insanity seizes you. The lights, the colours, the explosions, the shrieks, the feathered hats, the pretty faces as they fly past, the gilding, the statuary, the August night, and the mingling of a thousand melodies in a counterpoint beyond the dreams of Wagner—these things have stirred the sap of life in you, have shown you how fine it is to be alive, and, careless and free, have caught up your spirit into a heaven from which you scornfully survey the year of daily toil between one Wakes and another as the eagle scornfully surveys the potato-field. Your nostrils dilate—nay, matters reach such a pass that, even if you are genteel, you forget to condescend.

III

AFTER Ellis had had the correct drink in the private bar up the passage at the Turk's Head, and after he had plunged into the crowd and got lost in it, and submitted good-humouredly to the frequent ordeal of the penny squirt as administered by adorable creatures in bright skirts, he found himself cast up by the human ocean on the macadam shore near a shooting-gallery. This was no ordinary shooting-gallery. It was one of Jenkins's affairs (Jenkins of Manchester), and on either side of it Jenkins's Venetian gondolas and Jenkins's Mexican mustangs were whizzing round two of Jenkins's orchestras at twopence a time, and taking thirty-two pounds an hour. This gallery was very different from the old galleries, in which you leaned against a brass bar and shot up a kind of a drain. This gallery was a large and brilliant room, with the front wall taken out. It was hung with mirrors and cretonnes, it was richly carpeted, and, of course, it was lighted by electricity. Carved and gilded tables bore a whole armoury of weapons. You shot at tobacco-pipes, twisting and stationary, at balls poised on jets of water, and at proper targets. In the corners of the saloon, near the open, were large crimson plush lounges, on which you lounged after the fatigue of shopping.

A pink-clad girl, young and radiant, had the concern in charge.

She was speeding a party of bankrupt shooters, when she caught sight of Ellis. Ellis answered her smile, and strolled up to the booth with a countenance that might have meant anything. You can never tell what a dog is thinking.

" 'Ello ! " said the girl prettily (or, rather, she shouted prettily, having to compete with the two orchestras). " You here again ? "

The truth was that Ellis had been there on the previous night, and he had come again to-night expressly in order to see her ; but he would not have admitted, even to himself, that he had come expressly in order to see her ; in his mind it was just a chance that he might see her. She was a jolly girl. (We are gradually approaching the scandalous part.)

" What a jolly frock ! " he said, when he had shot five celluloid balls in succession off a jet of water.

Smiling, she mechanically took a ball out of the basket and let it roll down the conduit to the fountain.

" Do you think so ? " she replied, smoothing the fluffy muslin apron with her small hands, black from contact with the guns. " That one I wore last night was my second-best. I only wear this on Saturdays and Mondays."

He nodded like a connoisseur. The sixth ball had sprung up to the top of the jet. He removed it with the certainty of a King's Prize winner, and she complimented him.

" Ah ! " he said, " you should have seen me before I took to smoking and drinking ! "

She laughed freely. She was always showing her fine teeth. And she had such a frank, jolly countenance, not exactly pretty—better than pretty. She was a little short and a little plump, and she wore a necklace round her neck, a ring on her dainty, dirty finger, and a watch-bracelet on her wrist.

" Why ! " she exclaimed. " How old are you ? "

" How old are *you* ? " he retorted.

Dogs do not give things away like that.

" I'm nineteen," she said submissively. " At least, I shall be come Martinmas."

And she yawned.

" Well," he said, " a little girl like you ought to be in bed."

" Sunday to-morrow," she observed.

" Aren't you glad you're English ? " he remarked. " If you were in Paris you'd have to work Sundays too."

" Not me ! " she said. " Who told you that ? Have you been to Paris ? "

" No," he admitted cautiously ; " but a friend of mine has, and he told me. He came back only last week, and he says they keep open Sundays, and all night sometimes. Sunday is the great day over there."

"Well," said the girl kindly, "don't you believe it. The police wouldn't allow it. I know what the police are."

More shooters entered the saloon. Ellis had finished his dozen ; he sank into a lounge, and elegantly lighted a cigarette, and watched her serve the other marksmen. She was decidedly charming, and so jolly—with him. He noticed with satisfaction that with the other marksmen she showed a certain high reserve.

They did not stay long, and when they were gone she came across to the lounge and gazed at him provocatively.

"Dashed if she hasn't taken a fancy to me ! "

The thought ran through him like lightning.

"Well ? " she said.

"What do you do with yourself Sundays ? " he asked her.

"Oh, sleep."

"All day ? "

"All morning."

"What do you do in the afternoon ? "

"Oh, nothing."

She laughed gaily.

"Come out with me, eh ? "

"To-morrow ?   Oh, I should LOVE TO ! " she cried.

Her voice expanded into large capitals because by a singular chance both the neighbouring orchestras stopped momentarily together, and thus gave her shout a fair field. The effect was startling. It startled Ellis. He had not for an instant expected that she would consent. Never, dog though he was, had he armed a girl out on any afternoon, to say nothing of Sunday afternoon, and Knype's Wakes Sunday at that ! He had talked about girls at the club. He understood the theory. But the practice——

The foundation of England's greatness is that Englishmen hate to look fools. The fear of being taken for a ninny will spur an Englishman to the most surprising deeds of courage. Ellis said " Good ! " with apparent enthusiasm, and arranged to be waiting for her at half-past two at the Turk's Head. Then he left the saloon and struck out anew into the ocean. He wanted to think it over.

Once, painful to relate, he had thoughts of failing to keep the appointment. However, she was so jolly and frank. And what a fancy she must have taken to him ! No, he would see it through.

IV

IF anybody had prophesied to Ellis that he would be driving out a Wakes girl in a dogcart that Sunday afternoon he would have laughed at the prophet ; but so it occurred. He arrived at the Turk's Head at two twenty-five. She was there before him, dressed all in blue, except the white shoes and stockings, weighing herself on the machine in the yard. She showed her teeth, told him she weighed nine stone one, and abruptly asked him if he could drive. He said he could. She clapped her hands and sprang off the machine. Her father had bought a new mare the day before, and it was in the Turk's Head stable, and the yardman said it wanted exercise, and there was a dogcart and harness idling about, and, in short, Ellis should drive her to Sneyd Park, which she had long desired to see.

Ellis wished to ask questions, but the moment did not seem auspicious.

In a few moments the new mare, a high and somewhat frisky bay, with big shoulders, was in the shafts of a high, green dogcart. When asked if he could drive, Ellis ought to have answered : " That depends—on the horse." Many men can tool a fifteen-year-old screw down a country lane who would hesitate to get up behind a five-year-old animal (in need of exercise) for a spin down Broad Street, Hanbridge, on Knype Wakes Sunday. Ellis could drive ; he could just drive. His father had always steadfastly refused to keep horses, but the fathers of other dogs were more progressive, and Ellis had had opportunities. He knew how to take the reins, and get up, and give the office ; indeed, he had read a handbook on the subject. So he took the reins and got up, and the Wakes girl got up.

He chirruped. The mare merely backed.

" Give 'er 'er mouth," said the yardman disgustedly.

" Oh ! " said Ellis, and slackened the reins, and the mare pawed forward.

Then he had to turn her in the yard, and get her and the dogcart down the passage. He doubted whether he should do it, for the passage seemed a size too small. However, he did it, or the mare did it, and the entire organism swerved across a portion of the foot-path into Broad Street.

For quite a quarter of a mile down Broad Street Ellis blushed, and kept his gaze between the mare's ears. However, the mare went beautifully. You could have driven her with a silken thread, so it seemed. And then the dog, growing accustomed to his prominence up there on the dogcart, began to be a bit doggy. He knew the little thing's age and weight, but, really, when you take a girl out for a Sunday spin you want more information about her than that. He asked her name, and her name was Jenkins—Ada. She was the great Jenkins's daughter.

(" Oh," thought Ellis, " the deuce you are ! ")

" Father's gone to Manchester for the day, and aunt's looking after me," said Ada.

" Do they know you've come out—like this ? "

" Not much ! " She laughed deliciously. " How lovely it is ! "

At Knype they drew up before the Five Towns Hotel and descended. The Five Towns Hotel is the greatest hotel in North Staffordshire. It has two hundred rooms. It would not entirely disgrace Northumberland Avenue. In the Five Towns it is august, imposing, and unique. They had a lemonade there, and proceeded. A clock struck ; it was a near thing. No more refreshments now until they had passed the three-mile limit !

Yes ! Not two hundred yards farther on she spied an ice-cream shop in Fleet Road, and Ellis learnt that she adored ice-cream. The mare waited patiently outside in the thronged street.

After that the pilgrimage to Sneyd was punctuated with ice-creams. At the Stag at Sneyd (where, among ninety-and-nine dogcarts, Ellis's dogcart was the brightest green of them all) Ada had another lemonade, and Ellis had something else. They saw the Park, and Ada giggled charmingly her appreciation of its beauty. The conversation throughout consisted chiefly of Ada's teeth. Ellis said he would return by a different route, and he managed to get lost. How anyone driving to Hanbridge from Sneyd could arrive at the mining village of Silverton is a mystery. But Ellis arrived there, and he ultimately came out at Hillport, the aristocratic suburb of Bursley, where he had always lived till the last year. He feared recognition there, and his fear was justified. Some silly ass, a schoolmate, cried, " Go it ! " as the machine bowled along, and the mischief was that the mare, startled, went it.

She went it down the curving hill, and the vehicle after her, like a kettle tied to a dog's tail.

Ellis winked stoutly at Ada when they reached the bottom, and gave the mare a piece of his mind, to which she objected. As they crossed the railway-bridge a goods-train ran underneath and puffed smoke into the mare's eyes. She set her ears back.

"Would you!" cried Ellis authoritatively, and touched her with the whip (he had forgotten the handbook).

He scarcely touched her, but you never know where you are with any horse. That mare, which had been a mirror of all the virtues all the afternoon, was off like a rocket. She overtook an electric car as if it had been standing still. Ellis sawed her mouth; he might as well have sawed the funnel of a locomotive. He had meant to turn off and traverse Bursley by secluded streets, but he perceived that safety lay solely in letting her go straight ahead up the very steep slope of Oldcastle Street into the middle of the town. It would be an amazing mare that galloped to the top of Oldcastle Street! She galloped nearly to the top, and then Ellis began to get hold of her a bit.

"Don't be afraid," he said masculinely to Ada.

And, conscious of victory, he jerked the mare to the left to avoid an approaching car. . . .

The next instant they were anchored against the roots of a lamp-post. When Ellis saw the upper half of the lamp-post bent down at right angles, he could not believe that he and his dogcart had done that, especially as neither the mare, nor the dogcart, nor its freight, was damaged. The machine was merely jammed, and the mare, satisfied, stood quiet, breathing rapidly.

But Ada Jenkins was crying.

And the car stopped a moment to observe. And then a number of chapel-goers on their way to the Sytch Chapel, which the Carter family still faithfully attended, joined the scene; and then a policeman.

Ellis sat like a stuck pig in the dogcart. He knew that speech was demanded of him, but he did not know where to begin.

The worst thing of all was the lamp-post, bent, moveless, unnatural, atrociously comic, accusing him.

The affair was over the town in a minute; the next morning it reached Llandudno. Ellis Carter had been out on the spree

with *a Wakes girl* in a dogcart on Sunday afternoon, and had
got into such a condition that he had driven into a lamp-post
at the top of Oldcastle Street just as people were going into
chapel.

The lamp-post remained bent for three days—a fearful
warning to all dogs that doggishness has limits.

If it had not been a dogcart, and such a high, green dogcart ; if it had been, say, a brougham, or even a cab ! If it
had not been Sunday ! And, granting Sunday, if it had not
been just as people were going into chapel ! If he had not
chosen that particular lamp-post, visible both from the market-
place and St Luke's Square ! If he had only contrived to
destroy a less obtrusive lamp-post in some unfrequented
street ! And if it had not been a Wakes girl—if the reprobate
had only selected for his guilty amours an actress from one
of the touring companies, or even a star from the Hanbridge
Empire—yea, or even a local barmaid ! But *a Wakes girl !*

Ellis himself saw the enormity of his transgression. He
lay awake astounded by his own doggishness.

And yet he had seldom felt less doggy than during that
trip. It seemed to him that doggishness was not the glorious
thing he had thought. However, he cut a heroic figure at
the dogs' club. Every admiring face said : " Well, you *have*
been going the pace ! We always knew you were a hot 'un,
but, really——"

V

ON the following Friday evening, when Ellis jumped off the
car opposite his home on the Hawkins, he saw in the road,
halted, a train of vast and queer-shaped waggons in charge of
two traction-engines. They were painted on all sides with
the great name of Jenkins. They contained Jenkins's round-
abouts and shooting-saloons, on their way to rouse the joy
of life in other towns. And he perceived in front of the portico
the high, green dogcart and the lamp-post-destroying mare.

He went in. The family had come home that afternoon.
Sundry of his sisters greeted him with silent horror on their
faces in the hall. In the breakfast-room, which gave off the
drawing-room, was his mother in the attitude of an intent
listener. She spoke no word.

And Ellis listened, too.

" Yes," a very powerful and raucous voice was saying in

the drawing-room, " I reckoned I'd call and tell ye myself,
Mister Carter, what I thought on it. My gell, a motherless
gell, but brought up respectable ; sixth standard at Whalley
Range Board School ; and her aunt a strict God-fearing
woman ! And here your son comes along and gets hold of
the girl while her aunt's at the special service for Wakes folks
in Bethesda Chapel, and runs off with her in my dogcart with
one of my hosses, and raises a scandal all o'er the Five Towns.
God bless my soul, mister ! I tell'n ye I hardly liked to open
o' Monday afternoon, I was that ashamed ! And I packed
Ada off to Manchester. It seems to me that if the upper
classes, as they call 'em—the immoral classes *I* call 'em—'ud
look after themselves a bit instead o' looking after other people
so much, things might be a bit better, Mister Carter. I dare
say you think it's nothing as your son should go about ruining
the reputation of any decent, respectable girl as he happens
to fancy, Mister Carter ; but this is what I say. I say——"

Mr Carter was understood to assert, in his most pacific
and pained public-meeting voice, that he regretted, infinitely
regretted——

Mrs Carter, weeping, ran out of the breakfast-room.

And soon afterwards the traction-engines rumbled off, and
the high, green dogcart followed them.

Ellis sat spell-bound.

He heard the parlour maid go into the drawing-room and
announce, " Tea is ready, sir ! " and then his father's dry
cough.

And then the parlour maid came into the breakfast-room :
" Tea is ready, Mr Ellis ! "

Oh, the meal !

GEORGE WARWICK DEEPING (1877-)
*abandoned, while still a young man, his career as
a doctor for that of a successful novelist. When
war broke out he joined the R.A.M.C. and
served in Gallipoli, Egypt, and France. It is
interesting to note that his best seller "Sorrell
and Son," which has been adapted both as a
silent and a talking film, owes much of its
fine realism to his early training in medicine.*

THE GIRL ON THE MOUNTAIN

IT was hot on the steep mule-path that zigzagged up the
southern slope of Monte Verde to the sanctuary of Santa
Maria in Montorio, and David Flemming, with all his artist's
gear upon his back, paused every hundred yards or so to catch
the sea breeze, and to look back upon Villadoro, that pleasant,
frivolous, and rather artificial little town lying white at the
edge of its blue bay. There was shade here and there where
the grey, stone-paved path ran under old ilexes and stone
pines. The olive terraces were purpled with violets. Ever
and again the white pinnacles of Santa Maria glimmered above
the rocks and trees.

David Flemming broke the climb to drink a glass of
vermouth at the little green-shuttered osteria lying half-way
up the mountain. He sat under a pergola covered with roses
and vines, and his lean and rather humorous face was sad.
For even the pleasant comedies of life were tinged with pathos,
and Flemming's laughter was often tempted to end in tears.
He had discovered the utter loneliness of life, the loneliness
that overtakes a man when death has snatched from him the
other half of his soul. It was more than a year since his wife
had died. The first anguish had passed, but the loneliness
remained. They had been comrades ; life had been an
intimate interweaving of the sensitive threads of two person-
alities. Then fate had torn the fabric of life asunder, and left
Flemming's career all loose and ravelled.

Moving on again, he reached at last the broad walk between
huge ilexes that led to the soaring steps and the white façade
of Santa Maria. But Flemming did not stop at the sanctuary ;
he crossed the forecourt, passed round under an arch, and

struck a path that climbed to the top of Monte Verde, three hundred feet nearer the clouds.

The path was steep, mere flat rocks and stones piled together, and it ran through a pine wood where the wind made a plaintive murmuring. And more than once, as he climbed through sunlight and shadow, Flemming fancied that he heard the sound of someone singing. It was just a voice that came and went, uttering a few wayward notes, like the deep throat notes of a bird.

Then the sanctuary bells started jangling just as Flemming saw the blue summit sky through the trees. There would be all the glory of the view up yonder, the snow peaks, the turquoise sea, the wooded headlands, the rocky valley black with shadows. Moreover, lunch and a bottle of wine were not to be scoffed at after such a scramble.

The summit came suddenly, a smooth cap of turf with a big flat stone perched in the centre like some primitive altar. All around the sky seemed to hang like a blue tent, but that grey stone on the top of Monte Verde was coloured red, as though someone had lit a sacrificial fire.

Flemming stopped dead. Here was the unexpected on the top of a mountain, a woman kneeling by the great stone, her body flung forward over it, her head hidden in her arms. She was wearing some loose sort of red jacket, and her skirt was of white linen, short, and showing bare ankles. A mass of black hair was stirred by the wind, but she herself was absolutely motionless, save for the slight fluttering of her white skirt.

Flemming was posed. He took her to be a peasant girl who had climbed to the top of Monte Verde to cry her heart out over some love affair. Her back was towards him, and the choice seemed to be his, the choice of leaving her in possession, and losing the crown of the morning's climb.

But chance saved him that. The girl raised herself, turned, saw him, and started to her feet. And Flemming, if he had been surprised at finding her there on the top of Monte Verde, was doubly astonished when he saw her face.

For she was the child of another hemisphere, an islander, dark skinned, with a mass of dusky hair, large eyes, and a splendid throat. And Flemming, in his astonishment, was conscious of two things—that he had surprised her in some tragic moment, and that her eyes were empty of tears.

He was conscious of having blundered, conscious of a kind of resentfulness in her expression, and with an Englishman's habit of blurting out things in his own language, he tried to put her and himself at ease.

"I'm sorry. I didn't know anyone would be on the top of Monte Verde."

He realised instantly that the chances were against her knowing English, and that a man of more poise would have strolled to the edge of the plateau and admired the view.

"Monte Verde does not belong to me. The mountains should be free to us all, should they not?"

She answered him in English ; spoke it, indeed, as though it were her natural tongue. And she smiled slightly, perhaps at his most obvious astonishment.

"No doubt you have come from Villadoro, and you have come to paint."

Again Flemming was shocked by the discovery that it was the girl who was smoothing away the embarrassment of the moment and putting him at his ease. Her voice sounded very deep and rich, and though she was quite young there was a maturity about her that hinted at the woman of the world. Flemming, a "sensitive" himself, was aware of the palpable breed in her, a frank and gracious ease of manner that could keep its dignity in the face of such a coincidence. He awoke to the fact that here was something amazing and unique, a mere child who could carry off all the bizarrerie of her clothes, of her loose, black hair and her bare ankles, and remain convincing, natural, absolutely herself.

"It is a long climb from Villadoro," he said, "and I wanted to try and make a rather unique sketch."

By way of settling the situation, he began to unload himself, to pull out the legs of his collapsible easel, and to prepare ostentatiously for work. The way lay open for the girl to smile at him and retreat. But she did nothing of the kind. She sat herself down on the flat stone and watched him with perfect composure.

"Is it not funny, I met an English girl up here one day, two of us on the top of the mountain, and we did not speak? Two intelligent creatures with tongues ! And yet—I like the English."

He glanced at her and was struck by the soft charm of her manner. She seemed to have put some sad thing behind her ; her face had cleared, and for the first time he realised her beauty. There was nothing negroid about her. Her skin had a dusky pallor ; her face was refined in spite of its breadth ; her eyes were a clear blue and heavily lashed. But it was the physical perfection of her that appealed to the artist in him, the splendid throat, the modelling of the forearm and ankle, the generous grace of her very feminine figure. And she seemed quite unconscious of it all, a kind of dusky island queen, with all the subtle charm of a fine culture added to the simple insouciance of her southern nature.

She was amazing. The loose hair, the bare ankles, the red and white of her clothes seemed inevitable. Somehow he could not imagine her in a Paris frock, and yet he had an idea that she wore such creations.

" I think we are two very sensible people," he said suddenly.

He was recovering his poise, his sympathetic sense of humour.

Her eyes brightened to his.

" Well—perhaps. And I am glad you came. I wanted some distraction."

He saw a tremor as of pain pass over her face, but it cleared instantly.

" Oh, the sun—the sun—and the sea ! I was born on an island, a surf child."

" Is it rude to be curious ? "

" Why should it be ? Isn't life worth living as long as one remains inquisitive ? I was born at Hawaii."

He nodded. His little easel was set up, and he had rolled a round stone forward from the edge of the plateau to serve as a seat.

" I say, I am going to be very forward. But there is only one really inevitable thing for me to do."

" And that ? "

" Paint you—there—on that rock. May I ? "

She gave a charming lift of the head.

" Why not ? And may I talk ? It is such a silent world sometimes. I chatter to the mountains, but they cannot answer me back."

So Flemming painted her, while the bells of Santa Maria in Montorio began their midday chiming. It was a merry sanctuary, and the bells seemed to dance in the mountain air, riotously, and with gay abandonment. The Lady of the Mountain was no joyless prude, and seemed to love laughter rather than melancholy.

The chiming came to an end with one long, deep-tongued boom of the big bell.

" And I have kept still through it all. Now, listen ; it is noon."

She held up her hand, and through the silence they heard all the mountain and valley bells striking, like so many distant voices. Each white campanile for miles around took up the cry, and the echoes seemed to tremble in the deep valleys between the mountains.

Not only did Flemming paint her portrait, but he discovered her name and where she lived. She had been christened Eulalie, and the name had been changed to Lalia by her Hawaiian playmates. She lived at Acqua Dolce, a rather famous little villa in the river valley below, and Flemming remembered that Acqua Dolce was let to one Fenton Bale. He noticed that she was wearing a plain gold ring, and the obvious inference was that she was Bale's wife.

He seized a chance thought that suggested itself.

" I have wanted to paint in the gardens of Acqua Dolce. I am wondering if I can get leave."

She was silent a moment and her face became overclouded.

" My husband is not fond of strangers. I will ask him."

" But I am not going to thrust myself in——"

" I will ask him. Where are you staying ? "

" At the Hotel Regina, Villadoro—David Flemming."

She smiled at him rather wistfully, and in a short while he was alone on the summit of Monte Verde.

David Flemming went and sat on the big stone where he had seen her prostrate, her head in her arms. That there was some great sorrow in her life he felt convinced. Her courage had set it aside for the moment, and she faced him as though life hid no tragedy, no sinister shadows that darkened the sun.

Why had she come to such a lonely place ? And how strange the whole business seemed—a Hawaiian girl on the summit of an Italian mountain !

If the great stone could have spoken it might have startled Flemming with strange words, the words of a woman in anguish, who had fled to some solitary place where passions might cool themselves.

" O God, I shall kill him. Help me, or I shall kill him ! "

While Flemming ate his lunch and looked at the snow peaks and the sea, Lalia Bale raced down the mule-path, her string-soled shoes giving her a grip of the stones. She moved like a wild thing, agile, graceful, and with all the suppleness of an island child taught to swim through the surf. It was an hour after noon when she reached the bridge across the stream in the valley, and found herself at the iron gates of Acqua Dolce. An avenue of cypresses led up towards the villa hidden in its gardens which were full of the sound of running water.

" Hallo ! Where the devil have you been ? "

A man was leaning over the balustrade at the top of a terrace where clipped box trees grew in huge stone jars. He was a thin, yellow-faced man, with sunken cheeks and dull eyes. The muscles showed in his throat, and there was something about him that suggested a predaceous and hungry bird. His face was not the face of a healthy man ; it was unwholesome, irritable, violent, with shadows under his eyes, and a kind of loose and cynical cruelty hanging about the mouth.

The girl answered him very quietly, though his voice had sent a shiver of anger through her, that discordant voice like the harsh cry of a bird.

" I have been up Monte Verde."

" Damn it—what rot ! I've been waiting an hour for lunch——"

" You need not have waited."

She knew that he had done it to gain a grievance against her. That was Fenton Bale's way. He would spite himself in order to scold at her—and worse.

She climbed the steps leading to the terrace, and his panama hat moved along above the balustrade. Her pallor had increased. She was holding herself in, clenching her hands till the nails hurt her palms.

That jeering profile of his waited at the top of the steps.

" Come on ! "

His eyes flared.

" You've been out again in that get-up. Why don't you dress like a Christian ? You might be doing a cinema show."

She knew the man was ill, that he had drugged himself into evil decrepitude. And once she had thought she had loved him, in those Hawaiian days when she could swim and sail a boat.

" Don't, Fenton. I am so tired of it all."

" Tired ! "

He laughed.

" Tired ! And what have I spent on you ? Paris, London, Vienna—damn it, and you cannot dress to please me. Here, I'll settle it——"

He snatched at the sleeve of her loose red jacket, and his thin fingers pinched the flesh of her arm. She twisted away, but she did not cry out, though her lips went white. The sleeve gave at the seam, and he continued to drag at it, laughing like a malicious child.

" I'll settle the thing."

The whole sleeve came away in his hand, leaving her full white arm showing, with the marks of his fingers upon it. For a moment there was a kind of madness in her eyes, but she mastered herself and turned towards the house.

" You will be rough with me once too often, Fenton," she said. " I am not one of your soft Englishwomen—my blood is hotter than theirs."

Three days later David Flemming went down from the Regina Hotel to a dance at a little casino that was built on a headland that jutted into the bay. The night was superb, warm, and ablaze with stars, and the sea made no more than a moist murmur among the rocks. The casino gardens were brightly lit ; the string band was playing in the rotunda ; the cosmopolitan crowd had scattered itself round the little tables in the alcove ; only a few couples were dancing.

A gay little German widow was chattering in the vestibule. She nodded and smiled at David Flemming, for he was a favourite of hers.

" Ach, Mr. Flemming, I have a quarrel with you. You did not dance with me last week."

" Why, Baroness, then it was I who was the loser."

" So you have a smooth tongue, you wicked prevaricator. I was here—you not ask me."

She shrugged her plump shoulders and looked up at him provokingly, but found that Flemming was staring over her head with a surprised and innocent intentness that could not be quarrelled with. For, seated at one of the little tables in one of the recesses leading from the ball-room were Lalia Bale and her husband. The girl was wearing a brilliant wine-coloured gown and a string of pearls in her hair. She was no longer the child of the mountain, but a woman of the world, a Parisian creature, cosmopolitan and yet unique.

The German lady turned her smile upon someone else, and Flemming went to leave his hat and coat in the cloakroom.

And here a tall man, bald, clean-shaven, with ironical blue eyes, was stuffing a white scarf into an overcoat pocket.

" Hallo, Flemming ! "

" You here, as usual, Locker ? "

" Part of my business. I prescribe dancing for some of my patients, and I have to be here to see that they take it. Have you seen the sensation of the evening ? "

" No."

" Come along. I'll show you."

He took Flemming by the arm, and so piloted him that one of the doorways leading from the vestibule served as a picture frame to Lalia and the man seated at the table.

" There's a problem for you, Flemming ! What do you make of it ? "

Flemming's eyes were studying the man. Fenton Bale was lounging in his chair, his dress shirt bulging forward, his yellow face lined and haggard, his right hand twirling a liqueur glass by the stem. He seemed to be sneering at life, a malicious decadent, whose restless eyes saw little that was good, but very much that was evil.

" Who is the man, Locker ? "

" Fenton Bale, and that bit of milk and charcoal is his wife."

Flemming's mouth hardened.

" Yes, I have met her, but I have not met the man. What is he ? "

Locker was pulling on a pair of white gloves.

" A polyglot gentleman, a cosmopolitan—a bit of American, a bit of English and a bit of French mixed up into a very nasty mess, my dear Flemming. Plenty of money, a liver, and a devilish temper. Excuse me, there's the Marchesa ; I must go and pay my respects."

Flemming was left alone in the doorway, where he was partly screened by a palm. Lalia Bale had not seen him, so he felt no guilt in remaining there for a while to watch her and the man who was her husband.

Lalia looked splendid, but it was a mute and haughty splendour that scornfully suffered some ordeal. She did not speak to Bale, did not look at him ; her eyes seemed to be gazing at something a long way off ; she was there, and she was not there. The soul of the woman had withdrawn itself to some inaccessible proud height where no one could follow.

Flemming was puzzled, but in a little while he understood. That Hawaiian girl was the dominant figure in the room; a glowing thing with an ice-cold face, a woman who drew men and rebuffed them when they sought her. Her beauty was like no other kind of beauty that Flemming had ever seen. She was the sex spirit idealised, mysterious, strangely pure.

The casino etiquette was easy; introductions were not demanded, and Flemming saw several men go up to the girl, bow, and ask her to dance. And each time she refused, and each time a yellow gleam of mocking self-satisfaction seemed to light up Fenton Bale's face. He had brought his wife there to show her off, like some rare gem that he flashed in the eyes of other men, boastfully, and with an ironical sneer. He had forbidden her to dance. She should sit there—and be his.

David Flemming understood, and the man in him was angered. Bale's gloating sense of possession was so patent, so offensive, that no one could have watched him without appreciating the truth. And Flemming felt a sudden disgust at the sight of this wreck of a man flashing this child's beauty in the eyes of the world, like some Jew dog mocking the Gentiles with the yellow leer of his own wealth.

There was more than anger in Flemming's mood. He was touched, stirred to an imaginative pity, able to feel the supreme humiliation that was being laid upon the woman.

Then their eyes met across the length of the long room. Lalia's face seemed to float for a moment in a tremulous haze of hesitation. Then she smiled. It was as though she asked to be rescued.

The band had struck up a waltz. Couples floated out and began to circle the room. Flemming made his way round, and found himself bowing to Lalia Bale.

" Will you dance with me ? "

Her eyes flashed a rebellious " yes." As they glided away to the music Flemming caught a glimpse of Fenton Bale's face, and for the moment he was sorry that he had tempted Lalia to rebel. She would be made to suffer for it ; Fenton Bale would see to that.

But there were other things besides the music to carry him away—to make him forget that shrivelled, yellow-cheeked man by the window. For the girl had risen to him with a rush of recklessness ; her warm blood was afire, her supple body thrilling to the sinuous moan of the violins. Her eyes looked into his ; her throat seemed full of laughter and joy ;

if he was to match her physical exultation he would have no leisure to brood over the vicious jealousy of a sick and decadent man. Flemming was a fine dancer, but he had never danced with such a partner as this. She moved like a rhapsody, and Flemming's blood took fire. He was young again. He was the movement to her music, though some wild devil piped the tune.

They did not speak. There was an exultation in the flowing of their steps, and mere words would have marred the rhythm. People stopped to watch them, though it was doubtful whether they were conscious of anything but the music and their two selves. Then it became a *danse à deux*, the red and the black figure holding the room.

It was over. The leader of the band stood up, bowing in answer to a burst of applause. People began to talk ; waiters came hurrying to take orders ; the rooms and galleries were full of the shifting colours of the feminine crowd.

" That was splendid."

Her arm was resting in his and her eyes shone. He was about to lead her back to that table in the window recess.

" How hot it is in here ! "

He changed his mind of a sudden, though there was more than a mere sensuous drift in the impulse that prompted him.

" It would be cooler in the gardens."

" Yes, let's go out. I don't want to dance again."

They passed through the crowded vestibule and down the steps into the garden. Men and women watched them, and then smiled at each other. A waiter came hurrying, a little round-eyed man with a worried, deprecating smile.

" Monsieur, monsieur, please ! Ze gen'leman wish me to say——"

Flemming turned sharply.

" What is it ? "

" Ze gen'leman wish me to say he go home, sir, and will madame put on her cloak."

Flemming glanced at Lalia. She looked pale and uncompromising.

" I shall not go yet. Tell Signor Bale that I will come later, *plus tard*, you understand ? "

" Yes, madame."

She withdrew her arm from Flemming's, and there was the light of revolt in her eyes.

" Let him wait for me. I will please myself—for once."

Flemming was sobered. The waltz tune had changed to a sadder and more sinister movement. The glare of the casino had given place to the shadows of pines, cypresses, ilexes, and palms. Winding paths disappeared into the shadows. Here and there a light flickered, and they could hear the soft wash of the sea.

She put her head back, and seemed to draw in deep breaths, as though the night air cooled some inward flame within her. Her white throat showed. To Flemming there was something tragic in the poise of her head.

" Let's go down to the sea."

She swept on, and he followed ; the path was narrow, so that they could not walk abreast.

" I am afraid the blame is mine."

She answered him quickly over her shoulder.

" What blame ? Did you not see—you must have seen."

" You mean——"

" Oh, I must talk—I must talk, and somehow I feel that I know you—that I have known you for years. What fools we humans are—what cowards ! But I saw by your eyes that you understood. How gross and hateful life can be made ! "

She turned suddenly and faced him under the over-spreading canopy of a pine.

" I can talk to you—I must talk to you. And you are not afraid of me ? I am not like those women in there—who feed on a man's folly."

He answered her impulsively.

" I know that. We are children, you and I ; we can understand each other."

She turned and walked on.

" The other day—on Monte Verde—what did you think ? "

" That you were suffering."

He saw her put her hand to her throat.

" Oh, my God ! is a woman to have no pride ? Is she to be bullied, exposed like a tame beast—shown off before other men, to be made the creature of a man's evil whims ? I was just a child when he married me. I did not know then. And he is clever ; he has taken care to keep me at his mercy. Men are like that, but one might bear it from some men."

Flemming was mute for a moment. This passionate outburst of hers, so poignantly sincere, so vital, smote him like a wave of the sea. Its salt strength smothered him, lifted him away from the familiar rock of a man's habitual outlook

upon life. He had a feeling of breathlessness, of being seized
on and possessed by a rush of emotion that no amount of cool
and selfish reasoning could withstand.

The path broadened out, and ended in a rough terrace
built up on the rocks where the Italians bathed in spring and
summer. The sea was very calm, with just a soft heaving
that fringed each black rock with a little circle of foam. Across
the bay the lights of the old town glittered in a clustering fringe
that spread and thinned and died away upon the mountains.
A couple of sailing boats were gliding in towards the harbour,
mere grey ghosts upon the water.

Lalia and Flemming were quite alone. They stood and
leant upon the parapet, and watched each heave of the sea
pouring a gush of foam into each little pot-hole and crevasse
in the rocks below.

" How calm it is here ! It makes me think of Hawaii."

He was silent awhile.

" Why not go back ? "

By the way she glanced at him he knew that he had said
a foolish thing.

" That is what makes life so difficult ; one cannot go back.
I should not be happy there ; I have learnt too much, seen
too much. I should seem a stranger to them, and they would
seem strange to me. Besides, there are the Americans ; I do
not love them. What is more, I have no money."

She laughed suddenly and rested her chin on her hands.

" Do you know, I never have more than a franc in my
purse. No, my friend, I am not going to ask you for money."

He answered hotly.

" It never crossed my mind."

" I believe you. He keeps me without money, so that I am
tied to him by a golden rope. Oh, but it is hateful, talking
like this ; it sounds mean, horribly mean. Let's be just ourselves. Tell me about yourself. I feel—somehow—that you
have suffered, that you are not a beast of prey—like other men."

He betrayed a gleam of humour.

" I don't know that I am so interested in myself."

" No ? But I may be. Shall I read your character ?
I am rather good at reading people."

" Try."

" Let me feel one of your hands."

He gave her his left hand, and she ran the tips of her fingers
over it, touching it lightly here and there.

"Sensitive, rather diffident, reserved—and a little obstinate."

"Oh, come!"

"An artist; I know that, and yet you are not an egoist. Not good at business; inclined to be too generous. That's strange; I feel you have lost someone who was very dear to you."

He answered her quietly.

"I lost my wife. Oh, about a year ago or more. I haven't been quite alive since then. Marriages are happy sometimes, you know."

And then she showed him another aspect of herself, a phase that proved that she was not a devourer, that she could give—as well as take.

"Won't you tell me about her?"

"I don't know. I have never talked about her to anybody."

"Perhaps it hurts too much?"

"It is not that. There are parts of one's life into which one never takes a third person."

She stretched out a hand and touched his arm.

"Oh, but I never asked for that. I would never desire to pry into the sacred things that belonged to another woman. But now I know why your voice sounds lonely. It struck me that way up on Monte Verde; it was like the voice of someone who was always remembering in the middle of saying something—that there was no one to listen, no one—I mean—who mattered. The one who mattered was no longer there."

He looked over the sea.

"That's true, utterly true. In the middle of doing things even now—painting a picture, for instance—I suddenly realise she is not here, and life seems to break in the middle. Things do not seem worth while. I was ambitious. Yes, I suppose we were everything to each other."

"I can picture her. May I try?"

"Yes."

"She was rather fragile, pale, with large eyes and dark hair. But she had plenty of spirit, plenty of fun. She did not talk very much, but she was full of cleverness, understanding. She was one of those fragile, graceful women who make a man feel very protective, very tender. And yet she had an immense courage, more courage than you have. She helped you."

He turned to her in astonishment.

"How do you know all that?"

" How ? It is what you make me feel, that is all I can say. Perhaps your loneliness paints a thought picture, for you were very lonely."

" Lonely ? Good God ! no one knows how awful that loneliness can be till they have been through it. I didn't want to go on living ? "

" But you did go on living."

" Somehow. I was very near ending it once or twice." She sighed.

" Oh, I know. But perhaps it is worse to have to go on living with the dead body of the past in the same house with one. I think I know what loneliness means—a loneliness that has even no dreams left to it."

Flemming looked at her, and as he watched her pale face a strange thing happened to him. For suddenly his dead wife seemed to rise before him and to enter into the body of this island girl. The two women seemed to become mysteriously mingled. All the old poignant tenderness awoke in him and reached out towards the living as well as towards the dead.

" You and I seem to have drunk of the same cup. I am going to be your friend, Lalia. You can say things to me that you would say to your own self."

She remained motionless, brooding.

" Would she mind—if she knew ? "

" I think not. She was always generous. And somehow I feel her—the eternal woman—in you."

Again she sighed.

" I cannot help hating him. And sometimes he drives me mad, for I am not like your passive white women ; I have fire in my blood, and there are times when I feel that I shall do some desperate thing."

" You mean——"

" Kill myself—or kill him."

She uttered the words with the quietness of one who knew that she was uttering the truth. And Flemming looked at her with a sense of helplessness, feeling that he had been drawn into some inevitable and tragic current that was life itself, remorseless yet pathetic.

He turned and leant slightly towards her, resting his right arm along the wall.

" I should be a prig and a fool if I doubted that. But is he worth it ? "

She shrugged her shoulders.

" Oh, he is a devil, an ingenious, tormenting devil. Whisky
—and drugs. I try to think of him as he was, to realise that
the thing that lives is a kind of caricature of the thing that is
dead. And yet there is a horrible likeness in the caricature.
He was always cruel, a little unscrupulous, but, then, it seemed
a natural audacity, a masterfulness that appealed to a mere girl.
I misread it all then ; now I am wiser."

Suddenly they heard a harsh voice calling, the voice of a
man who had lost all self-restraint.

" Lalia ! Are you there ? Where the devil are you ? "

They looked at each other meaningly.

" I had better go. It maddens him to be kept waiting."

" I've been responsible. I am coming with you. I want
you to introduce me."

" He will be rude to you."

" Let him be rude. What does it matter ? "

She called to her husband.

" Is that you, Fenton ? Where are you ? "

" Up here, of course. Hurry along."

They found him at the top of the path that led down the
cliff to the terrace above the bathing place. A solitary lamp
burnt here, and a few iron chairs were ranged in a half-circle
under a stone pine, and Fenton Bale was sitting on one of
these iron chairs, the lamplight making his face look all shadowy
and haggard.

He started up jerkily, unsteadily.

" Where the devil have you been ? Didn't you get that
message ? "

" Yes, I got it, Fenton, but I meant to stay on a little
longer. I want to introduce you to Mr. Flemming."

" Oh ! And who the——"

He glared at Flemming, and for an instant these two men
stood face to face, eyeing each other, measuring each other.
Then Flemming held out a hand.

" Glad to meet you, sir. I must confess that I am the
sinner. I'm an artist, and you have to make allowances for
artists. We're infernal fools, of course."

He was easy, debonair, but that facile politeness of his was
a grip laid on the throat of Bale's evil temper. He was determined that the fellow should behave himself, and not fall to
snarling like a spoilt dog.

" You've kept me waiting, anyway. I'm an invalid, a sick
man, sir."

" I'm sorry. Your wife and I have met before, and the casino was so confoundedly hot that we strolled down here. Are you driving back ? "

" We shouldn't be walking, should we ? "

" Hardly. Shall I get hold of a carriage for you ? "

" Much obliged ; the porter fellow's paid for that."

Flemming laughed, but there was an edge to his laughter.

" Your husband won't let me be officious, Mrs. Bale. Shall I lead the way ? I know all these winding paths."

" Oh, there's my cloak. I left it in the cloakroom."

" Give me your number and I'll get it for you."

Flemming found them waiting at the entrance gates when he walked across the garden with Lalia's black velvet cloak over his arm. A powerful electric light hung from the iron arch over the gates, throwing a pale glare that made the foliage of the palms and the grass look a hard, metallic green. There were other people waiting, and there appeared to be a shortage of carriages, for Fenton Bale was kicking up a row with the concierge and not gaining in dignity thereby.

" Didn't I tell you to reserve me a carriage ? Well, and why the blazes isn't there a carriage here ? You won't get the ghost of a tip out of me."

The concierge was a big Frenchman who spoke English, and who had no intention of being bullied.

" Monsieur must wait his turn. The carriage is coming."

" Look here, my man, I don't want any impertinence. I ordered a carriage to be here at eleven ; other people have got their carriages."

" That is so, monsieur." And the concierge's tone suggested that the other people had better manners, and that Mr. Bale might wait till midnight so far as he was concerned.

Flemming was helping Lalia with her cloak. His hands touched hers. She looked at him over her shoulder.

" Oh, I am used to this. Try if you can get us away."

Bale had pounced on a carriage that had driven up and was attempting to annex it, but a bearded Austrian with two ladies refused to be hustled out of his rights. He was very polite, but very determined. It was his private carriage ; he managed to make Fenton Bale appreciate the fact.

People were smiling. Lalia drew aside under one of the palms and stood there haughtily. Flemming tackled the concierge, and dropped a two-lire piece into the man's hand.

He spoke to him in French and tapped his forehead suggestively.

"Monsieur is a little—— You understand. I apologise for him ; you are quite in the right."

The concierge smiled.

" I am ready to oblige monsieur. He shall have the third carriage."

Flemming turned, and discovered that Bale had rejoined his wife and was making a further exhibition of himself by scolding at her.

" It's all your damned fault. What did you want to go gallivanting off for ? You know it knocks me up to be out late."

Flemming felt very much tempted to take Bale by the scruff of the neck and shake him. The fellow seemed to have no self-control, no sense of the fitness of things. He let himself be carried away by any animal impulse. The whole thing was absurd ; but, like many absurd things, it was tragic.

" All right, sir, a carriage is coming."

He caught a flash of Lalia's eyes, a flash of gratitude and of appeal, and he went and stood by her, looking at Fenton Bale with mesmeric intentness. He would stare the little cad into behaving himself, and his attitude succeeded.

In another moment he was handing Lalia into a carriage though Bale had made a move to get in first.

" Good-night."

She had pressed his hand, and her eyes looked for a moment into his.

" Good-night."

" Acqua Dolce, cocchiere."

The carriage moved away, and Flemming stood under one of the palms, watching it. The band was still playing in the casino, Chaminade's " Autumn," and the music seemed to entangle itself with the emotions of the moment. How would that little beast behave now that he had her alone with him ? And Flemming found that he had no delusions as to Fenton Bale's most probable attitude towards his wife.

What a monstrous thing it was that she should be made the victim of a decadent sot's vile humours ! He was angry, generously angry, and mingled with his anger was a compassion that was not content to stand and philosophise. The vehemence and the drive of life had come back to David Flemming. The spirit of his dead wife seemed to have spoken to him by the mouth of Lalia Bale.

The carriage was rattling along the road that skirted the bay. There was the moist swish of the sea upon the shingle. From the windows of a tall house came the sound of laughter and the shrilling of a mandoline. The ilexes that lined the road met overhead and made a black tunnel.

Lalia was leaning back in her corner. Bale had begun before they had driven thirty yards, and she had let him snarl at her and given him not a word in return. He could rave like an hysterical woman, fling the most monstrous taunts at her, show all that malignant unreason that drives the most patient of mortals to despair.

" A nice fool you made of me. I suppose you think I'm a yellow dog, done for, a blasted corpse in trousers. Damn it, I'm not dead yet. I'm not going to die for a long time. You keep away from the men."

She did not answer, and her silence exasperated him.

" Who's this artist chap, anyway ? Short of money, is he ? You haven't given him those pearls, have you, to raise money on ? Don't you try that game ; I'm not going to be boobied into passing out the shekels for some other chap to pocket. Where are those pearls ? "

She twisted the rope out of her hair and tossed them to him.

" Take them. But be very careful, Fenton, or some day you may discover that I have taken you at your word."

" Ah, would you ? Yes, get yourself into the gutter, my dear. You know where those sort of adventures end."

" Fenton, do you know the kind of woman I am ? No, I think not."

" Women—they're all alike ; toss a man over when they've dragged all the fun out of him."

" Silence ! "

She leant towards him and spoke so fiercely that he crumpled in his corner.

" Fenton, I shall kill you—some day ; yes, kill you, if you talk to me like this."

David Flemming had not seen Lalia Bale for days, though he had climbed Monte Verde and wandered along the valley paths on the steep hillsides above the river. The image of her did not fade ; it was no day's fancy, no momentary infatuation. On the contrary, it grew more distinct and compelling ; he began to feel very lonely, and in his loneliness his thoughts turned to her.

Vineyards and olive groves surrounded Acqua Dolce, and grey stone walls shut in the villa grounds. The road ran along the eastern boundary, and there were paths that went up through the terraces where the olives grew. And Flemming began to haunt these paths, innocently enough. He would take his sketch-book with him and make studies of olives and cypresses and the river running in its rocky bed below. Only once did he see Lalia or have speech with her. Things were going badly; Bale had developed a new mania; he would hardly let her out of his sight.

Flemming was cutting down close to the wall one morning when he heard someone hailing him. It was a sneering and ironical voice, and had the same effect on Flemming as the sound of a file grating upon steel.

"Hallo! Mr. Gamboge. You seem to find a dashed lot of material round here."

Flemming glanced up and saw Bale looking down at him under the shade of a loquat tree.

"Good morning, sir."

Bale mimicked him.

"Good morning, sir. I'm not so damned polite as you are, sir. In fact, I see a dashed sight too much of you, sir."

Flemming smiled.

"Is that so?" he said.

"That is so, Mr. Gamboge. And my wife isn't on view— see. And if you try climbing over my wall you may get a jolly lot more than you bargain for."

It was not the face of a sane man that looked down at Flemming from under the shade of the loquat tree. It was all lined and yellow, with a cunning leer in the eyes, the face of a malicious faun.

Bale's insolence was ridiculous and vulgar, and Flemming was inclined to ignore it.

"You seem to have got some sort of prejudiced idea into your head."

Bale grinned at him.

"Look here, Mr. Juan; I'll show you what I carry in my pocket."

He dangled a nickel-plated revolver over the wall, and pointed it half-playfully at Flemming.

"I used to be a dead shot, old sport."

Flemming looked at him steadily.

"If you go walking about with toys like that you'll get

yourself into trouble, Mr. Fenton Bale. I should lock it up if I were you."

"Not me. You haven't lived out West, in Mexico, and in some of those dirty republics. You dress with your pistol ; it's part of the costume—see ? "

He waved his hat.

"Good-bye, Gamboge. You keep on the right side of my wall, old fellow."

Flemming left him and walked on, but his face was a little grim. Bale's antics struck him as serious.

"The man's mad. He ought to be watched. Good God ! he might take it into his brain to shoot her ! "

Flemming took one of the mule-paths back to Villadoro, and on reaching the town he went straight to a little white villa that stood amid palms and camellias and mimosa on the hillside just above the Regina Hotel. Here James Locker and his wife lived for eight months of the year, two very popular healers, without whom the English who wintered at Villadoro would have to pour out their woes in German or Italian.

Dr. Locker was at home, rolling a supply of cigarettes as he sat in the loggia that overlooked the sea.

"Hallo, Leonardo ! Stay to lunch ? Glad to see you. Sit down."

"I have got a problem for you, Locker."

"Oh, good heavens ! What is it, the disappearance of Mona Lisa ? "

"I'll tell you."

Locker was no fool, though he sauntered through life rather like a pierrot. He listened seriously enough, rolling his cigarettes, and glancing now and again at Flemming with a kind of affectionate irony.

"You have got to look into this, Locker. No ; I'm not a sentimental fool. You know something of Bale."

"Quite enough. He tried to choke me once in one of his riots. The man's a degenerate beast. I told him that he would drink and drug himself into Bedlam."

"Well, what are you going to do ? "

Locker got up.

"Call Grace in," he said dryly. "It's a case for consultation. You didn't know that Grace ran the practice, did you, Leonardo ? "

"I have a great admiration for your wife, Locker."

"She deserves it, my friend. Try rolling a few cigarettes

while I go and explain things. I think she is writing letters in that room of hers under the tiles."

Grace Locker was an exceptional woman, a woman whose appearance made strangers imagine that she spent all her time and energy elaborating new dresses, putting a superfine polish upon her nails, and massaging that smooth and handsome face of hers in a triumphant revolt against wrinkles. She contrived to be immensely busy without ever appearing in a hurry. Her very charm owed much to its suggestion of leisureliness. She was amazingly efficient, that was the secret of it all. She contrived to be both the busiest and the best-dressed woman in Villadoro, simply because she knew what to do—and did it —while other women were talking.

" What a sensible man you are, David. Of course, you were thinking of me when you came to appeal to Jim."

She sat down in a basket chair, looking fresh and delightfully young for a woman of forty. She was a fair woman, but she could still wear white in the morning without it making her look faded.

Flemming smiled at her.

" Of course, I had you in my thoughts. But I'm serious, Grace."

" Don't be a prig and assume that I'm frivolous because I don't moan. Jim has told me. I have been interested in that girl all the winter. She's one of the most fascinating things I've ever seen."

" And David wants to rescue her."

Flemming stared between the stone pillars of the loggia at the blue of the sea.

" Anyone would think, Locker, that you just trifled through life, and that you couldn't be in earnest about anything. I happen to know you. Grace couldn't have married a fool. I want you to go up to Acqua Dolce——"

" But I'm not going, David."

" But—look here——"

" I'm leaving it to Grace."

Flemming turned eagerly to Grace Locker.

" Will you go ? "

" Of course. I've been thinking things over. The girl wants rescuing, bringing out among people ; it is enough to make her morbid, being shut up with a man like Bale. He may be only a whimsical curmudgeon. People have cut him ; a little human flattery might work wonders with the man. I'll try it ; I'll just be charming to him, and get him to let the girl come and help with that fête of ours at the Villa Scala. That can serve as an excuse, and I can see what's to be made of Mr. Fenton Bale."

Flemming looked grateful but troubled.

" I suppose it's safe—for you——"

Locker laughed shrewdly.

" Grace would be safe anywhere. You need not picture Bale threatening her with a revolver. I'd trust her to manage a case of homicidal mania."

" If you think it's all right——"

" Of course, it's all right. Grace has struck an idea. Let her try her cunning on Mr. Fenton Bale."

So Grace Locker drove up the winding valley round to Acqua Dolce and called on the Bales.

She found herself in a long salon paved with marble, its windows opening upon a loggia all overgrown with vines and bougainvillea and Banksia roses. A little Italian garden lay below the loggia, with two fountains throwing plumes of water into the sunlight. The salon was full of fine old furniture ; it was plain that Fenton Bale had money.

And then Lalia came in, dressed in a simple white dress, with a red rose and a scarf of the same colour. She looked depressed and tired, for even her superb physique could not carry her through such a life as she was leading without betraying signs of strain.

The two women looked at each other interestedly. They were such utter contrasts—Grace Locker with her slim, fair elegance ; Lalia with her rich and dusky comeliness and her sad eyes. They were attracted to each other, and Grace Locker knew how to make the most of such a tendency.

" What a lovely place you have here ! Of course, you know its history. I have often felt that I should like to live here—in a house of actual romance."

" I suppose they were happy——"

" I have always heard so. I know an old padre who knew them, and he said they were like a pair of children, even when they had grown grey. I have come to ask you if you will do something for me."

" Oh ! "

" We are getting up a fête for the Italian hospital ; it is going to be held in the grounds of the Villa Scala. I am wondering if you would help me."

Lalia hesitated.

" I should love to, but——"

" Put the ' buts ' on one side."

She seemed to force herself to speak.

" Mrs. Locker, my husband is an invalid—with queer whims and prejudices——"

" Well, let me ask him."

" You might try.   I should love to help."

" I am quite ready to be importunate."

Her opportunity was on the threshold, for Fenton Bale came in, looking shrunken and yellow, a sloven who had not been shaved. He glanced sulkily at Mrs. Locker, and gave her a curt nod when Lalia introduced him.

Bale was not a promising subject, but Grace Locker attacked him with all her delightful guile.   Very few men could withstand her, but Bale had become something less than a man, and this refined and clever woman seemed to irritate him, even while she was being charming.   The brute in him refused to be fascinated, and in asserting its independence contrived to be insolent.

" I suppose it's a question of money, isn't it ?   All right. I'll give you a subscription—if that's what you want."

" It's your wife I want, Mr. Bale."

He grinned maliciously.

" Then you won't get her, ma'am.   The fact is, my wife doesn't know how to behave, so I keep her at home, except when I go out myself."

Grace Locker flushed slightly.   She glanced at Lalia, and felt humiliated for the girl's sake.

" I don't agree with you, Mr. Bale.   In fact——"

He interrupted her rudely.

" What's that matter, anyhow ?   My wife's not going to swank round at your show, but I'll give you a hundred francs and leave it at that.   I don't want to be in with the Villadoro crowd."

It was Lalia who rose with a meaning look at Grace Locker

" You see," her eyes said, " he will only insult us both. He is quite impossible."

Grace rose also.   She looked steadily at Fenton Bale, but she was too wise, too much herself, to squabble with such a man.   He was what he had made himself, a shrunk and bedrugged thing, a rotten apple ready to drop from the tree.

" I cannot take money that is given in such a spirit."

He laughed, showing his teeth.

" Oh, all right. Then I save a hundred francs."

She shook hands with Lalia, gave her a compassionate smile, and walked back to the carriage.

But she was angry. Grace Locker was not the woman to be pleased at being balked by a little blackguard, even though he might not be responsible for his actions.

She had reached the flight of steps leading down to the iron gates when she heard someone behind her.

" Mrs. Locker ! "

Grace turned and saw Lalia in her white dress, the sunlight striking through the olives and making a patterning of shadow all about her.

" I wanted to say I'm sorry. I couldn't help him being rude to you."

Grace's eyes lit up.

" My dear, of course I understand that. And really—I'm very angry with that husband of yours. I like you."

Lalia's lips quivered, and she seemed to be struggling to hide her emotion.

" And I like you—too. Somehow—you made me feel good directly I saw you."

" Well, see more of me ; I should welcome it. Why let your husband tyrannise ? "

Lalia shrugged her shoulders.

" He is not reasonable ; it is impossible to argue with him. And if I anger him—I know that I shall be afraid—not of him, but of myself. I have to set my teeth and keep my patience. Good-bye, I must go now."

She turned abruptly and made her way back towards the house, leaving Grace Locker full of a new compassion.

" The little beast ! Why doesn't he poison himself or shoot himself, and have done with it ? "

But she was in a serious mood when she described her experiences to her husband.

" David Flemming is right," she confessed. " I am half afraid of something tragic happening at Acqua Dolce."

The same evening David Flemming heard the result of the attempt to rescue Lalia. He was sitting in the loggia of the Lockers' villa, with the lights of Villadoro strung across the bay, and Grace Locker a dim figure in white lying back in a cane chair beside him. Locker had been called out to see a patient at one of the hotels, an athletic lady who had broken her ankle on the steep path to Monte Cavallo.

Close to Flemming a big camellia growing in a stone vase was starred with white flowers that looked like snowy rosettes on a cloak of black velvet. The night was supremely still. They could hear the band playing in the casino gardens.

" What can one do in such a case, my friend ? You cannot rush up, take the little wretch by the scruff of the neck and threaten to shake the life out of him if he doesn't mend his ways. Besides, I don't think Fenton Bale is capable of changing. He is just one of those wretched, fateful little figures that go bobbing through life, exasperating everybody and causing endless trouble. It's sordid and tragic and utterly puzzling."

Flemming was leaning forward, his hands clasped between his knees.

" Would one keep a leopardess and some miserable and depraved ape in the same cage ? And yet we humans persist in such inhumanity."

" You cannot reason on those lines, David. We are not mere animals. There are some things that have to be borne, and sometimes we are the better for bearing them."

" The old moral, that because a thing is nasty it helps to build up character. Let's get down to the tragic facts. Do you think that girl can go on living with that little blackguard and not revolt ? She is not English ; she is prouder, cleaner than most Englishwomen."

" What do you mean, David ? "

" Oh—well, she may kill him. That's what I mean."

Grace Locker raised herself in her chair.

" Then you, too, have felt that ? "

" I have."

" And what can one do ? I don't want to persuade you, my friend, into thrusting yourself into a tragedy."

" Do you know that she reminds me of Norah ? "

" What—this girl ? "

" Yes. There is the same impulsiveness, the same naïveté, the same psychical colour. Strange, isn't it ? Something has been reawakened in me. It was as though Norah were alive and married to that little beast."

Grace Locker looked at him in the dusk.

" David, don't be mad. You may make things worse."

He answered her with quiet passion :

" No, I am not that selfish sort of scoundrel. But I am

not going to stand aside and do nothing. Surely I can be a friend to her, a comrade."

" Oh, be very careful. Where do such friendships end— in many cases ? No ; I'm not an opportunist and a cynic, but people get hurt when trying to be heroic. And yet——"

" Well ? "

" You must follow your own calling. The fact is, I like you, David ; you are my very good friend ; I'm quite a motherly person. Why not let things drift a little, and wait in patience ? "

" Because," and his voice was solemn, " I am afraid of what might happen—while I waited."

When Flemming left the Lockers' villa he did not turn straight towards his hotel, but took the road that crossed to the old Roman bridge and led beside the river towards Acqua Dolce. He felt irresistibly drawn towards the white house among the palms and cypresses, with its garden full of the noise of running water and olive trees softening the grey walled terraces. Compassion possessed him, and something deeper than compassion. He was re-dreaming the dreams of fifteen years ago.

The villa gates were locked, but he climbed one of the rough walls and went wandering about the garden with its dusky alleyways and its turf walks between rose hedges and trellised vines. There was a light in one of the upper windows, but Flemming dared not go too near the house, though his imagination set that light in Lalia's room and made him think of her as wakeful and very lonely. He greeted her in his heart, this child of the south nurtured in London, Rome, Paris, and Vienna.

If Flemming gained anything by that midnight ramble— he gained a certain decision, and the sulky stare of the porter who had to let him into the hotel. Nor did the morning put an end to the night's mood. He took his artist's baggage under his arm and started for the woods on the hill slope above Acqua Dolce.

So steep was the hillside that Flemming was able to see down into the villa garden ; in fact, it was set out like a toy stage below him, with its terraces and statues, its groves of cypresses, its rose walks and stone fish ponds, its little Grecian theatre partly hidden by the encircling mystery of the towering trees. Acqua Dolce had been a house of romance. Love had planned all those quaint and formal terraces, those fountains and pools, those secret paths through green glooms, that little classic theatre open to the blue heaven. Flemming found himself thinking of the woman who had danced in that theatre, that wonderful woman who had set half Italy afire.

And then he saw Lalia, a little white figure moving along one of the terraces where orange trees grew in stone pots. He saw her pause and bend over one of the pools, and then disappear up a stone stairway under a smother of roses. For a while he lost sight of that thread of white, but suddenly she appeared within the grey curve of the Grecian theatre. He could see her above and between the cypresses, a figure that moved to no rhythmic music, but a figure that went hither and thither restlessly, pausing now and again to lean against the balustrade and look up at Monte Verde and the woods upon the hills.

Flemming stood up and willed her to see him. And presently she turned and stared fixedly in his direction. He had chosen a place where he was screened from the windows of the villa.

For fully half a minute the distant figure did not move.

He waved his arm. She waved back. Then she appeared to be pointing towards the top of the cypresses, and Flemming guessed what he wished to guess.

They met at the low stone wall that shut off the garden from the woods above. A row of cypresses threw a mass of shadow here, their sharp spires motionless against the blue of the sky.

" I wondered whether I should see you again."

She was wearing a red camellia in her white dress, and the flower was the colour of blood.

" Well, I had to come."

Her eyes met his with perfect frankness. There was no guile in her attitude towards him, none of the self-conscious cunning of the feminine intriguer.

" You can trust me, Lalia. I should not be here—but for that."

She smiled at him.

" Trust you ! Of course I trust you. I am quick in such things. Do you think I should have let you paint me that day on Monte Verde if I had not known instantly what sort of man you were ? Should I have danced with you that night ? Should we have talked—as we talked—down there by the sea ? "

" Do you know—I began to live again—that night ? We seemed to come together out of our two lonely lives. I want to know how things are with you."

A swift change came over her face. She rested her arms on the top of the wall and stared up at the pinewoods.

" I feel that I can talk to you as I might talk to myself."

" Talking helps us. You saw Grace Locker yesterday ? "

" You sent her ? I guessed it."

" I thought she might get you out into the life down yonder. She is a sort of queen in Villadoro."

Lalia rested her chin on her wrists.

" It was good of you, David. But, then—he is mad, and yet most horribly sane. It is like living with a cunning and malicious devil, to whom nothing is too petty or too monstrous. He is asleep—now. I am trying to be patient."

" I know."

" You must have no will of your own. Every maddening freak of his has to be humoured. It would be funny if it weren't horrible. One moment he is in an absurd rage about nothing, the next he is trying to be affectionate. Oh, my God ; it is that which is so difficult to bear ! "

She hid her face suddenly in her arms, as though ashamed and utterly humiliated. It was a mute anguish, poignant, silent, motionless. Her woman's pride, all the intimate delicacies of life were in voiceless revolt.

And Flemming was stirred to the deeps. This was no melodrama, no piece of play-acting, no pretty tale dreamed in a dreamer's brain. The figure in the white dress was terribly real, terribly appealing. He wanted to touch her, to feel his hand smoothing that dark brown hair of hers, to raise her head and make her look into his eyes.

" Lalia, I have got to help you—somehow."

She lifted her head.

" No one can help me. I have taken a fate and I must live it through. And yet you do help me."

She stretched out a hand and he held it fast.

" You can talk to me ; tell me everything. I understand. I don't ask for anything. I'll just come here, and you shall talk. It is something to have a listener."

" But I don't know whether I shall let you come here. It will be utter selfishness on my part."

" Then I am guilty of selfishness."

" Yes, but you don't realise——"

It was Flemming who saw Bale's grinning face appear from behind one of the cypresses, and by an effort he restrained himself and did not let go of Lalia's hand.

"What the devil are you two playing at—anyhow?"

Lalia went white as her dress. She glanced over her shoulder and tried to withdraw her hand. But there was a touch of the divine madness in David Flemming, a spirit that rebelled at the thought of compromise or of shrinking from a crisis in which the enemy was so contemptible. He found himself refusing to feel embarrassed or to confess that Fenton Bale had any right to mouth at him.

"If you want to know the truth, sir, I came here with the express purpose of seeing your wife. She did not know that I was coming."

Fenton Bale flourished his arms.

"I like your infernal insolence."

Flemming put Lalia's hand away and, leaning over the wall, looked steadily at Fenton Bale.

"You happen to have a very charming wife, Mr. Bale. Other men realise it—if you do not. And supposing I were to tell you that I had just asked her to leave you—and that she had refused."

Bale stared at him, like a dog who has made up his mind to bite an intruder and is astonished by the intruder attacking instead of waiting to be attacked. His yellow face looked flat, inept and puzzled.

"Well, this is the funniest darned situation I ever fell into —anyway!"

He glanced rancorously at Lalia.

"Let's have no more of this fooling. I'm not the sort of child to stand it—see? I've lived in rough countries——"

Lalia turned to Flemming :

"Please leave it to me."

Her eyes appealed to him, willed him to go. The whole situation seemed so impossible, for there were no hidden generosities in Fenton Bale that could be aroused by rivalry. He was not sane ; he was not even human in any reasonable sense, and Lalia knew him better than David Flemming did.

Bale's hand went into the side pocket of his coat ; he was grinning.

"I've got something here that can talk, old sport."

Flemming seemed to hesitate, but a glance from Lalia warned him against meddling.

"Oh, run away, Mr. Flemming, or my husband will be taking all this seriously. What an innocent you are, Fenton, not to see that Mr. Flemming has been ragging you ! "

She laughed quite merrily, and caught Bale by the arm.

"Good-bye. Next time please come in by the gate."

Bale had begun to mutter something, but that shrunken, bedrugged body of his was incapable of much physical independence. This girl from the south could have lifted him in her arms and carried him off like a child. She pushed him through the cypresses, laughing, and calling back to Flemming:

"Good-bye. It really was wrong of you to try and hold my hand."

Flemming did not move, but stood leaning against the wall and staring at the row of cypresses through which those two had disappeared. He had more than a suspicion that he had blundered on to the edge of a tragedy, and that the steel-bright thing that lay in Bale's pocket might have spoken with irresponsible violence. He had seen a momentary panic in Lalia's eyes. He realised that he had been at the mercy of a morphomaniac's savage whim.

But Lalia ! It was monstrous that she should have to live on the edge of a possible fatality. The man was irresponsible. He might shoot her, shoot himself. He was like so much dynamite, with a candle burning close by.

For a moment he felt tempted to climb the wall and follow them, but saner thoughts prevailed. She knew Bale, she knew how to handle him. He had only made things more difficult for her by trying to thrust a chivalrous sympathy into her life. And so he climbed back into the woods to get a view of the villa garden. No one was to be seen there save a man in bright blue trousers hoeing one of the lower terraces where olives grew.

All that evening Fenton Bale sat brooding in the loggia like a little yellow god staring at nothing with sullen and expressionless eyes. His face was a mere wrinkled mask. He neither moved nor spoke nor took notice of anything. Coffee, liqueurs, his Russian cigarettes were left untouched on the ebony and mother of pearl table beside him. He just stared and stared like a corpse propped in a chair.

Lalia had brought a book and a reading-lamp out into the loggia, but he had repulsed her sullenly when she had suggested that she should read to him.

"Put that dashed light out. I don't want to hear that sort of twaddle."

And so they sat on together while the darkness fell, and the green leaves of the vines on the trellises turned black. Stars glittered above the mountains. They could hear the river in the valley rushing over its rocky bed.

To Lalia this silence became charged with a feeling of fatality. She could not escape from a strange sense of impending dread. The man in the chair had become a vague blur, but his grey face was like the dim face of a ghost. There was something frightening in his immobility, in his utter silence. She wondered what was passing in his mind, whether this mood was the last sinister phase of his soul's madness.

They had not spoken of the affair of the morning. She had just laughed it aside, and her laughter seemed to have dominated him, though she had caught him watching her with a kind of sinister and secret interest.

She yawned and stretched out her arms.

"You are not gay company, Fenton."

He did not answer her for a moment.

"Not like your artist friend."

"Why worry about that ? Am I never to speak to a living creature ? "

"Go to bed," he said laconically.

And she left him there sunk in his chair.

Lalia's room communicated with her husband's, but she locked both doors that night. She was brushing her hair when she heard him come upstairs, and she remained motionless, expecting him to speak to her. But he passed her door without pausing and went to his room, and for a long while she heard him moving restlessly to and fro. Roberts, his English servant, had been fastening the shutters and locking the doors downstairs. Bale was still moving about his room when she got into bed, but presently his restlessness seemed to come to an end. The sense of tension relaxed, and she fell asleep.

This sleep of hers was not to last through the night, and she awoke from it suddenly with a sense of clamour in her brain. Someone had been calling, calling, and the voice had tangled itself up in the bizarrerie of a restless dream.

She sat up, chilled, vaguely disturbed. For the moment the house seemed silent ; a full moon was shining ; there was no wind to rattle the shutters. And then she understood.

A sudden outcry came from her husband's room, and the

voice was like the voice of a frightened child terrified by some dream. It was shrill, querulous and insistent, suggestive of panic.

Lalia slipped out of bed, put on a dressing-jacket, lit a candle, and went out into the passage. The childish outcry continued. She tried the door and found it unlocked.

" Fenton, what is it ? "

" I'm dying—I'm dying."

She closed the door, set the candle on a table and sat down on the edge of the bed. For the first few seconds she was confused and not a little frightened, for he was breathing jerkily and tossing his arms to and fro, his jacket wide open, the muscles showing in his throat. She laid a hand over his heart ; it was beating rapidly, but not like the heart of a dying man.

Her intuition helped her to sum up the situation. The man was hysterical—something had thrown him into a panic.

" What has frightened you, Fenton ? "

He bleated the same cry.

" I'm dying."

" No, no, lie still ; you have had nightmare."

He gave her one queer, half-cunning, half-agonised look, and then burst into tears. His hands came clutching at her ; he dragged himself round in the bed and tried to snuggle his face into her bosom.

" I was choking ; I woke up choking. I was dying—and no one cares. Why don't you send for a doctor ? You don't care—you'll be glad——"

He clung to her, convulsed, pitiable, like a scared child. And the first spasm of repulsion quivered out of her throat ; she held him in her arms—this little wreck of a man who sobbed and complained.

" There—there, I'm here ; I'll stay with you. You're frightened, that's all. I'll stay here with you."

" It was awful. I couldn't breathe. You won't leave me —you won't run away——"

" No, no."

" I've been a beast sometimes. I'm so cold, I'm shivering."

She made him lie down.

" There—get warm. I'll sit here—and hold your hand. You'll feel better soon."

Hers was no affectation of compassion. She had no love for the man, but his terror, the very misery of his cowardice, even his pitiable selfishness, called to the woman in her. Some primitive instinct answered his child's wail. She laid a hand on his forehead.

" You've been dreaming. Doesn't that feel cool and soft ? I'll sit here with you and you must go to sleep. Try and go to sleep. I'll frighten the bad dreams away."

Her presence seemed to soothe him, and presently he fell asleep, clutching her hand tightly so that she could not move without awaking him. She decided not to leave him, but to sit the night out beside him, and her compassion carried her through.

That vigil brought her new thoughts and a new inspiration as she listened to her husband's breathing, and to the rushing of the river over the rocks below. She had a vision of a further effort, of a further struggle to bear with the man. Life had meant a renunciation of all that youth desires. She would still strive to play her part, to humour him, to save him from his meaner self.

So the dawn came ; yellow light slanted through the shutters ; a mule team went up the road with a jingling of bells. The sanctuary on Monte Verde sent out a morning chime.

When Fenton Bale awoke he found himself holding Lalia's hand. For a moment he did not remember the scene he had made in the night. He blinked at her as though bemused and puzzled.

" So you slept after all, Fenton ? I kept the dreams away."

" Slept ! Did I call you up ? "

" I have been sitting here for about five hours."

" Good Lord ! "

She saw by his eyes that he remembered.

" I've been thinking, Fenton ; thinking hard."

" What, all the night ? "

" Part of it."

She freed her hand and went and opened one of the shutters. The morning sun poured in, and the white walls of the villa seemed washed by a sea of green.

" It is a wonderful morning, Fenton. The olives are all blue and there is not a cloud in the sky."

He lay there apathetically and did not answer her.

" Just the morning to start on a holiday. Why shouldn't we start on a holiday ? "

" What sort of a holiday do you think I'm fit for ? I don't want to go gallivanting about."

She sat on the window-ledge and the sunlight played in her hair.

" I don't mean an actual holiday, Fenton. Why shouldn't we make a new beginning—start a new bit of life ? It's possible."

He pulled himself up in bed.

" What d'you mean ? "

" We haven't been very happy—have we, Fenton ? I'm ready to let bygones be bygones and to start afresh. Let us try."

" So I'm to blame, am I ? "

" I never spoke of blame. Everybody has something to forgive. My quarrel is with that thing—over there."

She pointed to a little rosewood cabinet that stood on the top of a chest of drawers. Bale's eyes followed the pointing of her hand. He grunted.

" Can't do without it—now."

She went and stood facing him.

" Don't you realise that you have got to choose—to choose between me—and the stuff in that cabinet ? Make a fight for it. I'll help ; I'll do all that I can."

" It's no use," he said sullenly ; " you can't fight against a thing that has become a food."

But she would not let him surrender, and she set out to make a last effort to save her husband from the curse of the crave he had created. Perhaps the man's better self shone out momentarily through the fog of opium ; perhaps her pleading proved even more powerful than a potent drug. At all events she won him over, though he joined her sullenly like a man who misdoubted his own strength.

" All right. Chuck it away. The key's in my purse—there—on the table."

She found the key and unlocked the rosewood cabinet. In it were rows of little bottles, a pile of chip boxes, and a couple of hypodermic syringes in gilt cases. She gathered all the plunder in a fold of her night-dress, and stood looking compassionately at her husband.

" Promise me that is all, Fenton."

" Yes ; that's the lot."

" I will make it up to you. I am going to throw these into the river."

In half an hour she was standing on a rocky bank above one of the deep pools in the valley. The stream foamed into it from above, but where the rush had spent itself the pool was wonderfully clear and the colour of green glass. She had brought a little bright-coloured leather bag with her, and she stood on an outjutting rock and tossed bottles and syringes into the water. She was very solemn over it, and her eyes looked sad ; perhaps she doubted the permanence of her triumph.

Climbing back to the road and rounding the corner where the terrace wall jutted out, she walked straight into David Flemming. He was standing in the shade of an overhanging pine and looking up towards the house whose red roof showed through the foliage.

" You are out early."

She noticed at once how serious his eyes were.

" I was worried ; I admit it."

" Yes, but I have news for you. I must not stay more than two minutes. He is waiting for me, and he is just like a child this morning."

She told him all that she had to tell, but Flemming's eyes did not brighten to hers. He, too, misdoubted the value of this victory.

" He has let you throw all his drugs away ? "

" Yes. I mean to stand by him and help him to fight through."

He looked at her gravely, compassionately, for there was an air of sadness and resignation about her, as though she were none too sanguine, but had made up her mind to go through with it to the end.

" It's splendid of you."

" Oh, no, it's nothing of the kind. Perhaps it's despair. Good-bye. I must go. I'll—I'll write to you sometimes."

" I shall be down at Villadoro. Send for me—if——"

She gave him one look and hurried on as though she could not trust herself to say more.

" Good-bye. I shan't forget you."

Dr. Locker, driving along the sea-front of his smart car-rozza, sighted a man leaning over the parapet and watching the waves playing over the rocks below. Locker ordered the driver to stop and, jumping out, crossed the footpath and leant over the parapet close to Flemming, but the artist was so absorbed in some thoughts of his own that he did not glance at the man at his side.

Locker looked at him shrewdly.

" Hallo ! Leonardo."

Flemming turned sharply.

" Hallo ! I didn't realise who it was. In a way you are opportune."

" Thanks. Get in and drive ; I have to go to San Pietro."

They went bowling along the dusty road overhung by pines and ilexes and mimosa trees, with villa gardens on one side and the blue of the sea on the other. For a while they chatted about the Villa Scala bazaar, the tennis tournament in the casino gardens, and the expected visit of the English Mediterranean fleet. But this was mere dust so far as David Flemming was concerned, though he was shy with the shyness of a man who is fiercely in earnest.

" I say, Locker, I want to ask you something."

" Well, ask away."

" When a man who has the drug craving has the drug suddenly taken away from him, what happens ? "

" Sometimes he collapses, even dies."

" Yes ? "

" Or goes off his head and does something violent."

" That's what I thought. I may as well tell you the truth, Locker. Mrs. Bale has persuaded her husband to let her throw all the stuff away, and I tell you—I'm worried."

Locker was in a cynical mood.

" I shouldn't worry. He has another hoard hidden away somewhere. That is always the way. They are very cunning —the poor devils."

" Then you think he only made a pretence——"

" I'd swear to it. The only way to make sure that such a man as Bale does not get his particular drug is to shut him up in a nursing-home with people he can't bribe round him. I expect there is morphia hidden in every corner of that house."

" You may be right."

" My dear man, I have had to deal with a good many drug-maniacs in my time."

Flemming might be outreasoned, but he was not reassured. A peculiar restlessness took possession of him that day ; it was as though telepathic suggestion were at work, beating a mysterious warning into his brain. Towards evening it grew more imperious, more suggestive. He dined as usual at his hotel, took his coffee under a palm in the garden ; chatted to a couple of American women, and then broke away. Something was driving him up towards Acqua Dolce, something born of a restless imagination, or of a mysterious sympathy that no mechanical theory could explain.

It was a rare night ; a full moon was shining, and the road lay white between dark walls and gardens. The mountains were sharp ridged and black against a sky of steel. The river running in the valley made a noise like thunder.

It took Flemming half an hour to reach Acqua Dolce. The white walls of the house gleamed between the palms, cypresses, and ilexes ; the iron gates were closed.

On the opposite side of the road rose a grass bank topped by a few old olive trees, whose delicate foliage caught the moonlight and made a lacework of silver and jet. Flemming climbed the bank, and sat down on a gnarled root of one of the trees. He could see the upper windows of the villa ; the shutters were not closed, and the moonlight played upon the glass. Here and there a stone figure on the balustrades of the terrace walks shone white amid the gloom of shrubs and trees. The river thundered below, but no wind stirred the leaves of the olives.

Was it a mere superstitious whim that had brought him here—a mysterious voice speaking in the air ? He wondered. Nothing could have seemed more peaceful than this Italian valley, sleeping in the moonlight. It suggested no possible tragedy. And the sound of the bells ringing in the campaniles on the hills shivered through it with a thrill of mystery and of awe.

Flemming's eyes fixed themselves suddenly on a path that came winding down through the garden from one of the upper terraces. He thought he had seen something move there, gliding along the curves that were sometimes in the shadow, sometimes in the moonlight.

He sat at gaze, his face sharpening. The path ended in a formal walk along the terrace at the top of the boundary wall. A figure appeared there—a figure in a white dress, with hair black as the shadows under the trees. It was Lalia.

She threw a hurried glance up and down the road below, but she did not notice the man sitting under the olive tree, for he kept quite still, and his dark clothes merged into the outlines of the tree trunks. Flemming saw her climb the low wall, and let herself down by her hands. There was a drop of some five feet, but she landed lightly in the road below.

Flemming did not move. A kind of intuitive and tragic curiosity possessed him. What was she about to do ?

Lalia did not hesitate. Some very definite purpose seemed to possess her, for she started up the road with quick, silent steps. She had come out barefooted—that was why her feet made no sound.

As she disappeared round the curve of the road Flemming sprang down the bank and followed her. He had realised with sudden vividness what this escapade of hers might mean.

Lalia had heard him. He had a glimpse of her looking back as he came in view, her face white in the moonlight. He shouted to reassure her.

" It's Flemming. I want to speak to you."

But she gave a strange cry, turned, and started running up the road away from him.

Flemming went in pursuit. He had been something of an athlete as a youngster, but he found himself being left behind by this child of the Pacific. Never had he seen a girl run as she ran—beautifully, like a wild thing, lissome and very strong. Her short, loose skirt did not hinder her, and her bare feet seemed to give her grip and speed.

He hailed her once more :

" Lalia—stop ! "

But she paid no heed, and he saved his breath to make a race of it, a race that hinted at some tragic goal. He began to gain on her a little along one of the straight grey stretches of the mountain road.

Suddenly he saw her swerve to one side and take a path that led downwards through a plantation of olives. Flemming knew that path, and whither it led. Someone had built a rough stone belvedere at the top of a precipice that overhung the river, where a magnificent view could be had right down the valley, with Villadoro lying white on the edge of the sea.

He had been running like a man ; now he ran as a desperate lover. It was to be a battle of wills, and of bodies. He was racing her for her life.

The path ran about two hundred yards before it reached the plateau overhanging the river, and Flemming was some thirty yards behind the figure in the white dress. Yet Lalia looked like beating him in that death race, for her bare feet seemed to give her a better grip.

"Thank God!"

She had stumbled and fallen forward, and the cry burst from him impulsively. But she was up again before he could reach her.

"Go back—go back!"

"Lalia—give in!"

She dashed on, with Flemming after her. He gained, and caught her at the bottom of the short flight of rough steps that led down to the platform.

"Lalia!"

She struggled with him, and her strength almost overmatched his.

"Let me go, David—let me go!"

"No—no!"

He had his arms around her and she tried to break his grip, her hair clouding in his face.

"Let me go—do let me go!"

"I cannot!"

She panted:

"I cannot bear it! I must kill myself before he drives me to madness."

"You shall not kill yourself; neither shall he drive you mad."

"David—I shall kill him."

"No. Give in to me, dear. I am stronger than death."

The despair seemed to go out of her quite suddenly. She surrendered, and he felt her limp in his arms. He had to hold her. Her arms went round his neck; her head lay on his shoulder.

"Oh—my dear—what shall I do?"

She broke down, and all her passionate soul seemed to dissolve in anguish. He held her close and smoothed her hair. He was touching a woman and a child.

"Tell me——"

She shivered.

"Oh, I was wrong. A devil seemed to seize him when he had lost his drugs. I cannot tell you, David. I cannot go on living with him. He fell asleep, and I seized my chance."

Flemming was deeply moved.

"Lalia, you and I are strangers to each other, and yet somehow you have given me back the will to live. Sit down here with me, and let us see what we can make out of this tangle."

He led her to the belvedere overlooking the valley. They could see Villadoro shining white in the moonlight and the river flashing and foaming in the valley below. Flemming kept hold of her hand, and held it so firmly that she smiled at him with her wet eyes.

"I shan't throw myself over, David. That mood has gone."

He did not let her hand go, nor did she try to withdraw it.

"We must face things, Lalia. You cannot go on living this life."

"But what am I to do?"

He was silent for some while, thinking.

"Listen to me. I happen to be fairly well off, so far as money goes. I am going to ask you to let me give you what you need. I'm not making a bargain; I'm not asking for anything in return. You must go away and live your own life, and I can help you to begin it."

She looked at him with shining eyes.

"But I can't take your money."

"Why not?"

"Because it is yours."

"Oh, nonsense!" he broke out passionately. "Of course you can take it. I'm not making any cad's bargain with you. What is money for but to be used, and I have more than I know what to do with. I might send it to a charity, or write a cheque for some relative I don't care twopence about. Lalia, you'll take it?"

"No."

"Yes. Because I shall know that you don't trust me if you refuse."

She covered her eyes with her hand.

"Oh, what problems! But to escape! Yes, I'll take it, David. I'll go to Vienna. I had friends there. I'm not afraid to work. I can speak four languages, and I could teach. But how shall I go?"

He thought a moment.

"Go back to-night; bear one more night there. Then to-morrow morning come down to Villadoro; I will meet you in the Casino gardens at eleven. I can manage things; you shall have enough to carry you along for the moment. Go to Genoa, buy a trunk and some clothes, and then go on to Milan and Vienna. Write to me from there, and I will arrange to have more money sent to you. Is not that very simple?"

She sighed.

"It sounds so simple. I will go back to-night and think it over. I promise to meet you in the morning and tell you what I have decided."

She rose, hesitated, and then looked straight into his eyes as she stood beside her.

"You have willed me to live, David. You have been very good to me. And there is nothing that I can do in return."

"But there is, Lalia. Go on living, and so helping me to live. A month ago I did not care whether I lived or died ; in fact, I think I would rather have had death. But I do care now."

She laid a hand on his shoulder.

"And I care, too. Do you doubt it ? Something sang in my heart that night when we danced together. But there, we must just be comrades, and I must be going back."

They wandered slowly through the olive groves, where the moonlight sifted through and made delicate patterns on the ground. Silence had fallen upon them—a silence that was intimate and mysterious. Now and again they looked into each other's eyes and smiled.

The road lay white and empty before them, with a black shadow falling across it here and there where a pine or cypress intercepted the moonlight. They reached the wall where Lalia had let herself drop from the terrace below.

"The gates are locked."

"Then I must help you up."

An old fig tree hung down in one place. Flemming took Lalia in his arms and lifted her up till she could get a grip of the tree. He made a stirrup with his hands for one of her bare feet. She drew herself up, stood for a moment on his shoulder, and then scrambled to the top of the wall.

Flemming was looking at one of his hands.

"I say, you have cut your foot."

"Have I ? It can't be very much. I did not feel it. I must creep in now. Good night."

She leant over to him, her hair hanging down.

"I trust you, David."

"Till to-morrow," he answered her.

She disappeared, and he stood there at the foot of the wall, listening, determined to stay there till he was sure that she had succeeded in getting back into the house. If Bale had fallen into a drugged sleep, well and good ; but if the little beast——

He threw his head back sharply like a man challenged, for a cry came from the direction of the villa. He heard a man shouting angrily, and with a shrill and almost screaming self-abandonment. Another voice answered him—also a man's voice—scared and appealing.

Flemming made a leap for the fig tree, pulled himself up, and was over the wall like a man scaling a redoubt. He took the first path that showed in the moonlight; it led him uphill and towards the villa, and that was all he desired. And suddenly he found himself in the main way from the iron gates to the house, with a broad flight of steps going up under the shade of cypresses and firs.

A revolver-shot rang out, the sound echoing across the valley.

" Good God ! he's shot her ! "

Flemming ran on, and as he reached the flight of steps a man came blundering down them. It was Roberts, Bale's English valet, unnerved and in a panic.

He swerved to one side when he saw Flemming, and threw up his hands dramatically.

" Help ! Help ! "

" What has happened, man ? Are you hurt ? "

He stared into the valet's white face.

" No, sir. I was running for assistance, sir. He's up there with a revolver, and she's with him. He shot at me.".

" Come along, then ! Come on ! "

Flemming raced up the steps, and the valet followed him, flustered and out of breath, but ready to follow when there was another man in front.

" Be careful, sir. He's clean mad."

" All right."

Flemming had reached the last steps leading to the main terrace in front of the villa. He came to a sudden halt, stood staring, and then turned to the valet and signalled to him to hold back, for Flemming had seen enough in that one glance to realise that any meddling would mean death for the woman whom he loved.

On the terrace Lalia and her husband were facing each other in the moonlight, the woman absolutely motionless, the man wagging a revolver up and down as though he were wagging a monster forefinger. Then Fenton Bale began to shuffle round in a circle, and as he moved Lalia turned also, but more slowly, so that her eyes never left his face. Flemming had crouched down so that he could just see over the top step. He knew that if he made a dash for Bale the fellow would fire at Lalia.

It was a dumb show that Flemming watched—a play of mutes in the moonlight—and yet he could size up the tragic horror of the thing, and realise how disastrously it might end. Fenton Bale had nothing to say. He just grinned, and went shuffling round and round with that revolver of his, possessed by all the cunning ferocity of his madness, determined to kill, yet gloating over the prospect, and holding his hand for a while. And Lalia kept pace with him while he circled round her, so that he had to meet her eyes and look into her white face.

It had become a battle of wills, silent and problematical. When Bale's back was towards him Flemming could see Lalia's face. There seemed to be no fear upon it, but a kind of intense and youthful vitality that challenged Bale's idiot spite and dared it to act. She held her head high and her throat showed, and as she moved she looked like a statue turning on a pedestal.

Flemming was in a savage dilemma. He longed to jump up, make a dash for Bale, and risk the consequences so far as he himself was concerned, but he had an uncanny feeling that the madman's first shot would be fired at Lalia.

The valet came crawling up behind him and started to whisper. Flemming silenced him with a jab of the foot.

For Fenton Bale had stopped his shuffling round in a circle, and was standing staring at his wife as though the clock of madness in his brain had struck the hour.

Their profiles were turned towards Flemming. He heard Lalia speaking.

" Put that thing away, Fenton. It does not frighten me."

He gave a sort of chuckle.

" I can see a little hole in your head, and there will be a bigger hole at the back to match it. Gosh ! I can shoot ; I could shoot the moon."

She went three steps towards him.

" I dare you to shoot me, Fenton. I am not afraid of you."

The devil of madness in him mocked her.

" You wait. I'll make a pretty white angel of you. Don't you hear the bells ringing ? "

He stooped and leered at her, the revolver pointed.

" There's nobody here but you and me, no one at all. Isn't it quiet ? We are going away together ; I shan't stay behind you, my dear ; I'll lie down and hold your hand. Then, bang

For Fenton Bale had stopped his shuffling round in a circle, and was standing staring at his wife as though the clock of madness in his brain had struck the hour.

and I shall be with you again. I wonder whether it will be cold."

She faced him as though he were some wild beast that had to be magnetised.

" No, you are going to bed, Fenton, and you are going to give me——"

Flemming sprang up with a fierce cry, for he saw Bale poke his hand forward and a jet of flame start from the black muzzle. Lalia went swaying back, but Flemming's first business was with Bale. He made a wild dash across the terrace, and Bale, catching sight of him, stood faltering with an idiot indecision, the hand that held the revolver swaying like a bough in a wind. Then, with a gesture of impatience, he thrust the muzzle into his own face and fired.

Flemming saw Bale fall forward and crumple up in a heap, the revolver striking the stones. But when he looked towards Lalia, she was still erect, a white figure in the moonlight.

" Lalia——"

He went towards her as though he expected to see her totter and fall.

She stretched out her hands to him.

" Oh, dear God ! I'm not touched. It went by me."

Flemming and the man Roberts carried Fenton Bale into the house and laid him on a sofa in one of the ground floor rooms. He was dead, with a bullet in his brain.

A couple of scared Italian servants were whispering on the stairs. Flemming spoke to them, told them that " il signor " had shot himself, that he would go down to Villadoro for a doctor, and that the best thing they could do was to go back to bed.

Flemming found Lalia sitting on a stone seat at the edge of the terrace. She turned a dazed white face to him, and her eyes had a shadowy and lost look. The place seemed strangely still, with the mountains clear and sharp under the full moon, the hillsides brilliantly lit or lost in deep shadows. Not a leaf stirred. The trees and shrubs might have been obelisks cut out of black marble.

Flemming went and stood beside her.

" He is dead."

She echoed the last words as though her brain had been numbed by the shock.

" Dead ! But how strange."

" I don't want you to stay here, Lalia."

" Not stay here ? Where shall I go ? "

He realised how the tragedy had shocked her, that she was dazed, that she had no power for the moment either to choose or to will.

" I am going to take you back to Villadoro. I have friends here—Mrs. Locker; you remember her. She will be very kind."

Lalia rose like a child, holding out a hand to him.

" Yes, take me away from here, David. I will do just what you wish."

" I'll tell your husband's man."

He returned to the house and found Roberts waiting in the vestibule.

" I'm taking Mrs. Bale to Dr. Locker's. She ought not to stay here."

" Yes, sir."

" I shall ask Dr. Locker to come up to see the body. You will stay here, of course ? "

Flemming and Lalia did not remember that the iron gates were locked till Roberts came running after them with the key. He had been somewhat officious and familiar as Fenton Bale's servant, but he had taken Flemming's measure and stepped into his proper place.

" Leave the gates unlocked and wait up for Dr. Locker."

" Yes, sir."

Flemming was never likely to forget that walk down to Villadoro in the moonlight, for Lalia took his hand like a child, and seemed to give her fate into his keeping. And all that is admirable in a man's love realised itself in Flemming's heart that night. Had his dead wife come back from the grave to walk with them, he could have looked in her eyes, and spoken : " Dear, you will not condemn me because of this child. She will give me much that I lost when you were taken from me. ∎

The lights of Villadoro began to glimmer in the valley.

Flemming felt Lalia's hand stir in his.

" They will not be cross with you for bringing me ? "

" You don't know Grace Locker as I do. Put such thoughts out of your head, dear."

She drew closer to him.

" I should feel so lost without you, David. My soul seems to have dried up. I can't think of things."

" Keep hold of my hand," he said simply, " and leave life to me."

Lights were still burning in the Lockers' villa when Flemming and Lalia came up through the garden to the stone loggia running along the front of the house. A chair had been left in the loggia, and Flemming made Lalia sit down there.

" Wait. I'll go and tell them."

He found Grace writing letters, and her husband rolling cigarettes. They just looked at him, and waited after the first words, for his face had news graven upon it.

" Fenton Bale has shot himself. He tried to shoot his wife first, but missed her. I wonder if you will go up to Acqua Dolce, Locker ? "

Locker jumped up.

" Of course. Is he badly hurt ? "

" He's dead."

" Good God ! "

" I came really to see Grace. I've brought Lalia Bale down here. I'm wondering whether you could take her in ? "

Grace Locker left her bureau.

" David, you are a man of sense. Of course. Where is she ? "

" I left her sitting in the loggia. The shock has dazed her. She was worrying about being a bother to you."

Grace glanced at her husband

" We can dispense with you, Jim. You had better run up to Acqua Dolce. I'll go to her, David."

Flemming's eyes thanked her.

" You see, I knew who to come to. She will want you, Grace. I'll walk up with your man."

" Yes. I shall be glad to have both of you out of the way."

She hurried out into the loggia where Lalia's white figure showed in the gloom.

" You poor dear, come in at once ; come up to my room."

" David said that you would be kind to me."

" That shows that he is a very sensible man."

In half an hour Grace Locker had Lalia in bed, and had given her a dose of veronal to make her sleep.

Flemming was out early next day buying flowers at the little stall under the church wall in the market square. Grace Locker was taking her café au lait in the loggia when he arrived. She noticed his flowers and smiled brightly.

" Jim wants to see you. He's in the study. I'll take those flowers for you."

Locker had news for Flemming.

"That's a fine girl, Leonardo. She has sent us on a mission, though I fail to see why she should want to be generous to that beggar's reputation."

"What do you mean?"

"She wants to hide the fact that he tried to shoot her. If that valet has not been gossiping, and if we get in before the good Italian officials——"

"That's generous of her, Locker. Come along, we'll get hold of Roberts and persuade him to forget a few details. Bale shot himself; that's enough for anybody."

They started for Acqua Dolce together, and found that the police had not yet put in an appearance, and that the man Roberts was to be persuaded to forget that Fenton Bale had attempted murder.

"I've been with him five years, gentlemen, and he was generous to me—in his way. The drugs did it. God knows I've pitied his wife and I've pitied him. Well, he was mad, clean mad. It's good of her to want to cover it up."

Meanwhile, Lalia lay abed in a little room whose window overlooked the sea, that blue sea upon whose edge little white towns glistened. And between the blue of the sea and the blue of the sky the soft purple of the distant Apennines hung like a mysterious cloud.

But Lalia lay in a kind of daze, with eyes half closed, and her breathing hardly perceptible. The reaction had come upon her, and she felt weary with the weariness of one whose heart has been heavy for many a long month.

Her eyes looked at the flowers in the vase on a table beside her. Grace Locker had put them there, and Lalia knew that Flemming had brought them. She smiled, but there was a questioning wistfulness in the smile, for this lethargy of her brought with it a mood of doubt and of sensitive self-abasement. No doubt he pitied her, but then, she would not let him sacrifice himself. And a sudden fear of love itself seized her. She felt herself a child of tragedy. Supposing she brought unhappiness into his life?"

Grace Locker came in and found her lying there mute, and still, and sorrowful.

"I wonder if you will see someone?"

There was a start of fear in Lalia's eyes.

"Who is it?"

"Why, the sender of those flowers."

She turned her face away.

" No—no, not yet. I'm—I'm thinking. I'm afraid of myself. It may mean so much to me—and to him."

Three weeks later David Flemming arrived at the little town of Felice, and, hiring a carriage outside the station, ordered the man to drive to the Villa Merula.

But Mrs. Locker was not at the Villa Merula when Flemming pulled the iron bell-handle. Yet a neat, black-eyed Italian maid seemed to have expected him.

" The ladies have gone to the Capo, sir."

Flemming's Italian was fairly serviceable. He asked to be directed to the Capo.

" Follow the road, sir, and take the first path on the left. It will take you to the Capo. You cannot miss your way."

In the midst of a thicket of wild rosemary he met Grace Locker, and her kind eyes lit up under the shade of her white parasol.

" I was coming back to the villa. I thought my letter would bring you."

She gave him her hand.

" What a friend you have been. How is she ? "

" I left her there at the end of the Capo, under a big fir. Oh, she is happier, I think. There were days when she thought that she never ought to see you again—for your sake, not hers."

" I think I am a judge of that. May we come back to lunch ? "

" Better still. I will make up a picnic basket for two, and send it out to you."

" No, you must join us."

" Very well. But I shall not hurry back."

She smiled as she left him to go upon his way.

The path ran under the wall of a garden that was smothered with passion flower, roses, and climbing geranium. The whole headland smelt with rosemary, and thyme, and the resinous pines. And in a short while Flemming came to a place where the path ended in a little plateau of grass screened by rocks, and shaded by two or three old pines.

Lalia was sitting there with her back against one of the trees, her hands locked about her knees.

" So I have found you."

She started round, her hands dropping from her knees.

" David ! "

" And what a tyrant you have been to me. I had begun to wonder whether I should have to rebel."

He threw himself down beside her on the grass, and for a moment her eyes seemed afraid to meet his. She was breathing deeply, her fine throat quivering with emotion.

" It was Grace who persuaded me. She said she knew you so well, and that——"

He reached out and took one of her hands.

" Grace is splendid, but I can speak for myself. I want to forget everything but these pines, that bit of blue sea and sky, the foam down yonder, and you."

She turned and looked at him with grave and appealing eyes.

" David, do you mean——"

" I want you to want me. Why, dear heart, you can give me back life. I see colour, and joy, and sunlight again. You can teach me to work. You don't know what a hell of loneliness I have been through."

" I know. But am I the mate for you ? Some of your good English think me half a savage."

" Oh, good God ! let them think what they please. Am I asking for a little colourless, bloodless girl with no ideas beyond what is supposed to be nice and pretty ? I want someone to share life with me, someone who is just a little wild and adventurous, and impulsive. What do most of the English know about you island people, you who are natural aristocrats ? Look at the blue sea, and the mountains, and smell these pines, and tell me that we are not born comrades. Lalia, I love you, love you, and nothing is going to stop me loving you."

She looked at him with head thrown back, eyes half closed. And suddenly her eyes seemed to open and to fill with tawny light.

" I can't help it, David. You will have to take me. I'm a wild girl, in spite of Paris and Vienna."

" I want the surf child, the girl with the red flowers in her hair."

GUY DE MAUPASSANT (1850–1893), though one of the world's supreme "artists of the short story," was only forty-three when he died. His life of tragic misfortune is reflected in the cynicism and morbidity of many of his tales. "Happiness," however, reveals De Maupassant in a more optimistic mood. The story is told with such delicate perception that this simple romance becomes a living human document.

HAPPINESS

IT was tea-time, just before the lights were brought in. The sky was all rosy with sunset and shimmering with gold dust. The villa looked down upon the Mediterranean, which lay without ripple or quiver, like a vast sheet of burnished metal, smooth and shining in the fading daylight. The irregular outline of the distant mountains on the right stood out black against the pale purple background of the western sky.

The conversation turned on love, that old familiar topic, and remarks that had been made many times before were being offered once again. The gentle melancholy of the twilight diffused a languorous charm and created an atmosphere of tender emotion. The word "love," constantly reiterated, now in a man's virile voice, now in a woman's delicate tones, seemed to dominate the little drawing-room, hovering like a bird, brooding like a spirit.

"Is it possible to remain faithful to one love year after year?"

Some said yes, some said no. Distinctions were made, limits defined, and instances cited. The minds of all, men and women alike, were surging with a host of disturbing memories, which trembled on their lips, but which they dared not utter. Their emotion expressed itself in the deep and ardent interest with which they discussed this commonplace, yet sovereign, passion, this tender and mysterious bond between two beings.

Suddenly someone, with his eyes on the distant prospect, exclaimed :

"Oh, look over there. What can it be?"

On the sky-line, a great blurred mass of grey was rising out of the sea. The ladies sprang to their feet and gazed in surprise at this startling thing that they had never seen before.

"It is Corsica," someone explained. "It is visible two or three times a year in certain exceptional atmospheric conditions. When the air is perfectly clear the mists of water vapour, which usually veil the horizon, are lifted."

The ridges of the mountains could be faintly discerned, and some thought that they could make out even the snow on the peaks.

This sudden apparition of a phantom world, emerging from the sea, produced on those who witnessed it a disquieting impression, a feeling of uneasiness, almost of consternation.

An old gentleman, hitherto silent, exclaimed :

"That very island which has risen from the waters as if in response to our conversation, reminds me of a curious experience. It was there that I came upon a wonderful instance of faithful love, a love that was incredibly happy. This is the story :

"Five years ago I paid a visit to Corsica. Although visible now and then, like to-day, from the coast of France, less is known of that wild island than of America, and it seems almost more remote. Picture to yourselves a world still in a state of chaos, a raging sea of mountains, intersected by narrow gorges with rushing torrents. Instead of plains, there are vast, rolling sweeps of granite and gigantic undulations of the earth, overgrown with bush and great forests of chestnut trees and pines. It is a virgin country, desolate, uncultivated, in spite of an occasional village planted like a heap of rocks on a mountain top. There is no agriculture, industry, or art. You never come upon a scrap of wood-carving or sculpture, or any relic, showing in the Corsicans of old a taste, whether primitive or cultured, for graceful and beautiful things. It is this that strikes you most forcibly in that superb but austere country, its hereditary indifference to that striving after exquisite forms, which we call Art. In Italy, every palace is not only full of masterpieces, but is itself a masterpiece ; in Italy, marble, wood, bronze, iron, metals, stone, all testify to the genius of man, and even the humblest relics of antiquity, that lie about in old houses, reveal this divine passion for beauty. Italy is to all of us a beloved and sacred land, because it displays convincingly the energy, grandeur, power and triumph of creative intelligence.

"And opposite her shores lies wild Corsica, just as she was in her earliest days. There a man leads his own life in his rude cottage, indifferent to everything that does not directly concern himself or his family quarrels. And he still retains the defects and qualities of primitive races. Passionate, vindictive, frankly bloodthirsty, he is at the same time hospitable, generous, faithful, ingenuous. He opens his door to the stranger and repays the most trifling act of kindness with loyal friendship.

"For a whole month I had been wandering all over this magnificent island, and I had a feeling of having reached the end of the world. There were no inns, no taverns, no roads. Mule tracks lead up to hamlets that cling to the mountain sides and look down upon winding cañons, from whose depths rises of an evening the deep, muffled roar of torrents. The wanderer knocks at the door of a house and asks for a night's hospitality. He takes his place at his host's frugal board, sleeps beneath his humble roof, and the next day the master of the house escorts his guest to the outskirts of the village, where they shake hands and part.

"One evening, after a ten hours' tramp, I reached a little solitary dwelling at the upper end of a valley, which, a mile lower, fell away abruptly to the sea. It was a ravine of intense dreariness, walled in by bleak mountains, rising steeply on either side, and covered with bush, fallen rocks, and lofty trees. Near the hut there were some vines and a small garden, and at a little distance, some tall chestnut trees. It was enough to support life, and indeed amounted to a fortune on that poverty-stricken island.

"I was met by an old woman of severe aspect and unusual cleanliness. Her husband rose from a straw-bottomed chair, bowed to me, and then resumed his seat without a word.

"'Pray excuse him,' said his wife. 'He is deaf. He is eighty-two.'

"To my surprise, she spoke French like a Frenchwoman.

"'You are not a native of Corsica?' I asked.

"'No, we are from the mainland, but we have lived here for fifty years.'

"A wave of horror and dismay swept over me at the thought of those fifty years spent in that gloomy cranny, so far from towns and places where men live. An old shepherd entered, and we all sat down to supper, which consisted of a single course, thick broth containing potatoes, bacon, and cabbages

all cooked together. When the short meal was over I took a
seat before the door. I was weighed down by the melancholy
aspect of that forbidding landscape and by that feeling of
depression which at times overtakes the traveller on a dismal
evening in dreary surroundings, a foreboding that the end of
everything, the end of existence, the end of the world, is at
hand. Suddenly the appalling wretchedness of life is borne
in upon us ; the isolation of each one of us ; the hollowness
of everything ; the black loneliness of the heart, which is
lulled and deceived by its own imaginings to the brink of
the grave.

" Presently the old woman rejoined me, and with the curiosity which lingers even in the serenest soul, she began to
question me.

" ' So you come from France ? '

" ' Yes, I am on a pleasure trip.'

" ' I suppose you live in Paris.'

" ' No, my home is Nancy.'

" At this she seemed to be seized by some violent emotion,
and yet I cannot explain how it was that I saw, or rather felt,
her agitation.

" ' Your home is Nancy ? ' she repeated slowly.

" Her husband appeared in the doorway, with the impassive
air that deaf people have.

" ' Never mind about him," she continued, ' he cannot
hear us.' After a pause she resumed :

" ' Then you know people at Nancy ? '

" ' Yes, nearly everyone.'

" ' Do you know the Sainte-Allaizes ? '

" ' Very well indeed. They were friends of my father's.'

" ' What is your name ? '

" I told her. She looked at me searchingly. Then, in the
low voice of one conjuring up the past :

" ' Yes, yes, I remember perfectly. And what has become
of the Brisemares ? '

" ' They are all dead.'

" ' Ah ! And did you know the Sirmonts ? '

" ' Yes, the last of them is a General now.'

" She was quivering with excitement, with pain, with
mingled emotions, strong, sacred, impossible to describe, with
a strange yearning to break the silence, to utter all the secrets
hitherto locked away in her heart, to speak about those people,
whose very names shook her to the soul.

" ' Henri de Sirmont. Yes, I know,' she exclaimed. ' He is my brother.'

" I glanced at her in amazement. Suddenly I remembered.

" Long ago there had been a terrible scandal among the Lorraine aristocracy. Suzanne de Sirmont, a beautiful and wealthy girl, had eloped with a non-commissioned officer in the Hussar regiment commanded by her father. The son of a peasant, but for all that a fine figure in his blue pelisse, this common soldier had captivated his Colonel's daughter. No doubt she had had opportunities of seeing him, admiring him, and falling in love with him, as she watched the squadrons trooping past. But how had she contrived to speak to him ? How had they managed to meet and come to an understanding ? How had she ventured to convey to him that she loved him ? No one ever knew.

" No suspicion had been aroused. At the end of the soldier's term of service they disappeared together one night. A search was made for them, but without result. Nothing was ever heard of them again and the family looked upon her as dead.

" And now I had found her in this desolate valley.

" ' I remember perfectly,' I said at last. ' You are Mademoiselle Suzanne.'

" She nodded. Tears welled from her eyes. Then, with a glance towards the old man, who was standing motionless on the threshold of his hut :

" ' And that is my husband.'

" Then I realised that she still loved him, that she still beheld him with eyes that had not lost their illusion.

" ' I trust that you have been happy ? ' I ventured.

" In a voice straight from the heart she answered :

" ' Yes, very happy. He has made me very happy. I have never regretted anything.'

" I gazed at her in sympathetic surprise, marvelling at the power of love. This well-bred, wealthy girl had followed that humble peasant, and had stooped to his level. She had submitted to an existence destitute of all the graces, luxuries, and refinements of life. She had conformed to his simple ways. And she still loved him. She had become a peasant woman, in bonnet and cotton gown. She sat on a straw-bottomed chair at a wooden table, and supped on a broth of cabbages, potatoes, and bacon, served in an earthenware dish. At night she lay on a palliasse by his side. She had never had a thought for anything but her lover. And she regretted nothing, neither jewels, silks and satins, luxuries, cushioned chairs, the warmth and perfume of tapestried rooms, nor downy couches so grateful to weary limbs. He was her one desire. As long as he was there she asked no more of life.

"A mere girl, she had sacrificed her whole future, the world, and those who had brought her up and loved her. All alone with him, she had come to this wild ravine. And he had been all in all to her. He had satisfied her heart's desires, its dreams, its endless longings, its undying hopes. He had filled her whole life with bliss from beginning to end. She could not possibly have been happier.

"I lay awake all night, listening to the old soldier's stertorous breathing, as he slept on his pallet by the side of her who had followed him to the ends of the earth, and I pondered on their strange, yet simple story ; their happiness, so perfect, yet founded on so little.

"At sunrise I shook hands with the old couple and bade them farewell."

．　　．　　．　　．　　．　　．　　．

The speaker was silent.

"You may say what you please," one of the women exclaimed, "her ideals were paltry. Her wants and desires were absurdly primitive. She was just a fool."

"What did that matter ? " replied another woman pensively. "She was happy."

On the horizon, Corsica was vanishing in the gloom of night, sinking slowly back into the sea, as if its vast shadowy form had manifested itself for no other purpose than to tell its tale of those two simple lovers who had found a refuge on its shores.

ELEANOR FARJEON *has written de-lightful and distinctive poems for children. Her first novel was " Ladybrook," a tale of Sussex country life which, while innocent of fantasy and allegory, retained that delicate humorous touch which characterises the work she does for children. Her sensitiveness to beauty and true understanding of the essential qualities of romance find expression in this charming rhapsody.*

ANTHONY IN BLUE ALSATIA

SKIPPING his breakfast paper one day, bewildered, as he always was, by vital facts about Home Rails, Questions in the House, and Three-Piece Suits : facts grasped, as he knew, instantaneously in their full import all over England by different orders of mind from his, through which they slipped as through gauze : Anthony's roving eye was captured by certain words in a paragraph headed

MOUCHARD (NEAR THE JURA MOUNTAINS)

Jura Mountains . . . Blue smoke . . . a blue-eyed Alsatian . . . a Concertina . . . the Blue Alsatian Express . . . many miles from nowhere . . . haymaking damsels in white sunbonnets . . . hayrakes . . . laughing at us . . .

A MINOR MYSTERY

Anthony's eye roved no more. He felt that the gauze, which could not contain the torrents of the world's activities, might house this butterfly and not brush off its bloom. He read the paragraph with attention. It described the break-down " many miles from nowhere " of the Blue Alsatian Express at the foot of the Jura Mountains. It described the blue smoke rising from a heated axle, the engine-driver sprint-ing along the lines like a madman, soldiers jumping out on the line and playing a concertina, a nervous woman-passenger wondering what had happened ; it indicated the plutocratic luxury of the corridor train with its restaurant ; it told of the blue mountains and the blue sky, and " the hay-making damsels in white sunbonnets and hay-forks on their shoulders " who " are laughing at us over the hedgerows."

357

And then came the paragraph headed " A Minor Mystery " which ended the account of the accident.

" One mystery about this train will never be solved. When it first came to a standstill a quiet little man, who looked like a country farmer, packed up his things, climbed out of the train, and deliberately walked away from it without any outward sign of annoyance, hesitation, or distraction, crossing the fields and disappearing into a wood.

Had the breakdown occurred within easy reach of his own home or destination ? "

" Oh, no," said Anthony, answering the journalist, " of course not ! "

Why should it ? It was most unlikely. And—annoyance ? Why should the little man be annoyed ? And where was the Mystery, Minor or Major ?

Railways—it is their drawback—compel you to travel to somewhere. You, who desire to travel to Anywhere, must take your ticket to Stroud or Stoke, and chance it. The safest plan is to choose some place with a name like Lulworth, Downderry, or Nether Wallop ; such places surely cannot go far wrong. But even though they prove to be heaven in its first, second, or third degree, still, there you must go, and nowhere else ;—and think of the Seventh Heavens you flash through continually on your way there, Heavens with no names and no stations, Heavens to which no tickets are issued. To whom has it not happened, time and again, on his way to the Seaside, the Moors, or the Highlands, to cry in his heart, at some glimpse of Paradise from the carriage windows : " *That* is where I really wanted to go—*that* is where I would like to get out ! That valley of flowers, that cottage in the birch-glade, that buttercup field with the little river and a kingfisher—if only the train would stop ! "—But it never does.

Never ? Once it did. Anthony laughed aloud at that Minor Mystery in his morning paper. Where was the Mystery ? Luck had been with the quiet little man, and he did the only thing there was to do.

" Why have we stopped ? " asked the nervous lady who sat opposite Anthony in the stuffy carriage.

" Ha-ha-ha ! Ha-ha-ha ! " laughed a fresh young voice outside.

" Preposterous, preposterous !   I shall be late ! " snorted
a fat millionaire.

" I want my lunch," puffed his fat wife.   " I refuse to go
without my lunch ! "

Anthony looked out of the window.   A hedgerow bowed
with blossom, beyond it a meadow in full flower, long flowering
grass, threaded with flowering stems, lace-white, chicory-blue
flowers, a profusion of flowers shimmering in the long grass.
In one part of the meadow the grass lay mowed in swathes,
the sweet flowers with it.   A party of young peasants, in
loose white shirts and embroidered jackets and aprons, lay
in the grass munching honey-cake and drinking light beer.
One tall young fellow, splendid as a god, stood edgeways in
the sunlight, his bright scythe shining.   A few girls stood and
stooped in the long grass, picking the flowers ; some wore
wreaths of the blue and white flowers, some were laughing
under their white sunbonnets, some used, some rested on,
their rakes, all were sweet and fresh and frank.

" Oh, why *don't* we go on ? " moaned the nervous lady.
" Oh, *what* has happened ? "

Passengers spoke on all sides.   " We are held up ! "
" We   have   broken   down ! "   " Bandits !—these   dreadful
foreign parts ! "   " The engine is on fire ! "   " The engine-
driver has gone mad ! "

" Oh, oh, oh ! " moaned the nervous lady in the carriage.

" Ha-ha-ha ! " laughed the gay young voices in the air.

" I shall be late, I tell you ! " fumed the fat millionaire.

" Are we *never* going to eat ? " puffed his wife.

Beyond the meadow of flowers and haymakers lay the
blue mountains, as blue as dreams, as Paradise.   Soft dim
woods lay between the meadow and the slope.   At the very
edge of the woods, as though it had just stepped out of the
trees and set foot on the grass, was a tiny cottage with a balcony.
In the fringe of trees meandered little paths and a little stream,
and some goats.   The scent of hay and flowers and aromatic
trees filled the carriage.

" La-la-la-LA, ti-TI-ti-TI ! "   A soldier sitting on the
rails was singing *The Blue Danube* to a concertina played by
another soldier.

The girls in the meadow began to dance.

" Oh, what is it, what is it ? " wailed the nervous lady.

" Food, food ! " puffed the fat one.

" How late, how *late* I shall be ! " repeated her husband.

" Keep the doors shut—don't let them come in ! " implored the nervous lady, wringing her hands.

" Ha-ha-ha ! " laughed the dancing girls, " ha-ha-ha ! "

" *Swish !* " sang the young god's scythe.

Anthony got his little bag from the rack and opened the carriage door.   The nervous lady gave a tiny shriek.

" Ah ! don't let them in ! "

" Late ! late ! late ! "

" Lunch is served.   Come ! "

Anthony crossed the rail and found a gap in the blossoming hedge.   In the hayfield, nearly hidden in flowers, was a crooked footpath.   It led over the meadows to the little wood at the foot of the blue mountains.   He followed it unhesitatingly. He left behind him the dancing laughing flower-gatherers, the young god mowing, the peasants drinking, the soldiers playing, the Blue Alsatian Express containing the millionaire who would be late—for what ?   For what could one be late ? One was in Blue Alsatia.   To which there are no tickets.

He entered the little wood and was lost to sight.

At the back of the cottage, barefoot by the little stream, stood a girl of sixteen, a lovely grey-eyed child, feeding her kids from a bundle of hay in her apron, at which they pushed and pulled.   She wore a white chemise and a blue embroidered skirt.   When the kids were rough she thrust them from her with her brown toes, and laughed like music.   On a bench by the cottage stood a pitcher and a wooden bowl.

Her eyes met Anthony's.· She let fall her apron, and the sweet hay tumbled down, a full feast for the kids.   She went to the bench, filled the bowl with milk, and offered it to Anthony with a bit of honey-cake, her grey eyes smiling.   As he drank, she made a simple gesture.

" Stay," she said.

The Blue Alsatian Express went on without him.

Anthony stirred his tea-cup.   In the next column was an account of Last Night's Debate on——

He skipped it.

JEFFERY FARNOL (1878—   ) *was for two years a theatrical scene-painter, though his literary career may be said to have started at the age of nineteen. With very few exceptions his work is " in costume," and he has a particular fondness for the Regency period, which is the setting for his best-loved books, " The Amateur Gentleman " and " The Broad Highway." Boxing is his favourite sport.*

FORTUNE'S FOOL

CHAPTER I

UPON a certain Christmas Eve I chanced to be seated very securely in the stocks for some small matter or another—which, if I remember rightly, was a duck.

I was very thirsty, and faint with cold and hunger, for I had sat there since early morning. Nevertheless, despite all this, despite the crick in my back and the ache in my legs, I endeavoured to preserve that serene indifference and philosophic calm behind which I had sought shelter from those unkind buffets with which Fate had beset me, these latter evil days. To the which end I settled my aching back against the hard, unsympathetic wall behind me, and gave all my attention to the battered volume in my hand.

Now, as I read in the book, with my hat pulled down over my face—for the sun was low, and its level rays dazzled my eyes—as I perused those thumbed pages, seeking consolation from the wisdom therein set down, I became suddenly aware of an unpleasantly hard object which had obtruded itself into my ribs, and, looking down, I beheld an ebony stick or staff, and, glancing along this, I saw in turn a white, veinous hand, an elegant ruffle, a blue coat-sleeve and, lastly, a face—a face seamed by numberless small lines and wrinkles, out of which looked a pair of the very brightest, twinkling blue eyes I had ever seen ; and though the lips were solemn, it almost seemed that those eyes smiled at me, notwithstanding my threadbare, dusty exterior, and somewhat undignified situation. Therefore I checked my indignation at being thus rudely disturbed, and smiled back at my visitor, while, because of his years, I uncovered my head.

"Pray, young man," said he, standing very upright and square of shoulder for all his age, "pray, what is it you read there?"

"Ancient sir," I answered, bowing as well as my cramped position would allow, "I read, for one thing, that it is easier to grow cabbages than to govern an empire."

"True, true," nodded my inquisitor, smiling with eyes and lips now, "but how came you with Marcus Aurelius?"

"Ancient sir," said I, "I have at all times found him to be a most pleasant companion, more especially in times of any little—unpleasantness, such as you behold me now enduring."

"It was a—duck, I think?" inquired the ancient gentleman.

"Sir, I believe it was."

"Just so," he nodded; "you were accused and convicted of—shall we say?—gathering it to yourself by the wayside."

"An excellent phrase, sir," said I, with another attempt at a bow. "And I am free to admit the impeachment, for, sir, a man will live if he can, and, to live, needs must he eat—now and then."

"The argument is unanswerable, young sir."

"Moreover," I continued, closing my book, for the ancient gentleman had seated himself upon the stocks, "moreover, I am extremely partial to roast duck, at all times."

"That also is very natural, young sir; ducks in their season are very fit and proper for eating. But in this instance, young sir, may I be permitted to point out to you that this particular duck was my property?"

"Then, ancient sir, I take the liberty of congratulating you on having once possessed a bird so remarkably fine and tender."

Here my companion threw back his head, and laughed so unfeignedly that even I was constrained to smile.

"By all the gods," he exclaimed, shaking his head at me, "by all the gods of Olympus, you may be a vasty rogue, but 'tis a shame you should sit here any longer—even for such a matchless duck."

"In that, ancient sir," said I, straightening my aching back, with a sigh, "in that I cannot help but agree with you."

The ancient gentleman laughed again, and, setting a silver whistle to his lips, blew two shrill blasts; whereupon I presently heard the measured tread of feet, and, glancing over my shoulder, beheld another ancient man, also very stiff as to back and square as to shoulder, who, halting suddenly, faced about, touched the brim of his hat, and stood at attention ; then I noticed that he wore a black patch over one eye.

"Sergeant !"

"Sir ?"

"Tell Giles to bring the keys."

"Yessir."

"And, Sergeant—tell him I'm waiting."

"Yessir ! "

Saying which, the Sergeant wheeled, and strode back with measured step, as though giving time to a file of invisible Grenadiers.

"Only one eye, you'll notice," said my companion, nodding after the upright figure of the Sergeant. " Sir, my name is Bulstrode—Pertinax Bulstrode. I was wounded and left for dead at Corunna, but my Sergeant—Sergeant Battle, sir— brought me off and lost his eye in the doing of it ; nevertheless, he manages to see as much with that one eye as most people can with two—ah ! and a great deal more. A remarkable man, you'll say ? Sir, you are right. Sergeant Battle is the most remarkable man I know. I have a prodigious regard for his opinion. And now, may I see your book, young sir ? " my companion inquired abruptly.

For answer I put the volume into his outstretched hand. He took the book and opened its worn pages with that deft and gentle touch which only the true lover of books can possess ; then glanced up at me sharply from under his thick eyebrows.

"You read in the Latin ? " he inquired.

"Yes, sir."

"And the Greek ? "

"Yes, sir."

"And yet—you sit in the stocks."

"Occasionally," I sighed.

At this he smiled again, but thereafter grew suddenly grave, and shook his head.

"A scholar—so young, and yet sits in the stocks ! " said he, as though to himself, and so fell to turning the pages of the book.

"This is a very rare edition ? " he exclaimed, all at once.

"Yes, ancient sir."

"A most valuable book, and—Ha, there is a name written

here ! " And his bright, piercing eyes were sharper than ever under his thick brows.

" Ancient sir," said I, meeting his look, " let me assure you that, so far, I steal only ducks, or an occasional rabbit. The book is my own—like the name written in it."

" Sir, sir," said my companion, staring harder than ever, " do you mean that you are—Martin Fanshawe—Fanshawe of Revelsdown ? "

" I was once, sir."

" You—you ? The admired Corinthian, the idol of the fashionable world—the second Brummell ! "

" Sir," said I bitterly, " indeed you embarrass me ! "

" Nay, young sir, your fame was widespread three years ago—you were the ' bang-up Blood '—the dashing Buck who gambled away his fortune in a single night ! "

" No, sir," said I, shaking my head. " It took me three nights to do it."

" Furthermore, young sir, you are the man who—so Rumour says—won the love of the beautiful Diana Chalmers."

" But Rumour is generally a vasty liar, sir ; nobody could win this woman's love, because, first, she doesn't know the meaning of the word, and, secondly, she has no heart."

" Are you sure of that ? Are you quite sure of that ? " regarding me under drawn brows.

" Yes ; to my cost, ancient sir ! " I answered, frowning down at my imprisoned legs.

" Your name is doubly familiar," said my companion, after a while, " for, young sir, I knew your father in the Peninsula. He is dead, I trust ? "

" Long before his son became—what you see him," I answered gloomily.

After this we fell silent again, until there came once more the tread of feet, the first slow and deliberate, the others very quick and hasty, and the tall Sergeant marched up, accompanied by the short-legged beadle, who puffed with haste and jingled his keys officiously as he came.

" Here I be, Sir Pertinax. The rogue should have sat there another two hours ; but if 'tis your wishes, why, out 'e comes ! " And he jingled his keys again.

These the ancient gentleman now took from him, and, despite his obsequious remonstrance, freed me from my galling bonds with his own hands.

" Sir," said I, as I rose, somewhat clumsily because of the

painful stiffness in my limbs, " permit me to offer you the
thanks of a most unworthy fellow, yet one who will cherish the
memory of your charitable action. Believe me, I am most
sincerely grateful."

So saying, I slipped the book into my pocket, and, lifting
my hat, turned to go upon my way. But now, all at once, I
was seized with a sudden giddiness ; a deadly faintness came
over me. I stumbled, and should have fallen but for the
Sergeant's ready arm.

" Why, how now ? " exclaimed Sir Pertinax, laying his
hand upon my shoulder.

" It is nothing, sir," said I, forcing a laugh, " nothing in
the world, I thank you. A little giddiness—the long confinement."

" And want o' food, sir ! " added the Sergeant.

" Food ! " cried Sir Pertinax. " By all the gods, you're
right, Sergeant—you're always right ! Why, he's been sitting
here since early morning ! Why, damme ! take his arm,
Sergeant Battle ! "

" No, indeed," said I. " It will pass in a moment ; and
I am not wholly destitute."

" Be that as it may, young sir, the Sergeant here has
taken a fancy to you—the Sergeant is a remarkable man—for
so have I, sir. You shall sup with me to-night—roast duck
again, sir, but with apple sauce and a bottle of burgundy this
time. Sergeant Battle—forward—march ! "

CHAPTER II

SUPPER was nearly over—such a supper as I had not enjoyed
for many a long day. The candlelight glittered upon
silver and cut glass ; it glowed in the wine, and shone upon
the kindly face of my host. And, contrasting all this with my
own miserable estate, remembering I must soon exchange this
warmth and luxury for the bleak and lonely road, I stifled the
sigh upon my lips, and swallowed my wine at a gulp.

" Young sir," said my host, glancing across at me with his
quick, bright eyes, " you sighed, I think ? "

" Folly never sighs, sir," I answered.

" Of that I am not by any means sure, young sir."

" Sighs," I continued, " are for the ambitious, the remorseful
and the lovesick."

" And are you—none of these ? "

" No, sir—I am merely a fool."

" And would you have me think, then, that a fool never sighs ? "

" Not if he is a consistent fool, since folly must needs laugh on until—either it dies, or has suffered sufficiently. And thus, ancient sir, this fool, having eaten and drunk and laughed with you, will bid you good-night, and take himself off about his business."

" Which is to find wisdom, I trust, young sir—and self-respect."

" Ancient sir," said I, rising, " a few days since I stole a duck of yours, and cooked and ate it in a barn, and found it not amiss ; to-day I endured the stocks for it, as philosophically as might be ; to-morrow I may be clapped in the stocks of some other village, for hunger is a recurrent evil, and must be supplied."

" And what, young sir—what of your self-respect ? "

" That died, sir, three years ago, with my name."

" And yet," said Sir Pertinax, watching me under his brows, " you wear your father's signet still ! " And he pointed to the ring on my finger. " Ay, look at it—look at it, and read the motto engraved there : ' Resurgam—I shall arise ! ' You see, I knew your father years ago."

Now, as I stood there, staring down at the ring, there came to me a memory of other days, when the Fool—though always the Fool—was young in his folly—when ambition ran high and failure was unknown. And as I looked, remembering him who had given the ring, my sight grew dim and blurred. " Resurgam ! " I muttered, and, clenching my hands, I thrust them deep down into my pockets, and, lifting my head, I faced Sir Pertinax across the table.

" Sir," said I, " if a man's self-respect, once gone, can ever be regained, it must be sought for by darksome roads, by laborious days and sleepless nights, it seems to me."

" True, true, young sir ! "

" Then, sir, I thank you humbly—deeply ; and now I'll be gone upon my way—to seek it." And, turning hastily, I caught up my hat.

" Stay," said Sir Pertinax, leaning across the table ; " supposing I could put you in the way of it—would you accept my help—for the sake of your father ? "

" Yes, sir ! " said I, " for you have brought back forgotten memories."

"Memory," said Sir Pertinax, shaking his head ; " 'tis a blessing bitter-sweet. I have two memories, very fair and tender, young sir, of one who died, and one who—ran away. It was never my lot to call a woman ' wife,' for she died, as I say, but I might have made a very excellent uncle, only that she—ran away. And it is of her that I would speak to you, though I think—yes, I think her letter might best explain the matter. Sit down, young sir, and I will read it to you." And forthwith, drawing the candles nearer, Sir Pertinax took the letter from his pocket, and, unfolding it with gentle fingers, read as follows :

"The spoiled child is weary of her toy ; she has had her way, and is wretched. London is become hateful ; society, fashions, even admiration, palls ; she sighs for the country, for you and for the Sergeant.

"But then you may not have forgiven her ; you may not want this foolish, disobedient child. And yet, because she knows you so well, she thinks you may. So she is coming back to you—to be forgiven—for Christmas is near, and this is a season of sweet memories and of forgiveness. But, because she has been so cruel to you in the past, she is a little afraid ; therefore if you want her, needs must you come and fetch her, though indeed you need not come far ; she will await you at the posting-house, here at Cranbrook, from nine o'clock this Christmas Eve until midnight.

"But, should you not come, then will she go back again ; and because hope will be dead—as her poor heart has been these many months—she will give herself to the beast whom you know. Therefore, if you have any love yet remaining for your wayward child, come ; because she is lonely—lonely and very wretched, and because Christmas is at hand. Her heart, alas ! is dead. Yet, indeed, indeed she would strive to make this a happy season for you—like those of the past that seem so far away. You should find her very loving and very humble, and never, never more would she run away and leave you solitary. So does she pray you come and fetch her—home.

"And, though she is afraid, nevertheless she thinks you may come, because you were all the father and mother she ever knew, and because you loved her once, and would not see her wedded to a beast."

Sir Pertinax folded up the letter very tenderly, watching me under his brows all the time.

" Young sir," said he, " there are the words of one I dearly love—the child of my dead sister. But she was young and high-spirited, and—this is but a dreary place, perhaps. So she fled to an aunt in London. And there in the world of fashion she met and loved one who proved unworthy—poor child ! But hearts seldom die. What do you think ? "

" I think, sir, that you will go to her."

" Then, young sir, therein you are wrong."

" Wrong ? Then you mean——"

" I mean, young sir, that you shall go for me, if you will."

" Sir," said I, starting up to my feet, " you surely jest ! "

" Will you go, young sir ? "

" But why ? " I demanded. " Why entrust such a mission to me—a stranger ? "

" Perhaps because of the ring you wear."

" But, sir, remember an hour ago you took me from the stocks ! I am a vagrant, and worse ! "

" But, peradventure you may find your self-respect upon the road ; I humbly pray it may be so. And now, young sir, it is already eight o'clock, and there, I think, is the Sergeant with your horse."

" My horse ? " I exclaimed, as the sound of hoofs struck my ear.

" The Sergeant, as I told you, is a very remarkable man ; Cranbrook is ten miles away, and it is already eight o'clock, sir ; you must ride hard—I would not have you late."

" But—but, sir," I stammered, " what would you have me do ? "

" I would ask you to bear a message for me."

" A message, sir ? "

" A letter, young sir. Come, will you undertake this mission ? "

" But, sir, I—don't understand ! "

" Will you go, young sir—yes or no ? "

For a moment I stood irresolute ; then, raising my head, I looked into the sharp, kindly eyes of my host.

" Since you honour me with your trust, I will go, sir," said I ; " and though I am only what I am, you shall find me worthy."

Hereupon Sir Pertinax seated himself at a small writing-table and scrawled a hasty note. And having sanded and folded it, he handed it to me. As one in a dream I thrust it into my bosom, and as one in a dream I followed him out into the forecourt. Here was the Sergeant, with a cloak upon his arm, which he proceeded to put about my shoulders ; and here also was a groom, holding a horse that champed its bit and pawed impatient hoof. So, still like one in a dream, I mounted, drew the cloak about me, and, giving the horse his head, galloped away upon my mission.

CHAPTER III

THE clock in the great square tower of the church was striking nine as I rode into Cranbrook and dismounted in the yard of the inn which is called the posting-house. And, being come into the house, I beheld a fire that roared merrily up the chimney, while before it, in a great elbow-chair, sat a large, rotund man, nodding drowsily at the blaze, but who roused himself sufficiently to glance at me, murmuring sleepily :

" G'd-evening, sir ! Merry Chris'mas ! " Saying which he rang a bell which stood upon a small table beside him, whereupon a trim young dame appearing, he rolled his heavy head at me, and murmured :

" Gen'l'man's orders, Nancy ! " And so, apparently forgetting all about me, nodded at the fire again.

The trim dame smiled, and dropped me a curtsey, but in so doing, she chanced to espy my boots beneath my cloak— a sorry pair, worn and broken, and immediately her smile vanished, and it seemed to me that she began to eye me and my fine cloak with suspicion.

Now this, trifling though it was, added to my embarrassment ; for as she stood waiting my orders, and staring at my boots, I suddenly remembered that I knew not whom to ask for, since Sir Pertinax had never once mentioned his niece's name. Therefore, while the trim dame continued to eye me and my sorry boots very much askance, I took the letter from my pocket, but finding it bore no superscription, I stood, wholly at a loss, staring at the blank sides of the letter in deep perplexity.

" What'll you take ? " demanded the trim dame, grim-voiced, as her supercilious eyes stared now at my threadbare coat, which my open cloak revealed in all its shabbiness.

" Come, what d'ye want ? " she demanded.

" Thank you," I answered, " you may bring me a mug of ale."

She turned away with a toss of her head, and presently returned with a foaming tankard, which she took care not to relinquish until I had paid the money into her hand ; whereupon she tossed her head again, and left me to the fat, drowsy man, who still nodded at the fire. After he had nodded, and I had watched him awhile, I spoke.

" Have you many guests in the house ? "

" Guests, sir ? " said he, rolling a somnolent eye at me. " Now and then, sir, they comes and they goes, sir—goes. Ah ! seems t'me as they goes oftener than they comes."

" There is a lady here, I think, who came about an hour ago ? "

" Ah ! " nodded the man. " But she'll go again, bless ye. They allus does ; they comes and they goes. There's a gen'l'man in the coffee-room, too—one of the quality. Ah ! to 'ear 'im swearin' at the ostlers is a eddication. Come in about a 'our ago, but 'e'll go again, like all the rest on 'em."

But now I spied a pleasant-faced maid, who, tripping up beside the landlord's chair, laid her hand upon his shoulder and shook him gently :

" Lady in number six wants to know if Sir Pertinax Bulstrode has come yet, father ? " But before the sleepy landlord could speak, I rose, drawing my cloak about me.

" I come from Sir Pertinax," said I.

" Then this way, sir," she answered ; and, leading the way up the wide oak stairway, she paused at a certain door, knocked and stood aside.

So, hat in hand, I entered the room, but beholding her whom I sought, I stopped, all at once.

" Diana ! " said I ; and thereafter we stood gazing upon each other, silent and utterly still. As I looked upon her loveliness, the recollection of the long days and weary months rolled from me, and I forgot all things but her triumphant beauty, took a sudden eager step towards her ; then as suddenly checked myself. For memory rushed back upon me, and with it a great and bitter rage.

" Martin ! " she whispered. " Oh, Martin, is it really you ? "

" Indeed, yes," said I. " Though I wonder you should recognise me, for I am a little—altered, perhaps."

"Thank God!" she whispered. "You are come back from the dead! And—oh, Martin, it is Christmas Eve!"

And now her eyes were hid beneath their curling lashes, and her pale cheeks glowed all at once.

"Christmas Eve!" I repeated, and frowned.

"Yes, Martin. And I—I have prayed for this." And, speaking, she reached out her hands to me. Then, looking from those appealing hands to the tender smile upon her lips, I clenched my fists, and stooped my head that I might not look upon temptation; and thus beholding my broken boots, my soiled and shabby garments, I laughed and shook my head.

"Madame," said I, "here is only a poor rascal, a paltry rogue, not worth a proud lady's prayers. Nor would he have them. For if you could not love him when Fortune was his friend, do not pity him because you see him what he is; for pity is akin to love, they say, and he desires—neither!"

"But, Martin, you loved me once?"

"Did I so, madame? Ah, well, youth is ever foolish!"

"Foolish!" said she. And, sighing, turned away.

"To love so madly one who proved she had no heart!" said I bitterly.

"I was so young, Martin, and you had many enemies. They lied, and I believed them; they poisoned my mind against you. I was so very young."

"But we are older now. All this was ages since."

"But you have not forgotten. You have come back, Martin."

"How?" I exclaimed. "You never think I sought you out knowingly? You never think that I came to meet the proud and beautiful Lady Diana—the toast of London?"

"Don't!" she cried, shrinking away. "Ah, don't." And she covered her face.

"Dear Lady Diana," said I, bowing, "believe me, I would have died rather than you should have seen me as I am. I have sunk very low, but I have some shred of pride left—even yet."

"Yes, you were always over-proud, Martin, and a little cruel," she said, with her face still hidden. "And I have hoped—prayed that you might come back to me some day, to tell me that you forgive."

"Forgive!" I exclaimed. "Of what avails forgiveness now? It is too late! Who am I to forgive? I am become an outcast, a discredited wretch hiding himself in out-of-the-way places. Indeed, it would be folly to seek forgiveness of such a pitiful wretch."

"Ah, no, Martin—no, no! Poverty is no sin, it cannot debase a man."

"No, but hunger may. Who will not steal that he may live? And, my Lady Diana, thus low have I sunk—a pilferer, a petty thief. Yes," said I, seeing her stricken look, "' thief ' is an ugly word, but ' famine ' is far worse; and hunger is a pain that may drag a man to the uttermost depths. Remember me as I was three years ago, and believe, I pray you, that I could not knowingly have sought you out to confront you with the thing I am!"

"Then why—why are you here?"

"I came on a mission for Sir Pertinax."

"Then you know my uncle?"

"He made my acquaintance as I sat in the stocks."

"The stocks! Oh, Martin!"

"I had stolen a duck, you see—a grave offence, madame. I had also cooked and eaten it—which was graver still."

"And he sent you to me?"

"To his niece, madame, naming no names. Even the letter, as you see, bears no superscription. And thus I came in ignorance."

So I gave her the letter. And now, turning to look at her —for I had kept my face averted hitherto—I saw that her lashes were thick with tears, and that her hands trembled as she unfolded the letter. Now, as she read, her cheeks all at once became suffused with a rosy glow, and, when she looked at me again, there was a new light in her eyes.

"Do you know what is written here, Martin?"

"No. My mission is only to bring you back to Sir Pertinax; and so, with your permission, I'll go and see your chaise got ready."

"Stay!" said she, intercepting me. "Sir Charles Trefusis is below, Martin."

"Trefusis?" said I, frowning. "Well, what of that?"

"He has sworn that—that I shall go back to London."

"Ah!" said I, smiling. "But were Trefusis twenty times the man he is, he should not stop you to-night!"

"He would create a disturbance. And he has a man watching my chaise. Oh, I cannot go this way!"

"Then what will you do?"

"Run away, Martin."

"How?"

"You must ride on ahead, and wait for me on the road."

"And what of Trefusis? If he is so earnestly bent on creating a disturbance, I've no mind to deny him."

"Martin, it is Christmas Eve."

"Well," said I, as she hesitated.

"And, oh, I would not have you meet each other!"

"Why, I have a long account to settle with him."

"Yes, Martin. And I have heard he tried to kill you once."

"That was three years ago!" said I bitterly. "No one would take the trouble now."

"Then go, Martin—go, I beg of you—and wait for me on the road!"

Now, as she spoke, in her earnestness, she rested her hands on my arm; and the touch of her thrilled me, as, indeed, it had ever done, so that needs must I obey her.

"I will wait," said I. "But if you keep me long, I shall come back and bring you away, Trefusis or no."

It was a frosty night, but the wind had died away, while, overhead, the moon rose very bright and clear; therefore, I drew rein in the shade of some trees, and, as I waited the coming of my lady it almost seemed that I could still feel the touch of her fingers on my arm. Presently, growing impatient, I set my horse for Cranbrook again, and had already gone some distance when I spied my lady afoot, and hurrying towards me; therefore I checked my career, and, as I prepared to dismount, she was beside me.

"Quick!" she cried, and reached up her hands to me. "Quick! Take me up before you!"

Scarcely knowing what I did, I stooped and caught her up to the saddle before me, and in this posture we began our journey, with never a word between us.

And now indeed I rode as one in a dream who realises the impossible; and this dream of mine was a blending of joy and sorrow, of pleasure and torment; for needs must I keep one arm about her, and needs must she rest in that embrace, so that with every movement of the horse I could feel the sway of that supple, yielding body, and the warm sweet tenderness of her; and, though her hood was close drawn, yet could I hear the quick, soft pant of her breath, while over my senses stole the fragrance of her hair.

But when we had ridden some while in silence, she spoke, very softly :

" Are you cold, Martin ? "

" No," I said. " No, I thank you."

" Yet you tremble, Martin ? "

" I—it was a passing chill," I stammered. " The wind is keen here among the hills."

" Yes, it is freezing, I think. Do you remember that last Christmas, Martin—when you told me that you loved me ? "

" Yes, I remember."

" We were to have been married in January. You were very impatient always, Martin. And then I wrote that cruel letter, that wicked——"

" That altered our lives," said I.

" Martin, oh, Martin, can you ever forgive me ? "

" Yes," said I ; " the past is over and done with. I forgive you."

" Then, look at me, Martin. Bend closer. I cannot see your eyes."

Obediently I stooped my head, and, in that moment, her arms were about my neck, and her lips were pressed to mine Then, borne away beyond my strength, I caught her close against my heart, and held her there.

" Oh, woman ! " I cried. " Oh, woman that I love, and always must. You that I have dreamed of in my misery and degradation ; you that I have hungered for, thirsted for— why do you tempt me ? Can't you see that I can never come back to you the pitiful wreck of what I was—the broken, penniless outcast ? Ah, why—why couldn't you pretend to forget, as I did ? "

" Because I love you, Martin ; from the first, yes, even when I wrote you that cruel letter."

" Stop," I groaned. " It were shame in me to listen ; there is the future."

As I spoke, I started, and turned my head.

" Listen," said I ; " here, I think, comes one who might solve this problem for us, and in the only way. Listen ! '

Faint with distance, yet growing rapidly nearer, was the wild beat of hoof-strokes drumming upon the frosty road.

" Trefusis ! " she exclaimed breathlessly ; and then, " Ride—spur, Martin, spur ! "

" Useless," said I, " he is but one, and we are two."

" Then what—oh, what shall we do ? "

" This," said I ; and kicking free of the stirrups I slid down from the saddle. " Now ride on, 'tis but half a mile to the house. Diana, ride I say ! "

" And leave you ? Never ! "

" I would but stay him a while."

" Stay him ! How ? And what of the old quarrel between you ? No ; my place is here ! "

Then, before I could stay her, she was down in the road beside me, and thus we awaited our pursuer. On he came, with a thunder of hoofs, and at the same wild pace—nearer and nearer, until I could see the gleaming buckle in his hat-band, until I could distinguish the eyes below. Nearer and nearer, and so reined in with a jerk, and saluted us with a mocking flourish of his hat.

" Ah, Trefusis," said I, stepping up to him, " this is very well met. You will remember our last meeting, perhaps ? " Now, watching him, I saw him start at this.

" Egad, it's Fanshawe ! " he exclaimed.

" And entirely at your service ! " said I.

" Stay, though," he drawled. " Can this be Fanshawe— Fanshawe the Corinthian, the ' glass of fashion and mould of form ? ' Fanshawe in such a hat ? Preposterous ! But, whoever you happen to be, sir, stand aside—my business is with this lady."

" The lady is bound for Tenterden, sir," said I, folding my arms.

" She rides for London, sir ! "

" I think not," said I.

" Think as you please ! " he retorted. " But stand aside ! D'you hear ? For the last time, will you stand aside ? "

For answer I smiled and shook my head. I saw his brows twitch together as, wheeling his horse, he rode at me with upraised whip. But as he came I leapt aside, avoiding the blow, and, as his horse reared, leapt in and catching him in a sudden, passionate grip, dragged him from the saddle.

" You were always a liar, and a coward, Trefusis ! " said I, smiling down at him as he lay.

Very slowly he came to his elbow, and, watching him, I saw what I had expected, the gleam of the weapon he had drawn and levelled. But I only smiled, and nodded my head at him.

" A liar and coward ! " I repeated. " And a murderer, too, it seems ! Shoot, man, and be done ! "

For a moment we remained thus, staring into each other's eyes above the levelled pistol. Then, reading my purpose in my look, he suddenly altered his aim to her who stood at my elbow ; but as the weapon flashed I leapt between, felt a sudden, jarring shock, and, staggering back against grassy bank, leaned there.

" Yes, Trefusis," I said, through stiffening lips, " a liar—and a—murderer ! And being so—you have resolved for us—the problem, and so—I thank you."

But even while I spoke he sprang to his feet, tossed aside the smoking pistol, and, leaping into the saddle, spurred galloping down the road, and I heard his hoof-strokes die rapidly into the distance.

And now a deadly faintness came over me, with a growing numbness, and my sight failed. But in the dark her voice called to me from far away.

" Diana," said I, " oh, my love — the problem is — solved for us. We need not trouble for — the future — after all."

And so, as it seemed, I fell into the dark.

CHAPTER IV

SIR PERTINAX stood over me, his blue coat laid aside, his shirt-sleeves rolled up, while at the bed's foot was the Sergeant with bowl and sponge.

Having seen thus much, I closed my eyes again, and lay utterly still, for a great weariness oppressed me.

Then I became conscious of a hand that stroked my hair and caressed my brow with a touch ineffably gentle ; therefore, opening my eyes again, I saw that my lady leaned above me. Glancing up at Sir Pertinax, I smiled.

" Ancient sir," said I, " my mission is accomplished. I have brought back your child to you, and so—can die in peace very comfortably, which, under the circumstances, is the very wisest thing I ever did."

" Die ! " exclaimed Sir Pertinax. " Die, young sir ? Pooh ! I've seen many gunshot wounds in my time, and I'm surgeon enough to promise you shall be up by New Year's Day. We found you in time, you see—that is, the Sergeant did ; the Sergeant, as I think I mentioned before, is a very remarkable man, young sir. Die ? A fiddlestick, sir ! Life for you is but just beginning, it seems."

"Life, sir?" said I. "And what can life bring—to the Fool? What of the future?"

"The future? Nay, ask this maid of ours, she shall answer you best," and he laid his hand upon my lady's bent head. "Speak to him, child, tell him."

Then my lady took from her bosom a certain letter, and, unfolding it, read aloud in her sweet, low voice:

"Poor child, and is thy heart dead? Yet am I sending with these poor lines a Christmas present that, methinks, shall bring to it a joyful resurrection.

"He is very proud in his abasement, but all things are possible to Love. Thus, with this happy season, this time of forgiveness, a new life may begin for each one of you, fuller, richer than you have ever known. Such is my prayer."

Now, even as she ended, suddenly upon the stillness of the room the bells in the church tower, hard by, began to ring a merry peal.

"Hark!" cried Sir Pertinax. "The chimes have begun already. Hark to the Christmas bells!" And in a little he turned to me, and his blue eyes were wondrous kind.

"Martin," said he, "a man's self-respect is better than riches. To-day you are poor, but you are a man again, such a man as your father would have been proud to acknowledge. So, Martin, lad, give me your hand. A merry Christmas, Martin!" Then, as he spoke, he took my heavy hand, and set within its feeble clasp my lady's slender fingers.

"Sergeant," said he, "attention! Sergeant Battle, we have dreamed of this. Have we, or have we not, Sergeant Battle?"

"Ay, sir, many a time; a new line o' march for all on us, as you might say, sir."

"The Sergeant is right, as usual; it *is* a new line of march. Children, to-day, this Christmas Day, a new life begins for each one of us. But for you the future holds greater and more enduring joys than any you have known. Am I not right, children, am I not right?"

And looking into my lady's dear eyes, I knew that he was. Thus Sorrow fled away from me, and was lost in the merry clamour of the bells.

GILBERT FRANKAU (1884—   ) *is the eldest son of the late Julia Frankau, better known as Frank Danby, whose novels were as popular with her generation as are those of her gifted son with his.   After a distinguished military career, Captain Frankau produced in 1919 "Peter Jackson, Cigar Merchant," a brilliant success which has been sustained by his later novels, "Masterson," "Everywoman," etc.*

ONE WEEK AT THE RITZ

"*A wealthy corporation requires for a mission demanding tact rather than experience a British subject, about thirty years of age and of unimpeachable social position. Remuneration lavish but according to results. Preference will be given to one who is married, to one who speaks Spanish, and to an ex-officer of the Royal Flying Corps. Applicants must present themselves in person to Mr. Cyrus P. Dreschler at 27a, Cornhill, E.C., between the hours of 11 and 1 to-day,*" read out Charlie Torrance across the débris of the lodging-house breakfast ; and he added, the skin round his blue eyes puckering in thought, " It sounds like a spoof to me."

" You ought to make certain, oughtn't you ? " retorted Mrs. Charlie. " After all, we can't afford to leave anything to chance these days."

" These days " were being pretty bad ones for the Torrances. Somehow or other, ever since Charlie left the Flying Service, things had been going from worse to worst with them ; so that already they were reduced—this young man of good family but no prospects, and this young woman who had abandoned her own prospects of making a living as a play-actress to marry him—to the last hundred pounds of his wound-gratuity and her savings.

" Of course I'll go if you think I ought to," went on the young man, fingering the clipped tawn of his moustache. " Perhaps—if the thing isn't a spoof—the fact that I can speak a little Spanish and handle a joy-stick may help."

He rose to his full height (not quite the proverbial six-foot

378

of heroic fiction) and making his way round the untidy table, kissed his wife's sleek dark head.

" You're always the optimist of the family, Meg," he told her, " though how you can be optimistic in this kind of place beats me."

" It *is* pretty awful, isn't it ? " Mrs. Charlie glanced at the window beyond whose uncleaned panes the suburban trams went slushing down the hill, at the scratched wallpaper and the botched furniture and the patched carpet and the general beastliness of Number 47, Boundary Road, S.E. 28. " But we'll get out of it somehow or other, won't we ? "

" Of course we will," chorused Charlie ; and went off to get ready for what he secretly regarded as a forlorn hope with a little of his old jauntiness.

Mrs. Charlie called to him through the flimsy door which led to their airless bedroom, " I should put on my tail-coat if I were you, darling," and began to tidy up the breakfast things preparatory to their removal, probably about mid-day, by the frowsy landlady's one frowsier servant.

She was still very beautiful, was Mrs. Charlie ; though worry, which is akin to old age, had already pencilled little lines on her broad forehead, and housework roughened ever so slightly her managing hands. Moreover, her face, an almost perfect oval under the smooth sweep of her hair, showed character. The lips were red and decisive, the chin firm and full-moulded, the eyes—dark as her hair—truthful and truth-compelling.

They clouded a little, those truth-compelling eyes, as the managing hands finished their distasteful task ; and even when Charlie—the pre-war tail-coat clipping him tightly at the waist-line, the pre-war top-hat in his hand—came in to kiss good-bye, apprehension still dwelt dark in their pupils. " He won't get the job," thought Charlie's wife, responding to his kiss, " he never does get any job."

And Charlie's thoughts as he swung himself on to the crowded tram paralleled his wife's. " I'm no good," he said to himself. " No earthly good for civilian life." From which, reacting to the unpleasant stimulus of his travelling-companions, his mind re-visualized those easy pre-war days when—first in the motor-car business and after that in the just-developing business of the air—he had always managed to pick up a good living for himself. " Two's different, though," he mused, paying for his tram-ticket. " Besides—

everything's so infernally dear nowadays." All the same—went on thought—other people managed to pick up a living. He began to think of Mrs. Charlie ; saw, in his mind's eye, her face actually outlined against the blurred windows. Whereupon his resolution, which had wilted a little under constant misfortune, stiffened again. " Damn it ! " he said to himself, " damn it, I *will* make good."

The tram jolted on, endlessly through endless suburbs. At last it made Westminster Bridge. Big Ben pointed twenty minutes to eleven. " I must be there to the tick," thought Charlie. The car jolted on again, down the Embankment. The weather seemed to be clearing, and by the time they reached Blackfriars, a thin gleam of London's sunlight shone over the river.

The sunlight invigorated the ex-officer, making him reckless. He hailed a taxi, and told the driver, " Twenty-seven, A, Cornhill." " May as well do the thing in style," he mused, jingling the scanty change in the pocket of his home-pressed trousers. . . .

§ 2

BUT the " style " of an eighteen-penny taxi-cab seemed a poor thing to Charlie Torrance when, some five minutes later, his be-spatted feet carried him dubiously up seven red marble steps, through a gun-metal and plate-glass door, towards a desk whereat a uniformed commissionaire sat Cerberus-like beween two rows of shining gadgets and a mahogany board lettered in gold, " Enquiries." Beyond this Cerberus stretched a vast hall among whose marble columns bareheaded clerks passed on swift errands ; while up and down, to and from, the tessellated floor of this hall, three lifts hurried with a ceaseless clash of bronze gates and a ceaseless shimmer of indicator lights.

" I came to see Mr. Cyrus P. Dreschler," said Charlie ; and he added, " This is 27a, Cornhill, isn't it ? "

" It is," vouchsafed the commissionaire. " Have you a card ? "

The ex-officer fumbled in his pocket and produced the necessary pasteboard.

" Write your address on it, please," said the commissionaire. More fumbling produced a pencil with which, rather shame-facedly, Charlie Torrance confessed his temporary domicile.

The commissionaire took the card and, inserting it in the rubber carrier of a pneumatic tube, whisked it to some unknown destination with the pull of a lever. " Wait here, please," he said ; and shortly afterwards, having answered one of the sharply-tinkling telephones, " Mr. Dreschler will see you. It's room 217, third floor. Any of the liftmen will direct you."

Within seventy-two seconds, Charlie Torrance, by now convinced that whatever the strange advertisement might be, it was no spoof, found himself in a large unfriendly room, distempered olive-green and furnished with that particular breed of green leather, red mahogany woodwork and Turkey carpet which typifies finance the world over.

There were some dozen other men in the room—all, as Charlie realized in a flash, after the same job. Of these young men some seemed to be already acquainted with one another ; and the newcomer, listening to their conversation, recognized without difficulty that, in whatever other particular most of them might fail, it would not be in their own estimate of their social position.

" Not much use to me, I'm afraid," murmured a confirmatory voice at Charlie's side ; and, turning, he saw a broad-shouldered, shabbily dressed man with a humorous face, obviously a ranker officer.

" Why not ? " asked Charlie, putting his hat, stick and gloves on the mahogany table.

" Too many nobs," confided the other.

At which precise moment, the further door of the big room opened, and a commissionaire even more resplendent than the one on the ground floor asked pompously for, " The Honourable Alan Livermore."

The Honourable Alan, a weak-lipped youngster in the short black coat and sponge-bag trousers of the post-war Stock Exchange blood, stepped forward and disappeared through the door.

" Too many nobs," repeated the ranker.

Apparently, however, the Honourable Alan's interview lasted less than three minutes ; as, at the end of that time, the commissionaire reappeared to call another applicant, and went on doing so at five- or ten-minute intervals for the best part of an hour. Meanwhile, the room continued to fill.

At last Charlie's turn came ; and, picking up his impedimenta from the table, he followed the commissionaire into the presence of a little man, domed of bald forehead, bushy of eyebrow and resolute of chin, who perched on a big swivel-chair behind a big bare desk set in the middle of a big bare apartment.

" Sit down," commanded the little man.

Charlie took the indicated chair, which faced a strong north light, and Cyrus P. Dreschler looked at him in absolute silence for thirty full seconds.

" So you came in answer to my advertisement ? " he said at last.

" Yes. I was here at eleven."

" Something in your favour, anyway," snapped the American. " Any other qualifications ? "

" Well," Charlie couldn't help one of his ingratiating smiles, " well, I'm married, I was a member of the Royal Air Force, and I do speak Spanish."

" *Habla bien ?* " asked the other, with the most surprising accent Charlie had ever heard.

" *Si, señor. Lo hablo desed niño.*"

" H'm ! That's more than most of them do." The eyes under the bushy brows glinted and the thin lips relaxed to a smile.

After a short pause, Dreschler went on to talk of half a dozen subjects which seemed to Charlie Torrance utterly irrelevant to the matter in hand. " Funny people, you English," he said. " Most of you don't seem able to read your own language. I should have thought that advertisement was as clear as daylight." He broke off and gazed ruminatingly out of the window. Then, suddenly, he began to rap out question after purposeful question. " What was Mr. Torrance's rank ? Where had Flight - Commander Torrance been educated ? Had he any business experience ? What war-service had he seen ? What makes of machine had he flown ? What age was his wife ? Had they any children ? "

Answering, Charlie's heart rose. He looked surreptitiously at the watch on his wrist and saw that he had already been in Mr. Dreschler's room a quarter of an hour—longer than any of the other candidates. Somehow or other, he rather liked Mr. Dreschler. But that gentleman's next question, " Now tell me what you've been doing since you were demobilized," dropped his heart into his pre-war boots.

" Taking it easy, more or less," he prevaricated.

" H'm ! " Again Mr. Dreschler fell silent. After a

while he said, as though speaking to himself, " I can't make head or tail of this country. I'm staying at the Ritz ; and when I look round the dining-room there, it seems to me as though every other young man I set eyes on is exactly the person I'm looking for. But when I get 'em down here——" He broke off, waving a large well-manicured hand as though to say, " When I get 'em down here they don't cut any ice."

By now Charlie's heart had oozed clean through the soles of his boots on to the Turkey carpet, so that it was only with supreme difficulty he managed to say, " I hope you'll excuse me for mentioning it, Mr. Dreschler, but you haven't yet told me what the job is."

" Of course I haven't." The American laughed. " The job's a secret till I find the right man for it." And a few minutes afterwards, with the usual vague promise, " Well, I'll let you know my decision," Charlie Torrance found himself footing it down Cornhill. " Another wash-out," he thought.

Nor was the thought any less bitter because of the instinctive liking he had taken to Mr. Cyrus P. Dreschler. " I'm sure *he's* no spoofer," said Charlie to himself, and so saying, remembered the American's remark about the young men he had seen at the Ritz.

§ 3

Eating his frugal lunch, tubing and tramming it home, that remark stuck like wax in Charlie Torrance's mind. " The Ritz," he kept on thinking ; " the Ritz ! If only I could meet Cyrus P. there instead of at those unfriendly offices of his, I believe I really could persuade him to give me this mysterious job."

But it was not until he arrived at Boundary Road, not until—Meg having gone out to purchase their tea—he sat alone in his oldest clothes (one does not wear one's pre-war kit more than is absolutely necessary when one is down to one's last hundred pounds) that the Great Idea took shape in Charlie Torrance's brain.

This Great Idea, like all Great Ideas, was daring, so daring that, when Meg came back, he was almost afraid to broach it to her.

" Well," she asked. " What happened ? "

" Only the usual promise."

" To let you know ? "

" Yes."

Meg took off her coat and took the purchased cakes out of their paper bag. He could see by the look in her eyes that she was disappointed, and her disappointment once more stiffened his resolution : so that, after tea had been cleared away and his pipe was lit, he gave her the gist of the morning's interview, ending :

" And that's that ! You see, old thing, the trouble with this sort of job, as with all decent jobs, is that one wants influence to get them. If one hasn't got influence, one's got to have cheek. The devil's own cheek ! Now, if only I knew somebody who knew Dreschler. If only I could afford to stay at the sort of hotel he stays at. If only I could meet him socially——"

He broke off, puffing furiously at his pipe, and his wife watched him in wonder. This was a new Charlie, a Charlie— as she phrased it to herself—out for blood. " Go on," she prompted.

He went on diffidently. " I've got an idea. Of course you'll think it crazy, and I suppose in a way it is. My idea's this. We've got to put our best goods in the window. We've got to get out of these rotten lodgings. We've got to get back into London. We've got to meet people—people who'll do us a bit of good. We've got to go somewhere—somewhere where we'll be seen—somewhere like," gaining courage, he exploded his bombshell, " like the Ritz."

" The Ritz ! " Meg stared at this new husband of hers across the stained tablecloth. " But we couldn't afford to stay at the Ritz for a week."

" Yes, we could." Charlie got up from the lodging-house chair, which creaked at the release of his weight, and began to stride purposefully up and down the room. " Oh yes, we could. We could stay there for a whole fortnight, if necessary, on a hundred."

" And after that ? " Meg's dark eyes were sheer panic.

" Oh, after that the deluge."

" But, Charlie—I don't understand. Why should we go to the Ritz ? "

" So as to meet Dreschler."

" But you've met Dreschler."

" No. I haven't." Irritation crisped the voice. " I haven't met him. I've only been interviewed by him."

They argued things out till their tempers frayed. To

Meg, the Great Idea was the idea of a lunatic : to Charlie, the more he discussed it, the greater it became. He had " a hunch," he told her, his eyes alight with the instinct of the gambler, " an absolute hunch." Dreschler was their man. If only Dreschler could be persuaded to give him this job . . .

" But you don't even know what the job is," countered Meg.

" I'm sure it's a good one," he said stubbornly.

" Supposing you don't get it ? "

" But I shall get it."

They continued to argue, till supper-time, through supper-time ; till the frowsy landlady, fearful of her gas-bill, came knocking at their door to tell them it was high time all virtuous lodgers were a-bed. . . .

§ 4

AT four-o'clock in the afternoon of the day following the insertion of Mr. Cyrus P. Dreschler's advertisement in the *Times*, there arrived at the Arlington Street entrance of the Ritz Hotel an unostentatious taxi from which—followed by a small cascade of pre-war leather luggage—there emerged Flight-Commander and Mrs. Charles Torrance, whose first-floor suite, reserved by telephone, was even then—so the *chef de réception* informed them—ready.

" And the flowers I ordered," asked Flight-Commander Torrance haughtily, " are they in the sitting-room ? "

" Certainly, sir. The fires have been lit also."

" Good." Charlie allowed himself to be conducted across the two-hundred-and-fifty-thousand-franc ? Aubusson carpet to the lift.

The lift glided upwards, and Mrs. Charlie's heart sank with the gliding of it. Even though she had permitted herself, at about three o'clock of a sleepless morning, to be over-persuaded into it, all her love of truth revolted at what Charlie insisted on describing as their " big bluff." " Supposing we fail ? " she thought. " What then ? "

A vision of that " then," a penniless, hopeless " then," affrighted her as she followed the blue-clad and obsequious page-boy down the long silent corridor to their suite ; affrighted her still more as she sank into the gilt armchair in front of the crackling wood-fire.

B.G.S.S.   N

But nothing seemed to affright Charlie. In this atmosphere
of Louis Seize panelling, bronze wall-lights and brocade
curtains, he appeared to recover all that daredeviltry which
had first fascinated her in him. " Buck up, old thing," he
whispered, tipping the luggage-porters, " buck up. We're
going to have tea, then we're going to have cocktails, then
we're going to have our baths, and then we're going to see if
we can find Cryus P."

" And my clothes ? " faltered Meg.

" My dear, your clothes " (they had inspected them together, timorously, before starting) " are perfectly all right."
And Flight-Commander Charles Torrance rang for the valet
and the chamber-maid, bidding them in his most martial
manner to unpack.

Tea and the subsequent cocktails (" Martini with a dash "
—one of the most potent known to man) raised Meg's spirit
more than a little. She began to forget her apprehensions.
Her nature, too, expanded—play-actress-wise—to the luxury
of their surroundings. It seemed a far, an impossibly far
cry from the outer suburbs to Piccadilly.

Soon, S.E. 28 and its lodging-house faded like a nightmare
from her mind. She lit a cigarette, one of the new gold-tipped
cigarettes which Charlie had purchased that morning. " I
wonder if I could have a manicurist and a hairdresser ? " she
asked.

" Of course, my dear. I'll telephone down for them."

Followed for Meg a delirious two hours. She had her
hair washed, waved. She had her nails manicured, polished.
She had a bath, a real bath, creamy with perfumed soap and
perfumed tablets. All the while her spirits lifted and lifted.
So that by the time she issued tall and lovely from the fragrant
waters, she was singing, actually singing to herself, as she had
sung in the old days when Charlie's pay had made life
possible.

Listening to that singing as he shaved—he, too, had taken
just such a bath—Charlie felt like a lion. " If she'll only keep
that mood up," he thought, " if we can only both keep it
up——"

But dressing for dinner scraped a little of the temporary
gilt off their gingerbread—for her black frock, good though
the cut of it, seemed more than a little old-fashioned ; while
as for his dress-suit, not even the valet's sedulous iron could
restore its pristine nap. Nevertheless, at seven fifty-seven to

the second, they issued from their suite and rang bravely enough for the lift.

§ 5

AT eight o'clock in the evening of the day following the insertion of his advertisement in the *Times*, Mr. Cyrus P. Dreschler, of the Pan-American Aerial Transport Company, sat ruminant in the glass-roofed marble-pillared rotunda of his hotel. All afternoon, in the big offices at Cornhill, he had been weighing the merits of his various applicants. None of them, on mature consideration, seemed much good. They lacked snap, decision, force. " These Britishers look all right on the surface, but they don't seem to have anything to them underneath," he mused, his keen eyes flickering from group to cocktail-drinking group at the porphyry-topped tables, and appraising from his own commercial and individualistic standpoint the various young men whose immaculate black evening clothes contrasted so adequately with the bare shoulders and coloured frocks of their female companions.

At which precise moment in his ruminations, Mr. Cyrus P. Dreschler looked up to see a tall tawny-moustached youth accompanied by an almost equally tall young woman, dark-haired and almost jewelless in a black close-fitting gown, proceeding nonchalantly dinnerwards.

As this couple passed, the tall tawny-moustached youth turned his head ever so slightly, and his blue eyes lit as though with surprised recognition. Cyrus P., fumbling in his memory, answered the semi-greeting, and a moment afterwards found himself on his feet being introduced to the tall dark young woman as " my wife, Mrs. Torrance."

Looking back on that introduction from the sure-knowledged standpoint of the after-years, Meg is prepared to swear that she noticed a sudden gleam, half-hopeful, half-humourous, under Cyrus P.'s shaggy eyebrows. But it is more credible that, at the time, she was conscious only of an American voice begging her and her husband to take a cocktail with him.

Charlie accepted the cocktail, and the three of them sat sipping.

" You're just dining here, I presume ? " said the American after the usual banalities.

" No, Mr. Dreschler." Charlie's *aplomb* was superb. " We've been turned out of our house—the painters, you know—so we're putting up here for a day or two till we can get back to it again." And he went on embroidering the impromptu story until Meg, her truthful soul shocked to the core, heard him invite the American, " if, by any chance, he were at a loose end," to take dinner with them.

" Now, that's very kind of you, Mr. Torrance," replied Dreschler. " As a matter of fact, I am at a loose end, and I'll be more than glad to accept your hospitality. You'll have another cocktail first, though, won't you ? "

" Thanks."

That cocktail, third of the series, stimulated Charlie Torrance's imagination nearly to genius-point. To see him as he led his little party into the princely restaurant, one would have thought him millionaire indeed. And the dinner of his ordering matched his momentary millionairedom. There was caviare, brought heaven knows how from the Volga ; pink Bortsch a-swim with pale cream ; delicate blue trout with butter-soaked potatoes ; baby-lamb ; giant asparagus which melted between one's lips ; and a *soufflé, surprise*, crisply warm without, icily cold within. While as for the wine-list, Charlie's scrutinizing eye scarcely found Pommery's best and the Napoleon brandy good enough.

To Dreschler, whose dyspeptic interior had hitherto contented itself with the plainest of grills and the lightest of light wines, the meal was as great an amazement as its provider. Almost, listening to the care-free conversation of his host and hostess (once launched, Meg, despite her truth-loving instincts, fell no whit behind Charlie in inventiveness) he decided himself to have found his Britisher at last. But—the memory of a certain recently perused document coming suddenly into his mind—he refrained from business talk ; and even after the Cabinet cigars had been kindled, no mention of the Pan-American Aerial Transport Company passed the barrier of his big square teeth. Instead, he talked London from the casual visitor's standpoint.

" For a stranger," he opined, switching his cigar financier-wise from the right-hand to the left-hand corner of his mouth, " this is a pretty dull town."

" Only because you don't *know* London, Mr. Dreschler." Charles lifted his brandy-glass to the light and inspected the dark amber of it with the eye of a connoisseur. " To a Londoner, it's the cheeriest place on earth. There are the theatres, for instance."

" Theatres ? " Dreschler nearly sniffed. " I can't say I think much of the theatres. Now, a good vaudeville show——"

" Vaudeville ? " said a puzzled Charlie.

" Mr. Dreschler means a music-hall," interpreted Meg.

Whereupon Charlie insisted upon telephoning for a box at the Hippodrome ; and thither, in a taxi for which he insisted on paying, the three of them proceeded.

But even England's highest-paid comedian failed to crinkle Meg's red lips with laughter. For Meg, despite Charlie's concealing hand, had seen the sum total of the dinner-bill, and at that sight all her apprehensions had returned fifty-fold. " Eight pounds," she mused, " and he gave the waiter ten shillings. Then there's the taxi-cab, and this box, and the suite, and the flowers he ordered, and the fires, and my manicurist, and my hairdresser. Why, we must have spent twenty-five pounds since four o'clock this afternoon ! "

All the same, Meg kept it up bravely enough until the end of the performance, until the last whisky-and-soda (" we'd better have them up in my stiting-room," decided Charlie) had been drunk and they were once more alone. Then, angrily, she turned to her husband.

" You've gone crazy," she told him. " Crazy ! A week of this will see us on the streets. And what have you done ? Nothing. Nothing at all. Why, you didn't even mention the job to Mr. Dreschler."

" Don't panic, my dear, don't panic." Charlie patted her knee. " There's plenty of time to mention the job. To-morrow, for instance, when we take him to one of the night-clubs."

" Night-clubs ? "

" Rather. He's terribly keen on dancing."

" When did he tell you that ? "

" Just now, while you were powdering your nose."

" And what will to-morrow night cost ? "

" Never you mind what it'll cost." He laughed, the old reckless laugh she had once loved. " We're in this game, and we've got to see it through."

That night, sleepless despite the perfection of the perfect box-mattress, Meg Torrance gave herself up for lost. " He's mad," she thought, listening to the easy, child-like breathing of her husband, " quite mad. He'll ruin us. He'll spend every penny we've got, and then there'll be nothing for it but for me to go on the stage again."

§ 6

MORNING with its closed curtains, its shaded bed-lights, its crisp rolls and steaming coffee gave Meg back a little of her courage. "Perhaps he's right after all," she mused, hearing Charlie's merry whistle from the near-by bathroom. "Perhaps this *is* the way to get that job."

But as the morning wore on—Charlie, a-search for some friend who could procure them admittance to one of the only three reputable night-clubs, left her alone till lunch-time—Meg's spirits sank once again to zero : and by the evening, when Harry Vigers, a sporty-looking but impecunious youth who had consented to play host at Ciro's on condition that Charlie recouped him for the bill, led the three of them to a corner table where the smoked salmon already showed pink beside the ice-frosted wine-coolers, she would gladly have given the last few pounds they possessed to be back in the old frowsy lodgings at S.E. 28. Nor did it improve matters when, at the end of dinner, the American, with a peculiar inflection of his courteous voice, said to her : " You look as though something were worrying you, Mrs. Torrance."

" Worrying me, Mr. Dreschler ? " With an effort, she managed a stage smile. " Why, I'm the happiest woman in London. Who wouldn't be, with three cavaliers ? "

" That's the spirit." Again the peculiar inflection crept into Dreschler's voice. " That's the spirit. Never say die. Even when things are looking their worst——" He broke off the sentence ; and, the music suddenly beginning, invited her to dance.

As they moved off across the floor, Charlie Torrance, even as his wife, began to grow apprehensive. The American had been at his office all day. He might have engaged somebody else for the mysterious job. There might not even be a job. " In which case," said Charlie to himself, " I shall have played a mug's game."

Nevertheless, the game had to be played out to the end— even if that end meant ruin. It seemed funny to think of ruin, here, among the lights and the rich food and the thumping music and the bejewelled women.

" You'll give me the next dance, won't you, Mrs. Torrance ? "

" If you like, Mr. Vigers."

Harry's and his wife's voices interrupted the gloomer's

musing; and a little later, as the pair glided away, he found himself alone with Dreschler, who said : " This is a great place, and your wife's a great dancer."

They talked aimlessly of this and that for a few sentences ; till, surprisingly, the American remarked.

" Do you know, I can't help wondering why any young man in your position should have troubled to answer that advertisement of mine."

The query, as Dreschler had intended, came like a bolt from blue skies. For a moment Charlie hesitated. Then, determined at all costs to bluff the limit, he answered, " Well, you see, Mr. Dreschler, this sort of life—night-clubs, you know—is all very well for a time. But one gets tired of it."

" I get you. I get you perfectly." Dreschler's tone gave no hint of the thought in Dreschler's brain. " And you're not afraid of a job of work ? "

" Rather not."

" Well, if that's so, you'd better come and see me at Cornhill again. I'm going away in a friend's automobile for the week-end, but I'll be back by Tuesday night."

Tuesday night ! " For one second, Charlie's face exposed Charlie's bluff. Tuesday, you see, was ninety-six solid hours away, and during those entire ninety-six hours, to say nothing of the night to follow them, he would be chained, as surely as though with links of steel, to the Ritz.

Yet, after that first paralysing second, Flight-Commander Charles Torrance never batted an eyelid. He would be charmed, said Flight-Commander Charles Torrance, absolutely charmed to have another business talk with Mr. Dreschler, say on the Wednesday, if Wednesday would be suitable.

" Wednesday at half-past ten will do me," snapped the American ; and making a note of the appointment in a tiny diary which he drew from his waistcoat pocket, closed the topic.

§ 7

" MR. DRESCHLER," said the hall-porter, " has just wired that he is not coming back till to-morrow."

It was already ten o'clock on Tuesday night, and the Torrances had just finished dining, as inexpensively as they might, in the uncrowded grill-room.

" What time to-morrow ? " asked Charlie.

"I don't know, sir. Mr. Dreschler does not say."

Crestfallen, the two young people wandered back into the rotunda, and there sat down. It was better to be in the rotunda with its lights, its music and its people than in their own suite, in those luxurious rooms which the past four days had made utterly hateful to both of them.

"I don't believe he's ever coming back," said Meg. "I believe you were right. I believe the whole thing's a spoof."

Charlie tried to answer her cheerfully, but the cheerfulness had gone out of him. Every hour since that night at Ciro's had chipped a fragment from the stucco of his self-confidence. This last blow completed the chipping process. "I've been a fool," he thought, "an utter fool." And so thinking, his mind reverted to the morrow's nightmare—his bill.

How much money would there be in the bank after paying his bill? That was the problem, the one maddening problem. For their expenses had scarcely diminished with Dreschler's departure. Try as they might to be careful about what they ordered, to remember themselves almost at the end of their financial tether, carefulness—in that atmosphere—was almost an impossibility. Quite apart, too, from the growing liability of their bill, it seemed as though ready money actually oozed from their pockets.

"Your appointment was supposed to be half-past ten, wasn't it?" broke in Meg.

"Yes, dear."

"Will you keep it?"

"I don't know. In view of what that porter fellow said, it hardly seems worth while. And yet, somehow or other, I believe that Dreschler will be there."

"And supposing he isn't?"

"God knows." Charlie sighed, one of the old hopeless sighs of S.E. 28. "The unemployment dole, probably."

And that night, neither of them slept.

§ 8

THE little gilt clock on the cream-panelled wall of the Louis Seize sitting-room showed half an hour after midday; but there was no sign of a returning Charlie. "Even if it's off," thought Meg, "even if he's failed, he might have telephoned."

The unkindness of his silence hurt—hurt more than the apprehensions of failure, of poverty. What did failure, what did poverty matter so long as Charlie went on loving her ? Besides, they weren't really poor. Hadn't they their health, their youth, all their lives in which to make good ? Even if there wasn't much left in the bank after paying their hotel bill she could pawn her last remaining bits of jewellery, her last remaining furs. The furs and the jewellery would see them through till February. After that, if Charlie still hadn't got a job, she could go back to the stage and earn enough for them both. " But I can't do it if he leaves off caring for me," she thought, " I just can't."

A knock and a page-boy interrupted.

" Yes ? " she said, her brain still muzzy with thought.

For answer, the page-boy handed her an envelope. There was no stamp and no address on the envelope, only her husband's name. Staring at it, she knew its contents. " It's our bill," she thought, " our bill ! "

The page-boy had long since departed, but Meg still stood upright by the fireless hearth, the unopened envelope in her hand. " I daren't," she thought, " I daren't open this till Charlie comes back or telephones." But there was still no sign of Charlie, and the telephone on the little Empire desk was still dumb—dumb as Fate itself. The electrically-controlled clock-hands jerked and jerked round the face of the dial. Twelve-forty. Twelve-forty-five. Twelve-fifty. Now a darker apprehension clouded her mind. Supposing Charlie had failed, and failing . . . made an end of things. Men, desperate men, men at the end of their tether, did sometimes . . . make an end of things. Charlie was so proud, so terribly proud : not like Harry Vigers. . . . Supposing, supposing Charlie's pride had driven him to . . . to the worst.

Would he never come ? Would the telephone-bell never ring ? Would nothing, nothing break this intolerable suspense ?

A sunray, slanting in through the filmy lace *brise-bise*, showed Meg's face whiter than the unopened envelope between her pale fingers. . . .

And then suddenly, rapturously, Charlie burst in on her. His blue eyes were all alight, shining with hope and happiness. " I've got it," he shouted, " I've got the job " ; and before Meg had time to realize the miracle, he was holding her in his arms. " I've got the job," he shouted again, kissing her on the lips, on the forehead, on the creamy skin behind her ears.

Half in tears, half in laughter, dumb with sheer reaction from her long suspense, Meg answered his kisses. " But what *is* the job ? " she stammered at last.

" The job of a lifetime, my dear. Organizing an air-service for one of the South American Governments, and selling 'em 'planes into the bargain. We're to have a thousand a year whatever happens. And a commission on every 'plane I sell. And our expenses. Expenses for the two of us. Dreschler says you've got to go with me. Dreschler says you'll be *terribly* useful when it comes to entertaining the Dago politicians. Dreschler's taken a frightful fancy to you. Dreschler's a ripper. He drove straight to his office instead of coming here, so as not to miss our appointment. Dreschler's offered to advance me a quarter's salary if I need it."

" Need it ! " Abruptly, the thought of that unopened envelope flashed through Meg's mind. " Of course we'll need it. There's," she stretched the thing out to him, " there's our bill, Charlie. I didn't dare open it till you came back."

But when Flight-Commander Charles Torrance, still jubilant beyond self-control, opened that envelope, there fell from it, not a bill but a letter, a letter in cold typewriting, which read :

" The Pan-American Aerial Transport Company,
Wednesday, May 27.

" *Dear Torrance,*

" *This letter should meet you on your return. I'm a bit of a gambler myself, and can appreciate a good bluff, which yours surely was, as well as the next fellow. You forgot, though, that you gave me your address at our first interview ; and that landladies, especially when approached by a tactful Enquiry Agent, are apt to gossip about their lodgers !*

" *Yours sincerely,*

" Cyrus P. Dreschler.

" *P.S.—I'm just telephoning the hotel-people to charge your bill to me. Buy your wife some new clothes with the money. She needs them.*"

Meg always says it was the last three words of that postscript which sent her off in a faint.

FRANCIS BRET HARTE (1839–1910), who was born of Anglo-Dutch parents, spent his childhood in California, where he absorbed much of the atmosphere of the old prospecting days. He was the originator of "Wild West" literature and of characters with whom we have now been familiarised through the medium of the Cinema. "The Luck of Roaring Camp" and "Mliss" are perhaps his finest short stories.

MLISS

CHAPTER I

JUST where the Sierra Nevada begins to subside in gentler undulations, and the rivers grow less rapid and yellow, on the side of a great red mountain, stands "Smith's Pocket." Seen from the red road at sunset, in the red light and the red dust, its white houses look like the outcroppings of quartz on the mountain-side. The red stage, topped with red-shirted passengers, is lost to view half-a-dozen times in the tortuous descent, turning up unexpectedly in out-of-the-way places, and vanishing altogether within a hundred yards of the town. It is probably owing to this sudden twist in the road that the advent of a stranger at Smith's Pocket is usually attended with a peculiar circumstance. Dismounting from the vehicle at the stage-office, the too-confident traveller is apt to walk straight out of town under the impression that it lies in quite another direction. It is related that one of the tunnel-men, two miles from town, met one of these self-reliant passengers with a carpet-bag, umbrella, *Harper's Magazine*, and other evidences of "civilisation and refinement," plodding along over the road he had just ridden, vainly endeavouring to find the settlement of Smith's Pocket.

An observant traveller might have found some compensation for his disappointment in the weird aspect of that vicinity. There were huge fissures on the hillside, and displacements of the red soil, resembling more the chaos of some primary elemental upheaval than the work of man ; while, half-way down, a long flume straddled its narrow body and disproportionate legs over the chasm, like an enormous fossil of some forgotten antediluvian. At every step smaller ditches crossed the road, hiding in their sallow depths unlovely streams that crept away to a clandestine union with the great yellow torrent below, and here and there were the ruins of some cabin with the chimney alone left intact, and the hearthstone open to the skies.

The settlement of Smith's Pocket owed its origin to the finding of a " pocket " on its site by a veritable Smith. Five thousand dollars were taken out of it in one half-hour by Smith. Three thousand dollars were expended by Smith and others in erecting a flume and in tunnelling. And then Smith's Pocket was found to be only a pocket, and subject, like other pockets, to depletion. Although Smith pierced the bowels of the great red mountain, that five thousand dollars was the first and last return of his labour. The mountain grew reticent of its golden secrets, and the flume steadily ebbed away the remainder of Smith's fortune. Then Smith went into quartz-mining ; then into quartz-milling ; then into hydraulics and ditching, and then by easy degrees into saloon-keeping. Presently it was whispered that Smith was drinking a great deal ; then it was known that Smith was a habitual drunkard, and then people began to think, as they are apt to, that he had never been anything else. But the settlement of Smith's Pocket, like that of most discoveries, was happily not dependent on the fortune of its pioneer, and other parties projected tunnels and found pockets. So Smith's Pocket became a settlement, with its two fancy stores, its two hotels, its one express-office, and its two first families. Occasionally its one long straggling street was overawed by the assumption of the latest San Francisco fashions, imported per express, exclusively to the first families ; making outraged Nature, in the ragged outline of her furrowed surface, look still more homely, and putting personal insult on that greater portion of the population to whom the Sabbath, with a change of linen, brought merely the necessity of cleanliness, without the luxury of adornment. Then there was a Methodist Church, and hard by a Monte-Bank, and a little beyond, on the mountain-side, a graveyard ; and then a little schoolhouse.

" The Master," as he was known to his little flock, sat alone one night in the schoolhouse, with some open copy-books before him, carefully making those bold and full characters which are supposed to combine the extremes of chirographical and moral excellence, and had got as far as " Riches are deceitful," and was elaborating the noun with an insincerity of flourish that was quite in the spirit of his text, when he heard a gentle tapping. The woodpeckers had been busy about the roof during the day, and the noise did not disturb his work. But the opening of the door, and the tapping continuing from the inside, caused him to look up. He was slightly startled by the figure of a young girl, dirty and shabbily clad. Still, her great black eyes, her coarse, uncombed, lustreless black hair falling over her sunburned face, her red arms and feet streaked with the red soil, were all familiar to him. It was Melissa Smith,—Smith's motherless child.

"What can she want here?" thought the master. Everybody knew "Mliss," as she was called, throughout the length and height of Red Mountain. Everybody knew her as an incorrigible girl. Her fierce, ungovernable disposition, her mad freaks, and lawless character, were in their way as proverbial as the story of her father's weaknesses, and as philosophically accepted by the townsfolk. She wrangled with and fought the schoolboys with keener invective and quite as powerful arm. She followed the trails with a woodman's craft, and the master had met her before, miles away, shoeless, stockingless, and bareheaded on the mountain road. The miners' camps along the stream supplied her with subsistence during these voluntary pilgrimages in freely-offered alms. Not but that a larger protection had been previously extended to Mliss. The Rev. Joshua McSnagley, "stated" preacher, had placed her in the hotel as servant, by way of preliminary refinement, and had introduced her to his scholars at Sunday-school. But she threw plates occasionally at the landlord, and quickly retorted to the cheap witticisms of the guests, and created in the Sabbath-school a sensation that was so inimical to the orthodox dullness and placidity of that institution, that, with a decent regard for the starched frocks and unblemished morals of the two pink-and-white-faced children of the first families, the reverend gentleman had her ignominiously expelled. Such were the antecedents and such the character of Mliss as she stood before the master. It was shown in the ragged dress, the unkempt hair, and bleeding feet, and asked his pity. It flashed from her black, fearless eyes, and commanded his respect.

"I come here to-night," she said rapidly and boldly, keeping her hard glance on his, "because I knew you was alone. I wouldn't come here when them gals was here. I hate 'em and they hates me. That's why. You keep school, don't you? I want to be teached!"

If to the shabbiness of her apparel and uncomeliness of her tangled hair and dirty face she had added the humility of tears, the master would have extended to her the usual moiety of pity, and nothing more. But, with the natural though illogical instincts of his species, her boldness awakened in him something of that respect which all original natures pay unconsciously to one another in any grade. And he gazed at her the more fixedly as she went on still rapidly, her hand on that door-latch, and her eyes on his :—

" My name's Mliss,—Mliss Smith ! You can bet your life on that. My father's Old Smith,—Old Bummer Smith,— that's what's the matter with him. Mliss Smith,—and I'm coming to school ! "

" Well ? " said the master.

Accustomed to be thwarted and opposed, often wantonly and cruelly, for no other purpose than to excite the violent impulses of her nature, the master's phlegm evidently took her by surprise. She stopped ; she began to twist a lock of her hair between her fingers ; and the rigid line of upper lip, drawn over the wicked little teeth, relaxed and quivered slightly. Then her eyes dropped, and something like a blush struggled up to her cheek, and tried to assert itself through the splashes of redder soil, and the sunburn of years. Suddenly she threw herself forward, calling on God to strike her dead, and fell quite weak and helpless, with her face on the master's desk, crying and sobbing as if her heart would break.

The master lifted her gently and waited for the paroxysm to pass. When, with face still averted, she was repeating between her sobs the *mea culpa* of childish penitence,—that " she'd be good, she didn't mean to," etc., it came to him to ask her why she had left Sabbath-school.

Why had she left the Sabbath-school ?—why ? Oh, yes ! What did he (McSnagley) want to tell her she was wicked for ? What did he tell her that God hated her for ? If God hated her, what did she want to go to Sabbath-school for ? *She* didn't want to be " beholden " to anybody who hated her.

Had she told McSnagley this ?

Yes, she had.

The master laughed. It was a hearty laugh, and echoed so oddly in the little schoolhouse, and seemed so inconsistent and discordant with the sighing of the pines without, that he shortly corrected himself with a sigh. The sigh was quite as sincere in its way, however, and after a moment of serious silence he asked about her father.

Her father ? What father ? Whose father ? What had he ever done for her ? Why did the girls hate her ? Come now ! what made the folks say, " Old Bummer Smith's Mliss ! " when she passed ? Yes ; oh, yes ! She wished he was dead,— she was dead,—everybody was dead ; and her sobs broke forth anew.

The master then, leaning over her, told her as well as he could what you or I might have said after hearing such un-natural theories from childish lips ; only bearing in mind perhaps better than you or I the unnatural facts of her ragged dress, her bleeding feet, and the omnipresent shadow of her drunken father. Then, raising her to her feet, he wrapped his shawl around her, and bidding her come early in the morning, he walked with her down the road. There he bade her " good night." The moon shone brightly on the narrow path before them. He stood and watched the bent little figure as it stag-gered down the road, and waited until it had passed the little graveyard and reached the curve of the hill, where it turned and stood for a moment, a mere atom of suffering outlined against the far-off patient stars. Then he went back to his work. But the lines of the copy-book thereafter faded into long parallels of never-ending road, over which childish figures seemed to pass sobbing and crying into the night. Then, the little schoolhouse seeming lonelier than before, he shut the door and went home.

The next morning Mliss came to school. Her face had been washed, and her coarse black hair bore evidence of recent struggles with the comb, in which both had evidently suffered. The old defiant look shone occasionally in her eyes, but her manner was tamer and more subdued. Then began a series of little trials and self-sacrifices, in which master and pupil bore an equal part, and which increased the confidence and sympathy between them. Although obedient under the master's eye, at times during recess, if thwarted or stung by a fancied slight, Mliss would rage in ungovernable fury, and many a palpitating young savage, finding himself matched with his own weapons of torment, would seek the master with torn jacket and scratched face, and complaints of the dreadful Mliss. There was a serious division among the townspeople on the subject ; some threatening to withdraw their children from such evil com-panionship, and others as warmly upholding the course of the master in his work of reclamation. Meanwhile, with a steady persistence that seemed quite astonishing to him on looking back afterward, the master drew Mliss gradually out of the shadow of her past life, as though it were but her natural progress down the narrow path on which he had set her feet the moonlit night of their first meeting. Remembering the experience of the evangelical McSnagley, he carefully avoided that Rock of Ages on which that unskilful pilot had shipwrecked her young faith. But if, in the course of her reading, she chanced to stumble upon those few words which have lifted such as she above the level of the older, the wiser, and the more prudent,—if she learned something of a faith that is symbolised by suffering, and the old light softened in her eyes, it did not take the shape of a lesson. A few of the plainer people had made up a little sum by which the ragged Mliss was enabled to assume the garments of respect and civilisation ; and often a rough shake of the hand and words of homely commendation from a red-shirted and burly figure sent a glow to the cheek of the young master, and set him to thinking if it was altogether deserved.

Three months had passed from the time of their first meeting, and the master was sitting late one evening over the moral and sententious copies, when there came a tap at the door, and again Mliss stood before him. She was neatly clad and clean-faced, and there was nothing perhaps but the long black hair and bright black eyes to remind him of his former apparition. " Are you busy ? " she asked. " Can you come with me ? "—and on his signifying his readiness, in her own wilful way she said, " Come, then, quick ! "

They passed out of the door together and into the dark road. As they entered the town the master asked her whither she was going. She replied, " To see my father."

It was the first time he had heard her call him by that filial title, or indeed anything more than " Old Smith " or the " Old man." It was the first time in three months that she had spoken of him at all, and the master knew she had kept resolutely aloof from him since her great change. Satisfied from her manner that it was fruitless to question her purpose, he passively followed. In out-of-the-way places, low groggeries, restaurants, and saloons, in gambling-hells and dance-houses, the master preceded by Mliss, came and went. In the reeking smoke and blasphemous outcries of low dens, the child, holding the master's hand, stood and anxiously gazed, seemingly unconscious of all in the one absorbing nature of her pursuit. Some of the revellers, recognising Mliss, called to the child to sing and dance for them, and would have forced liquor upon her but for the interference of the master. Others, recognising him, mutely made way for them to pass. So an hour slipped by. Then the child whispered in his ear that there was a cabin on the other side of the creek crossed by the long flume where she thought he still might be. Thither they crossed,—a toilsome half-hour's walk,—but in vain. They were returning by the ditch at the abutment of the flume, gazing at the lights of the town on the opposite bank, when suddenly, sharply, a quick report rang out on the clear night air. The echoes caught it, and carried it round and round Red Mountain, and set the dogs to barking all along the streams. Lights seemed to dance and move quickly on the outskirts of the town for a few moments, the stream rippled quite audibly beside them, a few stones loosened themselves from the hillside and splashed into the stream, a heavy wind seemed to surge the branches of the funereal pines, and then the silence seemed to fall thicker, heavier, and deadlier. The master turned towards Mliss with an unconscious gesture of protection, but the child had gone. Oppressed by a strange fear, he ran quickly down the trail to the river's bed, and jumping from boulder to boulder, reached the base of Red Mountain and the outskirts of the village. Midway of the crossing he looked up and held his breath in awe. For high above him on the narrow flume he saw the fluttering little figure of his late companion crossing swiftly in the darkness.

He climbed the bank, and, guided by a few lights moving about a central point on the mountain, soon found himself breathless among a crowd of awestricken and sorrowful men.

Out from among them the child appeared, and, taking the master's hand, led him silently before what seemed a ragged hole in the mountain. Her face was quite white, but her excited manner gone, and her look that of one to whom some long-expected event had at last happened,—an expression that to the master in his bewilderment seemed almost like relief. The walls of the cavern were partly propped by decaying timbers. The child pointed to what appeared to be some ragged, cast-off clothes left in the hole by the late occupant. The master approached nearer with his flaming dip, and bent over them. It was Smith, already cold, with a pistol in his hand and a bullet in his heart, lying beside his empty pocket.

CHAPTER II

THE opinion which McSnagley expressed in reference to a
" change of heart " supposed to be experienced by Mliss was
more forcibly described in the gulches and tunnels. It was
thought there that Mliss had " struck a good lead." So when
there was a new grave added to the little enclosure, and at the
expense of the master a little board and inscription put above
it, the *Red Mountain Banner* came out quite handsomely, and
did the fair thing to the memory of one of " our oldest
pioneers," alluding gracefully to that " bane of noble in-
tellects," and otherwise genteelly shelving our dear brother
with the past. " He leaves an only child to mourn his loss,"
says the *Banner*, " who is now an exemplary scholar, thanks
to the efforts of the Rev. Mr. McSnagley." The Rev. McSnagley, in fact, made a strong point of Mliss's conversion, and,
indirectly attributing to the unfortunate child the suicide of her
father, made affecting allusions in Sunday-school to the bene-
ficial effects of the " silent tomb," and in this cheerful contemplation drove most of the children into speechless horror,
and caused the pink-and-white scions of the first families to
howl dismally and refuse to be comforted.

The long dry summer came. As each fierce day burned
itself out in little whiffs of pearl-grey smoke on the mountain
summits, and the upspringing breeze scattered its red embers
over the landscape, the green wave which in early spring up-
heaved above Smith's grave grew sere and dry and hard. In
those days the master, strolling in the little churchyard of a
Sabbath afternoon, was sometimes surprised to find a few
wild flowers plucked from the damp pine-forests scattered
there, and oftener rude wreaths hung upon the little pine
cross. Most of these wreaths were formed of a sweet-scented
grass, which the children loved to keep in their desks, inter-
twined with the plumes of the buckeye, the syringa, and the
wood-anemone ; and here and there the master noticed the
dark blue cowl of the monk's hood, or deadly aconite. There
was something in the odd association of this noxious plant with
these memorials which occasioned a painful sensation to the
master deeper than his æsthetic sense. One day, during a long
walk, in crossing a wooded ridge he came upon Mliss in the
heart of the forest, perched upon a prostrate pine, on a fantastic throne formed by the hanging plumes of lifeless branches,

her lap full of grasses and pine-burrs, and crooning to herself one of the negro melodies of her younger life. Recognising him at a distance, she made room for him on her elevated throne, and with a grave assumption of hospitality and patronage that would have been ridiculous had it not been so terribly earnest, she fed him with pine-nuts and crab-apples. The master took that opportunity to point out to her the noxious and deadly qualities of the monk's hood, whose dark blossoms he saw in her lap, and extorted from her a promise not to meddle with it as long as she remained his pupil. This done,—as the master had tested her integrity before,—he rested satisfied, and the strange feeling which had overcome him on seeing them died away.

Of the homes that were offered Mliss when her conversion became known, the master preferred that of Mrs. Morpher, a womanly and kind-hearted specimen of South-Western efflorescence, known in her maidenhood as the " Per-rairie Rose." Being one of those who contend resolutely against their own natures, Mrs. Morpher, by a long series of self-sacrifices and struggles, had at last subjugated her naturally careless disposition to principles of " order," which she considered, in common with Mr. Pope, as " Heaven's first law." But she could not entirely govern the orbits of her satellites, however regular her own movements, and even her own " Jeemes " sometimes collided with her. Again her old nature asserted itself in her children. Lycurgus dipped into the cupboard " between meals," and Aristides came home from school without shoes, leaving those important articles on the threshold, for the delight of a barefooted walk down the ditches. Octavia and Cassandra were " keerless " of their clothes. So with but one exception, however much the " Prairie Rose " might have trimmed and pruned and trained her own matured luxuriance, the little shoots came up defiantly wild and straggling. That one exception was Clytemnestra Morpher, aged fifteen. She was the realisation of her mother's immaculate conception,— neat, orderly, and dull.

It was an amiable weakness of Mrs. Morpher to imagine that " Clytie " was a consolation and model for Mliss. Following this fallacy, Mrs. Morpher threw Clytie at the head of Mliss when she was " bad," and set her up before the child for adoration in her penitential moments. It was not, therefore, surprising to the master to hear that Clytie was coming to school, obviously as a favour to the master and as an example for Mliss and others. For " Clytie " was quite a young lady. Inheriting her mother's physical peculiarities, and in obedience to the climatic laws of the Red Mountain region, she was an early bloomer. The youth of Smith's Pocket, to whom this kind of flower was rare, sighed for her in April and languished in May. Enamoured swains haunted the schoolhouse at the hour of dismissal. A few were jealous of the master.

Perhaps it was this latter circumstance that opened the master's eyes to another. He could not help noticing that Clytie was romantic ; that in school she required a great deal of attention ; that her pens were uniformly bad and wanted fixing ; that she usually accompanied the request with a certain expectation in her eye that was somewhat disproportionate to the quality of service she verbally required ; that she sometimes allowed the curves of a round, plump white arm to rest on his when he was writing her copies ; that she always blushed and flung back her blonde curls when she did so. I don't remember whether I have stated that the master was a young man,—it's of little consequence, however ; he had been severely educated in the school in which Clytie was taking her first lesson, and, on the whole, withstood the flexible curves and factitious glance like the fine young Spartan that he was. Perhaps an insufficient quality of food may have tended to this asceticism. He generally avoided Clytie ; but one evening, when she returned to the schoolhouse after something she had forgotten, and did not find it until the master walked home with her, I hear that he endeavoured to make himself particularly agreeable,—partly from the fact, I imagine, that his conduct was adding gall and bitterness to the already overcharged hearts of Clytemnestra's admirers.

The morning after this affecting episode Mliss did not come to school. Noon came, but not Mliss. Questioning Clytie on the subject, it appeared that they had left the school together, but the wilful Mliss had taken another road. The afternoon brought her not. In the evening he called on Mrs. Morpher, whose motherly heart was really alarmed. Mr. Morpher had spent all day in search of her, without discovering a trace that might lead to her discovery. Aristides was summoned as a probable accomplice, but that equitable infant succeeded in impressing the household with his innocence. Mrs. Morpher entertained a vivid impression that the child would yet be found drowned in a ditch, or, what was almost as terrible, muddied and soiled beyond the redemption of soap and water.

Sick at heart, the master returned to the schoolhouse. As he lit his lamp and seated himself at his desk, he found a note lying before him addressed to himself in Mliss's handwriting. It seemed to be written on a leaf torn from some old memorandum-book, and, to prevent sacrilegious trifling, had been sealed with six broken wafers. Opening it almost tenderly, the master read as follows :—

" RESPECTED SIR,—When you read this, I am run away. Never to come back. *Never*, NEVER, NEVER. You can give my beeds to Mary Jennings, and my Amerika's Pride [a highly coloured lithograph from a tobacco-box] to Sally Flinders. But don't you give anything to Clytie Morpher. Don't you dare to. Do you know what my opinion is of her : it is this, she is perfekly disgustin. That is all and no more at present from Yours respectfully,   MELISSA SMITH."

The master sat pondering on this strange epistle till the moon lifted its bright face above the distant hills and illuminated the trail that led to the schoolhouse, beaten quite hard with the coming and going of little feet. Then, more satisfied in mind, he tore the missive into fragments and scattered them along the road.

At sunrise the next morning he was picking his way through the palm-like fern and thick underbrush of the pine forest, starting the hare from its form, and awakening a querulous protest from a few dissipated crows, who had evidently been making a night of it, and so came to the wooded ridge where he had once found Mliss. There he found the prostrate pine and tasselled branches, but the throne was vacant. As he drew nearer, what might have been some frightened animal started through the crackling limbs. It ran up the tossed arms of the fallen monarch and sheltered itself in some friendly foliage. The master, reaching the old seat, found the nest still warm ; looking up in the intertwining branches, he met the black eyes of the errant Mliss. They gazed at each other without speaking. She was first to break the silence.

" What do you want ? " she asked curtly.

The master had decided on a course of action. " I want some crab-apples," he said humbly.

" Shan't have 'em ! go away ! Why don't you get 'em of Clytemnerestera ? " (It seemed to be a relief to Mliss to express her contempt in additional syllables to that classical young woman's already long-drawn title.) " Oh, you wicked thing ! "

"I am hungry, Lissy. I have eaten nothing since dinner yesterday. I am famished!" and the young man in a state of remarkable exhaustion leaned against the tree.

Melissa's heart was touched. In the bitter days of her gipsy life she had known the sensation he so artfully simulated. Overcome by his heartbroken tone, but not entirely divested of suspicion, she said—

"Dig under the tree near the roots, and you'll find lots; but mind you don't tell!" (for Mliss had *her* hoards as well as the rats and squirrels).

But the master, of course, was unable to find them, the effects of hunger probably blinding his senses. Mliss grew uneasy. At length she peered at him through the leaves in an elfish way, and questioned—

"If I come down and give you some, you'll promise you won't touch me?"

The master promised.

"Hope you'll die if you do?"

The master accepted instant dissolution as a forfeit. Mliss slid down the tree. For a few moments nothing transpired but the munching of the pine-nuts. "Do you feel better?" she asked with some solicitude. The master confessed to a recuperated feeling, and then, gravely thanking her, proceeded to retrace his steps. As he expected, he had not gone far before she called him. He turned. She was standing there quite white, with tears in her widely opened orbs. The master felt that the right moment had come. Going up to her, he took both her hands, and, looking in her tearful eyes, said, gravely, "Lissy, do you remember the first evening you came to see me?"

Lissy remembered.

"You asked me if you might come to school, for you wanted to learn something and be better, and I said——"

"Come," responded the child, promptly.

"What would *you* say if the master now came to you and said that he was lonely without his little scholar, and that he wanted her to come and teach him to be better?"

The child hung her head for a few moments in silence. The master waited patiently. Tempted by the quiet, a hare ran close to the couple, and raising her bright eyes and velvet forepaws, sat and gazed at them. A squirrel ran half-way down the furrowed bark of the fallen tree, and there stopped.

"We are waiting, Lissy," said the master in a whisper,

and the child smiled. Stirred by a passing breeze, the tree-tops rocked, and a long pencil of light stole through their interlaced boughs full on the doubting face and irresolute little figure. Suddenly she took the master's hand in her quick way. What she said was scarcely audible, but the master, putting the black hair back from her forehead, kissed her ; and so, hand in hand, they passed out of the damp aisles and forest odours into the open sunlit road.

CHAPTER III

SOMEWHAT less spiteful in her intercourse with other scholars, Mliss still retained an offensive attitude in regard to Clytemnestra. Perhaps the jealous element was not entirely lulled in her passionate little breast. Perhaps it was only that the round curves and plump outline offered more extended pinching surface. But while such ebullitions were under the master's control, her enmity occasionally took a new and irrepressible form.

The master in his first estimate of the child's character could not conceive that she had ever possessed a doll. But the master, like many other professed readers of character, was safer in *a posteriori* than *a priori* reasoning. Mliss had a doll, but then it was emphatically Mliss's doll,—a smaller copy of herself. Its unhappy existence had been a secret discovered accidentally by Mrs. Morpher. It had been the old-time companion of Mliss's wanderings, and bore evident marks of suffering. Its original complexion was long since washed away by the weather and anointed by the slime of ditches. It looked very much as Mliss had in days past. Its one gown of faded stuff was dirty and ragged as hers had been. Mliss had never been known to apply to it any childish term of endearment. She never exhibited it in the presence of other children. It was put severely to bed in a hollow tree near the schoolhouse, and only allowed exercise during Mliss's rambles. Fulfilling a stern duty to her doll, as she would to herself, it knew no luxuries.

Now Mrs. Morpher, obeying a commendable impulse, bought another doll and gave it to Mliss. The child received it gravely and curiously. The master, on looking at it one day, fancied he saw a slight resemblance in its round red cheeks and mild blue eyes to Clytemnestra. It became evident before long that Mliss had also noticed the same resemblance. Accordingly she hammered its waxen head on the rocks when she was alone, and sometimes dragged it with a string round its neck to and from school. At other times, setting it up on her desk, she made a pincushion of its patient and inoffensive body. Whether this was done in revenge of what she considered a second figurative obtrusion of Clytie's excellences upon her, or whether she had an intuitive appreciation of the rites of certain other heathens, and, indulging in that " fetish " ceremony, imagined that the original of her wax model would pine away and finally die, is a metaphysical question I shall not now consider.

In spite of these moral vagaries, the master could not help noticing in her different tasks the working of a quick, restless, and vigorous conception. She knew neither the hesitancy nor the doubts of childhood. Her answers in class were always slightly dashed with audacity. Of course she was not infallible. But her courage and daring in passing beyond her own depth and that of the floundering little swimmers around her, in their minds outweighed all errors of judgment. Children are not better than grown people in this respect, I fancy ; and whenever the little red hand flashed above her desk, there was a wondering silence, and even the master was sometimes oppressed with a doubt of his own experience and judgment.

Nevertheless, certain attributes which at first amused and entertained his fancy began to afflict him with grave doubts. He could not but see that Mliss was revengeful, irreverent, and wilful. That there was but one better quality which pertained to her semi-savage disposition,—the faculty of physical forti-tude and self-sacrifice ; and another, though not always an attribute of the noble savage,—truth. Mliss was both fearless and sincere ; perhaps in such a character the adjectives were synonymous.

The master had been doing some hard thinking on this subject, and had arrived at that conclusion quite common to all who think sincerely, that he was generally the slave of his own prejudices, when he determined to call on the Rev. McSnagley for advice. This decision was somewhat humiliat-ing to his pride, as he and McSnagley were not friends. But he thought of Mliss and the evening of their first meeting ; and perhaps with a pardonable superstition that it was not chance alone that had guided her wilful feet to the schoolhouse, and perhaps with a complacent consciousness of the rare mag-nanimity of the act, he choked back his dislike and went to McSnagley.

The reverend gentleman was glad to see him. Moreover, he observed that the master was looking " peartish," and hoped he had got over the " neuralgy " and " rheumatiz." He himself had been troubled with a dumb " ager " since last Conference. But he had learned to " rastle and pray."

Pausing a moment to enable the master to write his certain method of curing the dumb " ager " upon the book and volume of his brain, Mr. McSnagley proceeded to inquire after Sister Morpher. " She is an adornment to Christe*w*anity, and has a likely growin' young family," added Mr. McSnagley ; " and there's that mannerly young gal, so well behaved,— Miss Clytie." In fact, Clytie's perfections seemed to affect him to such an extent that he dwelt for several minutes upon them. The master was doubly embarrassed. In the first place, there was an enforced contrast with poor Mliss in all this praise of Clytie. Secondly, there was something unpleasantly confidential in his tone of speaking of Mrs. Morpher's earliest born. So that the master, after a few futile efforts to say something natural, found it convenient to recall another engagement, and left without asking the information required, but in his after reflections somewhat unjustly giving the Rev. Mr. McSnagley the full benefit of having refused it.

Perhaps this rebuff placed the master and pupil once more in the close communion of old. The child seemed to notice the change in the master's manner, which had of late been constrained, and in one of their long post-prandial walks she stopped suddenly, and mounting a stump, looked full in his face with big, searching eyes. " You ain't mad ? " said she, with an interrogative shake of the black braids. " No." " Nor bothered ? " " No." " Nor hungry ? " (Hunger was to Mliss a sickness that might attack a person at any moment.) " No." " Nor thinking of her ? " " Of whom, Lissy ? " " That white girl." (This was the latest epithet invented by Mliss, who was a very dark brunette, to express Clytemnestra.) " No." " Upon your word ? " (A substitute for " Hope you'll die ? " proposed by the master.) " Yes." " And sacred honour ? " " Yes." Then Mliss gave him a fierce little kiss, and, hopping down, fluttered off. For two or three days after that she condescended to appear more like other children, and be, as she expressed it, " good."

Two years had passed since the master's advent at Smith's Pocket, and as his salary was not large, and the prospects of Smith's Pocket eventually becoming the capital of the State not entirely definite, he contemplated a change. He had informed the school trustees privately of his intentions, but, educated young men of unblemished moral character being scarce at that time, he consented to continue his school term through the winter to early spring. None else knew of his intention except his one friend, a Dr. Duchesne, a young Creole physician, known to the people of Wingdam as "Duchesny." He never mentioned it to Mrs. Morpher, Clytie, or any of his scholars. His reticence was partly the result of a constitutional indisposition to fuss, partly a desire to be spared the questions and surmises of vulgar curiosity, and partly that he never really believed he was going to do anything before it was done.

He did not like to think of Mliss. It was a selfish instinct, perhaps, which made him try to fancy his feeling for the child was foolish, romantic, and unpractical. He even tried to imagine that she would do better under the control of an older and sterner teacher. Then she was nearly eleven, and in a few years, by the rules of Red Mountain, would be a woman. He had done his duty. After Smith's death he addressed letters to Smith's relatives, and received one answer from a sister of Melissa's mother. Thanking the master, she stated her intention of leaving the Atlantic States for California with her husband in a few months. This was a slight superstructure for the airy castle which the master pictured for Mliss's home, but it was easy to fancy that some loving, sympathetic woman, with the claims of kindred, might better guide her wayward nature. Yet, when the master had read the letter, Mliss listened to it carelessly, received it submissively, and afterwards cut figures out of it with her scissors, supposed to represent Clytemnestra, labelled "the white girl," to prevent mistakes, and impaled them upon the outer walls of the schoolhouse.

When the summer was about spent, and the last harvest had been gathered in the valleys, the master bethought him of gathering in a few ripened shoots of the young idea, and of having his harvest-home, or examination. So the savants and professionals of Smith's Pocket were gathered to witness that time-honoured custom of placing timid children in a constrained position, and bullying them as in a witness-box. As usual in such cases, the most audacious and self-possessed were the lucky recipients of the honours. The reader will imagine that in the present instance Mliss and Clytie were pre-eminent, and divided public attention ; Mliss with her clearness of material perception and self-reliance, Clytie with her placid self-esteem and saint-like correctness of deportment. The other little ones were timid and blundering. Mliss's readiness and brilliancy, of course, captivated the greatest number and provoked the greatest applause. Mliss's antecedents had unconsciously awakened the strongest sympathies of a class whose athletic forms were ranged against the walls, or whose handsome bearded faces looked in at the windows. But Mliss's popularity was overthrown by an unexpected circumstance.

McSnagley had invited himself, and had been going through the pleasing entertainment of frightening the more timid pupils by the vaguest and most ambiguous questions delivered in an impressive funereal tone ; and Mliss had soared into astronomy, and was tracking the course of our spotted ball through space, and keeping time with the music of the spheres, and defining the tethered orbits of the planets, when McSnagley impressively arose. " Meelissy ! ye were speaking of the revolutions of this yere yearth and the move-*ments* of the sun, and I think ye said it had been a doing of it since the creashun, eh ? " Mliss nodded a scornful affirmative. " Well, war that the truth ? " said McSnagley, folding his arms. " Yes," said Mliss, shutting up her little red lips tightly. The handsome outlines at the windows peered farther in the schoolroom, and a saintly Raphael face, with blonde beard and soft blue eyes, belonging to the biggest scamp in the diggings, turned toward the child and whispered, " Stick to it, Mliss ! " The reverend gentleman heaved a deep sigh, and cast a compassionate glance at the master, then at the children, and then rested his look on Clytie. That young woman softly elevated her round white arm. Its seductive curves were enhanced by a gorgeous and massive specimen bracelet, the gift of one of her humblest worshippers, worn in honour of the occasion. There was a momentary silence. Clytie's round cheeks were very pink and soft. Clytie's big eyes were very bright and blue. Clytie's low-necked white book-muslin rested softly on Clytie's white, plump shoulders. Clytie looked at the master, and the master nodded. Then Clytie spoke softly :—

" Joshua commanded the sun to stand still, and it obeyed him ! " There was a low hum of applause in the schoolroom, a triumphant expression on McSnagley's face, a grave shadow on the master's, and a comical look of disappointment reflected from the windows. Mliss skimmed rapidly over her astronomy, and then shut the book with a loud snap. A groan burst from

McSnagley, an expression of astonishment from the school-room, a yell from the windows as Mliss brought her red fist down on the desk with the emphatic declaration—

"It's a d——n lie. I don't believe it!"

CHAPTER IV

THE long wet season had drawn near its close. Signs of spring were visible in the swelling buds and rushing torrents. The pine forests exhaled the fresher spicery. The azaleas were already budding, the ceanothus getting ready its lilac livery for spring. On the green upland which climbed Red Mountain at its southern aspect the long spike of the monk's hood shot up from its broad-leaved stool, and once more shook its dark-blue bells. Again the billow above Smith's grave was soft and green, its crest just tossed with the foam of daisies and butter-cups. The little graveyard had gathered a few new dwellers in the past year, and the mounds were placed two by two by the little paling until they reached Smith's grave, and there there was but one. General superstition had shunned it, and the plot beside Smith was vacant.

There had been several placards posted about the town, intimating that, at a certain period, a celebrated dramatic company would perform, for a few days, a series of " side-splitting " and " screaming " farces ; that, alternating pleas-antly with this, there would be some melodrama and a grand divertisement, which would include singing, dancing, etc. These announcements occasioned a great fluttering among the little folk, and were the theme of much excitement and great speculation among the master's scholars. The master had promised Mliss, to whom this sort of thing was sacred and rare, that she should go, and on that momentous evening the master and Mliss " assisted."

The performance was the prevalent style of heavy medi-ocrity ; the melodrama was not bad enough to laugh at nor good enough to excite. But the master, turning wearily to the child, was astonished, and felt something like self-accusation in noticing the peculiar effect upon her excitable nature. The red blood flushed in her cheeks at each stroke of her panting little heart. Her small passionate lips were slightly parted to give vent to her hurried breath. Her widely opened lids threw up and arched her black eyebrows. She did not laugh at the dismal comicalities of the funny man, for Mliss seldom laughed.

Nor was she discreetly affected to the delicate extremes of the corner of a white handkerchief, as was the tender-hearted " Clytie," who was talking with her " feller " and ogling the master at the same moment. But when the performance was over, and the green curtain fell on the little stage, Mliss drew a long deep breath, and turned to the master's grave face with a half-apologetic smile and wearied gesture. Then she said, " Now take me home ! " and dropped the lids of her black eyes, as if to dwell once more in fancy on the mimic stage.

On their way to Mrs. Morpher's the master thought proper to ridicule the whole performance. Now he shouldn't wonder if Mliss thought that the young lady who acted so beautifully was really in earnest, and in love with the gentleman who wore such fine clothes. Well, if she were in love with him, it was a very unfortunate thing ! " Why ? " said Mliss, with an upward sweep of the drooping lid. " Oh ! well, he couldn't support his wife at his present salary, and pay so much a week for his fine clothes, and then they wouldn't receive as much wages if they were married as if they were merely lovers,—that is," added the master, " if they are not already married to somebody else ; but I think the husband of the pretty young countess takes the tickets at the door, or pulls up the curtain, or snuffs the candles, or does something equally refined and elegant. As to the young man with nice clothes, which are really nice now, and must cost at least two and a half or three dollars, not to speak of that mantle of red drugget, which I happen to know the price of, for I bought some of it for my room once,—as to this young man, Lissy, he is a pretty good fellow, and if he does drink occasionally, I don't think people ought to take advantage of it and give him black eyes and throw him in the mud. Do you ? I am sure he might owe me two dollars and a half a long time before I would throw it up in his face, as the fellow did the other night at Wingdam."

Mliss had taken his hand in both of hers and was trying to look in his eyes, which the young man kept as resolutely averted. Mliss had a faint idea of irony, indulging herself sometimes in a species of sardonic humour, which was equally visible in her actions and speech. But the young man continued in this strain until they had reached Mrs. Morpher's, and he had deposited Mliss in her maternal charge. Waiving the invitation of Mrs. Morpher to refreshment and rest, and shading his eyes with his hand to keep out the blue-eyed Clytemnestra's siren glances, he excused himself and went home.

For two or three days after the advent of the dramatic company, Mliss was late at school, and the master's usual Friday afternoon ramble was for once omitted, owing to the absence of his trustworthy guide. As he was putting away his books and preparing to leave the schoolhouse, a small voice piped at his side, " Please, sir ! " The master turned, and there stood Aristides Morpher.

" Well, my little man," said the master impatiently, " what is it ?—quick ! "

" Please, sir, me and ' Kerg ' thinks that Mliss is going to run away agin."

" What's that, sir ? " said the master, with that unjust testiness with which we always receive disagreeable news.

" Why, sir, she don't stay home any more, and ' Kerg ' and me see her talking with one of those actor fellers, and she's with him now ; and please, sir, yesterday she told ' Kerg ' and me she could make a speech as well as Miss Cellerstina Mont-moressy, and she spouted right off by heart," and the little fellow paused in a collapsed condition.

" What actor ? " asked the master.

" Him as wears the shiny hat. And hair. And gold pin. And gold chain," said the just Aristides, putting periods for commas to eke out his breath.

The master put on his gloves and hat, feeling an unpleasant tightness in his chest and thorax, and walked out in the road. Aristides trotted along by his side, endeavouring to keep pace with his short legs to the master's strides, when the master stopped suddenly, and Aristides bumped up against him. " Where were they talking ? " asked the master, as if continuing the conversation.

" At the Arcade," said Aristides.

When they reached the main street the master paused. " Run down home," said he to the boy. " If Mliss is there, come to the Arcade and tell me. If she isn't there, stay home ; run ! " And off trotted the short-legged Aristides.

The Arcade was just across the way,—a long, rambling building containing a bar-room, billiard-room, and restaurant. As the young man crossed the plaza he noticed that two or three of the passers-by turned and looked after him. He looked at his clothes, took out his handkerchief and wiped his face before he entered the bar-room. It contained the usual number of loungers, who stared at him as he entered. One of them looked at him so fixedly and with such a strange expression that the master stopped and looked again, and then saw it was only his own reflection in a large mirror. This made the master think that perhaps he was a little excited, and so he took up a copy of the *Red Mountain Banner* from one of the tables, and tried to recover his composure by reading the column of advertisements.

He then walked through the bar-room, through the restaurant, and into the billiard-room. The child was not there. In the latter apartment a person was standing by one of the tables, with a broad-brimmed glazed hat on his head. The master recognised him as the agent of the dramatic company ; he had taken a dislike to him at their first meeting, from the peculiar fashion of wearing his beard and hair. Satisfied that the object of his search was not there, he turned to the man with the glazed hat. He had noticed the master, but tried that common trick of unconsciousness, in which vulgar natures always fail. Balancing a billiard-cue in his hand, he pretended to play with a ball in the centre of the table. The master stood opposite to him until he raised his eyes ; when their glances met, the master walked up to him.

He had intended to avoid a scene or quarrel, but when he began to speak, something kept rising in his throat and retarded his utterance, and his own voice frightened him, it sounded so distant, low, and resonant.

" I understand," he began, " that Melissa Smith, an orphan, and one of my scholars, has talked with you about adopting your profession. Is that so ? "

The man with the glazed hat leaned over the table, and made an imaginary shot, that sent the ball spinning round the cushions. Then walking round the table he recovered the ball and placed it upon the spot. This duty discharged, getting ready for another shot, he said—

" S'pose she has ? "

The master choked up again, but, squeezing the cushion of the table in his gloved hand, he went on—

" If you are a gentleman, I have only to tell you that I am her guardian, and responsible for her career. You know as well as I do the kind of life you offer her. As you may learn of any one here, I have already brought her out of an existence worse than death,—out of the streets and the contamination of vice. I am trying to do so again. Let us talk like men. She has neither father, mother, sister, or brother. Are you seeking to give her an equivalent for these ? "

The man with the glazed hat examined the point of his cue, and then looked around for somebody to enjoy the joke with him.

" I know that she is a strange, wilful girl," continued the master, " but she is better than she was. I believe that I have some influence over her still. I beg and hope, therefore, that you will take no further steps in this matter, but as a man, as a gentleman, leave her to me. I am willing——" But here something rose again in the master's throat, and the sentence remained unfinished.

The man with the glazed hat, mistaking the master's silence, raised his head with a coarse, brutal laugh, and said in a loud voice—

" Want her yourself, do you ? That cock won't fight here, young man ! "

The insult was more in the tone than the words, more in the glance than tone, and more in the man's instinctive nature than all these. The best appreciable rhetoric to this kind of animal is a blow. The master felt this, and, with his pent-up, nervous energy finding expression in the one act, he struck the brute full in his grinning face. The blow sent the glazed hat one way and the cue another, and tore the glove and skin from the master's hand from knuckle to joint. It opened up the corners of the fellow's mouth, and spoilt the peculiar shape of his beard for some time to come.

There was a shout, an imprecation, a scuffle, and the trampling of many feet. Then the crowd parted right and left, and two sharp quick reports followed each other in rapid succession. Then they closed again about his opponent, and the master was standing alone. He remembered picking bits of burning wadding from his coatsleeve with his left hand. Some one was holding his other hand. Looking at it, he saw it was still bleeding from the blow, but his fingers were clenched around the handle of a glittering knife. He could not remember when or how he got it.

The man who was holding his hand was Mr. Morpher. He hurried the master to the door, but the master held back, and tried to tell him as well as he could with his parched throat about " Mliss." " It's all right, my boy," said Mr. Morpher. " She's home ! " And they passed out into the street together. As they walked along Mr. Morpher said that Mliss had come running into the house a few moments before, and had dragged him out, saying that somebody was trying to kill the master at

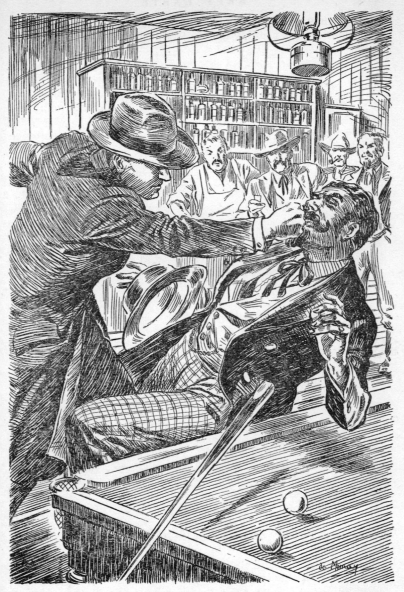

*The blow sent the glazed hat one way and the cue another, and tore
the glove and skin from the master's hand from knuckle to joint.*

the Arcade. Wishing to be alone, the master promised Mr.
Morpher that he would not seek the agent again that night,
and parted from him, taking the road toward the schoolhouse.
He was surprised on nearing it to find the door open,—still
more surprised to find Mliss sitting there.

The master's nature, as I have hinted before, had, like most
sensitive organisations, a selfish basis. The brutal taunt thrown
out by his late adversary still rankled in his heart. It was
possible, he thought, that such a construction might be put
upon his affection for the child, which at best was foolish and
Quixotic. Besides, had she not voluntarily abnegated his
authority and affection? And what had everybody else said
about her? Why should he alone combat the opinion of all,
and be at last obliged tacitly to confess the truth of all they
had predicted? And he had been a participant in a low bar-
room fight with a common boor, and risked his life, to prove
what? What had he proved? Nothing! What would the
people say? What would his friends say? What would
McSnagley say?

In his self-accusation the last person he should have wished
to meet was Mliss. He entered the door, and, going up to his
desk, told the child, in a few cold words, that he was busy and
wished to be alone. As she rose he took her vacant seat, and,
sitting down, buried his head in his hands. When he looked
up again she was still standing there. She was looking at his
face with an anxious expression.

" Did you kill him? " she asked.

" No! " said the master.

" That's what I gave you the knife for! " said the child,
quickly.

" Gave me the knife? " repeated the master, in bewilderment.

" Yes, gave you the knife. I was there under the bar.
Saw you hit him. Saw you both fall. He dropped his old
knife. I gave it to you. Why didn't you stick him? " said
Mliss rapidly, with an expressive twinkle of the black eyes and
a gesture of the little red hand.

The master could only look his astonishment.

" Yes," said Mliss. " If you'd asked me, I'd told you I
was off with the playactors. Why was I off with the playactors? Because you wouldn't tell me you was going away. I
knew it. I heard you tell the Doctor so. I wasn't agoin' to
stay here alone with those Morphers. I'd rather die first."

With a dramatic gesture which was perfectly consistent with her character, she drew from her bosom a few limp green leaves, and, holding them out at arm's-length, said in her quick vivid way, and in the queer pronunciation of her old life, which she fell into when unduly excited—

" That's the poison plant you said would kill me. I'll go with the playactors, or I'll eat this and die here. I don't care which. I won't stay here, where they hate and despise me ! Neither would you let me, if you didn't hate and despise me too ! "

The passionate little breast heaved, and two big tears peeped over the edge of Mliss's eyelids, but she whisked them away with the corner of her apron as if they had been wasps.

" If you lock me up in jail," said Mliss fiercely, " to keep me from the playactors, I'll poison myself. Father killed himself,—why shouldn't I ? You said a mouthful of that root would kill me, and I always carry it here," and she struck her breast with her clenched fist.

The master thought of the vacant plot beside Smith's grave, and of the passionate little figure before him. Seizing her hands in his and looking full into her truthful eyes, he said—

" Lissy, will you go with *me ?* "

The child put her arms around his neck, and said joyfully, " Yes."

" But now—to-night ? "

" To-night ! "

And, hand in hand, they passed into the road,—the narrow road that had once brought her weary feet to the master's door, and which it seemed she should not tread again alone. The stars glittered brightly above them. For good or ill the lesson had been learned, and behind them the school of Red Mountain closed upon them for ever.

NATHANIEL HAWTHORNE (1804–1864) *came of Puritan stock. While he was never able completely to free himself from his New England background the artist in him rebelled against it. From the conflict emerged his most famous book, " The Scarlet Letter," the subject of which suggested itself to him while he was a Customs official in Salem. Hawthorne is also famous for his " Tanglewood Tales."*

DROWNE'S WOODEN IMAGE

ONE sunshiny morning, in the good old times of the town of Boston, a young carver in wood, well known by the name of Drowne, stood contemplating a large oaken log, which it was his purpose to convert into the figure-head of a vessel. And while he discussed within his own mind what sort of shape or similitude it were well to bestow upon this excellent piece of timber, there came into Drowne's workshop a certain Captain Hunnewell, owner and commander of the good brig called the *Cynosure*, which had just returned from her first voyage to Fayal.

" Ah ! that will do, Drowne, that will do ! " cried the jolly captain, tapping the log with his rattan. " I bespeak this very piece of oak for the figure-head of the *Cynosure*. She has shown herself the sweetest craft that ever floated, and I mean to decorate her prow with the handsomest image that the skill of man can cut out of timber. And, Drowne, you are the fellow to execute it."

" You give me more credit than I deserve, Captain Hunnewell," said the carver, modestly, yet, as one conscious of eminence in his heart. " But, for the sake of the good brig, I stand ready to do my best. And which of these designs do you prefer ? Here,"—pointing to a staring, half-length figure, in a white wig and scarlet coat,—" here is an excellent model, the likeness of our gracious king. Here is the valiant Admiral Vernon. Or, if you prefer a female figure, what say you to Britannia with the trident ? "

" All very fine, Drowne ; all very fine," answered the mariner. " But as nothing like the brig ever swam the ocean, so I am determined she shall have such a figure-head as old

421

Neptune never saw in his life. And what is more, as there is a secret in the matter, you must pledge your credit not to betray it."

"Certainly," said Drowne, marvelling, however, what possible mystery there could be in reference to an affair so open, of necessity, to the inspection of all the world as the figure-head of a vessel. "You may depend, Captain, on my being as secret as the nature of the case will permit."

Captain Hunnewell then took Drowne by the button, and communicated his wishes in so low a tone that it would be unmannerly to repeat what was evidently intended for the carver's private ear. We shall, therefore, take the opportunity to give the reader a few desirable particulars about Drowne himself.

He was the first American who is known to have attempted —in a very humble line, it is true—that art in which we can now reckon so many names already distinguished, or rising to distinction. From his earliest boyhood he had exhibited a knack,—for it would be too proud a word to call it genius,— a knack, therefore, for the imitation of the human figure in whatever material came most readily to hand. The snows of a New England winter had often supplied him with a species of marble as dazzlingly white, at least, as the Parian or the Carrara, and if less durable, yet sufficiently so to correspond with any claims to permanent existence possessed by the boy's frozen statues. Yet they won admiration from maturer judges than his schoolfellows, and were, indeed, remarkably clever, though destitute of the native warmth that might have made the snow melt beneath his hand. As he advanced in life, the young man adopted pine and oak as eligible materials for the display of his skill, which now began to bring him a return of solid silver as well as the empty praise that had been an apt reward enough for his productions of evanescent snow. He became noted for carving ornamental pump-heads, and wooden urns for gate-posts, and decorations, more grotesque than fanciful, for mantel-pieces. No apothecary would have deemed himself in the way of obtaining custom, without setting up a gilded mortar, if not a head of Galen or Hippo-crates, from the skilful hand of Drowne.

But the great scope of his business lay in the manufacture of figure-heads for vessels. Whether it were the monarch himself, or some famous British admiral or general, or the governor of the province, or perchance the favourite daughter of the ship-owner, there the image stood above the prow, decked out in gorgeous colours, magnificently gilded, and staring the whole world out of countenance, as if from an innate consciousness of its own superiority. These specimens of native sculpture had crossed the sea in all directions, and been not ignobly noticed among the crowded shipping of the Thames, and wherever else the hardy mariners of New England had pushed their adventures. It must be confessed that a family likeness pervaded these respectable progeny of Drowne's skill; that the benign countenance of the king resembled those of his subjects, and that Miss Peggy Hobart, the merchant's daughter, bore a remarkable similitude to Britannia, Victory, and other ladies of the allegoric sisterhood; and, finally, that they all had a kind of wooden aspect, which proved an intimate relationship with the unshaped blocks of timber in the carver's workshop. But at least there was no inconsiderable skill of hand, nor a deficiency of any attribute to render them really works of art, except that deep quality, be it of soul or intellect, which bestows life upon the lifeless and warmth upon the cold, and which, had it been present, would have made Drowne's wooden image instinct with spirit.

The captain of the *Cynosure* had now finished his instructions.

"And, Drowne," said he, impressively, "you must lay aside all other business and set about this forthwith. And as to the price, only do the job in first-rate style, and you shall settle that point yourself."

"Very well, Captain," answered the carver, who looked grave and somewhat perplexed, yet had a sort of smile upon his visage; "depend upon it, I'll do my utmost to satisfy you."

From that moment the men of taste about Long Wharf and the Town Dock who were wont to show their love for the arts by frequent visits to Drowne's workshop, and admiration of his wooden images, began to be sensible of a mystery in the carver's conduct. Often he was absent in the daytime. Sometimes, as might be judged by gleams of light from the shop-windows, he was at work until a late hour of the evening; although neither knock nor voice, on such occasions, could gain admittance for a visitor, or elicit any word of response. Nothing remarkable, however, was observed in the shop at those hours when it was thrown open. A fine piece of timber, indeed, which Drowne was known to have reserved for some work of especial dignity, was seen to be gradually assuming shape. What shape it was destined ultimately to take was a problem to his friends and a point on which the carver himself preserved a rigid silence. But day after day, though Drowne was seldom noticed in the act of working upon it, this rude form began to be developed until it became evident to all observers that a female figure was growing into mimic life. At each new visit they beheld a larger pile of wooden chips and a nearer approximation to something beautiful. It seemed as if the hamadryad of the oak had sheltered herself from the unimaginative world within the heart of her native tree, and that it was only necessary to remove the strange shapelessness that had incrusted her, and reveal the grace and loveliness of a divinity. Imperfect as the design, the attitude, the costume, and especially the face of the image still remained, there was already an effect that drew the eye from the wooden cleverness of Drowne's earlier productions and fixed it upon the tantalizing mystery of this new project.

Copley, the celebrated painter, then a young man and a resident of Boston, came one day to visit Drowne ; for he had recognized so much of moderate ability in the carver as to induce him, in the dearth of professional sympathy, to cultivate his acquaintance. On entering the shop the artist glanced at the inflexible image of king, commander, dame, and allegory that stood around, on the best of which might have been bestowed the questionable praise that it looked as if a living man had here been changed to wood, and that not only the physical, but the intellectual and spiritual part, partook of the stolid transformation. But in not a single instance did it seem as if the wood were imbibing the ethereal essence of humanity. What a wide distinction is here ! and how far would the slightest portion of the latter merit have outvalued the utmost degree of the former !

" My friend Drowne," said Copley, smiling to himself, but alluding to the mechanical and wooden cleverness that so invariably distinguished the images, " you are really a remarkable person ! I have seldom met with a man in your line of business that could do so much ; for one other touch might make this figure of General Wolfe, for instance, a breathing and intelligent human creature."

" You would have me think that you are praising me highly, Mr. Copley," answered Drowne, turning his back upon Wolfe's image in apparent disgust. " But there has

come a light into my mind.   I know, what you know as well,
that the one touch which you speak of as deficient is the only
one that would be truly valuable, and that without it these
works of mine are no better than worthless abortions.   There
is the same difference between them and the works of an
inspired artist as between a sign-post daub and one of your
best pictures."

"This is strange," cried Copley, looking him in the face,
which now, as the painter fancied, had a singular depth of
intelligence, though hitherto it had not given him greatly the
advantage over his own family of wooden images.   "What
has come over you ?   How is it that, possessing the idea which
you have now uttered, you should produce only such works as
these ? "

The carver smiled, but made no reply.   Copley turned
again to the images, conceiving that the sense of deficiency
which Drowne had just expressed, and which is so rare in a
merely mechanical character, must surely imply a genius, the
tokens of which had heretofore been overlooked.   But no ;
there was not a trace of it.   He was about to withdraw when
his eyes chanced to fall upon a half-developed figure which
lay in a corner of the workshop, surrounded by scattered chips
of oak.   It arrested him at once.

"What is here ?   Who has done this ? " he broke out,
after contemplating it in speechless astonishment for an
instant.   "Here is the divine, the life-giving touch.   What
inspired hand is beckoning this wood to arise and live ?   Whose
work is this ? "

"No man's work," replied Drowne.   "The figure lies
within that block of oak, and it is my business to find it."

"Drowne," said the true artist, grasping the carver fervently by the hand, "you are a man of genius ! "

As Copley departed, happening to glance backward from
the threshold, he beheld Drowne bending over the half-created
shape, and stretching forth his arms as if he would have
embraced and drawn it to his heart ; while, had such a miracle
been possible, his countenance expressed passion enough to
communicate warmth and sensibility to the lifeless oak.

"Strange enough ! " said the artist to himself.   "Who
would have looked for a modern Pygmalion in the person of a
Yankee mechanic ! "

As yet, the image was but vague in its outward present-
ment ; so that, as in the cloud-shapes around the western

sun, the observer rather felt, or was led to imagine, than really saw what was intended by it. Day by day, however, the work assumed greater precision, and settled its irregular and misty outline into distincter grace and beauty. The general design was now obvious to the common eye. It was a female figure, in what appeared to be a foreign dress ; the gown being laced over the bosom, and opening in front so as to disclose a skirt or petticoat, the folds and inequalities of which were admirably represented in the oaken substance. She wore a hat of singular gracefulness, and abundantly laden with flowers, such as never grew in the rude soil of New England, but which, with all their fanciful luxuriance, had a natural truth that it seemed impossible for the most fertile imagination to have attained without copying from real prototypes. There were several little appendages to this dress, such as a fan, a pair of earrings, a chain about the neck, a watch in the bosom, and a ring upon the finger, all of which would have been deemed beneath the dignity of sculpture. They were put on, however, with as much taste as a lovely woman might have shown in her attire, and could therefore have shocked none but a judgment spoiled by artistic rules.

The face was still imperfect ; but gradually, by a magic touch, intelligence and sensibility brightened through the features, with all the effect of light gleaming forth from within the solid oak. The face became alive. It was a beautiful, though not precisely regular, and somewhat haughty aspect, but with a certain piquancy about the eyes and mouth, which, of all expressions, would have seemed the most impossible to throw over a wooden countenance. And now, so far as carving went, this wonderful production was complete.

"Drowne," said Copley, who had hardly missed a single day in his visits to the carver's workshop, "if this work were in marble it would make you famous at once ; nay, I would almost affirm that it would make an era in the art. It is as ideal as an antique statue, and yet as real as any lovely woman whom one meets at a fireside or in the street. But I trust you do not mean to desecrate this exquisite creature with paint, like those staring kings and admirals yonder ? "

"Not paint her ! " exclaimed Captain Hunnewell, who stood by ; "not paint the figure-head of the *Cynosure* ! And what sort of a figure should I cut in a foreign port with such an unpainted oaken stick as this over my prow ! She must, and she shall, be painted to the life, from the topmost flower in her hat down to the silver spangles on her slippers."

" Mr. Copley," said Drowne, quietly, " I know nothing of marble statuary, and nothing of the sculptor's rules of art ; but of this wooden image, this work of my hands, this creature of my heart,"—and here his voice faltered and choked in a very singular manner,—" of this—of her—I may say that I know something. A wellspring of inward wisdom gushed within me as I wrought upon the oak with my whole strength, and soul, and faith. Let others do what they may with marble, and adopt what rules they choose. If I can produce my desired effect by painted wood, those rules are not for me, and I have a right to disregard them."

" The very spirit of genius," muttered Copley to himself. " How otherwise should this carver feel himself entitled to transcend all rules, and make me ashamed of quoting them ? "

He looked earnestly at Drowne, and again saw that expression of human love which, in a spiritual sense, as the artist could not help imagining, was the secret of the life that had been breathed into this block of wood.

The carver, still in the same secrecy that marked all his operations upon this mysterious image, proceeded to paint the habiliments in their proper colours, and the countenance with nature's red and white. When all was finished he threw open his workshop, and admitted the townspeople to behold what he had done. Most persons, at their first entrance, felt impelled to remove their hats, and pay such reverence as was due to the richly dressed and beautiful young lady who seemed to stand in a corner of the room, with oaken chips and shavings scattered at her feet. Then came a sensation of fear ; as if, not being actually human, yet so like humanity, she must therefore be something preternatural. There was, in truth, an indefinable air and expression that might reasonably induce the query, Who and from what sphere this daughter of the oak should be ? The strange, rich flowers of Eden on her head ; the complexion, so much deeper and more brilliant than those of our native beauties ; the foreign, as it seemed, and fantastic garb, yet not too fantastic to be worn decorously in the street ; the delicately wrought embroidery of the skirt ; the broad gold chain about her neck ; the curious ring upon her finger ; the fan, so exquisitely sculptured in open-work, and painted to resemble pearl and ebony ;—where could Drowne, in his sober walk of life, have beheld the vision here so matchlessly embodied ! And then her face ! In the dark eyes and around the voluptuous mouth there played a look made up of pride, coquetry, and a gleam of mirthfulness, which impressed Copley with the idea that the image was secretly enjoying the perplexing admiration of himself and other beholders.

" And will you," said he to the carver, " permit this masterpiece to become the figure-head of a vessel ? Give the honest captain yonder figure of Britannia,—it will answer his purpose far better,—and send this fairy queen to England, where, for aught I know, it may bring you a thousand pounds."

" I have not wrought it for money," said Drowne.

" What sort of a fellow is this ? " thought Copley. " A Yankee, and throw away the chance of making his fortune ! He has gone mad ; and thence has come this gleam of genius."

There was still further proof of Drowne's lunacy, if credit were due to the rumour that he had been seen kneeling at the feet of the oaken lady, and gazing with a lover's passionate ardour into the face that his own hands had created. The bigots of the day hinted that it would be no matter of surprise if an evil spirit were allowed to enter this beautiful form and seduce the carver to destruction.

The fame of the image spread far and wide. The inhabitants visited it so universally that after a few days of exhibition there was hardly an old man or a child who had not become minutely familiar with its aspect. Even had the story of Drowne's wooden image ended here, its celebrity might have been prolonged for many years by the reminiscences of those who looked upon it in their childhood, and saw nothing else so beautiful in after life. But the town was now astounded by an event the narrative of which has formed itself into one of the most singular legends that are yet to be met with in the traditionary chimney-corners of the New England metropolis, where old men and women sit dreaming of the past, and wag their heads at the dreamers of the present and the future.

One fine morning, just before the departure of the *Cynosure* on her second voyage to Fayal, the commander of that gallant vessel was seen to issue from his residence in Hanover Street. He was stylishly dressed in a blue broadcloth coat, with gold-lace at the seams and buttonholes, an embroidered scarlet waistcoat, a triangular hat, with a loop and broad binding of gold, and wore a silver-hilted hanger at his side. But the good captain might have been arrayed in the robes of a prince or the rags of a beggar, without in either case attracting notice, while obscured by such a companion as now leaned on his arm. The people in the street started, rubbed their eyes, and either leaped aside from their path, or stood as if transfixed to wood or marble in astonishment.

" Do you see it ?—do you see it ? " cried one, with tremulous eagerness. " It is the very same ! "

" The same ? " answered another, who had arrived in town only the night before. " Who do you mean ? I see only a sea-captain in his shore-going clothes, and a young lady in a foreign habit, with a bunch of beautiful flowers in her hat. On my word, she is as fair and bright a damsel as my eyes have looked on this many a day ! "

" Yes ; the same !—the very same ! " repeated the other. " Drowne's wooden image has come to life ! "

Here was a miracle indeed ! Yet, illuminated by the sunshine, or darkened by the alternate shade of the houses, and with its garments fluttering lightly in the morning breeze, there passed the image along the street. It was exactly and minutely the shape, the garb, and the face which the townspeople had so recently thronged to see and admire. Not a rich flower upon her head, not a single leaf, but had had its prototype in Drowne's wooden workmanship, although now their fragile grace had become flexible, and was shaken by every footstep that the wearer made. The broad gold chain upon the neck was identical with the one represented on the image, and glistened with the motion imparted by the rise and fall of the bosom which it decorated. A real diamond sparkled on her finger. In her right hand she bore a pearl and ebony fan, which she flourished with a fantastic and bewitching coquetry, that was likewise expressed in all her movements as well as in the style of her beauty and the attire that so well harmonized with it. The face, with its brilliant depth of complexion, had the same piquancy of mirthful mischief that was fixed upon the countenance of the image, but which was here varied and continually shifting, yet always essentially the same, like the sunny gleam upon a bubbling fountain. On the whole, there was something so airy and yet so real in the figure, and withal so perfectly did it represent Drowne's image, that people knew not whether to suppose the magic wood etherealized into a spirit or warmed and softened into an actual woman.

" One thing is certain," muttered a Puritan of the old

stamp, " Drowne has sold himself to the Devil ; and doubtless this gay Captain Hunnewell is a party to the bargain."

" And I," said a young man who overheard him, " would almost consent to be the third victim, for the liberty of saluting those lovely lips."

" And so would I," replied Copley, the painter, " for the privilege of taking her picture."

The image, or the apparition, whichever it might be, still escorted by the bold captain, proceeded from Hanover Street through some of the cross lanes that make this portion of the town so intricate, to Ann Street, thence into Dock Square, and so downward to Drowne's shop, which stood just on the water's edge. The crowd still followed, gathering volume as it rolled along. Never had a modern miracle occurred in such broad daylight, nor in the presence of such a multitude of witnesses. The airy image, as if conscious that she was the object of the murmurs and disturbance that swelled behind her, appeared slightly vexed and flustered, yet still in a manner consistent with the light vivacity and sportive mischief that were written in her countenance. She was observed to flutter her fan with such vehement rapidity that the elaborate delicacy of its workmanship gave way, and it remained broken in her hand.

Arriving at Drowne's door, while the captain threw it open, the marvellous apparition paused an instant on the threshold, assuming the very attitude of the image, and casting over the crowd that glance of sunny coquetry which all remembered on the face of the oaken lady. She and her cavalier then disappeared.

" Ah ! " murmured the crowd, drawing a deep breath, as with one vast pair of lungs.

" The world looks darker now that she has vanished," said some of the young men.

But the aged, whose recollections dated as far back as witch times, shook their heads, and hinted that our forefathers would have thought it a pious deed to burn the daughter of the oak with fire.

" If she be other than a bubble of the elements," exclaimed Copley, " I must look upon her face again."

He accordingly entered the shop ; and there, in her usual corner, stood the image, gazing at him, as it might seem, with the very same expression of mirthful mischief that had been the farewell look of the apparition when, but a moment before, she turned her face towards the crowd. The carver stood beside his creation, mending the beautiful fan, which by some accident was broken in her hand. But there was no longer any motion in the life-like image, nor any real woman in the workshop, nor even the witchcraft of a sunny shadow, that might have deluded people's eyes as it flitted along the street. Captain Hunnewell, too, had vanished. His hoarse, sea-breezy tones, however, were audible on the other side of a door that opened upon the water.

"Sit down in the stern sheets, my lady," said the gallant captain. "Come, bear a hand, you lubbers, and set us on board in the turning of a minute-glass."

And then was heard the stroke of oars.

"Drowne," said Copley, with a smile of intelligence, "you have been a truly fortunate man. What painter or statuary ever had such a subject! No wonder that she inspired a genius into you, and first created the artist who afterwards created her image."

Drowne looked at him with a visage that bore the traces of tears, but from which the light of imagination and sensibility, so recently illuminating it, had departed. He was again the mechanical carver that he had been known to be all his lifetime.

"I hardly understand what you mean, Mr. Copley," said he, putting his hand to his brow. "This image! Can it have been my work? Well, I have wrought it in a kind of dream; and now that I am broad awake I must set about finishing yonder figure of Admiral Vernon."

And forthwith he employed himself on the stolid countenance of one of his wooden progeny, and completed it in his own mechanical style, from which he was never known afterwards to deviate. He followed his business industriously for many years, acquired a competence, and in the latter part of his life attained to a dignified station in the church, being remembered in records and traditions as Deacon Drowne, the carver. One of his productions, an Indian chief, gilded all over, stood during the better part of a century on the cupola of the Province House, bedazzling the eyes of those who looked upward, like an angel of the sun. Another work of the good deacon's hand—a reduced likeness of his friend Captain Hunnewell, holding a telescope and quadrant—may be seen to this day, at the corner of Broad and State Streets, serving in the useful capacity of sign to the shop of a nautical-instrument maker. We know not how to account for the inferiority of this quaint old figure as compared with the recorded excellence of the Oaken Lady, unless on the supposition that in every human spirit there is imagination, sensibility, creative power, genius, which, according to circumstances, may either be developed in this world, or shrouded in a mask of dullness until another state of being. To our friend Drowne there came a brief season of excitement, kindled by love. It rendered him a genius for that one occasion, but, quenched in disappointment, left him again the mechanical carver in wood, without the power even of appreciating the work that his own hands had wrought. Yet who can doubt that the very highest state to which a human spirit can attain, in its loftiest aspirations, is its truest and most natural state, and that Drowne was more consistent with himself when he wrought the admirable figure of the mysterious lady, than when he perpetrated a whole progeny of blockheads ?

There was a rumour in Boston, about this period, that a young Portuguese lady of rank, on some occasion of political or domestic disquietude, had fled from her home in Fayal and put herself under the protection of Captain Hunnewell, on board of whose vessel, and at whose residence, she was sheltered until a change of affairs. This fair stranger must have been the original of Drowne's Wooden Image.

EDEN PHILLPOTTS (1862–), *an Anglo-Indian by birth, was for ten years a clerk in an insurance office. On coming to London he studied for the stage, but " abandoned the art on finding his ability did not justify perseverance." Nevertheless this training enabled him to write one of the most successful comedies of modern times—" The Farmer's Wife." His literary work includes novels of Devonshire and poetry.*

MADONNA OF THE FIREFLIES

A IR had fallen in love with earth, and though all was silvery and the sky clouded, yet it seemed that the gold of past sunshine lingered interwoven as a permanent possession of mountain and vale. Vegetation draped rather than clothed this earth. The emerald and jade spread no heavy vesture over plain and hill, but transparently covered them, as though in these haunts of sunlight no pelt was needed to keep the brown earth warm.

Spring danced through Tuscany, and where her twinkling footfall passed, the bud broke and the flower bloomed. Here was radiant green of vine, pear and apple, peach and almond ; while darker foliage of plum and fig spattered the golden verdure, and, darker yet, seen far off, reigned the cypress, splashing earth with its solitary notes of exclamation, now dotted singly, now clustering about some lifted campanile, or marking boundaries between land and land. Ringed in with mountains, that fell broadly to their foothills, lapped in milky air, its din silenced, its detail hidden, there spread a city, levelled like a low island of corals and bright lavas in the midst of a dim green sea. It broke out of the verdant plain, and by the russet and amber of it, by the mellow tincture kneaded into every roof, by its mighty dome and that silver stalk beside it ; by the lesser cupolas and turrets and by the tower of towers, that breaks like a brown flower from a brown sheath, one marked Firenze, queen and enchantress of the olden time.

John Travers gazed upon this scene from a tiny piazza five miles distant, and his troubled face grew softer. He lifted it to the blue-robed Apennine, then turned to gaze at a podere a mile away. The place rose perched on its proper knap, like a thousand others. Under old terra-cotta, whose warmth was bleached by a century of sunshine and fretted with orange and ebony lichens, the white walls stood. No cypress crowned this hill, but a great loquat massed against the dwelling, a hayrick, reduced to a mere wedge of gold about its stake, flashed sunbright beside the farm, and beneath, subtending the homestead, there rolled out familiar cultivation. Hay was being saved, and pale ribbons of fallen grass spread shining between the rows of vine and fruit-trees.

Hither went the watcher presently. It was his home for a season. Life had crossed the man's hopes and derided his ambitions of late, had put to him harsh questions, only to be answered after intervals of dismay and doubt. For here was one who had dictated to fate and turned his back on fortune. With full hands she came to him, and he had sent her with full hands away, counting dearer than her obvious gifts of peace and plenty, one little, doubtful, personal possession born with him—a glimmer from remote, ancestral flames.

The son of a prosperous physician, John Travers might have followed in the safe footsteps trampled by his father, and with no more than fair measure of steady work and application have succeeded to the parental name and renown. Nor in his earlier youth did it occur to him to question a career so indicated. As a matter of course, John Travers the elder assumed that his son—a man of good presence and fine ability—would carry on his own work, succeed to his practice and pursue his original field of inquiry, which was the eye ; indeed, the lad for long years accepted the situation as expedient in every aspect, and not until he had been at a hospital for nearly five years, filled the position of indresser and begun to read for his finals, awakened the doubts that waxed into ultimate denial.

He had always drawn with accuracy, and his father, no draughtsman, was wont to impress on the lad how valuable this gift must prove ; but the instinct grew with use ; the studies in anatomy became less and less a means and more of an end ; some subtle seed of art, that had not perished but only slept through certain generations, now found a congenial temperament, or modelled it ; and at twenty-five years of age John Travers the younger knew that he must be a painter.

Life for him meant art, not science ; the spirit awoke and cried to him that he must indeed use his own eyes, that the sight of other men might be bettered, but not as his father had done before him. He was called into the world to make beautiful things from his own sense of beauty ; and now he had been striving to do so for six years, and the goal was far distant still. He followed the uphill path of the painter of ideas. No conventional road lured him ; he answered to his own vision ; but as yet it was not perfected, and he stood upon the bleak plateau-lands of doubt, where difficulties crowd the horizon like mountain peaks, and the climber, chilled and wearied by his last effort, finds each point gained but the vantage ground that shows a loftier one.

To Firenze he had come, smarting and wounded, for his year's work and his masterpiece had been rejected by the Royal Academy—a trial unforeseen after three years of acceptance. And for a moment art tasted bitter to his palate ; the kinship of friends in the city was vain ; their enthusiasm and undying hope appeared but folly.

He walked amid figures of the mind, that beckoned and promised much ; and others that also beckoned and promised nothing. Like Lucian before him, he dreamed and saw two women, and doubted between them, while his heart beat low and hope went hungry. The one was thin, worn, labour-stained, with deep lines on her face and a great wistfulness in her wonderful eyes. Gaunt she was, and her hands were made ugly by eternal labour ; her garment was earth-coloured and ragged, so that it hardly served to hide her lean bosom and thin arms. But the other minced in her going, and was round and very fair. Her garment owned neither stain nor tatter ; she went sleekly in purple and fine linen, and she moved with smiles confidently, daintily, as one for ever welcome, from whom no lover of beauty could turn away. Art was the first woman, and culture was the second ; and Travers remembered how Lucian, with a cynical indifference, had flouted the spirit for the substance, disowned the creator, and thrown in his lot as jurist and literary trifler with her who promised the fruits and the joys of earth.

But Art had won this man for ever, and there was no turning back for him. Though the loaf that she offered was lean and her flask of wine but thin, they held that nourishment of the soul no other food could promise him.

He had turned his back on Firenze, and removed from

sight and sound of his fellow-labourers. At a little podere in Bagni di Ripoli, Travers came by sure stages to himself, while his unconquerable ideal, dimmed for a while, now, in the dreaming vales of Arno, trembled out again, daily to grow brighter and steadier. His purposes were assured, his mind affirmed, and patience visited him as a welcome guest.

Life at the podere, unutterably fine in its stern simplicity, was well qualified to help the painter. Here generation after generation of one race laboured upon land that they could never own. Yet it sustained them, and they lived and toiled in contentment and family friendship. Here were twelve men, women, and children, all knit together in relationships ; and with them lived one old man, who had known another world than this, and come by accident of fallen fortunes to home at Ripoli with a dead wife's kindred. They made room for him without question, recognized his superior birth and education, lifted him to a place above themselves and loved him for his tribulations and his bravery. Now he also worked with his hands and earned his few daily pence ; but in the fields he could not labour, therefore he did lesser tasks about the home, for he was a good carpenter and house-painter ; he had made the podere fair with green shutters, and drawn beneath the deep eaves a frescoed pattern of purple grapes upon a golden lattice. These were his holiday tasks, and he spent his pennies on the colours that went to make them ; but at other times he mended the picks and ploughs, repaired the hedges, and used his needle upon the clothes of the men.

Amedio Brogi was the head of the family—a grandfather whose wife was dead. Then came Giacomo, his eldest son, with a living wife and two children, and Luigi, his second son, a bachelor. Giacomo's eldest boy, Gustavo, was wedded to his cousin, Emilia, and their offspring had brought beauty into the Brogi race—a quality until her advent lacking.

But Bice was fairer than a lap of spring flowers—all woman at sixteen, with innocent brown eyes that made the heart of man glad, a small red mouth, and fair hair that still dwelt in twin-plaited tails upon her back, though Emilia declared that it should be lifted to its proper crown.

Concerning the rest of the family, Travers as yet knew little. It took time to appreciate the clan and master the relation-ships, but for the present his first friends were Amedio, the grandfather, Gustavo, Emilia's husband and Bice's father, and Bice herself. For she was that loveliest of artists' dreams, an Italian girl at once beautiful and fair. " My skin is the colour of the filbert nuts, when the sun just touches them ; and my hair is the colour of the ripe maize, and my eyes are the colour of the wine of Orvieto," explained Bice to the artist, when he talked about painting her. The last simile he declined to accept. " No," he said, " your eyes are more beautiful than wine ; they are the colour of the autumn woods, when the leaves change to amber."

Bice was betrothed to Carlo Brogi, a distant cousin, who dwelt with the clan ; but here was a dark and difficult matter, for Carlo—now twenty years of age, a skilled vine-dresser, and a man of gentle disposition and good character—was not strong. He suffered, and there were days that followed on sleepless nights when Carlo could do no work. Sometimes he coughed ; sometimes his strength seemed to leave him, and his heart beat too fast. Then he could only sit in the sun and plait straw, like a girl. His folk whispered the grave word " consumption " among themselves, and were very tender to Carlo ; but a local physician, who had seen him, uttered no definite pronouncement, though he shook his head and declined to give any hopeful promise. He bade Carlo be stirring, eat well, take much olive oil, and work in the air when he could do so.

Lastly, of the friends of John Travers was Virgilio Torrigiani, the old kinsman of the clan, who loved beautiful things. His very name bespoke some culture, and there was extraordinary dignity about his bent figure. Ugliness triumphed in him and achieved the lovable and picturesque. He had a great nose and a bulldog mouth, large grey eyes that never lacked puzzledom and wonder for all his fourscore years, and a head as bald as head could be. He had lost all his money by going surety for a friend, who betrayed him ; and he had lost his wife, Amedia Brogi's sister, and three daughters, who had all died in youth. And now he himself stood on the verge, very busy, uncomplaining, childlike, full of stories and full of interest in the life of his wife's people. He had found her a serving woman in a friend's family, and fallen in love with her and married her. Visitors from England and America knew Virgilio. He could speak English, and was fond of bringing from an under-recess in his garments a Christmas card sent to him three years earlier by a British lady of high degree.

" I mended her travelling-bag with a silver clasp," he said.

" And she was by birth honourable, though she scorned to claim the fact. You can see her name written by herself upon this card of Christmas memory. It was to show that, while moving amidst honourable people, like herself, she still could remember Virgilio Torrigiani and his silver clasp."

Among these peace-lovers, to a home where not one harsh word was ever heard or voice lifted in anger; into a sunlit habitation of human souls as poor and contented as the lizards on their threshing-floor, had come John Travers; and little by little his larger interests faded, his deeper cares died. The trivial concerns and fleeting hopes and fears of the Brogi gathered weight for him; politics were narrowed to their affairs; ambition descended upon the promise of the vines; and, for excitement, was the plan of a fresco on the side of the barn; for intrigue, certain matters hatched in secret with Virgilio concerning the welfare of Carlo Brogi and his sweetheart.

II

AT first Travers had felt a sort of contempt for these people. Smarting and writhing under the heavy hand of chance, he scorned a folk who could " take life lying down," as he phrased it; but presently he began to accept the point of view, and to perceive not only the limitations, but also the compensation of an existence represented by the temporal return of four centimes a day. The Brogi farmed the podere for its owner, and received roughly one-half of the profits that accrued from all sources. It was a prosperous enterprise, and averaged a return of from five to seven and even eight per cent. upon the outlay. But not all the family was content to have no hand in their own fate. Bice had a will, and the artist, whose Italian sufficed for the purpose, presently found that, added to beauty, the girl possessed character. It expressed itself naturally in the terms of her religion, and an intellect, bright enough, found in superstition food that chimed with her ambitions and her hopes. She had an active mind, as opposed to the passive instincts of her kindred; it was not enough that the saints should smile upon her dreams and help her to be good; she looked to them to help her to be happy also.

Dark as a cave opened the mouth of a lower chamber upon a little piazza before the dwelling-house of the Brogi, and

from within, there issued the savour of cattle. Four beasts
dwelt there—milch cows which Bice attended. They never
grazed, for their food was served to them daily ; but Bice took
them for a walk sometimes after the evening milking, that
they might stretch their legs and take pleasure in the fresh
air at sunset time. Then best the artist liked to talk with
her, because the spirit of rest and contemplation haunted that
hour ; and when Carlo did not walk beside his sweetheart,
Travers would sometimes do so, and mark her moods, now
gay, now sad. She uttered surprising things sometimes, and
dumbly felt the poetry of life.

" It is because my lover is not strong," she explained. " If
he was like me—hard and tough and always ready to work,
and hungry and knowing no pain—then I should never think
of sad, strange things, but just be like other girls :
full of joy of being a girl and having a lover. But it makes
you old and wise very quickly if there is doubt. It brings
curious thoughts into your mind. The thoughts are not themselves funny, but it is funny that I, Bice, should think them.
For instance, I wondered last night in my bed what had become of all the smiles of all the beautiful, dead women that
have ever lived. A smile frightens away the ugliness of the
ugliest people. A girl's face is never ugly when it is smiling.
But the smiles of a pretty girl are like the cornflowers and
poppies in the corn : you cannot see them without smiling
back."

" The smiles of the fair, dead women have all warmed
somebody's hearts in their time, perhaps."

" It is not enough. What becomes of them ? There are
things that are too beautiful for God to let them die. I tell
you, smiles are treasured up, as we treasure up the grapes,
and when we lovely girls die and go to heaven, our smiles are
given back to us again—they are all there waiting for us."

So would the girl chatter beside the kine, and presently,
with growing intimacy, she began to give the painter a larger
glimpse of the secrets of her heart. Returning one day to his
mid-day meal, which he ate with the family, who were now
accustomed to his presence, Travers found Bice dragging a
haycart as though she had been a pony. Her sleeves were
pulled up, and her feet were naked. He helped her with this
burden up the hill. A path wound here steeply, flanked by
whispering wheat, whose glaucous blue made harmony with
the olives about it ; and half-way up the track was a shrine

of ripe, red brick, faced with crumbling mortar. The niche
held a little marble Virgin and Child, and behind them dabs
of russet and rose, faded and fallen from the mouldering
plaster, told of a perished fresco there. Above was a penthouse of sun-dried tiles, and in the niche stood a green bowl
that held a bouquet of wild flowers—blue sage, the gladiolus
of the corn, nigella, and sweet, sad-coloured broom-rapes. A
vine clambered up the little sanctuary, and presently amber
bunches of fruit would cluster there.

" Your patron saint, Bice. I am always wishing that you
would tell me about her. There are fresh flowers for her
every day, and the place where you kneel has no grass left
upon it."

Bice rested, and wiped her forehead with her blue skirt.
She looked at the speaker and nodded.

" I may tell you," she said. " I cannot tell you all there
is to tell at one moment ; but in pieces perhaps. She is my
saint, and sometimes I think she is going to be strong, and
sometimes I doubt about it. I am not very sure of her yet.
Time will tell. I am being very good to her. I look at her
with four eyes every day, and I pray to her with two hearts.
A girl cannot do more than that. Sometimes I call her
Madonna delle Lucciole, and sometimes Madonna delle Lucer-
tole. Because certainly the lizards love her. I have seen them
lift up their paws and pray to her."

Travers nodded gravely.

" The good St. Francis taught them to do that. You remember how he wanted all the world to know the best thing
he had ever heard, and how he talked to the birds and fishes
and told them about Christ ? So the fireflies and the lizards
no doubt heard too."

She doubted it not.

" The fireflies love this place best in the whole podere.
They much like the irises, that make so great a brightness
under the trees when they are in flower, and they love the
olives, and signal backwards and forwards and wave their
little lamps to each other ; but they burn brightest at the
shrine, and I have seen them light up the face of Mary
Madonna till it shone. And I think, because she is so tiny,
that they understand her and she talks to them. And I kneel
sometimes and hope they will come to me from her and tell
me something—something about Carlo."

" Perhaps it will happen."

" One has to be patient with the saints and the Blessed Mother. They take their own time. But she will give me a sign presently."

" I believe Carlo is going to be strong again, Bice."

" It must be one way or the other soon. We want to marry, but if he is to die before long, we must not."

" I don't think he is going to die."

" It is not what you think, or what I hope. It is what will happen," she said. " And nothing ever happens till it has happened. Corn is not bread till it has gone into the oven. So I pray a great deal here—far oftener than anybody knows—and I am a very good girl in other ways—exceedingly good."

" I know you are. It is a most deserving case, Bice, and if Madonna of the Fireflies does not take some trouble about it soon, I shall feel very much surprised."

" It is certainly her turn now—one must give and take, I suppose, even if one is the Mother of Christ," said Bice.

" The saints themselves get nothing for nothing in this weary world," he admitted.

" Why should they ? " she asked. " We Brogi say it is not honest to take without giving. But there are plenty of people in Italy who think it the great cleverness to do that."

" And everywhere else," he assured her.

They went on presently and entered the house-place, where a mighty chimney yawned over an open hearth and the food was spread for the workers. Amedio Brogi and Virgilio Torrigiani sat in the places of honour—snug chairs on either side of the fire, lifted above the floor—while Giacomo took the head of the table and Luigi, the foot. Emilia, Giacomo's daughter-in-law, stirred a great red, copper pot upon the charcoal fire and presently served broth of beans and fennel. Then followed black bread, with oil and some red wine. And that was all. They ate much bread, but butter they did not know, nor tea, nor coffee. Water, and wine made on the podere was all their drink, and of meat they took but little ; yet they celebrated delicate feasts sometimes at the season of fruits, and Travers had already tasted alpine strawberries and curds and ewes' milk—a dish that no gourmet might scorn.

So the stranger lived among the people and found his heart go out to them at last and peace return to him. And she came not empty-handed, for, as his wounded spirit healed and disappointments faded behind this foreground of beauty and human content, the normal desire to create awoke, and he girt up his loins and answered the voice that called.

III

ROUND about the old shrine the flowering vines were hung on little maple trees that lifted them above the corn, and a strip of soft sward, newly shorn, passed behind the ancient holy place. This accident led to an inspiration, and John Travers, returning in the crepuscule through dusk of the olives silently, marked Bice at her orisons. She knelt upright with her hands together, and it happened that above her head the fireflies twinkled. So absorbed was she that his footfall passed unheeded, and he stood awhile marking her profile fitfully outlined as the golden green lights spangled the darkness behind it. A magic picture came and went in the wavering illumination, and Bice remained visible even when the living lights quivered away amid the trees and above the wheat. For during these June nights there was no darkness —only a tender, ineffable grey and blue mingled. The sun loved teeming earth too well to leave her long, and after midnight the aura above his secret way could be seen, where he dallied a little behind the Apennine before returning.

Travers waited motionless until the girl was done ; then, when she rose, he appeared and declared his purpose.

" I must paint you in this beautiful, dim light—just your head against the smoke-colour of the olives in the dark," he said. " But there shall be the glimmer of one firefly behind your hair throwing up a little halo, and perhaps two or three other fireflies—one far off and one passing by in front of you. I see a beautiful picture if I am clever enough to paint it ; and I shall call you ' La Madonna delle Lucciole.' "

" It would be better to paint the saint herself. I gave her a bunch of tassel hyacinths to-day ; but yesterday a bad thing happened. The rose I put there had a green beetle hid in the midst of it, and all the heart of the rose was eaten out by the greedy beetle. It was a stupid thing to happen, and Madonna will be vexed. I should have seen the beetle."

As they went up through the glimmering orchards, Bice expounded the folk-lore by which she unconsciously guided many of her actions ; while the listener made pretence to listen and learn as he studied the outlines of her head, long neck, and straight back. She was so fresh and virginal. For a moment he contemplated an " Annunciation," painting it as none had painted it yet—a night piece with a moony spirit on silver wings bending before the Virgin, where she wandered under the tender and transparent gloom of olives. But he returned to the earlier vision—the girl's head lit by the little living fires.

She was busy the next day, and he sat beside her and offered his help while she shelled a dish of peas for market. The delicate green of them, in a red copper bowl beside Bice's dark blue dress, made fragrant colour, and he, in good humour, told her so. But she was pensive and full of a great matter. He tuned himself to her mood, therefore, and begged to learn what had befallen her.

" I have had a dream," she said, " a deep dream, and it was a happy dream, but it was also very difficult."

" Dreams never come true, they say, in my country."

" Dreams are sent," she answered, " and it is silly of your country to say that they never come true. Dreams are sent to help us and to warn us and to save us sometimes. They do come true. This dream was sent to save Carlo. I am perhaps wrong to say that it was a dream at all. It may have happened."

" Tell me about it, Bice."

Her thumb ceased not from tumbling the peas into the pan while she talked to him, so that little pops of the splitting peascods punctuated the wonders of her dream.

" It was the middle of the night, Senor, when I woke suddenly to hear a tiny tapping and a tiny voice talking to me. ' Lift me up, Bice,' said the little voice, and I looked down upon the floor and saw my white Madonna delle Lucciole standing there ! She had come all the way from her shrine to me ; but she had left the Bambino there, and her arms were empty. And in each hand she carried a firefly, as a man or woman might hold a candle, and the flies understood that they were to light Madonna to me through the darkness of the sleeping house. I lowered down my open hand to the ground, and the wee Lady rested her foot upon it, so that I lifted her up gently to the coverlet ; and she set her fireflies on my knee, and she sat down near my shoulder and talked to me.

" Of Carlo she talked, and it was thus. ' Bice Brogi,' said Madonna. ' I am come to tell thee how thy betrothed shall win health and strength again and be strong of his hands and thy joyful husband and the father of thy children ' ; and I said : ' Blessed Mother of Christ, I knew it was possible to thee ; and I am sorry for the green beetle in the rose.' She held up her little hand, because, you see, she had come to talk to me, and didn't want me to talk to her. Then she went on again, in a voice like the ' glu-glu ' of the nightingale. ' Bice, there is a crucifix at the first shop over the Ponte Vecchia—an old, old crucifix. It is in the window beside a gold and crystal snuff-box and a piece of old lace.' And that nearly made me jump out of bed with wonder, because I have longed and longed for that crucifix since I was a little girl. It has been in the window for three years. It is black and silver, curiously carved and fretted, and though very small, so wonderful that you see the drops of blood on the Hands and Feet and Side. And at the head and foot and upon each arm is a round bead of red coral, most beautiful to see. I interrupted Madonna again, because I was so excited. ' Blessed Mother,' I said, ' I have wanted the crucifix for long years, and I have talked with all my might to that old toad of a man in the shop and tried to make him say forty lire, though I haven't got them if he did ; but year after year he tells me sixty lire, for too well he knows that I want the crucifix.'

" Then the little Lady spoke again. ' You must win it for Carlo, because it is life and health for Carlo to have that precious thing. It belonged to a saint, and if your lover but holds it to his breast each night and prays to the suffering Lord with faith, his sickness will pass from him, and he will be whole again. But single-handed and by your own strength and through your own fortune unaided must you win the price of it. None shall help you ; none can help you but I.' It is true that I am a very business-like girl, Senor—even old Virgilio Torrigiani has said that. Now I blessed the little Virgin again and asked her if she would help me and put it into the heart of the old toad of a man to take less ; but she did not seem to be interested in that. It was too small a thing for her holy mind. ' Remember ! ' she said. ' Carlo must have the crucifix, and you alone can get it for him. None must help you. Now lift me down, for the dawn is making ready and I must go.' I did as the Lady bade me, and she tripped away, with the fireflies flying in front of her to light the darkness. I heard her little feet tapping on the stone floor, and then everything was silent again. And when the morning came I woke up all one puzzle—because I have to do this great thing alone."

A tame white chicken came close to Bice, and she held out some green peas for the bird to peck out of her hand.

" It was a beautiful dream, and of course it has got to come true, Bice. Don't you think I might help ? "

" No, no, no," she declared vehemently. " If that had been possible, I should not have told you, because it would have been begging. None can help me, and if anybody gave me a single lira of the price, the crucifix would be useless to Carlo."

" How much have you saved ? "

Bice shrugged her shoulders.

" I have got no money in the world," she said. " My last lira went to buy a pipe for my grandfather on his birthday."

" And the crucifix is sixty lire ? "

She nodded.

" I do not think Madonna delle Lucciole will trouble to make the old toad man's heart softer."

" Then the grand thing is to know how you are going to earn the money. Well, I see a very easy way out of the fix."

" Impossible, Senor."

" You sit to me for my picture, and I pay you sixty lire for the sittings."

" No, that is charity. I know an old man at Firenze. He is a friend of Virgilio's. He has a white beard, like flax, and brown eyes, that he can lift to heaven, so that you would think he saw God's Throne and the angels round it. It is his great art to look like a saint, and he is run after in the studios and does very well. He makes three lire a day, and he is a fine man and can be turned into fine pictures, and has the art to keep as still as a sleeping cat for hours. But I cannot earn sixty centimes that way. It would not be honest, and the crucifix would not work."

" You're a purist, Bice. But think twice. How can you do what the Madonna wants you to do if you raise objections of this sort ? If you're worth sixty lire to me as a model, there's an end of it."

She shook her head.

" A thing is only worth what you have to pay to get it," she told him. " I would sit to you for nothing."

" But suppose I sell the picture of you for a thousand lire ? "

" That is your affair, and I should not suppose anything so silly. I only tell you this dream because it is so beautiful and interesting. The Madonna would not have bade me do it if there was no way to do it. I trust her. There will come a way. Only I must be better than ever, and do good things, and think good thoughts, and tempt her with all my strength to come and talk to me again."

She rose and picked up the bowl of peas, while Travers, as interested as a child in the story, considered the problem and could see no immediate solution. He allowed Bice's affairs to take possession of his mind to the exclusion of his own.

The drift and drizzle of time in this haunt of amity and frugal peace had come between him and the realities and problems of his own life. He was conscious of it, and happy that it should be so. When he picked up reality again it should be with a strong grasp. For the moment here was other reality and the problem of a girl's happiness.

He sought Virgilio Torrigiani and talked with him. Roses, white and red, climbed a trellis on the western face of the farmhouse ; but the woodwork had failed here and there, so that Virgilio was called to mend it. A new lattice had been erected, and now the ancient man gave it a coat of paint before placing it in position.

" May I talk to you, Virgilio ? Here's a puzzle that Bice Brogi has set me. She is a brave and honest girl, with faith enough to move mountains."

"Her dream ? "

" Yes. Now we must fix the way out for her."

Virgilio set down his brush and nodded. To him the subject possessed infinite charm. But he put his finger to his lip.

" Not here—the walls listen and there are windows behind the rose trees. Sometimes, too, I think that the cows overhear one and tell people things, for secrets are hard to keep if a man is poor. The poor have no privacy. But I am going to the valley presently to mend a plough. The metal tongue is worn out, and we have a new one that I screw to the wooden share for Luigi. Then we will talk."

" You'll find a way—such a wise and clever man as you are."

" I am wise," admitted Virgilio, patting his forehead, " but I am not clever. If I was clever, I should not be painting this lattice and living with the Brogi."

They met by the plough, and the old man asked a question.

" Is it not true that you have considered Carlo and think he may get better ? "

" Yes ; I was a doctor once—or very nearly. I have

thought a great deal about Carlo. It's only a typical case of anæmia, and I have got a chemist in Firenze to make him some very special physic. It's a food rather than a physic."

" He is very much better for it already."

" Much. He will be absolutely well and hearty in six months. In fact, I've found out what is the matter with him, Virgilio ; but the point is that neither he nor Bice will ever believe that he can be cured now without the crucifix. It is vital that he should have it. There is a thing called Faith Healing, and, if you give it another name, Science will recognize it and admit its significance. I'm doing wonders with Carlo. The truth is that he has nothing radically the matter. He is tall and has grown too fast. I am fattening him and getting blood into him. But, given the crucifix, my task is lightened and we hasten the cure. Of course what we have to do is to put sixty lire into Bice's pocket—in such a way that she will consider it has fallen honestly and properly to her, either as a result of work, or good fortune. But she's so punctilious that I don't see any way."

Virgilio regarded the painter with mild astonishment.

" Do you not ? There are a great many ways really. We are a subtle people and quick in such things. Yes, there are plenty of ways—if you will pay the money. For instance, Enrico Cardoso is dying. He will be dead and in his grave in two—three weeks. He has known the Brogi and cared for them. He might leave Bice sixty, or even a hundred lire under his will. It would be surprising, but not beyond possibility."

" A stroke of genius, Virgilio ! Could you manage it ? "

" Yes, but it is clumsy. There is a better way. This little Madonna in the shrine. Why should not she find the money ? "

Old Torrigiani winked and then laughed. His amusement brought tears to his eyes and he wiped them away. Travers broke a black Tuscan cigar in half and they smoked it together.

" How on earth can the little puppet find sixty lire ? She's not worth a franc herself," he said.

" Come and look at her," answered the other. " I'm glad you approached me with this matter, for it takes an Italian to outwit an Italian. You would never have been too clever for Bice. But I shall show you how easy it will be to hoodwink her and give her the desire of her heart."

They went to the shrine, where Bice's last offering of flowers flagged a little in a blaze of afternoon sunshine. A great jar of asphodel she had set there, with a spike or two of Mary's thistle—the plant upon whose leaf fell milk from the Virgin Mother's breast to stain it with ivory whiteness evermore. Virgilio elaborated a plan, and the painter listened and applauded.

" Do it not too swiftly, else she may suspect," he said ; " but wait until the next festa, and then let the thing happen. Carlo will be getting still stronger by that time, and his eye brighter, and his power to pull and carry greater. And meanwhile you shall hurry to old Giacomo Rossi, the man of the antiquity shop, and buy the crucifix yourself for fear of accidents. But explain to him that when Bice Brogi comes to pay for it, she may take it away."

IV

BICE was not self-conscious, and since the painter wished it, she did not mind him making sketches of her at her prayers. He studied her in the morning sometimes, when the low sun burned through the vines and set great dew drops glittering upon every green thing ; but best he liked to see her when twilight sucked the form and colour out of the orchards, and the filigrane of foliage was gone. Then only dim masses, amorphous and vast, marked the roll of the land, where it spread darkling to the starry skies of summer nights, while a cool breath moved through the glades and amid the trees like a presence, and the fireflies trickled their little lamps in the network of the flowering olives.

On such a night came Bice to her shrine and, unknown to her, John Travers kept watch, for the plot was afoot, and the trap set. He had, at the inspiration of Virgilio, purchased an ancient vessel of bronze—hard and sharp-edged—and when the girl was safely out of the way, with his old friend's aid, Travers carefully buried the curio where Bice's knees had worn away the grass before her shrine. Then in the dry dust was the old vase hidden, so that the edge of it must salute the suppliant's touch when next she knelt. The thing was worth two hundred lire, and it seemed to Virgilio and the painter that by no possibility could Bice deny her little Lady's direct interposition, for had not her own patient knees worn down the earth until the vase proclaimed its presence ?

"It is a gift from Madonna to her, and she must accept it as the reward of prayer," explained Virgilio. His old eyes blinked innocently as he spoke ; but his mouth twitched.

And now the bronze lip of the vase bit gently on Bice's rounded knee, and she, thinking it a stone, bent to dislodge it. But the obstacle would not be moved, and presently she began scraping away the soil. She felt the rim of the vase now, and talked aloud to herself.

"What is it ? What is this under the earth ? " she said.

Stones had been thrust in with the vase, to make the disposal of it seem more natural, and now, impatient, Bice hurt her hand, and uttered a little cry, whereon Travers, as though by chance, came past on his way to the house, and asked her what she was doing. She explained, and soon between them they unearthed the treasure. Then the girl flew homeward, to learn what she had found, while John hastened beside her a little way and warned her not to be too sanguine that the metal was of any worth. She had fallen straightway into the snare ; she assured him that the treasure must be precious ; she accepted it as a gift from the saint.

"I know, I feel how it is," she said. "The good, little white Madonna's heart has gone out to me and Carlo. This heavy thing will go to Rossi, and he will give me the crucifix in exchange for it. Miracles can still be made to happen, if a girl has faith."

Then she outsped him, and when Travers arrived, he found Bice in the midst of her family with Amedio Brogi holding the treasure in his hands, and Giacomo, Gustavo, Emilia, and the rest, in conclave about the elder. Only old Virgilio Torrigiani sat in his chimney corner apart and showed no enthusiastic interest.

"I love not croaking," he said, "but it is wise not to count too much upon promises. Things do not keep their promises any more than men do. We must not taste the wine at sight of the flower buds."

Invited to give an opinion, Travers was equally cautious.

"It may be worth plenty of money—hundreds of lire for all I can tell," he said. "On the other hand, you may not find anybody to buy it. Of course, I would buy it at any price you liked to ask ; but I know you won't let me. Still, it must be worth something, for it is very old, surely. If it doesn't fetch sixty lire, it might at least fetch thirty."

But Bice scorned their prudence.

"You know nothing at all," she said. "It is a miracle, and there's an end of it. The vase was not there yesterday, and it was there to-day, and Madonna knows to a soldo the value of it. And if you are so dull that you do not feel in your heads what will happen to-morrow, I will tell you what will happen. It is this. The old, toad-faced Rossi at the shop will claw the vase and tap it and shrug his shoulders and sigh and say it is a great sacrifice ; and then he will give me the crucifix and keep the vase. That is going to happen to-morrow."

They were silent before her assurance ; and when the family rose next day with the sun, to go about their business before breakfast, Bice had already set out for Firenze with her vase.

Descending the orchard, Travers marked that she had put fresh flowers on the shrine before starting. A mauve spike of dalmatian iris and a white rose and a red rose were laid at the foot of the image.

And two hours later the radiant Bice returned with her crucifix and fifty lire.

Rossi, with a sudden, rare generosity, had been content to make no more than a hundred per cent. on the exchange.

"There is no doubt that my marriage with Carlo is in sight," declared Bice, "for now that the crucifix sent to me by Madonna of the Fireflies shall lie on his breast every night, he will grow stronger and stronger, so fast that he will soon do a man's work again. And I shall keep the money for our wedding. And where the vase was hidden in the earth is most holy evermore, so I shall plant a loquat seed there, and it will spring up and grow faster than common trees, and bear fruit in five years, and make good money for my children."

The fate of the loquat tree, John Travers never learned, though it is certain that before he left Bagni di Ripoli, Carlo was nearly restored to health. But neither the artist's physics nor his council had much to do with the cure, in the opinion of the Brogi. They doubted little that Bice had saved her lover from an early grave, and to the black and silver crucifix with the coral beads they gave the praise. Only Virgilio understood ; but he never contradicted the clan. He was too wise for that.

"You must let me know when the wedding happens," John said to Bice during the last sitting that she gave him, "for I will send you both a wedding present."

She promised to tell him.

"You have been already far too good to us, but you are yourself happier and fatter than when you came, and happiness and fatness are great gifts," she said, "because they keep out care and cold, which are the saddest things in the world. So we have done something."

"Not to mention your picture. It is finished now. Look at yourself with your head dark against the night-hidden olive trees, and the shrine all dim, and the fireflies just lighting your hair like a halo."

"It is wonderful to make such a thing out of those little tubes of paint. I hope somebody will love it well enough to buy it," said Bice.

"It has been a rest and a joy and a blessing to make it, and none can ever love it as much as I do."

"Ah! That is the way with all we make ourselves. Only God understands what work may be to the worker," said old Virgilio.

SHEILA KAYE SMITH *has written a series of novels and short stories, mostly dealing with Sussex. Among the best known are " Tamarisk Town " and " Joanna Godden." After the Brontës and Mary Webb she is the most successful woman interpreter of the powerful workings— sometimes tragic, sometimes mirthful—of the forces of nature upon the native, and, as in " The Mockbeggar," upon those who " go native."*

THE MOCKBEGGAR

Mr. and Mrs. Reginald Dalrymple were walking along the high road that leads from Iden to Wittersham, across the Isle of Oxney. They were very particular about being given their full name of Reginald Dalrymple, to distinguish them from Mr. and Mrs. Charley Dalrymple, who were in North-ampton Workhouse ; from the Peter Dalrymples, who tramped in Wales ; from the Stanley Dalrymples, who were in prison ; and from Serena Dalrymple, who had put herself outside the pale of decent society on the roads by marrying a nigger.

Mr. Reginald Dalrymple was about sixty-five years old, and his back was bent. Otherwise he looked hale enough, and his face, at least as much as could be seen of it through a thatch of brown whiskers, was red as an autumn pear. He wore a frock coat, grey flannel trousers, a pair of brown beach shoes with rather inadequate uppers, and a bowler hat.

Mrs. Reginald Dalrymple was about three years younger than her husband, and was inclined to stoutness, though she looked an able-bodied woman. She wore a very handsome cape trimmed with jet ; a woollen muffler that might have been grey but to which she referred as " my white scarf," and a man's cap set at a rakish angle. She wheeled a perambulator, which did not, however, contain a baby, but the Reginald Dalrymples' luggage—indeed, it may be said their entire household equipment, which at a first glance would appear to consist entirely of old rags. However, a more sympathetic inspection would reveal a really excellent kettle (the leak was only just below the spout), a very suspicious-looking rug, an assortment of cups, a tin plate, a screw-driver, an ancient copy of *Tit-Bits*, a photograph of a robust young woman with a hat full of feathers, and another photograph of a sailor.

" I'm beginning to feel my feet," said Mrs. Reginald Dalrymple to her husband.

" And I'm thinking it's coming on to rain," said he, with a look up at the lowering sky.

It was autumn, and the red leaves were shaking against soft clouds of October grey which the wind brought down from Benenden in the west.

" Where's our next chance of a doss ? " asked Mrs. Dalrymple.

" There's the Throws, up at Potman's Heath," replied her husband, " but I reckon they'll be —— damp to-night."

" Reg ! Don't use words," said Mrs. Dalrymple with dignity. " You forget my mother was a Stanley."

" I'm never likely to forget it the way you go on about it. Anyone 'ud think she'd been Queen Victoria on her throne to hear you talk. But what I say is, it's coming on to rain, and there ain't no Union within fifteen miles. Besides, you're feeling your feet," he added kindly.

" I've walked twelve miles since dinner, Reg," said Mrs. Dalrymple with a little plaintive sigh.

" Hook on then," said he, extending a ragged elbow.

She hooked, and for some moments they walked on in silence. Then he said : " It'll be awkward for you pushing the pram with one hand," and took it from her, though Mr. Reginald Dalrymple had often boasted that he had never come down to wheeling a perambulator, and never would.

" I've been thinking," said she a few minutes later, by which time the rain was spattering freely in the dust, " I've been thinking we must have come near that Mockbeggar place by the Stocks Road. The house was standing there five year ago when we was on the roads with Sue and her lot, and if it hasn't tumbled down since, there's one good room in it anyway, with the ceiling tight, and there's water in the well at the bottom of the yard."

Mr. Dalrymple reflected. " You're right, Hannah—I believe you're right this once. We should be coming to that Mockbeggar in half an hour. It'll be raining the skies down by that time, so we might go in and light a fire and not trouble about getting farther to-night. It's a good way from the nearest place, and we're not like to be meddled with."

Mrs. Dalrymple was feeling her feet more and more, in

spite of the supporting elbow and the removal of the pram. She was also beginning to get wet, though this did not worry her, as she was accustomed to it. She was far more preoccupied with the thought that she could not walk a twelve-mile stretch without getting tired—and she'd been able to walk twice that as a girl, when she and Reginald had tramped all round the country by Chichester. She had had the children then as well—one slung at her breast, and the other hanging on her skirt when his dad did not carry him. She was glad when she saw three sharp gables suddenly draw themselves against the sky, which sagged low over the fields, squirting rain.

" That's it," she said, " that's the Mockbeggar. I knew it was somewhere in these parts, though we haven't been here since Sue was on the roads with her man. D'you remember that time we dossed under the stack at Wassall ? "

Mr. Dalrymple grunted. He was looking for a gap in the hedge, for it struck him that it would be best to go straight across the fields to shelter instead of walking round by the road. He soon found what he thought was a proper opening, and proceeded to enlarge it to meet the ample requirements of his wife by pushing the perambulator through it. He then gallantly offered a hand to Mrs. Dalrymple, and, after much gasping and effort and crackling of twigs, she was at his side in the paddock which belonged to the Mockbeggar.

" A Mockbeggar House " in Kent is any large-sized house which stands empty close to a high road, and seems to mock the beggar who plods along thinking he will find charity at those doors which, on his close arrival, are found to be either swinging on their hinges or barred on emptiness. The Mockbeggar at Wittersham was an especially large house which, owing to want of repairs, a poor landlord, and a defective water supply, had stood empty for some time.

" A downstairs room 'ud be best," said Mrs. Reginald.

They went into one next the passage on the ground floor. It was full of dead leaves and bits of glass from a broken window, but there was a grate in it where a fire might possibly burn, and the rain was confined to a small pool under the window-sill.

" You unpack here, Hannah, and I'll go and get some water for the kettle."

Mrs. Dalrymple extracted the kettle from the pram, carefully wrapped in a piece of newspaper, and while her husband went off she proceeded to arrange her various belongings. The sinister-looking rug she put in the corner with a nice, comfortable bit of sacking—that was the bedroom. The cups, the plate, and a broken knife she put on the remains of a shelf— that was the kitchen ; while the two photographs she set proudly among the dust and cobwebs on the mantelpiece— that was the parlour. She was then, according to custom, going on to make herself really comfortable by taking off her shoes when she was startled by a noise overhead.

An empty house is full of noises, and Mrs. Dalrymple had a wide experience of empty houses. Mere scuttlings of rats or hootings of owls or rustlings of crickets or howlings of wind in chimneys could not alarm her, but this sound she knew at once was none of these. It was a footstep, a human footstep, which moved in the room overhead, and she held her breath to listen. The next minute she heard more and worse—that murmur coming to her through the boards was a human voice. She stuck her head out of the window (no need to open it first), and made a sign to Reginald, who was coming up the yard with the kettle. The sign urged both silence and attention, also haste. His response was immediate ; they had often been together in these emergencies demanding a quick stealth. He did not speak a word till he was back beside her in the room.

" It's people ! " said Mrs. Dalrymple in a hoarse whisper, " there's people here ! "

" How d'you know ? Where are they ? "

" They're up above. I heard 'em talking. Listen ! "

They both listened. The sounds in the upper room con- tinued—voices and footsteps.

" There's two," said Mrs. Dalrymple, " I can tell by their feet. Who can it be ? It's road people like ourselves, most like. No one else 'ud ever come here."

" I wonder if it's anyone we know. It might be the Lovells—you know Lance and Aurelia Lovell are walking in Kent."

" I hope it ain't folk in the house after repairs," said Mr. Dalrymple, struck by a sudden thought. " You never know your luck, and someone may have bought the place."

" I hope it's not that stuck-up Eleanor Ripley and her husband," said Mrs. Dalrymple. " We had enough of their airs when we met them at Maidstone. She's got saucers to all her cups."

" Well, I'd sooner it was her than gaujos," returned Mr. Dalrymple, " it 'ud never do for us to get found here, and it 'ud mean a-spoiling of the place for visitors."

" You go and have a look," suggested his wife. " Take off your shoes."

Mr. Dalrymple shuffled them off without undoing the laces, and left the room with extreme caution. His progress upstairs and along the passage was as silent as only his kind know how to make it.

Mrs. Dalrymple strained her ears, which were as quick as they were when she was seventeen. The voices continued, but she detected more than conversation—she thought she heard a sound of sobbing. Time went on. Reginald was evidently manœuvring with his usual discretion, for the flow of talk above remained uninterrupted. Indeed, so velvet-footed was he that he was back at her side before she expected him, and, old stager though she was, nearly made her jump.

" It's gaujos," he said in a low voice. " There's two of 'em, mighty queer——"

" How queer ? "

" Oh, the girl's got short hair like a boy, and the boy—he's soft looking. They're only a boy and girl ; maybe we could scare 'em out."

" I don't want to scare them," said Mrs. Dalrymple. " The night ain't fit for a dog, and I'd be sorry to turn 'em out in it. But if they ain't road people, what are they doing here ? "

" They're quarrelling," said Mr. Dalrymple, " quarrelling and crying."

" I thought I heard crying."

" It's the girl's crying into a handkerchief. She's got a white handkerchief with a blue border."

" Are they gentry ? "

" Fine gentry, I should say, by their clothes, but I don't think they're after repairs or taking the house or anything."

" What are they doing then ? "

" Sheltering from the rain like us, and I don't think they've got much money, for they're talking a lot of words about the price of a ticket to London."

" Is that what the trouble's about ? "

" No, I don't know as it is. I can't make out a lot of their foolish words, but it seems as either he wants to marry her and she won't, or else as they are married and she wants to get shut of him, and he won't have it."

" I should think not ! " said Mrs. Dalrymple. " I'm all for sticking to your lawful certificated husband, and that's why I'd never go to the workhouse except just now and again for a rest."

" Well, maybe they ain't married—I don't rightly know. They had too many words for me to be able to make out the lot of them. But hold your tongue, Hannah ; they're coming down."

Steps sounded on the rickety stairs of the Mockbeggar— unskilful, gaujo steps that made every stair creak.

Mrs. Dalrymple made a hasty movement as if to gather up her possessions, and thrust them back under the rags in the perambulator—stirred perhaps by some dim instinct of far-off ancestors who must not let the stranger look upon their household gods.

Her husband laid hold of her arm. " Don't be scared ; they're nothing—hardly cut their teeth yet ! "

At the same moment a young man appeared in the doorway. He was tall and loosely knit, with a heavy coltishness about him as of one not full grown. Behind him a girl's face stood out of the shadows framed in a queer little stiff mane of cropped hair. Her eyes were bright and resolute, but at the same time frightened.

" Hullo ! " said the youth truculently to Mr. Dalrymple, " what are you doing here ? "

Mr. Dalrymple looked the aggressor up and down. " This place belongs to us as much as you."

" *More* than you," said Mrs. Dalrymple, " seeing as we're road people and you're house people who have no business here ! "

" Well, I might ask what your business is ? "

" Our business is to have a supper and a doss on a wet night, and if you keep clear and don't come round talking foolishness we won't meddle with you, and there's room enough for the lot of us."

" It's all right, Bob," said the girl ; " let's go back." Her face was flushed and the eyes were a little swollen under the straight line of her fringe.

Mrs. Dalrymple suddenly became professional.

" I'm not the one to interfere with a real lady and gentleman," she whined, putting on the manner which she kept for well-dressed strangers. " I'm sure you're a real fine lady and gentleman, and if the lady will only cross my hand with silver I'll tell her some gorgeous things about herself, and maybe about the gentleman, too. I can see a lot of money coming to you, lady—even more than the price of a ticket to London."

The girl darted a surprised look at her companion.

"Come, lady," wheedled Mrs. Dalrymple. "I'll tell you a high-class tale about husbands."

The girl turned away with a heightening of her flush. "I can't bear this nonsense," she said in a low voice to the young man. "These people needn't interfere with us, nor we with them. Let's go upstairs."

The youth looked sulky.

"It's all very well," he said, "but they've got the only decent room ; the rain's coming through all the ceilings above."

"You should have put your traps in here," said Mr. Dalrymple, "then we should have kept out of it ; but as we're here, we mean to stick. My old woman's wet through, and she's going to have a dry doss, I'm blowed if she ain't."

"Oh, well, come on," said the young man. "It may clear up before night, and then we'll start again."

He turned away, following the girl upstairs, and the Reginald Dalrymples were left in peace.

"There's queer things you meets on the roads," said Mrs. Dalrymple, "and it isn't so much the people you meet as the places where you meets 'em. Now, what are those two doing here ? I'm beat."

"You're curious," retorted Mr. Dalrymple—"fair eat up with curiosity—because you're a woman. Now, I don't think twice about 'em as long as they leaves me alone, and nor won't you, Hannah, if you've got sense. Here, let us have a fire and get ourselves dry."

He turned to the all-providing pram, and from its depths drew forth its last treasures—some blocks of wood and a bundle of sticks. The Dalrymples always carried a supply of dry firewood about with them, for they were getting old, and considered themselves entitled to a certain amount of luxury in their old age.

A fire was soon lit and the kettle put on to boil ; once it was blazing, the addition of a few damp sticks gathered outside no longer mattered. The room grew warm, and Mrs. Dalrymple's clothes began to steam. Her husband took off his coat and put it over her shoulders.

"There you are, Hannah," he said. "I don't want it. This weather makes me sweat, but you've got to take care of your bones."

They made tea, which they ate in great comfort, with half a stale loaf and a lump of lard. Outside, the rain was hissing down, while the wind howled in the chimney.

"It'll be wet upstairs," said Mrs. Dalrymple pleasantly.

The fire was beginning to die down, and Mr. Dalrymple did not fancy going outside to get in more sticks.

"I'll go and have a look at the banisters," he said, "and maybe there's a bit of a cupboard door."

The banisters looked satisfactory as fuel, and he was in the act of wrenching a couple of them out when he saw the young man on the staircase above him.

"Hi!" said the latter dejectedly, "we're half flooded out upstairs. I was going to suggest that we come in with you till it stops raining. We'll clear out as soon as the weather lets us."

"We're poor people," said Mr. Dalrymple, "Mrs. Reginald Dalrymple and I are poor people, and we can't afford to take lodgers at our fire without a bit of silver."

"We aren't asking you to take us as lodgers, damn it! I'm just asking you to let the young lady come and sit in a dry place. It's what you wouldn't refuse a dog."

"I would certainly refuse a dog," returned Mr. Dalrymple with dignity. "My wife and I never allows no dogs to sit with us, it being well known as dogs have fleas, and my wife being a lady as'll have nothing to do with fleas."

The young man surveyed Mr. Dalrymple as if he himself belonged to that species.

"Well, if you want money," he said, "I suppose you must have it. Will a shilling do you?"

"A shilling will do me very well," said Mr. Dalrymple loftily, "and it includes the fire. We have a very excellent fire!"

"So I gather," said the young man as he coughed in the smoke that was eddying upstairs.

But even the Dalrymples' quarters, full of smoke and the smell of ancient rags, were better than the leaking, dripping rooms where he and Meave Anstey had been struggling in vain to keep warm and dry. Meave was shivering now, and her little face was not pink but blue as she sat down gingerly beside Mrs. Dalrymple's fire.

" Cross my hand with silver, lady," said that good woman returning unabashed to the attack, " and I'll tell you the prettiest fortune that ever was spoke."

" I don't want your lies," said the girl angrily, with a sudden gulp.

" Lies, lady ! I never tells lies ! May I be struck dead if I does ! "

" My wife is well known as a truth-telling woman," said Mr. Dalrymple, " and I'll thank you not to miscall her ! "

For some reason Meave felt rebuked, though she believed neither of them.

" I'm sorry," she said. " Well, you may tell my fortune if you like, but I've only got sixpence."

" Thank you, lady. Thank you kindly, lady. Sixpence will buy me a packet of tea at the next village, lady. And I'll drink your very good health in it, for I never drinks nothing stronger than tea, which is well known."

Meave held out a soft, artistic-looking hand, which was by this time more than a little grimy.

" I likes dirt on the hand," remarked Mrs. Dalrymple, " it helps me to see the lines better. Now what I see is this : I see a railway line, with a train on it going to London, and you and a gentleman are in that train, and when you get to London I see a church, and a priest, and a great crowd of people, and rice, and slippers. I see all that, and you in the middle of it, beautiful as an angel, and beside you a tall, handsome young gentleman with light hair and brown eyes."

The girl pulled her hand away angrily. " Don't talk such nonsense, please ! I can't stand it."

" You don't want to get married ! "

" No, I don't. As if I'd—Rice ! Slippers ! White veil ! " The scorn grew in her voice.

" There's a wedding cake," encouraged Mrs. Dalrymple, " with sugar all over it."

" I don't want to hear any more. Look here, you're a fortune-teller, aren't you ? I suppose I'm the first girl you've ever met who hasn't wanted to hear about marriage ? "

" You would be the first if I believed you," said Mrs. Dalrymple, who had dropped her company manner in the familiarity of the scene.

" Well, you can believe it. I don't want to get married— I don't believe in marriage," and she threw a defiant glance, not at Mrs. Dalrymple, but at the young man.

" But a girl can't never live by herself ; it ain't natural."

" And it ain't safe," said Mr. Dalrymple. " I've known more than one time when my wife here might have got copped if it hadn't been for having me handy to show her the right trick."

" I don't mean to be alone," said the girl. " I don't believe in that either. What I hate is the hypocrisy and slavery of marriage "—her voice rose and warmed, she became a little lecturer—" it's the idea of losing my freedom which I can't bear. If women hadn't been slaves for centuries none of them could bear it. When I choose my mate we shall both of us be free—free to love and free to part. There shall be no keeping of the outer husk when the kernel has rotted."

Mr. and Mrs. Dalrymple stared silently with their mouths open, and the young man looked uneasy.

" You see me and my friend here now," continued Meave, " and even you, a woman outside the ordinary conventions of society, immediately form the idea that we're going to be married. I tell you you're utterly wrong. If we were going to be married we shouldn't be running away, we should be sitting at home, unpacking wedding presents. We are going to join our lives together, but in freedom, not in bondage. We shall be free to part whenever we choose, free to work, free to go our own ways——" She had almost forgotten that she had not got her debating society before her.

" Well," said Mrs. Dalrymple, " I don't want to part and I don't want to work, and I don't want to go any different ways from Mr. Dalrymple, so I can't see the sense of what you're saying. Mr. Dalrymple and me has been married close on forty years, and we've got a daughter, Sue, who's been married twenty years to a fine feller in the osier trade. She has a caravan with brass rods on the door and lace curtains in the windows, and five of the dearest little children you could think of, leastways the eldest's nearly grown up now. And we've got a son, Jerome, who's a sailor, and has had two wives one after the other. The wife he's got now lives in the house and has a china tea service. We're proud of our children, but they've gone away from us, and I don't know what we'd do if we hadn't got each other."

" She's uncommon set on her children," said Mr. Dalrymple ; " that's their likenesses up there on the shelf, what we carries about with us everywhere. My daughter Sue 'ud have us stay with her, and once we went and stopped with my son and daughter at Portsmouth, and slept in a bed. But we'd just as soon be along of each other here."

"Reckon you want your husband more when you're old than when you're young," said Mrs. Dalrymple. "I'm getting too old to do most of the things I used, and I don't know what I'd do if it wasn't for Mr. Dalrymple, who does them for me. Our idea is to keep on the roads till we're old enough to go into the Married Quarters at the Workhouse. It 'ud break our hearts if we was to be separated after all this time. I don't hold with being parted from your certificated husband."

"You gets used to each other like," said Mr. Dalrymple. "If I was to go on the roads with anyone else I'd be so bothered and vexed I shouldn't know what to do."

"If I was ever to see you on the roads with anyone else——" said Mrs. Dalrymple menacingly.

"Not likely, old lady," replied he, pushing her cap over one eye in playful affection.

"Now, now," said she, "none of your larks." But she looked pleased and a little proud of him.

The rain had become a storm, with a rush of wind in the chimneys of the Mockbeggar. Dead leaves flew rustling round the yard, and the pool under the window was a little lake. But beside the fire it was warm and dry, though the smoke, as it eddied and waved under the low ceiling, made Meave choke a little and strange tears come into her eyes. Of course that was the smoke; she felt proud and thrilled. She had broken free at last, and she was saving Bob, who otherwise would have become a slave, having all the instincts of one.

"Ooo—ooo—yah!" A loud yawn from Mr. Dalrymple made her start. "I'm —— sleepy," he added conversationally.

"Now don't start using words again," said his wife. "I'm not accustomed to them, being a Stanley, and I reckon the young lady ain't either, for all her uncertificated ideas. If you wants to go to sleep—go."

"I'm going," said Mr. Dalrymple.

"Then take back your coat. I've dried under it nicely."

"I don't want any coat. I'm warm as toast."

"You want it, and you'll take it—here now."

An amiable tussle followed, which ended in Mr. Dalrymple putting on his coat, while his wife had the piece of sacking in addition to her share of the rug. They took no more notice

Mr. and Mrs. Dalrymple stared silently with their mouths open,
and the young man looked uneasy.

of Meave Anstey and Bob Pettigrew, but were soon asleep, with the queer, stiff, silent sleep of animals who rest among foes.

" Rum old pair ! " said Bob under his breath. " I'm sorry you've been let in for this, Meave, but it's better than being swamped upstairs."

" Oh, they're all right. I rather like them, though, of course, they're frauds. They're decent to each other, which is odd. I rather thought that type of man always bullied his wife."

" Men aren't quite such rotters as you think, even tramps."

He spoke irritably, for the sordid side of the adventure was unpleasantly obvious on this night of wind and rain without and stuffiness and teasing smoke within. To his surprise she did not take up his challenge. She sat watching the old couple as they lay huddled in the corner, a confused blot of rags and shadows.

" It's love that holds them together," she said in her debating-society voice hushed down to a whisper, " not the mere fact of marriage."

" I dunno," said he truculently. " I don't believe they'd be together now if they weren't married—anyhow, not together like this."

" Why not ? Why shouldn't lovers be faithful ? "

" It's different, as I've told you a hundred times, especially when you're old. I'd think nothing of it if they were young or middle-aged. But they're old, and there must have been lots of times when they were tired of loving and tired of life, and would never have gone on if they hadn't belonged to each other."

" That's just it—they were tied."

" And the tie kept them together over the bad places. It's like being roped on a climb. When one or another of them went down there was always the rope, and as soon as they were on their legs again they didn't notice it. I believe people who aren't married—no matter how much they love each other—somehow they're hardly ever in together at the finish. You generally find that if the going's rough they drift apart. Why, you yourself say you'd hate to belong to a man all your life ; you want the one great Moment, and then not to spoil it by going on together. I think there's a good deal to be said for that, though, as I've told you dozens of times, I want to marry you."

He looked very young as he sat there beside her in the dying firelight. He was only a boy, or he wouldn't have come with her ; he wouldn't have let her force her adventure on him like that. He was very young, but he would grow old, like Mr. Dalrymple. That soft brown lock of hair on his forehead would be grey, his face a little worn, perhaps. Should she see it then, or would they have gone their separate ways ? She wondered what he would look like when he was old—what he would be like ? Kind, protective, unselfish, like Mr. Dalrymple ? A strong arm to lean on when she needed it most ? Growing old together—together not only at the start, but at the journey's end—but tied, as Mr. and Mrs. Dalrymple were tied, by the memories of struggles and toils together, by adventures and hardships shared, by long years of companionship in wayfaring, by the love of their children.

She bowed her head suddenly over her lap and tears fell into her hands.

" Meave, darling, what is it ?   Tell me."

His arm was round her, his shoulder under her cheek.

" Bob—Bob—will you always love me—when we're old ? "

" Of course, I shall always love you."

" As much as that——? "   She waved her hand towards the indefinite mass of Mr. and Mrs. Dalrymple.

" I should hope so "—with a little contempt.

" Then—Bob—let's go back."

" Go back where ? "

" Home—I want us to get married."

" My little Meave.   But you said—— "

" It's seeing them. They're so happy—they're so true. They're dirty, terrible, shameless old things, but they're happy. They've got something that we haven't got, that we can't ever have, unless we're married."

He had the wisdom to be silent, hugging her without a word.

" Let's go back home. It's not ten o'clock yet, and we can tell Mother we were caught in the rain and waited to see if it would stop.   She need never know."

" And we'll get married ? "

" Yes—though you know she'll make us go in for everything—bridesmaids and rice and church bells and all that."

" Never mind ! It'll make Mrs. Dalrymple's fortune come true."

They both laughed a little.

" When shall we start ? " he asked her.

" Oh, soon—now."

" But it's coming down in buckets ! "

" Never mind. We're only an hour from home. We haven't got to face all that walk into Rye, and then the journey into London."

She shivered a little, and he drew her close in sudden, fierce protection.

" I shouldn't have let you come. I've been a fool about all this. I didn't believe in it, and yet I gave way because I was afraid of losing you. I should have had sense enough for both of us, and made you go my way instead of yours."

" Is that what you're going to do in future ? "

" Yes—when you're a silly little thing ! "

She laughed with her mouth close to his.

It was he who remembered the need for quick action.

" Come, we must be getting off, or we shan't be home till it's too late to explain. Are you ready ? "

" Quite. I'm glad we didn't bring any luggage, except in our ulster pockets. It would have been difficult to explain why we'd gone for a walk with two suitcases."

They giggled light-heartedly, and went out on tip-toe.

They were off, but just as they were leaving the Mockbeggar she remembered something that had been left undone.

" Bob, we ought to tell them. I want them to know."

" For heaven's sake don't go back and wake them up. What do you want them to know ? "

" That we're going to be married."

" What on earth has that got to do with them ? "

" Oh, nothing, of course, but I thought—— Give me a leaf out of your pocket-book, there's a darling."

He gave it, and she scribbled on it : " We are going to be married," and creeping back into the room, put it on the mantelpiece beside the pictures of the blowsy girl and the sailor.

" And look here," she added, " as we're not going to London, we might just leave the price of our tickets with them. It may help them a lot."

" They'll probably spend it on drink."

" Well, let them. I don't care. I can't bear to think of people without proper boots on their feet."

The firelight was playing reproachfully on the toe of Mr. Dalrymple's shoe.

" Nor can I. Well, here's the money. It'll be a surprise for them when they wake up."

He put it beside the paper on the mantelpiece, and they both went out.

It was daylight when Mr. and Mrs. Reginald Dalrymple awoke ; the storm had ceased.

" Hullo ! They've gone ! " said he.

" Not taken any of our things with them, have they, Reg ? " asked his wife, looking round anxiously.

" Not they—they're gentry. Gentry don't take poor people's things without a lawyer. What's this ? "

Her husband had found the treasure on the mantelpiece.

" I'm blowed if they haven't left their money behind 'em— a pound, if it's a tanner ! "

" That's luck for us, anyway, if it ain't exactly luck for them."

" Oh, I reckon they done it on purpose. They'd never have put their dough just there by our Jack's likeness. It's Christian charity, that's what it is."

" I don't believe it's Christian charity—that 'ud be tuppence. A pound's nothing but an accident. Howsumever, it makes no difference to me what it is so long as it's there. I could do with a plate o' ham."

" A plate o' ham and a cup o' coffee, and a bottle o' whisky to come along with us to Tonbridge."

" That's it. But look there, Reg—there's writing on the paper ! "

" So there is. Pity we ain't scollards."

" Maybe it's a word for us."

" That's what it is, I reckon."

She picked up the paper and inspected it solemnly, then passed it on to her husband, who did the same.

" Pity we never got no school-learning, Reg."

" I've never felt the want."

" But I'd like to be able to read the word they've left us."

" That's because you're a woman and made of curiosity. I, being a man, says let's take the money and be thankful. And now, old lady, pack up your traps, for, thanks to this bit of luck, we'll have our breakfast at the ' Blue Boar.' "

HENRY DE VERE STACPOOLE, *an Irishman with a heritage of French blood, was a doctor until he felt the call to literature. He joined deep sea expeditions, founded a society for the protection of sea birds, and wove stories rich in colour and romance around his beloved South Sea Islands. "The Blue Lagoon," "The Pearl Fishers" "Vanderdecken," and "Drums of War" are among his best-known novels.*

MARU

THE night was filled with vanilla and frangipani odours, and the endless sound of the rollers on the reef. Somewhere away back amidst the trees a woman was singing ; the tide was out, and from the veranda of Lygon's house, across the star-shot waters of the lagoon, moving yellow points of light caught the eye. They were spearing fish by torch-light in the reef pools.

It had been a shell lagoon once, and in the old days men had come to Tokahoe for sandal wood ; now there was only copra to be had, and just enough for one man to deal with. Tokahoe is only a little island, where one cannot make a fortune but where you may live fortunately enough if your tastes are simple and beyond the lure of whisky and civilization.

The last trader had died in this paradise of whisky—or gin—I forget which, and his ghost was supposed to walk the beach on moonlit nights, and it was apropos of this that Lygon suddenly put the question to me, " Do you believe in ghosts ? "

" Do you ? " replied I.

" I don't know," said Lygon. " I almost think I do, because every one does. Oh, I know a handful of hard-headed super-civilized people say they don't, but the mass of humanity does. The Polynesians and Micronesians do ; go to Japan, go to Ireland, go anywhere and everywhere you will find ghost believers."

Lombroso has written something like that," said I.

" Has he ? Well, it's a fact, but all the same it's not evidence ; the universality of a belief seems to hint at reality in the thing believed in—yet what is more wanting in real reason than Tabu ? Yet Tabu is universal. You find men

here who daren't touch an artu tree because artu trees are
Tabu to them ; or eat turtle or touch a dead body. Well,
look at the Jews ; a dead body is Tabu to a Cohen ; India is
riddled with the business, so's English Society—it's all the
same thing under different disguises.

"Funny that talking of ghosts we should have touched
on this, for when I asked you did you believe in ghosts,
I had a ghost story in mind, and Tabu comes into it. This
is it."

And this is the story somewhat as told by Lygon :

Some fifty years back, when Pease was a pirate bold, and
Hayes in his bloom, and the top-sails of the *Leonora* a terror
to all dusky beholders, Maru was a young man of twenty. He
was son of Malemake, King of Fukariva, a kingdom the size
of a soup plate, nearly as round and without a middle ; an
atoll island, in short ; just a ring of coral, sea beaten and
circling, like a bezel, a sapphire lagoon.

Fukariva lies in the Paumotus or Dangerous Archipelago,
where the currents run every way, and the winds are un-
accountable. The underwriters to this day fight shy of a
Paumotus trader, and in the '60's few ships came here, and
the few that came were on questionable business. Maru, up
to the time he was twenty years of age, only remembered
three.

There was the Spanish ship that came into the lagoon
when he was only seven. The picture of her remained with
him, burning and brilliant, yet tinged with the atmosphere of
nightmare ; a big top-sail schooner, that lay for a week mirroring herself on the lagoon water whilst she refitted ; fellows
with red handkerchiefs tied round their heads crawling aloft,
and laying out on the spars. They came ashore for water,
and what they could find in the way of taro and nuts, and made
hay on the beach, insulting the island women till the men
drove them off. Then, when she was clearing the lagoon,
a brass gun was run out and fired, leaving a score of dead and
wounded on that salt white beach.

That was the Spaniard. Then came a whaler, who took
what she wanted, and cut down trees for fuel and departed,
leaving behind the smell of her as an enduring recollection ;
and lastly, when Maru was about eighteen, a little old schooner
slank in one early morning.

She lay in the lagoon like a mangy dog, a humble ship,

very unlike the Spaniard or the blustering whale-man ; she only wanted water and a few vegetables, and her men gave no trouble ; then, one evening, she slank out again with the ebb, but she left something behind her—small-pox. It cleared the island, and of the hundred and fifty subjects of King Malemake, only ten were left—twelve people in all, counting the king and Maru.

The king died of a broken heart and age, and of the eleven people left, three were women, widows of men who had died of the small-pox.

Maru was unmarried, and as king of the community he might have collected the women for his own household. But he had no thought of anything but grief ; grief for his father and the people who were gone. He drew apart from the others, and the seven widowers began to arrange matters as to the distribution of the three widows. They began with arguments and ended with clubs ; three men were killed, and one of the women killed another man because he had brained the man of her fancy.

Then the dead were buried in the lagoon—Maru refusing to help because of his Tabu—and the three newly-married couples settled down to live their lives, leaving Maru out in the cold. He was no longer king. The women despised him because he hadn't fought for one of them, and the men because he had failed in brutality and leadership. They were a hard lot, true survivals of the fittest, and Maru, straight as a palm tree, dark-eyed, gentle, and a dreamer, seemed, amongst them, like a man of another tribe and time.

He lived alone, and sometimes in the sun blaze on that great ring of coral he fancied he saw the spirits of the departed walking as they had walked in life, and sometimes it might be thought he heard the voice of his father chiding him.

When the old man died Maru had refused to touch the body or help in its burial. Filial love, his own salvation, nothing would have induced Maru to break his Tabu, which barred him from touching a dead body.

It was part of him, an iron reef in his character beyond the influence of will.

II

ONE morning, some six weeks after all this marrying and settling down, a brig came into the lagoon. She was a Blackbirder, the *Portsoy*, owned and captained by Colin

Robertson, a Banffshire man, hence the name of his brig. Robertson and his men landed, took off water, coco-nuts, bananas, and everything else they could find worth taking. Then they turned their attention to the population. Four men were not a great find, but Robertson was not above trifles ; he recruited them ; that is to say, he kicked them into his boat and took them on board the *Portsoy*, leaving the three widows, grass widows now—wailing on the shore. He had no finer feelings about the marriage tie, and he reckoned they would make out somehow. They were no use to him as labour, and they were ill-favoured ; all the same, being a man of gallantry and some humour, he dipped his flag to them as the *Portsoy* cleared the lagoon and breasted the tumble at the break.

Maru, standing aft, saw the island with the white foam fighting the coral and the gulls threshing around the break ; saw the palms cut against the pale aquamarine of the skyline that swept up into the burning blue of noon ; heard the long rumble and boom of the surf on the following wind, and watched and listened till the sound of the surf died to nothingness, and of the island nothing remained but the palm tops, like pin-heads above the sea dazzle.

He felt no grief. But there came to him a new and strange thing, a silence, that the ship-board sounds could not break. Since birth the eternal boom of the waves on coral had been in his ears, night and day, and day and night, louder in storms, but always there. It was gone. That was why, despite the sound of the bow wash, and boost of the waves, and the creak of cordage and block, the brig seemed to have carried Maru into the silence of a new world.

They worked free of the Paumotus into the region of settled winds and accountable currents passing atolls, and reefs that showed like the threshing of a shark's tail in the blue, heading north-west in a world of wind and waves and sky, desolate of life, and, for Maru, the land of Nowhere.

So it went on from week to week, and, as far as he was concerned, so it might have gone on for ever. He knew nothing of the world into which he had been suddenly snatched, and land, which was not a ring of coral surrounding a lagoon, was for him unthinkable.

He knew nothing of navigation, and the brass-bound wheel, at which a sailor was always standing with his hands on the spokes, now twirling it this way, now that, had for him a fascination beyond words, the fascination of a strange toy for a little child, and something more. It was the first wheel he had ever seen, and its movements about its axis seemed magical, and it was never left without some one to hold it and move it—why ? The mystery of the binnacle into which the wheel-mover was always staring, as a man stares into a rock pool after fish, was almost as fascinating.

Maru peeped into the binnacle one day, and saw the fish, something like a star fish, that still moved and trembled. Then some one kicked him away, and he ran forward and hid, feeling that he had pried into the secrets of the white men's gods, and fearing the consequences.

But the white men's gods were not confined to the wheel and binnacle ; down below they had a god that could warn them of the weather, for that day at noon, and for no apparent reason, the sailors began to strip the brig of her canvas. Then the sea rose, and two hours later the cyclone seized them. It blew everything away, and then took them into its calm heart, where, dancing like giants in dead still air, and with the sea for a ballroom floor, the hundred foot high waves broke the *Portsoy* to pieces.

Maru alone was saved, clinging to a piece of hatch cover, half stunned, confused, yet unafraid and feeling vaguely that the magic wheel and little trembling fish god had somehow betrayed the white men. He knew that he was not to die, because this strange world that had taken him from his island had not done with him yet, and the sea, in touch with him like this and half washing over him at times, had no terror for him, for he had learned to swim before he had learned to walk. Also his stomach was full ; he had been eating biscuits whilst the *Portsoy's* canvas was being stripped away, and though the wind was strong enough almost to whip the food from his hands.

The peaceful swell that followed the cyclone was a thing enough to have driven an ordinary man mad with terror. Now lifted hill high on a glassy slope, the whole wheel of the horizon came to view under the breezing wind and blazing sun, then gently down—sliding, the hatch cover would sink to a valley bottom only to climb again a glassy slope, and rise again hill high into the wind and sun. Foam flecks passed on the surface, and in the green sun-dazzled crystal of the valley floors, he glimpsed strips of fucus floating far down, torn by the storm from their rock attachments, and through the sloping wall of glass, up which the hatch cover was climbing, he once glimpsed a shark, lifted and cradled in a ridge of the great swell, strange to see as a fly in amber or a fish in ice.

The hatch cover was sweeping with a four-knot current, moving with a whole world of things concealed, or half-seen or hinted at. A sea current is a street ; it is more, it is a moving pavement for the people of the sea ; jelly fish were being carried with Maru on the great swell running with the current, a turtle broke the water close to him and plunged again, and once a white roaring reef passed by only a few cable lengths away. He could see the rock exposed for a moment, and the water closing on it in a tumble of foam.

III

FOR a day and a night and a day and a night the voyage continued, the swell falling to a gentle heave, and then in the dawn came a sail, the mat-sail of a canoe like a brown wing cut against the haliotis-shell coloured sky.

In the canoe was a girl, naked as the new moon. Paddle in hand, and half crouching, she drove the canoe towards him, the sail loose and flapping in the wind. Then he was on board the canoe, but how he got there he scarcely knew ; the whole thing was like a dream within a dream.

In the canoe there was nothing, neither food nor water, only some fishing lines, and as he lay exhausted, consumed with thirst and faint with hunger, he saw the girl resetting the sail. She had been fishing last evening from an island up north, and blown out to sea by a squall had failed to make the land again, but she had sighted an island in the sou-west, and was making for it, when she saw the hatch cover and the brown, clinging form of Maru.

As he lay half dead in the bottom of the canoe, he watched her as she crouched with eyes fixed on the island and the steering paddle in hand, but before they could reach it, a squall took them, half-filling the canoe with rain-water, and Maru drank and drank till his ribs stood out, and then, renewed, half rose, as the canoe, steered by the girl, rushed past tumbling green seas and a broken reef to a beach white as salt, towards which the great trees came down with the bread-fruits dripping with the new-fallen rain, and the palms bending like whips in the wind.

IV

TALIA, that was her name, and though her language was different from the tongue of Maru, it had a likeness of a sort. In those days that little island was uncharted and entirely desolate but for the gulls of the reef and the birds of the woods, and it was a wonderland to Maru, whose idea of land as a sea-beaten ring of coral was shattered by woods that bloomed green as a sea-cave to the moonlight, high ground, where rivulets danced amidst the ferns, and a beach protected from the outer seas by a far-flung line of reefs. Talia to him was as wonderful as the island ; she had come to him out of the sea ; she had saved his life ; she was as different from the women of the Paumotus as day from night. A European would have called her beautiful, but Maru had no thought of her beauty or her sex ; she was just a being, beneficent, almost divorced from earth ; the strangest thing in the strange world that Fate had seized him into, part with the great heaving swell he had ridden so long, the turtle that had broken up to look at him, the spouting reef, the sunsets over wastes of water, and the stars spread over wastes of sky.

He worshipped her in his way, and he might have worshipped her at a greater distance, only for the common bond of youth between them, and the incessant call of the world around them. Talia was practical ; she seemed to have forgotten her people, and that island up north, and to live entirely in the moment. They made two shacks in the bushes, and she taught him island woodcraft, and the uses of berries and fruit that he had never seen before ; also when to fish in the lagoon ; for a month after they reached the island the poisonous season arrived, and Talia knew it, how, who can tell ? She knew many things by instinct, the approach of storms, and when the poisonous season had passed, the times for fishing, and little by little their tongues, that had almost been divided at first, became almost one so that they could chatter together on all sorts of things, and she could tell him that her name was Talia, the daughter of Tepairu, that her island was named Makea, that her people had twenty canoes, big ones, and many little ones, and that Tepairu was not the name of a man, but a woman. That Tepairu was queen or chief woman of her people, now that her husband was dead.

And Maru was able to tell her by degrees of what he would remember, of the old Spanish ship, and how she spouted smoke and thunder, and killed the beach people, of his island and its shape—he drew it on the sand, and Talia, who knew nothing of atolls, at first refused to believe in it, thinking he was jesting—of his father, who was chief man or king of Fukariva, and of the destruction of the tribe. Then he told of the ship with the little wheel—he drew it on the sand—and the little fish god ; of the centre of the cyclone, where the waves where like white dancing men, and of his journey on the hatch cover across the blue heaving sea.

They would swim in the lagoon together, right out to the reefs where the great rollers were always breaking, and out there Talia always seemed to remember her island, pointing north with her eyes fixed across the sea dazzle, as though she could see it, and her people, and the twenty canoes beached on the spume white beach beneath the palms.

" Some day they will come," said Talia. She knew her people, those sea rovers, inconsequent as the gulls. Some day, for some reason or none, one of the fishing canoes would fish as far as this island, or be blown there by some squall. She would take Maru back with her. She told him this.

The thought began to trouble Maru. Then he grew gloomy. He was in love. Love had hit him suddenly. Somehow, and in some mysterious manner, she had changed from a beneficent being, and part of a dream, to a girl of flesh and blood. She knew it, and at the same moment he turned for her into a man.

Up to this she had had no thought of him except as an individual, for all her dreams about him, he might as well have been a palm-tree, but now it was different, and in a flash he was everything. The surf on the reef said, Maru, and the wind in the trees, Maru, and the gulls fishing and crying at the break had one word, Maru ! Maru ! Maru !

Then, one day, swimming out near the bigger break in the reefs, a current drove them together, their shoulders touched, and Maru's arm went round her, and amidst the blue laughing sea and the shouting of the gulls, he told her that the whole world was Talia, and as he told her and as she listened, the current of the ebb, like a treacherous hand, was drawing them through the break towards the devouring sea.

They had to fight their way back, the ebb just beginning would soon be a mill-race, and they knew, and neither could help the other. It was a hard struggle for love and life against the enmity against life and love that hides in all things from the heart of man to the heart of the sea, but they won. They had reached calm waters, and were within twenty strokes of the beach when Talia cried out suddenly and sank.

Maru, who was slightly in front, turned and found her gone ; she had been seized with cramp, the cramp that comes from over-exertion, but he did not know that ; the lagoon was free of sharks, but, despite that fact, and the fact that he did not fear them, he fancied for one fearful moment that a shark had taken her.

Then he saw her below, a dusky form on the coral floor, and he dived.

He brought her to the surface, reached the sandy beach, and, carrying her in his arms, ran with her to the higher level of the sands, and placed her beneath the shade of the trees. She moved in his arms as he carried her, and when he laid her down, her breast heaved in one great sigh, water ran from her mouth, her limbs stiffened, and she moved no more.

Then all the world became black for Maru ; he knew nothing of the art of resuscitating the drowned. Talia was dead.

He ran amongst the trees crying out that Talia was dead ; he struck himself against tree boles and was tripped by ground lianas ; the things of the forest seemed trying to kill him too. Then he hid amongst the ferns, lying on his face, and telling the earth that Talia was dead. Then came sundown, and after that the green moonlight of the woods, and suddenly sleep, with a vision of blue laughing sea and Talia swimming beside him, and then day again, and with the day the vision of Talia lying dead beneath the trees. He could not bury her. He could not touch her. The iron reef of his Tabu held firm, indestructible, unalterable as the main currents of the sea.

He picked fruits and ate them like an animal, and without knowing that he ate, torn towards the beach by the passionate desire to embrace once more the form that he loved, but held from the act by a grip ten thousand years old, and immutable as gravity or the spirit that lives in religions.

He must not handle the dead. Through all his grief came a weird touch of comfort ; she had not been dead when he carried her ashore. He had not touched the dead.

Then terrible thoughts came to him of what would happen to Talia if he left her lying there. Of what predatory gulls might do. He had some knowledge of these matters, and past visions of what had happened on Fukariva when the dead were too numerous for burial came to him, making him shiver like a whipped dog. He could, at all events, drive the birds away, without touching her, without even looking at her his presence on the beach would keep the birds away. It was near noon when this thought came to him. He had been lying on the ground, but he sat up now as though listening to this thought. Then he rose up and came along cautiously amongst the trees. As he came, the rumble of the reef grew louder, and the sea-wind began to reach him through the leaves ; then the light of day grew stronger, and slipping between the palm boles, he pushed a great bread-fruit leaf aside and peeped, and there, on the blinding beach, under the forenoon sun, more clearly even than he had seen the ghosts of men on Fukariva, he saw the ghost of Talia walking by the sea and wringing its hands.

Then the forest took him again, mad, this time, with terror.

When on Fukariva he had seen the ghosts of men walking in the sun-blaze on the coral, he had felt no terror ; he had never seen them except on waking from sleep beneath some tree, and the sight of them had never lasted for more than a moment. He had said to himself, " they are the spirits of the departed," and they had seemed to him part of the scheme of things, like reflections cast on the lagoon, or the spirit voices heard in the wind, or dreams, or the ships that had come from Nowhere and departed Nowhere.

But the ghost of Talia was different from these. It was in some tremendous way real, and it wept because the body of Talia lay unburied.

He had made it weep.

He alone could give it rest.

Away, deep in the woods, hiding amongst the bushes, springing alive with alarm at the slightest sound, he debated this matter with himself, and curiously, now, love did not move him at all or urge him ; it was as though the ghost of Talia had stepped between him and his love for Talia, not destroying it, but obscuring it. Talia for him had become two things : the body he had left lying on the sand under the trees, and the ghost he had seen walking on the beach ; the real Talia no longer existed for him, except as the vaguest wraith. He lay in the bushes, facing the fact that so long as the body lay unburied the ghost would walk. It might even leave the beach and come to him.

This thought brought him from his hiding-place ; he could not be alone with it amongst the bushes, and then he found that he could not stand alone with it amongst the trees, for at any moment she might appear, wringing her hands, in one of the glades, or glide to his side from behind one of the tree boles.

He made for the southern beach.

Although unused to woods, till he reached this island he had the instinct for direction, a brain compass more mysterious than the little trembling fish that had directed the movements of the wheel on board the *Portsoy*. Making due south, amidst the gloom of the trees, he reached the beach where the sun was blazing on the sands and the birds flying and calling over the lagoon. The reef lay far out, a continuous line, unlike the reefs to the north, continuous but for a single break through which the last of the ebb was flowing out oilily, mirroring a palm-tree that stood there like the warden of the lagoon. The sound of the surf was low, the wind had died away, and as Maru stood watching and listening, peace came to his distracted soul.

He felt safe here. Even when Talia had been with him the woods had always seemed to him peopled with lurking things, unused as he was to trees in great masses ; and now released from them and touched again by the warmth of the sun he felt safe. It seemed to him that the ghost could not come here. The gulls said it to him and the flashing water, and as he lay down on the sands, the surf on the reef said it to him. It was too far away for the ghost to come. It seemed to him that he had travelled many thousand miles from a country remote as his extreme youth, losing everything on the way but a weariness greater than Time could hold or thought take recognition of.

Then he fell asleep and he slept whilst the sun went down into the west and the flood swept into the lagoon and the stars broke out above. That tremendous sleep unstirred by the vaguest dream lasted till the dawn was full.

Then he sat up, renewed as though God had remade him in mind and body.

A gull was strutting on the sands by the water's edge, its long shadow strutting after it, and the shadow of the gull flew straight as a javelin into the renewed mind of Maru. Talia was not dead. He had not seen her ghost. She had come to life and had been walking by the sea wringing her hands for

him thinking him drowned.   For the form he had seen walking
in the sands had cast a shadow.   He remembered that now.
Ghosts do not cast shadows.

And instantly his mind, made reasonable by rest and
sleep, revisualized the picture that had terrified his mind
distraught by grief.   That was a real form, what folly could
have made him doubt it ?   Talia was alive—alive, warm, and
waiting for him on the northern beach, and the love for her
that fear had veiled rushed in upon him and seized him with a
great joy that made him shout aloud as he sprang to his feet,
yet with a pain at his heart like the pain of a rankling spear-
wound as he broke through the trees shouting as he ran :
" Talia ! Talia ! Talia ! "

He passed the bushes where he had hidden, and the ferns.
He heard the sounds of the surf coming to meet him, he saw
the veils of the leaves divide and the blaze of light and morning
splendour on the northern sands and lagoon and sea.

He stood and looked.

Nothing.

He ran to the place where he had laid her beneath the
trees, there was still faintly visible the slight depression made
by her body, and close by, strangely and clearly cut, the
imprint of a little foot.

Nothing else.

He stood and called and called, and no answer came
but the wood echo and the sound of the morning wind ; then
he ran to the sea edge.   Then he knew.

The sand was trodden up and on the sand, clear cut and
fresh, lay the mark left by a beached canoe and the marks left
by the feet of the men who had beached her and floated her
again.

They had come—perhaps her own people—come, maybe,
yesterday whilst he was hiding from his fears, debating with
his Tabu—come, and found her, and taken her away.

He plunged into the lagoon and, swimming like an otter
and helped by the out-going tide, reached the reef.   Scrambling
on to the rough coral, bleeding from cuts but feeling nothing
of his wounds, he stood with wrinkled eyes facing the sea blaze
and with the land-breeze blowing past him out beyond the
thundering foam of the reef to the blue and heaving sea.

Away to the north, like a brown wing-tip, showed the sail
of a canoe.   He watched it.   Tossed by the lilt of the swell it
seemed beckoning to him.   Now it vanished in the sea dazzle,

now reappeared, dwindling to a point, to vanish at last like a dream of the sea, gone, never to be recaptured.

" And Maru ? " I asked of Lygon, " did he ever——"

" Never," said Lygon. " The islands of the sea are many. Wait." He struck a gong that stood close to his chair, struck it three times, and the sounds passing into the night mixed with the voices of the canoe men returning from fishing on the reef.

Then a servant came on to the veranda, an old, old man, half bent like a withered tree.

" Maru," said Lygon, " you can take away these glasses— but one moment, Maru, tell this gentleman your story."

" The islands of the sea are many," said Maru, like a child repeating a lesson. He paused for a moment as though trying to remember some more, then he passed out of the lamplight with the glasses.

" A year ago he remembered the whole story," said Lygon.

But for me the whole story lay in those words, that voice, those trembling hands that seemed still searching for what the eyes could see no more.

ERNEST TEMPLE THURSTON (1879—1933) *has sometimes been styled a sentimentalist—largely because of his chivalrous treatment of women in his novels. If this is so, then it is a sentimentality that has stirred and delighted the hearts of thousands. "The City of Beautiful Nonsense" and "The Greatest Wish in the World" are rich in tolerant humour, idealism and quaint and gentle beauty.*

SOME ONE ELSE'S ROMANCE

IT is not always your own romance that is interesting. Your own romance is sometimes a very grey affair, with ugly threads that protrude in ragged ends, and then—it is as well to look to some one else.

Some one else will always have something in their lives that will make your own worth living. If you can but learn the art of looking for it, you will find colour everywhere. That is romance-colour. It is romance when you see blue and purple in the distant hills ; it is romance when you see deep violet beneath in the shade beneath the trees.

All this is romance, because, if you climb up to the distant hills they are green ; and if you stroll beneath the shadows of the trees, all is green there too. But there are colours in life as well—if not just now in your own, then in some one else's. It is not all so grey as it looks when you peer into it.

Personally, I am very fond of some one else. If it were not for some one else, I don't think I could quite go on. For whenever things are very grey with me, when my day is misty, when there is only a crude foreground and the blue distant is lost in grey—then I go to some one else.

But I am no master at the art. There are very few of us who are. Sometimes I find it very hard to obliterate myself entirely. It is recognised to be a difficult thing to do.

There was a pretty little romance once ; but I lost it. I lost it because, in the midst of it all, I tumbled across myself.

Some one else was in an A B C shop. A wee mouse of a thing she was, with a white face and pretty lips that you knew must feel quite cold when you touched them. The lips of a woman are the petals of a rose.   That is a commonplace simile, but it is true.

Every woman's lips are like that ; but some are the petals in the early morning before the sun has warmed them—some are the petals in the heavy, languorous heat of the day, and some—some are the withered petals when the summer is gone. I don't like to think of those.

Anyhow hers were the early morning ones—so early that the dew still chilled them.   She waited on me in a whisper, I don't know how else to describe it.   Her feet whispered ; her skirt whispered.   She whispered, " What are you going to have ? "   Yes, she waited on me in a whisper.

Sometimes I used to talk to her, asking her if she felt well that day and when she was going to take her holidays—silly questions expressing nothing more than my desire to draw her into conversation and discover her romance.

" I want you to give me a photograph of yourself," I said boldly one day.

The cup and saucer that she was carrying nearly tumbled from her hand.   I had never made such a brazen remark before.   She was quite unprepared for it.

" I did have one taken once," she said in sudden confidence, leaning down over the table, so that her voice might reach me.   " It was in evening dress.   But I haven't got any copies now.   I sent the last one away to Auntie when Uncle died."

" Did it help her to bear her loss ? " I asked—a facetious, ridiculous question.   The fact is, I was thinking of myself. I wanted her to find me funny.

In that respect I failed.   Her china eyes gazed at me, and she whispered, " Auntie died a fortnight later."

You see, she was much funnier than I was.   I could not have thought of anything so humorous as that, if I had tried for a year.

" Well, will you get one taken," I suggested seriously—" if I—if I pay for it ? "

She caught in a little breath of amazed delight between her lips.   Then she squeezed her hands together.

" Oh, wouldn't that be lovely ! " she exclaimed, so loud that she did not have to bend down over the table, and I heard her quite plainly.

" Then you can give one to me," I continued—" and you can give one to him."   I paused meaningly.

Her eyebrows went up in an arch like a rainbow.

" How did you know ? " she whispered.

" I can see a picture of him in your eyes," said I—" and I want to know all about him."

" I can't talk now," she replied, with a frightened glance over her shoulder. She looked like a mouse peering up fearfully from a piece of cake. Yes—and such a piece of cake ! She was just longing to tell me everything.

" When will you tell me then ? " I persisted.

" I don't know."

" What are you doing next Sunday ? "

" We're going out to Epping together."

" Ah—and the Sunday after that ? "

" He works every other Sunday."

" Then you're free the Sunday after next ? "

" Yes."

" We go to Kew Gardens then. All the woods are open to the public now, and when you've got your eyes full of bluebells, then you can tell me all about him. Don't forget —Charing Cross Underground at three o'clock, the Sunday after next. Tell him you're coming ; don't keep a secret from him. I'll send him my photograph if he wants to know what I'm like. And when you clear away my plate you will find something that will make glad the heart of your photographer. Sunday after next—three o'clock—Charing Cross."

Well—there was colour ! Ah, yes—but there was too much of it. I lost it all—and just because I tumbled up against myself.

There are few Sundays that I have looked forward to more than that one. There are few Sundays that I look back to with more regret and shame.

I was there at five minutes to three. I could see the blue-bells already. I could hear that little mouse's voice whispering through them all about him, when they were going to be married, where they were going to live.

And then—down Villiers Street she came. Oh, but she was a mouse no longer. She was a cockatoo ! The small, white face and the dusty-coloured hair were all crowned with a violent magenta-coloured hat, adorned with violent magenta-coloured feathers. It was immense. The colour alone filled the whole street. It dragged remarks from little boys. It received all that it asked for ; and it asked in such stentorian tones, that the little boys had to shriek at the top of their voice in order to be heard. I thought of it in the middle of the bluebells, and I wanted to run away.

And she—she bore it with the pride of a Cleopatra carrying off Antony in her arms in the eyes of the whole world. It was her best hat. Are there many things a woman is more proud of ?

It was then that I tumbled against myself. I forgot all about romance. How could I be seen with a hat like that ! So wrapped was I in my own feelings that I did not realise how much of the whole spirit of romance that hat meant to her.

I hid behind the bookstall and watched her come in. There she waited with an expectant, triumphant look upon her little face.

When people stared at her, she almost smiled back in pleasure, as though she would like to tell them all about it.

At last I emerged from my retreat. I came up timidly to her side. I had determined what to do. I raised my hat.

" Well," said I—" how are you ? You're looking splendid. Will you just run and get the tickets while I buy a paper ? " and I slipped a sovereign into her hand.

I often wonder what she did with those tickets. I often wonder whether she went alone to look at the bluebells. I can just imagine the bluebells staring at her.

ANTHONY TROLLOPE (1815–1882) *was
a Government official attached to the Post Office
and was directly responsible for many reforms
including a proper supply of pillar-boxes. He
wrote more than forty novels, of which the
Barsetshire series are the most famous. In his
Autobiography he made no secret of his mechanical
method of composition, and in this way
prejudiced many contemporary critics against him.*

THE JOURNEY TO PANAMA

THERE is perhaps no form of life in which men and women
of the present day frequently find themselves for a time
existing, so unlike their customary conventional life, as that
experienced on board the large ocean steamers. On the
voyages so made, separate friendships are formed and separate
enmities are endured. Certain lines of temporary politics are
originated by the energetic, and intrigues, generally innocent
in their conclusions, are carried on with the keenest spirit by
those to whom excitement is necessary ; whereas the idle and
torpid sink into insignificance and general contempt,—as it is
their lot to do on board ship as in other places. But the enjoy-
ments and activity of such a life do not display themselves till
the third or fourth day of the voyage. The men and women
at first regard each with distrust and ill-concealed dislike.
They by no means anticipate the strong feelings which are to
arise, and look forward to ten, fifteen, or twenty days of gloom
or sea-sickness. Sea-sickness disappears, as a general condition, on the evening of the second day, and the gloom about
noon on the fourth. Then the men begin to think that the
women are not so ugly, vulgar, and insipid ; and the women
drop their monosyllables, discontinue the close adherence to
their own niches, which they first observed, and become
affable, perhaps even beyond their wont on shore. And
alliances spring up among the men themselves. On their
first entrance to this new world, they generally regard each
other with marked aversion, each thinking that those nearest to
him are low fellows, or perhaps worse ; but by the fourth day,
if not sooner, every man has his two or three intimate friends
with whom he talks and smokes, and to whom he communicates

those peculiar politics, and perhaps intrigues, of his own voyage. The female friendships are slower in their growth, for the suspicion of women is perhaps stronger than that of men; but when grown they also are stronger, and exhibit themselves sometimes in instances of feminine affection.

But the most remarkable alliances are those made between gentlemen and ladies. This is a matter of course on board ship quite as much as on shore, and it is of such an alliance that the present tale purports to tell the story. Such friendships, though they may be very dear, can seldom be very lasting. Though they may be full of sweet romance—for people become very romantic among the discomforts of a sea voyage—such romance is generally short-lived and delusive, and occasionally is dangerous.

There are several of these great ocean routes, of which, by the common consent, as it seems, of the world, England is the centre. There is the Great Eastern line, running from Southampton across the Bay of Biscay and up the Mediterranean. It crosses the Isthmus of Suez, and branches away to Australia, to India, to Ceylon, and to China. There is the great American line, traversing the Atlantic to New York and Boston with the regularity of clockwork. The voyage here is so much a matter of every-day routine, that romance has become scarce upon the route. There are one or two other North American lines, perhaps open to the same objection. Then there is the line of packets to the African coast—very romantic as I am given to understand; and there is the great West Indian route, to which the present little history is attached —great, not on account of our poor West Indian Islands, which cannot at the present moment make anything great, but because it spreads itself out from thence to Mexico and Cuba, to Guiana and the republics of Grenada and Venezuela, to Central America, the Isthmus of Panama, and from thence to California, Vancouver's Island, Peru and Chili.

It may be imagined how various are the tribes which leave the shores of Great Britain by this route. There are Frenchmen for the French sugar islands, as a rule not very romantic; there are old Spaniards, Spaniards of Spain, seeking to renew their fortunes amidst the ruins of their former empire; and new Spaniards—Spaniards, that is, of the American republics, who speak Spanish, but are unlike the Don both in manners and physiognomy—men and women with a touch perhaps of Indian blood, very keen after dollars, and not much given to the graces of life. There are Dutchmen too, and Danes, going out to their own islands. There are citizens of the stars and stripes, who find their way everywhere—and, alas ! perhaps, now also citizens of the new Southern flag, with the palmetto leaf. And there are Englishmen of every shade and class, and Englishwomen also.

It is constantly the case that women are doomed to make the long voyage alone. Some are going out to join their husbands, some to find a husband, some few peradventure to leave a husband. Girls who have been educated at home in England, return to their distant homes across the Atlantic, and others follow their relatives who have gone before them as pioneers into a strange land. It must not be supposed that these females absolutely embark in solitude, putting their feet upon the deck without the aid of any friendly arm. They are generally consigned to some prudent elder, and appear as they first show themselves on the ship to belong to a party. But as often as not their real loneliness shows itself after a while. The prudent elder is not, perhaps, congenial ; and by the evening of the fourth day a new friendship is created.

Not a long time since such a friendship was formed under the circumstances which I am now about to tell. A young man—not very young, for he had turned his thirtieth year, but still a young man—left Southampton by one of the large West Indian steam-boats, purposing to pass over the Isthmus of Panama, and thence up to California and Vancouver's Island. It would be too long to tell the cause which led to these distant voyagings. Suffice to say, it was not the accursed hunger after gold—*auri sacra fames*—which so took him ; nor had he any purpose of permanently settling himself in those distant colonies of Great Britain. He was at the time a widower, and perhaps his home was bitter to him without the young wife whom he had early lost. As he stepped on board he was accompanied by a gentleman some fifteen years his senior, who was to be the companion of his sleeping apartment as far as St. Thomas. The two had been introduced to each other, and therefore appeared as friends on board the *Serrapiqui* ; but their acquaintance had commenced in Southampton, and my hero, Ralph Forrest by name, was alone in the world as he stood looking over the side of the ship at the retreating shores of Hampshire.

" I say, old fellow, we'd better see about our places," said his new friend, slapping him on his back. Mr. Matthew Morris was an old traveller, and knew how to become intimate with his temporary allies at a very short notice. A long course of travelling had knocked all bashfulness out of him, and when he had a mind to do so he could make any man his brother in half an hour, and any woman his sister in ten minutes.

" Places ? what places ? " said Forrest.

" A pretty fellow you are to go to California. If you don't look sharper than that you'll get little to drink and nothing to eat till you come back again. Don't you know the ship's as full as ever she can hold ? "

Forrest acknowledged that she was full.

" There are places at table for about a hundred, and we have a hundred and thirty on board. As a matter of course those who don't look sharp will have to scramble. However I've put cards on the plates and taken the seats. We had better go down and see that none of these Spanish fellows oust us." So Forrest descended after his friend, and found that the long tables were already nearly full of expectant dinner-eaters. When he took his place a future neighbour informed him, not in the most gracious voice, that he was encroaching on a lady's seat ; and when he immediately attempted to leave that which he held, Mr. Matthew Morris forbade him to do so. Thus a little contest arose, which, however, happily was brought to a close without bloodshed. The lady was not present at the moment, and the grumpy gentleman agreed to secure for himself a vacant seat on the other side.

For the first three days the lady did not show herself. The grumpy gentleman, who, as Forrest afterwards understood, was the owner of stores in Bridgetown, Barbadoes, had other ladies with him also. First came forth his daughter, creeping down to dinner on the second day, declaring that she would be unable to eat a morsel, and prophesying that she would be forced to retire in five minutes. On this occasion, however, she agreeably surprised herself and her friends. Then came the grumpy gentleman's wife, and the grumpy gentleman's wife's brother—on whose constitution the sea seemed to have an effect quite as violent as on that of the ladies ; and lastly, at breakfast on the fourth day, appeared Miss Viner, and took her place as Mr. Forrest's neighbour at his right hand.

He had seen her before on deck, as she lay on one of the benches, vainly endeavouring to make herself comfortable, and had remarked to his companion that she was very unattractive and almost ugly. Dear young ladies, it is thus that men always speak of you when they first see you on board ship ! She was disconsolate, sick at heart, and ill at ease in body also. She did not like the sea. She did not in the least like the grumpy gentleman, in whose hands she was placed. She did not especially like the grumpy gentleman's wife ; and she altogether hated the grumpy gentleman's daughter, who was the partner of her berth. That young lady had been very sick and very selfish ; and Miss Viner had been very sick also, and perhaps equally selfish. They might have been angels, and yet have hated each other under such circumstances. It was no wonder that Mr. Forrest thought her ugly as she twisted herself about on the broad bench, vainly striving to be comfortable.

" She'll brighten up wonderfully before we're in the tropics," said Mr. Morris. " And you won't find her so bad then. It's she that is to sit next you."

" Heaven forbid ! " said Forrest. But, nevertheless, he was very civil to her when she did come down on the fourth morning. On board the West Indian Packets, the world goes down to its meals. In crossing between Liverpool and the States, the world goes up to them.

Miss Viner was by no means a very young lady. She also was nearly thirty. In guessing her age on board the ship the ladies said that she was thirty-six, but the ladies were wrong. She was an Irish woman, and when seen on shore, in her natural state, and with all her wits about her, was by no means without attraction. She was bright-eyed, with a clear dark skin, and good teeth ; her hair was of a dark brown and glossy, and there was a touch of feeling and also of humour about her mouth, which would have saved her from Mr. Forrest's ill-considered criticism, had he first met her under more favourable circumstances.

" You'll see a good deal of her," Mr. Morris said to him, as they began to prepare themselves for luncheon, by a cigar immediately after breakfast. " She's going across the Isthmus and down to Peru."

" How on earth do you know ? "

" I pretty well know where they're all going by this time. Old Grumpy told me so. He has her in tow as far as St. Thomas, but knows nothing about her. He gives her up there to the captain. You'll have a chance of making yourself very agreeable as you run across with her to the Spanish main."

Mr. Forrest replied that he did not suppose he should know her much better than he did now ; but he made no further remark as to her ugliness. She had spoken a word or two to him at table, and he had seen that her eyes were bright, and had found that her tone was sweet.

"I also am going to Panama," he said to her, on the morning of the fifth day. The weather at that time was very fine, and the October sun as it shone on them, while hour by hour they made more towards the South, was pleasant and genial. The big ship lay almost without motion on the bosom of the Atlantic, as she was driven through the waters at the rate of twelve miles per hour. All was as pleasant now as things can be on board a ship, and Forrest had forgotten that Miss Viner had seemed so ugly to him when he first saw her. At this moment, as he spoke to her, they were running through the Azores, and he had been assisting her with his field-glass to look for orange-groves on their sloping shores, orange-groves they had not succeeded in seeing, but their failure had not disturbed their peace.

"I also am going to Panama."

"Are you, indeed?" said she. "Then I shall not feel so terribly alone and disconsolate. I have been looking forward with such fear to that journey on from St. Thomas."

"You shall not be disconsolate, if I can help it," he said. "I am not much of a traveller myself, but what I can do I will."

"Oh, thank you!"

"It is a pity Mr. Morris is not going on with you. He's at home everywhere, and knows the way across the Isthmus as well as he does down Regent Street."

"Your friend, you mean?"

"My friend, if you call him so; and indeed I hope he is, for I like him. But I don't know more of him than I do of you. I also am as much alone as you are. Perhaps more so."

"But," she said, "a man never suffers in being alone."

"Oh! does he not? Don't think me uncivil, Miss Viner, if I say that you may be mistaken in that. You feel your own shoe when it pinches, but do not realize the tight boot of your neighbour."

"Perhaps not," said she. And then there was a pause, during which she pretended to look again for the orange-groves. "But there are worse things, Mr. Forrest, than being alone in the world. It is often a woman's lot to wish that she were let alone." Then she left him and retreated to the side of the grumpy gentleman's wife, feeling perhaps that it might be prudent to discontinue a conversation which, seeing that Mr. Forrest was quite a stranger to her, was becoming particular.

"You're getting on famously, my dear," said the lady from Barbadoes.

"Pretty well, thank you, ma'am," said Miss Viner.

"Mr. Forrest seems to be making himself quite agreeable. I tell Amelia,"—Amelia was the young lady to whom in their joint cabin Miss Viner could not reconcile herself—"I tell Amelia that she is wrong not to receive attentions from gentlemen on board ship. If it is not carried too far," and she put great emphasis on the "too far "—" I see no harm in it."

"Nor I, either," said Miss Viner.

"But then Amelia is so particular."

"The best way is to take such things as they come," said Miss Viner,—perhaps meaning that such things never did come in the way of Amelia. "If a lady knows what she is about she need not fear a gentleman's attentions."

"That's just what I tell Amelia ; but then, my dear, she has not had so much experience as you and I."

Such being the amenities which passed between Miss Viner and the prudent lady who had her in charge, it was not wonderful that the former should feel ill at ease with her own "party," as the family of the Grumpy Barbadian was generally considered to be by those on board.

"You're getting along like a house on fire with Miss Viner," said Matthew Morris, to his young friend.

"Not much fire I can assure you," said Forrest.

"She ain't so ugly as you thought her ? "

"Ugly !—no ; she's not ugly. I don't think I ever said she was. But she is nothing particular as regards beauty."

"No ; she won't be lovely for the next three days to come, I dare say. By the time you reach Panama, she'll be all that is perfect in woman. I know how these things go."

"Those sort of things don't go at all quickly with me," said Forrest, gravely. "Miss Viner is a very interesting young woman, and as it seems that her route and mine will be together for some time, it is well that we should be civil to each other. And the more so, seeing that the people she is with are not congenial to her."

"No ; they are not. There is no young man with them. I generally observe that on board ship no one is congenial to unmarried ladies except unmarried men. It is a recognized

nautical rule. Uncommon hot, isn't it ? We are beginning to
feel the tropical air. I shall go and cool myself with a cigar in
the fiddle." The " fiddle " is a certain part of the ship devoted
to smoking, and thither Mr. Morris betook himself. Forrest,
however, did not accompany him, but going forward into the
bow of the vessel, threw himself along upon the sail, and medi-
tated on the loneliness of his life.

On board the *Serrapiqui*, the upper tier of cabins opened
on to a long gallery, which ran round that part of the ship,
immediately over the saloon, so that from thence a pleasant
inspection could be made of the viands as they were being
placed on the tables. The custom on board these ships is for
two bells to ring preparatory to dinner, at an interval of half
an hour. At the sound of the first, ladies would go to their
cabins to adjust their toilets ; but as dressing for dinner is
not carried to an extreme at sea, these operations are generally
over before the second bell, and the lady passengers would
generally assemble in the balcony for some fifteen minutes
before dinner. At first they would stand here alone, but by
degrees they were joined by some of the more enterprising of
the men, and so at last a kind of little drawing-room was
formed. The cabins of Miss Viner's party opened to one side
of this gallery, and that of Mr. Morris and Forrest on the
other. Hitherto Forrest had been contented to remain on his
own side, occasionally throwing a word across to the ladies on
the other ; but on this day he boldly went over as soon as he
had washed his hands and took his place between Amelia and
Miss Viner.

" We are dreadfully crowded here, ma'am," said Amelia.

" Yes, my dear, we are," said her mother. " But what
can one do ? "

" There's plenty of room in the ladies' cabin," said Miss
Viner. Now if there be one place on board a ship more distasteful to ladies than another, it is the ladies' cabin. Mr.
Forrest stood his ground, but it may be doubted whether he
would have done so had he fully understood all that Amelia
had intended.

Then the last bell rang. Mr. Grumpy gave his arm to Mrs.
Grumpy. The brother-in-law gave his arm to Amelia, and
Forrest did the same to Miss Viner. She hesitated for a
moment, and then took it, and by so doing transferred herself
mentally and bodily from the charge of the prudent and
married Mr. Grumpy to that of the perhaps imprudent, and

certainly unmarried Mr. Forrest. She was wrong. A kind-hearted, motherly old lady from Jamaica, who had seen it all, knew that she was wrong, and wished that she could tell her so.

But there are things of this sort which kind-hearted old ladies cannot find it in their hearts to say. After all, it was only for the voyage. Perhaps Miss Viner was imprudent, but who in Peru would be the wiser? Perhaps, indeed, it was the world that was wrong, and not Miss Viner. *Honi soit qui mal y pense*, she said to herself, as she took his arm, and leaning on it, felt that she was no longer so lonely as she had been. On that day she allowed him to give her a glass of wine out of his decanter. " Hadn't you better take mine, Miss Viner? " asked Mr. Grumpy, in a loud voice, but before he could be answered, the deed had been done.

" Don't go too fast, old fellow," Morris said to our hero that night, as they were walking the deck together before they turned in. " One gets into a hobble in such matters before one knows where one is."

" I don't think I have anything particular to fear," said Forrest.

" I dare say not, only keep your eyes open. Such harridans as Mrs. Grumpy allow any latitude to their tongues out in these diggings. You'll find that unpleasant tidings will be put on board the ship going down to Panama, and everybody's eye will be upon you." So warned, Mr. Forrest did put himself on his guard, and the next day and a half his intimacy with Miss Viner progressed but little. These were, probably, the dullest hours that he had on the whole voyage.

Miss Viner saw this and drew back. On the afternoon of that second day she walked a turn or two on deck with the weak brother-in-law, and when Mr. Forrest came near her, she applied herself to her book. She meant no harm ; but if she were not afraid of what people might say, why should he be so ? So she turned her shoulder towards him at dinner, and would not drink of his cup.

" Have some of mine, Miss Viner," said Mr. Grumpy, very loudly. But on that day Miss Viner drank no wine.

The sun sets quickly as one draws near to the tropics, and the day was already gone, and the dusk had come on, when Mr. Forrest walked out upon the deck that evening a little after six. But the night was beautiful and mild, and there was a hum of many voices from the benches. He was already uncomfortable, and sore with a sense of being deserted. There was but one person on board the ship that he liked, and why should he avoid her and be avoided ? He soon perceived where she was standing. The Grumpy family had a bench to themselves, and she was opposite to it, on her feet, leaning against the side of the vessel. " Will you walk this evening, Miss Viner ? " he asked.

" I think not," she answered.

" Then I shall persevere in asking till you are sure. It will do you good, for I have not seen you walking all day."

" Have you not ? Then I will take a turn. Oh, Mr. Forrest, if you knew what it was to have to live with such people as those." And then, out of that, on that evening, there grew up between them something like the confidence of real friendship. Things were told such as none but friends do tell to one another, and warm answering words were spoken such as the sympathy of friendship produces. Alas, they were both foolish ; for friendship and sympathy should have deeper roots.

She told him all her story. She was going out to Peru to be married to a man who was nearly twenty years her senior. It was a long engagement, of ten years' standing. When first made, it was made as being contingent on certain circumstances. An option of escaping from it had then been given to her, but now there was no longer an option. He was rich, and she was penniless. He had even paid her passage-money and her outfit. She had not at last given way and taken these irrevocable steps till her only means of support in England had been taken from her. She had lived the last two years with a relative who was now dead. " And he also is my cousin,—a distant cousin—you understand that."

" And do you love him ? "

" Love him ! What ; as you loved her whom you have lost ?—as she loved you when she clung to you before she went ? No ; certainly not. I shall never know anything of that love."

" And is he good ? "

" He is a hard man. Men become hard when they deal in money as he has done. He was home five years since, and then I swore to myself that I would not marry him. But his letters to me are kind."

Forrest sat silent for a minute or two, for they were up in the bow again, seated on the sail that was bound round the bowsprit, and then he answered her, "A woman should never marry a man unless she loves him."

"Ah," says she, "of course you will condemn me. That is the way in which women are always treated. They have no choice given them, and are then scolded for choosing wrongly."

"But you might have refused him."

"No; I could not. I cannot make you understand the whole,—how it first came about that the marriage was proposed, and agreed to by me under certain conditions. Those conditions have come about, and I am now bound to him. I have taken his money and have no escape. It is easy to say that a woman should not marry without love, as easy as it is to say that a man should not starve. But there are men who starve, —starve although they work hard."

"I did not mean to judge you, Miss Viner."

"But I judge myself, and condemn myself so often. Where should I be in half an hour from this if I were to throw myself forward into the sea? I often long to do it. Don't you feel tempted sometimes to put an end to it all?"

"The waters look cool and sweet, but I own I am afraid of the bourne beyond."

"So am I, and that fear will keep me from it."

"We are bound to bear our burden of sorrow. Mine, I know, is heavy enough."

"Yours, Mr. Forrest! Have you not all the pleasures of memory to fall back on, and every hope for the future? What can I remember, or what can I hope? But, however, it is near eight o'clock, and they have all been at tea this hour past. What will my Cerberus say to me? I do not mind the male mouth, if only the two feminine mouths could be stopped." Then she rose and went back to the stern of the vessel; but as she slid into a seat, she saw that Mrs. Grumpy was standing over her.

From thence to St. Thomas the voyage went on in the customary manner. The sun became very powerful, and the passengers in the lower part of the ship complained loudly of having their portholes closed. The Spaniards sat gambling in the cabin all day, and the ladies prepared for the general move which was to be made at St. Thomas. The alliance between Forrest and Miss Viner went on much the same as ever, and Mrs. Grumpy said very ill-natured things. On one occasion she ventured to lecture Miss Viner; but that lady knew how to take her own part, and Mrs. Grumpy did not get

" A woman should never marry a man unless she loves him."

the best of it. The dangerous alliance, I have said, went on the same as ever ; but it must not be supposed that either person in any way committed aught that was wrong. They sat together and talked together, each now knowing the other's circumstances ; but had it not been for the prudish caution of some of the ladies there would have been nothing amiss. As it was there was not much amiss. Few of the passengers really cared whether or no Miss Viner had found an admirer. Those who were going down to Panama were mostly Spaniards, and as the great separation became nearer, people had somewhat else of which to think.

And then the separation came. They rode into that pretty harbour of St. Thomas early in the morning, and were ignorant, the most of them, that they were lying in the very worst centre of yellow fever among all those plague-spotted islands. St. Thomas is very pretty as seen from the ships ; and when that has been said, all has been said that can be said in its favour. There was a busy, bustling time of it then. One vessel after another was brought up alongside of the big ship that had come from England, and each took its separate freight of passengers and luggage. First started the boat that ran down the Leeward Islands to Demerara, taking with her Mr. Grumpy and all his family.

" Good-bye, Miss Viner," said Mrs. Grumpy. " I hope you'll get quite safely to the end of your voyage ; but do take care."

" I'm sure I hope everything will be right," said Amelia, as she absolutely kissed her enemy. It is astonishing how well young women can hate each other, and yet kiss at parting.

" As to everything being right," said Miss Viner, " that is too much to hope. But I do not know that anything is going especially wrong.—Good-bye, sir," and then she put out her hand to Mr. Grumpy. He was at the moment leaving the ship laden with umbrellas, sticks, and coats, and was forced to put them down in order to free his hand.

" Well, good-bye," he said. " I hope you'll do, till you meet your friends at the Isthmus."

" I hope I shall, sir," she replied ; and so they parted.

Then the Jamaica packet started.

" I dare say we shall never see each other again," said Morris, as he shook his friend's hand heartily. " One never does. Don't interfere with the rights of that gentleman in Peru, or he might run a knife into you."

"I feel no inclination to injure him on that point."

"That's well; and now good-bye." And thus they also were parted. On the following morning the branch ship was dispatched to Mexico; and then, on the afternoon of the third day that for Colon—as we Englishmen call the town on this side of the Isthmus of Panama. Into that vessel Miss Viner and Mr. Forrest moved themselves and their effects; and now that the three-headed Cerberus was gone, she had no longer hesitated in allowing him to do for her all those little things which it is well that men should do for women when they are travelling. A woman without assistance under such circumstances is very forlorn, very apt to go to the wall, very ill able to assert her rights as to accommodation; and I think that few can blame Miss Viner for putting herself and her belongings under the care of the only person who was disposed to be kind to her.

Late in the evening the vessel steamed out of St. Thomas' harbour, and as she went Ralph Forrest and Emily Viner were standing together at the stern of the boat looking at the retreating lights of the Danish town. If there be a place on the earth's surface odious to me, it is that little Danish isle to which so many of our young seamen are sent to die,—there being no good cause whatever for such sending. But the question is one which cannot well be argued here.

"I have five more days of self and liberty left me," said Miss Viner. "That is my life's allowance."

"For heaven's sake do not say words that are so horrible."

"But am I to lie for heaven's sake, and say words that are false; or shall I be silent for heaven's sake, and say nothing during these last hours that are allowed to me for speaking? It is so. To you I can say that it is so, and why should you begrudge me the speech?"

"I would begrudge you nothing that I could do for you."

"No, you should not. Now that my incubus has gone to Barbadoes, let me be free for a day or two. What chance is there, I wonder, that the ship's machinery should all go wrong, and that we should be tossed about in the seas here for the next six months? I suppose it would be very wicked to wish it?"

"We should all be starved; that's all."

"What, with a cow on board, and a dozen live sheep, and thousands of cocks and hens! But we are to touch at Santa

Martha and Cartagena.   What would happen to me if I were to run away at Santa Martha ? ''

" I suppose I should be bound to run with you."

" Oh, of course.   And therefore, as I would not wish to destroy you, I won't do it.   But it would not hurt you much to be shipwrecked, and wait for the next packet."

" Miss Viner," he said after a pause,—and in the meantime he had drawn nearer to her, too near to her considering all things—" in the name of all that is good, and true, and womanly, go back to England.   With your feelings, if I may judge of them by words which are spoken half in jest——"

" Mr. Forrest, there is no jest."

" With your feelings a poorhouse in England would be better than a palace in Peru."

" An English workhouse would be better, but an English poorhouse is not open to me.   You do not know what it is to have friends—no, not friends, but people belonging to you—just so near as to make your respectability a matter of interest to them, but not so near that they should care for your happiness. Emily Viner married to Mr. Gorloch in Peru is put out of the way respectably.   She will cause no further trouble, but her name may be mentioned in family circles without annoyance. The fact is, Mr. Forrest, that there are people who have no business to live at all."

" I would go back to England," he added, after another pause.   " When you talk to me with such bitterness of five more days of living liberty you scare my very soul.   Return, Miss Viner, and brave the worst.   He is to meet you at Panama. Remain on this side of the Isthmus, and send him word that you must return.   I will be the bearer of the message."

" And shall I walk back to England ? " said Miss Viner.

" I had not quite forgotten all that," he replied, very gently.   " There are moments when a man may venture to propose that which under ordinary circumstances would be a liberty.   Money, in a small moderate way, is not greatly an object to me.   As a return for my valiant defence of you against your West Indian Cerberus, you shall allow me to arrange that with the agent at Colon."

" I do so love plain English, Mr. Forrest.   You are pro-posing, I think, to give me something about fifty guineas."

" Well, call it so if you will," said he, " if you will have plain English that is what I mean."

" So that by my journey out here, I should rob and deceive

the man I do know, and also rob the man I don't know. I am afraid of that bourne beyond the waters of which we spoke ; but I would rather face that than act as you suggest."

" Of the feelings between him and you, I can of course be no judge."

" No, no ; you cannot. But what a beast I am not to thank you ! I do thank you. That which it would be mean in me to take, it is noble, very noble, in you to offer. It is a pleasure to me—I cannot tell why—but it is a pleasure to me to have had the offer. But think of me as a sister, and you will feel that it would not be accepted ;—could not be accepted, I mean, even if I could bring myself to betray that other man."

Thus they ran across the Caribbean Sea, renewing very often such conversations as that just given. They touched at Santa Martha and Cartagena on the coast of the Spanish main, and at both places he went with her on shore. He found that she was fairly well educated, and anxious to see and to learn all that might be seen and learned in the course of her travels. On the last day, as they neared the Isthmus, she became more tranquil and quiet in the expression of her feelings than before, and spoke with less of gloom than she had done.

" After all ought I not to love him ? " she said. " He is coming all the way up from Callao merely to meet me. What man would go from London to Moscow to pick up a wife ? "

" I would—and thence round the world to Moscow again —if she were the wife I wanted."

" Yes ; but a wife who has never said that she loved you ! It is purely a matter of convenience. Well ; I have locked my big box, and I shall give the key to him before it is ever again unlocked. He has a right to it, for he has paid for nearly all that it holds."

" You look at things from such a mundane point of view."

" A woman should, or she will always be getting into difficulty. Mind, I shall introduce you to him, and tell him all that you have done for me. How you braved Cerberus and the rest of it."

" I shall certainly be glad to meet him."

" But I shall not tell him of your offer ;—not yet at least. If he be good and gentle with me, I shall tell him that too after a time. I am very bad at keeping secrets,—as no doubt you have perceived. We go across the Isthmus at once ; do we not ? "

" So the Captain says."

" Look ! "—and she handed him back his own field-glass.
" I can see the men on the wooden platform. Yes ; and I can
see the smoke of an engine." And then, in little more than
an hour from that time the ship had swung round on her
anchor.

Colon, or Aspinwall as it should be called, is a place in
itself as detestable as St. Thomas. It is not so odious to an
Englishman, for it is not used by Englishmen more than is
necessary. We have no great depot of traffic there, which we
might with advantage move elsewhere. Taken, however, on
its own merits, Aspinwall is not a detestable place. Luckily,
however, travellers across the Isthmus to the Pacific are never
doomed to remain there long. If they arrive early in the day,
the railway thence to Panama takes them on at once. If it be
not so, they remain on board ship till the next morning. Of
course it will be understood that the transit line chiefly affects
Americans, as it is the highroad from New York to California.

In less than an hour from their landing, their baggage had
been examined by the Custom House officers of New Grenada,
and they were on the railway cars, crossing the Isthmus. The
officials in those out-of-the-way places always seem like apes
imitating the doings of men. The officers at Aspinwall open
and look at the trunks just as monkeys might do, having clearly
no idea of any duty to be performed, nor any conception that
goods of this or that class should not be allowed to pass. It is
the thing in Europe to examine luggage going into a new
country ; and why should not they be as good as Europeans ?

" I wonder whether he will be at the station ? " she said,
when the three hours of the journey had nearly passed. Forrest
could perceive that her voice trembled as she spoke, and that
she was becoming nervous.

" If he has already reached Panama, he will be there. As
far as I could learn the arrival up from Peru had not been
telegraphed."

" Then I have another day,—perhaps two. We cannot
say how many. I wish he were there. Nothing is so intolerable
as suspense."

" And the box must be opened again."

When they reached the station at Panama they found that
the vessel from the South American coast was in the roads,
but that the passengers were not yet on shore. Forrest,
therefore, took Miss Viner down to the hotel, and there remained with her, sitting next to her in the common drawing-

room of the house, when she had come back from her own bedroom. It would be necessary that they should remain there four or five days, and Forrest had been quick in securing a room for her. He had assisted in taking up her luggage, had helped her in placing her big box, and had thus been recognized by the crowd in the hotel as her friend. Then came the tidings that the passengers were landing, and he became nervous as she was. " I will go down and meet him," said he, " and tell him that you are here. I shall soon find him by his name." And so he went out.

Everybody knows the scrambling manner in which passengers arrive at an hotel out of a big ship. First came two or three energetic, heated men, who, by dint of screeching and bullying, have gotten themselves first disposed. They always get the worst rooms at the inns, the housekeepers having a notion that the richest people, those with the most luggage, must be more tardy in their movements. Four or five of this nature passed by Forrest in the hall, but he was not tempted to ask questions of them. One, from his age, might have been Mr. Gorloch, but he instantly declared himself to be Count Sapparello. Then came an elderly man alone, with a small bag in his hand. He was one of those who pride themselves on going from pole to pole without encumbrance, and who will be behoved to no one for the carriage of their luggage. To him, as he was alone in the street, Forrest addressed himself. " Gorloch," said he. " Gorloch : are you a friend of his ? "

" A friend of mine is so," said Forrest.

" Ah, indeed ; yes," said the other. And then he hesitated. " Sir," he then said, " Mr. Gorloch died at Callao, just seven days before the ship sailed. You had better see Mr. Cox." And then the elderly man passed in with his little bag.

Mr. Gorloch was dead. " Dead ! " said Forrest, to himself, as he leaned back against the wall of the hotel, still standing on the street pavement. " She has come out here ; and now he is gone ! " And then a thousand thoughts crowded on him. Who should tell her ? And how would she bear it ? Would it in truth be a relief to her to find that that liberty for which she had sighed had come to her ? Or now that the testing of her feelings had come to her, would she regret the loss of home and wealth, and such position as life in Peru would give her ? And above all would this sudden death of one who was to have been so near to her, strike her to the heart ?

But what was he to do ? How was he now to show his

friendship? He was returning slowly in at the hotel door, where crowds of men and women were now thronging, when he was addressed by a middle-aged, good-looking gentleman, who asked him whether his name was Forrest. " I am told," said the gentleman, when Forrest had answered him, " that you are a friend of Miss Viner's. Have you heard the sad tidings from Callao ? " It then appeared that this gentleman had been a stranger to Mr. Gorloch, but had undertaken to bring a letter up to Miss Viner. This letter was handed to Mr. Forrest, and he found himself burdened with the task of breaking the news to his poor friend. Whatever he did do, he must do at once, for all those who had come up by the Pacific steamer knew the story, and it was incumbent on him that Miss Viner should not hear the tidings in a sudden manner and from a stranger's mouth.

He went up into the drawing-room, and found Miss Viner seated there in the midst of a crew of women. He went up to her, and taking her hand, asked her in a whisper whether she would come out with him for a moment.

" Where is he ? " said she. " I know that something is the matter. What is it ? "

" There is such a crowd here. Step out for a moment." And he led her away to her own room.

" Where is he ? " said she. " What is the matter ? He has sent to say that he no longer wants me. Tell me; am I free from him ? "

" Miss Viner, you are free."

Though she had asked the question herself, she was astounded by the answer; but, nevertheless, no idea of the truth had yet come upon her. " It is so," she said. " Well, what else ? Has he written ? He has bought me, as he would a beast of burden, and has, I suppose, a right to treat me as he pleases."

" I have a letter; but, dear Miss Viner——"

" Well, tell me all,—out at once. Tell me everything."

" You are free, Miss Viner; but you will be cut to the heart when you learn the meaning of your freedom."

" He has lost everything in trade. He is ruined."

" Miss Viner, he is dead ! "

She stood staring at him for a moment or two, as though she could not realize the information which he gave her. Then gradually she retreated to the bed, and sat upon it. " Dead, Mr. Forrest ! " she said. He did not answer her, but handed her the letter, which she took and read as though it were mechanically. The letter was from Mr. Gorloch's partner, and told her everything which it was necessary that she should know.

"Shall I leave you now ? " he said, when he saw that she had finished reading it.

"Leave me ; yes,—no. But you had better leave me, and let me think about it. Alas me, that I should have so spoken of him ! "

"But you have said nothing unkind."

"Yes ; much that was unkind. But spoken words cannot be recalled. Let me be alone now, but come to me soon. There is no one else here that I can speak to."

He went out, and finding that the hotel dinner was ready, he went in and dined. Then he strolled into the town, among the hot, narrow, dilapidated streets ; and then, after two hours' absence, returned to Miss Viner's room. When he knocked, she came and opened the door, and he found that the floor was strewed with clothes. "I am preparing, you see, for my return. The vessel starts back for St. Thomas the day after to-morrow."

"You are quite right to go,—to go at once. Oh, Miss Viner ! Emily, now at least you must let me help you."

He had been thinking of her most during those last two hours, and her voice had become pleasant to his ears, and her eyes very bright to his sight.

"You shall help me," she said. "Are you not helping me when at such a time you come to speak to me ? "

"And you will let me think that I have a right to act as your protector ? "

"My protector ! I do know that I want such aid as that. During the days that we are here together you shall be my friend."

"You shall not return alone. My journeys are nothing to me. Emily, I will return with you to England."

Then she rose up from her seat and spoke to him.

"Not for the world," she said. "Putting out of question the folly of your forgetting your own objects, do you think it possible that I should go with you, now that he is dead ? To you I have spoken of him harshly ; and now that it is my duty to mourn for him, could I do so heartily if you were with me ? While he lived, it seemed to me that in those last days I had a right to speak my thoughts plainly. You and I were to part and meet no more, and I regarded us both as people apart, who for a while might drop the common usages of the world. It is so no longer. Instead of going with you farther, I must ask you to forget that we were ever together."

" Emily, I shall never forget you."

" Let your tongue forget me. I have given you no cause to speak good of me, and you will be too kind to speak evil."

After that she explained to him all that the letter had contained. The arrangements for her journey had all been made ; money also had been sent to her ; and Mr. Gorloch in his will had provided for her, not liberally, seeing that he was rich, but still sufficiently.

And so they parted at Panama. She would not allow him even to cross the Isthmus with her, but pressed his hand warmly as he left her at the station. " God bless you ! " he said. " And may God bless you, my friend ! " she answered.

Thus alone she took her departure for England, and he went on his way to California.

TALES OF HIGH ADVENTURE

How good is man's life, the mere living !
how fit to employ
All the heart and the soul and the senses
for ever in joy.

ROBERT BROWNING.   *The Wild Joys of Living.*

A. J. ALAN *is the famous broadcaster of stories whose real identity is " the best kept secret in England." Whoever he is, no one will deny him a place among the best short story writers of to-day. His disarming confidence and the cleverly casual way in which he develops his stories lend an air of reality to the most improbable plots. " My Adventure in Norfolk" is a fine example of the author's inimitable style.*

MY ADVENTURE IN NORFOLK

I DON'T know how it is with you, but during February *my* wife generally says to me : " Have you thought at all about what we are going to do for August ? " And, of course, I say " No," and then she begins looking through the advertisements of bungalows to let.

Well, this happened last year, as usual, and she eventually produced one that looked possible. It said : " Norfolk—Hickling Broad — Furnished Bungalow — Garden — Garage, Boathouse," and all the rest of it—— Oh—*and* plate and linen. It also mentioned an exorbitant rent. I pointed out the bit about the rent, but my wife said : " Yes, you'll have to go down and see the landlord, and get him to come down. They always do." As a matter of fact, they always don't, but that's a detail.

Anyway, I wrote off to the landlord and asked if he could arrange for me to stay the night in the place to see what it was really like. He wrote back and said : " Certainly," and that he was engaging Mrs. So-and-so to come in and " oblige me," and make up the beds and so forth.

I tell you, we do things thoroughly in our family—I have to sleep in all the beds, and when I come home my wife counts the bruises and decides whether they will do or not.

At any rate, I arrived, in a blinding snowstorm, at about *the* most desolate spot on God's earth. I'd come to Potter Heigham by train, and been driven on—(it was a good five miles from the station). Fortunately, Mrs. Selston, the old lady who was going to " do " for me, was there, and she'd

511

lighted a fire, and cooked me a steak, for which I was truly thankful.

I somehow think the cow, or whatever they get steaks off, had only died that morning. It was very—er—obstinate. While I dined, she talked to me. She *would* tell me all about an operation her husband had just had. *All* about it. It was almost a lecture on surgery. The steak was rather underdone, and it sort of made me feel I was illustrating her lecture. Anyway, she put me clean off my dinner, and then departed for the night.

I explored the bungalow and just had a look outside. It was, of course, very dark, but not snowing quite so hard. The garage stood about fifteen yards from the back door. I walked round it but didn't go in. I also went down to the edge of the broad, and verified the boathouse. The whole place looked as though it might be all right in the summertime, but just then it made one wonder why people ever wanted to go to the North Pole.

Anyhow, I went indoors, and settled down by the fire. You've no idea how quiet it was ; even the water-fowl had taken a night off—at least, they weren't working.

At a few minutes to eleven I heard the first noise there'd been since Mrs. What's-her-name—Selston—had cleared out. It was the sound of a car. If it had gone straight by I probably shouldn't have noticed it at all, only it didn't go straight by ; it seemed to stop farther up the road, before it got to the house. Even that didn't make much impression. After all, cars *do* stop.

It must have been five or ten minutes before it was borne in on me that it hadn't gone on again. So I got up and looked out of the window. It had left off snowing, and there was a glare through the gate that showed that there were headlamps somewhere just out of sight. I thought I might as well stroll out and investigate.

I found a fair-sized limousine pulled up in the middle of the road about twenty yards short of my gate. The light was rather blinding, but when I got close to it I found a girl with the bonnet open, tinkering with the engine. Quite an attractive young female, from what one could see, but she was so muffled up in furs that it was rather hard to tell.

I said :

" Er—good evening—anything I can do ? "

She said she didn't know what was the matter. The engine

had just stopped, and wouldn't start again. And it *had*! It wouldn't even turn, either with the self-starter or the handle. The whole thing was awfully hot, and I asked her whether there was any water in the radiator. She didn't see why there shouldn't be, there always had been. This didn't strike me as entirely conclusive. I said, we'd better put some in, and see what happened. She said, why not use snow? But I thought not. There was an idea at the back of my mind that there was some reason why it was unwise to use melted snow, and it wasn't until I arrived back with a bucketful that I remembered what it was. Of course—goitre.

When I got back to her she'd got the radiator cap off, and inserted what a Danish friend of mine calls a "funeral." We poured a little water in. . . . Luckily I'd warned her to stand clear. The first tablespoonful that went in came straight out again, red-hot, and blew the "funeral" sky-high. We waited a few minutes until things had cooled down a bit, but it was no go. As fast as we poured water in it simply ran out again into the road underneath. It was quite evident that she'd been driving with the radiator bone dry, and that her engine had seized right up.

I told her so. She said:

"Does that mean I've got to stop here all night?"

I explained that it wasn't as bad as all that; that is, if she cared to accept the hospitality of my poor roof (and it *was* a poor roof—it let the wet in). But she wouldn't hear of it. By the by, she didn't know the—er—circumstances, so it wasn't that. No, she wanted to leave the car where it was and go on on foot.

I said:

"Don't be silly, it's miles to anywhere."

However, at that moment we heard a car coming along the road, the same way as she'd come. We could see its lights, too, although it was a very long way off. You know how flat Norfolk is—you can see a terrific distance.

I said:

"There's the way out of all your troubles. This thing, whatever it is, will give you a tow to the nearest garage, or at any rate a lift to some hotel."

One would have expected her to show some relief, but she didn't. I began to wonder what she jolly well *did* want. She wouldn't let me help her to stop where she was, and she didn't seem anxious for anyone to help her to go anywhere else.

B.G.S.S. R

She was quite peculiar about it. She gripped hold of my arm, and said :

" What do you think this is that's coming ? "

I said :

" I'm sure I don't know, being a stranger in these parts, but it sounds like a lorry full of milk cans."

I offered to lay her sixpence about it (this was before the betting-tax came in). She'd have had to pay, too, because it *was* a lorry full of milk cans. The driver had to pull up because there wasn't room to get by.

He got down and asked if there was anything he could do to help. We explained the situation. He said he was going to Norwich, and was quite ready to give her a tow if she wanted it. However, she wouldn't do that, and it was finally decided to shove her car into my garage for the night, to be sent for next day, and the lorry was to take her along to Norwich.

Well, I managed to find the key of the garage, and the lorry-driver—Williams, his name was—and I ran the car in and locked the door. This having been done—(ablative absolute)—I suggested that it was a very cold night. Williams agreed, and said he didn't mind if he did. So I took them both indoors and mixed them a stiff whisky and water each. There wasn't any soda. And, naturally, the whole thing had left *me* very cold, too. I hadn't an overcoat on.

Up to now I hadn't seriously considered the young woman. For one thing it had been dark, *and* there had been a seized engine to look at. Er—I'm afraid that's not a very gallant remark. What I mean is that to anyone with a mechanical mind a motor-car in that condition is much more interesting than—er—well, it *is* very interesting—but why labour the point ? However, in the sitting-room, in the lamplight, it was possible to get more of an idea. She was a little older than I'd thought, and her eyes were too close together.

Of course, she wasn't a—how shall I put it ? Her manners weren't quite easy and she was careful with her English. *You* know. But that wasn't it. She treated us with a lack of friendliness which was—well, we'd done nothing to deserve it. There was a sort of vague hostility and suspicion, which seemed rather hard lines, considering. Also, she was so anxious to keep in the shadow that if I hadn't moved the lamp away she'd never have got near the fire at all.

And the way she hurried the wretched Williams over his drink was quite distressing ; and foolish, too, as *he* was going to drive, but that was her—funnel. When he'd gone out to start up his engine I asked her if she was all right for money, and she apparently was. Then they started off, and I shut up the place and went upstairs.

There happened to be a local guide-book in my bedroom, with maps in it. I looked at these and couldn't help wondering where the girl in the car had come from ; I mean my road seemed so very unimportant. The sort of road one might use if one wanted to avoid people. If one were driving a stolen car, for instance. This was quite a thrilling idea. I thought it might be worth while having another look at the car. So I once more unhooked the key from the kitchen dresser and sallied forth into the snow. It was as black as pitch, and so still that my candle hardly flickered. It wasn't a large garage, and the car nearly filled it. By the by, we'd backed it in so as to make it easier to tow it out again.

The engine I'd already seen, so I squeezed past along the wall and opened the door in the body part of the car. At least, I only turned the handle, and the door was pushed open from the inside and—something—fell out on me. It pushed me quite hard, and wedged me against the wall. It also knocked the candle out of my hand and left me in the dark— which was a bit of a nuisance. I wondered what on earth the thing was—barging into me like that—so I felt it, rather gingerly, and found it was a man—a dead man—with a moustache. He'd evidently been sitting propped up against the door. I managed to put him back, as decorously as possible, and shut the door again.

After a lot of grovelling about under the car I found the candle and lighted it, and opened the opposite door and switched on the little lamp in the roof—and then—oo-er !

Of course, I had to make some sort of examination. He was an extremely tall and thin individual. He must have been well over six feet three. He was dark and very cadaverous looking. In fact, I don't suppose he'd ever looked so cadaverous in his life. He was wearing a trench coat.

It wasn't difficult to tell what he'd died of. He'd been shot through the back. I found the hole just under the right scrofula, or scalpel—what is shoulder-blade, anyway ? Oh, clavicle — stupid of me — well, that's where it was, and the bullet had evidently gone through into the lung. I say " evidently," and leave it at that.

There were no papers in his pockets, and no tailor's name

on his clothes, but there was a note-case, with nine pounds in it. Altogether a most unpleasant business. Of course, it doesn't do to question the workings of Providence, but one couldn't help wishing it hadn't happened. It was just a little mysterious, too—er—who had killed him ? It wasn't likely that the girl had or she wouldn't have been joy-riding about the country with him ; and if someone else had murdered him why hadn't she mentioned it ? Anyway, she hadn't and she'd gone, so one couldn't do anything for the time being. No telephone, of course. I just locked up the garage and went to bed. That was two o'clock.

Next morning I woke early, for some reason or other, and it occurred to me as a good idea to go and have a look at things —by daylight, and before Mrs. Selston turned up. So I did. The first thing that struck me was that it had snowed heavily during the night, because there were no wheel tracks or footprints, and the second was that I'd left the key in the garage door. I opened it and went in. The place was completely empty. No car, no body, no nothing. There was a patch of grease on the floor where I'd dropped the candle, otherwise there was nothing to show I'd been there before. One of two things must have happened : either some people had come along during the night and taken the car away, or else I'd fallen asleep in front of the fire and dreamt the whole thing.

Then I remembered the whisky glasses.

They should still be in the sitting-room. I went back to look, and they were, all three of them. So it *hadn't* been a dream and the car *had* been fetched away, but they must have been jolly quiet over it.

The girl had left her glass on the mantelpiece, and it showed several very clearly defined finger-marks. Some were mine, naturally, because I'd fetched the glass from the kitchen and poured out the drink for her, but hers, her finger-marks, were clean, and mine were oily, so it was quite easy to tell them apart. It isn't necessary to point out that this glass was very important. There'd evidently been a murder, or something of that kind, and the girl must have known all about it, even if she hadn't actually done it herself, so anything she had left in the way of evidence ought to be handed over to the police ; and this was all she *had* left. So I packed it up with meticulous care in an old biscuit-box out of the larder.

When Mrs. Selston came, I settled up with her and came

back to Town. Oh, I called on the landlord on the way and told him I'd " let him know " about the bungalow. Then I caught my train, and in due course drove straight to Scotland Yard. I went up and saw my friend there. I produced the glass and asked him if his people could identify the marks. He said, " Probably not," but he sent it down to the finger-print department and asked me where it came from. I said : " Never you mind ; let's have the identification first." He said : " All right."

They're awfully quick, these people—the clerk was back in three minutes with a file of papers. They knew the girl all right. They told me her name and showed me her photo-graph ; not flattering. Quite an adventurous lady, from all accounts. In the early part of her career she'd done time twice for shoplifting, chiefly in the book department. Then she'd what they call " taken up with " a member of one of those race-gangs one sometimes hears about.

My pal went on to say that there's been a fight between two of these gangs, in the course of which her friend had got shot. She'd managed to get him away in a car, but it had broken down somewhere in Norfolk. So she'd left it and the dead man in someone's garage, and had started off for Norwich in a lorry. Only she never got there. On the way the lorry had skidded, and both she and the driver—a fellow called Williams—had been thrown out, and they'd rammed their heads against a brick wall, which everyone knows is a fatal thing to do. At least, it was in their case.

I said : " Look here, it's all very well, but you simply can't know all this ; there hasn't been time—it only happened last night."

He said : " Last night be blowed ! It all happened in February, nineteen nineteen. The people you've described have been dead for years."

I said : " Oh ! "

And to think that I might have stuck to that nine pounds !

ALPHA OF THE PLOUGH (1865—   )
*is a journalist and a skilled biographer as well
as a writer of fiction. He has also produced
several important books on affairs of the day
under his own name of A. G. Gardiner, of
which the best known is "The Pillars of
Society." The charming essays of "Alpha
of the Plough" were written during the War
as a diversion from the anxiety of the times.*

ON A MAP OF THE OBERLAND

I WAS rummaging among my books this morning when I
came across Frey's map of the Bernese Oberland, and
forthwith forgot the object of my search in the presence of this
exhilarating discovery. Mr. Chesterton, I think, once described how he evoked the emotions of a holiday by calling a
cab, piling it up with luggage, and driving to the station.
Then, having had his sensation, he drove home again. It
seemed to me rather a poor way of taking an imaginative holiday.
One might as well heat an empty oven in order to imagine a
feast. The true medium of the spiritual holiday is the map.
That is the magic carpet that whisks you away from this sodden
earth and unhappy present to sunny lands and serener days.

There are times when books offer no escape from the burden
of things, when, as Mr. Biglow says

> *I'm as unsoshul as a stone,*
> *And kind o' suffercate to be alone;*

but there are no circumstances in which a map will not do the
trick. I do not care whether it is a map of the known or the
unknown, the visited or the unvisited, the real or the fanciful.
It was the jolly map which Stevenson invented in an idle hour
which became the seed of *Treasure Island*. That is how a map
stimulated his fancy and sent it out on a career of immortal
adventure. And though you have not Stevenson's genius for
describing the adventure, that is what a map will do for you
if you have a spark of the boy's love of romance left in your
soul. It is the " magic casement " of the poet. I have never
crossed the Atlantic in the flesh, but, lord, what spiritual
adventures I have had with maps in the enchanted world on

the other side! I have sailed with Drake in Nombre Dios Bay, and navigated the grim straits with Magellan, and lived with the Incas of Peru and the bloody Pizarro, and gone up the broad bosom of the Amazon into fathomless forests, and sailed through the Golden Gates on golden afternoons, and stood with Cortes " silent upon a peak in Darien." I know the Shenandoah Valley far better than I know Wimbledon Common, and have fought over every inch of it by the side of Stonewall Jackson, just as I have lived in the mazes of the Wilderness with Grant and Lee.

Do not tell me I have never been to these places and a thousand others like them. I swear that I have. I have traversed them all in the kingdom of the mind, and if you will give me a map and a rainy day (like this) I will go on a holiday more entrancing than any that Mr. Cook ever planned. It is not taking tickets that makes the traveller. I have known people who have gone round the world without seeing anything, while Thoreau could stay in his back garden and entertain the universe.

But if maps of the unvisited earth have the magic of romance in them, maps of the places you have known have a fascination no less rich and deep. They, too, take you out on a holiday, but it is a holiday of memory and not of the imagination. You are back with yourself in other days and in other places and with other friends. You may tell me that this was a dreary, rainy morning, sir, and that I spent it looking out over the dismal valley and the sad cornfields with their stricken crops. Nothing of the sort. I spent it in the Bernese Oberland, with an incomparable companion. Three weeks I put in, sir, three weeks on the glaciers. See, there, on this glorious map of Frey's, is Mürren, from whence we started. In front is the mighty snow mass of the Jungfrau, the Mönch and the Eiger, shutting out the glacier solitudes whither we are bound.

There goes our track up the ravine to Obersteinberg and there is the Mütthorn hut, standing on the bit of barren rock that sticks out from the great ice-billows of the Tschingelhorn glacier. Do you remember, companion of mine, the mighty bowls of steaming tea we drank when we reached that haven of refuge? And do you remember our start from the hut at two o'clock in the morning, roped with our guide and with our lanterns lit—and the silence of our march over the snow and ice beneath the glittering stars, and the hollow boom of distant avalanches, and the breaking of the wondrous dawn over the ice-fields, and the unforgettable view as we reached the ridge

of the Petersgrat and saw across the Rhone Valley the great
mountain masses beyond—the Weisshorn, the Matterhorn,
Mont Blanc, and the rest—touched to an unearthly beauty by
the flush of the new-risen sun ? And the scramble up the
Tschingelhorn, and the long grind down the ice slopes and the
moraine to the seclusion of the Lötschenthal ? And then the
days that followed in the great ice region behind the Jungfrau ;
the long, silent marches over pathless snows and by yawning
crevasses, the struggle up peaks in the dawn, and the nights
in the huts, sometimes with other climbers who blew in across
the snows from some remote adventure, sometimes alone as in
that tiny hut on the Finsteraarhorn, where we paid three and a
half francs for a bunch of wood to boil our kettle ?

There is the Oberaar hut standing on the ledge of a dizzy
precipice. Do you remember the sunset we saw from thence,
when out of the general gloom of the conquering night one
beam from the vanished sun caught the summit of the Dom
and made it gleam like a palace in the heavens or like the towers
of the radiant city that Christian saw across the dark river ?
And there at the end of the journey is the great glacier that
leaps down, seven thousand feet, between the Schreckhorn and
the Wetterhorn, to the gracious valley of Grindelwald. How
innocent it looks on this map, but what a day of gathering
menace was that when we got caught between the impassable
crevasses, and night came on and the rain came down and . . .
But let the magic carpet hasten slowly here. . . .

It was still dark when Heinrich of the Looking Glass leapt
up from our bed of hay in the Dolfuss hut, lit the candle and
began to prepare the breakfast. Outside, the rain fell in torrents
and the clouds hung thick and low over glacier and peaks.
Our early start for the Gleckstein hut was thwarted. Night
turned to dawn and dawn to day, and still the rain pelted
down on that vast solitude of rock and ice. Then the crest of
the Finsteraarhorn appeared through a rent in the clouds,
patches of blue broke up the grey menace of the sky, the
rain ceased. Otmar and Heinrich hastily washed the iron cups
and plates and swept the floor of the hut, and then, shouldering
our rucksacks and closing the door of the empty hut, we
scrambled down the rocks to the glacier.

It was 8.15 and the guide-books said it was a seven hours'
journey to the Gleckstein. That seemed to leave ample
margin ; but do not trust guide-books in a season of drought
when the crevasses are open.

This wisdom, however, came later. All through the morning we made excellent progress. The sun shone, the clouds hung lightly about the peaks, the ice was in excellent condition. Heinrich, who brought up the rear, occasionally broke into song. Now, when Heinrich sings you know that all is well. When he whistles you are in a tight place. For the rest he is silent. Otmar, his brother, is less communicative. He goes on ahead silently under all conditions, skirting crevasses, testing snow-bridges to see if they will bear, occasionally pausing to consult his maps. Once only did he burst into song that day—but of that later. Otmar is an autocrat on the ice or the rocks. In the hut he will make your tea and oil your boots and help Heinrich to wash your cups and sweep the floor. But out in the open he is your master. If you ask him inconvenient questions he does not hear. If you suggest a second breakfast before it is due his silence as he pounds forward ahead humiliates you. If your pace slackens there is a rebuke in the taut insistence of the rope.

It was eleven when we halted for our cold tea and sardines (white wine for Otmar and Heinrich). The pause gave Heinrich an opportunity of taking out his pocket looking-glass and touching up his moustache ends and giving a flick to his eyebrows. Heinrich is as big and brawny as an ox, but he has the soul of a dandy.

It had been easy going on the furrowed face of the ice, but when we came to the snow slope that leads to the Lauteraar saddle our pace slackened. The snow was soft, and we sank at each step up to our shins. Otmar eased the passage up the slope by zigzagging, but it was one o'clock when we came face to face with the wall of snow, flanked by walls of rock, which form the " saddle." Otmar led my companion over the rocks ; but decided that Heinrich should bring me up the snow face. Step cutting is slow work, and though Otmar, having reached the top of the saddle, threw down a second rope, which Heinrich lashed round his waist, it was two o'clock before that terrible wall was surmounted, and we could look down the great glacier that plunged seven thousand feet down into the hollow where Grindelwald lay with its red roofs and pleasant pastures, its hotels and its tourists.

We had taken nearly six hours to surmount the pass ; but we seemed, nevertheless, to have the day well in hand. Four thousand feet down on a spur of the Wetterhorn we could see the slate roof of the Gleckstein hut. It seemed an easy walk over the glacier, but in these vast solitudes of ice and snow and rock, vision is deceptive. The distant seems incredibly near, for the familiar measurements of the eye are wanting.

The weather had changed again. Clouds had settled on the mighty cliffs of the Schreckhorn on our left and the Wetterhorn on our right. Mist was rolling over the pass ; rain began to fall. We cut short our lunch (cold tea, cold veal, bread and jam), and began our descent, making a wide detour of the glacier to the right in the direction of the Wetterhorn. We descended a rocky precipice that cleaves the glacier, crossed an ice slope on which Otmar had to cut steps, and came in view of Grindelwald, lying like a picture postcard far down below—so immediately below that it seemed that one might fling a stone down into its midst.

At half-past three it began to dawn on me that things were not going well. Otmar had, during the past three weeks, been the most skilful of guides over most of the great glacier passes of the Oberland and up many a peak ; but so far we had seen nothing like the condition of the Grindelwaldfirn. The appalling slope of this great sea of ice makes a descent in normal times a task of difficulty. But this year the long drought had left open all the yawning crevasses with which it is seamed, and its perils were infinitely increased.

Again and again Otmar sought a way out of the maze, taking us across perilous snow-bridges and cutting steps on knife-edges of ice where one looked down the glittering slope on one side, and into the merciless green-blue depths of the crevasse on the other. But wherever he turned he was baulked. Always the path led to some vast fissure which could be neither leapt nor bridged. Once we seemed to have escaped and glissaded swiftly down. Then the slope got steeper and we walked—steeper and Otmar began cutting steps in the ice— steeper and Otmar paused and looked down the leap of the glacier. We stood silent for his verdict. " It will not go." We turned on the rope without a word, and began remounting our steps.

It was half-past four. The mist was thickening, the rain falling steadily. Below, the red roofs and green pastures of Grindelwald gleamed in the sunlight of the valley. Nearer, the slate roof of the Gleckstein on its spur of rock was still visible. Two hours before it had seemed but a step to either. Now they seemed to have receded to another hemisphere.

For the first time there flashed through the mind the thought that possibly we should not reach the hut after all. A night on the glacier, or rather on the dark ridges of the Wetterhorn ! A wet night, too.

The same thought was working in Otmar's mind. No word came from him, no hint that he was concerned. But the whole bearing of the man was changed. In the long hours of the morning he had led us listlessly and silently ; now he was like a hound on the trail. The tug of the rope became more insistent. He made us face difficulties that he had skirted before ; took us on to snow-bridges that made the mind reel ; slashed steps with his ice axe with a swift haste that spoke in every stroke of the coming night. Once I failed to take a tricky snow ridge that came to a point between two crevasses, slipped back and found myself in the crevasse, with my feet dancing upon nothing. The rope held ; Otmar hauled me out without a word, and we resumed our march.

Heinrich had been unroped earlier and sent to prospect from above for a possible way out. We followed at his call, but he led us into new mazes, down into a great cavern in the glacier, where we passed over the ruined walls and buttresses of an ice cathedral, emerging on the surface of the glacier again, only to find ourselves once more checked by impassable gulfs.

It was now half-past five. We had been three and a half hours in vainly attempting to find a way down the ice. The mist had come thick upon us. The peaks were blotted out, Grindelwald was blotted out ; the hut was no longer visible. Only an hour and a half of light remained, and the whole problem was still unsolved. The possibility of a night on the ice or the rocks began to approach the sphere of certainty. My strength was giving out, and I slipped again and again in the ice steps. A kind of dull resignation had taken possession of the mind. One went forward in a stupor, responsive to the tug of the rope, but indifferent to all else.

Otmar was now really concerned. He came from a valley south of the Rhone, and was unfamiliar with this pass ; but he is of a great strain of Alpine guides, is proud of his achievements—he had led in the first ascent of the Zmutt ridge of the Matterhorn that year—and to be benighted on a glacier would have been a deadly blow to his pride.

He unroped himself, and dashed away in the direction of the ridge of the Wetterhorn, that plunged down on our right. We watched him skimming across crevasses, pausing here and there to slash a step in the ice for foothold, balancing himself on icy ridges and vanishing into a couloir of the mountain—first depositing his rucksack on the rocks to await his return. Five minutes passed—ten. Heinrich startled the silence with an halloo—no answer. A quarter of an hour—then, from far below, a faint cry came.

" It will go," said Heinrich, " get on." We hurried across the intervening ice, and met Otmar returning like a cat up the rocks. Down that narrow slit in the mountain we descended with headlong speed. There were drops of thirty and fifty feet, slabs of rock to cross with negligible foot and hand holds, passages of loose rock where a careless move would have sent great stones thundering on the heads of those before. Once Heinrich lowered me like a bale of goods down a smooth-faced precipice of fifty feet. Once he cried : " Quick : it is dangerous," and looking up at the crest of the Wetterhorn I saw a huge block of ice poised perilously above our downward path.

The night was now upon us. We were wet to the skin. A thunderstorm of exceptional violence added to the grimness of the setting. But we were down the ridge at last. We raced across a narrow tongue of the glacier and were safe on the spur of rocks where we knew the Gleckstein hut to be. But there was no light to guide us. We scrambled breathlessly over boulders and across torrents from the Wetterhorn, each of us hardly visible to the other in the thickening mist, save when the blaze of lightning flashed the scene into sudden and spectral clearness. At last we struck a rough mountain path, and five minutes later we lifted the latch of the hut.

" What is the time, Heinrich ? "

" Half-past eight."

" What would you have done, Otmar, if we had been benighted ? "

Otmar did not hear. But as he got the wood and made the fire, and emptied the rucksacks of our provisions, he began to sing in a pleasant tenor voice. And Heinrich joined in with his full bass.

And presently, stripped of our wet clothes and wrapped in blankets, we sat down to a glorious meal of steaming tea—in an iron teapot as large as a pail—tongue, soup, potted chicken, and jam.

" That was a narrow escape from a night on the mountains," I said.

" It is a very foolish glacier," said Heinrich.

Otmar said nothing.

Five hours later Otmar woke us from our bed of hay.

" It is fine," he said.   " The Wetterhorn will go."

.   .   .   .

As I look up it is still raining and the sad sheaves still stand in the sodden fields.   But I have been a journey.   I have had three weeks in the Oberland—three weeks of summer days with a world at peace, the world that seems like a dream we once had, so remote has it become and so incredible.   I roll up my magic carpet and bless the man who invented maps for the solace of men.

"BARTIMEUS" (1886–   ) *is the Biblical pen-name adopted by Paymaster Commander L. A. da Costa Ricci, whose books about the Navy are enjoyed by everyone in tune with the magic of the sea. His first book, "Naval Occasions," from which this story is taken, appeared in 1914, and received a warm welcome as one of the few authentic accounts of life in "The Silent Service" during the Great War.*

THE GREATER LOVE

THE sun was setting behind a lurid bank of cloud above the hills of Spain, and, as is usual at Gibraltar about that hour, a light breeze sprang up. It eddied round the Rock and scurried across the harbour, leaving dark cat's-paws in its trail : finally it reached the inner mole, alongside which a cruiser was lying.

A long pendant of white bunting, that all day had hung listlessly from the main topmast, stirred, wavered, and finally bellied out astern, the gilded bladder at the tail bobbing uneasily over the surface of the water.

The Officer of the Watch leaned over the rail and watched the antics of the bladder, round which a flock of querulous gulls circled and screeched. "The paying-off pendant [1] looks as if it were impatient," he said laughingly to an Engineer Lieutenant standing at his side.

The other smiled in his slow way and turned seaward, nodding across the bay towards Algeciras. "Not much longer to wait—there's the steamer with the mail coming across now." He took a couple of steps across the deck and turned. "Only another 1200 miles. Isn't it ripping to think of, after three years . . . ? " He rubbed his hands with boyish satisfaction. " All the coal in and stowed—boats turned in, funnels smoking —that's what I like to see ! Only the mail to wait for now : and the gauges down below "—he waggled his forefinger in the air, laughing—" like that . . . ! "

The Lieutenant nodded and hitched his glass under his arm. "Your middle watch, Shortie ? Mine too : we start

---

[1] A pendant, one-and-a-quarter times the length of the ship, flown by ships homeward bound under orders to pay off.

working up for our passage trial then, don't we ? Whack her up, lad—for England, Home, and Beauty ! "

The Engineer Lieutenant walked towards the hatchway. " What do *you* think ! " and went below humming—

" *From Ushant to Scilly* . . ."

The Lieutenant on watch turned and looked up at the Rock, towering over the harbour. Above the green-shuttered, pink and yellow houses, and dusty, sun-dried vegetation, the grim pile was flushing rose-colour against the pure sky. How familiar it was, he thought, this great milestone on the road to the East, and mused awhile, wondering how many dawns he had lain under its shadow : how many more sunsets he would watch and marvel at across the purple Bay.

" British as Brixton ! " He had read the phrase in a book once, describing Gibraltar. So it was, when you were homeward bound. He resumed his measured pacing to and fro. The ferry steamer had finished her short voyage and had gone alongside the wharf, out of sight behind an arm of the mole. Not much longer to wait now. He glanced at his wrist-watch. " Postie " wouldn't waste much time getting back. Not all the beer in Waterport Street nor all the glamour of the " Ramps " would lure him astray to-night. The Lieutenant paused in his measured stride and beckoned a side-boy. " Tell the signalman to let me know directly the postman is sighted coming along the mole."

He resumed his leisurely promenade, wondering how many letters there would be for him, and who would write. His mother, of course . . . and Ted at Charterhouse. His speculations roamed afield. Any one else ? Then he suddenly remembered the Engineer Lieutenant imitating the twitching gauge-needle with his forefinger. Lucky beggar he was. There was some one waiting for him who mattered more than all the Teds in the world. More even than a Mother—at least, he supposed. . . . His thoughts became abruptly sentimental and tender.

A signalman, coming helter-skelter down the ladder, interrupted them, as the Commander stepped out of his cabin on to the quarter-deck.

" Postman comin' with the mail, sir."

A few minutes later a hoist of flags whirled hurriedly to the masthead, asking permission to proceed " in execution of previous orders." What those orders were, even the paying-off pendant knew, trailing aft over the stern-walk in the light wind.

. . . .

The Rock lay far astern like a tinted shadow, an opal set in a blue-grey sea. Once beyond the Straits the wind freshened, and the cruiser began to lift her lean bows to the swell, flinging the spray aft along the forecastle in silver rain. The Marine bugler steered an unsteady course to the quarter-deck hatchway and sounded the Officers' Dinner Call.

> " *Officers' wives eat puddings and pies,*
> *But sailors' wives eat skilly . . .*"

chanted the Lieutenant of the impending first watch, swaying to the roll of the ship as he adjusted his tie before the mirror. He thumped the bulkhead between his cabin and the adjoining one.

" Buck up, Shortie ! " he shouted ; " it's Saturday Night at Sea ! Your night for a glass of port."

" Sweethearts and wives ! " called another voice across the flat. " You'll get drunk to-night, Snatcher, if you try to drink to all——" The voice died away and rose again in expostulation with a Marine servant. " . . . Well, does it *look* like a clean shirt . . . ! "

" Give it a shake, Pay, and put it on like a man ! " Some one else had joined in from across the flat. The Engineer Lieutenant pushed his head inside his neighbour's cabin : " Come along—come along ! You'll be late for dinner. Fresh grub to-night : no more ' Russian Kromeskis ' and ' Fanny Adams ' ! "

" One second. . . . Right ! " They linked arms and entered the Wardroom as the President tapped the table for grace. The Surgeon scanned the menu with interest. " Jasus ! Phwat diet ! " he ejaculated, quoting from an old Service story. " Listen ! " and read out—

" Soup : Clear."

" That's boiled swabs," interposed the Junior Watchkeeper.

" Mr. President, sir, I object—this Officer's unladylike conversation."

" Round of port—fine him ! " interrupted several laughing voices.

" Go on, Doc. ; what next ? "

" Fish : ' Mullets.' "

" Main drain loungers," from the Junior Watch-keeper.
" Isn't he a little Lord Fauntleroy—two rounds of port ! "

" *Entrée* : Russian Kromeskis——" A roar of protest.

" And—— ? "

" Mutton cutlets."

" Goat, he means. What an orgie ! Go on ; fain would
we hear the worst, fair chirurgeon," blathered the Paymaster.
" Joint ? "

" Joint ; mutton or——"

" Princely munificence," murmured the First Lieutenant.
" He's not a messman : he's a—a—what's the word ? "

" Philanthropist. What's the awful alternative ? "

" There isn't any ; it's scratched out." The A.P. and the
Junior Watch-keeper clung to each other. " The originality of
the creature ! And the duff ? "

" Rice-pudding."

" Ah me ! alack-a-day ! alas ! " The Paymaster tore his
hair. " I must prophesy . . . *must* prophesy,—shut up,
every one ! *Shut* up ! " He closed his eyes and pawed the air
feebly. " I'm a medium. I'm going to prophesy. I feel it
coming. . . . The savoury is . . . the savoury is "—there was
a moment's tense silence—" sardines on toast." He opened
his eyes. " Am I right, sir ? Thank you."

The Surgeon leaned forward, and picking up the massive
silver shooting trophy that occupied the centre of the table,
handed it to a waiter.

" Take that to the Paymaster, please. First prize for divina-
tion and second sight. And you, Snatcher—you'll go down
for another round of port if you keep on laughing with your
mouth full."

So the meal progressed. The " mullets " were disentangled
from their paper jackets amid a rustling silence of interrogation.
The Worcester sauce aided and abetted the disappearance of
the Russian Kromeskis, as it had so often done before. The
mutton was voted the limit, and the rice-pudding held evidences that the cook's hair wanted cutting. The Junior Watch-
keeper—proud officer of that functionary's division—vowed
he'd have it cut in a manner which calls for no description in
these pages. There weren't any sardines on toast. The
Philanthropist appeared in person, with dusky, upturned
palms, to deplore the omission.

" Ow ! signor—olla fineesh ! I maka mistake ! No have
got sardines, signor . . . ! "

" Dear old Ah Ying ! " sighed the Engineer Lieutenant, " I never really loved him till this minute. Why did we leave him at Hong-Kong and embark this snake-in-the-grass. . . . No sardines . . . ! "

But for all that every one seemed to have made an admirable meal, and the Chaplain's " For what we have received, thank God ! " brought it to a close. The table was cleared, the wine decanters passed round, and once again the President tapped with his ivory mallet. There was a little silence—

" Mr. Vice—the King ! "

The First Lieutenant raised his glass. " Gentlemen—the King ! "

" The King ! " murmured the Mess, with faces grown suddenly decorous and grave. At that moment the Corporal of the Watch entered ; he glanced down the table, and approaching the Junior Watch-keeper's chair saluted and said something in an undertone. The Junior Watch-keeper nodded, finished his port, and rose, folding his napkin. His neighbour, the Engineer Lieutenant, leaned back in his chair, speaking over his shoulder—

" Your First Watch, James ? "

The other nodded.

" Then," with mock solemnity, " may I remind you that our lives are in your hands till twelve o'clock ? Don't forget that, will you ? "

The Junior Watch-keeper laughed. " I'll bear it in mind." At the doorway he turned with a smile : " It won't be the first time your valuable life has been there."

" Or the last, we'll hope."

" We'll hope not, Shortie."

The buzz of talk and chaff had again begun to ebb and flow round the long table. The First Lieutenant lit a cigarette and began collecting napkin-rings, placing them eventually in a row, after the manner of horses at the starting-post. " Seven to one on the field, bar one—Chief, your ring's disqualified. It would go through the ship's side. Now, wait for the next roll—stand by ! Clear that flower-pot——"

" Disqualified be blowed ! Why, I turned it myself when I was a student, out of a bit of brass I stole——"

" Can't help that ; it weighs a ton—scratched at the post ! "

The Commander tapped the table with his little hammer—

" May I remind you all that it's Saturday Night at Sea ? " and gave the decanters a little push towards his left-hand neighbour. The First Lieutenant brushed the starters into a heap at his side ; the faintest shadow passed across his brow.

" So it is ! " echoed several voices.

" Now, Shortie, fill up ! Snatcher, you'd better have a bucket. . . . ' There's a Burmah girl a-settin' an' I know she thinks,'—port, Number One ? " The First Lieutenant signed an imperceptible negation and pushed the decanter round, murmuring something about hereditary gout.

It was ten years since he had drunk that toast : since a certain tragic dawn, stealing into the bedroom of a Southsea lodging, found him on his knees at a bedside. . . . They all knew the story, as men in Naval Messes afloat generally do know each other's tragedies and joys. And yet his right-hand neighbour invariably murmured the same formula as he passed the wine on Saturday nights at sea. In its way it was considered a rather subtle intimation that no one wanted to pry into his sorrow—even to the extent of presuming that he would never drink that health again.

In the same way they all knew that it was the one occasion on which the little Engineer Lieutenant permitted himself the extravagance of wine. He was saving up to get married ; and perhaps for the reason that he had never mentioned the fact, every one not only knew it, but loved and chaffed him for it.

The decanters travelled round, and the First Lieutenant leaned across to the Engineer Lieutenant, who was contemplatively watching the smoke of his cigarette. There was a whimsical smile in the grave, level eyes.

" I suppose we shall have to think about rigging a garland [1] before long, eh ? "

The other laughed half-shyly. " Yes, before long, I hope, Number One."

Down came the ivory hammer—

" Gentlemen—Sweethearts and Wives ! "

" And may they never meet ? " added the Engineer Commander. In reality the most domesticated and blameless of husbands, it was the ambition of his life to be esteemed a sad dog, and that men should shake their heads over him crying " Fie ! "

The First Lieutenant gathered together his silver rings. " Now then, clear the table. She's rolling like a good 'un. Seven to one on the field, bar——"

[1] A garland of evergreens is triced up to the triatic stay between the masts on the occasion of an officer's marriage.

" Speech ! " broke in the Paymaster. " Speech, Shortie ! Few words by a young officer about to embark on the troubled sea of matrimony. Hints on the Home——"

The prospective bridegroom shook his head, laughing, and coloured in a way rather pleasant to see. He rose, pushing in his chair. In the inside pocket of his mess-jacket was an unopened letter, saved up to read over a pipe in peace.

" My advice to you all is——"

" ' Don't,' " from the Engineer Commander.

" Mind your own business," and the Engineer Lieutenant fled from the Mess amid derisive shouts of " Coward ! " The voice of the First Lieutenant rose above the hubbub——

" Seven to one on the field—and what about a jump or two ? Chuck up the menu-card, Pay. Now, boys, roll, bowl, or pitch . . . ' Every time a blood-orange or a good see-gar ' . . . ! "

.   .   .   .

The Officer of the First Watch leaned out over the bridge rails, peering into the darkness that enveloped the forecastle, and listening intently. The breeze had freshened, and the cruiser slammed her way into a rising sea, labouring with the peculiar motion known as a " cork-screw roll " : the night was very dark. Presently he turned and walked to the chart-house door : inside, the Navigation Officer was leaning over the chart, wrinkling his brows as he pencilled a faint line.

" Pilot," said the other, " just step out here a second."

The Navigator looked up, pushing his cap from his forehead. " What's up ? "

" I think the starboard anchor is ' talking.' I wish you'd come and listen a moment." The Navigator stepped out on to the bridge, closing the chart-house door after him, and paused a moment to accustom his eyes to the darkness. " Dark night, isn't it ? Wind's getting up, too. . . ." He walked to the end of the bridge and leaned out. The ship plunged into a hollow with a little shudder and then flung her bows upwards into a cascade of spray. A dull metallic sound detached itself from the sibilant rushing of water and the beat of waves against the ship's side, repeating faintly with each roll of the ship from the neighbourhood of the anchor-bed. The Navigator nodded : " Yes, . . . one of the securing chains wants tautening, I should say. ' Saltash Luck ' [1] for some one ! " He moved back into the chart-house and picked up the parallel-rulers again.

[1] A thorough wetting.

The Lieutenant of the Watch went to the head of the ladder and called the Boatswain's Mate, who was standing in the lee of the conning-tower yarning with the Corporal of the Watch—

"Pipe the duty sub. of the watch to fall in with oilskins on ; when they're present take them on to the forecastle and set up the securing chain of the starboard bower-anchor. Something's worked loose. See that any one who goes outside the rail has a bowline on."

"Aye, aye, sir." The Boatswain's Mate descended the ladder, giving a few preliminary " cheeps " with his pipe before delivering himself of his tidings of " Saltash Luck " to the duty sub. of the port watch.

The Officer of the Watch gave an order to the telegraph-man on the bridge, and far below in the Engine-room they heard the clang of the telegraph gongs. He turned into the chart-house and opened the ship's log, glancing at the clock as he did so. Then he wrote with a stumpy bit of pencil—

"9.18. Decreased speed to 6 knots. Duty Sub. secured starboard bower-anchor."

He returned to the bridge and leaned over the rail, straining his eyes into the darkness and driving spray towards the indistinct group of men working on the streaming forecastle. In the light of a swaying lantern he could make out a figure getting out on to the anchor-bed ; another was turning up with a rope's end ; he heard the faint click of a hammer on metal. The ship lurched and plunged abruptly into the trough of a sea. An oath, clear-cut and distinct, tossed aft on the wind, and a quick shout.

He turned aft and rushed to the top of the ladder, bawling down between curved palms with all the strength of his lungs.

.　　.　　.　　.　　.　　.　　.

The Engineer Lieutenant who left the Wardroom after dinner did not immediately go on deck. He went first to his cabin, where he filled and lit a pipe, and changed his mess-jacket for a comfortable, loose-fitting monkey-jacket. Then he settled down in his arm-chair, wedged his feet against the bunk to steady himself against the roll of the ship, and read his letter. Often as he read he smiled, and once he blinked a little, misty-eyed. The last sheet he re-read several times.

" . . . Oh, isn't it good to think of ! It was almost worth the pain of separation to have this happiness now—to know that every minute is bringing you nearer. I wake up in the morning with that happy sort of feeling that something nice is

going to happen soon—and then I realise : you are coming
Home ! I jump out of bed and tear another leaf off the calendar,
—there are only nine left now, and then comes one marked
with a big cross. . . . Do you know the kind of happiness that
hurts ? Or is it only a girl who can feel it ? . . . I pray every
night that the days may pass quickly, and that you may come
safely."

It was a very ordinary little love-letter, with its shy admixture of love and faith and piety : the sort so few men ever earn,
and so many (in Heaven's mercy) are suffered to receive. The
recipient folded it carefully, replaced it in its envelope, and
put it in his pocket. Then he lifted his head suddenly,
listening. . . .

Down below, the Engine-room telegraph gong had clanged,
and the steady beat of the engines slowed. With an eye on his
wrist-watch, he counted the muffled strokes of the piston. . . .
Decreased to 6 knots. What was the matter ? Fog ? He rose
and leaned over his bunk, peering through the scuttle. Quite
clear. He decided to light a pipe and go on deck for a
" breather " before turning in, and glanced at the little clock
ticking on the bulkhead. Twenty past nine ; ten minutes walk
on the quarter-deck and then to bed. It was his middle watch.

As he left his cabin some one in the Wardroom began
softly playing the piano, and the Paymaster's clear baritone
joined in, singing a song about somebody's grey eyes watching
for somebody else. The Mess was soaking in sentiment
to-night : must be the effect of Saturday Night at Sea, he
reflected.

He reached the quarter-deck and stood looking round,
swaying easily with the motion of the ship. The sea was getting
up, and the wind blew a stream of tiny sparks from his pipe.
Farther aft the sentry on the life-buoys was mechanically
walking his beat, now toiling laboriously up a steep incline,
now trying to check a too precipitous descent. The Engineer
Lieutenant watched him for a moment, listening to the notes
of the piano tinkling up through the open skylight from the
Wardroom.

> *"I know of two white arms*
> *Waiting for me . . ."*

The singer had started another verse ; the Engineer Lieutenant
smiled faintly, and walked to the ship's side to stare out into the
darkness. Why on earth had they slowed down ? A sudden

impatience filled him. Every minute was precious now. Why——

"MAN OVERBOARD. AWAY LIFEBOAT'S CREW!" Not for nothing had the Officer of the Watch received a "Masts and Yards" upbringing; the wind forward caught the stentorian shout and hurled it along the booms and battery, aft to the quarter-deck where the little Engineer Lieutenant was standing, one hand closed over the glowing bowl of his pipe, the other thrust into his trousers pocket.

The Engine-room telegraph began clanging furiously, the sound passing up the casings and ventilators into the night; then the Boatswain's Mate sent his ear-piercing pipe along the decks, calling away the lifeboat's crew. The sentry on the life-buoys wrenched at the releasing knob of one of his charges and ran across to the other.

The leaden seconds passed, and the Engineer Lieutenant still stood beside the rail, mechanically knocking the ashes from his pipe. . . . Then something went past on the crest of a wave: something white that might have been a man's face, or broken water showing up in the glare of a scuttle. . . . A sound out of the darkness that might have been the cry of a low-flying gull.

Now it may be argued that the Engineer Lieutenant ought to have stayed where he was. Going overboard on such a night was too risky for a man whose one idea was to get home as quickly as possible—who, a moment before, had chafed at the delay of reduced speed. Furthermore, he had in his pocket a letter bidding him come home safely; and for three years he had denied himself his little luxuries for love of her who wrote it. . . .

All the same—would she have him stand and wonder if that was a gull he had heard . . . ?

Love of women, Love of life. . . . ! Mighty factors—almost supreme. Yet a mortal has stayed in a wrecked stoke-hold, amid the scalding steam, to find and shut a valve; Leper Settlements have their doctors and pastor; and "A very gallant Gentleman" walks unhesitatingly into an Antarctic blizzard, to show there is a love stronger and higher even than these.

The Engineer Lieutenant was concerned with none of these fine thoughts. For one second he did pause, looking about as if for somewhere to put his pipe. Then he tossed it on to the deck, scrambled over the rail, took a deep breath, and dived.

The Marine sentry ran to the side of the ship.

" *Christ !* " he gasped, and forsook his post, to cry the tale aloud along the seething battery.

The ship shuddered as the engines were reversed, and the water under the stern began to seethe and churn. The Commander had left his cabin, and was racing up to the bridge, as the Captain reached the quarter-deck. A knot of officers gathered on the after-bridge.

" Pin's out, sir ! " shouted the Coxswain of the sea-boat, and added under his breath, " Oars all ready, lads ! Stan' by to pull like bloody 'ell—there's two of 'em in the ditch. . . ." The boat was hanging a few feet above the tumbling water.

" Slip ! " shouted a voice from the invisible fore-bridge. An instant's pause, and the boat dropped with a crash on to a rising wave. There was a clatter and a thud of oars in rowlocks ; the clanking of the chain-slings, and the boat, with her motley-clad [1] life-belted crew, slid off down the slant of a wave. For a moment the glare of an electric light lit the faces of the men, tugging and straining grimly at their oars ; then she vanished, to reappear a moment later on the crest of a sea, and disappeared again into the darkness.

The Commander on the fore-bridge snatched up a megaphone, shouting down-wind—

" Pull to starboard, cutter ! Make for the life-buoy light ! "

The watchers on the after-bridge were peering into the night with binoculars and glasses. The A.P. extended an arm and forefinger : " There's the life-buoy—there ! . . . Now—there ! D'you see it ? You can just see the flare when it lifts on a wave. . . . Ah ! That's better ! "

The dazzling white beam from a search-light on the fore-bridge leaped suddenly into the night. " Now we can see the cutter—" the beam wavered a moment and finally steadied. " Yes, there they are. . . . I say, there's a devil of a sea running."

" Ripping sea-boats our Service cutters are," said another, staring through his glasses. " They'll live in almost anything ; but this isn't a dangerous sea. The skipper 'll turn in a minute and make a lee for them."

" Think old Shortie reached the buoy ? "

" Probably swimming about looking for the other fellow, if I know anything of him ; who did he go in after ? "

" One of the duty sub.—they were securing the anchor or something forward, and the bowline slipped——"

[1] Any one near the boat responds to the call " Away Lifeboat's crew ! "

. . . and Willy Sparling, with a broken collar-bone, collapsed dramatically enough.

" By gad ! He's got him ! There's the buoy—yes, two of
them. *Good* old Shortie. . . . My God ! *Good* old Shortie ! "
The speaker executed a sort of war-dance and trod on the
Paymaster's toes.

" When you've quite finished, Snatcher. . . . By the way,
what about hot-water bottles—blankets—stimulants. . . . First
aid : come along ! ' Assure the patient in a loud voice that he
is safe.' . . . ' Aspect cheerful but subdued.' . . . I learned
the whole rigmarole once ! "

From the fore upper bridge the Captain was handling his
ship like a picket-boat.

" 'Midships—steady ! Stop both ! " He raised his mouth
from the voice-pipe to the helmsman, and nodded to the
Officer of the Watch. " She'll do now. . . . The wind 'll
take her down."

The Commander leaned over the rail and called the Boatswain's Mate—

" Clear lower deck ! Man the falls ! "

The ranks of men along the ship's side turned inboard, and
passed the ropes aft, in readiness to hoist the boat. There
were three hundred men on the falls, standing by to whisk the
cutter to the davit-heads like a cockle-shell.

" They've got 'em—got 'em both ! " murmured the deep
voices : they spat impatiently. " What say, lads ? Stamp an'
go with 'er ? "

" Silence in the battery ! *Marry* ! "

The Commander was leaning over the bridge rails ; the
Surgeon and two Sick-berth Stewards were waiting by the
davits. Alongside the cutter was rising and falling on the
waves.

" All right, sir ! " The voice of the Coxswain came up
as if from the deep. They had hooked the plunging boat on
somehow, and his thumb-nail was a pulp. . . .

Three hundred pairs of eyes turned towards the fore-
bridge.

" *Hoist away !* "

No need for the Boatswain's Mate to echo the order ; no
need for the Petty Officers' " With a will, then, lads ! " They
rushed aft in a wild stampede, hauling with every ounce of
beef and strength in their bodies. The cutter, dripping and
swaying, her crew fending her off the rolling ship with their
stretchers, shot up to the davits.

" High 'nough ! "

The rush stopped like one man. Another pull on the after-fall—enough. She was hoisted. " *Walk back !* . . . *Lie to !* "

A tense silence fell upon the crowded battery : the only sound that of men breathing hard. A limp figure was seen descending the Jacob's ladder out of the boat, assisted by two of the crew. Ready hands were outstretched to help, and the next moment Willie Sparling, Ordinary Seaman, Official Number 13728, was once more on the deck of a man-of-war—a place he never expected to see again.

" Ow ! " He winced, " Min' my shoulder—its 'urted. . . . " He looked round at the familiar faces lit by the electric lights, and jerked his head back at the boat hanging from her davits. " *'E* saved my life—look after 'im. 'E's a . . . 'e's a—bleedin' 'ero, . . . " and Willie Sparling, with a broken collar-bone, collapsed dramatically enough.

The Engineer Lieutenant swung himself down on to the the upper deck and stooped to wring the water from his trousers. The Surgeon seized him by the arm—

" Come along, Shortie—in between the blankets with you ! "

The hero of the moment disengaged his arm and shook himself like a terrier. " Blankets be blowed—it's my Middle Watch."

The Surgeon laughed. " Plenty of time for that : it's only just after half-past nine. What about a hot toddy ? "

" Lord ! I thought I'd been in the water for hours. . . . Yes, by Jove ! a hot toddy——" He paused and looked round, his face suddenly anxious. " By the way, . . . any one seen a pipe sculling about . . . ? "

Down below the telegraph gongs clanged, and the ship's bows swung round on to her course, heading once more for England, Home, and Beauty.

J. D. BERESFORD (1873–) *became famous with the publication before the Great War of an autobiographical novel-trilogy, "Jacob Stahl." His work shows remarkable powers of psychological analysis and command over his medium—be it the short story, detective fiction, sketch or novel. His precision of style and consummate craftsmanship have placed him right in the front rank of living novelists.*

REPARATION

THE belief in fate is as old as the history of man. It looms as a stupendous threat in the life of the savage, a dark influence challenging his every action with the menaces of taboo and totem. But we men and women of this twentieth century, with our knowledge of physics, our chemical theories of a mechanical cosmogony, our ready explanation of every natural and abnormal phenomenon, have won a partial freedom from the old slavery. We stand erect, defying the lightning of the gods and challenging the probability of any super-natural interference with the deliberate course of our ordered existences. We have new words for fate. We speak of chance, of coincidence, or, with a shrug of the shoulders, of luck. We look down with condescension at the feeble savage who cowers before the incomprehensible mandates of his intimate gods.

Even Angus Whitley himself, in these later, successful days of his, has come to smile whimsically at the idea that he could have been driven by the direct interference of any supernormal influence. His blue eyes have lost their old expression of wondering speculation. He is a made man, happily married, happily employed, and he prefers to believe, now, in chance or luck as the sole director of his destiny during those two years in which he worked his passage around the full circumference of the earth. He has almost forgotten, though I have not, the harried youngster of twenty-five who surged desperately through the streets of New York, hag-ridden by his furious urgency to end the amazing quest that was then speeding him to the close of his Odyssey.

But I remember his haunted face and the awed intonations

of his voice when he first told me his story ; and, while I
cannot definitely assert that throughout those two adventurous
years the spirit of Fuller Herbert stood at Whitley's elbow,
prodding him on to complete his mission, I do claim that some
deeper, more esoteric influence than luck must be postulated
to account for the apparent coincidences. Chance ? Yes ;
but what lies behind the appearance of chance ?

Whitley, the young failure of twenty-three, was returning,
temporarily defeated, from Cape Town to London, when the
thing began. He had gone out eighteen months before as an
engineer, and somehow failed to make good. One could find
half a dozen reasons to account for his failure—his inexperience,
his lack of influence, the conditions of South Africa—it was
that uneasy period between the Jameson raid and the Boer
War. There is no need in any case to assume that the blight
had already settled upon him.

He had, it is true, known Fuller Herbert in Johannesburg,
as everybody knew him—that is to say, very slightly. In all
his seven years in South Africa, Herbert had never come
within sight of making a friend. He was a man apart from
the other competitors in the diamond-market, respected both
for his knowledge and his shrewdness, but passively disliked ;
until in the last six months of his stay that feeling was a trifle
mitigated by a feeling of pity. Everyone else but himself
knew that he was doomed, and he must have known it, subconsciously, though he fought against the realization until—
for his own purposes—it was too late. His trouble was some
complicated and rather mysterious disease of the liver, variously
diagnosed by Cape Town specialists as due to tuberculosis
and a malignant growth. Whatever it was, there can be no
question that during his last days the disease very seriously
affected his naturally eccentric mind.

He was a tall, thin man, with a long and prominent nose,
a little spiteful mouth, and a small but noticeably aggressive
chin. Even before the colour of his skin turned to a high
and bitter yellow he was remarkable for his ugliness. There
was something mediæval about it. He was like the incarnation
of some revolting caricature by Rowlandson or Gilray.

Young Whitley ran across him in Cape Town the day
before they sailed, and Herbert did what was for him an
unprecedented thing—he made what seemed to be a generous
offer when he heard that Angus was going to travel third class.

" No, no," he said. " Don't do that. You're just the

man I want for a secretary on the voyage. I'm going home
for good. No end of stuff to settle up. I want someone
badly."

In the surprise of the moment, Angus never thought of
refusing. He did not like Fuller Herbert—no one did—but
he anticipated no difficulty in putting up with him for three
weeks as an employer. Moreover, there was a queer urgency
about Fuller, then, that would brook no denial. He did
nothing, he seemed to have nothing to do, but his actions and
speech were those of a man who had a critical, even a vital,
engagement, five minutes ahead—an engagement that was
always waiting for him, that engrossed all his attention and
never matured.

His air of expectation was not less marked on the boat ;
indeed, it was rather exaggerated. Angus's duties as secretary
were purely imaginary. Herbert would take him down into
his cabin in the morning and begin by making some pretence
of business. He would stand by the port-hole—they steamed
north through a flat calm until they passed Las Palmas—and
mutter to himself, as if collecting his thoughts. Occasionally
a sentence or two would be addressed directly to Angus.

" There's a lot to be done," Herbert would say. " Everything ought to be rearranged. This afternoon . . ." Then
his glance would wander out through the port-hole, over
the diminished expanse of gleaming water, and he would add
absently, " This afternoon, perhaps—a few letters." It
seemed as if that immense appointment must be waiting for
him on the sky-line ; that it might come in sight, now, at
any minute.

Angus had his moments of uneasiness, at first. He was a
conscientious lad, and he felt that he was not earning his
passage. He even tried to make up for his idleness as a
secretary by offering his services as personal servant. But
Herbert was obviously bothered by these attentions, and
presently Angus settled down to doing nothing, with the
consolation that it was not *his* fault. He was young ; he was
on his way home ; he was going to see the girl he was engaged
to, after eighteen months' absence ; and if he had any presenti-
ment at all, it was that his luck would change, that he would
get a job in England, that everything was going to be—all
right.

Meanwhile Fuller Herbert's preoccupation increased with
every day's run northward. The record of that run was, in

fact, his sole interest. He never put into the sweep that the financiers continued to organise daily, despite the monotonous regularity of the readings, but he was invariably among the first to get the news. After that, he would stalk away to the quietest corner of the deck—it was too hot to go below—and watch out for that approaching crisis which might at any instant, one inferred, show itself on the horizon.

It was the day after passing Las Palmas that Fuller's reserve was suddenly broken. The boat was running, full steam, into an Atlantic gale. Angus had been in high spirits at dinner. His employer had not put in an appearance at that meal, but Angus's excitement was not due to any lack of restraint on that account, but rather to what seemed to him a welcome change after the deadly monotony of the weather during the earlier part of the trip. It pleased him to see the " fiddles " on the table, to anticipate a more than usually violent gale, to be taking part in some kind of adventure. He was talking eagerly about mining machinery to a man whose acquaintance he had recently made—a man who might be useful, Angus thought, congratulating himself on his worldly wisdom—when a steward summoned him to Herbert's cabin.

Herbert was in his bunk, lying on his side, and he did not open his eyes when Angus came in. For a minute, perhaps, Angus stood uncertainly awaiting his instructions. A sense of oppression and urgency had unexpectedly come to him as he entered that confined space. He laid a hand on the edge of the bunk to steady himself against the roll of the boat, which was getting the force of the increasing gale full on her quarter. But it was not the roaring of the sea smashing now and again passionately at the deadlight that disconcerted him. That fury outside was the splendid, natural vigour of the elements, a revel in which he would willingly have joined. It was the tense, in some way rigid, atmosphere of the cabin that dismayed him. It seemed as if that repulsive yellow figure in the bunk was tremendously holding this one little bubble of his surroundings, starkly stiff and resistant against the whole tumult of the earth ; as if by some incredible effort of will he was even defying the movement of time.

And when he spoke, his words came from him with an effect both of effort and of restraint that bespoke a double purpose. There was something that had to be done, while with the better part of his will and attention he kept back the entire forces of the universe from prematurely thrusting upon him the pressure of that long-expected appointment he had so anxiously awaited.

" Can you hear, Whitley ? " he began, still with his eyes closed, and the sound of his voice had a quality at once hard and shrill, like the twanging of a strained wire.

When Angus had reassured him he went on more rapidly, in broken, uneven sentences : " I've an important mission for you—a charge. Think of it as sacred—sacred. I shall know."

What he meant by that " I shall know " Angus did not pause to inquire. The sentence went straight down into his subconsciousness and stayed there for nearly two years. Only at the last did he wonder vaguely whether it were possible that Fuller could, indeed, have *known*.

" I knew a young woman—in England. I've written her name and address and put them inside the bag," Herbert continued. " All my fault—she was barely eighteen—and I couldn't forget—never could forget. . . . Good reasons— my brother—family. . . . Always wanted the family to think that I . . . My brother would make trouble—dispute the will if I put her down in it. He mustn't know. I've been putting diamonds aside for her. They're all right. The receipts are in the bag. I saved them for her, here and there. She may have a child. The diamonds for them both. But my brother mustn't know. All my other papers in order. There's nothing to show. I meant to give them to her myself. I was going home for that. Reparation . . . to make repara- tion. Couldn't forget . . ."

Angus, clutching the edge of the bunk, heard every syllable spoken by Herbert. His thin, intense voice seemed to occupy the cabin and drive out the multitudinous clamour of the storm. When he stopped speaking, all the noise of the sea and the ship came back with the rush of a sudden cataract.

" But do you mean that you want me to . . ." Angus began, and was surprised to find that he had to shout in order to make himself heard.

Herbert opened his eyes for the first time, and with a quick jerk shot his hand under his pillow. He produced a small leather bag and tendered it to Angus.

" Diamonds," he said, in a relaxed voice that broke weakly against the tumult. Then, raising himself slightly on his elbows, he closed his eyes again and made one more heroic effort to stay the procession of time.

"A sacred trust for you," he said, in those former shrill tones that made Angus think of a fine escape of highly compressed air. "Sacred. I was afraid I might not—be strong enough—deliver it myself. Chose you—Cape Town—deliberately—in case. Diamonds for Sarah Browning and her child—my child. Deliver as soon as you reach England. Tell no one. No one. My brother raise objections. Go now. See you again in the morning—complete arrangements."

He sank back with a long sigh, as if the pressure had been removed and the balance with the universe restfully stabilised.

Angus slipped the leather bag into his hip pocket and left the cabin with the solemnity of one afraid of disturbing a religious ceremony. But as soon as he had closed the door behind him he remembered his social duty and harried out the ship's doctor.

The doctor was in Herbert's cabin within a few minutes, but he was too late. Herbert had already gone to keep his appointment.

Angus Whitley's feeling with regard to his "sacred trust" when he landed at Southampton was mainly one of boredom. He should have been free to go to the girl he was engaged to and discuss their plans for the future; and instead of that he had to undertake a tedious journey to the Midlands to make this vicarious reparation. His one consolation was to be found in the romantic posings natural to his age and temperament. He saw himself definitely as the hero in the coming interview. He heard himself modestly disclaiming praise or reward. He came and showered amazing wealth on the head of Sarah Browning. He chose to picture her as a patient, beautiful woman, bowing her head to poverty and the slurs of evil reputation for the sake of her child—and when he had disposed upon her the priceless gift of freedom he retired, unassuming, almost bashful, but with the consciousness of having been the chance instrument of her happiness. He rehearsed that scene until he grew tired of it, and then thanked Heaven that with this one mission his connection with Fuller Herbert's past was finally closed. For all Herbert's other affairs were in strict order—papers, will, instructions, the address of his lawyer in London and that of his brother in Devonshire. The captain of the boat had charge of that. Not even Angus's testimony was required. When he had delivered the fortune in uncut stones, secretly deducted by the testator from the Herbert inheritance, Angus's work was finished.

He was certainly eager to get the job over. He had, as an offset to his romantic conception of himself as the delivering hero, an uneasy sense of doing something slightly illegal. He was aware of a new distrust of his fellow-travellers in the train that was taking him to the village home of the ill-used Sarah Browning. It is not every man of Angus's appearance who can afford to carry uncut diamonds to the value of perhaps fifty thousand pounds in his hip pocket. If, by some unhappy accident, that hoard were discovered, Angus realised that he might find it difficult to account for his possession of that little leather bag.

Besides that condensed wealth, the bag contained nothing but the official receipts for the money paid for the stones—a certificate of legal buying—and Sarah Browning's name and address on a slip of paper. Herbert had cautiously omitted any legal instrument, such as a deed of gift, that would have involved the admission of a fourth person into the secret. At the last, when his disease had got hold of him, he had without question been suffering from some kind of obsession with regard to this act of reparation. He had even kept it from Angus, his chosen messenger, until the very hour of his august engagement had actually sounded. . . .

Angus arrived at the little village of Halton, four miles from the cathedral city of Medboro', in the early afternoon. Now that he had actually reached his goal, his doubts had momentarily slipped from him. As he made his way toward the village post office, in order to discover the precise situation of Sarah Browning's house or cottage, he warmed again to his part of the glorious messenger.

The postmistress was a stout, communicative woman, with the inquisitive eyes of an official fully conscious of her importance in the management of village affairs.

" Sarah Browning," she repeated cautiously, with the air of one prepared to temporise. " Well, of course everyone knows Sally Browning. Why, she was 'ousemaid at the Rectory for—'ow long was it, four years or five ? "

" Isn't she there, now ? " Angus asked.

" No ! " the postmistress returned, and somehow succeeded in making a whole report out of her monosyllable. Her expression was a little coy, as if she asked whether this stranger was not poking fun at her. She obviously deemed it incredible that anyone should believe that Sally Browning was still housemaid at the Rectory.

Angus misread the ingenuousness of one absorbed in local affairs.

" You mean that she *had* to leave ? " he asked.

" Well, no, she didn't *'ave* to," the postmistress replied, still scrutinising him warily. " She went to better 'erself."

" How long ago ? " Angus inquired.

" Now let me think," the postmistress began, and did her thinking aloud in an immense paragraph of corroborative evidence, finally clinching her date as " three years last 'arvest," with a triumphant parallel.

Angus was giving her little attention. Quite early in the postmistress's speech that approximate date of a little more than three years had loomed convincingly, and yet he remembered to have heard that Herbert had been in South Africa for seven. Could his mistress, then, have continued, or returned to her work at the Rectory after her child was born ? A fragment of Herbert's last speech welled up in his mind. " She was barely eighteen," he had said.

" How old would Miss Browning be now, about ? " Angus asked.

" Ah, now that I *can* tell you," his informant said, pouncing on the opportunity for a display of accuracy, " for she was born the same week as my Lizzie, who'll be twenty-six come the nineteenth o' next month. Dear, dear, 'ow the time flies ! Why, I remember . . ." Like most village folk in England, she was more eager to give than to receive information. She had no curiosity concerning the unimaginable world whose affairs moved vaguely beyond the focus of her centred attention. To her the little village of Halton was a complete universe.

" But she hadn't . . . she didn't, then . . ." Angus interrupted her, and paused, unable to pose his question with the tact he felt was demanded of him.

" 'Adn't what ? " the postmistress encouraged him, softly, her head a little askew in her lust for the delivery of knowledge.

" She—she was never in trouble of any sort, I suppose ? " Angus asked.

The plump figure of the postmistress fairly quivered with emotion, and her voice dropped to a purring note that conveyed the ultimate expression of confidence. " N-no. Well, there, to be quite fair, she never was. We used to say as Sally knew 'er way about as well as most. Bless you, there was talk enough, one time. Sure to be with a good-looking wench like she was—more particular about seven or eight years ago, when there was a gentleman stayed at the Royal Oak one summer, as went off later to foreign parts, Africa, or somewheres, I heard. But nothin' never 'appened to Sally ; leastways not as anyone knows of. . . ."

But Angus, his head bowed confidentially over the counter of the little shop, was not attending. His knight-errantry was taking new shape. This good-looking wench who knew her way about as well as most, made no appeal to his sympathies. The feeling of boredom at the prospect of an immense and futile service to the wishes of Fuller Herbert, was growing upon him. He had, without doubt, now, another journey before him, and with no certainty at the end of it. In these three years Sarah Browning might have " bettered " herself more than once. Already he had received the impression that she was a young woman with a marked capacity for betterment.

" You can give me her address, I suppose ? " he said.

A look of distress passed across the face of the postmistress. " She went—I'm pretty near sure—to Southampton," she replied, and glanced distrustfully, almost with dread, at a vast collection of untidy papers that littered the rough shelves behind her.

" Don't you forward her letters ? " Angus asked.

" Well, she did give me 'er address afore she went," the postmistress said, uneasily, " and I did forward one or two letters for 'er just at first, but there ain't been any, now, for years, as you might say—'er being an orphan out of an 'ome and 'avin' no people of 'er own, in a way of speakin'."

" Do you think you could find that address ? " Angus said. " It's—it's rather important. There is—some money for her. . . ."

" Indeed ! " commented the postmistress with her first sign of curiosity in the stranger's business.

A sudden spasm of impatience seized Angus. He felt that he could not endure another minute of inaction. He wanted passionately to be finished with this absurd " charge " of his ; to find this confounded woman at once and be free to get on with the affairs of his own life. He looked at the horrid litter of papers on the shelves, and in his mind he pictured an immense and intricate research, lasting perhaps for hours, while he tediously examined the deposit that represented Heaven knew how many years of scrupulous ineptitude. It was incredible that the postmistress could ever have destroyed a single document ; not less incredible that she could ever find one.

" I must know her address," Angus exclaimed, almost fiercely.

And then occurred the first of many coincidences, if they were coincidences, and not due to some direct interference with the dull, habitual movements of natural law. For the postmistress, turning with a sigh of forlorn distress to the awful muddle behind her, let her plump red hand hover for a moment like the beak of a fortune-telling love-bird, and then plunged with the convulsive jerk of an automaton at the very bunch of litter, sere-edged and brittle in places, that contained Sarah Browning's address.

" There you are, then, young man," she exclaimed, on a high note of triumph. " Sarah Browning, the Ocean Hotel, Southampton. She went as chambermaid, I remember."

She glowed to a very ecstasy in the contemplation of her ability for accurate reference, positively flaunting at him the precision and reliability of her official aptitude for business method.

Angus turned with a long sigh of impatience to the obligations of his " trust." He had been in Southampton not many hours before. He had even noticed, half-consciously, the façade of the Ocean Hotel—a new building with an effect of conscious cleanliness and rectitude ; well built and badly placed ; staring its boast of efficiency across a poor street. He might, for all he knew, have shouldered Sarah Browning on the footway. And now he had to face all the hesitations and interruptions of a return journey, with no certainty of concluding his mission at the end of it. Only he felt he must know, at once, how much farther he might have to go before that little bag of diamonds, snug and warm in his hip pocket, could be delivered. It was the uncertainty that irritated him. He saw himself tracking Herbert's heiress through England. But, no ! In the train that night between Waterloo and Southampton he came to a definite resolve. If she had gone from the Ocean Hotel he would go to Devonshire and write to her. His responsibilities went no farther than that. It was absurd and impossible to undertake any more of these fruitless journeys. She must come to him. She was, though she was still unaware of it, magnificently rich. She would be

fully compensated for all her trouble, whereas he could anticipate no reward—unless Sarah Browning were unexpectedly
generous. And even then he had a certainty that it was not
in her nature to be generous.

That resolve, with all its promise of ease and finality, was
an imminent goal to him as he bounded up the steps and burst
through the solemn doors of the Ocean Hotel. He was panting
with eagerness as he demanded the whereabouts of Sarah
Browning from the flashily demure woman at the bureau.

" Oh, she's left here years ago," was the expected reply.

" I know, I know," assented Angus, " but where's she
gone to ? " He was too anxious to remark then, what he
afterward recognised as the most important characteristic of
the woman he was seeking. She was always remembered.
Surely there must have been many chambermaids in service
at the hotel since that gaudily staid woman in the office had
first undertaken her duties. Yet she had shown no sign of
hesitation when Miss Browning's name was mentioned.
Though Sarah had left the place " years ago," she was remembered, instantly and with certainty.

" Oh, you'd better ask the manager," said the woman in
the bureau, with a toss of her yellow head. She somehow
managed to convey that it was no part of a woman's business
to inquire into the ultimate destination of Sarah Browning.

The manager, when found, had an air of almost religious
discretion. He seemed to summarise in his own person all
the salient aspects of his own hotel. He might have been
the model from which the place had been designed. He
was so ostentatiously clean and precise, and barrenly efficient ;
and yet his pale-blue eyes with their sandy lashes had a slightly
wistful look, as if he, too, was aware of being essentially the
right thing in a wrong position.

He regarded Angus with a touch of practised but half-
wistful inquiry.

" Yes, Miss Browning left here—ah—two years last April,"
he said, and added, as though to satisfy his own craving for the
punctilious, " Ah—on the twenty-third."

" Where did she go to ? " Angus asked. " She left her
address, I suppose ? "

The manager, disregarding the question, delicately picked
his teeth with a quill.

" There was a lady here, a Mrs. Cresswell, who took a—
ah—liking for her," he continued. " She—ah—found certain

qualities in Miss Browning. We—ah—for the matter of that, all found certain qualities in her. She went back with this lady to—ah—undertake the management of a boarding-house in—ah—Sydney, Australia. Her address is, or was, 307 Pike Street, Sydney—ah—Australia."

Angus laughed. " That's a long way to go to find any-one," he said.

The manager permitted himself no air of surprise. " It is, as you say, a long way," he agreed. " If I can—ah—help you in any other way . . . ? "

But the manager's functions, so far as Angus was con-cerned, were now exhausted. He thanked him and went, almost light-heartedly. The little bag of diamonds still nestled confidingly in his hip pocket, but it was outrageous to suppose that he could be called upon to deliver them in person to Sarah Browning, in Sydney. He would, however, do more than was actually required of him. He would send a cable-gram to 307 Pike Street, prepaying the reply, although he could ill afford the expense, and request Herbert's unofficial legatee to communicate with him at once in Devonshire.

And then Fate, deliberate but persistent, caught him at the Central Post Office in Southampton, while he was, with a touch of dismay, disbursing the charge of his cable. A hand was laid on his shoulder and a pleasant voice said, " Now I call this the most astonishing piece of luck, Mr. Whitley."

He turned to confront Graham Dixon, the man with whom he had been in conversation when that fateful message had been brought to him at dinner on the night that Fuller Herbert had died.

" I wanted your address and couldn't get it," Dixon con-tinued, with a friendly smile. " Since I landed I have found that it will be necessary to send a man, an engineer for choice, out to our works in Sydney, and I judged from our talk on the steamer that you might be willing to take the job. And if you are, you're just the very man I want. Now will you come to my hotel and talk things over ? "

Angus stared at him resentfully. " To Sydney ? " he said. " You want me to go to Sydney ? It's a devil of a long way to go."

For a moment he could not realise that Dixon was offering him what might prove to be a very promising job. He did not think of the job, but only of the " sacred charge " that was again being thrust upon him just when his resolve had relieved him from further effort. Dixon seemed to have come suddenly from nowhere, as if he had been the supernatural agent of Herbert, thrusting again upon Angus the awful urgency of that cursed commission.

Dixon did not appear to notice the gaucheness of the reply. "Sheer luck," he went on, evenly, as he led Angus out into the street. "Honestly, I don't know why I went into that post office. . . ."

Angus listened without appreciating the detail of Dixon's conversation. He did not want to go to Australia. He had been in South Africa for two years, and now, if he were but given a little time, he would, he was sure, find a job at home. But he knew, even as he tried desperately to refuse Dixon's offer, that he would be forced to accept it. He could not oppose Dixon's suave confidence that he would accept it. It was, of course, a chance for him.

"In a sense, a position of peculiar trust," Dixon explained. "Things are not going right over there. We have our suspicions of the manager. . . . I chose you because I felt when I first met you that you were essentially a man to be trusted. . . . I should send you in the first place as an assistant engineer at a salary of forty pounds a month, and I want you to report to me privately, on the general management. Later . . ."

"I must go home first, to Devonshire," Angus put in, and then realised that his stipulation was a form of acceptance.

"By all means," Dixon agreed. "Do you think you could be ready to sail in a fortnight's time ? If an advance for your outfit would be a convenience, don't hesitate to call upon me."

So Angus went to Devonshire to meet that girl of his and to wait for the answer to his cable. And no answer came. Herbert had warned him to tell nobody about the diamonds, but he disobeyed that injunction so far as his sweetheart was concerned. She could be trusted ; and together they revolted against the necessity of his going, and gave way not because they respected the sacredness of his trust, but because, when they examined the situation at their leisure, it seemed that to accept Dixon's offer was the shortest way to achieve their soul's desire. If things went well, she was to go out to him in a year's time.

And when, some months later, Angus called at 307 Pike Street, to find that the boarding-house had changed hands again since Mrs. Cresswell had taken it, being now in a rapid decline under the direction of a drunken proprietor who had been too apathetic to reply to the cable (Angus saw it lying on the shabby hall table among a litter that reminded him of the country post office), he shrugged his shoulders, patted his hip pocket with a nervous movement that was becoming habitual to him, and decided that he had done everything that was humanly possible. Sarah Browning had gone to Auckland, New Zealand, about eighteen months earlier. More than that the fuddled proprietor of the Pike Street boarding-house could not or would not tell him.

So Angus set his face toward his new work, and toward the making of his fortune and the great day when his sweetheart should join him in the new world. He did not know that he was snapping his fingers at Fate, and that Fate had responded to the insult with a contemptuous smile.

It would be a mistake, however, to credit Fate or the spirit of Fuller Herbert with the entire control of Angus's career in Sydney. Even if he had never received that arduous commission of his, he would almost certainly have come to grief over the Dixon job. Muller, the manager of the works, was too clever for Angus's straightforward habit ; and Muller, from the first, had decided that he had no use for this young emissary from England. Muller played his own game with discretion and foresight, outwitting and outpointing the simple honesty of Whitley, from his preliminary explanation (apparently a frank and, considering his position, a generous statement) of the firm's affairs, to the day, five months later, when, with a well-assumed reluctance, he handed to Angus his month's notice of dismissal.

So far, I cannot trace any direct interference with Angus's fortune, but there can be no question that the result would have been different if he had been a free man. For the truth is that from the day he abandoned his pursuit of Sarah Browning at the door of the Pike Street boarding-house he was, in some indefinable way, haunted. He would pause in the conduct of the most intricate undertaking, bewildered with the sudden sense of an important duty recently overlooked, of a vast and overwhelming responsibility, incredibly, almost criminally, forgotten. Then the thing would take him with a shock of horror, so that he would stand startled and aghast, searching his mind for a memory of the essential duty culpably omitted. At other times the suggestions came to him vaguely, distracting his attention from his work, with cloudy thoughts of some object in life that was greater and finer than his petty pre-occupation with the details of his chosen profession. At those moments he would pause, whatever he was doing, and stare blankly before him, as though his eyes were strained to see, through the semblances of his material surroundings, the figure of the obsessing purpose that would drive him through the world in the pursuit of the self-confident, capable woman whose fortune rested so securely in his hip pocket. Only by a great effort of will could he return to his work, cursing Sarah Browning, the diamonds, and the memory of Herbert's commission. But Muller would note those fits of abstraction and make use of them.

And the haunting steadily persisted, presently adding another cause of discomfort to Angus's life. For it seemed that he was subconsciously aware of the written word "Auckland" long before his eye could pick it out from a printed page. Whenever he took up *The Sydney Bulletin* he found himself constrained to hunt for that one name, and he could fix his attention on nothing else until he found it. Also, in the street, he would suddenly pause in his walk and look up to discover perhaps a bill of steamer sailings, or it might be the name of a café, but in either case the prominent word that had hailed him so stridently through the deepest abstraction was always that one word "Auckland."

Nevertheless, nearly five weeks elapsed after his dismissal from the Dixon works, and, having sent the greater part of his salary home to Devonshire, he was sinking rapidly toward the social stratum of the beachcomber, before he signed on as assistant engineer on the Sydney and Auckland packet. He had not, even then, surrendered his will to the power that was driving him across the world. He was merely relaxing into a condition of helplessness and apathy. He felt that luck was against him ; that he would never make good, never marry that girl in Devonshire who so steadfastly and magnificently loved him. He went to Auckland rather because the name so persistently haunted him, than because he had the least hope of fulfilling his "sacred trust." It is certainly more than a little remarkable that from the moment he left Sydney his obsession by the word Auckland finally left him.

He had a few hours' leave in the course of the boat's forty-eight hours' stay in port, and he went up to one of the better hotels in the town on the off-chance of getting news of Herbert's

heiress. He got it without difficulty. Sarah Browning had
never served in that particular house ; she had been desk clerk
at the Imperial, the swell place behind the town, but she was
remembered. She had left Auckland, however, " oh, twelve
months or more," Angus's informant told him. " Went to
America, to better herself.' "

Angus went up to the Imperial and discovered that Miss
Browning's last known address was " The Mountjoy," San
Francisco. He also learned from the cynical male clerk who
had succeeded her that " Sally " had expressed her intention of
marrying an American millionaire.

He had not made up his mind, then, to devote all his
energies to that absurd quest after the fugitive heiress. The
thought of it increasingly bothered him ; it came between
him and his every purpose, but no more than if it had been the
memory of some rather important letter he ought to have
written. It was the famous south-easterly gale that settled
him. It is still talked about in Auckland. Incidentally, that
gale wrecked Angus's packet, which turned turtle thirty miles
out from land and drove him back in the company of a capsized
lifeboat to his point of departure. He was in hospital for
three weeks, and in that time he had leisure to think things
over. He reviewed his past from the moment of Herbert's
death, and in his weak state he came to believe that the hand
of destiny lay heavily upon him and that he would know neither
security nor peace of mind until he had delivered Herbert's
diamonds to Sally Browning. And once he had got that idea
into his head, his duty became an obsession with him. He
retarded his recovery by his eagerness to set about the business
at once and be done with it. In his quieter moments he still
argued with himself, maintaining that no one could expect
him to devote his whole life to the casual service that had
been so unwarrantably thrust upon him, but his superstition
had become stronger than any logic.

When I met him about fifteen months later in New York
he had the eyes and the bearing of a fanatic. During the
interval he had been " working his way " round the world.
He had been in San Francisco and Los Angeles, Philadelphia
and Chicago. He had served on tramp steamers, done odd
jobs in the cities, " jumped the cars," and been near to total
destitution once or twice, while he made his furious pilgrimage
on the trail of the enterprising Sally Browning, who in her
vigorous exploration of the road to wealth seemed to have

been inspired by a mad desire to fly from the fortune that was so desperately pursuing her.

He had lost track of her in Chicago. She had left there under some kind of a cloud, and with a misplaced and, as it turned out, unnecessary ingenuity had obliterated her traces. For seven months Angus had earned his living in Chicago as a lift-boy, waiting impatiently for the clue that had come to him at last through the chance conversation of two passengers in his lift. At the sound of Sarah Browning's name the attentive lift-boy had suffered a transformation that must have considerably astonished his two passengers. He had stopped the lift between floors while he demanded particulars. He was no longer a servant, but a fanatic pilgrim who cared nothing for any man on earth if he could but fulfil his quest. Had he just found the clue to the finding of a quarter of a million dollars instead of the clue to getting rid of them, he would not have shown a tenth part of the excitement. I gather that he got his information without any hesitation. Perhaps that instinctive movement of the hand to his hip pocket had been misread? As a mark of gratitude he deposited his informants on their proper floor, and then left the building and, an hour later, Chicago, without further ceremony.

He ought to have caught Sally Browning in New York. He had, as it were, short-circuited her trail, for she had been West again in the interval, and if he had had enough money for his car-fare he would have found her before she sailed for Liverpool. As it was, he jumped a freight, got hung up on a side-track, and missed her by twenty-four hours. When I met him he had just signed on as a fireman in a White Star boat.

I tried to dissuade him from that ignominy, but he seemed quite unable to give me his attention, refusing my offer to lend him the amount of his second-class fare, as if I were putting some tricky impediment in his way. I did not know then what was driving him, and I remember wondering whether he had committed a crime and was flying from justice. He had much the air of a man haunted by terror and charging in panic through the least hint of obstruction. I could not be expected to guess that the lure which drew him was the longing to deliver himself of a fortune in diamonds to Mrs. Sarah Fulton at the Savoy Hotel in London. She had married her million-aire two days before she left New York, and had taken him to Europe for their honeymoon. The passengers in Angus's

lift had been discussing her wedding when he had overheard
them. The strange thing was that he should not have heard
of her engagement earlier ; but his prosecution of the quest
had not led him to study the New York journals.

He has told me that he received his first real shock in
the discharge of his precious mission when he spoke to the
suspicious attendant across the counter in the Savoy foyer.
He entered the place with no particular hope of reaching
the end of his journey. The habit of asking for Sally—almost
exclusively in the halls of hotels—had so grown upon him
that he never anticipated anything but the usual reply. So
far as he had thought about it at all, he had thought it probable
that the Fultons had gone to Paris, to Geneva, to Rome, to
Moscow. He may have had visions of following them by
the Trans-Siberian Railway to China and Japan. He was
certainly prepared to do that if necessary. He had discarded
every other impulse but this dogged pursuit of a fixed idea.
And when the attendant told him that Mrs. Fulton was not
only staying at the Savoy, but was at that very moment in
the hotel, Angus was staggered. In a single moment he had
to recast all his values. He was like a blind man who, having
patiently worked in darkness all his life, suddenly receives the
gift of sight and does not know what to do with it.

" Have you got a message for her ? " the attendant asked,
with a look of disgust at Angus's clothes. He had, as a matter
of fact, forgotten to change them since he emerged from the
stoke-hold of the liner.

The familiar sense of impediment braced him again.
" A message ? " he repeated. " By hell ! yes, I've got a
message for her." And his hand went back with its habitual
movement to the little bulge in his hip pocket.

The attendant backed. " What name ? " he asked, looking
round for help.

" Angus Whitley," was the reply, spoken as if that, to
Mrs. Fulton, unknown name was a combination to conjure
with. " You let her know I'm here," he added, and, turning
away from the counter, threw himself in his oil-stained canvas
into one of the luxurious armchairs of the Savoy foyer.

They probably sent up his name to Mrs. Fulton, because
they did not know what to do with him. Why she consented
to see him is a deeper mystery. But Sarah Browning had
much strange history behind her, and she may have thought
it best, in those early days of her marriage, to be reasonably

cautious. Her husband was out just then, and she hoped, no doubt, to deal with the intruder and get rid of him before Fulton returned. If he represented some less creditable episode in her moving past, he might, she probably imagined, be rapidly and easily bought. For all Sarah's history that had been, in a sense, doubtful, was solely connected with finance. Since that one strange affair of hers with Herbert, ten years earlier, she had, as she might have phrased it, " kept herself respectable." A little shuffling of accounts, such as she had been guilty of in Chicago, did not, in her opinion, impeach her cherished reputation for virtue.

So she gave directions that he was to be shown up to her sitting-room, and to my mind the queerest aspect of the whole affair is the change that came over Angus when, at last, he realised that his goal was achieved. He had perhaps three or four minutes in which to grasp that fact while he followed the supercilious but distinctly nervous flunkey through long passages and then up in the lift to the sixth floor. And his realisation breaking, now, into a clear retrospect of his tremendous Odyssey, showed him, as he said, that he had been " a most almighty fool."

One enormous question posed itself to the extinction of all other issues. " Why," he asked himself, " had he not got rid of the diamonds and kept the money for himself ? " He had only one answer ; he had never thought of it. The possibility had, quite simply, never occurred to him. And at that eleventh hour it seemed to him that he had missed the chance of his life. He was, by instinct and habit, an honest man, but in his tremendous reaction he cursed himself for his stupidity. He even contemplated the theft as still possible. As he stepped out of the lift on the sixth floor he was reviewing the possibilities of turning back, of hiding himself in London, and disposing of Sarah's diamonds—at however great a loss—to some " fence " in the East End. Sheer inertia carried him on to Mrs. Fulton's room ; that and his natural curiosity to see the woman whose life-history had been his single study for more than two years. And when he actually faced her the temptation passed. From the moment he entered Sarah's presence he recovered his sanity. The Angus Whitley of that interview was the Angus who had sailed hopefully enough from Cape Town in the autumn of '96. For the first time he was able to see the humour of the immense undertaking nto which he had been so curiously led.

Mrs. Fulton must not be judged too hardly for her share in the culminating scene of Angus's tragic comedy. He began with an obvious but unfortunate reference to Fuller Herbert. With his return to sanity had come also a return of his appreciation of ordinary values ; and he was intensely conscious of himself, he says, as being so absurdly " improbable," sprung out of nowhere in his stoker's outfit, and appearing in an elaborate hotel sitting-room, with no other credential than a bag of uncut diamonds. No one, least of all the practical Mrs. Fulton, could be expected to believe in so unlikely an apparition. And then he must needs open with that unhappy reference to Herbert, Sally's one slip from virtue. Inevitably she scented blackmail from the outset.

" You've made some mistake," she said, with decision. " I've never known anyone of that name."

" It's a long time ago," Angus admitted, with the natural but utterly misguided intention of proving his case. " Ten years or more. At Halton in Northamptonshire. You were in service at the Rectory."

Mrs. Fulton's face expressed contempt. " You've made some mistake, young man," she said. " I've never heard of the place."

For one moment he was staggered by her self-assurance. Was it possible, he wondered, that he had picked up the wrong trail, between Chicago and New York ; that there were two Sarah Brownings, and that, after all his travail, he had found the wrong one ?

" Were you ever at the Central in Chicago ? " he asked, testing his clues.

Mrs. Fulton showed a faint shade of disconcertion. It may have flashed through her mind that this queer stranger was a representative of Pinkerton's, that he had ferreted out her complete history, and that it might be as well to come to terms at once. She had little fear of the results of the Chicago affair ; that was nothing more than a question of financial settlement.

" I may have been. Why ? " she asked.

" And at the Mountjoy, 'Frisco ? " he continued.

" I was—for a time. Why ? " snapped Mrs. Fulton.

Angus heaved a long sigh of relief. This was, at all events, the right Sarah Browning. " Why ? Oh, it's a long story," he said. " You've taken two years out of my life."

Sally's eyebrows went up, but her expression was entirely non-committal.

" Let's cut the story," Angus said, desperately, and produced the little leather bag from his hip pocket. " The essentials are that Fuller Herbert thought he had ruined you. He was crazy to make reparation, and he died on the boat coming home from South Africa. He made his will and all that, but he hadn't mentioned you in it for fear of his family making a fuss, so he handed over this bag of diamonds to me to give to you. He—he made it a ' sacred trust ' ; and I've followed you clean round the world to discharge it. It's taken me, as I said, rather more than two years." He paused a moment, watching the cautious, reserved face of the still incredulous Sally, and then emptied the contents of the bag on to the table in front of her.

Mrs. Fulton regarded the diamonds with infinite suspicion.

" What's that ? " she asked, pointing to a little bundle of papers that had come out of the bag with the stones.

" The official certificates for the diamonds—to prove that they were not bought illicitly, you know," Angus explained. But the certificates were so soaked with sea-water as to be practically illegible.

Sarah pursed her handsome mouth and steadfastly declined to touch either the stones or the papers.

" You're sure they *are* diamonds ? " she asked.

" Quite sure," Angus returned, grimly.

" Where are you staying ? " she said, and continued : " I think there must be some mistake. I never knew anyone called Fuller Herbert. But if you'll leave the diamonds here I'll have them tested to see if they are genuine, and if they are I'll write to you."

Angus wondered whether she was momentarily stirred to a thought of generosity ; if she suffered a fugitive impulse to send him ten shillings for his trouble ?

" I'm not staying anywhere," he said. " Write to me Poste Restante at the General Post Office. My name is Angus Whitley."

It seemed a good moment to get out, but Herbert's heiress checked him at the door.

" What about the bag ? " she asked. " Aren't you going to leave that ? "

" No, by God ! I'll keep the bag ! " Angus replied. " As —as a reward."

"Very well," Sally returned, calmly generous.

He has that bag still. It is one of his favourite jokes to produce it and to ask a new acquaintance how much he thinks that little leather bag is worth. His own answer is, "Two years of my life." But, then, as a successful man, happily married, he can afford to laugh now at his amazing Odyssey ; just as in his security he can afford to attribute the change of his fortunes to luck. For, as he marched into the Strand, with his head up, a free and, as he protests, at that moment a supremely happy man, he met Dixon, who had been looking for him for eighteen months, and now found him for the second time by a happy coincidence.

But I am not sure. I feel that the little leather bag repre- sents far more than Whitley thinks when he jokingly says "Two years of my life." I believe that those two years of his were not, as he implies, wasted. They brought him strength of purpose, powers of endurance, and much experience.

Nor can I convince myself that luck or chance was the final arbiter of his wanderings. The coincidences seem to me too many and too marked for that explanation. For my own part, I prefer to believe that the spirit of Fuller Herbert was always at Whitley's elbow during that long probation of his ; that it could not seek its rest until it had achieved its perfectly futile purpose of reparation.

I must add a final paragraph to note that Angus never called at the General Post Office for Sarah Fulton's promised letter, so we shall never know whether or not it contained a postal order for ten shillings—the probable limit of her gener- osity. Also to say that he did once meet her again, twelve years later, at a great reception in a famous London house. She did not, of course, recognise him, and he did not think it tactful to recall their last interview ; but he swears that the magnificent and now famous tiara she was wearing was com- posed of the stones that he had once carried round the world in his hip pocket.

PHYLLIS BOTTOME (1884—   ) *had her first novel accepted when she was seventeen, but it was not until some years later that she scored an important success with " The Dark Tower."   She has lived in many different countries and mixed with people of all races, types and professions.   Her novels are as successful in America as they are in England.*

HENRY

For four hours every morning, and for twenty minutes before a large audience at night, Fletcher was locked up with murder.

It glared at him from twelve pairs of amber eyes ; it clawed the air close to him, it spat naked hate at him, and watched with uninterrupted intensity, to catch him for one moment off his guard.

Fletcher had only his will and his eyes to keep death at bay.

Of course outside the cage, into which Fletcher shut himself nightly with his twelve tigers, were the keepers, standing at intervals around it with concealed pistols ; but they were outside it.   The idea was, that if anything happened to Fletcher they would be able, by prompt action, to get him out alive ; but they had his private instructions to do nothing of the kind, to shoot straight at his heart, and pick off the guilty tiger afterwards to cover their intentions.   Fletcher knew better than to try to preserve anything the tigers left of him, if once they had started in.

The lion tamer in the next cage was better off than Fletcher ; he was intoxicated by a rowdy vanity which dimmed fear. He stripped himself half naked every night, covered himself with ribbons, and thought so much of himself that he hardly noticed his lions.   Besides, his lions had all been born in captivity, were slightly doped ; and were only lions.

Fletcher's tigers weren't doped, because dope dulled their fears of the whip and didn't dull their ferocity ; captivity softened nothing in them, and they hated man.

Fletcher had taught tigers since he was a child, his father

had started him on baby tigers, who were charming. They hurt you as much as they could with an absent-minded roguishness difficult to resist ; what was death to you was play to them, but as they couldn't kill him, all the baby tigers did was to harden Fletcher and teach him to move about quickly. Speed is the tiger's long suit and Fletcher learned to beat him at it. He knew by a long-trained instinct when a tiger was going to move, and moved quicker so as to be somewhere else. He learned that tigers must be treated like an audience, though for different reasons ; you must not turn your back upon them, because tigers associate backs with springs.

Fletcher's swift eyes moved with the flickering sureness of lightning—even quicker than lightning, for while lightning has the leisure to strike, Fletcher had to avoid being struck by something as quick as a flash and much more terrible.

After a few months the baby tigers could only be taught by fear, fear of a whip lash, fear of a pocket pistol which stung them with blank cartridges ; and above all the mysterious fear of the human eye. Fletcher's father used to make him sit opposite him for hours practising eyes. When he was only ten years old, Fletcher had learned never to show a tiger that he was afraid of him. " If you ain't afraid of a tiger, you're a fool," his father told him, " but if you show a tiger you're afraid of him, you won't even be a fool long ! "

The first thing Fletcher taught his tigers, one by one in their cages, was to catch his eye, then he stared them down. He had to show them that his power of mesmerism was stronger than theirs ; if once they believed this, they might believe that his power to strike was also stronger. Once Fletcher had accustomed tigers to be out-faced, he could stay in their cages for hours in comparative safety.

The next stage was to get them used to noise and light. Tigers dislike noise and light and they wanted to take it out of Fletcher when he exposed them to it.

When it came to the actual trick teaching, Fletcher relied on his voice and a long stinging whip. The lion tamer roared at his lions. Fletcher's voice was not loud ; but it was as noticeable as a warning bell, it checked his tigers like the crack of a pistol.

For four hours every morning, Fletcher, who was as kind as he was intrepid, frightened his tigers into doing tricks. He rewarded them as well ; after they had been frightened enough

to sit on tubs, he threw them bits of raw meat. He wanted
them to associate tubs with pieces of raw meat, and not sitting
on tubs with whips; attempting to attack him, which they
did during all transition stages, he wanted them to associate
with flashes from his pocket pistol, followed by the impact of
very unpleasant sensations. Their dislike of the pistol was
an important point; they had to learn to dislike it so much
that they would, for the sake of their dislike, sacrifice their
fond desire to obliterate Fletcher.

Fletcher took them one by one at first and then rehearsed
them gradually together. It was during the single lessons that
he discovered Henry.

Henry had been bought, rather older than the other tigers,
from a drunken sailor. The drunken sailor had tearfully
persisted that Henry was not as other tigers, and selling him
at all was like being asked to part with a talented and only
child.

" 'E 'as a 'eart ! " Henry's first proprietor repeated over
and over again.

Fletcher, however, suspected this fanciful statement of
being a mere ruse to raise Henry's price, and watchfully dis-
regarded its implications.

For some time afterwards, Henry bore out Fletcher's
suspicions. He snarled at all the keepers, showed his teeth
and clawed the air close to Fletcher's head exactly like the
eleven other tigers, only with more vim. He was a very fine
young tiger, exceptionally powerful and large; the polished
corners of the Temple did not shine more brilliantly than the
lustrous striped skin on Henry's back, and when his painted
impassive face, heavy and expressionless as a Hindoo idol's,
broke up into activity, the very devils believed and trembled.
Fletcher believed but he didn't tremble—he only sat longer and
longer, closer and closer to Henry's cage, watching.

The first day he went inside there seemed no good reason,
either to Henry or to himself, why he should live to get out.
The second day something curious happened. While he was
attempting to out-stare Henry and Henry was stalking him to
get between him and the cage door, a flash of something like
recognition came into Henry's eyes, a kind of " Hail fellow
well met ! " He stopped stalking and sat down. Fletcher
held him firmly with his eyes; the great painted head sank
down and the amber eyes blurred and closed under Fletcher's
penetrating gaze. A loud noise filled the cage . . . a loud, con-

tented, pleasant noise. Henry was purring ! Fletcher's voice changed from the sharp brief order like the crack of a whip into a persuasive companionable drawl. Henry's eyes re-opened, he rose, stood rigid for a moment, and then slowly the rigidity melted out of his powerful form. Once more that answering look came into the tiger's eyes. He stared straight at Fletcher without blinking and jumped on to his tub. He sat on it impassively, his tail waving, his great jaws closed. He eyed Fletcher attentively and without hate. Then Fletcher knew that this tiger was not as other tigers ; not as any other tiger.

He threw down his whip, Henry never moved ; he ap-proached Henry, Henry lifted his lip to snarl, thought better of it, and permitted the approach. Fletcher took his life in his hand and touched Henry. Henry snarled mildly, but his great claws remained closed, his eyes expressed nothing but a gentle warning, they simply said : " You know I don't like being touched ; be careful, I might have to claw you ! " Fletcher gave a brief nod ; he knew the margin of safety was slight, but he had a margin. He could do something with Henry.

Hour after hour every day he taught Henry, but he taught him without a pistol or a whip. It was unnecessary to use anything beyond his voice and his eyes. Henry read his eyes eagerly. When he failed to catch Fletcher's meaning, Fletcher's voice helped him out. Henry did not always understand even Fletcher's voice, but where he differed from the other tigers was that he wished to understand ; nor had he from the first the slightest inclination to kill Fletcher.

He used to sit for hours at the back of his cage waiting for Fletcher. When he heard far off—unbelievably far off—the sound of Fletcher's step, he moved forward to the front of his cage and prowled restlessly to and fro till Fletcher unlocked the door and entered. Then Henry would crouch back a little, politely, from no desire to avoid his friend, but as a mere tribute to the superior power he felt in Fletcher. Directly Fletcher spoke he came forward proudly and exchanged their wordless eye language.

Henry liked doing his tricks alone with Fletcher. He jumped on and off his tub following the mere wave of Fletcher's hand. He soon went further, jumped on a high stool and leapt through a large white paper disc held up by Fletcher. Although the disc looked as if he couldn't possibly go through it, yet the

clean white sheet always yielded to his impact ; he did get
through it, blinking a little, but feeling a curious pride that he
had faced the odious thing ; and pleased Fletcher.

He let Fletcher sit on his back, though the mere touch
of an alien creature was repulsive to him. But he stood perfectly still, his hair rising a little, his teeth bared, a growl half
suffocated in his throat. He told himself it was Fletcher.
He must control his impulse to fling him off and tear
him up.

In all the rehearsals and performances in the huge arena,
full of strange noises, blocked with alien human beings, Henry
led the other tigers ; and though Fletcher's influence over him
was weakened, he still recognised it. Fletcher seemed farther
away from him at these times, less sympathetic and godlike, but Henry tried hard to follow the intense persuasive
eyes and the brief emphatic voice ; he would not lose touch
even with this attenuated ghost of Fletcher.

It was with Henry and Henry alone that Fletcher dared
his nightly stunt, dropped the whip and stick at his feet and
let Henry do his tricks as he did them in his cage alone, with
nothing beyond Fletcher's eyes and voice to control him.
The other eleven tigers, beaten, glaring and snarling, on to
their tubs, sat impassively despising Henry's unnatural docility.
He had the chance they had always wanted, and he didn't take
it—what kind of a tiger was he ?

But Henry ignored the other tigers. Reluctantly, standing
with all four feet together on his tub, he contemplated a further
triumph. Fletcher stood before him, holding a stick between
his hands and above his head ; intimately, compellingly,
through the language of his eyes Fletcher told Henry to jump
from his tub over his head. What Fletcher said was : " Come
on, old thing ! Jump ! Come on ! I'll duck in time. You
won't hurt me ! It's my stunt ! Stretch your old paws together
and jump ! " And Henry jumped. He hated the dazzling
lights, loathed the hard, unexpected, senseless sounds which
followed his leap, and he was secretly terrified that he would
land on Fletcher. But it was very satisfactory when, after his
rush through the air, he found he hadn't touched Fletcher, but
had landed on another tub carefully prepared for him ; and
Fletcher said to him as plainly as possible before he did the
drawer trick with the other tigers : " Well ! You are a one-er
and no mistake ! "

The drawer trick was the worst of Fletcher's stunts.

He had to put a table in the middle of the cage, and whip each tiger up to it. When he had them placed each on his tub around the table, he had to feed them with a piece of raw meat deftly thrown at the exact angle to reach the special tiger for which it was intended, and to avoid contact with eleven other tigers ripe to dispute this intention. Fletcher couldn't afford the slightest mistake or a fraction of delay. Each tiger had to have in turn his piece of raw meat, and the drawer shut after it—opened—the next morsel thrown exactly into the grasp of the next tiger, and so on, until the twelve were all fed.

Fletcher always placed Henry at his back. Henry snatched in his turn his piece of raw meat, but he made no attempt, as the other tigers always did, to take any one else's ; and Fletcher felt the safer for knowing that Henry was at his back. He counted on Henry's power to protect him more than he counted on the four keepers standing outside the cage with their pistols. More than once, when one of the other tigers turned restive, Fletcher had found Henry, rigid, but very light on his toes, close to his side, between him and danger.

The circus manager spoke to Fletcher warningly about his foolish infatuation for Henry.

" Mark my words, Fletcher," he said, " the tiger doesn't live that wouldn't do you in if it could. You give Henry too many chances—one day he'll take one of them."

But Fletcher only laughed. He knew Henry ; he had seen the soul of the great tiger leap to his eyes and shine there in answer to his own eyes. A man does not kill his god ; at least not willingly. It is said that two thousand years ago he did some such thing, through ignorance ; but Fletcher forgot this incident. Besides, on the whole, he believed more in Henry than he did in his fellow-men. This was not surprising, because Fletcher had very little time for human fellowship. When he was not teaching tigers not to kill him, he rested from the exhaustion of the nerves which comes from a prolonged companionship with eager, potential murderers ; and the rest of the time Fletcher boasted of Henry to the lion tamer ; and taught Henry new tricks.

Macormack, the lion tamer, had a very good stunt lion, and he was extravagantly jealous of Henry. He could not make his lion go out backwards before him from the arena cage into the passage as Henry had learned to do before Fletcher ; and when he had tried, Ajax had, not seriously but with an intention rather more than playful, flung him against the bars of the cage.

Macormack brooded deeply on this slight from his pet, and determined to take it out of Fletcher's.

" Pooh ! " he said. " You call yourself damned plucky for laying your ole 'oof on 'Enry's scruff, and 'e don't 'alf look wicked while you're doin' it. Why don't yer put yer 'ead in 'is mouf and be done with it ? That 'ud be talking, that would ! "

" I wouldn't mind doing it," said Fletcher reflectively, after a brief pause, " once I get 'im used to the idea. 'Is jaw ain't so big as a lion's, still I could get the top of me 'ead in."

The lion tamer swaggered off jeering, and Fletcher thought out how best to lay this new trick before Henry for his approval.

But from the very first Henry didn't approve of it. He showed quite plainly that he didn't want his head touched. He didn't like his mouth held forcibly open and wouldn't have anything put between his teeth without crunching. Fletcher wasted several loaves of bread over the effort—and only succeeded once or twice gingerly and very ungracefully in getting portions of his own head in and out in safety. Henry roared long and loudly at him, clawed the air, and flashed all the language he could from his flaming eyes into Fletcher's, to explain that this thing wasn't done between tigers ! It was hitting below the belt ! An infringement of an instinct too deep for him to master ; and Fletcher knew that he was outraging Henry's instinct, and decided to refrain.

" It ain't fair to my tiger ! " he said to himself regretfully ; and he soothed Henry with raw meat and endearments, promising to refrain from his unnatural venture.

But when the hour for the performance came, Fletcher forgot his promise. He was enraged at Macormack's stunt lion for getting more than his share of the applause. He had the middle cage, and what with the way Macormack swaggered half naked in his scarlet ribbons, and the lion roared—that pulverising, deep-toned, desert roar—and yet did all his tricks one after the other like a little gentleman, it did seem as if Henry barely got a round of his due applause.

Henry jumped through his white disc—so did the stunt lion ! He took his leap over Fletcher's head—the stunt lion did something flashy with a drum, not half as dangerous, and the blind and ignorant populace ignored Henry and preferred the drum.

" I don't care ! " said Fletcher to himself. " Henry's got to take my head in his mouf whether he likes it or not—that'll startle 'em ! "

He got rid of all the other tigers. Henry was used to that, he liked it ; now he would do his own final stunt—walk out backwards into the passage which led to the cages, and Fletcher would hurry out through the arena and back to Henry's cage, give him a light extra supper, and tell him what a fine tiger he was.

But Fletcher called him into the middle of the stage instead and made him take that terrible attitude he had taught him for the new trick. His eyes said : " You'll do this once for me, old man, won't you ? "

Henry's eyes said : " Don't ask it ! I'm tired ! I'm hungry ! I want to get out ! "

But Fletcher wouldn't read Henry's eyes any more. He tried to force his head side-ways into the terrible open jaws, and Henry's teeth, instinctive, reluctant, compelled, closed on Fletcher's neck.

What Henry minded after the momentary relief of his instinctive action was the awful stillness of Fletcher. It wasn't the stillness of the arena—that was nothing, a mere deep indrawn breath. Fletcher lay limp between his paws, as if the trick were over, as if all tricks were over. He wouldn't get up, he didn't look at Henry. Henry's eyes gazed down unblinkingly into the blank eyes of Fletcher. All Henry's soul was in his eyes watching for Fletcher's soul to rise to meet them. And for an age nothing happened, until at last Henry realised that nothing ever would.

Before the nearest keeper shot Henry, Henry knew that he had killed his god. He lifted up his heavy painted head and roared out through the still arena, a loud despairing cry.

His heart was pierced before they reached his heart.

MRS. AGATHA CHRISTIE *is one of the few contemporary women writers of detective fiction with a world-wide reputation. Her master-creations are those books dealing with the adventures of Hercule Poirot, the great Belgian detective ; but her fresh and fertile invention has expressed itself in a bewildering variety of ways— tales of the supernatural, detective stories and parodies, fantastic mysteries, and light romances.*

THE SIGN IN THE SKY

THE Judge was finishing his charge to the jury.

"Now, gentlemen, I have almost finished what I want to say to you. There is evidence for you to consider as to whether this case is plainly made out against this man so that you may say he is guilty of the murder of Vivien Barnaby. You have had the evidence of the servants as to the time the shot was fired. They have one and all agreed upon it. You have had the evidence of the letter written to the defendant by Vivien Barnaby on the morning of that same day, Friday, September 13th—a letter which the defence has not attempted to deny. You have had evidence that the prisoner first denied having been at Deering Hill, and later, after evidence had been given by the police, admitted he had. You will draw your own conclusions from that denial. This is not a case of direct evidence. You will have to come to your own conclusions on the subject of motive—of means, of opportunity. The contention of the defence is that some person unknown entered the music room after the defendant had left it, and shot Vivien Barnaby with the gun which, by strange forgetfulness, the defendant had left behind him. You have heard the defendant's story of the reason it took him half an hour to get home. If you disbelieve the defendant's story and are satisfied beyond any reasonable doubt that the defendant did, upon Friday, September 13th, discharge his gun at close quarters to Vivien Barnaby's head with intent to kill her, then, gentlemen, your verdict must be Guilty. If, on the other hand, you have any reasonable doubt, it is your duty to acquit the prisoner. I will now ask you to retire to your room and consider and let me know when you have arrived at a conclusion."

The jury were absent a little under half an hour. They returned the verdict that to every one had seemed a foregone conclusion, the verdict of " Guilty."

Mr. Satterthwaite left the court after hearing the verdict, with a thoughtful frown on his face.

A mere murder trial as such did not attract him. He was of too fastidious a temperament to find interest in the sordid details of the average crime. But the Wylde case had been different. Young Martin Wylde was what is termed a gentleman—and the victim, Sir George Barnaby's young wife, had been personally known to the elderly gentleman.

He was thinking of all this as he walked up Holborn, and then plunged into a tangle of mean streets leading in the direction of Soho. In one of these streets there was a small restaurant, known only to the few of whom Mr. Satterthwaite was one. It was not cheap—it was, on the contrary, exceedingly expensive, since it catered exclusively for the palate of the jaded *gourmet*. It was quiet—no strains of jazz were allowed to disturb the hushed atmosphere—it was rather dark, waiters appeared soft-footed out of the twilight, bearing silver dishes with the air of participating in some holy rite. The name of the restaurant was Arlecchino.

Still thoughtful, Mr. Satterthwaite turned into the Arlecchino and made for his favourite table in a recess in the far corner. Owing to the twilight before mentioned, it was not until he was quite close to it that he saw it was already occupied by a tall dark man who sat with his face in shadow, and with a play of colour from a stained window turning his sober garb into a kind of riotous motley.

Mr. Satterthwaite would have turned back, but just at that moment the stranger moved slightly and the other recognised him.

" God bless my soul," said Mr. Satterthwaite, who was given to old-fashioned expressions. " Why, it's Mr. Quin ! "

Three times before he had met Mr. Quin, and each time the meeting had resulted in something a little out of the ordinary. A strange person, this Mr. Quin, with a knack of showing you the things you had known all along in a totally different light.

At once Mr. Satterthwaite felt excited—pleasurably excited. His rôle was that of the looker-on, and he knew it, but sometimes when in the company of Mr. Quin, he had the illusion of being an actor—and the principal actor at that.

" This is very pleasant," he said, beaming all over his

dried-up little face. " Very pleasant indeed. You've no
objection to my joining you, I hope ? "

" I shall be delighted," said Mr. Quin. " As you see I
have not yet begun my meal."

A deferential head waiter hovered up out of the shadows.
Mr. Satterthwaite, as befitted a man with a seasoned palate,
gave his whole mind to the task of selection. In a few minutes
the head waiter, a slight smile of approbation on his lips,
retired, and a young satellite began his ministrations. Mr.
Satterthwaite turned to Mr. Quin.

" I have just come from the Old Bailey," he began. " A
sad business, I thought."

" He was found guilty ? " said Mr. Quin.

" Yes, the jury were out only half an hour."

Mr. Quin bowed his head.

" An inevitable result—on the evidence," he said.

" And yet," began Mr. Satterthwaite—and stopped.

Mr. Quin finished the sentence for him.

" And yet your sympathies were with the accused ? Is
that what you were going to say ? "

" I suppose it was. Martin Wylde is a nice-looking young
fellow—one can hardly believe it of him. All the same, there
have been a good many nice-looking young fellows lately who
have turned out to be murderers of a particularly cold-blooded
and repellent type."

" Too many," said Mr. Quin quietly.

" I beg your pardon ? " said Mr. Satterthwaite, slightly
startled.

" Too many for Martin Wylde. There has been a tendency from the beginning to regard this as just one more of a
series of the same type of crime—a man seeking to free himself
from one woman in order to marry another."

" Well," said Mr. Satterthwaite doubtfully. " On the
evidence——"

" Ah ! " said Mr. Quin quickly. " I am afraid I have not
followed all the evidence."

" Mr. Satterthwaite's self-confidence came back to him
with a rush. He felt a sudden sense of power. He was
tempted to be consciously dramatic.

" Let me try to show it to you. I have met the Barnabys,
you understand. I know the peculiar circumstances. With
me, you will come behind the scenes—you will see the thing
from inside."

Mr. Quin leant forward with his quick encouraging smile. " If any one can show me that, it will be Mr. Satterthwaite," he murmured.

Mr. Satterthwaite gripped the table with both hands. He was uplifted, carried out of himself. For the moment he was an artist pure and simple—an artist whose medium was words.

Swiftly, with a dozen broad strokes, he etched in the picture of life at Deering Hill. Sir George Barnaby, elderly, obese, purse-proud. A man perpetually fussing over the little things of life. A man who wound up his clocks every Friday afternoon, and who paid his own housekeeping books every Tuesday morning, and who always saw to the locking of his own front door every night. A careful man.

And from Sir George he went on to Lady Barnaby. Here his touch was gentler, but none the less sure. He had seen her but once, but his impression of her was definite and lasting. A vivid defiant creature—pitifully young. A trapped child, that was how he described her.

" She hated him, you understand ? She had married him before she knew what she was doing. And now——"

She was desperate—that was how he put it. Turning this way and that. She had no money of her own, she was entirely dependent on this elderly husband. But all the same she was a creature at bay—still unsure of her own powers, with a beauty that was as yet more promise than actuality. And she was greedy. Mr. Satterthwaite affirmed that definitely. Side by side with defiance there ran a greedy streak—a clasping and a clutching at life.

" I never met Martin Wylde," continued Mr. Satterthwaite. " But I heard of him. He lived less than a mile away. Farming, that was his line. And she took an interest in farming—or pretended to. If you ask me, it was pretending. I think that she saw in him her only way of escape—and she grabbed at him, greedily, like a child might have done. Well, there could only be one end to that. We know what that end was, because the letters were read out in court. He kept her letters—she didn't keep his, but from the text of hers one can see that he was cooling off. He admits as much. There was the other girl. She also lived in the village of Deering Vale. Her father was the doctor there. You saw her in court perhaps ? No, I remember, you were not there, you said. I shall have to describe her to you. A fair girl—

very fair. Gentle. Perhaps—yes, perhaps a tiny bit stupid.
But very restful, you know. And loyal. Above all, loyal."
He looked at Mr. Quin for encouragement, and Mr. Quin
gave it him by a slow appreciative smile. Mr. Satterthwaite
went on.

"You heard that last letter read—you must have seen it ;
in the papers, I mean. The one written on the morning of
Friday, September 13th. It was full of desperate reproaches
and vague threats, and it ended by begging Martin Wylde to
come to Deering Hill that same evening at six o'clock. ' *I will
leave the side door open for you, so that no one need know you
have been here. I shall be in the music room.*' It was sent by
hand."

Mr. Satterthwaite paused for a minute or two.

"When he was first arrested, you remember, Martin Wylde
denied that he had been to the house at all that evening. His
statement was that he had taken his gun and gone out shooting
in the woods. But when the police brought forward their
evidence, that statement broke down. They had found his
fingerprints, you remember, both on the wood of the side door
and on one of the two cocktail glasses on the table in the music
room. He admitted then that he had come to see Lady
Barnaby, that they had had a stormy interview, but that it
had ended in his having managed to soothe her down. He
swore that he left his gun outside leaning against the wall
near the door, and that he left Lady Barnaby alive and well,
the time being then a minute or two after a quarter-past six.
He went straight home, he says. But evidence was called to
show that he did not reach his farm until a quarter to seven,
and as I have just mentioned, it is barely a mile away. It
would not take half an hour to get there. He forgot all about
his gun, he declares. Not a very likely statement—and
yet——"

"And yet ? " queried Mr. Quin.

"Well," said Mr. Satterthwaite slowly, " it's a possible
one, isn't it ? Counsel ridiculed the supposition, of course,
but I think he was wrong. You see, I've known a good many
young men, and these emotional scenes upset them very much
— especially the dark, nervous type like Martin Wylde.
Women now can go through a scene like that, and feel positively
better for it afterwards, with all their wits about them. It
acts like a safety valve for them, steadies their nerves down
and all that. But I can see Martin Wylde going away with

his head in a whirl, sick and miserable, and without a thought
of the gun he had left leaning up against the wall."

He was silent for some minutes before he went on.

"Not that it matters. For the next part is only too clear,
unfortunately. It was exactly twenty minutes past six when
the shot was heard. All the servants heard it, the cook, the
kitchen-maid, the butler, the housemaid, and Lady Barnaby's
own maid. They came rushing to the music room. She was
lying huddled over the arm of her chair. The gun had been
discharged close to the back of her head, so that the shot
hadn't a chance to scatter. At least two of them penetrated
the brain."

He paused again and Mr. Quin asked casually :

"The servants gave evidence, I suppose ? "

Mr. Satterthwaite nodded.

"Yes. The butler got there a second or two before the
others, but their evidence was practically a repetition of each
other's."

"So they *all* gave evidence," said Mr. Quin musingly.
"There were no exceptions ? "

"Now I remember it," said Mr. Satterthwaite, "the
housemaid was only called at the inquest. She's gone to
Canada since, I believe."

"I see," said Mr. Quin.

There was a silence, and somehow the air of the little
restaurant seemed to be charged with an uneasy feeling. Mr.
Satterthwaite felt suddenly as though he were on the defensive.

"Why shouldn't she ? " he said abruptly.

"Why should she ? " said Mr. Quin with a very slight
shrug of the shoulders.

Somehow the question annoyed Mr. Satterthwaite. He
wanted to shy away from it—to get back on familiar ground.

"There couldn't be much doubt who fired the shot. As
a matter of fact, the servants seemed to have lost their heads a
bit. There was no one in the house to take charge. It was
some minutes before any one thought of ringing up the police,
and when they did so, they found that the telephone was out
of order."

"Oh ! " said Mr. Quin. "The telephone was out of
order."

"It was," said Mr. Satterthwaite—and was struck suddenly
by the feeling that he had said something tremendously
"important. It might, of course, have been done on purpose,"

he said slowly. " But there seems no point in that. Death was practically instantaneous."

Mr. Quin said nothing, and Mr. Satterthwaite felt that his explanation was unsatisfactory.

" There was absolutely no one to suspect but young Wylde," he went on. " By his own account even, he was only out of the house three minutes before the shot was fired. And who else could have fired it ? Sir George was at a bridge party a few houses away. He left there at half-past six and was met just outside the gate by a servant bringing him the news. The last rubber finished at half-past six exactly—no doubt about that. Then there was Sir George's secretary, Henry Thompson. He was in London that day, and actually at a business meeting at the moment the shot was fired. Finally there is Sylvia Dale who, after all, had a perfectly good motive, impossible as it seems that she should have had anything to do with a crime. She was at the station of Deering Vale seeing a friend off by the 6.28 train. That lets her out. Then the servants. What earthly motive could any one of them have ? Besides, they all arrived on the spot practically simultaneously. No, it must have been Martin Wylde."

But he said it in a dissatisfied kind of voice.

They went on with their lunch. Mr. Quin was not in a talkative mood, and Mr. Satterthwaite had said all he had to say. But the silence was not a barren one. It was filled with the growing dissatisfaction of Mr. Satterthwaite, heightened and fostered in some strange way by the mere quiescence of the other man.

Mr. Satterthwaite suddenly put down his knife and fork with a clatter.

" Supposing that that young man is really innocent," he said. " He's going to be hanged."

He looked very startled and upset about it. And still Mr. Quin said nothing.

" It's not as though——" began Mr. Satterthwaite, and stopped. " Why shouldn't the woman go to Canada ? " he ended inconsequently.

Mr. Quin shook his head.

" I don't even know what part of Canada she went to," continued Mr. Satterthwaite peevishly.

" Could you find out ? " suggested the other.

" I suppose I could. The butler now. He'd know. Or possibly Thompson, the secretary."

B.G,S.S.   T

He paused again. When he resumed speech, his voice sounded almost pleading.

" It's not as though it were anything to do with me ? "

" That a young man is going to be hanged in a little over three weeks ? "

" Well, yes—if you put it that way, I suppose. Yes, I see what you mean. Life and death. And that poor girl too. It's not that I'm hard-hearted—but, after all—what good will it do ? Isn't the whole thing rather fantastic ? Even if I found out where the woman's gone to in Canada—why, it would probably mean that I should have to go out there myself."

Mr. Satterthwaite looked seriously upset.

" And I was thinking of going to the Riviera next week," he said pathetically.

And his glance towards Mr. Quin said as plainly as it could be said. " Do let me off, won't you ? "

" You have never been to Canada ? "

" Never."

" A very interesting country."

Mr. Satterthwaite looked at him undecidedly.

" You think I ought to go ? "

Mr. Quin leaned back in his chair and lighted a cigarette. Between puffs of smoke he spoke deliberately.

" You are, I believe, a rich man, Mr. Satterthwaite. Not a millionaire, but a man able to indulge a hobby without counting the expense. You have looked on at the dramas of other people. Have you never contemplated stepping in and playing a part ? Have you never seen yourself for a minute as the arbiter of other people's destinies—standing in the centre of the stage with life and death in your hands ? "

Mr. Satterthwaite leant forward. The old eagerness surged over him.

" You mean — if I go on this wild-goose chase to Canada——"

Mr. Quin smiled.

" Oh ! it was your suggestion, going to Canada, not mine," he said lightly.

" You can't put me off like that," said Mr. Satterthwaite earnestly. " Whenever I have come across you——" He stopped.

" Well ? "

" There is something about you I do not understand. Perhaps I never shall. The last time I met you——"

" On Midsummer's Eve."

Mr. Satterthwaite was startled, as though the words held a clue that he did not quite understand.

" Was it Midsummer's Eve ? " he asked confusedly.

" Yes. But let us not dwell on that. It is unimportant, is it not ? "

" Since you say so," said Mr. Satterthwaite courteously. He felt that elusive clue slipping through his fingers. " When I come back from Canada "—he paused a little awkwardly— " I—I—should much like to see you again."

" I am afraid I have no fixed address for the moment," said Mr. Quin regretfully. " But I often come to this place. If you also frequent it, we shall no doubt meet before very long."

They parted pleasantly.

Mr. Satterthwaite was very excited. He hurried round to Cook's and inquired about boat sailings. Then he rang up Deering Hill. The voice of a butler, suave and deferential, answered him.

" My name is Satterthwaite. I am speaking for a—er— firm of solicitors. I wished to make a few inquiries about a young woman who was recently housemaid in your establishment."

" Would that be Louisa, sir ? Louisa Bullard ? "

" That is the name," said Mr. Satterthwaite, very pleased to be told it.

" I regret she is not in this country, sir. She went to Canada six months ago."

" Can you give me her present address ? "

The butler was afraid he couldn't. It was a place in the mountains she had gone to—a Scotch name—ah ! Banff, that was it. Some of the other young women in the house had been expecting to hear from her, but she had never written or given them any address.

Mr. Satterthwaite thanked him and rang off. He was still undaunted. The adventurous spirit was strong in his breast. He would go to Banff. If this Louisa Bullard was there, he would track her down somehow or other.

To his own surprise, he enjoyed the trip greatly. It was many years since he had taken a long sea voyage. The Riviera, Le Touquet and Deauville, and Scotland had been his usual round. The feeling that he was setting off on an impossible mission added a secret zest to his journey. What an utter fool these fellow travellers of his would think him did they but know the object of his quest ! But then—they were not acquainted with Mr. Quin.

In Banff he found his objective easily attained. Louisa Bullard was employed in the large hotel there. Twelve hours after his arrival he was standing face to face with her.

She was a woman of about thirty-five, anæmic looking, but with a strong frame. She had pale brown hair inclined to curl, and a pair of honest brown eyes. She was, he thought, slightly stupid, but very trustworthy.

She accepted quite readily his statement that he had been asked to collect a few further facts from her about the tragedy at Deering Hill.

" I saw in the paper that Mr. Martin Wylde had been convicted, sir. Very sad it is too."

She seemed, however, to have no doubt as to his guilt.

" A nice young gentleman gone wrong. But though I wouldn't speak ill of the dead, it was her ladyship what led him on. Wouldn't leave him alone, she wouldn't. Well, they've both got their punishment. There's a text used to hang on my wall when I was a child, ' God is not mocked,' and it's very true. I knew something was going to happen that very evening—and sure enough it did."

" How was that ? " said Mr. Satterthwaite.

" I was in my room, sir, changing my dress, and I happened to glance out of the window. There was a train going along, and the white smoke of it rose up in the air, and, if you'll believe me, it formed itself into the sign of a gigantic hand. A great white hand against the crimson of the sky. The fingers were crooked-like, as though they were reaching out for something. It fair gave me a turn. ' Did you ever know ? ' I said to myself. ' That's a sign of something coming '— and sure enough at that very minute I heard the shot. ' It's come,' I said to myself, and I rushed downstairs and joined Carrie and the others who were in the hall, and we went into the music room, and there she was, shot through the head— and the blood and everything. Horrible ! I spoke up, I did, and told Sir George how I'd seen the sign beforehand, but he didn't seem to think much of it. An unlucky day, that was, I'd felt it in my bones from early in the morning. Friday, and the 13th—what could you expect ? "

She rambled on. Mr. Satterthwaite was patient. Again

and again he took her back to the crime, questioning her closely. In the end he was forced to confess defeat. Louisa Bullard had told all she knew, and her story was perfectly simple and straightforward.

Yet he did discover one fact of importance. The post in question had been suggested to her by Mr. Thompson, Sir George's secretary. The wages attached were so large that she was tempted, and accepted the job, although it involved her leaving England very hurriedly. A Mr. Denman had made all the arrangements this end and had also warned her not to write to her fellow-servants in England, as this might "get her into trouble with the immigration authorities," which statement she had accepted in blind faith.

The amount of the wages, casually mentioned by her, was indeed so large that Mr. Satterthwaite was startled. After some hesitation he made up his mind to approach this Mr. Denman.

He found very little difficulty in inducing Mr. Denman to tell all he knew. The latter had come across Thompson in London, and Thompson had done him a good turn. The secretary had written to him in September saying that for personal reasons Sir George was anxious to get this girl out of England. Could he find her a job? A sum of money had been sent to raise the wages to a high figure.

"Usual trouble, I guess," said Mr. Denman, leaning back nonchalantly in his chair. "Seems a nice quiet girl too."

Mr. Satterthwaite did not agree that this was the usual trouble. Louisa Bullard, he was sure, was not a cast-off fancy of Sir George Barnaby's. For some reason it had been vital to get her out of England. But why? And who was at the bottom of it? Sir George himself, working through Thompson? Or the latter working on his own initiative, and dragging in his employer's name.

Still pondering over these questions, Mr. Satterthwaite made the return journey. He was cast down and despondent. His journey had done no good.

Smarting under a sense of failure, he made his way to the Arlecchino the day after his return. He hardly expected to be successful the first time, but to his satisfaction the familiar figure was sitting at the table in the recess, and the dark face of Mr. Harley Quin smiled a welcome.

"Well," said Mr. Satterthwaite as he helped himself to a pat of butter, "you sent me on a nice wild-goose chase."

Mr. Quin raised his eyebrows.

" I sent you ? " he objected. " It was your own idea entirely."

" Whosever idea it was, it's not succeeded. Louisa Bullard has nothing to tell."

Thereupon Mr. Satterthwaite related the details of his conversation with the housemaid and then went on to his interview with Mr. Denman. Mr. Quin listened in silence.

" In one sense, I was justified," continued Mr. Satterthwaite. " She was deliberately got out of the way. But why ? I can't see it."

" No ? " said Mr. Quin, and his voice was, as ever, provocative.

Mr. Satterthwaite flushed.

" I dare say you think I might have questioned her more adroitly. I can assure you that I took her over the story again and again. It was not my fault that I did not get what we want."

" Are you sure," said Mr. Quin, " that you did not get what you want ? "

Mr. Satterthwaite looked up at him in astonishment, and met that sad, mocking gaze he knew so well.

The little man shook his head, slightly bewildered.

There was a silence, and then Mr. Quin said, with a total change of manner :

" You gave me a wonderful picture the other day of the people in this business. In a few words you made them stand out as clearly as though they were etched. I wish you would do something of that kind for the place—you left that in shadow."

Mr. Satterthwaite was flattered.

" The place ? Deering Hill ? Well, it's a very ordinary sort of house nowadays. Red brick, you know, and bay windows. Quite hideous outside, but very comfortable inside. Not a very large house. About two acres of ground. They're all much the same, those houses round the links. Built for rich men to live in. The inside of the house is reminiscent of a hotel—the bedrooms are like hotel suites. Baths and hot and cold basins in all the bedrooms and a good many gilded electric light fittings. All wonderfully comfortable, but not very country-like. You can tell that Deering Vale is only nineteen miles from London."

Mr. Quin listened attentively.

" The train service is bad, I have heard," he remarked.

" Oh ! I don't know about that," said Mr. Satterthwaite, warming to his subject. " I was down there for a bit last summer. I found it quite convenient for town. Of course, the trains only go every hour. 48 minutes past the hour from Waterloo—up to 10.48."

" And how long does it take to Deering Vale ? "

" Just about three-quarters of an hour. 28 minutes past the hour at Deering Vale."

" Of course," said Mr. Quin with a gesture of vexation, " I should have remembered. Miss Dale saw some one off by the 6.28 that evening, didn't she ? "

Mr. Satterthwaite did not reply for a minute or two. His mind had gone back with a rush to his unsolved problem. Presently he said :

" I wish you would tell me what you meant just now when you asked me if I was sure I had not got what I wanted ? "

It sounded rather complicated, put that way, but Mr. Quin made no pretence of not understanding.

" I just wondered if you weren't being a little too exacting. After all, you found out that Louisa Bullard was deliberately got out of the country. That being so, there must be a reason. And the reason must lie in what she said to you."

" Well," said Mr. Satterthwaite argumentatively. " What did she say ? If she'd given evidence at the trial, what could she have said ? "

" She might have told what she saw," said Mr. Quin.

" What did she see ? "

" A sign in the sky."

Mr. Satterthwaite stared at him.

" Are you thinking of *that* nonsense. That superstitious notion of its being the hand of God ? "

" Perhaps," said Mr. Quin, " for all you and I know it may have been the hand of God, you know."

The other was clearly puzzled at the gravity of his manner.

" Nonsense," he said. " She said herself it was the smoke of the train."

" An up train or a down train, I wonder ? " murmured Mr. Quin.

" Hardly an up train. They go at ten minutes to the hour. It must have been a down train—the 6.28—no, that won't do. She said the shot came immediately afterwards, and we know the shot was fired at twenty minutes past six. The train couldn't have been ten minutes early."

" Hardly, on that line," agreed Mr. Quin.

Mr. Satterthwaite was staring ahead of him.

" Perhaps a goods train," he murmured. " But surely, if so——"

" There would have been no need to get her out of England. I agree," said Mr. Quin.

Mr. Satterthwaite gazed at him, fascinated.

" The 6.28," he said slowly. " But if so, if the shot was fired then, why did every one say it was earlier ? "

" Obvious," said Mr. Quin. " The clocks must have been wrong."

" All of them ? " said Mr. Satterthwaite doubtfully. " That's a pretty tall coincidence, you know."

" I wasn't thinking of it as a coincidence," said the other. " I was thinking that it was Friday."

" Friday ? " said Mr. Satterthwaite.

" You did tell me, you know, that Sir George always wound the clocks on a Friday afternoon," said Mr. Quin apologetically.

" He put them back ten minutes," said Mr. Satterthwaite, almost in a whisper, so awed was he by the discoveries he was making. " Then he went out to bridge. I think he must have opened the note from his wife to Martin Wylde that morning—yes, decidedly he opened it. He left his bridge party at 6.30, found Martin's gun standing by the side door, and went in and shot her from behind. Then he went out again, threw the gun into the bushes where it was found later, and was apparently just coming out of the neighbour's gate when some one came running to fetch him. But the telephone —what about the telephone ? Ah ! yes, I see. He disconnected it so that a summons could not be sent to the police that way—they might have noted the time it was received. And Wylde's story works out now. The real time he left was five and twenty minutes past six. Walking slowly, he would reach home about a quarter to seven. Yes, I see it all. Louisa was the only danger with her endless talk about her superstitious fancies. Some one might realise the significance of the train and then—good-bye to that excellent *alibi*."

" Wonderful," commented Mr. Quin.

Mr. Satterthwaite turned to him, flushed with success.

" The only thing is—how to proceed now ? "

" I should suggest Sylvia Dale," said Mr. Quin.

Mr. Satterthwaite looked doubtful.

" I mentioned to you," he said, " she seemed to me a little
—er—stupid."

" She has a father and brothers who will take the necessary
steps."

" That is true," said Mr. Satterthwaite, relieved.

A very short time afterwards he was sitting with the girl
telling her the story. She listened attentively. She put no
questions to him, but when he had done she rose.

" I must have a taxi—at once."

" My dear child, what are you going to do ? "

" I am going to Sir George Barnaby."

" Impossible. Absolutely the wrong procedure. Allow
me to——"

He twittered on by her side. But he produced no impression. Sylvia Dale was intent on her own plans. She
allowed him to go with her in the taxi, but to all his remon-
strances she addressed a deaf ear. She left him in the taxi.
while she went into Sir George's city office.

It was half an hour later when she came out. She looked
exhausted, her fair beauty drooping like a waterless flower.
Mr. Satterthwaite received her with concern.

" I've won," she murmured, as she leant back with half-
closed eyes.

" What ? " he was startled. " What did you do ? What
did you say ? "

She sat up a little.

" I told him that Louisa Bullard had been to the police
with her story. I told him that the police had made inquiries
and that he had been seen going into his own grounds and out
again a few minutes after half-past six. I told him that the
game was up. He—he went to pieces. I told him that there
was still time for him to get away, that the police weren't
coming for another hour to arrest him. I told him that if he'd
sign a confession that he'd killed Vivien I'd do nothing, but
that if he didn't I'd scream and tell the whole building the
truth. He was so panicky that he didn't know what he was
doing. He signed the paper without realising what he was
doing."

She thrust it into his hands.

" Take it—take it. You know what to do with it so that
they'll set Martin free."

" He actually signed it," cried Mr. Satterthwaite, amazed.

" He is a little stupid, you know," said Sylvia Dale. " So am I," she added as an afterthought. " That's why I know how stupid people behave. We get rattled, you know, and then we do the wrong thing and are sorry afterwards."

She shivered, and Mr. Satterthwaite patted her hand.

" You need something to pull you together," he said. " Come, we are close to a very favourite resort of mine—the Arlecchino. Have you ever been there ? "

She shook her head.

Mr. Satterthwaite stopped the taxi and took the girl into the little restaurant. He made his way to the table in the recess, his heart beating hopefully. But the table was empty.

Sylvia Dale saw the disappointment in his face.

" What is it ? " she asked.

" Nothing," said Mr. Satterthwaite. " That is, I half expected to see a friend of mine here. It doesn't matter. Some day, I expect, I shall see him again. . . ."

WALTER DE LA MARE (1873–   )
*started life in a bank. He is the greatest
modern interpreter of that " border region "
between the natural and the supernatural. His
volume of short stories, " On the Edge," might
serve as a title to his collected works—poems,
novels, tales. No one, except perhaps Henry
James, has succeeded so well in conveying the
indefinable by suggestive and subtle use of symbols.*

ALL HALLOWS

*" And because time in itselfe . . . can receive no
alteration, the hallowing . . . must consist in the shape
or countenance which we put upon the affaires that
are incident in these days."*

RICHARD HOOKER.

IT was about half-past three on an August afternoon when
I found myself for the first time looking down upon All
Hallows. And at glimpse of it, fatigue and vexation passed
away. I stood " at gaze," as the old phrase goes—like the
two children of Israel sent in to spy out the Promised Land.
How often the imagined transcends the real. Not so All
Hallows. Having at last reached the end of my journey—
flies, dust, heat, wind—having at last come limping out upon
the green sea-bluff beneath which lay its walls—I confess the
actuality excelled my feeble dreams of it.

What most astonished me, perhaps, was the sense not so
much of its age, its austerity, or even its solitude, but its air
of abandonment. It lay couched there as if in hiding in its
narrow sea-bay. Not a sound was in the air ; not a jackdaw
clapped its wings among its turrets. No other roof, not even
a chimney, was in sight ; only the dark-blue arch of the sky ;
the narrow snowline of the ebbing tide ; and that gaunt coast
fading away into the haze of a West over which were already
gathering the veils of sunset.

We had met, then, at an appropriate hour and season.
And yet—I wonder. For it was certainly not the " beauty "
of All Hallows, lulled as if into a dream in this serenity of air
and heavens, which was to leave the sharpest impression upon

me. And what kind of first showing would it have made, I speculated, if an autumnal gale had been shrilling and trumpeting across its narrow bay—clots of wind-borne spume floating among its dusky pinnacles—and the roar of the sea echoing against its walls ! Imagine it frozen stark in winter, icy hoarfrost edging its every boss, moulding, finial, crocket, cusp !

Indeed, are there not works of man, legacies of a half-forgotten past, scattered across this human world of ours from China to Peru, which seem to daunt the imagination with their incomprehensibility ? Incomprehensible, I mean, in the sense that the passion that inspired and conceived them is incomprehensible. Viewed in the light of the passing day, they might be the monuments of a race of demi-gods. And yet, if we could but free ourselves from our timidities, and follies, we might realise that even we ourselves have an obligation to leave behind us similar memorials—testaments to the creative and faithful genius not so much of the individual as of Humanity itself.

However that may be, it was my own personal fortune to see All Hallows for the first time in the heat of the Dog Days, after a journey which could hardly be justified except by its end. At this moment of the afternoon the great church almost cheated one into the belief that it was possessed of a life of its own. It lay, as I say, couched in its natural hollow, basking under the dark dome of the heavens like some half-fossilised monster that might at any moment stir and awaken out of the swoon to which the wand of the enchanter had committed it. And with every inch of the sun's descending journey it changed its appearance.

That is the charm of such things. Man himself, says the philosopher, is the sport of change. His life and the life around him are but the flotsam of a perpetual flux. Yet, haunted by ideals, egged on by impossibilities, he builds his vision of the changeless ; and time diversifies it with its colours and its " effects " at leisure. It was drawing near to harvest now ; the summer was nearly over ; the corn would soon be in stook ; the season of silence had come, not even the robins had yet begun to practise their autumnal lament. I should have come earlier.

The distance was of little account. But nine flinty hills in seven miles is certainly hard commons. To plod (the occupant of a cloud of dust) up one steep incline and so see another ; to plod up that and so see a third ; to surmount

that and, half-choked, half-roasted, to see (as if in unbelievable
mirage) a fourth—and always stone walls, discoloured grass,
no flower but ragged ragwort, whited fleabane, moody nettle,
and the exquisite stubborn bindweed with its almond-burdened
censers, and always the glitter and dazzle of the sun—well,
the experience grows irksome.   And then that endless flint
erection with which some jealous Lord of the Manor had
barricaded his verdurous estate !   A fly-infested mile of the
company of that wall was tantamount to making one's way
into the infernal regions—with Tantalus for fellow-pilgrim.
And when a solitary and empty dung-wagon had lumbered by,
lifting the dumb dust out of the road in swirling clouds into
the heat-quivering air, I had all but wept aloud.

No, I shall not easily forget that walk—or the conclusion
of it—when footsore, all but dead beat—dust all over me,
cheeks, lips, eyelids, in my hair, dust in drifts even between
my naked body and my clothes—I stretched my aching limbs
on the turf under the straggle of trees which crowned the bluff
of that last hill still blessedly green and verdant, and feasted
my eyes on the cathedral beneath me.   How odd Memory is
—in her sorting arrangements.   How perverse her pigeon-
holes.

It had reminded me of a drizzling evening many years
ago.   I had stayed a moment to listen to an old Salvation
Army officer preaching at a street corner.   The sopped and
squalid houses echoed with his harangue.   His penitents'
drum resembled the block of an executioner.   His goatish
beard wagged at every word he uttered.   " My brothers and
sisters," he was saying, " the very instant our fleshly bodies
are born they begin to perish ; the moment the Lord has put
them together, time begins to take them to pieces again.   *Now*
at this very instant if you listen close, you can hear the nibblings
and frettings of the moth and rust within—the worm that never
dies.   It's the same with human causes and creeds and institu-
tions—just the same.   O then for that Strand of Beauty where
all that is mortal shall be shed away and we shall appear in the
likeness and verisimilitude of what in sober and awful truth
we are."

The light striking out of an oil and colourman's shop at
the street corner lay across his cheek and beard and glassed
his eye.   The soaked circle of humanity in which he was
gesticulating stood staring and motionless—the lassies, the
probationers, the melancholy idlers.   I had had enough.   I

went away. But it is odd that so utterly inappropriate a recollection should have edged back into my mind at this moment. There was, as I have said, not a living soul in sight. Only a few sea-birds—oyster catchers maybe—were jangling on the distant beach.

It was now a quarter to four by my watch, and the usual pensive " lin-lan-lone " from the belfry beneath me would soon no doubt be ringing to evensong. But if at that moment a triple bob-major had suddenly clanged its alarm over sea and shore, I couldn't have stirred a finger's breadth. Scanty though the shade afforded by the wind-shorn tuft of trees under which I lay might be—I was ineffably at peace.

No bell, as a matter of fact, loosed its tongue that stagnant half-hour. Unless then the walls beneath me already concealed a few such chance visitors as myself, All Hallows would be empty. A cathedral not only without a close but without a congregation—yet another romantic charm. The Deanery and the residences of its clergy, my old guide-book had long since informed me, were a full mile or more away. I determined in due time, first to make sure of an entry, and then having quenched my thirst, to bathe.

How inhuman any extremity—hunger, fatigue, pain, desire—makes us poor humans. Thirst and drouth so haunted my mind that again and again as I glanced towards it I supped up at one long draught that complete blue sea. But meanwhile, too, my eyes had been steadily exploring and searching out this monument of the bygone centuries beneath me.

The headland faced approximately due west. The windows of the Lady Chapel therefore lay immediately beneath me, their fourteenth-century glass showing flatly dark amid their traceries. Above it, the shallow V-shaped, leaden-ribbed roof of the chancel converged towards the unfinished tower, then broke away at right angles—for the cathedral was cruciform. Walls so ancient and so sparsely adorned and decorated could not but be inhospitable in effect. Their stone was of a bleached bone-gray ; a gray that none the less seemed to be as immaterial as flame—or incandescent ash. They were substantial enough, however, to cast a marvellously lucent shadow, of a blue no less vivid but paler than that of the sea, on the shelving sward beneath them. And that shadow was steadily shifting as I watched. But even if the complete edifice had vanished into the void, the scene would still have been of an incredible loveliness. The colours in air and sky on this dangerous coast seemed to shed a peculiar unreality even on the rocks of its own outworks.

So, from my vantage place on the hill that dominates it, I continued for a while to watch All Hallows ; to spy upon it ; and no less intently than a sentry who, not quite trusting his own eyes, has seen a dubious shape approaching him in the dusk. It may sound absurd, but I felt that at any moment I too might surprise All Hallows in the act of revealing what in very truth it looked like—and *was*, when no human witness was there to share its solitude.

Those gigantic statues, for example, which flanked the base of the unfinished tower—an intense bluish-white in the sunlight and a bluish-purple in shadow—images of angels and of saints, as I had learned of old from my guide-book. Only six of them at most could be visible, of course, from where I sat. And yet I found myself counting them again and yet again, as if doubting my own arithmetic. For my first impression had been that seven were in view—though the figure furthest from me at the western angle showed little more than a jutting fragment of stone which might perhaps be only part and parcel of the fabric itself.

But then the lights even of day may be deceitful, and fantasy plays strange tricks with one's eyes. With exercise, none the less, the mind is enabled to detect minute details which the unaided eye is incapable of particularising. Given the imagination, man himself indeed may some day be able to distinguish what shapes are walking during our own terrestrial midnight amid the black shadows of the craters in the noonday of the moon. At any rate, I could trace at last frets of carving, minute weather marks, crookednesses, incrustations, repairings, that had before passed unnoticed. These walls, indeed, like human faces, were maps and charts of their own long past.

In the midst of this prolonged scrutiny, the hypnotic air, the heat, must suddenly have overcome me. I fell asleep up there in my grove's scanty shade ; and remained asleep, too, long enough (as time is measured by the clocks of sleep) to dream an immense panoramic dream. On waking, I could recall only the faintest vestiges of it, and found that the hand of my watch had crept on but a few minutes in the interval. It was eight minutes past four.

I scrambled up—numbed and inert—with that peculiar sense of panic which sometimes follows an uneasy sleep. What folly to have been frittering time away within sight of my goal

at an hour when no doubt the cathedral would soon be closed
to visitors, and abandoned for the night to its own secret
ruminations. I hastened down the steep rounded incline of
the hill, and having skirted under the sunlit expanse of the
walls, came presently to the south door, only to discover that
my forebodings had been justified, and that it was already
barred and bolted. The discovery seemed to increase my
fatigue fourfold. How foolish it is to obey mere caprices.
What a straw is a man !

I glanced up into the beautiful shell of masonry above my
head. Shapes and figures in stone it showed in plenty—
symbols of an imagination that had flamed and faded, leaving
this signature for sole witness—but not a living bird or butterfly. There was but one faint chance left of making an entry.
Hunted now, rather than the hunter, I hastened out again
into the full blazing flood of sunshine—and once more came
within sight of the sea ; a sea so near at last that I could hear
its enormous sallies and murmurings. Indeed I had not
realised until that moment how closely the great western doors
of the cathedral abutted on the beach.

It was as if its hospitality had been deliberately designed,
not for a people to whom the faith of which it was the shrine
had become a weariness and a commonplace, but for the solace
of pilgrims from over the ocean. I could see them tumbling
into their cockle-boats out of their great hollow ships—sails
idle, anchors down ; see them leaping ashore and straggling
up across the sands to these all-welcoming portals—" Parthians
and Medes and Elamites ; dwellers in Mesopotamia and in the
parts of Egypt about Cyrene ; strangers of Rome, Jews and
Proselytes—we do hear them speak in our own tongue the
wonderful works of God."

And so at last I found my way into All Hallows—entering
by a rounded dwarfish side-door with zigzag mouldings.
There hung for corbel to its dripstone a curious leering face,
with its forked tongue out, to give me welcome. And an
appropriate one, too, for the figure I made !

But once beneath that prodigious roof-tree, I forgot myself
and everything that was mine. The hush, the coolness, the
unfathomable twilight drifted in on my small human consciousness. Not even the ocean itself is able so completely to
receive one into its solacing bosom. Except for the windows
over my head, filtering with their stained glass the last western
radiance of the sun, there was but little visible colour in those

great spaces, and a severe economy of decoration. The stone piers carried their round arches with an almost intimidating impassivity.

By deliberate design, too, or by some illusion of perspective the whole floor of the building appeared steadily to ascend towards the east, where a dark wooden multitudinously-figured rood-screen shut off the choir and the high altar from the nave. I seemed to have exchanged one universal actuality for another : the burning world of nature, for this oasis of quiet. Here, the wings of the imagination need never rest in their flight out of the wilderness into the unknown.

Thus resting, I must again have fallen asleep. And so swiftly can even the merest freshet of sleep affect the mind, that when my eyes opened, I was completely at a loss.

Where was I ? What demon of what romantic chasm had swept my poor drowsy body into this immense haunt ? The din and clamour of an horrific dream whose fainting rumour was still in my ear, became suddenly stilled. Then at one and the same moment, a sense of utter dismay at earthly surroundings no longer serene and peaceful, but grim and forbidding, flooded my mind, and I became aware that I was no longer alone. Twenty or thirty paces away, and a little this side of the rood-screen, an old man was standing.

To judge from the black and purple velvet and tassel-tagged gown he wore, he was a verger. He had not yet realised, it seemed, that a visitor shared his solitude. And yet he was listening. His head was craned forward and leaned sideways on his rusty shoulders. As I steadily watched him, he raised his eyes, and with a peculiar stealthy deliberation scanned the complete upper regions of the northern transept. Not the faintest rumour of any sound that may have attracted his attention reached me where I sat. Maybe a wild bird had made its entry through a broken pane of glass and with its cry had at the same moment awakened me and caught his attention. Or maybe the old man was waiting for some fellow-occupant to join him from above.

I continued to watch him. Even at this distance, the silvery twilight cast by the clerestory windows was sufficient to show me, though vaguely, his face : the high sloping nose, the lean cheekbones and protruding chin. He continued so long in the same position that I at last determined to break in on his reverie.

At sound of my footsteps his head sunk cautiously back

upon his shoulders ; and he turned ; and then motionlessly surveyed me as I drew near. He resembled one of those old men whom Rembrandt delighted in drawing : the knotted hands, the black drooping eyebrows, the wide thin-lipped ecclesiastical mouth, the intent cavernous dark eyes beneath the heavy folds of their lids. White as a miller with dust, hot and draggled, I was hardly the kind of visitor that any self-respecting custodian would warmly welcome, but he greeted me none the less with every mark of courtesy.

I apologised for the lateness of my arrival, and explained it as best I could. " Until I caught sight of you," I concluded lamely, " I hadn't ventured very far in : otherwise I might have found myself a prisoner for the night. It must be dark in here when there is no moon."

The old man smiled—but wryly. " As a matter of fact, sir," he replied, " the cathedral is closed to visitors at four— at such times, that is, when there is no afternoon service. Services are not as frequent as they were. But visitors are rare too. In winter, in particular, you notice the gloom—as you say, sir. Not that I ever spend the night here : though I am usually last to leave. There's the risk of fire to be thought of and . . . I think I should have detected your presence here, sir. One becomes accustomed after many years."

There was the usual trace of official pedantry in his voice, but it was more pleasing than otherwise. Nor did he show any wish to be rid of me. He continued his survey, although his eye was a little absent and his attention seemed to be divided.

" I thought perhaps I might be able to find a room for the night and really explore the cathedral to-morrow morning. It has been a tiring journey ; I come from B——"

" Ah, from B—— ; it *is* a fatiguing journey, sir, taken on foot. I used to walk in there to see a sick daughter of mine. Carriage parties occasionally make their way here, but not so much as once. We are too far out of the hurly-burly to be much intruded on. Not that them who come to make their worship here are intruders. Far from it. But most that come are mere sightseers. And the fewer of them, I say, in the circumstances, the better."

Something in what I had said or in my appearance seemed to have reassured him. " Well, I cannot claim to be a regular churchgoer," I said. " I am myself a mere sightseer. And yet—even to sit here for a few minutes is to be reconciled."

" Ah, reconciled, sir : " the old man repeated, turning
away. " I can well imagine it after that journey on such a
day as this. But to live here is another matter."

" I was thinking of that," I replied in a foolish attempt
to retrieve the position. " It must, as you say, be desolate
enough in the winter—for two-thirds of the year, indeed."

" We have our storms, sir—the bad with the good," he
agreed, " and our position is specially prolific of what they
call sea-fog. It comes driving in from the sea for days and
nights together—gale and mist, so that you can scarcely see
your open hand in front of your eyes even in broad daylight.
And the noise of it, sir, sweeping across overhead in that
wooliness of mist, if you take me, is most peculiar. It's
shocking to a stranger. No, sir, we are left pretty much to
ourselves when the fine weather birds are flown. . . . You'd
be astonished at the power of the winds here. There was a
mason—a local man too—not above two or three years ago
was blown clean off the roof from under the tower—tossed
up in the air like an empty sack. But "—and the old man at
last allowed his eyes to stray upwards to the roof again—" but
there's not much doing now." He seemed to be pondering.
" Nothing open."

" I mustn't detain you," I said, " but you were saying
that services are infrequent now. Why is that ? When one
thinks of——" But tact restrained me.

" Pray don't think of keeping me, sir. It's a part of my
duties. But from a remark you let fall I was supposing you
may have seen something that appeared, I understand, not
many months ago in the newspapers. We lost our Dean—
Dean Pomfrey—last November. To all intents and purposes,
I mean ; and his office has not yet been filled. Between you
and me, sir, there's a hitch—though I should wish it to go no
further. They are greedy monsters—those newspapers : no
respect, no discretion, no decency, in my view. And they
copy each other like cats in a chorus.

" We have never wanted to be a notoriety here, sir : and
not of late of all times. We must face our own troubles.
You'd be astonished how callous the mere sightseer can be.
And not only them from over the water whom our particular
troubles cannot concern—but far worse—parties as English
as you or me. They ask you questions you wouldn't believe
possible in a civilised country. Not that they care what
becomes of us—not one iota, sir. We talk of them masked-up

Inquisitors in olden times, but there's many a human being in
our own would enjoy seeing a fellow-creature on the rack if
he could get the opportunity.   It's a heartless age, sir."

This was queerish talk in the circumstances : and after
all I myself was of the glorious company of the sightseers.   I
held my peace.   And the old man, as if to make amends,
asked me if I would care to see any particular part of the building.   "The light is smalling," he explained, "but still if we
keep to the ground level there'll be a few minutes to spare ;
and we shall not be interrupted if we go quietly on our way."

For the moment the reference eluded me : I could only
thank him for the suggestion and once more beg him not to
put himself to any inconvenience.   I explained, too, that
though I had no personal acquaintance with Dr. Pomfrey, I
had read of his illness in the newspapers.   "Isn't he," I added.
a little dubiously, "the author of *The Church and the Folk* ?
If so, he must be an exceedingly learned and delightful man."

"Ay, sir."   The old verger put up a hand towards me ;
"you may well say it : a saint, if ever there was one.   But it's
worse than ' illness,' sir—it's oblivion.   And, thank God,
the newspapers didn't get hold of more than a bare outline."

He dropped his voice.   "This way, if you please ; " and
he led me off gently down the aisle, once more coming to a
standstill beneath the roof of the tower.   "What I mean, sir,
is that there's very few left in this world who have any place in
their minds for a sacred confidence—no reverence, sir.   They
would as lief All Hallows and all it stands for were swept
away to-morrow, demolished to the dust.   And that gives me
the greatest caution with whom I speak.   But sharing one's
troubles is sometimes a relief.   If it weren't so, why do those
Cartholics have their wooden boxes all built for the purpose ?
What else, I ask you, is the meaning of their fasts and
penances ?

"You see, sir, I am myself, and have been for upwards
of twelve years now, the Dean's verger.   In the sight of no
respecter of persons—of offices and dignities, that is, I take it
—I might claim to be even an elder brother.   And our Dean,
sir, was a man who was all things to all men.   No pride of
place, no vauntingness, none of your apron-and-gaiter high-
and-mightiness whatsoever, sir.   And then that !   And to
come on us without warning ; or at least without warning as
could be taken as *such*."   I followed his eyes into the darkening
stony spaces above us ; a light like tarnished silver lay over

the soundless vaultings. But so, of course, dusk, either of evening or daybreak, would affect the ancient stones. Nothing moved there.

"You must understand, sir," the old man was continuing, "the procession for divine service proceeds from the vestry over yonder out through those wrought-iron gates and so under the rood-screen and into the chancel there. Visitors are admitted on showing a card or a word to the verger in charge : but not otherwise. If you stand a pace or two to the right, you will catch a glimpse of the altar-screen—fourteenth-century work, Bishop Robert de Beaufort—and a unique example of the age. But what I was saying is that when we proceed for the services *out* of here *into* there, it has always been our custom to keep pretty close together ; more seemly and decent, sir, than straggling in like so many sheep.

"Besides, sir, aren't we at such times in the manner of an *array* ; 'marching as to war,' if you take me : it's a lesson in objects. The third verger leading : then the choristers, boys and men, though sadly depleted ; then the minor canons ; then any other dignitaries who may happen to be present, with the canon in residence ; then myself, sir, followed by the Dean.

"There hadn't been much amiss up to then, and on that afternoon, I can vouch—and I've repeated it *ad naushum*—there was not a single stranger out in this beyond here, sir—nave or transepts. Not within view, that is : one can't be expected to see through four feet of Norman stone. Well, sir, we had gone on our way, and I had actually turned about as usual to bow Dr. Pomfrey into his stall, when I found to my consternation, to my consternation, I say, he wasn't there ! It alarmed me, sir, and as you might well believe if you knew the full circumstances.

"Not that I lost my presence of mind. My first duty was to see all things to be in order and nothing unseemly to occur. My feelings were another matter. The old gentle-man had left the vestry with us : that I knew : I had myself robed 'im as usual, and he in his own manner, smiling with his 'Well, Jones, another day gone ; another day gone.' He was always an anxious gentleman for *time*, sir. How we spend it and all.

"As I say, then, he was behind me when we swepp out of the gates. I saw him coming on out of the tail of my eye—we grow accustomed to it, to see with the whole of the eye, I mean. And then—not a vestige ; and me—well, sir, non-plussed, as you may imagine. I gave a look and sign at Canon Ockham, and the service proceeded as usual, while I hurried back to the vestry thinking the poor gentleman must have been taken suddenly ill. And yet, sir, I was not surprised to find the vestry vacant, and him not there. I had been expecting matters to come to what you might call a head.

" As best I could I held my tongue, and a fortunate thing it was that Canon Ockham was then in residence, and not Canon Leigh Shougar, though perhaps I am not the one to say it. No, sir, our beloved Dean—as pious and harmless a gentleman as ever graced the Church—was gone for ever. He was not to appear in our midst again. He had been "—and the old man with elevated eyebrows and long lean mouth nearly whispered the words into my ear—" he had been absconded—abducted, sir."

" Abducted ! " I murmured.

The old man closed his eyes, and with trembling lids added, " He was found, sir, late that night up there in what they call the Trophy Room—sitting in a corner there, weeping. A child. Not a word of what had persuaded him to go or misled him there, not a word of sorrow or sadness, thank God. He didn't know us, sir—didn't know me. Just simple ; harmless ; memory all gone. Simple, sir."

It was foolish to be whispering together like this beneath these enormous spaces with not so much as a clothes-moth for sign of life within view. But I even lowered my voice still further : " Were there no premonitory symptoms ? Had he been failing for long ? "

The spectacle of grief in any human face is afflicting, but in a face as aged and resigned as this old man's—I turned away in remorse the moment the question was out of my lips ; emotion is a human solvent and a sort of friendliness had sprung up between us.

" If you will just follow me," he whispered, " there's a little place where I make my ablutions that might be of service, sir. We could converse there in better comfort. I am some-times reminded of those words in Ecclesiastes : ' And a bird of the air shall tell of the matter.' There is not much in our poor human affairs, sir, that was not known to the writer of that book."

He turned and led the way with surprising celerity, gliding along in his thin-soled, square-toed, clerical springside boots ;

and came to a pause outside a nail-studded door. He opened
it with a huge key, and admitted me into a recess under the
central tower. We mounted a spiral stone staircase and passed
along a corridor hardly more than two feet wide and so dark
that now and again I thrust out my fingertips in search of his
black velveted gown to make sure of my guide.

This corridor at length conducted us into a little room
whose only illumination I gathered was that of the ebbing
dusk from within the cathedral. The old man with trembling
rheumatic fingers lit a candle, and thrusting its stick into the
middle of an old oak table, pushed open yet another thick
oaken door. "You will find a basin and a towel in there, sir,
if you will be so kind."

I entered. A print of the Crucifixion was tin-tacked to
the panelled wall, and beneath it stood a tin basin and jug
on a stand. Never was water sweeter. I laved my face and
hands, and drank deep ; my throat like a parched river-course
after a drought. What appeared to be a tarnished censer lay
in one corner of the room ; a pair of seven-branched candle-
sticks shared a recess with a mouse-trap and a book. My
eyes passed wearily yet gratefully from one to another of these
mute discarded objects while I stood drying my hands.

When I returned, the old man was standing motionless
before the spike-barred grill of the window, peering out and
down.

"You asked me, sir," he said, turning his lank waxen
face into the feeble rays of the candle, "you asked me, sir, a
question which, if I understood you aright, was this : Was
there anything that had occurred *previous* that would explain
what I have been telling you ? Well, sir, it's a long story,
and one best restricted to them perhaps that have the good-
will of things at heart. All Hallows, I might say, sir, is my
second home. I have been here, boy and man, for close on
fifty-five years—have seen four bishops pass away and have
served under no less than five several deans, Dr. Pomfrey,
poor gentleman, being the last of the five.

"If such a word could be excused, sir, it's no exaggeration
to say that Canon Leigh Shougar is a greenhorn by com-
parison : which may in part be why he has never quite hit it
off, as they say, with Canon Ockham. Or even with Archdeacon Trafford, though he's another kind of gentleman
altogether. And *he* is at present abroad. He had what they
call a breakdown in health, sir.

"Now in my humble opinion, what was required was not only wisdom and knowledge but simple common sense. In the circumstances I am about to mention, it serves no purpose for any of us to be talking too much ; to be for ever sitting at a table with shut doors and finger on lip, and discussing what to most intents and purposes would hardly be called evidence at all, sir. What is the use of argufying, splitting hairs, objurgating about trifles, when matters are sweeping rapidly on from bad to worse. I say it with all due respect and not, I hope, thrusting myself into what doesn't concern me : Dr. Pomfrey might be with us now in his own self and reason if only common caution had been observed.

"But now that the poor gentleman is gone beyond all that, there is no hope of action or agreement left, none whatsoever. They meet and they meet, and they have now one expert now another down from London, and even from the continent. And I don't say they are not knowledgable gentlemen, either, nor a pride to their profession. But why not tell *all* ? Why keep back the very secret of what we know ? That's what I am asking. And, what's the answer ? Why simply that what they don't want to believe, what runs counter to their hopes and wishes and credibilities—and comfort— in this world, that's what they keep out of sight as long as decency permits.

"Canon Leigh Shougar *knows*, sir, what *I* know. And how, I ask, is he going to get to grips with it at this late day if he refuses to acknowledge that such things are what every fragment of evidence goes to prove that they are. It's *we*, sir, and not the rest of the heedless world outside, who in the long and the short of it are responsible. And what I say is : no power or principality here or hereunder can take possession of a place while those inside have faith enough to keep them out. But once let that falter—the seas are in. And when I say no power, sir, I mean—with all deference—even Satan himself." The lean lank face had set at the word like a wax mask. The black eyes beneath the heavy lids were fixed on mine with an acute intensity and—though more inscrutable things haunted them—with an unfaltering courage. So dense a hush hung about us that the very stones of the walls seemed to be of silence solidified. It is curious what a refreshment of spirit a mere tin basinful of water may be. I stood leaning against the edge of the table so that the candlelight still rested on my companion.

" What is *wrong* here ? " I asked him baldly.

He seemed not to have expected so direct an enquiry.
" Wrong, sir ? Why, if I might make so bold," he replied
with a wan, far-away smile and gently drawing his hand down
one of the velvet lapels of his gown, " if I might make so bold,
sir, I take it that you have come as a direct answer to prayer."

His voice faltered. " I am an old man now, and nearly
at the end of my tether. You must realise, if you please, that
I can't get any help that I can understand. I am not doubting
that the gentlemen I have mentioned have only the salvation of
the cathedral at heart—the cause, sir ; and a graver responsibility yet. But they refuse to see how close to the edge of
things we are : and how we are drifting.

" Take mere situation. So far as my knowledge tells me,
there is no sacred edifice in the whole kingdom—of a piece,
that is, with All Hallows not only in mere size and age but in
what I might call sanctity and tradition—that is so open—
open, I mean, sir, to attack of this peculiar and terrifying
nature."

" Terrifying ? "

" *Terrifying*, sir ; though I hold fast to what wits my Maker
has bestowed on me. Where else, may I ask, would you
expect the powers of darkness to congregate in open besiege-
ment than in this narrow valley ? First, the sea out there.
Are you aware, sir, that ever since living remembrance flood-tide
has been gnawing and mumbling its way into this bay to the
extent of three or four feet *per annum* ? Forty inches, and
forty inches, and forty inches corroding on and on : Watch it,
sir, man and boy as I have these sixty years past and then
make a century of it.

" And now, think a moment of the floods and gales that
fall upon us autumn and winter through and even in spring,
when this valley is liker paradise to young eyes than any place
on earth. They make the roads from the nearest towns well-
nigh impassable ; which means that for seven months of the
year we are to all intents and purposes clean cut off from the
rest of the world—as the Schindels out there are from the
mainland. Are you aware, sir, I continue, that as we stand
now we are above a mile from traces of the nearest human
habitation, and them merely the relics of a burnt-out old farm-
stead ? I warrant that if (and which God forbid) you had
been shut up here during the coming night, and it was a near
thing but what you weren't—I warrant you might have shouted

yourself dumb out of the nearest window if window you could reach—and not a human soul to heed or help you."

I shifted my hands on the table. It was tedious to be asking questions that received only such vague and evasive replies : and it is always a little disconcerting in the presence of a stranger to be spoken to so close, and with such positiveness.

"Well," I smiled, "I hope I should not have disgraced my nerves to such an extreme as that. As a small boy, one of my particular fancies was to spend a night in a pulpit. There's a cushion, you know ! "

The old man's solemn glance never swerved from my eyes. "But I take it, sir," he said, "if you had ventured to give out a text up there in the dark hours, your innocent young mind would not have been prepared for any kind of a congregation ? "

"You mean," I said a little sharply, "that the place is haunted ? " The absurd notion had flitted across my mind of some wandering tribe of gipsies chancing on a refuge so ample and isolated as this, and taking up its quarters in its secret parts. The old church must be honeycombed with corridors and passages and chambers pretty much like the one in which we were now concealed : and what does "cartholic " imply but an infinite hospitality within prescribed limits ? But the old man had taken me at my word.

"I mean, sir," he said firmly, shutting his eyes, "that there are devilish agencies at work here." He raised his hand. "Don't, I entreat you, dismiss what I am saying as the wanderings of a foolish old man." He drew a little nearer. "I have heard them with these ears ; I have seen them with these eyes ; though whether they have any positive substance, sir, is beyond my small knowledge to declare. But what indeed might we expect their substance to be ? First : ' I take it,' says the Book, ' to be such as no man can by learning define, nor by wisdom search out.' Is that so ? Then I go by the Book. And next : what does the same Word or very near it (I speak of the Apocrypha) say of their purpose ? It says— and correct me if I go astray—' Devils are creatures made by God, and that for vengeance.'

"So far, so good, sir. We stop when we can go no further. Vengeance. But of their power of what they can do, I can give you definite evidences. It would be a byword if once the rumour was spread abroad. And if it is not so, why, I ask, does every expert that comes here leave us in haste and in dismay ? They go off with their tails between their legs.

They see, they grope in, but they don't believe. They *invent* reasons. And they *hasten* to leave us ! " His face shook with the emphasis he laid upon the word. " Why ? Why, because the experience is beyond their knowledge, sir." He drew back breathless and, as I could see, profoundly moved.

" But surely," I said, " every old building is bound in time to show symptoms of decay. Half the cathedrals in England, half its churches, even, of any age, have been ' restored '—and in many cases with ghastly results. This new grouting and so on. Why, only the other day. . . . All I mean is, why should you suppose mere wear and tear should be caused by any other agency than——"

The old man turned away. " I must apologise," he interrupted me with his inimitable admixture of modesty and dignity, " I am a poor mouth at explanations, sir. Decay— stress—strain—settling—dissolution : I have heard those words bandied from lip to lip like a game at cup and ball. They fill me with nausea. Why, I am speaking not of dis- solution, sir, but of *repairs, restorations.* Not decay, *strengthen- ing.* Not a corroding loss, an awful *progress.* I could show you places—and chiefly obscured from direct view and difficult of a close examination, sir, where stones lately as rotten as pumice and as fretted as a sponge have been replaced by others fresh-quarried—and nothing of their kind within twenty miles.

" There are spots where massive blocks a yard or more square have been *pushed* into place by sheer force. All Hallows is safer at this moment than it has been for three hundred years. They meant well—them who came to see, full of talk and fine language, and went dumb away. I grant you they meant well. I allow that. They hummed and they hawed. They smirked this and they shrugged that. But at heart, sir, they were cowed—horrified : all at a loss. Their very faces showed it. But if you ask me for what purpose such doings are afoot— I have no answer ; none.

" But now, supposing you yourself, sir, were one of them, with *your* repute at stake, and you were called in to look at a house which the owners of it and them who had it in trust were disturbed by its being re-edificated and restored by some agency unknown to them. Supposing that ! *Why,*" and he rapped with his knuckles on the table, " being human *and not one of us* mightn't you be going away too with mouth shut, because you didn't want to get talked about to your disadvantage ?

And wouldn't you at last dismiss the whole thing as a foolish delusion, in the belief that living in out-of-the-way parts like these cuts a man off from the world, breeds maggots in the mind ?

" I assure you, sir, they don't—not even Canon Ockham himself to the full—they don't believe even me. And yet, when they have their meetings of the Chapter, they talk and wrangle round and round about nothing else. I can bear the other without a murmur. What God sends, I say, we humans deserve. We have laid ourselves open to it. But when you buttress up blindness and wickedness with downright folly, why then, sir, I sometimes fear for my own reason."

He set his shoulders as square as his aged frame would permit, and with fingers clutching the lapels beneath his chin, he stood gazing out into the darkness through that narrow inward window.

" Ah, sir," he began again, " I have not spent sixty years in this solitary place without paying heed to my own small wandering thoughts and instincts. Look at your newspapers, sir. What they call the Great War is over—and he'd be a brave man who would take an oath before heaven that *that* was only of human designing—and yet what do we see around us ? Nothing but strife and juggleries and hatred and contempt and discord wherever you look. I am no scholar, sir, but so far as my knowledge and experience carry me, we human beings are living to-day merely from hand to mouth. We learn to-day what ought to have been done yesterday, and yet are at a loss to know what's to be done to-morrow.

" And the Church, sir. God forbid I should push my way into what does not concern me ; and if you had told me half an hour gone by that you were a regular churchman, I shouldn't be pouring out all this to you now. It wouldn't be seemly. But being not so gives me confidence. By merely listening you can help me, sir ; though you can't help *us*. Centuries ago—and in my humble judgment, rightly—we broke away from the parent stem and rooted ourselves in our own soil. But, right or wrong, doesn't that of itself, I ask you, make us all the more open to attack from him who never wearies in going to and fro in the world seeking whom he may devour ?

" I am not wishing you to take sides. But a gentleman doesn't scoff ; you don't find him jeering at what he doesn't rightly understand. He keeps his own counsel, sir. And that's where, as I say, Canon Leigh Shougar sets me doubting. He refuses to make allowances ; though up there in London things may look different. He gets his company there ; and then for him the whole kallyidoscope changes, if you take me."

The old man scanned me an instant as if enquiring within himself whether, after all, I too might not be one of the outcasts. "You see, sir," he went on dejectedly, "I can bear what may be to come. I can, if need be, live on through what few years may yet remain to me and keep going, as they say. But only if I can be assured that my own inmost senses are not cheating and misleading me. Tell me the worst, and you will have done an old man a service he can never repay. Tell me, on the other hand, that I am merely groping along in a network of devilish *delusion*, sir—well, in that case I hope to be with my master, with Dr. Pomfrey, as soon as possible. We were all children once ; and now there's nothing worse in this world for him to come into, in a manner of speaking.

"Oh, sir, I sometimes wonder if what we call childhood and growing up isn't a copy of the fate of our ancient forefathers. In the beginning of time there were Fallen Angels, we are told ; but even if it weren't there in Holy Writ, we might have learnt it of our own fears and misgivings. I sometimes find myself looking at a young child with little short of awe, sir, knowing that within its mind is a scene of peace and paradise of which we older folk have no notion, and which will fade away out of it, as life wears in, like the mere tabernacling of a dream."

There was no trace of unction in his speech, though the phraseology might suggest it, and he smiled at me as if in reassurance. "You see, sir—if I have any true notion of the matter—then I say, heaven is dealing very gently with Dr. Pomfrey. He has gone back, and, I take it, his soul is elsewhere and at rest."

He had come a pace or two nearer, and the candlelight now cast grotesque shadows in the hollows of his brows and cheekbones, silvering his long scanty hair. The eyes, dimming with age, were fixed on mine as if in incommunicable entreaty. I was at a loss to answer him.

He dropped his hands to his sides. "The fact is," he looked cautiously about him, "what I am now being so bold as to suggest, though it's a familiar enough experience to me, may put you in actual physical danger. But then, duty's duty, and a deed of kindness from stranger to stranger quite another

matter. You seem to have come, if I may say so, in the nick
of time : that was all. On the other hand we can leave the
building at once if you are so minded. In any case we must
be gone well before dark sets in ; even mere human beings
are best not disturbed at any night-work they may be after.
The dark brings recklessness ; conscience cannot see as clear
in the dark. Besides, I once delayed too long myself. There
is not much of day left even now, though I see by the almanac
there should be a slip of moon to-night—unless the sky is
overclouded. All that I'm meaning is that our all-in-all, so to
speak, is the calm untrammelled evidence of the outer senses,
sir. And there comes a time when—well when one hesitates to
trust one's own."

I have read somewhere that it is only its setting—the shape,
the line, the fold, the angle of the lid and so on—that gives
its finer shades of meaning and significance to the human eye.
Looking into his, even in that narrow and melancholy illumination, was like pondering over a gray, salt, desolate pool—such
as sometimes neighbours the sea on a flat and dangerous coast.

Perhaps if I had been a little less credulous, or less exhausted, I should by now have begun to doubt this old creature's
sanity. And yet, surely, at even the faintest contact with the
insane, a sentinel in the mind sends up flares and warnings ;
the very landscape changes ; there is a sense of insecurity.
If, too, the characters inscribed by age and experience on a
man's face can be evidence of goodness and simplicity, then
my companion was safe enough. To trust in his sagacity was
another matter.

But then, there was All Hallows itself to take into account.
That first glimpse from my green headland of its louring yet
lovely walls had been strangely moving. There are buildings
(almost as though they were once copies of originals now half-
forgotten in the human mind) that have a singular influence
on the imagination. Even now in this remote candlelit room,
immured between its massive stones, the vast edifice seemed
to be gently and furtively fretting its impression on my mind.

I glanced again at the old man : he had turned aside as if
to leave me, unbiased, to my own decision. How would a
lifetime spent between these sombre walls have affected *me*,
I wondered ? Surely it would be an act of mere decency to
indulge their worn-out hermit ! He had appealed to me.
If I were ten times more reluctant to follow him, I could
hardly refuse. Not at any rate without risking a retreat as

humiliating as that of the architectural experts he had referred
to—with my tail between my legs.

" I only wish I could hope to be of any real help."

He turned about ; his expression changed, as if at the
coming of a light. " Why, then, sir, let us be gone at once.
You are with me, sir : that was all I hoped and asked. And
now there's no time to waste."

He tilted his head to listen a moment—with that large,
flat, shell-like ear of his which age alone seems to produce.
" Matches and candle, sir," he had lowered his voice to a
whisper, " but—though we mustn't lose each other ; you and
me, I mean—*not*, I think, a naked light. What I would
suggest, if you have no objection, is your kindly grasping my
gown. There is a kind of streamer here, you see—as if made
for the purpose. There will be a good deal of up-and-downing,
but I know the building blindfold and as you might say inch
by inch. And now that the bell-ringers have given up ringing
it is more in my charge than ever."

He stood back and looked at me with folded hands, a
whimsical childlike smile on his aged face. " I sometimes
think to myself I'm like the sentry, sir, in that play of William
Shakespeare's. I saw it, sir, years ago, on my only visit to
London—when I was a boy. If ever there was a villain for
all his fine talk and all, commend me to that ghost. I see him
yet."

Whisper though it was, a sort of chirrup had come into
his voice, like that of a cricket in a baker's shop. I took tight
hold of the velveted tag of his gown. He opened the door,
pressed the box of safety matches into my hand, himself
grasped the candlestick, and then blew out the light. We
were instantly marooned in an impenetrable darkness. " Now,
sir, if you would kindly remove your walking shoes," he
muttered close in my ear, " we should proceed with less noise.
I shan't hurry you. And please to tug at the streamer if you
need attention. In a few minutes the blackness will be less
intense."

As I stooped down to loose my shoe-laces I heard my heart
thumping merrily away. It had been listening to our conversation apparently ! I slung my shoes round my neck—as
I had often done as a boy when going paddling—and we set
out on our expedition.

I have endured too often the nightmare of being lost and
abandoned in the stony bowels of some strange and prodigious

building to take such an adventure lightly. I clung, I confess, desperately tight to my lifeline, and we groped steadily onward —my guide ever and again turning back to mutter warning or encouragement in my ear.

Now I found myself steadily ascending; and then in a while, feeling my way down flights of hollowly worn stone steps, and anon brushing along a gallery or corkscrewing up a newel staircase so narrow that my shoulders all but touched the walls on either side. In spite of the sepulchral cool in these bowels of the cathedral, I was soon suffocatingly hot, and the effort to see became intolerably fatiguing. Once, to recover our breath, we paused opposite a slit in the thickness of the masonry, at which to breathe the tepid sweetness of the outer air. It was faint with the scent of wild flowers and cool of the sea. And presently after, at a barred window, high overhead, I caught a glimpse of the night's first stars.

We then turned inward once more, ascending yet another spiral staircase. And now the intense darkness thinned a little, the groined roof above us becoming faintly discernible. A fresher air softly fanned my cheek; and then trembling fingers groped over my breast, and, cold and bony, clutched my own.

"Dead still here, sir, if you please." So close sounded the whispered syllables the voice might have been a messenger's within my own consciousness. "Dead still, here. There's a drop of some sixty or seventy feet a few paces on."

I peered out across the abyss, conscious, as it seemed, of the huge superincumbent weight of the noble fretted roof only a small space now immediately above our heads. As we approached the edge of this stony precipice, the gloom paled a little, and I guessed that we must be standing in some coign of the southern transept, for what light the evening skies now afforded was clearer towards the right. On the other hand, it seemed the northern windows opposite us were most of them boarded up, or obscured in some fashion. Gazing out, I could detect scaffolding poles—like knitting needles—thrust out from the walls and a balloon-like spread of canvas above them. For the moment my ear was haunted by what appeared to be the droning of an immense insect. But this presently ceased. I fancy it was internal only.

"You will understand, sir," breathed the old man close beside me—and we still stood, grotesquely enough, hand in hand—"the scaffolding over there has been in position a good

many months now. It was put up when the last gentleman
came down from London to inspect the fabric. And there it's
been left ever since. Now, sir !—though I implore you to be
cautious."

I hardly needed the warning. With one hand clutching
my box of matches, the fingers of the other interlaced with my
companion's, I strained every sense. And yet I could detect
not the faintest stir or murmur under that wide-spreading
roof. Only a hush as profound as that which must reign in
the Royal Chamber of the pyramid of Cheops faintly swirled
in the labyrinths of my ear.

How long we stayed in this position I cannot say ; but
minutes sometimes seem like hours. And then, without the
slightest warning, I became aware of a peculiar and incessant
vibration. It is impossible to give a name to it. It suggested
the remote whirring of an enormous mill-stone, or that—
though without definite pulsation—of revolving wings, or even
the spinning of an immense top.

In spite of his age, my companion apparently had ears as
acute as mine. He had clutched me tighter a full ten seconds
before I myself became aware of this disturbance of the air.
He pressed closer. "Do you see that, sir ? "

I gazed and gazed, and saw nothing. Indeed even in what
I had seemed to *hear* I might have been deceived. Nothing is
more treacherous in certain circumstances—except possibly
the eye—than the ear. It magnifies, distorts, and may even
invent. As instantaneously as I had become aware of it, the
murmur had ceased. And then—though I cannot be certain—
it seemed the dingy and voluminous spread of canvas over
there had perceptibly trembled, as if a huge cautious hand had
been thrust out to draw it aside. No time was given me to
make sure. The old man had hastily withdrawn me into the
opening of the wall through which we had issued ; and we
made no pause in our retreat until we had come again to the
narrow slit of window which I have spoken of and could refresh
ourselves with a less stagnant air. We stood here resting awhile.

"Well, sir ? " he enquired at last, in the same flat muffled
tones.

"Do you ever pass along here alone ? " I whispered.

"Oh, yes, sir. I make it a habit to be the last to leave—
and often the first to come ; but I am usually gone by this
hour."

I looked close at the dim face in profile against that narrow

oblong of night. " It is so difficult to be sure of oneself," I
said. " Have you ever actually *encountered* anything—near at
hand, I mean ? "

" I keep a sharp look-out, sir. Maybe they don't think
me of enough importance to molest—the last rat, as they say."

" But *have* you ? "—I might myself have been communicating with the phantasmal *genius loci* of All Hallows—our
muffled voices ; this intense caution and secret listening ;
the slight breathlessness, as if at any instant one's heart were
ready for flight : " But *have* you ? "

" Well yes, sir," he said. " And in this very gallery.
They nearly had me, sir. But by good fortune there's a recess
a little further on—stored up with some old fragments of
carving, from the original building, sixth-century, so it's said :
stone-capitals, heads and hands, and such like. I had had my
warning, and managed to lep in there and conceal myself.
But only just in time. Indeed, sir, I confess I was in such a
condition of terror and horror I turned my back."

" You mean you heard, but didn't look ? And—something
came ? "

" Yes, sir, I seemed to be reduced to no bigger than a
child, huddled up there in that corner. There was a sound
like clanging metal—but I don't think it was metal. It drew
near at a furious speed, then passed me, making a filthy gust
of wind. For some instants I couldn't breathe ; the air was
gone."

" And no other sound ? "

" No other, sir, except out of the distance a noise like the
sounding of a stupendous kind of gibberish. A calling ; or so
it seemed—no human sound. The air shook with it. You see,
sir, I myself wasn't of any consequence, I take it—unless a mere
obstruction in the way. But—I have heard it said somewhere
that the rarity of these happenings is only because it's a pain
and torment and not any sort of pleasure for such beings, such
apparitions, sir, good or bad, to visit our outward world. That's
what I have heard said ; though I can go no further.

" The time I'm telling you of was in the early winter—
November. There was a dense sea-fog over the valley, I
remember. It eddied through that opening there into the
candlelight like flowing milk. I never light up now : and, if
I may be forgiven the boast, sir, I seem to have almost forgotten
how to be afraid. After all, in any walk of life a man can only
do his best, and if there weren't such opposition and hindrances

in high places, I should have nothing to complain of. What is anybody's life, sir (come past the gaiety of youth) but marking time. . . . Did you hear anything *then*, sir ? "

His gentle monotonous mumbling ceased and we listened together. But every ancient edifice has voices and soundings of its own : there was nothing audible that I could put a name to, only what seemed to be a faint perpetual stir or whirr of grinding such as (to one's over-stimulated senses) the stablest stones set one on top of the other with an ever slightly varying weight and stress might be likely to make perceptible in a world of matter. A world which, after all, they say, is itself in unimaginably rapid rotation, and under the tyranny of time.

" No, I hear nothing," I answered : " but please don't think I am doubting what you say. Far from it. You must remember I am a stranger, and that therefore the influence of the place cannot but be less apparent to me. And you have no help in this now ? "

" No, sir. Not now. But even at the best of times we had small company hereabouts, and no money. Not for any substantial outlay, I mean. And not even the boldest suggests making what's called a public appeal. It's a strange thing to me, sir, but whenever the newspapers get hold of anything, they turn it into a byword and a sham. Yet how can they help themselves ?—with no beliefs to guide them and nothing to stay their mouths except about what for sheer human decency's sake they daren't talk about. But then, who am I to complain ? And now, sir," he continued with a sigh of utter weariness, " if you are sufficiently rested, would you perhaps follow me on to the roof ? It is the last visit I make—though by rights perhaps I should take in what there is of the tower. But I'm too old now for that—clambering and climbing over naked beams ; and the ladders are not so safe as they were."

We had not far to go. The old man drew open a squat heavily-ironed door at the head of a flight of wooden stairs. It was latched but not bolted, and admitted us at once to the leaden roof of the building and to the immense amphitheatre of evening. The last faint hues of sunset were fading in the west ; and silver-bright Spica shared with the tilted crescent of the moon the serene lagoon-like expanse of sky above the sea. Even at this height, the air was audibly stirred with the low lullaby of the tide.

The staircase by which we had come out was surmounted by a flat penthouse roof about seven feet high. We edged softly along, then paused once more ; to find ourselves now all but *tête-à-tête* with the gigantic figures that stood sentinel at the base of the buttresses to the unfinished tower.

The tower was so far unfinished, indeed, as to wear the appearance of the ruinous ; besides which, what appeared to be scars and stains as if of fire were detectable on some of its stones, reminding me of the legend which years before I had chanced upon, that this stretch of coast had more than once been visited centuries ago by pillaging Norsemen.

The night was unfathomably clear and still. On our left rose the conical bluff of the headland crowned with the solitary grove of trees beneath which I had taken refuge from the blinding sunshine that very afternoon. Its grasses were now hoary with faintest moonlight. Far to the right stretched the flat cold plain of the Atlantic—that enormous darkened looking-glass of space ; only a distant lightship ever and again stealthily signalling to us with a lean phosphoric finger from its outermost reaches.

The mere sense of that abysm of space—its waste powdered with the stars of the Milky Way ; the mere presence of the stony leviathan on whose back we two humans now stood, dwarfed into insignificance beside these gesturing images of stone, were enough of themselves to excite the imagination. And—whether matter-of-fact or pure delusion—this old verger's insinuations that the cathedral was now menaced by some inconceivable danger and assault had set my nerves on edge. My feet were numb as the lead they stood upon ; while the tips of my fingers tingled as if a powerful electric discharge were coursing through my body.

We moved gently on—the spare shape of the old man a few steps ahead, peering cautiously to right and left of him as we advanced. Once with a hasty gesture he drew me back and fixed his eyes for a full minute on a figure—at two removes —which was silhouetted at that moment against the starry emptiness : a forbidding thing enough, viewed in this vague luminosity, which seemed in spite of the unmoving stare that I fixed on it to be perceptibly stirring on its windworn pedestal.

But no ; " All's well ! " the old man had mutely signalled to me, and we pushed on. Slowly and cautiously ; indeed I had time to notice in passing that this particular figure held stretched in its right hand a bent bow, and was crowned with a high weather-worn stone coronet. One and all were frigid company. At last we completed our circuit of the tower, had come back to the place we had set out from, and stood eyeing one another like two conspirators in the clear dusk. Maybe there was a tinge of incredulity on my face.

"No, sir," murmured the old man, "I expected no other. The night is uncommonly quiet. I've noticed that before. They seem to leave us at peace on nights of quiet. We must turn in again and be getting home."

Until that moment I had thought no more of where I was to sleep or to get food, nor had even realised how famished with hunger I was. Nevertheless, the notion of fumbling down again out of the open air into the narrow inward blackness of the walls from which we had just issued was singularly uninviting. Across these wide flat stretches of roof there was at least space for flight, and there were recesses for concealment. To gain a moment's respite, I enquired if I should have much difficulty in getting a bed in the village. And as I had hoped, the old man himself offered me hospitality.

I thanked him; but still hesitated to follow, for at that moment I was trying to discover what peculiar effect of dusk and darkness a moment before had deceived me into the belief that some small animal—a dog, a spaniel, I should have guessed —had suddenly and surreptitiously taken cover behind the stone buttress nearby. But that apparently had been a mere illusion. The creature, whatever it might be, was no barker at any rate. Nothing stirred now; and my companion seemed to have noticed nothing amiss.

"You were saying," I pressed him, "that when repairs— restorations—of the building were in contemplation, even the experts were perplexed by what they discovered? What did they actually say?"

"Say, sir!" Our voices sounded as small and meaningless up here as those of grasshoppers in a noonday meadow. "Examine that balustrade which you are leaning against at this minute. Look at that gnawing and fretting—that furrowing above the lead. All that is honest wear and tear—constant weathering of the mere elements, sir—rain and wind and snow and frost. That's honest *nature*-work, sir. But now compare it, if you please, with this St. Mark here; and remember, sir, these images were intended to be part and parcel of the fabric as you might say, sentries on a castle—symbols, you understand."

I stooped close under the huge gray creature of stone until my eyes were scarcely more than six inches from its pedestal.

And, unless the moon deceived me, I confess I could find not the slightest trace of fret or friction. Far from it. The stone had been grotesquely decorated in low relief with a gaping crocodile—a two-headed crocodile ; and the angles, knubs and undulations of the creature were cut as sharp as with a knife in cheese. I drew back.

" Now cast your glance upwards, sir. Is that what you would call a saintly shape and gesture ? "

What I took to represent an eagle was perched on the image's lifted wrist—but louring and vulture-like. The head of the figure was poised at an angle of defiance—the ears unnaturally high up on the skull ; the lean right forearm extended with pointing forefinger as if in derision. Its stony gaze was fixed upon the stars ; its whole aspect was undeniably sinister and intimidating. The faintest puff of milk-warm air from over the sea stirred on my cheek. I drew aside.

" Ay, sir, and so with one or two of the rest of them," the old man commented, as he watched me, " there are other wills than the Almighty's."

At this, the pent-up excitement within me broke bounds. This nebulous insinuatory talk !—I all but lost my temper. " I can't, for the life of me, understand what you are saying," I exclaimed in a voice that astonished me with its shrill volume of sound in that intense lofty quiet. " One doesn't *repair* in order to destroy."

The old man met me without flinching. " No, sir ? Say you so ? And why not ? Are there not two kinds of change in this world ?—a building-up and a breaking-down ? To give strength and endurance for evil or misguided purposes, would that be time wasted, if such was your aim ? Why sir, isn't that true even of the human mind and heart ? We here are on the outskirts, I grant, but where would you expect the activity to show itself unless in the outer defences ? An institution may be beyond dying, sir : it may be being restored for a worse destruction. And a hundred trumpeting voices would make no difference when the faith and life within is tottering to its fall."

Somehow, this muddle of metaphors reassured me. Obviously the old man's wits had worn a little thin : he was the victim of an intelligible but monstrous hallucination.

" And yet you are taking it for granted," I expostulated, that, if what you say is true, a stranger could be of the slightest help. A visitor—mind you—who hasn't been inside the doors of a church, except in search of what is old and gone, for years."

The old man laid a trembling hand upon my sleeve. The folly of it—with my shoes hanging like ludicrous millstones round my neck !

" If you please, sir," he pleaded, " have a little patience with me. I'm preaching at nobody. I'm not even hinting that them outside the fold circumstantially speaking aren't of the flock. All in good time, sir ; the Almighty's time. Maybe—with all due respect—it's from them within we have most to fear. And indeed, sir, believe an old man : I could never express the gratitude I feel. You have given me the occasion to unbosom myself, to make a clean breast, as they say. All Hallows is my earthly home, and—well, there, let us say no more. You couldn't *help* me—except only by your presence here. God alone knows who can ! "

At that instant a dull enormous rumble reverberated from within the building—as if a huge boulder or block of stone had been shifted or dislodged in the fabric ; a peculiar grinding nerve-wracking sound. And for the fraction of a second the flags on which we stood seemed to tremble beneath our feet.

The fingers tightened on my arm. " Come, sir ; keep close ; we must be gone at once," the quavering old voice whispered ; " we have stayed too long."

But we emerged into the night at last without mishap. The little western door, above which the grinning head had welcomed me on my arrival, admitted us to *terra firma* again, and we made our way up a deep sandy track, bordered by clumps of herb agrimony and fennel and hemlock, with viper's bugloss and sea-poppy blooming in the gentle dusk of night at our feet. We turned when we reached the summit of this sandy incline and looked back. All Hallows, vague and enormous, lay beneath us in its hollow, resembling some natural prehistoric outcrop of that sea-worn rock-bound coast ; but strangely human and saturnine.

The air was mild as milk—a pool of faintest sweetnesses—gorse, bracken, heather ; and not a rumour disturbed its calm, except only the furtive and stertorous sighings of the tide. But far out to sea and beneath the horizon summer lightnings were now in idle play—flickering into the sky like the unfolding of a signal, planet to planet—then gone. That alone, and perhaps too this feeble moonlight glinting on the ancient glass, may have accounted for the faint vitreous glare that seemed ever and again to glitter across the windows of the northern transept far beneath. And yet how easily deceived is the imagination. This old man's talk still echoing in my ear, I could have vowed this was no reflection but the glow of some light shining fitfully from within outwards.

The old man paused beside a flowering bush of fuchsia at the wicket gate leading into his small square of country garden. " You'll forgive me, sir, for mentioning it ; but I make it a rule as far as possible to leave all my troubles and misgivings outside when I come home. My daughter is a widow, and not long in that sad condition, so I keep as happy a face as I can on things. And yet : well, sir, I wonder at times if—if a personal sacrifice isn't incumbent on them that have their object most at heart. I'd go out myself very willingly, sir, I can assure you, if there was any certainty in my mind that it would serve the cause. It would be little to me if——" He made no attempt to complete the sentence.

On my way to bed, that night, the old man led me in on tiptoe to show me his grandson. His daughter watched me intently as I stooped over the child's cot—with that bird-like solicitude which all mothers show in the presence of a stranger.

Her small son was of that fairness which almost suggests the unreal. He had flung back his bedclothes—as if innocence in this world needed no covering or defence—and lay at ease, the dews of sleep on lip, cheek, and forehead. He was breathing so quietly that not the least movement of shoulder or narrow breast was perceptible.

" The lovely thing ! " I muttered, staring at him. " Where is he now, I wonder ? " His mother lifted her face and smiled at me with a drowsy ecstatic happiness, then sighed.

And from out of the distance there came the first prolonged whisper of a wind from over the sea. It was eleven by my watch, the storm after the long heat of the day seemed to be drifting inland ; but All Hallows, apparently, had forgotten to wind its clock.

WASHINGTON IRVING (1783—1859), *whose education is said to have "suffered" owing to ill health in his youth, which caused him to travel in Europe, won a place in the foremost rank of American writers. He was called to the bar, tried politics and commerce, but eventually confined himself to literature. His classic works are, of course, "The Legend of Sleepy Hollow" and "Rip Van Winkle."*

THE ITALIAN BANDITTI

(Tales told to the Englishman and his Venetian friends at the Inn at Terracina).

THE BELATED TRAVELLERS

IT was late one evening that a carriage, drawn by mules, slowly toiled its way up one of the passes of the Apennines. It was through one of the widest defiles, where a hamlet occurred only at distant intervals, perched on the summit of some rocky height, or the white towers of a convent peeped out from among the thick mountain foliage. The carriage was of ancient and ponderous construction. Its faded embellishments spoke of former splendour, but its crazy springs and axle-trees creaked out the tale of present decline. Within was seated a tall, thin old gentleman, in a kind of military travelling dress, and a foraging cap trimmed with fur, though the grey locks which stole from under it hinted that his fighting days were over. Beside him was a pale, beautiful girl of eighteen, dressed in something of a northern or Polish costume. One servant was seated in front, a rusty, crusty-looking fellow, with a scar across his face, an orange-tawny *schnurbart*, or pair of moustaches, bristling from under his nose, and altogether the air of an old soldier.

It was, in fact, the equipage of a Polish nobleman ; a wreck of one of those princely families once of almost oriental magnificence, but broken down and impoverished by the disasters of Poland. The Count, like many other generous spirits, had been found guilty of the crime of patriotism, and was, in a manner, an exile from his country. He had resided for some time in the first cities of Italy, for the education of his daughter, in whom all his cares and pleasures were now centred. He had taken her into society, where her beauty and her accomplishments gained her many admirers ; and, had she not been the daughter of a poor broken-down Polish nobleman, it is more than probable many would have contended for her hand. Suddenly, however, her health became delicate and drooping ; her gaiety fled with the roses of her cheek, and she sank into silence and debility. The old Count saw the change with the solicitude of a parent. " We must try a change of air and scene," said he ; and in a few days the old family carriage was rumbling among the Apennines.

Their only attendant was the veteran Caspar, who had been born in the family, and grown rusty in its service. He had followed his master in all his fortunes ; had fought by his side ; had stood over him when fallen in battle ; and had received, in his defence, the sabre-cut which added such grimness to his countenance. He was now his valet, his steward, his butler, his factotum. The only being that rivalled his master in his affections was his youthful mistress. She had grown up under his eye, he had led her by the hand when she was a child, and he now looked upon her with the fondness of a parent. Nay, he even took the freedom of a parent in giving his blunt opinion on all matters which he thought were for her good ; and felt a parent's vanity at seeing her gazed at and admired.

The evening was thickening ; they had been for some time passing through narrow gorges of the mountains, along the edges of a tumbling stream. The scenery was lonely and savage. The rocks often beetled over the road, with flocks of white goats browsing on their brinks, and gazing down upon the travellers. They had between two and three leagues yet to go before they could reach any village ; yet the muleteer, Pietro, a tippling old fellow who had refreshed himself at the last halting-place with a more than ordinary quantity of wine, sat singing and talking alternately to his mules, and suffering them to lag on at a snail's pace, in spite of the frequent entreaties of the Count and maledictions of Caspar.

The clouds began to roll in heavy masses among the mountains, shrouding their summits from view. The air was damp and chilly. The Count's solicitude on his daughter's account overcame his usual patience. He leaned from the carriage, and called to old Pietro in an angry tone :

" Forward ! " said he. " It will be midnight before we
arrive at our inn."

" Yonder it is, signor," said the muleteer.

" Where ? " demanded the Count.

" Yonder," said Pietro, pointing to a desolate pile about a
quarter of a league distant.

" That the place ?—why, it looks more like a ruin than an
inn. I thought we were to put up for the night at a comfortable
village."

Here Pietro uttered a string of piteous exclamations and
ejaculations, such as are ever at the tip of the tongue of a
delinquent muleteer. " Such roads ! and such mountains !
and then his poor animals were wayworn, and leg-weary ;
they would fall lame ; they would never be able to reach the
village. And then what could his Excellenza wish for better
than the inn ; a perfect castello—a palazza—and such people !
—and such a larder !—and such beds !—His Excellenza might
fare as sumptuously, and sleep as soundly there as a prince ! "

The Count was easily persuaded, for he was anxious to get
his daughter out of the night air ; so in a little while the old
carriage rattled and jingled into the great gateway of the inn.

The building did certainly in some measure answer to the
muleteer's description. It was large enough for either castle
or palace ; built in a strong, but simple and almost rude
style ; with a great quantity of waste room. It had in fact
been, in former times, a hunting-seat of one of the Italian
princes. There was space enough within its walls and out-
buildings to have accommodated a little army. A scanty
household seemed now to people this dreary mansion. The
faces that presented themselves on the arrival of the travellers
were begrimed with dirt, and scowling in their expression.
They all knew old Pietro, however, and gave him a welcome as
he entered, singing and talking, and almost whooping, into
the gateway.

The hostess of the inn waited herself on the Count and his
daughter, to show them the apartments. They were conducted
through a long gloomy corridor, and then through a suite of
chambers opening into each other, with lofty ceilings, and great
beams extending across them. Everything, however, had a
wretched, squalid look. The walls were damp and bare,
excepting that here and there hung some great painting, large
enough for a chapel, and blackened out of all distinction.

They chose two bedrooms, one within another ; the inner

WASHINGTON IRVING

one for the daughter. The bedsteads were massive and mis-shapen ; but, on examining the beds so vaunted by old Pietro, they found them stuffed with fibres of hemp knotted in great lumps. The Count shrugged his shoulders, but there was no choice left.

The chilliness of the apartments crept to their bones ; and they were glad to return to a common chamber, or kind of hall, where was a fire burning in a huge cavern, miscalled a chimney. A quantity of green wood, just thrown on, puffed out volumes of smoke. The room corresponded to the rest of the mansion. The floor was paved and dirty. A great oaken table stood in the centre, immovable from its size and weight.

The only thing that contradicted this prevalent air of in-digence was the dress of the hostess. She was a slattern of course ; yet her garments, though dirty and negligent, were of costly materials. She wore several rings of great value on her fingers, and jewels in her ears, and round her neck was a string of large pearls, to which was attached a sparkling crucifix. She had the remains of beauty, yet there was something in the expression of her countenance that inspired the young lady with singular aversion. She was officious and obsequious in her attentions, and both the Count and his daughter felt relieved when she consigned them to the care of a dark, sullen-looking servant-maid, and went off to superintend the supper.

Caspar was indignant at the muleteer for having, either through negligence or design, subjected his master and mis-tress to such quarters ; and vowed by his moustaches to have revenge on the old varlet the moment they were safe out from among the mountains. He kept up a continual quarrel with the sulky servant-maid, which only served to increase the sinister expression with which she regarded the travellers, from under her strong dark eyebrows.

As to the Count, he was a good-humoured, passive traveller. Perhaps real misfortunes had subdued his spirit, and rendered him tolerant of many of those petty evils which make pros-perous men miserable. He drew a large broken arm-chair to the fireside for his daughter, and another for himself, and, seizing an enormous pair of tongs, endeavoured to rearrange the wood so as to produce a blaze. His efforts, however, were only repaid by thicker puffs of smoke, which almost overcame the good gentleman's patience. He would draw back, cast a look upon his delicate daughter, then upon the cheerless, squalid apartment, and, shrugging his shoulders, would give a fresh stir to the fire.

Of all the miseries of a comfortless inn, however, there is none greater than sulky attendance : the good Count for some time bore the smoke in silence, rather than address himself to the scowling servant-maid. At length he was compelled to beg for drier firewood. The woman retired muttering. On re-entering the room hastily, with an armful of faggots, her foot slipped ; she fell, and, striking her head against the corner of a chair, cut her temple severely.

The blow stunned her for a time, and the wound bled profusely. When she recovered, she found the Count's daughter administering to her wound, and binding it up with her own handkerchief. It was such an attention as any woman of ordinary feeling would have yielded ; but perhaps there was something in the appearance of the lovely being who bent over her, or in the tones of her voice, that touched the heart of the woman, unused to be ministered to by such hands. Certain it is, she was strongly affected. She caught the delicate hand of the Polonaise, and pressed it fervently to her lips :

" May San Francesco watch over you, signora ! " exclaimed she.

A new arrival broke the stillness of the inn. It was a Spanish Princess with a numerous retinue. The courtyard was in an uproar ; the house in a bustle. The landlady hurried to attend such distinguished guests ; and the poor Count and his daughter and their supper were for a moment forgotten. The veteran Caspar muttered Polish maledictions enough to agonize an Italian ear ; but it was impossible to convince the hostess of the superiority of his old master and young mistress to the whole nobility of Spain.

The noise of the arrival had attracted the daughter to the window just as the new-comers had alighted. A young cavalier sprang out of the carriage, and handed out the Princess. The latter was a little shrivelled old lady, with a face of parchment and sparkling black eye ; she was richly and gaily dressed, and walked with the assistance of a golden-headed cane as high as herself. The young man was tall and elegantly formed. The Count's daughter shrunk back at sight of him, though the deep frame of the window screened her from observation. She gave a heavy sigh as she closed the casement. What that sigh meant I cannot say. Perhaps it was at the contrast between the splendid equipage of the Princess, and the crazy rheumatic-looking old vehicle of her father, which stood hard by. Whatever might be the reason, the young lady closed the casement with a sigh. She returned to her chair,—a slight shivering passed over her delicate frame ; she leaned her elbow on the arm of the chair, rested her pale cheek in the palm of her hand, and looked mournfully into the fire.

The Count thought she appeared paler than usual.

" Does anything ail thee, my child ? " said he.

" Nothing, dear father ! " replied she, laying her hand within his, and looking up smiling in his face ; but as she said so, a treacherous tear rose suddenly to her eye, and she turned away her head.

" The air of the window has chilled thee," said the Count, fondly, " but a good night's rest will make all well again."

The supper-table was at length laid, and the supper about to be served, when the hostess appeared, with her usual obsequiousness, apologizing for showing in the new-comers ; but the night-air was cold, and there was no other chamber in the inn with a fire in it. She had scarcely made the apology when the Princess entered, leaning on the arm of the elegant young man.

The Count immediately recognized her for a lady whom he had met frequently in society, both at Rome and Naples ; and at whose conversaziones, in fact, he had constantly been invited. The cavalier, too, was her nephew and heir, who had been greatly admired in the gay circles both for his merits and prospects, and who had once been on a visit at the same time with his daughter and himself at the villa of a nobleman near Naples. Report had recently affianced him to a rich Spanish heiress.

The meeting was agreeable to both the Count and the Princess. The former was a gentleman of the old school, courteous in the extreme ; the Princess had been a belle in her youth, and a woman of fashion all her life, and liked to be attended to.

The young man approached the daughter, and began something of a complimentary observation ; but his manner was embarrassed, and his compliment ended in an indistinct murmur ; while the daughter bowed without looking up, moved her lips without articulating a word, and sank again into her chair, where she sat gazing into the fire, with a thousand varying expressions passing over her countenance.

This singular greeting of the young people was not perceived by the old ones, who were occupied at the time with
their own courteous salutations. It was arranged that they
should sup together ; and as the Princess travelled with her
own cook, a very tolerable supper soon smoked upon the
board. This, too, was assisted by choice wines, and liquors,
and delicate confitures brought from one of her carriages ; for
she was a veteran epicure, and curious in her relish for the
good things of this world. She was, in fact, a vivacious little
old lady, who mingled the woman of dissipation with the
devotee. She was actually on her way to Loretto to expiate a
long life of gallantries and peccadilloes by a rich offering at the
holy shrine. She was, to be sure, rather a luxurious penitent,
and a contrast to the primitive pilgrims, with scrip and staff,
and cockle-shell ; but then it would be unreasonable to expect
such self-denial from people of fashion ; and there was not a
doubt of the ample efficacy of the rich crucifixes, and golden
vessels, and jewelled ornaments, which she was bearing to the
treasury of the blessed Virgin.

The Princess and the Count chatted much during supper
about the scenes and society in which they had mingled, and
did not notice that they had all the conversation to themselves :
the young people were silent and constrained. The daughter
ate nothing, in spite of the politeness of the Princess, who continually pressed her to taste of one or other of the delicacies.
The Count shook his head.

"She is not well this evening," said he. "I thought she
would have fainted just now as she was looking out of the
window at your carriage on its arrival."

A crimson glow flushed to the very temples of the daughter ;
but she leaned over her plate, and her tresses cast a shade over
her countenance.

When supper was over, they drew their chairs about the
great fireplace. The flame and smoke had subsided, and a
heap of glowing embers diffused a grateful warmth. A guitar
which had been brought from the Count's carriage, leaned
against the wall ; the Princess perceived it : "Can we not
have a little music before parting for the night ? " demanded
she.

The Count was proud of his daughter's accomplishment,
and joined in the request. The young man made an effort of
politeness, and, taking up the guitar, presented it, though in
an embarrassed manner, to the fair musician. She would have

declined it, but was too much confused to do so ; indeed, she was so nervous and agitated, that she dared not trust her voice to make an excuse. She touched the instrument with a faltering hand, and, after preluding a little, accompanied herself in several Polish airs. Her father's eyes glistened as he sat gazing on her. Even the crusty Caspar lingered in the room, partly through a fondness for the music of his native country, but chiefly through his pride in the musician. Indeed, the melody of the voice, and the delicacy of the touch, were enough to have charmed more fastidious ears. The little Princess nodded her head and tapped her hand to the music, though exceedingly out of time ; while the nephew sat buried in profound contemplation of a black picture on the opposite wall.

"And now," said the Count, patting her cheek fondly, "one more favour. Let the Princess hear that little Spanish air you were so fond of. You can't think," added he, "what a proficiency she has made in your language ; though she has been a sad girl and neglected it of late."

The colour flushed the pale cheek of the daughter. She hesitated, murmured something ; but, with sudden effort, collected herself, struck the guitar boldly, and began. It was a Spanish romance, with something of love and melancholy in it. She gave the first stanza with great expression, for the tremulous, melting tones of her voice went to the heart ; but her articulation failed, her lip quivered, the song died away, and she burst into tears.

The Count folded her tenderly in his arms. "Thou art not well, my child," said he, "and I am tasking thee cruelly. Retire to thy chamber, and God bless thee ! " She bowed to the company without raising her eyes, and glided out of the room.

The Count shook his head as the door closed. "Something is the matter with that child," said he, "which I cannot divine. She has lost all health and spirits lately. She was always a tender flower, and I had much pains to rear her. Excuse a father's foolishness," continued he, "but I have seen much trouble in my family ; and this poor girl is all that is now left to me ; and she used to be so lively——"

"Maybe she's in love ! " said the little Princess, with a shrewd nod of the head.

"Impossible ! " replied the good Count artlessly. "She has never mentioned a word of such a thing to me."

How little did the worthy gentleman dream of the thousand

cares, and griefs, and mighty love concerns which agitate a
virgin heart, and which a timid girl scarcely breathes unto
herself !

The nephew of the Princess rose abruptly and walked about
the room.

When she found herself alone in her chamber, the feelings
of the young lady, so long restrained, broke forth with violence.
She opened the casement that the cool air might blow upon her
throbbing temples. Perhaps there was some little pride or
pique mingled with her emotions ; though her gentle
nature did not seem calculated to harbour any such angry
inmate.

" He saw me weep ! " said she, with a sudden mantling
of the cheek, and a swelling of the throat,—" but no matter !—
no matter ! "

And, so saying, she threw her white arms across the window-
frame, buried her face in them, and abandoned herself to an
agony of tears. She remained lost in a reverie, until the sound
of her father's and Caspar's voices in the adjoining room gave
token that the party had retired for the night. The lights
gleaming from window to window, showed that they were
conducting the Princess to her apartments, which were in the
opposite wing of the inn ; and she distinctly saw the figure
of the nephew as he passed one of the casements.

She heaved a deep heart-drawn sigh, and was about to
close the lattice, when her attention was caught by words
spoken below her window by two persons who had just turned
an angle of the building.

" But what will become of the poor young lady ? " said a
voice which she recognized for that of the servant-woman.

" Pooh ! she must take her chance," was the reply from
old Pietro.

" But cannot she be spared ? " asked the other entreatingly :
" she's so kind-hearted ! "

" *Cospetto !* what has got into thee ? " replied the other
petulantly : " would you mar the whole business for the sake
of a silly girl ? " By this time they had got so far from the
window that the Polonaise could hear nothing further.

There was something in this fragment of conversation
calculated to alarm. Did it relate to herself ?—and if so, what
was the impending danger from which it was entreated that
she might be spared ? She was several times on the point of
tapping at her father's door, to tell him what she had heard,

but she might have been mistaken ; she might have heard indistinctly ; the conversation might have alluded to some one else ; at any rate, it was too indefinite to lead to any conclusion. While in this state of irresolution, she was startled by a low knocking against the wainscot in a remote part of her gloomy chamber. On holding up the light, she beheld a small door there, which she had not before remarked. It was bolted on the inside. She advanced, and demanded who knocked, and was answered in the voice of the female domestic. On opening the door, the woman stood before it pale and agitated. She entered softly, laying her finger on her lips in sign of caution and secrecy.

" Fly ! " said she ; " leave this house instantly, or you are lost ! "

The young lady, trembling with alarm, demanded an explanation.

" I have no time," replied the woman, " I dare not—I shall be missed if I linger here—but fly instantly, or you are lost."

" And leave my father ? "

" Where is he ? "

" In the adjoining chamber."

" Call him, then, but lose no time."

The young lady knocked at her father's door. He was not yet retired to bed. She hurried into his room, and told him of the fearful warnings she had received. The Count returned with her into her chamber, followed by Caspar. His questions soon drew the truth out of the embarrassed answers of the woman. The inn was beset by robbers. They were to be introduced after midnight, when the attendants of the Princess and the rest of the travellers were sleeping, and would be an easy prey.

" But we can barricade the inn, we can defend ourselves," said the Count.

" What ! when the people of the inn are in league with the banditti ? "

" How, then, are we to escape ? Can we not order out the carriage and depart ? "

" San Francesco ! for what ? To give the alarm that the plot is discovered ? That would make the robbers desperate, and bring them on you at once. They have had notice of the rich booty in the inn, and will not easily let it escape them."

" But how else are we to get off ? "

"There is a horse behind the inn," said the woman, "from which the man has just dismounted who has been to summon the aid of part of the band at a distance."

"One horse; and there are three of us!" said the Count.

"And the Spanish Princess!" cried the daughter anxiously —"How can she be extricated from the danger?"

"*Diavolo!* what is she to me?" said the woman in sudden passion. "It is *you* I come to save, and you will betray me, and we shall all be lost! Hark!" continued she, "I am called —I shall be discovered—one word more. This door leads by a staircase to the courtyard. Under the shed, in the rear of the yard, is a small door leading out to the fields. You will find a horse there; mount it; make a circuit under the shadow of a ridge of rocks that you will see; proceed cautiously and quietly until you cross a brook, and find yourself on the road just where there are three white crosses nailed against a tree; then put your horse to his speed, and make the best of your way to the village—but recollect, my life is in your hands—say nothing of what you have heard or seen, whatever may happen at this inn."

The woman hurried away. A short and agitated consultation took place between the Count, his daughter, and the veteran Caspar. The young lady seemed to have lost all apprehension for herself in her solicitude for the safety of the Princess. "To fly in selfish silence, and leave her to be massacred!"—A shuddering seized her at the very thought. The gallantry of the Count, too, revolted at the idea. He could not consent to turn his back upon a party of helpless travellers, and leave them in ignorance of the danger which hung over them.

"But what is to become of the young lady," said Caspar, "if the alarm is given, and the inn thrown in a tumult? What may happen to her in a chance-medley affray?"

Here the feelings of the father were roused; he looked upon his lovely, helpless child, and trembled at the chance of her falling into the hands of ruffians.

The daughter, however, thought nothing of herself. "The Princess! the Princess!—only let the Princess know her danger." She was willing to share it with her.

At length Caspar interfered with the zeal of a faithful old servant. No time was to be lost—the first thing was to get the young lady out of danger. "Mount the horse," said he to the Count, "take her behind you, and fly! Make for the village, rouse the inhabitants, and send assistance. Leave me here to give the alarm to the Princess and her people. I am an old soldier, and I think we shall be able to stand siege until you send us aid."

The daughter would again have insisted on staying with the Princess.

" For what ? " said old Caspar bluntly. " You could do no good—you would be in the way ;—we should have to take care of you instead of ourselves."

There was no answering these objections ; the Count seized his pistols, and, taking his daughter under his arm, moved towards the staircase. The young lady paused, stepped back, and said, faltering with agitation—" There is a young cavalier with the Princess—her nephew—perhaps he may——"

" I understand you, Mademoiselle," replied old Caspar with a significant nod ; " not a hair of his head shall suffer if I can help it ! "

The young lady blushed deeper than ever ; she had not anticipated being so thoroughly understood by the blunt old servant.

" That is not what I mean," said she, hesitating. She would have added something, or made some explanation, but the moments were precious, and her father hurried her away.

They found their way through the courtyard to the small postern gate where the horse stood, fastened to a ring in the wall. The Count mounted, took his daughter behind him, and they proceeded as quietly as possible in the direction which the woman had pointed out. Many a fearful and anxious look did the daughter cast back upon the gloomy pile ; the lights which had feebly twinkled through the dusky casements were one by one disappearing, a sign that the inmates were gradually sinking to repose ; and she trembled with impatience, lest succour should not arrive until that repose had been fatally interrupted.

They passed silently and safely along the skirts of the rocks, protected from observation by their overhanging shadows. They crossed the brook, and reached the place where three white crosses nailed against a tree told of some murder that had been committed there. Just as they had reached this ill-omened spot they beheld several men in the gloom coming down a craggy defile among the rocks.

" Who goes there ? " exclaimed a voice. The Count put spurs to his horse, but one of the men sprang forward and seized the bridle. The horse started back, and reared, and, had not the young lady clung to her father, she would have been thrown off. The Count leaned forward, put a pistol to the very head of the ruffian, and fired. The latter fell dead. The horse sprang forward. Two or three shots were fired which whistled by the fugitives, but only served to augment their speed. They reached the village in safety.

The whole place was soon roused ; but such was the awe in which the banditti were held, that the inhabitants shrunk at the idea of encountering them. A desperate band had for some time infested that pass through the mountains, and the inn had long been suspected of being one of those horrible places where the unsuspicious wayfarer is entrapped and silently disposed of. The rich ornaments worn by the slattern hostess of the inn had excited heavy suspicions. Several instances had occurred of small parties of travellers disappearing mysteriously on that road, who, it was supposed at first, had been carried off by the robbers for the purpose of ransom, but who had never been heard of more. Such were the tales buzzed in the ears of the Count by the villagers, as he endeavoured to rouse them to the rescue of the Princess and her train from their perilous situation. The daughter seconded the exertions of her father with all the eloquence of prayers, and tears, and beauty. Every moment that elapsed increased her anxiety until it became agonizing. Fortunately there was a body of gendarmes resting at the village. A number of the young villagers volunteered to accompany them, and the little army was put in motion. The Count, having deposited his daughter in a place of safety, was too much of the old soldier not to hasten to the scene of danger. It would be difficult to paint the anxious agitation of the young lady while awaiting the result.

The party arrived at the inn just in time. The robbers, finding their plans discovered, and the travellers prepared for their reception, had become open and furious in their attack. The Princess's party had barricaded themselves in one suite of apartments, and repulsed the robbers from the doors and windows. Caspar had shown the generalship of a veteran, and the nephew of the Princess the dashing valour of a young soldier. Their ammunition, however, was nearly exhausted, and they would have found it difficult to hold out much longer, when a discharge from the musketry of the gendarmes gave them the joyful tidings of succour.

A fierce fight ensued, for part of the robbers were surprised in the inn, and had to stand siege in their turn ; while their comrades made desperate attempts to relieve them from under cover of the neighbouring rocks and thickets.

I cannot pretend to give a minute account of the fight, as I have heard it related in a variety of ways. Suffice to say, the robbers were defeated ; several of them killed, and several taken prisoners ; which last, together with the people of the inn, were either executed or sent to the galleys.

I picked up these particulars in the course of a journey which I made some time after the event had taken place. I passed by the very inn. It was then dismantled, excepting one wing, in which a body of gendarmes was stationed. They pointed out to me the shot-holes in the window-frames, the walls, and the panels of the doors. There were a number of withered limbs dangling from the branches of a neighbouring tree, and blackening in the air, which I was told were the limbs of the robbers who had been slain, and the culprits who had been executed. The whole place had a dismal, wild, forlorn look.

" Were any of the Princess's party killed ? " inquired the Englishman.

" As far as I can recollect, there were two or three."

" Not the nephew, I trust ? " said the fair Venetian.

" Oh no : he hastened with the Count to relieve the anxiety of the daughter by the assurances of victory. The young lady had been sustained throughout the interval of suspense by the very intensity of her feelings. The moment she saw her father returning in safety, accompanied by the nephew of the Princess, she uttered a cry of rapture, and fainted. Happily, however, she soon recovered, and, what is more, was married shortly afterwards to the young cavalier, and the whole party accompanied the old Princess in her pilgrimage to Loretto, where her votive offerings may still be seen in the treasury of the Santa Casa."

THE PAINTER'S ADVENTURE

I AM an historical painter by profession, and resided for some time in the family of a foreign Prince at his villa, about fifteen miles from Rome, among some of the most interesting scenery of Italy. It is situated on the heights of ancient Tusculum.

I assisted the Prince in researches which he was making among the classic ruins of his vicinity ; his exertions were highly successful. Many wrecks of admirable statues and fragments of exquisite sculpture were dug up : monuments of the taste and magnificence that reigned in the ancient Tusculan abodes. He had studded his villa and its grounds with statues, relievos, vases, and sarcophagi, thus retrieved from the bosom of the earth.

The mode of life pursued at the villa was delightfully serene, diversified by interesting occupations and elegant leisure. Every one passed the day according to his pleasure or pursuits ; and we all assembled in a cheerful dinner-party at sunset.

It was on the fourth of November, a beautiful serene day, that we had assembled in the saloon at the sound of the first dinner-bell. The family were surprised at the absence of the Prince's confessor. They waited for him in vain, and at length placed themselves at table. They at first attributed his absence to his having prolonged his customary walk ; and the early part of the dinner passed without any uneasiness. When the dessert was served, however, without his making his appearance, they began to feel anxious. They feared he might have been taken ill in some alley of the woods, or might have fallen into the hands of robbers. Not far from the villa, with the interval of a small valley, rose the mountains of the Abruzzi, the stronghold of banditti. Indeed, the neighbourhood had for some time past been infested by them ; and Barbone, a notorious bandit chief, had often been met prowling about the solitudes of Tusculum. The daring enterprises of these ruffians were well known : the objects of their cupidity or vengeance were insecure even in palaces. As yet they had respected the possessions of the Prince ; but the idea of such dangerous spirits hovering about the neighbourhood was sufficient to occasion alarm.

The fears of the company increased as evening closed in. The Prince ordered out forest guards and domestics with flambeaux to search for the confessor. They had not departed long when a slight noise was heard in the corridor of the ground-floor. The family were dining on the first floor, and the remaining domestics were occupied in attendance. There was no one on the ground-floor at this moment but the housekeeper, the laundress, and three field labourers, who were resting themselves, and conversing with the women.

I heard the noise from below, and, presuming it to be occasioned by the return of the absentee, I left the table and hastened downstairs, eager to gain intelligence that might relieve the anxiety of the Prince and Princess. I had scarcely reached the last step, when I beheld before me a man dressed as a bandit ; a carbine in his hand, and a stiletto and pistols in his belt. His countenance had a mingled expression of ferocity and trepidation : he sprang upon me, and exclaimed exultingly, " *Ecco il principe !* "

I saw at once into what hands I had fallen, but endeavoured to summon up coolness and presence of mind. A glance towards the lower end of the corridor showed me several ruffians, clothed and armed in the same manner with the one who had seized me. They were guarding the two females and the field labourers. The robber, who held me firmly by the collar, demanded repeatedly whether or not I were the Prince : his object evidently was to carry off the Prince, and extort an immense ransom. He was enraged at receiving none but vague replies, for I felt the importance of misleading him.

A sudden thought struck me how I might extricate myself from his clutches. I was unarmed, it is true, but I was vigorous. His companions were at a distance. By a sudden exertion I might wrest myself from him, and spring up the staircase, whither he would not dare to follow me singly. The idea was put in practice as soon as conceived. The ruffian's throat was bare ; with my right hand I seized him by it, with my left hand I grasped the arm which held the carbine. The suddenness of my attack took him completely unawares, and the strangling nature of my grasp paralysed him. He choked and faltered. I felt his hand relaxing its hold, and was on the point of jerking myself away, and darting up the staircase, before he could recover himself, when I was suddenly seized by some one from behind.

I had to let go my grasp. The bandit, once released, fell upon me with fury, and gave me several blows with the butt-end of his carbine, one of which wounded me severely in the forehead and covered me with blood. He took advantage of my being stunned to rifle me of my watch, and whatever valuables I had about my person.

When I recovered from the effect of the blow, I heard the voice of the chief of the banditti, who exclaimed, " *Quello e il principe ; siamo contente ; andiamo !* " (It is the Prince ; enough ; let us be off.) The band immediately closed round me and dragged me out of the palace, bearing off the three labourers likewise.

I had no hat on, and the blood flowed from my wound ; I managed to stanch it, however, with my pocket-handkerchief, which I bound round my forehead. The captain of the band conducted me in triumph, supposing me to be the Prince. We had gone some distance before he learnt his mistake from one of the labourers. His rage was terrible. It was too late to return to the villa and endeavour to retrieve his error, for by this time the alarm must have been given, and every one in arms. He darted at me a ferocious look—swore I had deceived him, and caused him to miss his fortune—and told me to prepare for death. The rest of the robbers were equally furious. I saw their hands upon their poniards, and I knew that death was seldom an empty threat with these ruffians. The labourers saw the peril into which their information had betrayed me, and eagerly assured the captain that I was a man for whom the Prince would pay a great ransom. This produced a pause. For my part, I cannot say that I had been much dismayed by their menaces. I mean not to make any boast of courage ; but I have been so schooled to hardship during the late revolutions, and have beheld death around me in so many perilous and disastrous scenes, that I have become in some measure callous to its terrors. The frequent hazard of life makes a man at length as reckless of it as a gambler of his money. To their threat of death, I replied, " that the sooner it was executed the better." This reply seemed to astonish the captain ; and the prospect of ransom held out by the labourers had, no doubt, a still greater effect on him. He considered for a moment, assumed a calmer manner, and made a sign to his companions, who had remained waiting for my death-warrant. "Forward!" said he ; "we will see about this matter by and by ! "

We descended rapidly towards the road of La Molara, which leads to Rocca Priori. In the midst of this road is a solitary inn. The captain ordered the troop to halt at the distance of a pistol-shot from it, and enjoined profound silence. He approached the threshold alone, with noiseless steps. He examined the outside of the door very narrowly, and then, returning precipitately, made a sign for the troop to continue its march in silence. It has since been ascertained, that this was one of those infamous inns which are the secret resorts of banditti. The inn-keeper had an understanding with the captain, as he most probably had with the chiefs of the different bands. When any of the patrols and gendarmes were quartered at his house, the brigands were warned of it by a preconcerted signal on the door ; when there was no such signal, they might enter with safety, and be sure of welcome.

After pursuing our road a little farther, we struck off towards the woody mountains which envelop Rocca Priori. Our march was long and painful, with many circuits and windings : at length we clambered a steep ascent, covered with a thick forest ; and when we had reached the centre, I was told to seat myself on the ground. No sooner had I done so than, at a sign from their chief, the robbers surrounded me, and, spreading their great cloaks from one to the other, formed a kind of pavilion of mantles, to which their bodies might be said to serve as columns. The captain then struck a light, and a flambeau was lit immediately. The mantles were extended to prevent the light of the flambeau from being seen through the forest. Anxious as was my situation, I could not look round upon this scene of dusky drapery relieved by the bright colours of the robbers' garments, the gleaming of their weapons, and the variety of strong-marked countenances, lit up by the flambeau, without admiring the picturesque effect of the scene. It was quite theatrical.

The captain now held an inkhorn, and, giving me pen and paper, ordered me to write what he should dictate. I obeyed. It was a demand, couched in the style of robber eloquence, " that the Prince should send three thousand dollars for my ransom ; or that my death should be the consequence of a refusal."

I knew enough of the desperate character of these beings to feel assured this was not an idle menace. Their only mode of ensuring attention to their demands is to make the infliction of the penalty inevitable. I saw at once, however, that the demand was preposterous, and made in improper language.

I told the captain so, and assured him that so extravagant a sum would never be granted.—" That I was neither a friend nor relative of the Prince, but a mere artist, employed to execute certain paintings. That I had nothing to offer as a ransom, but the price of my labours ; if this were not sufficient, my life was at their disposal ; it was a thing on which I set but little value."

I was the more hardy in my reply, because I saw that coolness and hardihood had an effect upon the robbers. It is true, as I finished speaking, the captain laid his hand upon his stiletto ; but he restrained himself, and, snatching the letter, folded it, and ordered me in a peremptory tone to address it to the Prince. He then dispatched one of the labourers with it to Tusculum, who promised to return with all possible speed.

The robbers now prepared themselves for sleep, and I was told that I might do the same. They spread their great cloaks on the ground, and lay down around me. One was stationed at a little distance to keep watch, and was relieved every two hours. The strangeness and wildness of this mountain bivouac among lawless beings, whose hands seemed ever ready to grasp the stiletto, and with whom life was so trivial and insecure, was enough to banish repose. The coldness of the earth, and of the dew, however, had a still greater effect than mental causes in disturbing my rest. The airs wafted to these mountains from the distant Mediterranean diffused a great chilliness as the night advanced. An expedient suggested itself. I called one of my fellow-prisoners, the labourers, and made him lie down beside me. Whenever one of my limbs became chilled, I approached it to the robust limb of my neighbour, and borrowed some of his warmth. In this way I was able to obtain a little sleep.

Day at length dawned, and I was roused from my slumber by the voice of the chieftain. He desired me to rise and follow him. I obeyed. On considering his physiognomy attentively, it appeared a little softened. He even assisted me in scrambling up the steep forest, among rocks and brambles. Habit had made him a vigorous mountaineer ; but I found it excessively toilsome to climb these rugged heights. We arrived at length at the summit of the mountain.

Here it was that I felt all the enthusiasm of my art suddenly awakened ; and I forgot in an instant all my perils and fatigues at this magnificent view of the sunrise in the midst of the mountains of the Abruzzi. It was on these heights that Hannibal first pitched his camp, and pointed out Rome to his followers. The eye embraces a vast extent of country. The minor height of Tusculum, with its villas and its sacred ruins, lies below ; the Sabine hills and the Albanian mountains stretch on either hand ; and beyond Tusculum and Frascati spreads out the immense Campagna, with its lines of tombs, and here and there a broken aqueduct stretching across it, and the towers and domes of the eternal city in the midst.

Fancy this scene lit up by the glories of a rising sun, and bursting upon my sight as I looked forth from among the majestic forests of the Abruzzi. Fancy, too, the savage foreground, made still more savage by groups of banditti, armed and dressed in their wild picturesque manner, and you will not wonder that the enthusiasm of a painter for a moment overpowered all his other feelings.

The banditti were astonished at my admiration of a scene which familiarity had made so common in their eyes. I took advantage of their halting at this spot, drew forth a quire of drawing-paper, and began to sketch the features of the landscape. The height on which I was seated was wild and solitary, separated from the ridge of Tusculum by a valley nearly three miles wide, though the distance appeared less from the purity of the atmosphere. This height was one of the favourite retreats of the banditti, commanding a look-out over the country ; while at the same time it was covered with forests, and distant from the populous haunts of men.

While I was sketching, my attention was called off for a moment by the cries of birds, and the bleatings of sheep. I looked around, but could see nothing of the animals which uttered them. They were repeated, and appeared to come from the summits of the trees. On looking more narrowly, I perceived six of the robbers perched in the tops of oaks, which grew on the breezy crest of the mountain, and commanded an uninterrupted prospect. They were keeping a look-out like so many vultures ; casting their eyes into the depths of the valley below us ; communicating with each other by signs, or holding discourse in sound which might be mistaken by the wayfarer for the cries of hawks and crows, or the bleating of the mountain flocks. After they had reconnoitred the neighbourhood, and finished their singular discourse, they descended from their airy perch, and returned to their prisoners. The captain posted three of them at three naked sides of the mountain, while he remained to guard us with what appeared his most trusty companion.

I had my book of sketches in my hand ; he requested to see it, and, after having run his eye over it, expressed himself convinced of the truth of my assertion that I was a painter. I thought I saw a gleam of good feeling dawning in him, and determined to avail myself of it. I knew that the worst of men have their good points and their accessible sides, if one would but study them carefully. Indeed, there is a singular mixture in the character of the Italian robber. With reckless ferocity he often mingles traits of kindness and good-humour. He is not always radically bad ; but driven to his course of life by some unpremeditated crime, the effect of those sudden bursts of passion to which the Italian temperament is prone. This has compelled him to take to the mountains, or, as it is technically termed among them, ' *andare in campagna.*' He has become a robber by profession ; but, like a soldier, when not in action he can lay aside his weapons and his fierceness, and become like other men.

I took occasion, from the observations of the captain on my sketchings, to fall into conversation with him, and found him sociable and communicative. By degrees I became completely at my ease with him. I had fancied I perceived about him a degree of self-love, which I determined to make use of. I assumed an air of careless frankness, and told him, that, as an artist, I pretended to the power of judging of the physiognomy ; that I thought I perceived something in his features and demeanour which announced him worthy of higher fortunes ; that he was not formed to exercise the profession to which he had abandoned himself ; that he had talents and qualities fitted for a nobler sphere of action ; that he had but to change his course of life, and, in a legitimate career, the same courage and endowments which now made him an object of terror, would assure him the applause and admiration of society.

I had not mistaken my man ; my discourse both touched and excited him. He seized my hand, pressed it, and replied with strong emotion—' You have guessed the truth ; you have judged of me rightly." He remained for a moment silent ; then with a kind of effort, he resumed : " I will tell you some particulars of my life, and you will perceive that it was the oppression of others, rather than my own crimes, which drove me to the mountains. I sought to serve my fellow-men, and they have persecuted me from among them." We seated ourselves on the grass, and the robber gave me the following anecdotes of his history.

THE STORY OF THE BANDIT CHIEFTAIN

I AM a native of the village of Prossedi. My father was easy enough in circumstances, and we lived peaceably and independently, cultivating our fields. All went on well with us until a new chief of the Sbirri was sent to our village to take command of the police. He was an arbitrary fellow, prying into everything, and practising all sorts of vexations and oppressions in the discharge of his office. I was at that time eighteen years of age, and had a natural love of justice and good neighbourhood. I had also a little education, and knew something of history, so as to be able to judge a little of men and their actions. All this inspired me with hatred for this paltry despot. My own family, also, became the object of his suspicion or dislike, and felt more than once the arbitrary abuse of his power. These things worked together in my mind, and I gasped after vengeance. My character was always ardent and energetic, and, acted upon by the love of justice, determined me, by one blow, rid the country of the tyrant.

Full of my project, I rose one morning before peep of day, and, concealing a stiletto under my waistcoat—here you see it!—and he drew forth a long keen poniard—I lay in wait for him in the outskirts of the village. I knew all his haunts, and his habits of making his rounds and prowling about like a wolf in the grey of the morning. At length I met him, and attacked him with fury. He was armed, but I took him unawares, and was full of youth and vigour. I gave him repeated blows to make sure work, and laid him lifeless at my feet.

When I was satisfied that I had done for him, I returned with all haste to the village, but had the ill-luck to meet two of the Sbirri as I entered it. They accosted me, and asked if I had seen their chief. I assumed an air of tranquillity, and told them I had not. They continued on their way, and within a few hours brought back the dead body to Prossedi. Their suspicions of me being already awakened, I was arrested and thrown into prison. Here I lay several weeks, when the Prince, who was Seigneur of Prossedi, directed judicial proceedings against me. I was brought to trial, and a witness was produced, who pretended to have seen me flying with precipitation not far from the bleeding body ; and so I was condemned to the galleys for thirty years.

" Curse on such laws ! " vociferated the bandit, foaming

with rage. " Curse on such a government ! and ten thousand
curses on the Prince who caused me to be adjudged so rigorously
while so many other Roman princes harbour and protect
assassins a thousand times more culpable ! What had I done
but what was inspired by a love of justice and my country ?
Why was my act more culpable than that of Brutus, when he
sacrificed Cæsar to the cause of liberty and justice ? "

There was something at once both lofty and ludicrous in
the rhapsody of this robber chief, thus associating himself with
one of the great names of antiquity. It showed, however, that
he had at least the merit of knowing the remarkable facts in the
history of his country. He became more calm, and resumed
his narrative.

I was conducted to Civita Vecchia in fetters. My heart
was burning with rage. I had been married scarce six months
to a woman whom I passionately loved, and who was pregnant.
My family was in despair. For a long time I made unsuccessful
efforts to break my chain. At length I found a morsel of iron,
which I hid carefully, and endeavoured, with a pointed flint,
to fashion it into a kind of file. I occupied myself in this work
during the night-time, and when it was finished, I made out,
after a long time, to sever one of the rings of my chain. My
flight was successful.

I wandered for several weeks in the mountains which
surround Prossedi, and found means to inform my wife of the
place where I was concealed. She came often to see me. I
had determined to put myself at the head of an armed band.
She endeavoured, for a long time, to dissuade me, but, finding
my resolution fixed, she at length united in my project of
vengeance, and brought me, herself, my poniard. By her
means I communicated with several brave fellows of the neighbouring villages, whom I knew to be ready to take to the mountains, and only panting for an opportunity to exercise their
daring spirits. We soon formed a combination, procured arms,
and we have had ample opportunities of revenging ourselves for
the wrongs and injuries which most of us have suffered.
Everything has succeeded with us until now, and, had it not
been for our blunder in mistaking you for the Prince, our
fortunes would have been made.

Here the robber concluded his story. He had talked himself
into complete companionship, and assured me he no longer
bore me any grudge for the error of which I had been the

innocent cause. He even professed a kindness for me, and wished me to remain some time with them. He promised to give me a sight of certain grottos which they occupied beyond Villetri, and whither they resorted during the intervals of their expeditions.

He assured me that they led a jovial life there ; had plenty of good cheer ; slept on beds of moss ; and were waited upon by young and beautiful females, whom I might take for models.

I confess I felt my curiosity roused by his descriptions of the grottos and their inhabitants : they realized those scenes in robber story which I had always looked upon as mere creations of the fancy. I should gladly have accepted his invitation, and paid a visit to these caverns, could I have felt more secure in my company.

I began to find my situation less painful. I had evidently propitiated the good-will of the chieftain, and hoped that he might release me for a moderate ransom. A new alarm, however, awaited me. While the captain was looking out with impatience for the return of the messenger who had been sent to the Prince, the sentinel posted on the side of the mountain facing the plain of La Molara came running towards us. " We are betrayed ! " exclaimed he. " The police of Frascati are after us. A party of carabineers have just stopped at the inn below the mountain." Then, laying his hand on his stiletto, he swore, with a terrible oath, that if they made the least movement towards the mountain, my life and the lives of my fellow-prisoners should answer for it.

The chieftain resumed all his ferocity of demeanour, and approved of what his companion said ; but when the latter had returned to his post, he turned to me with a softened air : " I must act as chief," said he, " and humour my dangerous subalterns. It is a law with us to kill our prisoners rather than suffer them to be rescued ; but do not be alarmed. In case we are surprised, keep by me ; fly with us, and I will consider myself responsible for your life."

There was nothing very consolatory in this arrangement, which would have placed me between two dangers. I scarcely knew, in case of flight, from which I should have the most to apprehend, the carbines of the pursuers, or the stilettos of the pursued. I remained silent, however, and endeavoured to maintain a look of tranquillity.

For an hour was I kept in this state of peril and anxiety. The robbers, crouching among their leafy coverts, kept an

eagle watch upon the carabineers below, as they loitered about
the inn ; sometimes lolling about the portal ; sometimes disappearing for several minutes ; then sallying out, examining
their weapons, pointing in different directions, and apparently
asking questions about the neighbourhood. Not a movement, a gesture, was lost upon the keen eyes of the brigands.
At length we were relieved from our apprehensions. The
carabineers, having finished their refreshment, seized their
arms, continued along the valley towards the great road, and
gradually left the mountain behind them. " I felt almost
certain," said the chief, " that they could not be sent after us.
They know too well how prisoners have fared in our hands on
similar occasions. Our laws in this respect are inflexible, and
are necessary for our safety. If we once flinched from them,
there would no longer be such a thing as a ransom to be
procured."

There were no signs yet of the messenger's return. I was
preparing to resume my sketching, when the captain drew a
quire of paper from his knapsack. " Come," said he, laughing,
" you are a painter,—take my likeness. The leaves of your
portfolio are small,—draw it on this." I gladly consented, for
it was a study that seldom presents itself to a painter. I recollected that Salvator Rosa in his youth had voluntarily
sojourned for a time among the banditti of Calabria, and had
filled his mind with the savage scenery and savage associates
by which he was surrounded. I seized my pencil with
enthusiasm at the thought. I found the captain the most
docile of subjects, and, after various shiftings of position,
placed him in an attitude to my mind.

Picture to yourself a stern muscular figure, in fanciful
bandit costume ; with pistols and poniards in belt ; his
brawny neck bare ; a handkerchief loosely thrown round it,
and the two ends in front strung with rings of all kinds, the
spoils of travellers ; relics and medals hanging on his breast ;
his hat decorated with various coloured ribands ; his vest and
short breeches of bright colours and finely embroidered ; his
legs in buskins or leggings. Fancy him on a mountain height,
among wild rocks and rugged oaks, leaning on his carbine, as
if meditating some exploit ; while far below are beheld villages
and villas, the scenes of his maraudings, with the wide Campagna dimly extending in the distance.

The robber was pleased with the sketch, and seemed to
admire himself upon paper. I had scarcely finished, when the

labourer arrived who had been sent for my ransom. He had reached Tusculum two hours after midnight. He brought me a letter from the Prince, who was in bed at the time of his arrival. As I had predicted, he treated the demand as extravagant, but offered five hundred dollars for my ransom. Having no money by him at the moment, he had sent a note for the amount, payable to whomsoever should conduct me safe and sound to Rome. I presented the note of hand to the chieftain ; he received it with a shrug. " Of what use are notes of hand to us ? " said he. " Who can we send with you to Rome to receive it ? We are all marked men ; known and described at every gate and military post and village church door. No ; we must have gold and silver ; let the sum be paid in cash, and you shall be restored to liberty."

The captain again placed a sheet of paper before me to communicate his determination to the Prince. When I had finished the letter, and took the sheet from the quire, I found on the opposite side of it the portrait which I had just been tracing. I was about to tear it off and give it to the chief.

" Hold ! " said he, " let it go to Rome ; let them see what kind of looking fellow I am. Perhaps the Prince and his friends may form as good an opinion of me from my face as you have done."

This was said sportively, yet it was evident there was vanity lurking at the bottom. Even this wary, distrustful chief of banditti forgot for a moment his usual foresight and precaution, in the common wish to be admired. He never reflected what use might be made of this portrait in his pursuit and conviction.

The letter was folded and directed, and the messenger departed again for Tusculum. It was now eleven o'clock in the morning, and as yet we had eaten nothing. In spite of all my anxiety, I began to feel a craving appetite. I was glad therefore to hear the captain talk something about eating. He observed that for three days and nights they had been lurking about among rocks and woods, meditating their expedition to Tusculum, during which time all their provisions had been exhausted. He should now take measures to procure a supply. Leaving me therefore in charge of his comrade, in whom he appeared to have implicit confidence, he departed, assuring me that in less than two hours we should make a good dinner. Where it was to come from was an enigma to me, though it was evident these beings had their secret friends and agents throughout the country.

Indeed, the inhabitants of these mountains, and of the valleys which they embosom, are a rude, half-civilized set. The towns and villages among the forests of the Abruzzi, shut up from the rest of the world, are almost like savage dens. It is wonderful that such rude abodes, so little known and visited, should be embosomed in the midst of one of the most travelled and civilized countries of Europe. Among these regions the robber prowls unmolested ; not a mountaineer hesitates to give him secret harbour and assistance. The shepherds, however, who tend their flocks among the mountains, are the favourite emissaries of the robbers, when they would send messages down to the valley either for ransom or supplies.

The shepherds of the Abruzzi are as wild as the scenes they frequent. They are clad in a rude garb of black or brown sheep-skin ; they have high conical hats, and coarse sandals of cloth bound round their legs with thongs, similar to those worn by the robbers. They carry long staves, on which, as they lean, they form picturesque objects in the lonely landscape, and they are followed by their ever-constant companion, the dog. They are a curious, questioning set, glad at any time to relieve the monotony of their solitude by the conversation of the passer-by ; and the dog will lend an attentive ear, and put on as sagacious and inquisitive a look as his master.

But I am wandering from my story. I was now left alone with one of the robbers, the confidential companion of the chief. He was the youngest and most vigorous of the band ; and though his countenance had something of that dissolute fierceness which seems natural to this desperate, lawless mode of life, yet there were traces of manly beauty about it. As an artist I could not but admire it. I had remarked in him an air of abstraction and reverie, and at times a movement of inward suffering and impatience. He now sat on the ground, his elbows on his knees, his head resting between his clinched fists, and his eyes fixed on the earth with an expression of sad and bitter rumination. I had grown familiar with him from repeated conversations, and had found him superior in mind to the rest of the band. I was anxious to seize any opportunity of sounding the feelings of these singular beings. I fancied I read in the countenance of this one traces of self-condemnation and remorse ; and the ease with which I had drawn forth the confidences of the chieftain encouraged me to hope the same with his follower.

After a little preliminary conversation, I ventured to ask him if he did not feel regret at having abandoned his family, and taken to this dangerous profession. " I feel," replied he, " but one regret, and that will end only with my life."

As he said this, he pressed his clinched fists upon his bosom, drew his breath through his set teeth, and added, with a deep emotion : " I have something within here that stifles me ; it is like a burning iron consuming my very heart. I could tell you a miserable story—but not now—another time."

He relapsed into his former position, and sat with his head between his hands, muttering to himself in broken ejaculations, and what appeared at times to be curses and maledictions. I saw he was not in a mood to be disturbed, so I left him to himself. In a little while the exhaustion of his feelings, and probably the fatigues he had undergone in this expedition, began to produce drowsiness. He struggled with it for a time, but the warmth and stillness of midday made it irresistible, and he at length stretched himself upon the herbage and fell asleep.

I now beheld a chance of escape within my reach. My guard lay before me at my mercy. His vigorous limbs relaxed by sleep—his bosom open for the blow—his carbine slipped from his nerveless grasp, and lying by his side—his stiletto half out of the pocket in which it was usually carried. Two only of his comrades were in sight, and those at a considerable distance on the edge of the mountain, their backs turned to us, and their attention occupied in keeping a look-out upon the plain. Through a strip of intervening forest, and at the foot of a steep descent, I beheld the village of Rocca Priori. To have secured the carbine of the sleeping brigand ; to have seized upon his poniard, and have plunged it in his heart, would have been the work of an instant. Should he die without noise, I might dart through the forest, and down to Rocca Priori before my flight might be discovered. In case of alarm, I should still have a fair start of the robbers, and a chance of getting beyond the reach of their shot.

Here, then, was an opportunity for both escape and vengeance ; perilous indeed, but powerfully tempting. Had my situation been more critical I could not have resisted it. I reflected, however, for a moment. The attempt, if successful, would be followed by the sacrifice of my two fellow-prisoners, who were sleeping profoundly, and could not be awakened in time to escape. The labourer who had gone after the ransom might also fall a victim to the rage of the robbers, without the money, which he brought being saved. Besides, the conduct of the chief towards me made me feel confident of speedy deliverance. These reflections overcame the first powerful impulse, and I calmed the turbulent agitation which it had awakened.

I again took out my materials for drawing, and amused myself with sketching the magnificent prospect. It was now about noon, and everything had sunk into repose, like the sleeping bandit before me. The noontide stillness that reigned over these mountains, the vast landscape below, gleaming with distant towns, and dotted with various habitations and signs of life, yet all so silent, had a powerful effect upon my mind. The intermediate valleys, too, which lie among the mountains, have a peculiar air of solitude. Few sounds are heard at midday to break the quiet of the scene. Sometimes the whistle of a solitary muleteer, lagging with his lazy animal along the road which winds through the centre of the valley ; sometimes the faint piping of a shepherd's reed from the side of the mountain, or sometimes the bell of an ass slowly pacing along, followed by a monk with bare feet, and bare, shining head, and carrying provisions to his convent.

I had continued to sketch for some time among my sleeping companions, when at length I saw the captain of the band approaching, followed by a peasant leading a mule, on which was a well-filled sack. I at first apprehended that this was some new prey fallen into the hands of the robbers ; but the contented look of the peasant soon relieved me, and I was rejoiced to hear that it was our promised repast. The brigands now came running from the three sides of the mountain, having the quick scent of vultures. Every one busied himself in unloading the mule, and relieving the sack of its contents.

The first thing that made its appearance was an enormous ham, of a colour and plumpness that would have inspired the pencil of Teniers ; it was followed by a large cheese, a bag of boiled chestnuts, a little barrel of wine, and a quantity of good household bread. Everything was arranged on the grass with a degree of symmetry ; and the captain, presenting me with his knife, requested me to help myself. We all seated ourselves round the viands, and nothing was heard for a time but the sound of vigorous mastication, or the gurgling of the barrel of wine as it revolved briskly about the circle. My long fasting, and the mountain air and exercise, had given me a keen appetite; and never did repast appear to me more excellent or picturesque.

From time to time one of the band was dispatched to keep a look-out upon the plain. No enemy was at hand, and the dinner was undisturbed. The peasant received nearly three times the value of his provisions, and set off down the mountain highly satisfied with his bargain. I felt invigorated by the hearty meal I had made, and, notwithstanding that the wound I had received the evening before was painful, yet I could not but feel extremely interested and gratified by the singular scenes continually presented to me. Everything was picturesque about these wild beings and their haunts. Their bivouacs; their groups on guard; their indolent noontide repose on the mountain-brow; their rude repast on the herbage among rocks and trees,—everything presented a study for a painter: but it was towards the approach of evening that I felt the highest enthusiasm awakened.

The setting sun, declining beyond the vast Campagna, shed its rich yellow beams on the woody summit of the Abruzzi. Several mountains crowned with snow shone brilliantly in the distance, contrasting their brightness with others, which, thrown into shade, assumed deep tints of purple and violet. As the evening advanced, the landscape darkened into a sterner character. The immense solitude around; the wild mountains broken into rocks and precipices, intermingled with vast oaks, corks, and chestnuts; and the groups of banditti in the foreground, reminded me of the savage scenes of Salvator Rosa.

To beguile the time, the captain proposed to his comrades to spread before me their jewels and cameos, as I must doubtless be a judge of such articles, and able to form an estimate of their value. He set the example, the others followed it; and in a few moments I saw the grass before me sparkling with jewels and gems that would have delighted the eyes of an antiquary or a fine lady.

Among them were several precious jewels, and antique intaglios and cameos of great value; the spoils, doubtless, of travellers of distinction. I found that they were in the habit of selling their booty in the frontier towns; but as these in general were thinly and poorly peopled, and little frequented by travellers, they could offer no market for such valuable articles of taste and luxury. I suggested to them the certainty of their readily obtaining great prices for these gems among the rich strangers with whom Rome was thronged.

The impression made upon their greedy minds was immediately apparent. One of the band, a young man, and the least known, requested permission of the captain to depart the following day, in disguise, for Rome, for the purpose of traffic ; promising, on the faith of a bandit (a sacred pledge among them), to return in two days to any place he might appoint. The captain consented, and a curious scene took place ; the robbers crowded round him eagerly, confiding to him such of their jewels as they wished to dispose of, and giving him instructions what to demand. There was much bargaining and exchanging and settling of trinkets among them ; and I beheld my watch, which had a chain and valuable seals, purchased by the young robber-merchant of the ruffian who had plundered me, for sixty dollars. I now conceived a faint hope, that if it went to Rome, I might somehow or other regain possession of it.[1]

In the meantime day declined, and no messenger returned from Tusculum. The idea of passing another night in the woods was extremely disheartening, for I began to be satisfied with what I had seen of robber-life. The chieftain now ordered his men to follow him that he might station them at their posts ; adding, that if the messenger did not return before night, they must shift their quarters to some other place.

I was again left alone with the young bandit who had before guarded me ; he had the same gloomy air and haggard eye, with now and then a bitter sardonic smile. I was determined to probe this ulcerated heart, and reminded him of a kind promise he had given me to tell me the cause of his suffering. It seemed to me as if these troubled spirits were glad of any opportunity to disburden themselves, and of having some fresh, undiseased mind, with which they could communicate. I had hardly made the request, when he seated himself by my side, and gave me his story in, as nearly as I can recollect, the following words.

---

[1] The hopes of the artist were not disappointed—the robber was stopped at one of the gates of Rome. Something in his looks or deportment had excited suspicion. He was searched, and the valuable trinkets found on him sufficiently evinced his character. On applying to the police, the artist's watch was returned to him.

THE STORY OF THE YOUNG ROBBER

I WAS born in the little town of Frosinone, which lies at the skirts of the Abruzzi. My father had made a little property in trade, and gave me some education, as he intended me for the Church ; but I had kept gay company too much to relish the cowl, so I grew up a loiterer about the place. I was a heedless fellow, a little quarrelsome on occasion, but good-humoured in the main ; so I made my way very well for a time, until I fell in love. There lived in our town a surveyor or land-bailiff of the Prince, who had a young daughter, a beautiful girl of sixteen ; she was looked upon as something better than the common run of our townsfolk, and was kept almost entirely at home. I saw her occasionally, and became madly in love with her—she looked so fresh and tender, and so different from the sunburnt females to whom I had been accustomed.

As my father kept me in money, I always dressed well, and took all opportunities of showing myself off to advantage in the eyes of the little beauty. I used to see her at church ; and, as I could play a little upon the guitar, I gave a tune sometimes under her window of an evening ; and I tried to have interviews with her in her father's vineyard, not far from the town, where she sometimes walked. She was evidently pleased with me, but she was young and shy ; and her father kept a strict eye upon her and took alarm at my attentions, for he had a bad opinion of me and looked for a better match for his daughter. I became furious at the difficulties thrown in my way, having been accustomed always to easy success among the women, being considered one of the smartest young fellows of the place.

Her father brought home a suitor for her, a rich farmer from a neighbouring town. The wedding-day was appointed, and preparations were making. I got sight of her at her window, and I thought she looked sadly at me. I determined the match should not take place, cost what it might. I met her intended bridegroom in the market-place, and could not restrain the expression of my rage. A few hot words passed between us, when I drew my stiletto and stabbed him to the heart. I fled to a neighbouring church for refuge, and with a little money I obtained absolution, but I did not dare to venture from my asylum.

At that time our captain was forming his troop. He had

known me from boyhood ; and, hearing of my situation, came to me in secret, and made such offers, that I agreed to enroll myself among his followers. Indeed, I had more than once thought of taking to this mode of life, having known several brave fellows of the mountains, who used to spend their money freely among us youngsters of the town. I accordingly left my asylum late one night, repaired to the appointed place of meeting, took the oaths prescribed, and became one of the troop. We were for some time in a distant part of the mountains, and our wild adventurous kind of life hit my fancy wonderfully, and diverted my thoughts. At length they returned with all their violence to the recollection of Rosetta ; the solitude in which I often found myself gave me time to brood over her image ; and, as I have kept watch at night over our sleeping camp in the mountains, my feelings have been roused almost to a fever.

At length we shifted our ground, and determined to make a descent upon the road between Terracina and Naples. In the course of our expedition we passed a day or two in the woody mountains which rise above Frosinone. I cannot tell you how I felt when I looked down upon the place, and distinguished the residence of Rosetta. I determined to have an interview with her ;—but to what purpose ? I could not expect that she would quit her home, and accompany me in my hazardous life among the mountains. She had been brought up too tenderly for that ; and when I looked upon the women who were associated with some of our troop, I could not have borne the thoughts of her being their companion. All return to my former life was likewise hopeless, for a price was set upon my head. Still I determined to see her ; the very hazard and fruitlessness of the thing made me furious to accomplish it.

About three weeks since, I persuaded our captain to draw down to the vicinity of Frosinone, suggesting the chance of entrapping some of its principal inhabitants, and compelling them to a ransom. We were lying in ambush towards evening, not far from the vineyard of Rosetta's father. I stole quietly from my companions, and drew near to reconnoitre the place of her frequent walks. How my heart beat when among the vines I beheld the gleaming of a white dress ! I knew it must be Rosetta's ; it being rare for any female of the place to dress in white. I advanced secretly and without noise, until, putting aside the vines, I stood suddenly before her. She uttered a piercing shriek, but I seized her in my arms, put my hand upon her mouth, and conjured her to be silent. I poured out all the frenzy of my passion ; offered to renounce my mode of life ; to put my fate in her hands ; to fly with her where we might live in safety together. All that I could say or do would not pacify her. Instead of love, horror and affright seemed to have taken possession of her breast. She struggled partly from my grasp, and filled the air with her cries.

In an instant the captain and the rest of my companions were around us. I would have given anything at that moment had she been safe out of our hands, and in her father's house. It was too late. The captain pronounced her a prize, and ordered that she should be borne to the mountains. I represented to him that she was my prize ; that I had a previous claim to her ! and I mentioned my former attachment. He sneered bitterly in reply ; observed that brigands had no business with village intrigues, and that, according to the laws of the troop, all spoils of the kind were determined by lot. Love and jealousy were raging in my heart, but I had to choose between obedience and death. I surrendered her to the captain, and we made for the mountains.

She was overcome by affright, and her steps were so feeble and faltering that it was necessary to support her. I could not endure the idea that my comrades should touch her, and, assuming a forced tranquillity, begged she might be confided to me, as one to whom she was more accustomed. The captain regarded me, for a moment, with a searching look, but I bore it without flinching, and he consented. I took her in my arms ; she was almost senseless. Her head rested on my shoulder ; I felt her breath on my face, and it seemed to fan the flame which devoured me. O God ! to have this glowing treasure in my arms, and yet to think it was not mine !

We arrived at the foot of the mountain ; I ascended it with difficulty, particularly where the woods were thick, but I would not relinquish my delicious burden. I reflected with rage, however, that I must soon do so. The thoughts that so delicate a creature must be abandoned to my rude companions maddened me. I felt tempted, the stiletto in my hand, to cut my way through them all, and bear her off in triumph. I scarcely conceived the idea before I saw its rashness ; but my brain was fevered with the thought that any but myself should enjoy her charms. I endeavoured to outstrip my companions by the quickness of my movements, and to get a little distance ahead, in case any favourable opportunity of escape should present. Vain effort! The voice of the captain suddenly ordered a halt. I trembled, but had to obey. The poor girl partly opened a languid eye, but was without strength or motion. I laid her upon the grass. The captain darted on me a terrible look of suspicion, and ordered me to scour the woods with my companions in search of some shepherd, who might be sent to her father's to demand a ransom.

I saw at once the peril. To resist with violence was certain death—but to leave her alone, in the power of the captain!—I spoke out then with a fervour, inspired by my passion and my despair. I reminded the captain that I was the first to seize her ; that she was my prize ; and that my previous attachment to her ought to make her sacred among my companions. I insisted, therefore, that he should pledge me his word to respect her ; otherwise I should refuse obedience to his orders. His only reply was to cock his carbine, and at the signal my comrades did the same. They laughed with cruelty at my impotent rage. What could I do ? I felt the madness of resistance. I was menaced on all hands, and my companions obliged me to follow them. She remained alone with the chief—yes, alone—and almost lifeless !

Here the robber paused in his recital, overpowered by his emotions. Great drops of sweat stood on his forehead ; he panted rather than breathed ; his brawny bosom rose and fell like the waves of the troubled sea. When he had become a little calm, he continued his recital.

I was not long in finding a shepherd, said he. I ran with the rapidity of a deer, eager, if possible, to get back before what I dreaded might take place. I had left my companions far behind, and I rejoined them before they had reached one half the distance I had made. I hurried them back to the place where we had left the captain. As we approached, I beheld him seated by the side of Rosetta. His triumphant look, and the desolate condition of the unfortunate girl, left me no doubt of her fate. I know not how I restrained my fury.

It was with extreme difficulty, and by guiding her hand, that she was made to trace a few characters, requesting her father to send three hundred dollars as her ransom. The letter was dispatched by the shepherd. When he was gone,

the chief turned sternly to me. " You have set an example,"
said he, " of mutiny and self-will, which, if indulged, would
be ruinous to the troop. Had I treated you as our laws
require, this bullet would have been driven through your
brain. But you are an old friend. I have borne patiently
with your fury and your folly. I have even protected you
from a foolish passion that would have unmanned you. As
to this girl, the laws of our association must have their course."
So saying, he gave his commands : lots were drawn, and the
helpless girl was abandoned to the troop.

Here the robber paused again, panting with fury, and it
was some moments before he could resume his story.

Hell, said he, was raging in my heart. I beheld the impossibility of avenging myself ; and I felt that, according to
the articles in which we stood bound to one another, the
captain was in the right. I rushed with frenzy from the place ;
I threw myself upon the earth ; tore up the grass with my
hands ; and beat my head and gnashed my teeth in agony and
rage. When at length I returned, I beheld the wretched
victim, pale, dishevelled, her dress torn and disordered. An
emotion of pity, for a moment, subdued my fiercer feelings.
I bore her to the foot of a tree, and leaned her gently against
it. I took my gourd, which was filled with wine, and, applying
it to her lips, endeavoured to make her swallow a little. To
what a condition was she reduced ! she, whom I had once
seen the pride of Frosinone ; who but a short time before I
had beheld sporting in her father's vineyard, so fresh, and
beautiful, and happy ! Her teeth were clinched ; her eyes
fixed on the ground ; her form without motion, and in a state
of absolute insensibility. I hung over her in an agony of
recollection at all that she had been, and of anguish at what
I now beheld her. I darted round a look of horror at my
companions, who seemed like so many fiends exulting in the
downfall of an angel ; and I felt a horror at myself for being
their accomplice.

The captain, always suspicious, saw, with his usual pene-
tration, what was passing within me, and ordered me to go
upon the ridge of the woods, to keep a look-out over the neighbourhood, and await the return of the shepherd. I obeyed, of
course, stifling the fury that raged within me, though I felt,
for the moment, that he was my most deadly foe.

On my way however, a ray of reflection came across my mind. I perceived that the captain was but following, with strictness, the terrible laws to which we had sworn fidelity. That the passion by which I had been blinded might, with justice, have been fatal to me, but for his forbearance; that he had penetrated my soul, and had taken precautions, by sending me out of the way, to prevent my committing any excess in my anger. From that instant I felt that I was capable of pardoning him.

Occupied with these thoughts, I arrived at the foot of the mountain. The country was solitary and secure, and in a short time I beheld the shepherd at a distance crossing the plain. I hastened to meet him. He had obtained nothing. He had found the father plunged in the deepest distress. He had read the letter with violent emotion, and then, calming himself with a sudden exertion, he had replied coldly : " My daughter has been dishonoured by those wretches ; let her be returned without ransom,—or let her die ! "

I shuddered at this reply. I knew that, according to the laws of our troop, her death was inevitable. Our oaths required it. I felt, nevertheless, that, not having been able to have her to myself, I could be her executioner.

The robber again paused with agitation. I sat musing upon his last frightful words, which proved to what excess the passions may be carried, when escaped from all moral restraint. There was a horrible verity in this story that reminded me of some of the tragic fictions of Dante.

We now come to a fatal moment, resumed the bandit. After the report of the shepherd, I returned with him, and the chieftain received from his lips the refusal of the father. At a signal which we all understood, we followed him to some distance from the victim. He there pronounced her sentence of death. Every one stood ready to execute his order, but I interfered. I observed that there was something due to pity as well as to justice. That I was as ready as any one to approve the implacable law, which was to serve as a warning to all those who hesitated to pay the ransoms demanded for our prisoners ; but that, though the sacrifice was proper, it ought to be made without cruelty. " The night is approaching," continued I ; " she will soon be wrapped in sleep ; let her then be dispatched. All I now claim on the score of former kindness is, let me strike the blow. I will do it as surely, though more tenderly than another." Several raised their voices against my proposition, but the captain imposed silence on them. He told me I might conduct her into a thicket at some distance, and he relied upon my promise.

I hastened to seize upon my prey. There was a forlorn kind of triumph at having at length become her exclusive possessor. I bore her off into the thickness of the forest. She remained in the same state of insensibility or stupor. I was thankful that she did not recollect me, for, had she once murmured my name, I should have been overcome. She slept at length in the arms of him who was to poniard her. Many were the conflicts I underwent before I could bring myself to strike the blow. But my heart had become sore by the recent conflicts it had undergone, and I dreaded lest, by procrastination, some other should become her executioner. When her repose had continued for some time, I separated myself gently from her, that I might not disturb her sleep, and, seizing suddenly my poniard, plunged it into her bosom. A painful and concentrated murmur, but without any convulsive movement, accompanied her last sigh.—So perished this unfortunate !

He ceased to speak. I sat, horror-struck, covering my face with my hands, seeking, as it were, to hide from myself the frightful images he had presented to my mind. I was roused from this silence by the voice of the captain : " You sleep," said he, " and it is time to be off. Come, we must abandon this height, as night is setting in, and the messenger is not returned. I will post some one on the mountain edge to conduct him to the place where we shall pass the night."

This was no agreeable news to me. I was sick at heart with the dismal story I had heard. I was harassed and fatigued, and the sight of the banditti began to grow insupportable to me.

The captain assembled his comrades. We rapidly descended the forest, which we had mounted with so much difficulty in the morning, and soon arrived in what appeared to be a frequented road. The robbers proceeded with great caution, carrying their guns cocked, and looking on every side with wary and suspicious eyes. They were apprehensive of encountering the civic patrol. We left Rocca Priori behind us. There was a fountain near by, and, as I was excessively thirsty,

I begged permission to stop and drink. The captain himself went and brought me water in his hat. We pursued our route, when, at the extremity of an alley which crossed the road, I perceived a female on horseback, dressed in white. She was alone. I recollected the fate of the poor girl in the story, and trembled for her safety.

One of the brigands saw her at the same instant, and, plunging into the bushes, he ran precipitately in the direction towards her. Stopping on the border of the alley, he put one knee to the ground, presented his carbine ready to menace her, or to shoot her horse if she attempted to fly, and in this way awaited her approach. I kept my eyes fixed on her with intense anxiety. I felt tempted to shout and warn her of her danger, though my own destruction would have been the consequence. It was awful to see this tiger crouching ready for a bound, and the poor innocent victim wandering unconsciously near him. Nothing but a mere chance could save her. To my joy the chance turned in her favour. She seemed almost accidentally to take an opposite path, which led outside of the wood, where the robber dared not venture. To this casual deviation she owed her safety.

I could not imagine why the captain of the band had ventured to such a distance from the height on which he had placed the sentinel to watch the return of the messenger. He seemed himself anxious at the risk to which he exposed himself. His movements were rapid and uneasy ; I could scarce keep pace with him. At length, after three hours of what might be termed a forced march, we mounted the extremity of the same woods, the summit of which we had occupied during the day ; and I learnt with satisfaction that we had reached our quarters for the night. " You must be fatigued," said the chieftain ; " but it was necessary to survey the environs, so as not to be surprised during the night. Had we met with the famous civic guard of Rocca Priori, you would have seen fine sport." Such was the indefatigable precaution and forethought of this robber chief, who really gave continual evidence of military talent.

The night was magnificent. The moon, rising above the horizon in a cloudless sky, faintly lit up the grand features of the mountain, while lights twinkling here and there, like terrestrial stars in the wide dusky expanse of the landscape, betrayed the lonely cabins of the shepherds. Exhausted by fatigue, and by the many agitations I had experienced, I prepared to sleep, soothed by the hope of approaching deliverance. The captain ordered his companions to collect some dry moss ; he arranged with his own hands a kind of mattress and pillow of it, and gave me his ample mantle as a covering. I could not but feel both surprised and gratified by such unexpected attentions on the part of this benevolent cut-throat ; for there is nothing more striking than to find the ordinary charities, which are matters of course in common life, flourishing by the side of such stern and sterile crime. It is like finding the tender flowers and fresh herbage of the valley growing among the rocks and cinders of the volcano.

Before I fell asleep I had some further discourse with the captain, who seemed to feel great confidence in me. He referred to our previous conversation of the morning ; told me he was weary of his hazardous profession ; that he had acquired sufficient property, and was anxious to return to the world, and lead a peaceful life in the bosom of his family. He wished to know whether it was not in my power to procure for him a passport to the United States of America. I applauded his good intentions, and promised to do everything in my power to promote its success. We then parted for the night. I stretched myself upon my couch of moss, which, after my fatigues, felt like a bed of down ; and, sheltered by the robber-mantle from all humidity, I slept soundly, without waking, until the signal to arise.

It was nearly six o'clock, and the day was just dawning. As the place where we had passed the night was too much exposed, we moved up into the thickness of the woods. A fire was kindled. While there was any flame, the mantles were again extended round it : but when nothing remained but glowing cinders, they were lowered, and the robbers seated themselves in a circle.

The scene before me reminded me of some of those described by Homer. There wanted only the victim on the coals, and the sacred knife to cut off the succulent parts, and distribute them around. My companions might have rivalled the grim warriors of Greece. In place of the noble repasts, however, of Achilles and Agamemnon, I beheld displayed on the grass the remains of the ham which had sustained so vigorous an attack on the preceding evening, accompanied by the relics of the bread, cheese, and wine. We had scarcely commenced our frugal breakfast, when I heard again an imitation of the bleating of sheep, similar to what I had heard the day before. The captain answered it in the same tone. Two men were soon after seen descending from the woody height, where we had passed the preceding evening. On nearer approach, they proved to be the sentinel and the messenger. The captain rose, and went to meet them. He made a signal for his comrades to join him. They had a short conference, and then returning to me with great eagerness, " Your ransom is paid," said he ; " you are free ! "

Though I had anticipated deliverance, I cannot tell you what a rush of delight these tidings gave me. I cared not to finish my repast, but prepared to depart. The captain took me by the hand, requested permission to write to me, and begged me not to forget the passport. I replied, that I hoped to be of effectual service to him, and that I relied on his honour to return the Prince's note for five hundred dollars, now that the cash was paid. He regarded me for a moment with surprise, then, seeming to recollect himself, " *E giusto*," said he, " *eccolo —adio !* " [1] He delivered me the note, pressed my hand once more, and we separated. The labourers were permitted to follow me, and we resumed with joy our road toward Tusculum.

[1] It is just—there it is—adieu !

EDGAR ALLAN POE (1809–1849) *re-mains unsurpassed as a writer of grotesque and fantastic stories. His comparatively short life was overshadowed by poverty, the bitterness that comes from non-recognition and a morbid craving for drugs that eventually destroyed his sanity. "A Descent into the Maelstrom" combines the wildest flights of nightmare fancy with the cold irrefutable facts of scientific laws.*

A DESCENT INTO
THE MAELSTROM

WE had now reached the summit of the loftiest crag. For some minutes the old man seemed too much exhausted to speak.

" Not long ago," he said at length, " and I could have guided you on this route as well as the youngest of my sons ; but, about three years past, there happened to me an event such as never happened before to mortal man—or at least such as no man ever survived to tell of—and the six hours of deadly terror which I then endured have broken me up body and soul. You suppose me a *very* old man—but I am not. It took less than a single day to change these hairs from a jetty black to white, to weaken my limbs, and to unstring my nerves, so that I tremble at the least exertion and am frightened at a shadow. Do you know I can scarcely look over this little cliff without getting giddy ? "

The " little cliff " upon whose edge he had so carelessly thrown himself to rest that the weightier portion of his body hung over it, while he was only kept from falling by the tenure of his elbow on its extreme and slippery edge—this " little cliff " arose, a sheer unobstructed precipice of black shining rock, some fifteen or sixteen hundred feet from the world of crags beneath us. Nothing would have tempted me to within half a dozen yards of its brink. In truth, so deeply was I excited by the perilous position of my companion, that I fell at full length upon the ground, clung to the shrubs around me, and dared not even glance upwards at the sky—while I struggled in vain to divest myself of the idea that the very foundations of the mountain were in danger from the fury of the winds. It was long before I could reason myself into sufficient courage to sit up and look out into the distance.

" You must get over these fancies," said the guide, " for I have brought you here that you might have the best possible view of the scene of that event I mentioned—and to tell you the whole story with the spot just under your eye.

" We are now," he continued, in that particularizing manner which distinguished him—" we are now close upon the Norwegian coast—in the sixty-eighth degree of latitude—in the great province of Nordland—and in the dreary district of Lofoden. The mountain upon whose top we sit is Helseggen, the Cloudy. Now raise yourself up a little higher—hold on to the grass if you feel giddy—so—and look out, beyond the belt of vapour beneath us, into the sea."

I looked dizzily, and beheld a wide expanse of ocean, whose waters wore so inky a hue as to bring at once to my mind the Nubian geographer's account of the *Mare Tenebrarum*. A panorama more deplorably desolate no human imagination can conceive. To the right and left, as far as the eye could reach, there lay outstretched, like ramparts of the world, lines of horridly black and beetling cliff, whose character of gloom was but the more forcibly illustrated by the surf which reared high up against its white and ghastly crest, howling and shrieking for ever. Just opposite the promontory upon whose apex we were placed, and at a distance of some five or six miles out at sea, there was visible a small, bleak-looking island ; or, more properly, its position was discernible through the wilderness of wild surge in which it was enveloped. About two miles nearer the land arose another of smaller size, hideously craggy and barren, and encompassed at various intervals by a cluster of dark rocks.

The appearance of the ocean, in the space between the more distant island and the shore, had something very unusual about it. Although, at the time, so strong a gale was blowing landward that a brig in the remote offing lay to under a double-reefed trysail, and constantly plunged her whole hull out of sight, still there was here nothing like a regular swell, but only a short, quick, angry cross dashing of water in every direction —as well in the teeth of the wind as otherwise. Of foam there was little except in the immediate vicinity of the rocks.

" The island in the distance," resumed the old man, " is called by the Norwegians Vurrgh. The one midway is Moskoe. That a mile to the north is Ambaaren. Yonder are Islesen, Hotholm, Keildhelm, Suarven and Buckholm. Farther off— between Moskoe and Vurrgh—are Otterholm, Flimen, Sandflesen and Stockholm. These are the true names of the places—but why it has been thought necessary to name them at all is more than either you or I can understand. Do you hear anything ? Do you see any change in the water ? "

We had now been about ten minutes upon the top of Helseggen, to which we had ascended from the interior of Lofoden, so that we had caught no glimpse of the sea until it had burst upon us from the summit. As the old man spoke, I became aware of a loud and gradually increasing sound, like the moaning of a vast herd of buffaloes upon an American prairie ; and at the same moment I perceived that what seamen term the *chopping* character of the ocean beneath us was rapidly changing into a current which set to the eastward. Even while I gazed, this current acquired a monstrous velocity. Each moment added to its speed—to its headlong impetuosity. In five minutes the whole sea, as far as Vurrgh, was lashed into ungovernable fury ; but it was between Moskoe and the coast that the main uproar held its sway. Here the vast bed of the waters, seamed and scarred into a thousand conflicting channels, burst suddenly into frenzied convulsion—heaving, boiling, hissing—gyrating in gigantic and innumerable vortices, and all whirling and plunging on to the eastward with a rapidity which water never elsewhere assumes, except in precipitous descents.

In a few minutes more, there came over the sea another radical alteration. The general surface grew somewhat more smooth, and the whirlpools, one by one, disappeared, while prodigious streaks of foam became apparent where none had been seen before. These streaks, at length, spreading out to a great distance, and entering into combination, took unto themselves the gyratory motion of the subsided vortices, and seemed to form the germ of another more vast. Suddenly— very suddenly—this assumed a distinct and definite existence, in a circle of more than a mile in diameter. The edge of the whirl was represented by a broad belt of gleaming spray ; but no particle of this slipped into the mouth of the terrific funnel, whose interior, as far as the eye could fathom it, was a smooth, shining and jet-black wall of water, inclined to the horizon at an angle of some forty-five degrees, speeding dizzily round and round with a swaying and sweltering motion, and sending forth to the winds an appalling voice, half shriek, half roar, such as not even the mighty cataract of Niagara ever lifts up in its agony to heaven.

The mountain trembled to its very base, and the rock
rocked. I threw myself upon my face, and clung to the scant
herbage in an excess of nervous agitation.

" This," said I at length to the old man, " this *can* be
nothing else than the great whirlpool of the Maelstrom."

" So it is sometimes termed," said he. " We Norwegians
call it the Moskoe-strom, from the island of Moskoe in the
midway."

The ordinary accounts of this vortex had by no means
prepared me for what I saw. That of Jonas Ramus, which
is perhaps the most circumstantial of any, cannot impart the
faintest conception either of the magnificence, or of the horror
of the scene—or of the wild bewildering sense of *the novel*
which confounds the beholders. I am not sure from what
point of view the writer in question surveyed it, nor at what
time ; but it could neither have been from the summit of
Helseggen, nor during a storm. There are some passages
of his description, nevertheless, which may be quoted for
their details, although their effect is exceedingly feeble in
conveying an impression of the spectacle.

" Between Lofoden and Moskoe," he says, " the depth of
the water is between thirty-six and forty fathoms ; but on the
other side, towards Ver (Vurrgh), this depth decreases so as
not to afford a convenient passage for a vessel, without the
risk of splitting on the rocks, which happens even in the
calmest weather. When it is flood, the stream runs up the
country between Lofoden and Moskoe with a boisterous
rapidity ; but the roar of its impetuous ebb to the sea is scarce
equalled by the loudest and most dreadful cataracts ; the
noise being heard several leagues off, and the vortices or pits
are of such an extent and depth, that if a ship comes within
its attraction, it is inevitably absorbed and carried down to
the bottom, and there beat to pieces against the rocks ; and
when the water relaxes, the fragments thereof are thrown up
again. But these intervals of tranquillity are only at the turn
of the ebb and flood, and in calm weather, and last but a quarter
of an hour, its violence gradually returning. When the stream
is most boisterous, and its fury heightened by a storm, it is
dangerous to come within a Norway mile of it. Boats, yachts,
and ships have been carried away by not guarding against it
before they were within its reach. It likewise happens frequently that whales come too near the stream, and are overpowered by its violence ; and then it is impossible to describe

their howlings and bellowings in their fruitless struggles to disengage themselves. A bear, once, attempting to swim from Lofoden to Moskoe, was caught by the stream and borne down, while he roared terribly, so as to be heard on shore. Large stocks of firs and pine trees, after being absorbed by the current, rise again broken and torn to such a degree as if bristles grew upon them. This plainly shows the bottom to consist of craggy rocks, among which they are whirled to and fro. This stream is regulated by the flux and reflux of the sea —it being constantly high and low water every six hours. In the year 1645, early in the morning of Sexagesima Sunday, it raged with such noise and impetuosity that the very stones of the houses on the coast fell to the ground."

In regard to the depth of the water, I could not see how this could have been ascertained at all in the immediate vicinity of the vortex. The " forty fathoms " must have reference only to portions of the channel close upon the shore either of Moskoe or Lofoden. The depth in the centre of the Moskoe-strom must be immeasurably greater ; and no better proof of this fact is necessary than can be obtained from even the sidelong glance into the abyss of the whirl which may be had from the highest crag of Helseggen. Looking down from this pinnacle upon the howling Phlegethon below, I could not help smiling at the simplicity with which the honest Jonas Ramus records, as a matter difficult of belief, the anecdotes of the whales and the bears ; for it appeared to me, in fact, a self-evident thing, that the largest ships of the line in existence, coming within the influence of that deadly attraction, could resist it as little as a feather the hurricane, and must disappear bodily and at once.

The attempts to account for the phenomenon—some of which, I remember, seemed to me sufficiently plausible in perusal—now wore a very different and unsatisfactory aspect. The idea generally received is that this, as well as three smaller vortices among the Ferroe islands, " have no other cause than the collision of waves rising and falling, at flux and reflux, against a ridge of rocks and shelves, which confines the water so that it precipitates itself like a cataract, and thus the higher the flood rises, the deeper must the fall be ; and the natural result of all is a whirlpool or vortex, the prodigious suction of which is sufficiently known by lesser experiments." These are the words of the *Encyclopædia Britannica*. Kircher and others imagine that in the centre of the channel of the Maelstrom is an abyss penetrating the globe, and issuing in some very remote part—the gulf of Bothnia being somewhat decidedly named in one instance. This opinion, idle in itself, was the one to which, as I gazed, my imagination most readily assented ; and, mentioning it to the guide, I was rather surprised to hear him say that, although it was the view almost universally entertained of the subject by the Norwegians, it nevertheless was not his own. As to the former notion, he confessed his inability to comprehend it ; and here I agreed with him —for, however conclusive on paper, it becomes altogether unintelligible, and even absurd, amid the thunder of the abyss.

" You have had a good look at the whirl now," said the old man ; " and if you will creep round this crag, so as to get in its lee, and deaden the roar of the water, I will tell you a story that will convince you I ought to know something of the Moskoe-strom."

I placed myself as desired, and he proceeded :

" Myself and my two brothers once owned a schooner-rigged smack of about seventy tons burthen, with which we were in the habit of fishing among the islands beyond Moskoe, nearly to Vurrgh. In all violent eddies at sea there is good fishing, at proper opportunities, if one has only the courage to attempt it ; but among the whole of the Lofoden coastmen, we three were the only ones who made a regular business of going out to the islands, as I tell you. The usual grounds are a great way lower down to the southward. There fish can be got at all hours, without much risk, and therefore these places are preferred. The choice spots over here among the rocks, however, not only yield the finest variety, but in far greater abundance ; so that we often got in a single day what the more timid of the craft could not scrape together in a week. In fact, we made it a matter of desperate speculation—the risk of life standing instead of labour, and courage answering for capital.

" We kept the smack in a cove about five miles higher up the coast than this ; and it was our practice, in fine weather, to take advantage of the fifteen minutes' slack to push across the main channel of the Moskoe-strom, far above the pool, and then drop down upon anchorage somewhere near Otter-holm, or Sandflesen, where the eddies are not so violent as elsewhere. Here we used to remain until nearly time for slack-water again, when we weighed and made for home. We never set out upon this expedition without a steady side wind for going and coming—one that we felt sure would not fail us before our return—and we seldom made a miscalculation upon this point.   Twice, during six years, we were forced to stay all night at anchor, on account of a dead calm, which is a rare thing indeed just about here ; and once we had to remain on the grounds nearly a week, starving to death, owing to a gale which blew up shortly after our arrival, and made the channel too boisterous to be thought of.   Upon this occasion we should have been driven out to sea in spite of everything (for the whirlpools threw us round and round so violently that at length we fouled our anchor and dragged it) if it had not been that we drifted into one of the innumerable cross currents—here to-day and gone to-morrow—which drove us under the lee of Flimen, where, by good luck, we brought up.

" I could not tell you the twentieth part of the difficulties we encountered ' on the ground '—it is a bad spot to be in, even in good weather—but we make shift always to run the gauntlet of the Moskoe-strom itself without accident ; although at times my heart has been in my mouth when we happened to be a minute or so behind or before the slack.   The wind sometimes was not as strong as we thought it at starting, and then we made rather less way than we could wish, while the current rendered the smack unmanageable.   My eldest brother had a son eighteen years old, and I had two stout boys of my own. These would have been of great assistance at such times in using the sweeps, as well as afterward in fishing—but, somehow, although we ran the risk ourselves, we had not the heart to let the young ones get into the danger—for, after all said and done, it *was* a horrible danger, and that is the truth.

" It is now within a few days of three years since what I am going to tell you occurred.   It was on the 10th of July 18—, a day which the people of this part of the world will never forget—for it was one in which blew the most terrible hurricane that ever came out of the heavens.   And yet all the morning, and indeed until late in afternoon, there was a gentle and steady breeze from the south-west, while the sun shone brightly, so that the oldest seaman amongst us could not have foreseen what was to follow.

" The three of us—my two brothers and myself—had crossed over to the islands about two o'clock p.m., and soon nearly loaded the smack with fine fish, which, we all remarked, were more plentiful that day than we had ever known them. It was just seven *by my watch* when we weighed and started for home, so as to make the worst of the Strom at slack water, which we knew would be at eight.

"We set out with a fresh wind on our starboard quarter, and for some time spanked along at a great rate, never dreaming of danger, for indeed we saw not the slightest reason to apprehend it. All at once we were taken aback by a breeze from over Helseggen. This was most unusual—something that had never happened to us before—and I began to feel a little uneasy, without exactly knowing why. We put the boat on the wind, but could make no headway at all for the eddies, and I was upon the point of proposing to return to the anchorage when, looking astern, we saw the whole horizon covered with a singular copper-coloured cloud that rose with the most amazing velocity.

"In the meantime the breeze that had headed us off fell away, and we were dead becalmed, drifting about in every direction. This state of things, however, did not last long enough to give us time to think about it. In less than a minute the storm was upon us—in less than two the sky was entirely overcast—and what with this and the driving spray, it became suddenly so dark that we could not see each other in the smack.

"Such a hurricane as then blew it is folly to attempt describing. The oldest seaman in Norway never experienced anything like it. We had let our sails go by the run before it cleverly took us ; but, at the first puff, both our masts went by the board as if they had been sawed off—the mainmast taking with it my youngest brother, who had lashed himself to it for safety.

"Our boat was the lightest feather of a thing that had ever sat upon water. It had a complete flush deck, with only a small hatch near the bow, and this hatch it had always been our custom to batten down when about to cross the Strom, by way of precaution against the chopping seas. But for this circumstance we should have foundered at once—for we lay entirely buried for some moments. How my elder brother escaped destruction I cannot say, for I never had an opportunity of ascertaining. For my part, as soon as I had let the foresail run, I threw myself flat on deck, with my feet against the narrow gunwale of the bow, and with my hands grasping a ring-bolt near the foot of the foremast. It was mere instinct that prompted me to do this—which was undoubtedly the very best thing I could have done—for I was too much flurried to think.

" For some moments we were completely deluged, as I say, and all this time I held my breath and clung to the bolt. When I could stand it no longer I raised myself upon my knees, still keeping hold with my hands, and thus got my head clear. Presently our little boat gave herself a shake, just as a dog does in coming out of the water, and thus rid herself, in some measure, of the seas. I was now trying to get the better of the stupor that had come over me, and to collect my senses so as to see what was to be done, when I felt somebody grasp my arm. It was my elder brother, and my heart leaped for joy, for I had made sure that he was overboard—but the next moment all this joy was turned into horror—for he put his mouth close to my ear, and screamed out the word ' *Moskoe-strom !* '

" No one ever will know what my feelings were at that moment. I shook from head to foot as if I had had the most violent fit of ague. I knew what he meant by that one word well enough—I knew what he wished to make me understand. With the wind that now drove us on, we were bound for the whirl of the Strom, and nothing could save us !

" You perceive that in crossing the Strom channel we always went a long way up above the whirl, even in the calmest weather, and then had to wait and watch carefully for the slack—but now we were driving right upon the pool itself, and in such a hurricane as this ! ' To be sure,' I thought, ' we shall get there just about the slack—there is some little hope in that ' —but in the next moment I cursed myself for being so great a fool as to dream of hope at all. I knew very well that we were doomed, had we been ten times a ninety-gun ship.

" By this time the first fury of the tempest had spent itself, or perhaps we did not feel it so much, as we scudded before it, but at all events the seas, which at first had been kept down by the wind, and lay flat and frothing, now got up into absolute mountains. A singular change, too, had come over the heavens. Around in every direction it was still as black as pitch, but nearly overhead there burst out, all at once, a circular rift of clear sky—as clear as I ever saw—and of a deep bright blue— and through it there blazed forth the full moon with a lustre that I never before knew her to wear. She lit up everything about us with the greatest distinctness—but, oh God, what a scene it was to light up !

" I now made one or two attempts to speak to my brother —but in some manner which I could not understand, the din had so increased that I could not make him hear a single word, although I screamed out at the top of my voice in his ear. Presently he shook his head, looking as pale as death, and held up one of his fingers, as if to say ' *listen*.'

" At first I could not make out what he meant—but soon a hideous thought flashed upon me. I dragged my watch from its fob. It was not going. I glanced at its face by the moonlight, and then burst into tears as I flung it far away into the ocean. *It had run down at seven o'clock? We were behind the time of the slack, and the whirl of the Strom was in full fury?*

" When a boat is well built, properly trimmed, and not deep laden, the waves in a strong gale, when she is going large, seem always to slip from beneath her—which appears very strange to a landsman—and this is called *riding*, in sea phrase.

" Well, so far we had ridden the swells very cleverly ! but presently a gigantic sea happened to take us right under the counter, and bore us with it as it rose—up—up—as if into the sky. I would not have believed that any wave could rise so high. And then down we came with a sweep, a slide, and a plunge, that made me feel sick and dizzy, as if I was falling from some lofty mountain-top in a dream. But while we were up I had thrown a quick glance around—and that one glance was sufficient. I saw our exact position in an instant. The Moskoe-strom whirlpool was about a quarter of a mile dead ahead, but no more like the everyday Moskoe-strom than the whirl as you now see it is like a mill-race. If I had not known where we were, and what we had to expect, I should not have recognized the place at all. As it was, I involuntarily closed my eyes in horror. The lids clenched themselves together as if in a spasm.

" It could not have been two minutes afterwards when we suddenly felt the waves subside, and were suddenly enveloped in foam. The boat made a short half-turn to larboard, and then shot off in its new direction like a thunderbolt. At the same moment the roaring noise of the waters was completely drowned in a shrill shriek—such a sound as you might imagine given out by the water-pipes of many thousand steam-vessels, letting off their steam all together. We were now in the belt of surf that always surrounds the whirl ! and I thought, of course, that another moment would plunge us into the abyss —down which we could only see indistinctly on account of the amazing velocity with which we were borne along. The boat did not seem to sink into the water at all, but to skim like an air-bubble on the surface of the surge. Her starboard side was next the whirl, and on the larboard arose the world of ocean we had left. It stood like a huge, writhing wall between us and the horizon.

" It may appear strange, but now, when we were in the very jaws of the gulf, I felt more composed than when we were only approaching it. Having made up my mind to hope no more, I got rid of a great deal of that terror which unmanned me at first. I supposed it was despair that strung my nerves.

" It may look like boasting—but what I tell you is truth—I began to reflect how magnificent a thing it was to die in such a manner, and how foolish it was in me to think of so paltry a consideration as my own individual life, in view of so wonderful a manifestation of God's power. I do believe that I blushed with shame when this idea crossed my mind. After a little while I became possessed with the keenest curiosity about the whirl itself. I positively felt a *wish* to explore its depths, even at the sacrifice I was going to make ! and my principal grief was that I should never be able to tell my old companions on shore about the mysteries I should see. These, no doubt, were singular fancies to occupy a man's mind in such extremity—and I have often thought since that the revolutions of the boat around the pool might have rendered me a little light-headed.

" There was another circumstance which tended to restore my self-possession ; and this was the cessation of the wind, which could not reach us in our present situation—for, as you saw yourself, the belt of surf is considerably lower than the general bed of the ocean, and this latter now towered above us, a high, black, mountainous ridge. If you have never been at sea in a heavy gale, you can form no idea of the confusion of mind occasioned by the wind and spray together. They blind, deafen, and strangle you, and take away all power of action or reflection. But we were now, in a great measure, rid of these annoyances—just as death-condemned felons in prison are allowed petty indulgences, forbidden them while their doom is yet uncertain.

" How often we made the circuit of the belt it is impossible to say. We careered round and round for perhaps an hour, flying rather than floating, getting gradually more and more into the middle of the surge, and then nearer and nearer to its horrible inner edge. All this time I had never let go of the ring-bolt. My brother was at the stern holding on to an empty water-cask, which had been securely lashed under the coop of the counter, and was the only thing on deck that had not been swept overboard when the gale first took us. As we approached the brink of the pit he let go his hold upon this, and made for the ring, from which, in the agony of his terror, he endeavoured to force my hands, as it was not large enough to afford us both a secure grasp. I never felt deeper grief than when I saw him attempt this act—although I knew he was a madman when he did it—a raving maniac through sheer fright. I did not care, however, to contest the point with him. I knew it could make no difference whether either of us held on at all; so I let him have the bolt and went astern to the cask. This there was no great difficulty in doing; for the smack went round steadily enough, and upon an even keel—only swaying to and fro with the immense swelters of the whirl. Scarcely had I secured myself in my new position, when we gave a wild lurch to starboard, and rushed headlong into the abyss. I muttered a hurried prayer to God, and thought all was over.

"As I felt the sickening sweep of the descent, I had instinctively tightened my hold upon the barrel, and closed my eyes. For some seconds I dared not open them—while I expected instant destruction, and wondered that I was not already in my death-struggles with the water. But moment after moment elapsed. I still lived. The sense of the falling had ceased; and the motion of the vessel seemed much as it had been before, while in the belt of the foam, with the exception that she now lay more along. I took courage and looked once again upon the scene.

"Never shall I forget the sensation of awe, horror, and admiration with which I gazed about me. The boat appeared to be hanging, as if by magic, midway down, upon the interior surface of a funnel, vast in circumference, prodigious in depth, and whose perfectly smooth sides might have been mistaken for ebony, but for the bewildering rapidity with which they spun around, and for the gleaming and ghastly radiance they shot forth, as the rays of the full moon, from that circular rift amid the clouds which I have already described, streamed in a flood of golden glory along the black walls and far away down into the inmost recess of the abyss.

"At first I was too much confused to observe anything accurately. The general burst of terrific grandeur was all that

I beheld. When I recovered myself a little, however, my gaze fell instinctively downward. In this direction I was able to obtain an unobstructed view, from the manner in which the smack hung on the inclined surface of the pool. She was quite upon an even keel—that is to say, her deck lay in a plain parallel with that of the water—but this latter sloped at an angle of more than forty-five degrees, so that we seemed to be lying upon our beam ends. I could not help observing, nevertheless, that I had scarcely more difficulty in maintaining my hold and footing in this situation than if we had been upon a dead level ; and this, I suppose, was owing to the speed at which we revolved.

" The rays of the moon seemed to search the very bottom of the profound gulf ; but still I could make out nothing distinctly, on account of a thick mist in which everything there was enveloped, and over which there hung a magnificent rainbow, like that narrow and tottering bridge which Mussulmen say is the only pathway between Time and Eternity. This mist, or spray, was no doubt occasioned by the clashing of the great walls of the funnel, as they all met together at the bottom—but the yell that went up to the heavens from out of that mist, I dare not attempt to describe.

" Our first slide into the abyss itself, from the belt of foam above, had carried us a great distance down the slope ; but our further descent was by no means proportionate. Round and round we swept—not in any uniform movement—but in dizzying swings and jerks that sent us sometimes only a few hundred yards—sometimes nearly the complete circuit of the whirl. Our progress downwards, at each revolution, was slow, but very perceptible.

" Looking about me upon the wide waste of liquid ebony on which we were thus borne, I perceived that our boat was not the only object in the embrace of the whirl. Both above and below us were visible fragments of vessels, large masses of building timber and trunks of trees, with many smaller articles, such as pieces of house furniture, broken boxes, barrels, and staves. I have already described the unnatural curiosity which had taken the place of my original terrors. It appeared to grow upon me as I drew nearer and nearer to my dreadful doom. I now began to watch, with a strange interest, the numerous things that floated in our company. I *must* have been delirious—for I even sought *amusement* in speculating upon the relative velocities of their several descents

*The boat appeared to be hanging, as if by magic, midway down,
upon the interior surface of a funnel.*

toward the foam below. ' This fir tree,' I found myself at one time saying, ' will certainly be the next thing that takes the awful plunge and disappears '—and then I was disappointed to find that the wreck of a Dutch merchant ship overtook it and went down before. At length, after making several guesses of this nature, and being deceived in all—this fact—the fact of my invariable miscalculation, set me upon a train of reflection that made my limbs again tremble, and my heart beat heavily once more.

" It was not a new terror that thus affected me, but the dawn of a more exciting *hope*. This hope arose partly from memory, and partly from present observation. I called to mind the great variety of buoyant matter that strewed the coast of Lofoden, having been absorbed and then thrown forth by the Moskoe-strom. By far the greater number of the articles were shattered in the most extraordinary way—so chafed and roughened as to have the appearance of having been stuck full of splinters—but then I distinctly recollected that there were *some* of them which were not disfigured at all. Now I could not account for this difference except by supposing that the roughened fragments were the only ones that had been *completely absorbed*—that the others had entered the whirl at so late a period of the tide, or, from some reason, had descended so slowly after entering, that they did not reach the bottom before the turn of the flood came, or of the ebb, as the case may be. I conceived it possible in either instance that they might thus be whirled up again to the level of the ocean, without under-going the fate of those which had been drawn in more early or absorbed more rapidly. I made, also, three important observations. The first was, that as a general rule, the larger the bodies were, the more rapid their descent—the second, that, between two masses of equal extent, the one spherical and the other *of any other shape*, the superiority in speed of descent was with the sphere—the third that, between two masses of equal size, the one cyclindrical and the other of any other shape, the cylinder was absorbed the more slowly. Since my escape, I have had several conversations on this subject with an old schoolmaster of the district ; and it was from him that I learned the use of the word ' cylinder ' and ' sphere.' He explained to me, although I have forgotten the explanation— how what I observed was, in fact, the natural consequence of the forms of the floating fragments—and showed me how it happened that a cylinder, swimming in a vortex, offered more resistance to its suction, and was drawn in with greater difficulty than an equally bulky body, of any form whatever.[1]

" There was one startling circumstance which went a great way in enforcing these observations, and rendering me anxious to turn them to account, and this was that, at every revolution, we passed something like a barrel, or else the yard or the mast of a vessel, while many of these things, which had been on our level when I first opened my eyes upon the wonders of the whirlpool, were now high up above us, and seemed to have moved but little from their original station.

" I no longer hesitated what to do. I resolved to lash myself securely to the water-cask upon which I now held, to cut it loose from the counter, and to throw myself with it into the water. I attracted my brother's attention by signs, pointed to the floating barrels that came near us, and did everything in my power to make him understand what I was about to do. I thought at length that he comprehended my design, but whether this was the case or not, he shook his head despairingly, and refused to move from his station by the ring-bolt. It was impossible to reach him ; the emergency admitted of no delay ; and so, with a bitter struggle, I resigned him to his fate, fastened myself to the cask by means of the lashings which secured it to the counter, and precipitated myself with it into the sea, without another moment's hesitation.

" The result was precisely what I had hoped it might be. As it is myself who now tells you this tale—as you see that I *did* escape—and as you are already in possession of the mode in which this escape was effected, and must therefore anticipate all that I have further to say—I will bring my story quickly to conclusion. It might have been an hour, or thereabout, after my quitting the smack, when, having descended to a vast distance beneath me, it made three or four wild gyrations in rapid succession, and, bearing my loved brother with it, plunged headlong, at once and for ever, into the chaos of foam below. The barrel to which I was attached sunk very little farther than half the distance between the bottom of the gulf and the spot at which I leaped overboard, before a great change took place in the character of the whirlpool. The slope of the sides of the vast funnel became momentarily less and less steep. The gyrations of the whirl grew, gradually, less and less violent. By degrees, the froth and the rainbow disappeared, and the bottom of the gulf seemed slowly to uprise. The sky

[1] See Archimedes, *De Incidentibus in Fluido*, lib. 2.

was clear, the winds had gone down, and the full moon was setting radiantly in the west, when I found myself on the surface of the ocean, in full view of the shores of Lofoden, and above the spot where the pool of the Moskoe-strom *had been*. It was the hour of the slack—but the sea still heaved in mountainous waves from the effects of the hurricane. I was borne violently into the channel of the Strom, and, in a few minutes, was hurried down the coast into the ' grounds ' of the fishermen. A boat picked me up—exhausted from fatigue—and (now that the danger was removed) speechless from the memory of its horror. Those who drew me on board were my old mates and daily companions—but they knew me no more than they would have known a traveller from the spirit-land. My hair, which had been raven-black the day before, was as white as you see it now. They say, too, that the whole expression of my countenance had changed. I told them my story—they did not believe it. I now tell it to *you*—and I can scarcely expect you to put more faith in it than did the merry fishermen of Lofoden."

RAFAEL SABATINI (1875—   ) *is
the son of an Italian father and an English
mother and was educated in Switzerland and
Portugal. Besides being the author of several
important studies of the Borgias, the In-
quisition and similar subjects, he is gifted with
a rare power of making historical fiction pulsate
with life. Several of his novels have been
filmed or dramatised, notably " Captain Blood."*

THE KING'S MESSENGER

ON a brilliant May morning of the year 1690 a gentleman
stepped ashore at Santiago de Porto Rico, followed by a
negro servant shouldering a valise. He had been brought to
the mole in a cock-boat from the yellow galleon standing in
the roadstead, with the flag of Spain floating from her main-
truck. Having landed him, the cock-boat went smartly about,
and was pulled back to the ship, from which circumstance the
gaping idlers on the mole assumed that this gentleman had
come to stay.

They stared at him with interest, as they would have stared
at any stranger. This, however, was a man whose exterior
repaid their attention, a man to take the eye. Even the wretched
white slaves toiling half-naked on the fortifications, and the
Spanish soldiery guarding them, stood at gaze.

Tall, straight, and vigorously spare, our gentleman was
dressed with sombre Spanish elegance in black and silver.
The curls of his black periwig fell to his shoulders, and his
keen shaven face with its high-bridged nose and disdainful lips
was shaded by a broad black hat about the crown of which
swept a black ostrich plume. Jewels flashed at his breast, a
foam of Mechlin almost concealed his hands, and there were
ribbons to the long gold-mounted ebony cane he carried. A
fop from the Alameda he must have seemed but for the manifest
vigour of him and the air of assurance and consequence with
which he bore himself. He carried his dark finery with an
indifference to the broiling tropical heat which argued an iron
constitution, and his glance was so imperious that the eyes of
the inquisitive fell away abashed before it.

He asked the way to the Governor's residence, and the

officer commanding the guard over the toiling white prisoners detached a soldier to conduct him.

Beyond the square, which architecturally, and saving for the palm trees throwing patches of black shadow on the dazzling white sun-drenched ground, might have belonged to some little town in Old Spain, past the church with its twin spires and marble steps, they came, by tall, wrought-iron gates, into a garden, and by an avenue of acacias to a big white house with deep external galleries all clad in jessamine. Negro servants in ridiculously rich red-and-yellow liveries admitted our gentleman, and went to announce to the Governor of Porto Rico the arrival of Don Pedro de Queiroz on a mission from King Philip.

Not every day did a messenger from the King of Spain arrive in this almost the least of his Catholic Majesty's overseas dominions. Indeed, the thing had never happened before, and Don Jayme de Villamarga, whilst thrilled to the marrow by the announcement, knew not whether to assign the thrill to pride or to alarm.

A man of middle height, big of head and paunch, and of less than mediocre intelligence, Don Jayme was one of those gentlemen who best served Spain by being absent from her, and this no doubt had been considered in appointing him Governor of Porto Rico. Not even his awe of majesty, represented by Don Pedro, could repress his naturally self-sufficient manner. He was pompous in his reception of him, and remained unintimidated by the cold haughty stare of Don Pedro's eyes—eyes of a singularly deep blue, contrasting oddly with his bronzed face. A Dominican monk, elderly, tall and gaunt, kept his excellency company.

"Sir, I give you welcome." Don Jayme spoke as if his mouth were full. "I trust you will announce to me that I have the honour to meet with his majesty's approbation."

Don Pedro made him a deep obeisance, with a sweep of his plumed hat, which, together with his cane, he thereafter handed to one of the negro lackeys. "It is to signify the royal approbation that I am here, happily, after some adventures. I have just landed from the 'San Tomas,' after a voyage of many vicissitudes. She has gone on to San Domingo, and it may be three or four days before she returns to take me off again. For that brief while I must make free with your excellency's hospitality." He seemed to claim it as a right rather than ask it as a favour.

"Ah!" was all that Don Jayme permitted himself to answer. And with head on one side, a fatuous smile on the thick lips under his grizzled moustache, he waited for the visitor to enter into details of the royal message.

The visitor, however, displayed no haste. He looked about him at the cool spacious room with its handsome furnishings of carved oak and walnut, its tapestries and pictures, all imported from the Old World, and inquired, in that casual manner of the man who is at home in every environment, if he might be seated. His excellency with some loss of dignity made haste to set a chair.

Composedly, with a thin smile which Don Jayme disliked, the messenger sat down and crossed his legs.

"We are," he announced, "in some sort related, Don Jayme."

Don Jayme stared. "I am not aware of the honour."

"That is why I am at the trouble of informing you. Your marriage, sir, established the bond. I am a distant cousin of Doña Hernanda."

"Oh! My wife!" His excellency's tone in some subtle way implied contempt for that same wife and her relations. "I had remarked your name : Queiroz." This also explained to him the rather hard and open accent of Don Pedro's otherwise impeccable Castilian. "You will, then, be Portuguese, like Doña Hernanda ?" and again his tone implied contempt of Portuguese, and particularly perhaps of Portuguese who were in the service of the King of Spain, from whom Portugal had re-established her independence a half-century ago.

"Half Portuguese, of course. My family——"

"Yes, yes." Thus the testy Don Jayme interrupted him. "But your message from his majesty ?"

"Ah yes. Your impatience, Don Jayme, is natural." Don Pedro was faintly ironical. "You will forgive me that I should have intruded family matters. My message, then. It will be no surprise to you, sir, that eulogistic reports should have reached his majesty, whom God preserve "—he bowed his head in reverence, compelling Don Jayme to do the same—" not only of the good government of this important island of Porto Rico, but also of the diligence employed by you to rid these seas of the pestilent rovers, particularly the English buccaneers who trouble our shipping and the peace of our Spanish settlements."

There was nothing in this to surprise Don Jayme. Not

even upon reflection. Being a fool, he did not suspect that Porto Rico was the worst governed of any Spanish settlement in the West Indies. As for the rest, he had certainly encouraged the extirpation of the buccaneers from the Caribbean. Quite recently, and quite fortuitously be it added, he had actually contributed materially to this desirable end as he was not slow to mention.

With chin high and chest puffed out, he moved, strutting, before Don Pedro as he delivered himself. It was gratifying to be appreciated in the proper quarter. It encouraged endeavour. He desired to be modest. Yet in justice to himself he must assert that under his government the island was tranquil and prosperous. Frey Luis here could bear him out in this. The Faith was firmly planted, and there was no heresy in any form in Porto Rico. And as for the matter of the buccaneers, he had done all that a man in his position could do. Not perhaps as much as he could have desired to do. After all, his office kept him ashore. Had Don Pedro remarked the new fortifications he was building ? The work was all but complete, and he did not think that even the infamous Captain Blood would have the hardihood to pay him a visit. He had already shown that redoubtable buccaneer that he was not a man with whom it was prudent to trifle. A party of this Captain Blood's men had dared to land on the southern side of the island a few days ago. But Don Jayme's followers were vigilant. He saw to that. A troop of horse was in the neighbourhood at the time. It had descended upon the pirates and had taught them a sharp lesson. He laughed as he spoke of it ; laughed at the thought of it ; and Don Pedro politely laughed with him, desiring with courteous and appreciative interest to know more of this.

" You killed them all, of course ? " he suggested, his contempt of them implicit in his tone.

" Not yet." His excellency spoke with a relish almost fierce. " But I have them under my hand. Six of them, who were captured. We have not yet decided upon their end. Perhaps the rope. Perhaps an auto-da-fé and the fires of the Faith for them. They are heretics all, of course. It is a matter I am still considering with Frey Luis here."

" Well, well," said Don Pedro, as if the subject began to weary him. " Will your excellency hear the remainder of my message ? "

The Governor was annoyed by this suggestion that his

lengthy exposition had amounted to an interruption. Stiffly he bowed to the representative of majesty. " My apologies," said he in a voice of ice.

But the lofty Don Pedro paid little heed to his manner. He drew from an inner pocket of his rich coat a folded parchment and a small flat leather case.

" I have to explain, your excellency, the condition in which this comes to you. I have said, although I do not think you heeded it, that I arrive here after a voyage of many vicissitudes. Indeed, it is little short of a miracle that I am here at all, considering what I have undergone. I, too, have been a victim of that infernal dog, Captain Blood. The ship on which I originally sailed from Cadiz was sunk by him a week ago. More fortunate than my cousin Don Rodrigo de Queiroz, who accompanied me and who remains a prisoner in that infamous pirate's hands, I made my escape. It is a long tale with which I will not weary you."

" It would not weary me," exclaimed his excellency, forgetting his dignity in his interest.

But Don Pedro waved aside the implied request for details. " Later ! Later, perhaps, if you care to hear of it. It is not important. What is important on your excellency's account is that I escaped. I was picked up by the ' San Tomas,' which has brought me here, and so I am happily able to discharge my mission." He held up the folded parchment. " I but mention it to explain how this has come to suffer by sea-water, though not to the extent of being illegible. It is a letter from his majesty's Secretary of State informing you that our Sovereign, whom God preserve, has been graciously pleased to create you, in recognition of the services I have mentioned, a knight of the most noble order of St. James of Compostella."

Don Jayme went first white, then red, in his incredulous excitement. With trembling fingers he took the letter and unfolded it. It was certainly damaged by sea-water. Some words were scarcely legible. The ink in which his own surname had been written had run into a smear, as had that of his government of Porto Rico, and some other words here and there. But the amazing substance of the letter was indeed as Don Pedro announced, and the royal signature was unimpaired.

As Don Jayme raised his eyes at last from the document, Don Pedro, proffering the leather case, touched a spring in it. It flew open, and the Governor gazed upon rubies that glowed like live coals against their background of black velvet.

"And here," said Don Pedro, "is the insignia; the cross of the most noble order in which you are invested."

Don Jayme took the case gingerly, as if it had been some holy thing, and gazed upon the smouldering cross. The friar came to stand beside him, murmuring congratulatory words. Any knighthood would have been an honourable, an unexpected, reward for Don Jayme's services to the crown of Spain. But that of all orders this most exalted and coveted order of St. James of Compostella should have been conferred upon him was something that almost defied belief. The Governor of Porto Rico was momentarily awed by the greatness of the thing that had befallen him.

And yet when a few minutes later the room was entered by a little lady, young and delicately lovely, Don Jayme had already recovered his habitual poise of self-sufficiency.

The lady, beholding a stranger, an elegant, courtly stranger, who rose instantly upon her advent, paused in the doorway, hesitating, timid. She addressed Don Jayme.

"Pardon. I did not know you occupied."

Don Jayme appealed, sneering, to the friar. "She did not know me occupied! I am the King's representative in Porto Rico, his majesty's Governor of this island, and my wife does not know that I am occupied, conceives that I have leisure. It is unbelievable. But come in, Hernanda. Come in." He grew more playful. "Acquaint yourself with the honours the King bestows upon his poor servant. This may help you to realise what his majesty does me the justice to realise, although you may have failed to do so: that my occupations here are onerous."

Timidly she advanced, obedient to his invitation. "What is it, Jayme?"

"What is it?" He seemed to mimic her. "It is merely this." He displayed the order. "His majesty invests me with the cross of Saint James of Compostella. That is all."

She grew conscious that she was mocked. Her pale, delicate face flushed a little. But there was no accompanying sparkle of her great, dark, wistful eyes to proclaim it a flush of pleasure. Rather, thought Don Pedro, she flushed from shame and resentment at being so contemptuously used before a stranger and at the boorishness of a husband who could so use her.

"I am glad, Jayme," she said in a gentle, weary voice. "I felicitate you. I am glad."

"Ah! You are glad. Frey Alonso, you will observe that Doña Hernanda is glad." Thus he sneered at her without even the poor grace of being witty. "This gentleman, by whose hand the order came, is a kinsman of yours, Hernanda."

She turned aside, to look again at that elegant stranger. Her gaze was blank. Yet she hesitated to deny him. Kinship when claimed by gentlemen charged by kings with missions of investiture is not lightly to be denied in the presence of such a husband as Don Jayme. And, after all, hers was a considerable family, and must include many with whom she was not personally acquainted.

The stranger bowed until the curls of his periwig met across his face. "You will not remember me, Doña Hernanda. I am, nevertheless, your cousin, and you will have heard of me from our other cousin Rodrigo. I am Pedro de Queiroz."

"You are Pedro?" She stared the harder. "Why, then . . ." She laughed a little. "Oh, but I remember Pedro. We played together as children. Pedro and I."

Something in her tone seemed to deny him. But he confronted her unperturbed.

"That would be at Santarem," said he.

"At Santarem it was." His readiness appeared now to bewilder her. "But you were a fat, sturdy boy then, and your hair was golden."

He laughed. "I have become lean in growing, and I favour a black periwig."

"Which makes your eyes a startling blue. I do not remember that you had blue eyes."

"God help us, ninny!" croaked her husband. "You never could remember anything."

She turned to look at him, and for all that her lip quivered, her eyes steadily met his sneering glance. She seemed about to speak, checked herself, and then spoke at last, very quietly. "Oh yes. There are some things a woman never forgets."

"And on the subject of memory," said Don Pedro, addressing the Governor with cold dignity, "I do not remember that there are any ninnies in our family."

"Faith, then, you needed to come to Porto Rico to discover it," his excellency retorted with his loud, coarse laugh.

"Ah!" Don Pedro sighed. "That may not be the end of my discoveries."

There was something in his tone which Don Jayme did not like. He threw back his big head and frowned. "You mean?" he demanded.

Don Pedro was conscious of an appeal in the little lady's dark, liquid eyes. He yielded to it, laughed, and answered:

"I have yet to discover where your excellency proposes to lodge me during the days in which I must inflict myself upon you. If I might now withdraw . . ."

The Governor swung to Doña Hernanda. "You hear? Your kinsman needs to remind us of our duty to a guest. It will not have occurred to you to make provision for him."

"But I did not know. . . . I was not told of his presence until I found him here."

"Well, well. You know now. And we dine in half an hour.

At dinner Don Jayme was in high spirits, which is to say that he was alternately pompous and boisterous, and occasionally filled the room with his loud jarring laugh.

Don Pedro scarcely troubled to dissemble his dislike of him. His manner became more and more frigidly aloof, and he devoted his attention and addressed his conversation more and more exclusively to the despised wife.

"I have news for you," he told her, when they had come to the dessert, "of our Cousin Rodrigo."

"Ah!" sneered her husband. "She'll welcome news of him. She ever had a particular regard for her Cousin Rodrigo, and he for her."

She flushed, keeping her troubled eyes lowered. Don Pedro came to the rescue, swiftly, easily. "Regard for one another is common among the members of our family. Every Queiroz owes a duty to every other, and is at all times ready to perform it." He looked very straightly at Don Jayme as he spoke, as if inviting him to discover more in the words than they might seem to carry. "And that is at the root of what I am to tell you, cousin Hernanda. As I have already informed his excellency, the ship in which Don Rodrigo and I sailed from Spain together was set upon and sunk by that infamous pirate Captain Blood. We were both captured, but I was so fortunate as to make my escape."

"You have not told us how. You must tell us how," the Governor interrupted him.

Don Pedro waved a hand disdainfully. "It is no great matter, and I soon weary of talking of myself. But . . . if

you insist . . . some other time. At present I am to tell you
of Rodrigo. He remains a prisoner in the hands of Captain
Blood. But do not be unduly alarmed."

There was need for his reassuring tone. Doña Hernanda,
who had been hanging on his words, had turned deathly
white.

"Do not be alarmed. Rodrigo is in good health, and his
life is safe. Also, from my own experience, I know that this
Blood, infamous pirate though he be, is not without chivalrous
ideals, and, piracy apart, he is a man of honour."

"Piracy apart?" Laughter exploded from Don Jayme.
"On my soul, that's humorous! You deal in paradox, Don
Pedro. Eh, Frey Alonso?"

The lean friar smiled mechanically. Doña Hernanda, pale
and piteous, suffered in silence the interruption. Don Pedro
frowned.

"The paradox is not in me, but in Captain Blood. An
indemoniated robber, yet he practises no wanton cruelty, and
he keeps his word. Therefore I say you need have no apprehension on the score of Don Rodrigo's fate. His ransom has
been agreed between himself and Captain Blood, and I have
undertaken to procure it. Meanwhile he is well and courteously
entreated, and, indeed, a sort of friendship has come to exist
between himself and his pirate captor."

"Faith, that I can believe!" cried the Governor, whilst
Doña Hernanda sank back in her chair with a sigh of relief.
"Rodrigo was ever ready to consort with rogues. Was he
not, Hernanda?"

"I . . ." She bridled indignantly; then curbed herself.
"I never observed it."

"You never observed it! I ask myself have you ever
observed anything? Well, well, and so Rodrigo's to be
ransomed. At what is his ransom fixed?"

"You desire to contribute?" cried Don Pedro with a
certain friendly eagerness.

The Governor started as if he had been stung. His
countenance became gravely blank. "Not I, by the Virgin!
Not I. That is entirely a matter for the family of Queiroz."

Don Pedro's smile perished. He sighed. "True! True!
And yet . . . I've a notion you'll come to contribute something before all is ended."

"Dismiss it," laughed Don Jayme, "for that way lies
disappointment."

They rose from table soon thereafter and withdrew to the noontide rest the heat made necessary.

They did not come together again until supper, which was served in that same room, in the comparative cool of eventide and by the light of a score of candles in heavy silver branches brought from Spain.

The Governor's satisfaction at the signal honour of which he was the recipient appeared to have grown with contemplation of it. He was increasingly jovial and facetious, but not on this account did he spare Doña Hernanda his sneers. Rather did he make her the butt of coarse humours, inviting the two men to laugh with him at the shortcomings he indicated in her. Don Pedro, however, did not laugh. He remained preternaturally grave, indeed almost compassionate, as he observed the tragic patience on that long-suffering wife's sweet face.

She looked so slight and frail in her stiff black satin gown, which rendered more dazzling by contrast the whiteness of her neck and shoulders, even as her lustrous, smoothly-dressed black hair stressed the warm pallor of her gentle countenance. A little statue in ebony and ivory she seemed to Don Pedro's fancy, and almost as lifeless until after supper he found himself alone with her in the deep jessamine-clad galleries that stood open to the cool night breezes blowing from the sea.

His excellency had gone off to indite a letter of grateful acknowledgment to the King, and had taken the friar to assist him. He had commended his guest to the attention of his wife, whilst commiserating with him upon the necessity. She had led Don Pedro out into the scented purple tropic night, and stepping now beside him came at last to life, and addressed him in a breathless anxiety.

" What you told us to-day of Don Rodrigo de Queiroz, is it true ? That he is a prisoner in the hands of Captain Blood, but unhurt and safe, awaiting ransom ? "

" Most scrupulously true in all particulars."

" You . . . you pledge your word for that ? Your honour as a gentleman ? For I must assume you a gentleman, since you bear commissions from the King."

" And on no other ground ? " quoth he, a little taken aback.

" Do you pledge me your word ? " she insisted.

" Unhesitatingly. My word of honour. Why should you doubt me ? "

" You give me cause. You are not truthful in all things. Why, for instance, do you say you are my cousin ? "

" You do not, then, remember me ? "

" I remember Pedro de Queiroz. The years might have given you height and slenderness ; the sun might have tanned your face, and under your black periwig your hair may still be fair, though I take leave to doubt it. But what, I ask myself, could have changed the colour of your eyes ? For your eyes are blue, and Pedro's were dark brown."

He was silent a moment, like a man considering, and she watched his stern, handsome face, made plain by the light beating upon it from the windows of the house. He did not meet her glance. Instead his eyes sought the sea, gleaming under the bright stars and reflecting the twinkling lights of ships in the roadstead, watched the fireflies flitting among the bushes in pursuit of moths, looked anywhere but at the little figure at his side.

At last he spoke, quietly, almost humorously, in admission of the imposture. " We hoped you would have forgotten such a detail."

" We ? " she questioned him.

" Rodrigo and I. He is at least my friend. He was hastening to you when this thing befell him. That is how we came to be on the same ship."

" And he desired you to do this ? "

" He shall tell you so himself when he arrives. He will be here in a few days, depend on it. As soon as I can ransom him, which will be very soon after my departure. When I was escaping—for, unlike him, I had given no parole—he desired that if I came here I should claim to be your cousin, so as to stand at need in his place until he comes."

She was thoughtful, and her bosom rose and fell in agitation. In silence they moved a little way in step.

" You took a foolish risk," she said, thereby showing her acceptance of his explanation.

" A gentleman," said he sententiously, " will always take a risk to serve a lady."

" Were you serving me ? "

" Does it seem to you that I could be serving myself ? "

" No. You could not have been doing that."

" Why question further, then ? Rodrigo wished it so. He will explain his motives fully when he comes. Meanwhile, as your cousin, I am in his place. If this boorish husband burdens you overmuch . . ."

" What are you saying ? " Her voice rang with alarm.

" That I am Rodrigo's deputy. So that you remember it, that is all I ask."

" I thank you, cousin," she said, and left him.

Three days Don Pedro continued as the guest of the Governor of Porto Rico, and they were much as that first day, saving that daily Don Jayme continued to increase in consciousness of his new dignity as a knight of Saint James of Compostella, and became, consequently, daily more insufferable. Yet Don Pedro suffered him with exemplary fortitude, and at times seemed even disposed to feed the Governor's egregious vanity. Thus, on the third night at supper, Don Pedro cast out the suggestion that his excellency should signalise the honour with which the King had distinguished him by some gesture that should mark the occasion and render it memorable in the annals of the island.

Don Jayme swallowed the suggestion avidly. " Ah yes ! That is an admirable thought. What do you counsel that I do ? "

Don Pedro smiled with flattering deprecation. " Not for me to counsel Don Jayme de Villamarga. But the gesture should be worthy of the occasion."

" Indeed, yes. That is true." The dullard's wits, however, were barren of ideas. " The question now is what might be considered worthy ? "

Frey Alonso suggested a ball at Government House, and was applauded in this by Doña Hernanda. Don Pedro, apologetically to the lady, thought a ball would have significance only for those who were bidden to it. Something was required that should impress all social orders in Porto Rico.

" Why not an amnesty ? " he inquired at last.

" An amnesty ? " The three of them looked at him in questioning wonder.

" Why not ? It is a royal gesture, true. But is not a governor in some sort royal, a viceroy, a representative of royalty, the one to whom men look for royal gestures ? To mark your accession to this dignity, throw open your gaols, Don Jayme, as do kings upon their coronation."

Don Jayme conquered his stupefaction at the magnitude of the act suggested, and smote the table with his fist, protesting that here was a notion worth adopting. To-morrow he would announce it in a proclamation, and set all prisoners free, their sentences remitted.

"That is," he added, "all but six, whose pardon would hardly please the colony."

"I think," said Don Pedro, "that exceptions would stultify the act. There should be no exceptions."

"But these are exceptional prisoners. Can you have forgotten that I told you I had made captive six buccaneers out of a party that had the temerity to land on Porto Rico?"

Don Pedro frowned, reflecting. "Ah, true!" he cried at last. "I remember."

"And did I tell you, sir, that one of these men is that dog Wolverstone?" He pronounced it Volverstohn.

"Wolverstone?" said Don Pedro, who also pronounced it Volverstohn. "You have captured Wolverstone!" It was clear that he was profoundly impressed; as well he might be, for Wolverstone, who was nowadays the foremost of Blood's lieutenants, was almost as well known to Spaniards and as detested by them as Blood himself. "You have captured Wolverstone!" he repeated, and for the first time looked at Don Jayme with eyes of unmistakable respect. "You did not tell me that. Why, in that case, my friend, you have clipped one of Blood's wings. Without Wolverstone he is shorn of half his power. His own destruction may follow now at any moment, and Spain will owe that to you."

Don Jayme spread his hands in an affectation of modesty. "It is something towards deserving the honour his majesty has bestowed upon me."

"Something!" echoed Don Pedro. "If the King had known this, he might have accounted the order of Saint James of Compostella inadequate."

Doña Hernanda looked at him sharply, to see whether he dealt in irony. But he seemed quite sincere, so much so that for once he had shed the hauteur in which he usually arrayed himself. He resumed after a moment's pause.

"Of course, of course, you cannot include these men in the amnesty. They are not common malefactors. They are enemies of Spain." Abruptly, with a hint of purpose, he asked: "How will you deal with them?"

Don Jayme thrust out a nether lip considering. "I am still undecided whether to hang them out of hand or to let Frey Alonso hold his auto-da-fé upon them and consign them to the fire as heretics. I think I told you so."

"Yes, yes. But I did not then know that Wolverstone is one of them. That makes a difference."

"What difference?"

"Oh, but consider. Give this matter thought. With thought you'll see for yourself what you should do. It's plain enough."

Don Jayme considered awhile as he was bidden. Then shrugged his shoulders.

"Faith, sir, it may be plain enough to you. But I confess that I see no choice beyond that of rope or fire."

"Ultimately, yes. One or the other. But not here in Porto Rico. That is to smother the effulgence of your achievement. Send them to Spain, Don Jayme. Send them to his majesty, as an earnest of the zeal for which he has been pleased to honour you. Show him thus how richly you deserve that honour and even greater honours. Let that be your acknowledgment."

Don Jayme was staring at him with dilating eyes. His face glowed. "I vow to Heaven I should never have thought of it," he said at last.

"Your modesty made you blind to the opportunity."

"It may be that," Don Jayme admitted.

"But you perceive it now that I indicate it?"

"Oh, I perceive it. Yes, the King of Spain shall be impressed."

Frey Alonso seemed downcast. He had been counting upon his auto-da-fé. Doña Hernanda was chiefly puzzled by the sudden geniality of her hitherto haughty and disdainful pretended cousin. Meanwhile Don Pedro piled Pelion upon Ossa.

"It should prove to his majesty that your excellency is wasted in so small a settlement as Porto Rico. I see you as governor of some more important colony. Perhaps as viceroy. . . . Who shall say? You have displayed a zeal such as has rarely been displayed by any Spanish governor overseas."

"But how and when to send them to Spain?" wondered Don Jayme, who no longer questioned the expediency of doing so.

"Why, that is a matter in which I can serve your excellency. I can convey them for you on the 'San Tomas,' which should call for me at any moment now. You will write another letter to his majesty, offering him these evidences of your zeal, and I will bear it together with these captives.

Your general amnesty can wait until I've sailed with them.
Thus there will be nothing to mar it. It will be complete
and properly imposing."

So elated and so grateful to his guest for his suggestion was
Don Jayme that he actually went the length of addressing him
as cousin in the course of thanking him.

The matter, it seemed, had presented itself for discussion
only just in time. For early on the following morning Santiago
was startled by the boom of a gun, and turning out to ascertain
the reason, beheld again the yellow Spanish ship which had
brought Don Pedro coming to anchor in the bay.

Don Pedro himself sought the Governor with the information that this was the signal for his departure, expressing a
polite regret that duty did not permit him longer to encroach
upon Don Jayme's princely hospitality.

Whilst his negro valet was packing his effects he went to
take his leave of Doña Hernanda, and again assured that
wistful little lady that she need be under no apprehension on
the score of her cousin Rodrigo, who would soon now be
with her.

After this Don Jayme, with an officer in attendance, carried
Don Pedro off to the town gaol, where the pirates were lodged.

In a dark, unpaved stone chamber, lighted only by a small,
heavily-barred, unglazed window set near the ceiling, they
were herded with perhaps a score of other malefactors of all
kinds and colours. The atmosphere of the place was so indescribably foul and noisome that Don Pedro recoiled as from
a blow when it first assailed him. Don Jayme's loud, coarse
laugh derided his fastidiousness. Nevertheless, the Governor
flicked out a handkerchief that was sprayed with verbena, and
thereafter at intervals held it to his nostrils.

Wolverstone and his five associates, heavily loaded with
irons, were in a group a little apart from their fellow-prisoners.
They squatted against the wall on the foul dank straw that was
their bedding. Unshaven, dishevelled and filthy, for no
means of grooming themselves had been allowed them, they
huddled together there as if seeking strength in union against
the common rogues with whom they were confined. Wolverstone, almost a giant in build, might from his dress have been
a merchant. Dyke, that sometime petty officer in the King's
Navy, had similarly been arrayed like a citizen of some consequence. The other four wore the cotton shirts and leather
breeches which had been the dress of the boucan-hunters

before they took to the sea, and their heads were swathed in coloured kerchiefs.

They did not stir when the door creaked on its ponderous hinges and a half-dozen corseletted Spaniards with pikes entered to form a guard of honour as well as a protection for the Governor. When that august personage made his appearance attended by his officer and accompanied by his distinguished-looking guest, the other prisoners sprang up and ranged themselves in awe and reverence. The pirates stolidly sat on. But they were not quite indifferent. As Don Pedro sauntered in, languidly leaning on his beribboned cane, dabbing his lips with a handkerchief, which he, too, had deemed it well to produce. Wolverstone stirred on his foul bed, and his single eye (he had lost the other one at Sedgmoor) rolled with almost portentous ferocity.

Don Jayme indicated the group by a wave of his hand. "There are your cursed pirates, Don Pedro, hanging together like a brood of carrion birds."

"These?" quoth Don Pedro haughtily, and pointed with his cane. "Faith, they look their trade, the villains."

Wolverstone glared more fiercely than ever, but was contemptuously silent. A stubborn rogue, it was plain.

Don Pedro advanced towards them, superb in his black and silver, seeming to symbolise the pride and majesty of Spain. The thick-set Governor, in pale green taffetas, kept pace with him, and presently, when they had come to a halt before the buccaneers, he addressed them.

"You begin to know, you English dogs, what it means to defy the might of Spain. And you'll know it better before all is done. I deny myself the pleasure of hanging you as I intended, so that you may go to Madrid, to feed a bonfire."

Wolverstone leered at him. "You are noble," he said, in execrable, but comprehensible Spanish. "Noble with the nobility of Spain. You insult the helpless."

The Governor raged at him, calling him the unprintably foul names that come so readily to an angry Spaniard's lips. This until Don Pedro checked him with a hand upon his arm.

"Is this waste of breath worth while?" He spoke disdainfully. "It but serves to detain us in this noisome place."

The buccaneers stared at him in a sort of wonder. Abruptly he turned on his heel.

"Come, Don Jayme." His tone was peremptory. "Have them out of this. The ' San Tomas ' is waiting, and the tide is on the turn."

The Governor hesitated, flung a last insult at them, then gave an order to the officer, and stalked after his guest, who was already moving away. The officer transferred the order to his men. With the butts of their pikes and many foul words the soldiers stirred the buccaneers. They rose with clank of gyves and manacles, and went stumbling out into the clean air and the sunshine, herded by the pikemen. Hangdog, foul and weary, they dragged themselves across the square, where the palms waved in the sea breeze, and the islanders stood to watch them pass, and so they came to the mole, where a wherry of eight oars awaited them.

The Governor and his guest stood by whilst they were being packed into the sternsheets, whither the pikemen followed them. Then Don Pedro and Don Jayme took their places in the prow with Don Pedro's negro, who carried his valise. The wherry pushed off and was rowed across the blue water to the stately ship from whose masthead floated the flag of Spain.

They came bumping along her yellow side at the foot of the entrance-ladder, to which a sailor hitched a boathook.

Don Pedro, from the prow of the wherry, called peremptorily for a file of musketeers to stand to order in the waist. A morioned head appeared over the bulwarks to answer him that it was done already. Then, with the pikemen urging them, and moving awkwardly and painfully in their irons, the buccaneer prisoners climbed the ladder and dropped one by one over the ship's side.

Don Pedro waved his black servant after them with the valise, and finally invited Don Jayme to precede him aboard. Himself, Don Pedro followed close, and when at the ladder's head Don Jayme came to a sudden halt, it was Don Pedro's continuing ascent that thrust him forward, and this so sharply that he almost tumbled headlong into the vessel's waist. There were a dozen ready hands to steady him, and a babble of voices to give him laughing welcome. But the voices were English, and the hands belonged to men whose garments and accoutrements proclaimed them buccaneers. They swarmed in the waist, and already some of them were at work to strike the irons from Wolverstone and his mates.

Gasping, livid, bewildered, Don Jayme de Villamarga

swung round to Don Pedro who followed. That very Spanish gentleman had paused at the head of the ladder and stood there steadying himself by a ratline, surveying the scene below him. He was calmly smiling.

" You have nothing to apprehend, Don Jayme. I give you my word for that. And my word is good. I am Captain Blood."

He came down to the deck under the stare of the bulging eyes of the Governor, who understood nothing. Before enlightenment finally came his dull, bewildered wits were to understand still less.

A tall, slight gentleman, very elegantly arrayed, stepped forward to meet the Captain. This, to the Governor's increasing amazement, was his wife's cousin, Don Rodrigo. Captain Blood greeted him in a friendly manner.

" I have brought your ransom, as you see, Don Rodrigo," and he waved a hand in the direction of the group of manacled prisoners. " You are free now to depart with Don Jayme. We'll cut short our farewells, for we take up the anchor at once. Hagthorpe, give the order."

Don Jayme thought that he began to understand. Furiously, he turned upon this cousin of his wife's.

" My God, are you in this ? Have you plotted with these enemies of Spain to—— ? "

A hand gripped his shoulder, and a boatswain's whistle piped somewhere forward. " We are weighing the anchor," said Captain Blood. " You were best over the side, believe me. It has been an honour to know you. In future be more respectful to your wife. Go with God, Don Jayme."

The governor found himself, as in a nightmare, bustled over the side and down the ladder. Don Rodrigo followed him after taking courteous leave of Captain Blood.

Don Jayme collapsed limply in the sternsheets of the wherry as it put off. But soon he roused himself furiously to demand an explanation whilst at the same time overwhelming his companion with threats.

Don Rodrigo strove to preserve his calm. " You had better listen. I was on that ship, the ' San Tomas,' on my way to San Domingo, when Blood captured her. He put the crew ashore on one of the Virgin Islands. But me he retained for ransom because of my rank."

" And to save your skin and your purse you made this infamous bargain with him ? "

"I have said that you had better listen. It was not so at all. He treated me honourably, and we became in some sort friends. He is a man of engaging ways, as you may have discovered. In the course of our talks he gleaned from me a good deal of my private life and yours, which in a way, through my Cousin Hernanda, is linked with it. A week ago, after the capture of the men who had gone ashore with Wolverstone, he decided to use the knowledge he had gained ; that and my papers, of which he had, of course, possessed himself. He told me what he intended to do, and promised me that if by the use of my name and the rest he succeeded in delivering those followers of his, he would require no further ransom from me."

"And you ? You agreed ? "

"Agreed ? Sometimes, indeed often, you are fatuous. My agreement was not asked. I was merely informed. Your own foolishness and the order of Saint James of Compostella did the rest. I suppose he conferred it upon you, and so dazzled you with it that you were prepared to believe anything he told you ? "

"You were bringing it to me ? It was among your papers ? " quoth Don Jayme, who thought he began to understand.

There was a grim smile on Don Rodrigo's long, sallow face. "I was taking it to the Governor of Hispaniola Don Jayme de Guzman, to whom the letter was addressed."

Don Jayme de Villamarga's mouth fell open. He turned pale. "Not even that, then ? The order was not intended for me ? It was part of his infernal comedy ? "

"You should have examined the letter more attentively."

"It was damaged by sea-water ! " roared the Governor furiously.

"You should have examined your conscience, then. It would have told you that you had done nothing to deserve the cross of Saint James."

Don Jayme was too stunned to resent the gibe. Not until he was home again and in the presence of his wife did he recover himself sufficiently to hector her with the tale of how he had been bubbled. Thus he brought upon himself his worst humiliation.

"How does it come, madam," he demanded, " that you recognised him for your cousin ? "

"I did not," she answered him, and dared at last to laugh

at him, taking payment in that moment for all the browbeating she had suffered at his hands.

" You did not ! You mean that you knew he was not your cousin ? "

" That is what I mean."

" And you did not tell me ? " The world was rocking about him.

" You would not allow me. When I told him that I did not remember that my Cousin Pedro had blue eyes, you told me that I never remembered anything, and you called me ninny. Because I did not wish to be called ninny again before a stranger I said nothing further."

Don Jayme mopped the sweat from his brow, and appealed in livid fury to her cousin Rodrigo, who stood by. " And what do you say to that ? " he demanded.

" For myself, nothing. But I might remind you of Captain Blood's advice to you at parting. I think it was that in future you be more respectful to your wife."

"SAKI" (1870–1916) *was the name taken from* "The Rubáiyât of Omar Khayyâm" *by H. H. Munro, one of the wittiest exponents of pre-war humour. His sketches, such as* "The Chronicles of Clovis," *are masterpieces of whimsical fun sharply contrasted with a deep and penetrating irony. He began his career as a journalist and also spent some years in Russia as a foreign correspondent. He refused a commission in the War and was killed at the front.*

A HOLIDAY TASK

KENELM JERTON entered the dining-hall of the Golden Galleon Hotel in the full crush of the luncheon hour. Nearly every seat was occupied, and small additional tables had been brought in, where floor space permitted, to accommodate late-comers, with the result that many of the tables were almost touching each other. Jerton was beckoned by a waiter to the only vacant table that was discernible, and took his seat with the uncomfortable and wholly groundless idea that nearly every one in the room was staring at him. He was a youngish man of ordinary appearance, quiet of dress and unobtrusive of manner, and he could never wholly rid himself of the idea that a fierce light of public scrutiny beat on him as though he had been a notability or a super-nut. After he had ordered his lunch there came the unavoidable interval of waiting, with nothing to do but to stare at the flower-vase on his table and to be stared at (in imagination) by several flappers, some maturer beings of the same sex, and a satirical-looking Jew. In order to carry off the situation with some appearance of unconcern he became spuriously interested in the contents of the flower-vase.

"What is the name of those roses, d'you know ?" he asked the waiter. The waiter was ready at all times to conceal his ignorance concerning items of the wine-list or *menu* ; he was frankly ignorant as to the specific name of the roses.

"*Amy Silvester Partington*," said a voice at Jerton's elbow.

The voice came from a pleasant-faced, well-dressed young woman who was sitting at a table that almost touched Jerton's. He thanked her hurriedly and nervously for the information, and made some inconsequent remark about the flowers.

696

" It is a curious thing," said the young woman, " that I should be able to tell you the name of those roses without an effort of memory, because if you were to ask me my name I should be utterly unable to give it to you."

Jerton had not harboured the least intention of extending his thirst for name-labels to his neighbour. After her rather remarkable announcement, however, he was obliged to say something in the way of polite inquiry.

" Yes," answered the lady, " I suppose it is a case of partial loss of memory. I was in the train coming down here ; my ticket told me that I had come from Victoria and was bound for this place. I had a couple of five-pound notes and a sovereign on me, no visiting cards or any other means of identification, and no idea as to who I am. I can only hazily recollect that I have a title ; I am Lady Somebody—beyond that my mind is a blank."

" Hadn't you any luggage with you ? " asked Jerton.

" That is what I didn't know. I knew the name of this hotel and made up my mind to come here, and when the hotel porter who meets the trains asked if I had any luggage I had to invent a dressing-bag and dress-basket ; I could always pretend that they had gone astray. I gave him the name of Smith, and presently he emerged from a confused pile of luggage and passengers with a dressing-bag and dress-basket labelled Kestrel-Smith. I had to take them ; I don't see what else I could have done."

Jerton said nothing, but he rather wondered what the lawful owner of the baggage would do.

" Of course it was dreadful arriving at a strange hotel with the name of Kestrel-Smith, but it would have been worse to have arrived without luggage. Anyhow, I hate causing trouble."

Jerton had visions of harassed railway officials and distraught Kestrel-Smiths, but he made no attempt to clothe his mental picture in words. The lady continued her story.

" Naturally, none of my keys would fit the things, but I told an intelligent page-boy that I had lost my key-ring, and he had the locks forced in a twinkling. Rather too intelligent, that boy ; he will probably end in Dartmoor. The Kestrel-Smith toilet tools aren't up to much, but they are better than nothing."

" If you feel sure that you have a title," said Jerton, " why not get hold of a peerage and go right through it ? "

" I tried that. I skimmed through the list of the House of

Lords in 'Whitaker,' but a mere printed string of names conveys awfully little to one, you know. If you were an army officer and had lost your identity you might pore over the Army Lists for months without finding out who you were. I'm going on another tack ; I'm trying to find out by various little tests who I am *not*—that will narrow the range of uncertainty down a bit. You may have noticed, for instance, that I'm lunching principally off lobster Newburg."

Jerton had not ventured to notice anything of the sort.

" It's an extravagance, because it's one of the most expensive dishes on the *menu*, but at any rate it proves that I'm not Lady Starping ; she never touches shell-fish, and poor Lady Braddleshrub has no digestion at all ; if I am *her* I shall certainly die in agony in the course of the afternoon, and the duty of finding out who I am will devolve on the press and the police and those sort of people ; I shall be past caring. Lady Knewford doesn't know one rose from another and she hates men, so she wouldn't have spoken to you in any case ; and Lady Mousehilton flirts with every man she meets—I haven't flirted with you, have I ? "

Jerton hastily gave the required assurance.

" Well, you see," continued the lady, " that knocks four off the list at once."

" It'll be rather a lengthy process bringing the list down to one," said Jerton.

" Oh, but, of course, there are heaps of them that I couldn't possibly be—women who've got grandchildren or sons old enough to have celebrated their coming of age. I've only got to consider the ones about my own age. I tell you how you might help me this afternoon, if you don't mind ; go through any of the back numbers of *Country Life* and those sort of papers that you can find in the smoking-room, and see if you come across my portrait with infant son or anything of that sort. It won't take you ten minutes. I'll meet you in the lounge about tea-time. Thanks awfully."

And the Fair Unknown, having graciously pressed Jerton into the search for her lost identity, rose and left the room. As she passed the young man's table she halted for a moment and whispered :

" Did you notice that I tipped the waiter a shilling ? We can cross Lady Ulwight off the list ; she would have died rather than do that."

At five o'clock Jerton made his way to the hotel lounge ;

he had spent a diligent but fruitless quarter of an hour among the illustrated weeklies in the smoking-room. His new acquaintance was seated at a small tea-table, with a waiter hovering in attendance.

" China tea or Indian ? " she asked as Jerton came up.

" China, please, and nothing to eat. Have you discovered anything ? "

" Only negative information. I'm not Lady Befnal. She disapproves dreadfully at any form of gambling, so when I recognized a well-known book-maker in the hotel lobby I went and put a tenner on an unnamed filly by William the Third out of Mitrovitza for the three-fifteen race. I suppose the fact of the animal being nameless was what attracted me."

" Did it win ? " asked Jerton.

" No, came in fourth, the most irritating thing a horse can do when you've backed it win or place. Anyhow, I know now that I'm not Lady Befnal."

" It seems to me that the knowledge was rather dearly bought," commented Jerton.

" Well, yes, it has rather cleared me out," admitted the identity-seeker ; " a florin is about all I've got left on me. The lobster Newburg made my lunch rather an expensive one, and, of course, I had to tip that boy for what he did to the Kestrel-Smith locks. I've got rather a useful idea, though. I feel certain that I belong to the Pivot Club ; I'll go back to town and ask the hall porter there if there are any letters for me. He knows all the members by sight, and if there are any letters or telephone messages waiting for me, of course that will solve the problem. If he says there aren't any, I shall say : ' You know who I am, don't you ? ' so I'll find out anyway."

The plan seemed a sound one ; a difficulty in its execution suggested itself to Jerton.

" Of course," said the lady, when he hinted at the obstacle, " there's my fare back to town, and my bill here and cabs and things. If you lend me three pounds that ought to see me through comfortably. Thanks ever so. Then there is the question of that luggage : I don't want to be saddled with that for the rest of my life. I'll have it brought down to the hall and you can pretend to mount guard over it while I'm writing a letter. Then I shall just slip away to the station, and you can wander off to the smoking-room, and they can do what they like with the things. They'll advertise them after a bit and the owner can claim them."

Jerton acquiesced in the manœuvre, and duly mounted guard over the luggage while its temporary owner slipped unobtrusively out of the hotel. Her departure was not, however, altogether unnoticed. Two gentlemen were strolling past Jerton, and one of them remarked to the other :

" Did you see that tall young woman in grey who went out just now ? She is the Lady——"

His promenade carried him out of earshot at the critical moment when he was about to disclose the elusive identity. The Lady Who ? Jerton could scarcely run after a total stranger, break into his conversation, and ask him for information concerning a chance passer-by. Besides, it was desirable that he should keep up the appearance of looking after the luggage. In a minute or two, however, the important personage, the man who knew, came strolling back alone. Jerton summoned up all his courage and waylaid him.

" I think I heard you say you knew the lady who went out of the hotel a few minutes ago, a tall lady, dressed in grey. Excuse me for asking if you could tell me her name ; I've been talking to her for half an hour ; she—er—she knows all my people and seems to know me, so I suppose I've met her somewhere before, but I'm blest if I can put a name to her. Could you—— ? "

" Certainly. She's a Mrs. Stroope."

" Mrs. ? " queried Jerton.

" Yes, she's the Lady Champion at golf in my part of the world. An awful good sort, and goes about a good deal in Society, but she has an awkward habit of losing her memory every now and then, and gets into all sorts of fixes. She's furious, too, if you make any allusion to it afterwards. Good day, sir."

The stranger passed on his way, and before Jerton had had time to assimilate his information he found his whole attention centred on an angry-looking lady who was making loud and fretful-seeming inquiries of the hotel clerks.

" Has any luggage been brought here from the station by mistake, a dress-basket and dressing-case, with the name Kestrel-Smith ? It can't be traced anywhere. I saw it put in at Victoria, that I'll swear. Why—there is my luggage ! and the locks have been tampered with ! "

Jerton heard no more. He fled down to the Turkish bath, and stayed there for hours.

ROBERT LOUIS STEVENSON (1850–1894) *had that enormous zest for life that seems to be the consolation of those whose existence is a perpetual struggle against death.* "*The Bottle Imp*" *is steeped in the glamour and mystery of the Southern Seas where he spent the last years of his life. It was first published in a Samoan translation and may surprise those who only know him as the author of* "*Treasure Island.*"

THE BOTTLE IMP

THERE was a man of the island of Hawaii, whom I shall call Keawe; for the truth is, he still lives, and his name must be kept secret; but the place of his birth was not far from Honaunau, where the bones of Keawe the Great lie hidden in a cave. This man was poor, brave, and active; he could read and write like a schoolmaster; he was a first-rate mariner besides, sailed for some time in the island steamers, and steered a whaleboat on the Kamakua coast. At length it came in Keawe's mind to have a sight of the great world and foreign cities, and he shipped on a vessel bound to San Francisco.

This is a fine town, with a fine harbour, and rich people uncountable; and, in particular, there is one hill which is covered with palaces. Upon this hill Keawe was one day taking a walk, with his pocket full of money, viewing the great houses upon either hand with pleasure. "What fine houses there are!" he was thinking, "and how happy must these people be who dwell in them, and take no care for the morrow!" The thought was in his mind when he came abreast of a house that was smaller than some others, but all finished and beautified like a toy; the steps of that house shone like silver, and the borders of the garden bloomed like garlands, and the windows were bright like diamonds; and Keawe stopped and wondered at the excellence of all he saw. So stopping, he was aware of a man that looked forth upon him through a window, so clear that Keawe could see him as you see a fish in a pool upon the reef. The man was elderly, with a bald head and a black beard; and his face was heavy with sorrow, and he bitterly sighed. And the truth of it is, that as Keawe looked in upon the man, and the man looked out upon Keawe, each envied the other.

All of a sudden the man smiled and nodded, and beckoned Keawe to enter, and met him at the door of the house.

" This is a fine house of mine," said the man, and bitterly sighed. " Would you not care to view the chambers ? "

So he led Keawe all over it, from the cellar to the roof, and there was nothing there that was not perfect of its kind, and Keawe was astonished.

" Truly," said Keawe, " this is a beautiful house ; if I lived in the like of it, I should be laughing all day long. How comes it, then, that you should be sighing ? "

" There is no reason," said the man, " why you should not have a house in all points similar to this, and finer, if you wish. You have some money, I suppose ? "

" I have fifty dollars," said Keawe ; " but a house like this will cost more than fifty dollars."

The man made a computation. " I am sorry you have no more," said he, " for it may raise you trouble in the future ; but it shall be yours at fifty dollars."

" The house ? " asked Keawe.

" No, not the house," replied the man ; " but the bottle. For I must tell you, although I appear to you so rich and fortunate, all my fortune, and this house itself and its garden, came out of a bottle not much bigger than a pint. This is it."

And he opened a lockfast place, and took out a round-bellied bottle with a long neck ; the glass of it was white like milk, with changing rainbow colours in the grain. Within-sides something obscurely moved, like a shadow and a fire.

" This is the bottle," said the man ; and, when Keawe laughed, " You do not believe me ? " he added. " Try, then, for yourself. See if you can break it."

So Keawe took the bottle up and dashed it on the floor till he was weary ; but it jumped on the floor like a child's ball, and was not injured.

" This is a strange thing," said Keawe. " For by the touch of it, as well as by the look, the bottle should be of glass."

" Of glass it is," replied the man, sighing more heavily than ever ; " but the glass of it was tempered in the flames of hell. An imp lives in it, and that is the shadow we behold there moving ; or, so I suppose. If any man buy this bottle the imp is at his command ; all that he desires—love, fame,

money, houses like this house, ay, or a city like this city—all
are his at the word uttered. Napoleon had this bottle, and by
it he grew to be the king of the world ; but he sold it at the
last and fell. Captain Cook had this bottle, and by it he
found his way to so many islands; but he too sold it, and
was slain upon Hawaii. For, once it is sold, the power goes
and the protection ; and unless a man remain content with
what he has, ill will befall him."

" And yet you talk of selling it yourself ? " Keawe said.

" I have all I wish, and I am growing elderly," replied the
man. " There is one thing the imp cannot do—he cannot
prolong life ; and it would not be fair to conceal from you
there is a drawback to the bottle ; for if a man die before he
sells it, he must burn in hell for ever."

" To be sure, that is a drawback and no mistake," cried
Keawe. " I would not meddle with the thing. I can do
without a house, thank God ; but there is one thing I could
not be doing with one particle, and that is to be damned."

" Dear me, you must not run away with things," returned
the man. " All you have to do is to use the power of the imp
in moderation, and then sell it to some one else, as I do to
you, and finish your life in comfort."

" Well, I observe two things," said Keawe. " All the
time you keep sighing like a maid in love—that is one ; and
for the other, you sell this bottle very cheap."

" I have told you already why I sigh," said the man. " It
it because I fear my health is breaking up ; and, as you said
yourself, to die and go to the devil is a pity for any one. As
for why I sell so cheap, I must explain to you there is a
peculiarity about the bottle. Long ago, when the devil
brought it first upon earth, it was extremely expensive, and
was sold first of all to Prester John for many millions of dollars ;
but it cannot be sold at all, unless sold at a loss. If you sell
it for as much as you paid for it, back it comes to you again
like a homing pigeon. It follows that the price has kept
falling in these centuries, and the bottle is now remarkably
cheap. I bought it myself from one of my great neighbours
on this hill, and the price I paid was only ninety dollars. I
could sell it for as high as eighty-nine dollars and ninety-nine
cents, but not a penny dearer, or back the thing must come to
me. Now, about this there are two bothers. First, when you
offer a bottle so singular for eighty-odd dollars, people suppose
you to be jesting. And second—but there is no hurry about

that—and I need not go into it. Only remember it must be coined money that you sell it for."

"How am I to know that this is all true?" asked Keawe.

"Some of it you can try at once," replied the man. "Give me your fifty dollars, take the bottle, and wish your fifty dollars back into your pocket. If that does not happen, I pledge you my honour I will cry off the bargain and restore your money."

"You are not deceiving me?" said Keawe.

The man bound himself with a great oath.

"Well, I will risk that much," said Keawe, "for that can do no harm," and he paid over his money to the man, and the man handed him the bottle.

"Imp of the bottle," said Keawe, "I want my fifty dollars back." And sure enough, he had scarce said the word before his pocket was as heavy as ever.

"To be sure this is a wonderful bottle," said Keawe.

"And now good-morning to you, my fine fellow, and the devil go with you for me," said the man.

"Hold on," said Keawe, "I don't want any more of this fun. Here, take your bottle back."

"You have bought it for less than I paid for it," replied the man, rubbing his hands. "It is yours now; and, for my part, I am only concerned to see the back of you." And with that he rang for his Chinese servant, and had Keawe shown out of the house.

Now, when Keawe was in the street, with the bottle under his arm, he began to think. "If all is true about this bottle, I may have made a losing bargain," thinks he. "But perhaps the man was only fooling me." The first thing he did was to count his money; the sum was exact—forty-nine dollars American money, and one Chili piece. "That looks like the truth," said Keawe. "Now I will try another part."

The streets in that part of the city were as clean as a ship's decks, and though it was noon, there were no passengers. Keawe set the bottle in the gutter and walked away. Twice he looked back, and there was the milky, round-bellied bottle where he left it. A third time he looked back and turned a corner; but he had scarce done so, when something knocked upon his elbow, and behold! it was the long neck sticking up; and as for the round belly, it was jammed into the pocket of his pilot-coat.

"And that looks like the truth," said Keawe.

The next thing he did was to buy a corkscrew in a shop, and go apart into a secret place in the fields. And there he tried to draw the cork, but as often as he put the screw in, out it came again, and the cork was as whole as ever.

" This is some new sort of cork," said Keawe, and all at once he began to shake and sweat, for he was afraid of that bottle.

On his way back to the port-side he saw a shop where a man sold shells and clubs from the wild islands, old heathen deities, old coined money, pictures from China and Japan, and all manner of things that sailors bring in their sea-chests. And here he had an idea. So he went in and offered the bottle for a hundred dollars. The man of the shop laughed at him at first, and offered him five ; but, indeed, it was a curious bottle, such glass was never blown in any human glass-works, so prettily the colours shone under the milky way, and so strangely the shadow hovered in the midst ; so, after he had disputed a while after the manner of his kind, the shopman gave Keawe sixty silver dollars for the thing and set it on a shelf in the midst of his window.

" Now," said Keawe, " I have sold that for sixty which I bought for fifty—or, to say truth, a little less, because one of my dollars was from Chili. Now I shall know the truth upon another point."

So he went back on board his ship, and when he opened his chest, there was the bottle, which had come more quicky than himself. Now Keawe had a mate on board whose name was Lopaka.

" What ails you," said Lopaka, " that you stare in your chest ? "

They were alone in the ship's forecastle, and Keawe bound him to secrecy, and told all.

" This is a very strange affair," said Lopaka ; " and I fear you will be in trouble about this bottle. But there is one point very clear—that you are sure of the trouble, and you had better have the profit in the bargain. Make up your mind what you want with it ; give the order, and it is done as you desire, I will buy the bottle myself ; for I have an idea of my own to get a schooner, and go trading through the islands."

" That is not my idea," said Keawe ; " but to have a beautiful house and garden on the Kona Coast, where I was born, the sun shining in at the door, flowers in the garden, glass in the windows, pictures on the walls, and toys and fine carpets on the tables, for all the world like the house I was in this day—only a story higher, and with balconies all about like the King's palace ; and to live there without care and make merry with my friends and relatives."

" Well," said Lopaka, " let us carry it back with us to Hawaii ; and if all comes true as you suppose, I will buy the bottle, as I said, and ask a schooner."

Upon that they were agreed, and it was not long before the ship returned to Honolulu, carrying Keawe and Lopaka, and the bottle. " They were scarce come ashore when they met a friend upon the beach, who began at once to condole with Keawe.

" I do not know what I am to be condoled about," said Keawe.

" Is it possible you have not heard," said the friend, " your uncle—that good old man—is dead, and your cousin—that beautiful boy—was drowned at sea ? "

Keawe was filled with sorrow, and, beginning to weep and to lament, he forgot about the bottle. But Lopaka was thinking to himself, and presently, when Keawe's grief was a little abated, " I have been thinking," said Lopaka, " had not your uncle lands in Hawaii, in the district of Kaü ? "

" No," said Keawe, " not in Kaü : they are on the mounttain side—a little be-south Kookena."

" These lands will now be yours ? " asked Lopaka.

" And so they will," says Keawe, and began again to lament for his relatives.

" No," said Lopaka, do not lament at present. I have a thought in my mind. How if this should be the doing of the bottle ? For here is the place ready for your house."

" If this be so," cried Keawe, " it is a very ill way to serve me by killing my relatives. But it may be, indeed ; for it was in just such a station that I saw the house with my mind's eye."

" The house, however, is not yet built," said Lopaka.

" No, nor like to be ! " said Keawe ; " for though my uncle has some coffee and ava and bananas, it will not be more than will keep me in comfort ; and the rest of that land is the black lava."

" Let us go to the lawyer," said Lopaka ; " I have still this idea in my mind."

Now, when they came to the lawyer's, it appeared Keawe's uncle had grown monstrous rich in the last days, and there was a fund of money.

' And here is the money for the house ! " cried Lopaka.

" If you are thinking of a new house," said the lawyer, " here is the card of a new architect of whom they tell me great things."

" Better and better ! " cried Lopaka. " Here is all made plain for us. Let us continue to obey orders."

So they went to the architect, and he had drawings of houses on his table.

" You want something out of the way," said the architect. " How do you like this ? " and he handed a drawing to Keawe.

Now, when Keawe set eyes on the drawing, he cried out aloud, for it was the picture of his thought exactly drawn.

" I am in for this house," thought he. " Little as I like the way it comes to me, I am in for it now, and I may as well take the good along with the evil."

So he told the architect all that he wished, and how he would have that house furnished, and about the pictures on the wall and the knick-knacks on the tables ; and he asked the man plainly for how much he would undertake the whole affair.

The architect put many questions, and took his pen and made a computation ; and when he had done he named the very sum that Keawe had inherited.

Lopaka and Keawe looked at one another and nodded.

" It is quite clear," thought Keawe, " that I am to have this house, whether or no. It comes from the devil, and I fear I will get little good by that ; and of one thing I am sure, I will make no more wishes as long as I have this bottle. But with the house I am saddled, and I may as well take the good along with the evil."

So he made his terms with the architect, and they signed a paper ; and Keawe and Lopaka took ship again and sailed to Australia ; for it was concluded between them they should not interfere at all, but leave the architect and the bottle imp to build and to adorn the house at their own pleasure.

The voyage was a good voyage, only all the time Keawe was holding in his breath, for he had sworn he would utter no more wishes, and take no more favours, from the devil. The time was up when they got back. The architect told them that the house was ready, and Keawe and Lopaka took a passage in the *Hall*, and went down Kona way to view the house, and see if all had been done fitly according to the thought that was in Keawe's mind.

Now, the house stood on the mountain side, visible to ships. Above, the forest ran up into the clouds of rain ; below, the black lava fell in cliffs, where the kings of old lay buried. A garden bloomed about the house with every hue of flowers ; and there was an orchard of papaia on the one hand and an orchard of bread-fruit on the other, and right in front, towards the sea, a ship's mast had been rigged up and bore a flag. As for the house, it was three stories high, with great chambers and broad balconies on each. The windows were of glass, so excellent that it was as clear as water and as bright as day. All manner of furniture adorned the chambers. Pictures hung upon the wall in golden frames—pictures of ships, and men fighting, and of the most beautiful women, and of singular places ; nowhere in the world are there pictures of so bright a colour as those Keawe found hanging in his house. As for the knick-knacks, they were extraordinarily fine : chiming clocks and musical boxes, little men with nodding heads, books filled with pictures, weapons of price from all quarters of the world, and the most elegant puzzles to entertain the leisure of a solitary man. And as no one would care to live in such chambers, only to walk through and view them, the balconies were made so broad that a whole town might have lived upon them in delight ; and Keawe knew not which to prefer, whether the back porch, where you get the land breeze and looked upon the orchards and the flowers, or the front balcony, where you could drink the wind of the sea, and look down the steep wall of the mountain and see the *Hall* going by once a week or so between Hookena and the hills of Pele, or the schooners plying up the coast for wood and ava and bananas.

When they had viewed all, Keawe and Lopaka sat on the porch.

" Well," asked Lopaka, " is it all as you designed ? "

" Words cannot utter it," said Keawe. " It is better than I dreamed, and I am sick with satisfaction."

" There is but one thing to consider," said Lopaka, " all this may be quite natural, and the bottle imp have nothing whatever to say to it. If I were to buy the bottle, and got no schooner after all, I should have put my hand in the fire for nothing. I gave you my word, I know ; but yet I think you would not grudge me one more proof."

" I have sworn I would take no more favours," said Keawe. " I have gone already deep enough."

" This is no favour I am thinking of," replied Lopaka.

"It is only to see the imp himself. There is nothing to be gained by that, and so nothing to be ashamed of, and yet, if I once saw him, I should be sure of the whole matter. So indulge me so far, and let me see the imp; and, after that, here is the money in my hand, and I will buy it."

"There is only one thing I am afraid of," said Keawe. "The imp may be very ugly to view, and if you once set eyes upon him you might be very undesirous of the bottle."

"I am a man of my word," said Lopaka. "And here is the money betwixt us."

"Very well," replied Keawe, "I have a curiosity myself. So come, let us have one look at you, Mr. Imp."

Now as soon as that was said, the imp looked out of the bottle, and in again, swift as a lizard; and there sat Keawe and Lopaka turned to stone. The night had quite come, before either found a thought to say or voice to say it with; and then Lopaka pushed the money over and took the bottle.

"I am a man of my word," said he, "and had need to be so, or I would not touch this bottle with my foot. Well, I shall get my schooner and a dollar or two for my pocket; and then I will be rid of this devil as fast as I can. For, to tell you the plain truth, the look of him has cast me down."

"Lopaka," said Keawe, "do not you think any worse of me than you can help; I know it is night, and the roads bad, and the pass by the tombs an ill place to go by so late, but I declare since I have seen that little face, I cannot eat or sleep or pray till it is gone from me. I will give you a lantern, and a basket to put the bottle in, and any picture or fine thing in all my house that takes your fancy; and be gone at once, and go sleep at Hookena with Nahinu."

"Keawe," said Lopaka, "many a man would take this ill; above all, when I am doing you a turn so friendly, as to keep my word and buy the bottle; and for that matter, the night and the dark, and the way by the tombs, must be all tenfold more dangerous to a man with such a sin upon his conscience and such a bottle under his arm. But for my part, I am so extremely terrified myself, I have not the heart to blame you. Here I go, then; and I pray God you may be happy in your house, and I fortunate with my schooner, and both get to heaven in the end in spite of the devil and his bottle."

So Lopaka went down the mountain; and Keawe stood in his front balcony, and listened to the clink of the horses' shoes, and watched the lantern go shining down the path, and along the cliff of caves where the old dead are buried ; and all the time he trembled and clasped his hands, and prayed for his friend, and gave glory to God that he himself was escaped out of that trouble.

But the next day came very brightly, and that new house of his was so delightful to behold that he forgot his terrors. One day followed another, and Keawe dwelt there in perpetual joy. He had his place on the back porch ; it was there he ate and lived, and read the stories in the Honolulu newspapers ; but when any one came by they would go in and view the chambers and the pictures. And the fame of the house went far and wide ; it was called *Ka-Hale Nui*—the Great House— in all Kona ; and sometimes the Bright House, for Keawe kept a Chinaman, who was all day dusting and furbishing ; and the glass, and the gilt, and the fine stuffs, and the pictures, shone as bright as the morning. As for Keawe himself, he could not walk in the chambers without singing, his heart was so enlarged ; and when ships sailed by upon the sea, he would fly his colours on the mast.

So time went by, until one day Keawe went upon a visit as far as Kailua to certain of his friends. There he was well feasted ; and left as soon as he could the next morning, and rode hard, for he was impatient to behold his beautiful house ; and, besides, the night then coming on was the night in which the dead of old days go abroad in the sides of Kona ; and having already meddled with the devil, he was the more chary of meeting with the dead. A little beyond Honaunau, looking far ahead, he was aware of a woman bathing in the edges of the sea ; and she seemed a well-grown girl, but he thought no more of it. Then he saw her white shift flutter as she put it on, and then her red holoku ; and by the time he came abreast of her she was done with her toilet, and had come up from the sea, and stood by the track-side in her red holoku, and she was all freshened with the bath, and her eyes shone and were kind. Now Keawe no sooner beheld her than he drew rein.

" I thought I knew every one in this country," said he. " How comes it that I do not know you ? "

" I am Kokua, daughter of Kiano," said the girl, " and I have just returned from Oahu. Who are you ? "

" I will tell you who I am in a little," said Keawe, dismounting from his horse, " but not now. For I have a thought in my mind, and if you knew who I was, you might have heard of me, and would not give me a true answer. But tell me, first of all, one thing : are you married ? "

At this Kokua laughed out aloud. " It is you who ask questions," she said. " Are you married yourself ? "

" Indeed, Kokua, I am not," replied Keawe, " and never thought to be until this hour. But here is the plain truth. I have met you here at the roadside, and I saw your eyes, which are like the stars, and my heart went to you as swift as a bird. And so now, if you want none of me, say so, and I will go on to my own place ; but if you think me no worse than any other young man, say so, too, and I will turn aside to your father's for the night, and to-morrow I will talk with the good man."

Kokua said never a word, but she looked at the sea and laughed.

" Kokua," said Keawe, " if you say nothing, I will take that for the good answer ; so let us be stepping to your father's door."

She went on ahead of him, still without speech ; only sometimes she glanced back and glanced away again, and she kept the strings of her hat in her mouth.

Now, when they had come to the door, Kiano came out on his veranda, and cried out and welcomed Keawe by name. At that the girl looked over, for the fame of the great house had come to her ears ; and, to be sure, it was a great temptation. All that evening they were very merry together ; and the girl was as bold as brass under the eyes of her parents, and made a mark of Keawe, for she had a quick wit. The next day he had a word with Kiano, and found the girl alone.

" Kokua," said he, " you made a mark of me all the evening ; and it is still time to bid me go. I would not tell you who I was, because I have so fine a house, and I feared you would think too much of that house and too little of the man that loves you. Now you know all, and if you wish to have seen the last of me, say so at once."

" No," said Kokua, but this time she did not laugh, nor did Keawe ask for more.

This was the wooing of Keawe ; things had gone quickly ; but so an arrow goes, and the ball of a rifle swifter still, and yet both may strike the target. Things had gone fast, but they had gone far also, and the thought of Keawe rang in the maiden's head ; she heard his voice in the breach of the surf upon the lava, and for this young man that she had seen but

twice she would have left father and mother and her native
islands.   As for Keawe himself, his horse flew up the path
of the mountain under the cliff of tombs, and the sound of
the hoofs, and the sound of Keawe singing to himself for
pleasure, echoed in the caverns of the dead.   He came to the
Bright House, and still he was singing.   He sat and ate in the
broad balcony, and the Chinaman wondered at his master, to
hear how he sang between the mouthfuls.   The sun went down
into the sea, and the night came ; and Keawe walked the
balconies by lamplight, high on the mountains, and the voice
of his singing startled men on ships.

" Here am I now upon my high place," he said to himself.
" Life may be no better ; this is the mountain top ; and all
shelves about me towards the worse.   For the first time I will
light up the chambers, and bathe in my fine bath with the hot
water and the cold, and sleep above in the bed of my bridal
chamber."

So the Chinaman had word, and he must rise from sleep
and light the furnaces ; and as he walked below, beside the
boilers, he heard his master singing and rejoicing above him
in the lighted chambers.   When the water began to be hot
the Chinaman cried to his master : and Keawe went into the
bathroom ; and the Chinaman heard him sing as he filled the
marble basin ; and heard him sing, and the singing broken,
as he undressed ; until of a sudden, the song ceased.   The
Chinaman listened, and listened ; he called up the house to
Keawe to ask if all were well, and Keawe answered him " Yes,"
and bade him go to bed ; but there was no more singing in
the Bright House ; and all night long the Chinaman heard
his master's feet go round and round the balconies without
repose.

Now, the truth of it was this : as Keawe undressed for his
bath, he spied upon his flesh a patch like a patch of lichen on
a rock, and it was then that he stopped singing.   For he knew
the likeness of that patch, and knew that he was fallen in the
Chinese Evil.[1]

Now, it is a sad thing for any man to fall into this sickness.
And it would be a sad thing for any one to leave a house so
beautiful and so commodious, and depart from all his friends
to the north coast of Molokai, between the mighty cliff and
the sea-breakers.   But what was that to the case of the man
Keawe, he who had met his love but yesterday and won her

[1] Leprosy.

but that morning, and now saw all his hopes break, in a moment, like a piece of glass ?

A while he sat upon the edge of the bath, then sprang, with a cry, and ran outside ; and to and fro, to and fro, along the balcony, like one despairing.

" Very willingly could I leave Hawaii, the home of my fathers," Keawe was thinking. " Very lightly could I leave my house, the high-placed, the many-windowed, here upon the mountains. Very bravely could I go to Molokai, to Kalaupapa by the cliffs, to live with the smitten and to sleep there, far from my fathers. But what wrong have I done, what sin lies upon my soul, that I should have encountered Kokua coming cool from the sea-water in the evening ? Kokua, the soul ensnarer ! Kokua, the light of my life ! Her may I never wed, her may I look upon no longer, her may I no more handle with my loving hand ; and it is for this, it is for you, O Kokua ! that I pour my lamentations ! "

Now you are to observe what sort of a man Keawe was, for he might have dwelt there in the Bright House for years, and no one been the wiser of his sickness ; but he reckoned nothing of that, if he must lose Kokua. And again he might have wed Kokua even as he was ; and so many would have done, because they have the souls of pigs ; but Keawe loved the maid manfully, and he would do her no hurt and bring her in no danger.

A little beyond the midst of the night, there came in his mind the recollection of that bottle. He went round to the back porch, and called to memory the day when the devil had looked forth ; and at the thought ice ran in his veins.

" A dreadful thing is in the bottle," thought Keawe, " and dreadful is the imp, and it is a dreadful thing to risk the flames of hell. But what other hope have I to cure my sickness or to wed Kokua ? What ! " he thought, " would I beard the devil once, only to get me a house, and not face him again to win Kokua ? "

Thereupon he called to mind it was the next day the *Hall* went by on her return to Honolulu. " There must I go first," he thought, " and see Lopaka. For the best hope that I have now is to find that same bottle I was so pleased to be rid of."

Never a wink could he sleep ; the food stuck in his throat ; but he sent a letter to Kiano, and about the time when the steamer would be coming, rode down beside the cliff of the tombs. It rained; his horse went heavily; he looked up at the black mouths of the caves, and he envied the dead that slept there and were done with trouble; and called to mind how he had galloped by the day before, and was astonished. So he came down to Hookena, and there was all the country gathered for the steamer as usual. In the shed before the store they sat and jested and passed the news; but there was no matter of speech in Keawe's bosom, and he sat in their midst and looked without on the rain falling on the houses, and the surf beating among the rocks, and the sighs arose in his throat.

"Keawe of the Bright House is out of spirits," said one to another. Indeed, and so he was, and little wonder.

Then the *Hall* came, and the whale-boat carried him on board. The after-part of the ship was full of Haoles [1]—who had been to visit the volcano, as their custom is; and the midst was crowded with Kanakas, and the forepart with wild bulls from Hilo and horses from Kaü; but Keawe sat apart from all in his sorrow, and watched for the house of Kiano. There it sat low upon the shore in the black rocks, and shaded by the cocoa-palms, and there by the door was a red holoku, no greater than a fly, and going to and fro with a fly's busyness. "Ah, queen of my heart," he cried, "I'll venture my dear soul to win you!"

Soon after darkness fell and the cabins were lit up, and the Haoles sat and played at the cards and drank whisky as their custom is; but Keawe walked the deck all night; and all the next day, as they steamed under the lee of Maui or of Molokai, he was still pacing to and fro like a wild animal in a menagerie.

Towards evening they passed Diamond Head, and came to the pier of Honolulu. Keawe stepped out among the crowd and began to ask for Lopaka. It seemed he had become the owner of a schooner—none better in the islands—and was gone upon an adventure as far as Pola-Pola or Kahiki; so there was no help to be looked for from Lopaka. Keawe called to mind a friend of his, a lawyer in the town (I must not tell his name), and inquired of him. They said he was grown suddenly rich, and had a fine new house upon Waikiki shore; and this put a thought in Keawe's head, and he called a hack and drove to the lawyer's house.

[1] Whites.

The house was all brand new, and the trees in the garden no greater than walking-sticks, and the lawyer, when he came, had the air of a man well pleased.

"What can I do to serve you ? " said the lawyer.

"You are a friend of Lopaka's," replied Keawe, "and Lopaka purchased from me a certain piece of goods that I thought you might enable me to trace."

The lawyer's face became very dark. "I do not profess to misunderstand you, Mr. Keawe," said he, "though this is an ugly business to be stirring in. You may be sure I know nothing, but yet I have a guess, and if you would apply in a certain quarter I think you might have news."

And he named the name of a man, which, again, I had better not repeat. So it was for days, and Keawe went from one to another, finding everywhere new clothes and carriages, and fine new houses, and men everywhere in great contentment, although, to be sure, when he hinted at his business their faces would cloud over.

"No doubt I am upon the track," thought Keawe. "These new clothes and carriages are all the gifts of the little imp, and these glad faces are the faces of men who have taken their profit and got rid of the accursed thing in safety. When I see pale cheeks and hear sighing, I shall know that I am near the bottle."

So it befell at last he was recommended to a Haole in Beritania Street. When he came to the door, about the hour of the evening meal, there were the usual marks of the new house, and the young garden, and the electric light shining in the windows ; but when the owner came, a shock of hope and fear ran through Keawe ; for here was a young man, white as a corpse, and black about the eyes, the hair shedding from his head, and such a look in his countenance as a man may have when he is waiting for the gallows.

"Here it is, to be sure," thought Keawe, and so with this man he noways veiled his errand. "I am come to buy the bottle," said he.

At the word, the young Haole of Beritania Street reeled against the wall.

"The bottle ! " he gasped. "To buy the bottle ! " Then he seemed to choke, and seizing Keawe by the arm, carried him into a room and poured out wine in two glasses.

"Here is my respects," said Keawe, who had been much about with Haoles in his time. "Yes," he added,

" I am come to buy the bottle. What is the price by now ? "

At that word the young man let his glass slip through his fingers, and looked upon Keawe like a ghost.

" The price," says he ; " the price ! You do not know the price ? "

" It is for that I am asking you," returned Keawe. " But why are you so much concerned ? Is there anything wrong about the price ? "

" It has dropped a great deal in value since your time, Mr. Keawe," said the young man, stammering.

" Well, well, I shall have the less to pay for it," said Keawe. " How much did it cost you ? "

The young man was as white as a sheet.

" Two cents," said he.

" What ! " cried Keawe, " two cents ? Why, then, you can only sell it for one. And he who buys it——" The words died upon Keawe's tongue ; he who bought it could never sell it again, the bottle and the bottle imp must abide with him until he died, and when he died must carry him to the red end of hell.

The young man of Beritania Street fell upon his knees. " For God's sake, buy it ! " he cried. " You can have all my fortune in the bargain. I was mad when I bought it at that price. I had embezzled money at my store ; I was lost else ; I must have gone to jail."

" Poor creature," said Keawe, " you would risk your soul upon so desperate an adventure, and to avoid the proper punishment of your own disgrace ; and you think I could hesitate with love in front of me. Give me the bottle, and the change which I make sure you have all ready. Here is a five-cent piece."

It was as Keawe supposed ; the young man had the change ready in a drawer ; the bottle changed hands, and Keawe's fingers were no sooner clasped upon the stalk than he had breathed his wish to be a clean man. And sure enough, when he got home to his room, and stripped himself before a glass, his flesh was whole like an infant's. And here was the strange thing : he had no sooner seen this miracle than his mind was changed within him, and he cared naught for the Chinese Evil, and little enough for Kokua ; and had but the one thought, that here he was bound to the bottle imp for time and for eternity, and had no better hope but to be a cinder for ever in the flames of hell. Away ahead of him he saw them blaze with his mind's eye, and his soul shrank, and darkness fell upon the light.

When Keawe came to himself a little, he was aware it was the night when the band played at the hotel. Thither he went, because he feared to be alone ; and there, among happy faces, walked to and fro, and heard the tunes go up and down, and saw Berger beat the measure, and all the while he heard the flames crackle and saw the red fire burning in the bottomless pit. Of a sudden the band played *Hiki-ao-ao* ; that was a song that he had sung with Kokua, and at the strain courage returned to him.

" It is done now," he thought, " and once more let me take the good along with the evil."

So it befell that he returned to Hawaii by the first steamer, and as soon as it could be managed he was wedded to Kokua, and carried her up the mountain side to the Bright House.

Now it was so with these two, that when they were together Keawe's heart was stilled ; but as soon as he was alone he fell into a brooding horror, and heard the flames crackle, and saw the red fire burn in the bottomless pit. The girl, indeed, had come to him wholly ; her heart leaped in her side at sight of him, her hand clung to his ; and she was so fashioned, from the hair upon her head to the nails upon her toes, that none could see her without joy. She was pleasant in her nature. She had the good word always. Full of song she was, and went to and fro in the Bright House, the brightest thing in its three stories, carolling like the birds. And Keawe beheld and heard her with delight, and then must shrink upon one side, and weep and groan to think upon the price that he had paid for her ; and then he must dry his eyes, and wash his face, and go and sit with her on the broad balconies, joining in her songs, and, with a sick spirit, answering her smiles.

There came a day when her feet began to be heavy and her songs more rare ; and now it was not Keawe only that would weep apart, but each would sunder from the other and sit in opposite balconies with the whole width of the Bright House betwixt. Keawe was so sunk in his despair, he scarce observed the change, and was only glad he had more hours to sit alone and brood upon his destiny, and was not so frequently condemned to pull a smiling face on a sick heart. But one day, coming softly through the house, he heard the sound of a child sobbing, and there was Kokua rolling her face upon the balcony floor, and weeping like the lost.

"You do well to weep in this house, Kokua," he said. "And yet I would give the head off my body that you (at least) might have been happy."

"Happy!" she cried. "Keawe, when you lived alone in your Bright House you were the word of the island for a happy man; laughter and song were in your mouth, and your face was as bright as the sunrise. Then you wedded poor Kokua; and the good God knows what is amiss in her—but from that day you have not smiled. Oh!" she cried, "what ails me? I thought I was pretty, and I knew I loved him. What ails me, that I throw this cloud upon my husband?"

"Poor Kokua," said Keawe. He sat down by her side, and sought to take her hand; but that she plucked away. "Poor Kokua," he said again. "My poor child—my pretty. And I had thought all this while to spare you! Well, you shall know all. Then, at least, you will pity poor Keawe; then you will understand how much he loved you in the past —that he dared hell for your possession—and how much he loves you still (the poor condemned one), that he can yet call up a smile when he beholds you."

With that he told her all, even from the beginning.

"You have done this for me?" she cried. "Ah, well, then what do I care!" and she clasped and wept upon him.

"Ah, child!" said Keawe, "and yet, when I consider of the fire of hell, I care a good deal!"

"Never tell me," said she, "no man can be lost because he loved Kokua, and no other fault. I tell you, Keawe, I shall save you with these hands, or perish in your company. What! you loved me and gave your soul, and you think I will not die to save you in return?"

"Ah, my dear, you might die a hundred times: and what difference would that make?" he cried, "except to leave me lonely till the time comes for my damnation?"

"You know nothing," said she. "I was educated in a school in Honolulu; I am no common girl. And I tell you I shall save my lover. What is this you say about a cent? But all the world is not American. In England they have a piece they call a farthing, which is about half a cent. Ah! sorrow!" she cried, "that makes it scarcely better, for the buyer must be lost, and we shall find none so brave as my Keawe! But, then, there is France; they have a small coin

there which they call a centime, and these go five to the cent,
or thereabout. We could not do better. Come, Keawe, let
us go to the French islands ; let us go to Tahiti as fast as ships
can bear us. There we have four centimes, three centimes,
two centimes, one centime ; four possible sales to come and
go on ; and two of us to push the bargain. Come, my
Keawe ! kiss me, and banish care. Kokua will defend you.''

" Gift of God ! " he cried. " I cannot think that God will
punish me for desiring aught so good. Be it as you will then,
take me where you please : I put my life and my salvation in
your hands."

Early the next day Kokua went about her preparations.
She took Keawe's chest that he went with sailoring ; and first
she put the bottle in a corner, and then packed it with the
richest of their clothes and the bravest of the knick-knacks in
the house. " For," said she, " we must seem to be rich
folks, or who would believe in the bottle ? " All the time of
her preparation she was as gay as a bird ; only when she looked
upon Keawe the tears would spring in her eye, and she must
run and kiss him As for Keawe, a weight was off his soul ;
now that he had his secret shared, and some hope in front of
him, he seemed like a new man, his feet went lightly on the
earth, and his breath was good to him again. Yet was terror
still at his elbow ; and ever and again, as the wind blows out
a taper, hope died in him, and he saw the flames toss and the
red fire burn in hell.

It was given out in the country they were gone pleasuring
in the States, which was thought a strange thing, and yet not
so strange as the truth, if any could have guessed it. So they
went to Honolulu in the *Hall*, and thence in the *Umatilla* to
San Francisco with a crowd of Haoles, and at San Francisco
took their passage by the mail brigantine, the *Tropic Bird*, for
Papeete, the chief place of the French in the south islands.
Thither they came, after a pleasant voyage, on a fair day of
the Trade Wind, and saw the reef with the surf breaking and
Motuiti with its palms, and the schooner riding withinside
and the white houses of the town low down along the shore
among green trees, and overhead the mountains and the
clouds of Tahiti, the wise island.

It was judged the most wise to hire a house, which they
did accordingly, opposite the British Consul's, to make a great
parade of money, and themselves conspicuous with carriages
and horses. This it was very easy to do, so long as they had

the bottle in their possession ; for Kokua was more bold than Keawe, and, whenever she had a mind, called on the imp for twenty or a hundred dollars. At this rate they soon grew to be remarked in the town ; and the strangers from Hawaii, their riding and their driving, the fine holokus, and the rich lace of Kokua, became the matter of much talk.

They got on well after the first with the Tahiti language, which is indeed like to the Hawaiian, with a change of certain letters ; and as soon as they had any freedom of speech, began to push the bottle. You are to consider it was not an easy subject to introduce ; it was not easy to persuade people you are in earnest, when you offer to sell them for four centimes the spring of health and riches inexhaustible. It was necessary besides to explain the dangers of the bottle ; and either people disbelieved the whole thing and laughed, or they thought the more of the darker part, became overcast with gravity, and drew away from Keawe and Kokua, as from persons who had dealings with the devil. So far from gaining ground, these two began to find they were avoided in the town ; the children ran away from them screaming, a thing intolerable to Kokua ; Catholics crossed themselves as they went by ; and all persons began with one accord to disengage themselves from their advances.

Depression fell upon their spirits. They would sit at night in their new house, after a day's weariness, and not exchange one word, or the silence would be broken by Kokua bursting suddenly into sobs. Sometimes they would pray together ; sometimes they would have the bottle out upon the floor, and sit all evening watching how the shadow hovered in the midst. At such times they would be afraid to go to rest. It was long ere slumber came to them, and, if either dozed off, it would be to wake and find the other silently weeping in the dark, or, perhaps, to wake alone, the other having fled from the house and the neighbourhood of that bottle, to pace under the bananas in the little garden, or to wander on the beach by moonlight.

One night it was so when Kokua awoke. Keawe was gone. She felt in the bed and his place was cold. Then fear fell upon her, and she sat up in bed. A little moonshine filtered through the shutters. The room was bright, and she could spy the bottle on the floor. Outside it blew high, the great trees of the avenue cried aloud, and the fallen leaves rattled in the veranda. In the midst of this Kokua was aware of another sound ; whether of a beast or of a man she could scarce tell, but it was as sad as death, and cut her to the soul. Softly she arose, set the door ajar, and looked forth into the moonlit yard. There, under the bananas, lay Keawe, his mouth in the dust, and as he lay he moaned.

It was Kokua's first thought to run forward and console him ; her second potently withheld her. Keawe had borne himself before his wife like a brave man ; it became her little in the hour of weakness to intrude upon his shame. With the thought she drew back into the house.

" Heaven," she thought, " how careless have I been—how weak ! It is he, not I, that stands in this eternal peril ; it was he, not I, that took the curse upon his soul. It is for my sake, and for the love of a creature of so little worth and such poor help, that he now beholds so close to him the flames of hell—ay, and smells the smoke of it, lying without there in the wind and moonlight. Am I so dull of spirit that never till now I have surmised my duty, or have I seen it before and turned aside ? But now, at least, I take up my soul in both the hands of my affection ; now I say farewell to the white steps of heaven and the waiting faces of my friends. A love for a love, and let mine be equalled with Keawe's ! A soul for a soul, and be it mine to perish ! "

She was a deft woman with her hands, and was soon apparelled. She took in her hands the charge—the precious centimes they kept ever at their side ; for this coin is little used, and they had made provision at a government office. When she was forth in the avenue clouds came on the wind, and the moon was blackened. The town slept, and she knew not whither to turn till she heard one coughing in the shadow of the trees.

" Old man," said Kokua, " what do you here abroad in the cold night ? "

The old man could scarce express himself for coughing, but she made out that he was old and poor, and a stranger in the island.

" Will you do me a service ? " said Kokua. " As one stranger to another, and as an old man to a young woman, will you help a daughter of Hawaii ? "

" Ah," said the old man. " So you are the witch from the Eight Islands, and even my old soul you seek to entangle. But I have heard of you, and defy your wickedness."

" Sit down here," said Kokua, " and let me tell you a

tale." And she told him the story of Keawe from the beginning to the end.

"And now," said she, " I am his wife, whom he bought with his soul's welfare. And what should I do ? If I went to him myself and offered to buy it, he will refuse. But if you go, he will sell it eagerly ; I will await you here ; you will buy it for four centimes, and I will buy it again for three. And the Lord strengthen a poor girl ! "

" If you meant falsely," said the old man, " I think God would strike you dead."

" He would ! " cried Kokua. " Be sure He would. I could not be so treacherous ; God would not suffer it."

" Give me the four centimes and await me here," said the old man.

Now, when Kokua stood alone in the street, her spirit died. The wind roared in the trees, and it seemed to her the rushing of the flames of hell ; the shadows towered in the light of the street lamp, and they seemed to her the snatching hands of evil ones. If she had had the strength, she must have run away, and if she had had the breath, she must have screamed aloud ; but, in truth, she could do neither, and stood and trembled in the avenue, like an affrighted child.

Then she saw the old man returning, and he had the bottle in his hand.

" I have done your bidding," said he. " I left your husband weeping like a child ; to-night he will sleep easy." And he held the bottle forth.

" Before you give it me," Kokua panted, " take the good with the evil—ask to be delivered from your cough."

" I am an old man," replied the other, " and too near the gate of the grave to take a favour from the devil. But what is this ? Why do you not take the bottle ? Do you hesitate ?"

" Not hesitate ! " cried Kokua. " I am only weak. Give me a moment. It is my hand resists, my flesh shrinks back from the accursed thing. One moment only ! "

The old man looked upon Kokua kindly. " Poor child ! " said he, " you fear : your soul misgives you. Well, let me keep it. I am old, and can never more be happy in this world, and as for the next——"

" Give it me ! " gasped Kokua. " There is your money. Do you think I am so base as that ? Give me the bottle."

" God bless you, child," said the old man.

Kokua concealed the bottle under her holoku, said farewell

to the old man, and walked off along the avenue, she cared not whither. For all roads were now the same to her, and led equally to hell. Sometimes she walked, and sometimes ran ; sometimes she screamed out loud in the night, and sometimes lay by the wayside in the dust and wept. All that she had heard of hell came back to her ; she saw the flames blaze, and she smelled the smoke, and her flesh withered on the coals.

Near day she came to her mind again, and returned to the house. It was even as the old man said—Keawe slumbered like a child. Kokua stood and gazed upon his face.

" Now, my husband," said she, " it is your turn to sleep. When you wake it will be your turn to sing and laugh. But for poor Kokua, alas ! that meant no evil—for poor Kokua no more sleep, no more singing, no more delight, whether in earth or heaven."

With that she lay down in the bed by his side, and her misery was so extreme that she fell in a deep slumber instantly.

Late in the morning her husband woke her and gave her the good news. It seemed he was silly with delight, for he paid no heed to her distress, ill though she dissembled 'it. The words stuck in her mouth, it mattered not ; Keawe did the speaking. She ate not a bite, but who was to observe it ? For Keawe cleared the dish. Kokua saw and heard him, like some strange thing in a dream ; there were times when she forgot or doubted, and put her hands to her brow ; to know herself doomed and hear her husband babble, seemed so monstrous.

All the while Keawe was eating and talking, and planning the time of their return, and thanking her for saving him and fondling her, and calling her the true helper after all. He laughed at the old man that was fool enough to buy that bottle.

" A worthy man he seemed," Keawe said. " But no one can judge by appearances. For why did the old reprobate require the bottle ? "

" My husband," said Kokua humbly, " his purpose may have been good."

Keawe laughed like an angry man.

" Fiddle-de-dee ! " cried Keawe. " An old rogue, I tell you ; and an old ass to boot. For the bottle was hard enough to sell at four centimes ; and at three it will be quite impossible. The margin is not broad enough, the thing begins to smell of scorching—brrr ! " said he, and shuddered. " It is true I bought it myself at a cent, when I knew not there were smaller coins. I was a fool for my pains ; there will never be found another, and whoever has that bottle now will carry it to the pit."

" O my husband ! " said Kokua. " Is it not a terrible thing to save oneself by the eternal ruin of another ? It seems to me I could not laugh. I would be humbled. I would be filled with melancholy. I would pray for the poor holder."

Then Keawe, because he felt the truth of what she said, grew the more angry. " Heighty-teighty ! " cried he. " You may be filled with melancholy if you please. It is not the mind of a good wife. If you thought at all of me, you would sit shamed."

Thereupon he went out, and Kokua was alone.

What chance had she to sell that bottle at two centimes ? None, she perceived. And if she had any, here was her husband hurrying her away to a country where there was nothing lower than a cent. And here—on the morrow of her sacrifice—was her husband leaving her and blaming her.

She would not even try to profit by what time she had, but sat in the house, and now had the bottle out and viewed it with unutterable fear, and now, with loathing, hid it out of sight.

By-and-by Keawe came back, and would have her take a drive.

" My husband, I am ill," she said. " I am out of heart. Excuse me, I can take no pleasure."

Then was Keawe more wroth than ever. With her, because he thought she was brooding over the case of the old man ; and with himself, because he thought she was right and was ashamed to be so happy.

" This is your truth," cried he, " and this your affection ! Your husband is just saved from eternal ruin, which he encountered for the love of you—and you can take no pleasure ! Kokua, you have a disloyal heart."

He went forth again furious, and wandered in the town all day. He met friends, and drank with them ; they hired a carriage and drove into the country, and there drank again. All the time Keawe was ill at ease, because he was taking this pastime while his wife was sad, and because he knew in his heart that she was more right than he ; and the knowledge made him drink the deeper.

Now there was an old brutal Haole drinking with him,

one that had been a boatswain of a whaler—a runaway, a digger in gold mines, a convict in prisons. He had a low mind and a foul mouth ; he loved to drink and to see others drunken ; and he pressed the glass upon Keawe. Soon there was no more money in the company.

" Here, you ! " says the boatswain, " you are rich, you have been always saying. You have a bottle or some foolishness."

" Yes," says Keawe, " I am rich ; I will go back and get some money from my wife, who keeps it."

" That's a bad idea, mate," said the boatswain. " Never you trust a petticoat with dollars. They're all as false as water ; you keep an eye on her."

Now this word struck in Keawe's mind ; for he was muddled with what he had been drinking.

" I should not wonder but she was false, indeed," thought he. " Why else should she be so cast down at my release ? But I will show her I am not the man to be fooled. I will catch her in the act."

Accordingly, when they were back in town, Keawe bade the boatswain wait for him at the corner by the old calaboose, and went forward up the avenue alone to the door of his house. The night had come again ; there was a light within, but never a sound ; and Keawe crept about the corner, opened the back door softly, and looked in.

There was Kokua on the floor, the lamp at her side ; before her was a milk-white bottle, with a round belly and a long neck ; and as she viewed it, Kokua wrung her hands.

A long time Keawe stood and looked in the doorway. At first he was struck stupid ; and then fear fell upon him that the bargain had been made amiss, and the bottle had come back to him as it came at San Francisco ; and at that his knees were loosened, and the fumes of the wine departed from his head like mists off a river in the morning. And then he had another thought ; and it was a strange one, that made his cheeks to burn.

" I must make sure of this," thought he.

So he closed the door, and went softly round the corner again, and then came noisily in, as though he were but now returned. And, lo ! by the time he opened the front door no bottle was to be seen ; and Kokua sat in a chair and started up like one awakened out of sleep.

" I have been drinking all day and making merry," said

Keawe. " I have been with good companions, and now I only came back for money, and return to drink and carouse with them again."

Both his face and voice were as stern as judgment, but Kokua was too troubled to observe.

" You do well to use your own, my husband," said she, and her words trembled.

" Oh, I do well in all things," said Keawe, and he went straight to the chest and took out money. But he looked besides in the corner where they kept the bottle, and there was no bottle there.

At that the chest heaved upon the floor like a sea-billow, and the house spun about him like a wreath of smoke, for he saw she was lost now, and there was no escape. " It is what I feared," he thought, " It is she who has bought it."

And then he came to himself a little and rose up ; but the sweat streamed on his face as thick as the rain and as cold as the well-water.

" Kokua," said he, " I said to you to-day what ill became me. Now I return to house with my jolly companions," and at that he laughed a little quietly. " I will take more pleasure in the cup if you forgive me."

She clasped his knees in a moment, she kissed his knees with flowing tears.

" Oh," she cried, " I ask but a kind word ! "

" Let us never one think hardly of the other," said Keawe, and was gone out of the house.

Now, the money that Keawe had taken was only some of that store of centime pieces they had laid in at their arrival. It was very sure he had no mind to be drinking. His wife had given her soul for him, now he must give his for hers ; no other thought was in the world with him.

At the corner, by the old calaboose, there was the boatswain waiting.

" My wife has the bottle," said Keawe, " and, unless you help me to recover it, there can be no more money and no more liquor to-night."

" You do not mean to say you are serious about that bottle ? " cried the boatswain.

" There is the lamp," said Keawe. " Do I look as if I was jesting ? "

" That is so," said the boatswain. " You look as serious as a ghost."

*There was Kokua on the floor, the lamp at her side ; before her
was a milk-white bottle with a round belly and a long neck ;
and as she viewed it Kokua wrung her hands.*

" Well, then," said Keawe, " here are two centimes ; you just go to my wife in the house, and offer her these for the bottle, which (if I am not much mistaken) she will give you instantly. Bring it to me here, and I will buy it back from you for one ; for that is the law with this bottle, that it still must be sold for a less sum. But whatever you do, never breathe a word to her that you have come from me."

" Mate, I wonder are you making a fool of me ? " asked the boatswain.

" It will do you no harm if I am," returned Keawe.

" That is so, mate," said the boatswain.

" And if you doubt me," added Keawe, " you can try. As soon as you are clear of the house, wish to have your pocket full of money, or a bottle of the best rum, or what you please, and you will see the virtue of the thing."

" Very well, Kanaka," says the boatswain. " I will try ; but if you are having your fun out of me, I will take my fun out of you with a belaying-pin."

So the whaler-man went off up the avenue ; and Keawe stood and waited. It was near the same spot where Kokua had waited the night before ; but Keawe was more resolved, and never faltered in his purpose ; only his soul was bitter with despair.

It seemed a long time he had to wait before he heard a voice singing in the darkness of the avenue. He knew the voice to be the boatswain's ; but it was strange how drunken it appeared upon a sudden.

Next the man himself came stumbling into the light of the lamp. He had the devil's bottle buttoned in his coat ; another bottle was in his hand ; and even as he came in view he raised it to his mouth and drank.

" You have it," said Keawe. " I see that."

" Hands off ! " cried the boatswain, jumping back. " Take a step near me, and I'll smash your mouth. You thought you could make a catspaw of me, did you ? "

" What do you mean ? " cried Keawe.

" Mean ? " cried the boatswain. " This is a pretty good bottle, this is ; that's what I mean. How I got it for two centimes I can't make out ; but I am sure you shan't have it for one."

" You mean you won't sell ? " gasped Keawe.

" No, sir," cried the boatswain. " But I'll give you a drink of the rum, if you like."

" I tell you," said Keawe, " the man who has that bottle goes to hell."

" I reckon I'm going anyway," returned the sailor ; " and this bottle's the best thing to go with I've struck yet. No, sir ! " he cried again, " this is my bottle now, and you can go and fish for another."

" Can this be true ? " Keawe cried. " For your own sake, I beseech you, sell it me ! "

" I don't value any of your talk," replied the boatswain. " You thought I was a flat, now you see I'm not ; and there's an end. If you won't have a swallow of the rum, I'll have one myself. Here's your health, and good-night to you ! "

So off he went down the avenue towards town, and there goes the bottle out of the story.

But Keawe ran to Kokua light as the wind ; and great was their joy that night ; and great, since then, has been the peace of all their days in the Bright House.

EDGAR WALLACE (1875–1932) *was perhaps the most successful writer of popular fiction who has ever lived. Crime, adventure, humour— all came alike to him. It is said that he was capable of writing in a week plays that would run for years, stories which would sell in their tens of thousands. He started from very humble beginnings, went into journalism and later became the most widely known writer in the world.*

SOLO AND THE LADY

" I'M naturally fond of children " (the steward speaking) " except when they're singletons. Only sons aren't so bad, except when they've got a mother who is strong enough to remind the old man that he was a boy once. That's a fatal thing to say to a father who's after a scalp, because whilst he's trying to think if he ever was a boy, the kid gets away without connecting his hide with pa's waist supporter. But only girls are worst. Man and boy, I've been following the sea for—I don't know how many years and I've got thoroughly acquainted with men, women, children and only children. I've known all the big statesmen and near statesmen in Europe and America and I've met every card baron from Lew Angus to Clink Smith. I've known missionaries and murderers—I had Stellman in one of my cabins when he was arrested on the high seas for killing Hannah Bontey—and I've looked after practically every big woman star from Hollywood. And they're easy people to get on with—if you only remember the names of their new husbands.

" But only daughters ! Mon Jew !—to use a foreign expression.

" The president of the Nation Line had one child—a daughter—and the only ship in the line that wasn't named after a nation was the *Winifred Wilford* which was named after her. But only for a year or so, when it was changed to the *Flemish*, Miss Wilford not liking the way the newspapers talked about the *Winifred Wilford* being scraped and the *Winifred Wilford* have a new refrigerating plant put into her. She said that it was vulgar and so Sir Ernest, her father, changed the name. I heard this from his valet, who used to be a bedroom steward on the *Italian*.

" I never saw the young lady, though it seemed that I couldn't very well miss seeing her, for every other voyage we got word that she was sailing with us next trip to visit her aunt in Chicago. The times the bridal suite went westward empty was because she'd changed her mind at the last minute. It used to be the joke of the ship. The old hands always asked when they came aboard if Winifred was sailing and the poor chap who had charge of the suite reckoned that she cost him the price of a row of houses through the best state-room in the *Flemish* going so often to New York without a passenger.

" I heard a whole lot about her from the valet. She used to go to Rome for a change and to Como for a rest. Then she'd have the Ascot house open and staffed and wouldn't be there a week before she'd skip over to Le Touquet for the golf or go down to Aix for the cure. She'd go to Paris because she was bored and to Switzerland because she had nerves, and Sir Ernest said it was natural that a high-spirited young girl wanted to get about a bit and thought she was the most wonderful thing that ever condescended to look like a human being.

" She was an only daughter, as I've said before.

" Card crooks are the easiest people to look after, and most stewards I know would sooner have a four-berth cabin-load of unlawfulness than the grandest ambassador that ever travelled in a bridal suite. I never blame card-sharps any more than I blame weasels and stoats. They're born to keep tag of the rabbits. If there wasn't any rabbits there would be no stoats. That's my idea of nature.

" Speaking generally, gangs are not so dangerous as the fellows who work lonesome. The lone man has got to be smart enough to do without partners and touts and stool pidgeons. It's the ideal way of working, because it reduces expenses and there is nobody to cut the loot with. That is the attraction which has split many a gang ; but the fellows who can work single-handed are few and far between and even Solo Smith, one of the cleverest, found it hard to make a living after he dropped his partner.

" There are a whole lot of games for two players and Solo knew them all, and his graft was good, because the people who play two-handed games are generally folks with money. Figure that out and think of your friends who play picquet and bezique and such-like games and you will see that I am right. What is more, a man who plays that kind of game reckons himself an expert. There are generally two or three experts in every passenger list and Solo managed to find one of them. There were voyages, of course, when he never made his fare, but on the whole Solo did very well and so long as he got a living he didn't mind, because he was sure and certain that one day he would get acquainted with the beautiful daughter of a Pittsburg millionaire and be honest ever after. He was the best-looking man I have ever met at the game. Fair, with curly yellow hair, fine-looking eyes and Roman nose. He was one of the few that got introduced to ladies, and surely the girls used to be crazy about him—I think that was one of the reasons he dropped Lila. He was the athletic sort you see in motor-car ads., sitting negligent at the wheel of a shiny car with a beautiful girl stroking the nose of a Russian bloodhound down-stage.

" One big film star tried to get him to play opposite her. Solo did the next best thing. He played opposite her husband and took a year's salary out of him in one sitting. The game was picquet and the husband was an expert.

" There was nothing novel about his method. He never wanted to play cards. It was always the sucker who said, ' Ah, gwan ! What are you scared about—think I'm a card-sharp ? '

" The easiest way to get money out of a sucker's pocket is to give him the free use of his hands. Al Lipski, who knew him very well, told me a lot about Solo.

" ' He's not the same man as he was when he had Lila Bowman as his partner. Lila had brains, if you want to know anything—she gave him all the education he's got. And then he double-crossed her in the only way a man can double-cross a woman—he said he would and he didn't.'

" ' What ? '

" ' Marry her,' said Al. ' Solo's got a pipe that one day he'll meet a million-dollar girl that'll fall for him. He always was a big thinker. Felix, have you ever noticed Solo going ashore in New York ? '

" I thought for a little while.

" ' No. I've taken his bag ashore, but I don't remember seeing him go.'

" Al Lipski gave a sort of laugh.

" ' I'll bet you haven't. He never goes ashore until all the passengers are off—he takes few risks, does Solo.'

" We had this talk on board the *Flemish*. She was a nice

ship, slow but sure. The cabin accommodation was good, the table was the best in the line, and if she took ten days to crawl from the Mersey to the Hudson it was a safe crawl. Our skipper in those days was Captain Grishway, one of the old school. That is to say he thought steam ought never to have been invented and that the sea had gone to the dogs since ships stopped carrying fore-to'-gallant sails. He hated crooks worse than poison, being a God-fearing man, but at the same time he didn't think passengers had any right to be on a ship. But he was a good seaman and never, as the saying goes, scratched a plate. I think he must have been Royal Navy before he came into the Western Ocean trade, for he was certainly full of navy ways. It was ' hands muster aft,' ' quartermaster stand by for going out of harbour ' and he had a bo'sun's mate to pipe him over the side just the same as if he was Captain of a blooming flagship.

" I was his steward for ten trips, and captain's steward is six of the seven sea-going jobs no man ever wants to hold down.

" But the skipper was a good fellow, apart from his navy ways, and when I got used to standing at attention and running instead of walking, and shaving before breakfast and other little fads, I got quite fond of him. He was a big fellow with a clean-shaven upper lip and a chin beard. And he was death to the card-men. The first voyage he made in the *Flemish* he had special notices printed and put in the smoke-room.

DON'T PLAY CARDS WITH ANY MAN UNLESS YOU KNOW HIS MOTHER.

" He followed this up by sending the master-at-arms to arrest Lew Grovener, one of the quickest men in the game. Lew's cabin was searched and about twenty packs of cards were found, and he was handed over to the New York police. On the eastward trip, he pinched young Harry Toler for running a chemmy bank in his private suite. For three voyages he kept the master-at-arms busy. We were lying alongside the pier at Liverpool one Saturday morning, waiting for the boat-trains, when I saw Sir Ernest Wilford's car come on to the jetty and I guessed there was going to be trouble.

" Sir Ernest was the President of the Nation Line and he was what every American thinks every Englishman is. He was a thin man with a long yellow moustache and he wore an eyeglass and a long-tailed coat and a top hat—winter and summer. When I saw his white spats come on to the bridge I knew that he hadn't driven over from his country house in Cheshire to wish Captain Grishway God-speed and a safe return. Ship owners don't do that sort of thing.

" I was in Grishway's cabin and the door leading to the office was ajar.

" ' Good-morning, Sir Ernest,' I heard the captain say.

" ' Good-morning, Captain. I called in at the smoke-room as I came along the promenade deck and I observed—ah —that—ah—you have a notice posted—ah :

" ' IF YOU MUST PLAY CARDS, USE YOUR OWN PACK. IF POKER IS YOUR FAVOURITE GAME, THERE'S ONE IN THE FIREPLACE—PLAY WITH THAT.'

" ' Yes, sir,' said the captain.

" ' And I read in the newspapers that you prosecuted three men at the Liverpool court for playing cards ? '

" ' They were sharpers, sir,' said the captain gruffly. ' They caught a young man from New Orleans—skinned him ! '

" ' Yes, yes,' said Sir Ernest. ' Very unpleasant—very unpleasant indeed, but you're getting the ship a bad name, Captain. People will soon think that the *Flemish* is the only ship these fellows travel by and they will give us a wide berth. It is quite sufficient to put the ordinary notice in the smoke-room, warning passengers not to play cards with strangers. There our responsibility ends. It is obviously outside our province to—ah—provide nursemaids for improvident and foolish young men.'

" There was a bit of silence after this and then the captain said :

" ' Do I understand that I am not to interfere with these thieves—that I am to allow them all the rope they want, Sir Ernest ? '

" ' Well—ah—yes. So long as they behave, they must be treated as though they were ordinary passengers. This is an instruction. If there is a complaint from a passenger, you may act. Otherwise . . .'

" ' Very good, sir,' said our old man in his happiest voice. ' It is not my business to clean up the Western Ocean.'

"'Exactly!' said Sir Ernest. 'Oh, by-the-way, I am thinking of sending my daughter with you next trip.'

"'We'll try to make her comfortable,' said our old man. He always said that.

"Now Captain Grishway was not the sort of man who would take a kick like this and forget all about it. He was hurt, and when a man like Grishway gets hurt he doesn't pass it on. I don't know how this kind of news spreads, but it was common talk in the stewards' quarters that the lid was off, and on the trip home we carried the grandest agglomeration of talent and science that has ever been brought together in one hull.

"Solo Smith had managed to stick to the ship all the time it was pure and he was on board, and one night when I was smoking one of his cigars on the boat deck, he told me that he thought that the captain was right and the owner wrong.

"'It has been paradise in the packet for the last six trips,' he said, 'especially to a refined player like myself. With Al Lipski and Tricky Taylor, and Boss Sullivan and all that kind of trash on board, there's no graft left for a man of my class. Sullivan and Doc Entwhistle want me to take a corner in their game, but, Felix, I've got a *repugnancio* to being No. 3 in any outfit. I'm a chief or nothing. My God!' he said, 'to think that a college man should come so low that he's got to take his share of a five-way cut!'

"However, it wasn't such a bad trip for him. He picked up a Boston hardware man who'd had a European education and played bezique and a game called Bushman's Poker with him, and by the thoughtful way this Boston man was looking when we came to the landing-stage, I guess Solo had packed a parcel.

"I had to go down to London to see a married sister of mine who'd had her first baby. I never dreamt I'd meet any of the boys; but one night when I was up west I ran into Solo Smith. He was staying at the Palace-Carlton and was on his way to a theatre when I saw him. There's nothing gives a man away quicker than evening dress, and Solo wore his as though he wasn't conscious that he had it on.

"'Why, Felix!' he said. 'What are you doing in town? Come and have a quick one!'

"He took me into a quiet bar off Piccadilly and he was in what I would call his college mood, for he was very bitter about an uncle of his who had died, leaving nothing much—except a few mortgages and a lot of enemies.

" ' That man made a solid hundred thousand a year and had a business worth two millions ! And he played every cent away on the races. Can you beat that, Felix, for selfishness ? He didn't think about his relations—me, I mean. He didn't worry about what would become of me. He just threw his money into the sea. Men like that ought to be . . . well, he's dead, anyway.'

" He told me that he was giving up ocean-going. He'd saved enough money to build an apartment-house in Los Angeles, and he was going into the real estate business, marry and settle down.

" ' I know a girl who's crazy about me,' he said. ' She's a lady and refined like me. I shouldn't be surprised if I didn't marry her when I get back home. Though I don't know. . . . I'm not like one of those cheap gangsters who can't sign their own names. There's some class to me and I ought to do better for myself than Lila.'

" Solo generally took a favourable view of himself. That was his one weakness.

" ' Who's Lila ? ' I asked him.

" ' She's a girl I know,' said Solo. ' She got ideas about me and we quarrelled. Not that I take notice of threats. I'm not afraid of any man or woman in the world, Felix. I'm that way. Nothing ever scared me. Al thinks I'm frightened of Lila, but what women say to me means nothing.'

" We drank up and went out on to Piccadilly. The roadway was pretty crowded because it was theatre time and we stood for a time waiting for the traffic cop to hold up the lines to let us get through.

" I didn't see the girl come up—she must have been following us and the first notion I had that anybody was around who knew Solo was when I heard somebody say :

" ' My ! Look who's here ! '

" Solo turned like as if he had been shot. His face was the colour of putty, and I could almost hear him shiver.

" ' Why—Lila,' he stammered, and if ever a man's voice said, ' I'm frightened,' it was Solo Smith's.

" This girl might have stepped out of a picture—she was that pretty—and I began to wonder what more a man wanted.

" ' Hello, Solo. My, you're all dolled up ! Going to a party ? '

" He blinked at her as though he had come out of the dark into a strong light.

B.G.S.S. 2 A

" ' Thought you were in—in New York,' he said.

" ' Sure you did.' She looked at him with a kind of smile. ' You're one big thinker ! Thought over that idea of ours ? '

" Solo pulled himself together.

" ' Why, yes,' he said, ' I was thinking—in fact, I was talking. . . .'

" ' Talking, yes,' she said, ' thinking, no ! Going back home soon ? Saw your name in the *Flemish* list, you'll be going back on that packet, I guess ? '

" Solo shook his head.

" ' No, Lila. I'm staying over for a month. Come and see me one day, Lila. I'm at the Palace-Carlton.'

" She nodded and walked away.

" ' Maybe I will,' she said, but I didn't like the way she said it. Neither did Solo.

" When I looked at him his face was wet, but he laughed.

" ' That's a real girl,' he said. ' My, that woman's mad at me ! I'm glad you didn't say I was going back on the *Flemish*. Not that I'm scared of Lila. All that stuff about shooting me up is fool talk.'

" ' Why don't you marry her—if that's what she wants ? ' I asked him.

" He didn't answer till we were crossing Piccadilly Circus.

" ' I might do better,' he said then.

" I thought that he might do worse.

" He seemed to have changed his mind about going to the theatre, and when I asked him if he'd like to come with me to the pictures, he said ' no, it was dark at the pictures.' He thought he'd go back to his hotel and asked me to walk with him. All the way he kept glancing over his shoulder, as if he expected to see somebody following him.

" ' I'm not scared of Lila,' he told me when we said ' Good-night,' ' I like her. I don't mind marrying her, but I'm not going to be frightened into it. Do you see what I mean, Felix ? If she'd cut out her letter-writing and that stuff about what she'll say to the judge when she comes up in court. That's bunk, and I simply pass it. There's no woman in the world can scare Solo Smith.'

" When I got back to the ship next morning I found the chief steward just about all in. I'd seen him that way before when he'd had a wire saying that Miss Winifred Wilford was sailing with us.

" ' She's coming this trip,' he said, and his hair was standing on end. ' Rush along to Jackson and give him a hand with the bridal suite—oh, no, you're captain's steward. I'm in such a state of mind that I don't know whether I'm on my head or my teeth ! "

" ' She won't come, sir,' I said.

" ' Won't she ? She's on the boat-train—left Euston half an hour ago in the director's private car ! And if she's anything like she was when she sailed to Madeira on the *Riff* there's going to be trouble ! '

" I didn't know until then that when she took the Madeira trip she ran the ship, had three of the officers suspended from duty, the purser and the chief steward fired and got the fourth officer, who was a sad-looking fellow with a secret sorrow, promoted to second on a cargo boat. I guess that his secret sorrow was that he didn't know much about navigation. In six months he piled up his ship on the Irish coast and lost his ticket.

" I went and took a look at the bridal suite. It was full of flowers and the writing table was piled up with telegrams from loving friends.

" Captain Grishway didn't worry ; he wasn't even down by the gangway when she arrived, but he sent the fourth officer.

" ' She's partial to fourth officers,' I heard him say to the chief.

" Having time to spare I dodged down to the gangway to look her over. A crowd of passengers came on board before she appeared and I was mightily interested in one who came up the first saloon gangway but had a second-class ticket. I showed her the way aft, but she didn't recognise me, or if she did she never made any sign. I wondered if Solo knew and guessed that he didn't. When the big rush of passengers was nearly through, Miss Wilford came up the gangway. I'm not good at describing dresses : she wore a sort of fluffy mauve with a fur coat. Pretty, with big dark eyes and a rather thinnish mouth and a beautiful complexion. That's how I'd describe her.

" The purser was there and the chief steward.

" ' Where is the captain ? ' she asked.

" ' He is on the bridge, Miss Wilford,' said the chief. ' We are casting off in a minute.'

" ' Go and tell him to come to my cabin at once, please,'

she said. 'He ought to be here — papa's captains always receive me. I shall wire to my papa right away and tell him.'

" The chief went straight up to the old man and gave him the message.

" The captain sort of played with his beard.

" ' Take stations for going out of harbour,' he said, very brief. ' Report to me when the mails are aboard. Send the pilot to the bridge.'

" I don't know who told Miss Wilford. Maybe she forgot all about the skipper and nobody told her at all. She was still alive when the ship turned into the Irish Sea. She had three maids and a lady secretary. Two of the maids were put into a first-class cabin and the other slept in the suite. Winifred had 'em on the move from the moment she came on board, but on the whole they had a better time than the secretary, who was a plain woman of thirty, but looked older.

" The same afternoon that we left port Miss Winifred strolled on to the bridge and rang the starboard engines astern. Captain was in the charthouse, but at the first sound of the bell he leapt out on to the bridge.

" ' What's wrong here ? ' he roared, and then he saw the girl.

" ' I wanted to see how this thing worked,' she said as cool as ice. ' Are you the captain ? '

" The captain's face was the colour of blood.

" ' Get off this bridge,' he said.

" She stared at him.

" ' I'm Miss Wilford——'

" ' I don't care if you're the Queen of Sheba—get off this bridge. Full ahead that starboard engine, Mr. Holdon, and don't allow passengers to meddle with the telegraph—what in blazes do you think you're here for ? '

" Winifred went red and white. She couldn't speak, but when she could :

" 'Take me back to Liverpool at once ! ' she screamed. ' You horrible man ! My papa will have you discharged. How dare you talk to me ! If you're a gentleman,' she said to the chief officer, ' you'll knock him down this very minute.'

" The poor chief could see his job going, but he was a good seaman.

" ' Sorry, Miss,' he said, ' but you're not allowed on the bridge unless you have the captain's invitation.' And when she had stamped down the companion ladder, he turned to the skipper. ' There goes forty pounds a month ! ' he said.

" The skipper said nothing.

" By all the laws of the sea he had done what was right. There wasn't a board, whether they were Trinity Masters or a Court of Inquiry that wouldn't have said that he was right. But right or wrong, he had lost his ship and he knew it. The wireless got working as soon as night fell and the first message that came to the captain was from Sir Ernest. I saw it on the skipper's desk. Did I lower myself to read it ? I did.

" ' Cannot understand your extraordinary conduct. Return from New York by first available steamer. Hand over your command to Captain Gillingham of *Ethiopia*. Chief officer returns with you.—WILFORD.'

" The old man just O.K.d the radio. I suppose he showed it to the chief, for the chief was mighty glum. He had a wife and three children. The skipper had two boys at the university. And Miss Winifred Wilford hadn't any children at all, only two little dogs like pen-wipers and a pet alligator which she kept at her home in Mentone.

" Her bedroom steward came to see me and asked me if I'd lend him a hand ; appears Miss didn't like the blue carpet in her bedroom and wanted a rose-pink.

" ' That woman,' he said, ' is the world's worst passenger. She treats everybody like a dog and she's given me half an hour to find a lady on the ship that plays pikky—now what in heat is pikky ? '

" ' Bill,' I said, ' you've got it wrong ; it's picquet — rhyming with ' hick ate ' you want. The only person on board that plays is Solo and he's a gentleman and wouldn't play against a lady.'

" ' She's no lady,' said Bill very vicious, ' and I'm going to lumber her on to Solo.'

" ' It's no good,' I said. ' Solo couldn't waste the time on her. He's paid four hundred and fifty dollars for his passage, and it stands to reason that he can't put pleasure before business.'

" I was a bit surprised later on when the captain sent for me.

" ' I hear that Miss Wilford is playing cards in her private parlour with that man Smith. Is he straight ? '

"Stewards never tell—except to ship's officers. I told him all I knew.

"'Humph,' he said. 'Wait whilst I write a radio—you can take it to the wireless house and tell the operator that if he can't get to England he must send by relay.'

"He was a long time writing the message, scratching out and beginning again a dozen times before he gave me a clean copy.

"'Your daughter insists upon playing cards with notorious sharp. Advise me what I am to do.'

"At midnight I was talking to the radio man when the answer came through :

"'My daughter is competent manage own affairs.'

"Just that and nothing more. I didn't see the radio till after the captain had it, because these wireless operators wouldn't tell you if Europe was burning, if the news came on a private message. I'm not blaming them—at the same time I'm not praising 'em. Amongst friends there ought to be give and take and I've told 'Lightning' more scandal than ten stewards on the ship.

"I saw the old man log the message in his private diary and I wouldn't have seen the radio at all only he made a copy for the chief.

"On the third day out the purser, thinking to get one in, stopped my lady as she was coming up the grand companion.

"'Excuse me, Miss,' he said, taking off his cap, as though he was speaking to royalty, 'but I understand that you've been playing cards with Mr. Smith.'

"She looked at him as though he was a hat she didn't like.

"'Well?' she says.

"'Well, Miss, this man Smith is a card-sharp. . . .'

"He got as far as that, when she walked past him. He was fired that night by radio. You wouldn't believe it possible ? It happened. This is a true story and there are a dozen men at the docks in New York who'll tell you it is true, and a hundred men on the line. A man will do a lot for his wife and a lot more for a lady who ought to be his wife, but when you want to see a real dam' fool, you've got to meet a rich man who idolises his only daughter.

" Now there was one man on board that ship who could get into the heart of the matter without upsetting the Queen of the Seas. And that man was a man of discretion and, if I may say so, experience. It's not for me to throw violets at myself, but—anyway I went along and saw Solo.

" Now a card-man is the most reasonable fellow in the world to deal with. You can make him do most anything except give you your money back. So far as we are concerned, they've got to be good, for one thirty-dollars-a-month steward can spoil a game worth thousands.

" ' I know what you've come to see me about, Felix,' he said when I went into his cabin. ' Miss Wilford and me are good friends. She admires me—I admire her. She's the woman of my dream and I'm the kind she's always thought about. She says she adores strong silent men.'

" I fell up against the wall, but before I could say anything he went on :

" ' You think I've been playing for money, Felix, but I haven't. We've been playing for almonds—the winner gets the kernels and the loser gets the shells. I've got enough shells in my cabin to start a war. I can't throw 'em away—they're sacred to me, Felix. . . .'

" ' Steady, Solo,' I said. ' What's all this stuff about admiring. Does she happen to know——? '

" ' She knows my past—I told her,' said Solo. ' She feels I haven't had my chance. If my uncle had died when he ought to have died, I'd have owned my own steam yacht and home on Long Island, and everything. She sees that. We're going to get married the day we make New York.'

" And it wasn't a joke. I nipped up and told the captain and he thought Solo had been stringing me along. But he wasn't taking any chances. He went down and saw Miss Wilford.

" ' That is entirely my own affair,' she said. ' Will you please leave my cabin ? '

" ' I don't like your father and I don't like you,' said the old man, ' but before I let you marry a professional thief I'll put you both in irons ! '

" He sent about a hundred dollars' worth of radio to Sir Ernest and got a $1.50 snub.

" ' Yours incomprehensible. Do not communicate further.'

" It appears that the president thought our old man had invented all this stuff to make it appear that he was looking after his daughter, so that he could get his job back.

" I thought the matter over and that night, when the smoke-room was empty, and Al Lipski was taking his evening walk on the promenade I went up to him and told him everything.

" ' Solo's dream has come true,' he said, ' and if you think you can get him to back out you're crazy. I know him. He's nearly through with business—since he left Lila he has hardly made enough money to pay expenses.'

" ' He may have left Lila, but she hasn't left him,' I said. ' She's on this ship.'

" He whistled.

" ' Does Solo know ? He doesn't ? Well, I'd tell him if I was a friend of his.'

" It wasn't until the next afternoon that the grand idea came to me. We had run into fine weather and the decks were crowded. Even the people who usually go to bed as soon as they get on board and don't get up until we stop to land emigrants at Ellis Island, had managed to crawl up to take a look at the gulf weed. I saw Miss Wilford and Solo sitting in a snug corner of the boat deck as I took the captain's after-noon tea to the bridge. Solo was talking, and by the earnest look on his face, I guessed he was talking about himself.

" The captain's cabin is behind the charthouse and I found him lying on his bed with a book in his hand. He wasn't reading. I've got an idea that he wasn't sleeping any too well, for Captain Grishway was a conscientious man.

" I put the tray on the table and then :

" ' I beg your pardon, sir,' I said. ' I'd like to pass a few remarks about Solo Smith if I may.'

" He scowled up at me.

" ' The more offensive they are, the better I shall like them, steward,' he said. And I gave him my views.

" He listened without saying a word, sipping his tea and looking down at the deck.

" ' Bring this Lila woman here,' he said, and I went down to the second-class deck and found her in her cabin.

" I think this time she recognised me.

" I didn't hear what she said to the captain or the captain said to her, because he shut both doors. It was nearly half an hour before the bell rang and I went in. Lila was sitting on the sofa and the old man was at his desk with a thick book in front of him, turning over the leaves as if he was looking for something.

" ' Go down and ask Mr. Smith to be kind enough to step up to my office,' he said, ' and listen, steward, you can stay with him whilst he's here. And give my compliments to the chief officer and ask him to come along.'

" I gave the message to the chief and went to look for Solo. He wasn't on the boat deck, nor yet in Miss Wilford's suite. I found him drinking a cocktail by himself in the smoke-room.

" ' Me ? ' he said. ' What does he want, Felix ? There's no trouble, is there ? He can't put me in irons—if he does I'll get a million dollars out of the company.'

" He was as nervous as a cat.

" I got him quiet and told him that the captain hadn't any idea of pinching him, and after a while he came with me, though I could see that he was in a blue funk.

" When I opened the captain's door and he saw Lila sitting there on the sofa I thought he would faint.

" ' Shut the door, steward. You know this lady, Smith ? '

" Solo nodded.

" He had another attack of the blinks he'd had in Piccadilly.

" ' This is the lady you promised to marry,' said the captain. ' I've seen your letters, and it seems to me that you're pretty well bound to carry out your promise.'

" ' Anyway, you're not marrying anybody else,' said Lila, but the captain told her not to interrupt.

" ' Sure, I'm marrying you, Lila,' said Solo. ' When we get back to New York——'

" ' There's no time like the present,' said the old man, taking up a book. ' By the laws of England I can marry anybody on the high seas.'

" Poor Solo looked one way and the other and then he must have seen Lila open her bag to take out a handkerchief. And if he saw that, he saw the grip of the little black automatic she carried around. I saw it and the captain saw it, so I guess Solo saw it, too.

" He was as pale as death. I've never known and don't know now what pull Lila had, or what Solo had done to keep this girl on his trail, but it must have been something pretty fierce to make him go under without a fight.

" ' I'm agreeable,' said Solo, and in ten minutes Lila and

he were man and wife, and I signed the log as witness, so did the chief officer.

" ' I've got a word to say to you, Captain,' said Solo when it was all over. ' I guess Lila knows about Miss Wilford ? '

" ' I certainly do,' said Lila. ' I've been wise to that picquet game. She had the secretary chaperone her—that's why you're alive, Solo.'

" For a second he seemed to be swallowing something, for his face was screwed up as if he was in pain.

" ' We're through with that,' he said, ' but I've been playing for almonds and I guess that doesn't pay expenses. She's been pestering me to play for real money—said she wanted me to win and she's got a fifty-thousand dollar credit at a New York bank.'

" ' Well ? ' said the captain.

" ' Well,' said Solo, ' there are two clear days before we get into port and I'd like to get a little of that fifty thousand.'

" Our old man didn't kick him out of the office as I expected. He just looked hard at Solo and smiled. I'd never seen him smile before.

" ' If you play cards for money with Miss Wilford, I shan't interfere,' he said. ' I have orders to that effect.'

.   .   .   .

" Miss Wilford didn't come home with us. She returned to England on a Cunard boat. The valet told me afterwards that the first thing she did when she found Solo had skipped with her fifty thousand was to send a long cable to her father and that same night the captain was reinstated and the chief officer and the purser and the four stewards she had fired on the westward trip.

" Even the fathers of only daughters have moments when they're sane ! "

P. C. WREN *met adventures in many parts of the world while serving in the British, French and Indian Armies. His powerful, romantic stories of the Foreign Legion have captured the imagination of thousands. The pages of "Beau Geste," "Beau Ideal" and "Beau Sabreur," and his stirring novels, are peopled with men who face strange dangers in cruel countries, yet keep certain ideals before them.*

BURIED TREASURE

"Poor old Cigale's pretty bad these days," said John Geste to his brothers Michael and Digby as he stepped into a tent of the standing camp some ninety kilometres south of Douargala.

"Yes," replied Digby, as he rose to help his brother remove and stow his kit in the tiny space which was allotted to each of the twelve men who lived in the little tent that could uncomfortably accommodate eight.

"Moon getting to the full," observed Michael. "We shall have to keep an eye on the poor old chap. What's his latest?"

"Seeing ghosts," replied John. "He's just been telling me all about it in the Guard Tent. When he was on sentry last night, he saw somebody approaching him. Such a very remarkable and extraordinary somebody that, instead of challenging, he rubbed his eyes and stared again. He told me all this in the most rational and convincing manner. It was really almost impossible to do anything but believe. He said :

"'When I looked again I hardly knew what to do. There undoubtedly was a man coming towards me out of the desert, from the direction of the ruins. Nothing strange in that, you may say, but the man was a soldier in uniform. And the uniform was not of this regiment, nor of this army, nor of this country—nor of this century—no, nor of this thousand years. His helmet was of shining metal, with ear-pieces and neckshield, but no visor—rather like a pompier's helmet, but with a horsehair crest and plume, and he had a gleaming cuirass of the same metal. In fact, I thought, for a moment, that he was a trooper of the Dragoon Guards until I saw that he carried a spear, at the slope, across his right shoulder, and for side-arms had a short sword—broad, but not much longer than a dagger. Under his cuirass he wore a sort of tunic that came down to his knees, and over this hung a fringe of broad strips of metal on leather. He wore metal greaves on his shins and sandals on his feet.

" ' In fact, he was a Roman soldier marching on patrol or doing sentry-go on his beat. For one foolish moment I thought of enemy tricks and stratagems and also of practical jokes, but then I realized that not only could I see him as plainly as I see you now, but that I could see *through* him. No, he was not nebulous and misty like a cloud of steam ; his outline was perfectly clear-cut, but, as he approached me, he came between me and one of the pillars of the ruins, and though I could see him perfectly clearly and distinctly, I could also see the pillar.

" ' I was in something of a quandary. As you know, I try to do my duty to the very best of my poor ability, and aim at being the perfect private soldier. But there is nothing laid down in Regulations on the subject of the conduct of a sentry when approached by a ghost.

" ' In the Regulations it says, " *Anyone* approaching," and at once the question arises as to whether a ghost is anyone. You see, it is the ghost *of* someone, and therefore cannot *be* someone, can it ? . . .'

" Thus spake the good Cigale," continued John, " and I assured him that personally I should not turn out the Guard nor rouse the camp to repel ghosts."

" No," agreed Digby. " I don't think I should, either. Sure to be a catch in it somewhere. The moment the Sergeant of the Guard came, the dirty dog would disappear—the ghost, I mean—and then you'd be for it.

" On the other hand," he continued, " if you didn't challenge him, he might go straight into the General's tent and give the old dear the fright of his life—and then you'd be for it again."

" Very rightly," agreed Michael. " What good would the General be at running a scrap next day, if he'd had a Roman soldier tickling him in the tummy with the butt-end of a spear all night ? "

" True," mused John. " It's a problem. There ought to be a section in the Regulations. They certainly provide for most other things."

And the uniform was not of this regiment, nor of this country—nor of this century—no, nor of this thousand years.

" And supposing it were the ghost of a most lovely *houri* approaching the General's tent ? " asked Digby. " Should it be left to the sentry's indiscretion ? And suppose the General came out and caught him turning her away—or turning unto her the other cheek also——"

" It's weird, though," Michael broke in upon these musings. " You can be absolutely certain that La Cigale thought he saw a Roman soldier, and if you think you see a thing, you *do* see it."

" What's that ? " inquired Digby incredulously. " If I think I see a pimple on the end of your nose, I *do* see one ? "

" Yes, you do, if you really think it. There is an image of it on the retina of your eye—and what is that but seeing ? "

" He did more than see him, too," put in John. " He had a long conversation with him. They compared notes as to their respective regiments—the Third Legion, and the French Foreign Legion."

" By Jove, that's interesting ! " observed Beau Geste. " I should have liked to hear them."

" I wonder if you'd have heard the ghost ? " said Digby. " Of course, if you *thought* you heard him, you *would* have heard him, eh ? "

" I say," he added. " I just thought I heard you ask me to have a cigarette. Therefore I *did* hear it."

" Yes," agreed Michael. " And you thought you saw me give you one. Therefore I did give you one. Smoke it."

The tent-flap was pulled aside, and La Cigale entered.

" Come along, old chap ! Splendid ! We were just talking about you and your interesting experience with the Roman legionary," Beau continued.

" Yes, yes," replied Cigale. " A charming fellow. We had a most interesting conversation. His depôt was here, and he'd served everywhere from Egypt to Britain, had sun-stroke twice in Africa, and frost-bite twice when stationed on The Wall, as he called it—Hadrian's Wall, that would be, between England and Scotland.

" He actually spoke of the Belgæ, and must have been stationed quite near my home at one time. A most intelligent chap, and with that education which comes from travel and experience. A little rocky on Roman history, I found, but who would expect a private soldier to be an authority on history— even that of his own country ? "

§ 2

LA CIGALE fell silent and mused awhile, breaking thereafter into mutterings, disjointed and fragmentary.

" Most interesting fellow. Rome in Africa, five centuries ; France in Africa, one century ; the sun the unconquerable enemy of both. Rome did not assimilate although she conquered. Will France assimilate, or be herself assimilated ? "

And turning to Michael Geste, said :

" He was stationed at Cæsarea once. They called it ' The Athens of the West.' We talked of Masinissa, the Berber King of Cæsarea and all Numidia. You will remember he fought against Rome, and then against Carthage in alliance with Rome. He was the grandfather of the great Jugurtha.

" We chatted also of his son Juba, who fought for Pompey in the civil war and committed suicide after Cæsar defeated him at Thapsus.

" *Most* interesting fellow. He told me that Antony's wife Octavia adopted Juba's little son and brought him up with Antony's own little daughter by Cleopatra—young Silene Cleopatra he called her. Quite a charming little romance he made of it, for the two kiddies grew up together at the Roman Court and fell in love with each other—married and lived happy ever after. They went back to Cæsarea and he ruled in the house of his fathers. Rather nice to think about when one considers those cruel times——"

§ 3

" OH, for God's sake, shut your jabbering row," growled The Treasure, from where he was lying on his blanket. " Enough to make a dog sick to listen to you."

" Then suppose the dog goes and is sick outside, and doesn't listen," suggested Digby.

" Yes, a charming little story," agreed Michael. " What else did your visitor talk about ? "

" Oh, places where he was stationed," replied La Cigale, " and about his Legion. He was frightfully proud of that—like we are of ours. He was in the Third African Legion. ' The Augustine,' he called it. He says it was three centuries in Africa. They only kept one legion in Africa, he tells me, though there were three in Britain. Great fellows, those

Romans, for system and organization. What do you think? In this Third Legion of his, the recruiting was almost purely hereditary. Think of that—hereditary drafts. When a man had served his time in the Legion they gave him land on the understanding that he married and settled down there, and sent his sons into the Legion. No wonder there was *esprit de corps* in the Augustine Legion. By the way, they built that place over there in A.D. 100, called it Sagunta Diana, and built it on the ground plan of a Roman camp.

"By Jove, he did a march that I envy him. First they marched right across North Africa, from here to Alexandria. There they embarked in triremes for Italy, and marched to Rome. Thence north, right up Italy, and all across France to a place whence they could see Britain. Then by transports again to Dover, whence they marched to London, and from there through the length of England to Hadrian's Wall. Twenty times 2,000 paces was their day's march—all marked off by regular camping-places.

"He tells me they had a frightful row in camp outside Alexandria with the Sixth Legion from Judea—the Ferrata Legion they called it. It seems the Third Legion hated the others coming into Africa to relieve them while they did their tour of foreign service ; they looked upon Africa as their own, and didn't want interlopers in their stations, such as Timgad, Lambæsis, Mascula, Verecundia and Sitifis. He called Timgad *Thamugadi*. I didn't recognize the word at first, as he pronounced it. He was awfully interested to hear that I'd been there and could identify some of the temples in which he had worshipped. It is still in a wonderful state of preservation, as you know. Lambæsis was his favourite camp, for some reason. He was delighted when I told him that the Arch of Septimus Severus is almost as perfect to-day as when he saw it last. That led us to speak of the Arch of Caracalla. That's at Theveste—about 200 miles from Carthage, you know. I'm afraid he began to think I was pulling his leg when I told him I knew it as well as his beloved Temple of Minerva. He got quite excited."

The Treasure growled, cursed, and spat.

"Told you all that, did he ? " he said. " Damn fine ghost ! Pity he couldn't have told you something useful. Where he'd buried a few bottles of wine, for example. D'you know what there was when you and your ghost was jabberin' ? Two village idiots together—that's what there was."

" If you interrupt again I'll put your face in the sand, and sit on your head till you die," murmured John Geste.

" But there wasn't two *crétins*," continued The Treasure. " There was only one barmy lunatic, and he was talkin' to hisself. 'E's talkin' to three others, 'e is, now."

John Geste rose to his feet, and The Treasure scrambled from the tent in haste.

" And this is a *most* interesting thing," continued La Cigale, still staring at the ground between his feet, as was his habit when not on duty or employed. " Very curious, too. He told me about a deserter from the Roman army—the Legionary Tacfrineas he called him, who went over to the enemy, and organized the Berber tribes against Rome. The Third Legion was frightfully sick about it. Of course, it was just as though one of us deserted and joined the Senussi or the Touareg or the Riffs, and taught them our drill and tactics, trained their artillerymen, gave them our plans and pass-words and generally made them about ten times as dangerous. as they are.

" I'd certainly never heard of this Tacfrineas before, so I couldn't have *imagined* all this, could I ? "

And he gazed appealingly at the faces of the three brothers.

" Of course not," said Beau Geste. " Extraordinarily interesting experience. It must give you great pleasure to think that, out of all the Battalion, it was you whom the Roman soldier chose to visit."

" Oh, yes. Indeed yes," agreed La Cigale, smiling. " I feel quite happy to-day, and can even bear the sight—and smell—of The Treasure. And the Roman soldier has promised to come and visit me again when I am on sentry, and he's going to tell me a great secret. I don't know what it is, but it's something about some gold."

La Cigale fell silent, pondering, and gradually the light of intelligence faded from his eyes, his mouth fell open, and he looked stupid, dull and miserable.

Digby Geste leant over and shook him by the knee.

" Splendid, old chap," he said. " You're a very remark-able man, you know. I envy you. What else did you and the other old *légionnaire* yarn about ? "

" Oh, we compared pay, rations, drill, marches and all that sort of thing, you know," replied La Cigale, brightening like a re-lighted lamp. " They had the same infernal road-making fatigues that we do.

"Why, he tells me they built one hundred and ninety miles of solid stone road from Thevesti to Carthage. Think of that—*stone !*

"Oh, yes, we exchanged grumbles. They had the same god-forsaken little outposts down in the South and much the same sort of tyranny from ' foreign ' N.C.O.'s, of whom they were more afraid than they were of the Centurions themselves. Yes, they had an iron discipline and even severer punishments. In a case where a man here might get *crapaudine*, because there were no cells in which to give him thirty days' solitary confinement, he would have been flogged to death in the Third Legion, or perhaps crucified.

"I say, I *do* hope he comes again. Do you think he will ? He gave me the happiest night I've had since I went—went—went——"

La Cigale groaned, and gazed stupidly around.

"Eh ? " he asked. " What's this ? " and lay down upon his blanket to sleep.

§ 4

LA CIGALE'S *bête noir* was a person who, in full possession of his faculties, had less understanding and intelligence than La Cigale at his maddest.

He was that curious product of the Paris slums, that seems to be less like a human being than are the criminal denizens of the underworld of any other city—Eastern or Western, civilized or savage. He was not so much a typical Paris apache, as an apache too bestial, degraded, evil and brutish to be typical even of the Parisian apache. Even the Geste brothers, who could find " tongues in trees, books in the running brooks, sermons in stones, and good in everything," could find no good in " The Treasure "—as Sergeant-Major Lejaune, with grim irony, had christened him. They had, individually and collectively, done their best, and had completely failed. That such a creature, personally filthy (inside his uniform), with foulest tongue and foulest habits, degraded and disgusting, a walking pollution and corruption, should be one's intimate companion at bed and board, was one of the many things that made life in the Legion difficult. One had to sleep, eat, march, and take one's ease (!) cheek by jowl with The Treasure, and could not escape him.

§ 5

AND the Treasure, by nature indescribably objectionable, deliberately made himself as personally and peculiarly objectionable to La Cigale as he possibly could. From the store of his vile, foul manners, he gave the sensitive ex-officer constant experience of the vilest and foulest of his filthy and revolting speech. Of his mean, low, injurious tricks, he reserved the worst for La Cigale. When accused by a non-commissioned officer of some offence, he invariably laid the blame upon La Cigale, in the reasoned belief and reasonable hope that the poor madman would have either too little wit or too much chivalry to defend himself and arraign his lying accuser.

On one occasion, at Ain Sefra, Beau Geste had seen The Treasure, just before kit inspection, direct the attention of La Cigale, by a sudden shout and pointing hand, to something else, while he snatched a belt from La Cigale's kit and placed it with his own. This saved him from eight days' prison and transferred the punishment to the bewildered La Cigale, who could only stammer to the roaring Sergeant-Major Lejaune that his show-down of kit had been complete a few seconds before. But it had earned The Treasure a worse punishment, for the indignant Beau Geste had soundly and scientifically hammered him, until he wept and begged for mercy, with profuse protestations that he had not done it, but would never do it again.

He never did, but he redoubled his efforts to render La Cigale's life insupportable, and showed something almost approaching intelligence in ascertaining which of his foul habits and fouler words most annoyed, shocked, disgusted and upset his unhappy victim.

For Beau Geste, The Treasure entertained a deep respect, a great fear and a sharp knife, the last-named to be taken as prescribed (in the back), and when opportunity and occasion should arise. These would have arisen long ago but that his enemy had two brothers and two horrible American friends who rendered an otherwise perfectly simple job not only difficult but extremely dangerous. . . . (Remember poor Bolidar !)

Like almost all of his kind, The Treasure was a drunkard, and there was nothing he would not do for money, inasmuch as money to him was synonymous with liquor. Having been, in private life, a professional pick-pocket and sneak-thief, he was able to keep himself modestly supplied with cash while avoiding the terrible retribution which overtakes the *légionnaire* who robs his comrades.

§ 6

"Do you know, young gentlemen," said John Geste, one afternoon, to his two brothers as they strolled from the parade ground whence they had just been dismissed to the tent where they would now settle down to the cleaning of their kit, " I've had an idea ? "

Digby seized John's wrist that he might feel his pulse, and observed :

"An idea, Beau ! He's had an idea. Hold him while I fetch some water."

"He's got plenty already," replied Michael unperturbed, " on the brain. Idea's probably drowned by now."

"No, no," said John. "It's still swimming around. It's this : La Cigale is for guard again to-night and simply bubbling with excitement at the thought of seeing his Roman soldier again."

"What ! Do you want to go and pal up with him ? " interrupted Digby. "Butt in and make up to La Cigale's old pal—severing two loving hearts—green-eyed jealousy——"

" No, the pup only wants to see a ghost," said Michael.

"Well, of course, I would," admitted John. " But what I was going to say, when you two—er—gentlemen began to bray, was this. Poor old Cigale may do anything under the disturbing influences of full moon and a private visit from this Shade."

"Shady business," murmured Digby. "He may go clean off the deep end in his excitement—start showing him round the camp, take him in to gaze upon the slumbering features of Lejaune, or even toddle off with him to visit a two-thousand-years-closed wine-shop in the forum at Sagunta Diana. It occurred to me that a few of us three might exchange with fellows who are for guard, and keep an eye on the poor old chap."

"Quite so," agreed Beau Geste. " Good lad. I fancy Lejaune would be only too glad of the chance to smash La Cigale for being a gentleman and an ex-officer. And if the doctor or the colonel or a court-martial officially pronounced him mad he might be put in a lunatic asylum. And that would be about the cruellest and most dreadful thing one could imagine, for he's half sane half the time, and as sane as we are occasionally."

"Oh, yes," agreed Digby. "Far saner than some people —John, for example."

§ 7

IN the early moonlit hours of the following morning, John Geste patrolled the beat which adjoined that of La Cigale, while Michael and Digby took turns to sit outside the guard tent to watch.

For an hour or so of his tour of sentry go, La Cigale behaved quite normally.

Suddenly John, marching on his beat towards where La Cigale stood staring in the direction of the ruins of Sagunta Diana, saw him spring to attention, present arms, hold himself erect and rigid as a statue, relax and stand at ease, change his rifle from his right hand to his left and then, bowing, warmly shake hands with some person invisible.

"I am so glad you've come again, my friend," John heard La Cigale say. "Most kind and charming of you. I'm awfully sorry I can't show myself as hospitable as I should like to be—but you know what it is. No, we shan't be disturbed until I'm relieved. Grand Rounds passed some time ago."

John Geste shivered slightly.

A most uncanny experience. It was perfectly obvious that La Cigale was talking to somebody whom he could see and hear and touch.

Could it be that ghosts really exist, and are visible to those who are what is called psychic?

He stared and stared at the place where anyone would be standing who was talking, face to face, with La Cigale. Nothing, of course.

He rubbed his eyes and, clasping the blade of the long bayonet in his hands, leant upon his rifle while he concentrated his gaze as though peering through a fog.

Nothing, of course.

But *was* there nothing? Was there a shadow confronting La Cigale? The shadow of a medium-sized thick-set man leaning upon his spear in the very attitude in which John was leaning upon his bayonet and rifle.

Or was it pure illusion ? All moonshine—a curious optical delusion enormously strengthened by La Cigale's conduct and the fact that he was talking so naturally.

Yes, a clear case of hetero-suggestion. Curious, though, that one's ears could so affect one's eyes that one could imagine one saw what one imagined one heard.

Would he hear the Roman soldier's voice in a moment ? If so, he would be perfectly certain that he *could* see the figure of a Roman soldier wearing a helmet like that of a fireman ; a moulded breast-plate from which depended heavy hangings ; metal greaves ; and high-laced sandals—a man who bore a longish shield curved at the sides and straight at the top and bottom, on which was painted an eagle, a capital A, and the figure III.

He only *thought* he saw him now, of course, and in a moment he would think he heard his voice. At present there was but one, and hearing it was like listening to a person who is using the telephone in the room in which one is.

"Were you really ? No ! How very interesting ! "

"Oh, yes ; I've been there several times. To think that we have trodden the same streets, entered the very same shops and dwelling-houses, temples and theatres, actually drunk from the same faucet and washed our hands in the same stone trough ! I think that one of the most interesting—the most *human* and real—things in all the wonderful Pompeii are those grooves worn in the edges of the troughs where thousands of people for hundreds of years all laid their right hands on the same spot to support themselves as they bent over the trough to put their lips to the faucet from which the water trickled."

"Yes, of course you have, many and many a time, and so did I once—just to be one with all those departed Romans."

"Yes, that's what makes it so wonderful. Not merely a case of my having been in a place which is only on the site of a place in which you have been. Yes, exactly. The very same actual and identical houses. You and I, my friend, have trodden on the same actual paving-blocks, and have sat upon the same stone seats. I have walked in the very ruts in which the wheels of your chariot rolled as you drove it down the stone-paved High Street of Pompeii, and I have stood in the wineshops in which you have drunk."

" Yes, a very funny picture, indeed. It is still there, the colours as perfect as when you saw it last. They've got glass, and a sort of blind over it now, and a custodian to guard it. To think you actually saw it being painted and remember roaring with laughter when Balbus drew your attention to it."

" Oh, didn't you ? A pity. History says that he was living there about that time."

" Yes, you must have hated returning from furlough just then even to the Third Legion."

" Well, no, we aren't supposed to do it—and there'd be precious little to be had if we were. One hears tales, of course. There's a place we call Fez where one or two are supposed to have got hold of a little."

" Really ? By Jove, that would be an interesting find for anybody who unearthed it now. . . ."

" *I* could ? I'm afraid it wouldn't be of much use to me—though it would be most awfully interesting to see it. There would probably be coins of which no known specimen exists at the present day. Priceless. Oh, yes, they would fetch any sum. . . ."

" By Jove, that was hard luck ! They don't seem to have changed much, from your day to ours. We call them Bedouin and Touareg. Attack us in much the same way. Stamp us flat occasionally, but discipline always tells. . . "

" Could you really ? The very spot ? Very kind of you —most charming. I should love to see the coins."

" Oh, no, I shouldn't wish to remove it, but if you could spare one or two specimens that are unknown to-day, I should love to have them as souvenirs. I should not part with them of course. One or two early Greek gold ones."

" Now at once ? Really most kind of you. A very great honour. Oh, no, I wouldn't dream of showing anybody else. I never betray a confidence. . . ."

.   .   .   .

And then John Geste rushed forward as La Cigale, throwing his rifle up on his right shoulder, marched off in the direction of Sagunta Diana. Digby Geste came hurrying from the direction of the Guard Tent.

Seizing La Cigale's arm, John swung him about.

" What are you doing, man ? " he expostulated. " You can't leave your post like this. You're a pretty sentry ! You don't want to be shot, do you ?—not at dawn by a firing party of your own comrades, at any rate ! "

Digby arrived and seized La Cigale's other arm.

" Come home, Bill Bailey," quoth he. " Setting us all a nice example, aren't you ? And I thought you were the model *légionnaire*."

" Good God, what am I doing ! " stammered La Cigale and passed his hand across his eyes as the brothers released him.

" Thank you so much, gentlemen. This absent-mindedness is terrible. Do you know, a friend of mine, a most interesting chap, strolled over from his lines and we fell into conversation. I actually forgot that I was on sentry. I am getting *so* absent-minded. When he invited me to come over and—er—look at something, I was just going to walk across with him. Thank you *so* much."

" All right now ? " asked Digby.

" Oh quite, thank you ! " replied La Cigale. " It was only a momentary aberration. I'd sooner die than leave my post, of course."

" What became of him ? " asked John.

" Oh, he went off without me," replied La Cigale. " There he goes, look. I hope he's not offended."

§ 8

THE brothers stared and stared in the direction of La Cigale's extended hand.

" See anything, John ? " whispered Digby.

" Well, do you know ? " answered John, " I couldn't absolutely swear that I didn't see a nebulous figure. And the astounding thing is that I saw or thought I saw something that La Cigale never mentioned."

"The shield?" whispered Digby. "With a capital A and the Roman III, and something at the top?"

"Did you see it, too?" inquired a voice from behind. Michael had joined them.

"Clearly," replied Digby. "Did you, Beau?"

"Absolutely distinctly," replied Michael. "I saw a Roman soldier. I could describe every detail of his kit; I could sketch him exactly as he was."

"I, too," affirmed Digby.

"You, John?" asked Michael.

"Couldn't swear to it," replied John. "Cigale was chatting away so naturally with *somebody*—that I couldn't help fancying that I saw the man to whom he was talking. I certainly didn't see anything clearly and definitely like you two seem to have done. And yet I fancied I dimly saw the III A shield. If nobody else had mentioned it I should have thought that I'd dreamed the whole thing."

"Rum business," murmured Digby.

"Not an ' absinthe ' business, anyhow," replied Michael, as John and La Cigale turned about and began to pace their respective beats.

"You and I are fey, Digby Geste," smiled Michael, linking his arm through that of his brother as they turned back to the guard-tent.

§ 9

THE Treasure lay hid in the black shadow of a crumbling arch watching with wolfish eyes a man who laboured to remove the light, loose sand that had collected at the base of a wall at a point twenty-five paces from a pillar—the fourth of a row that had once supported and adorned the front of a Temple of Diana. Something approaching excitement stirred the sluggish depths of his evil and avaricious soul as he once more assured himself that he was on the track of something good.

Yesterday—with his back turned to his comrades and an appearance of great absorption in his work—he had listened with close attention as this bloomin' lunatic told his blasted friends, those bestial Englishmen, about how he was going to sneak over to these ruddy ruins and dig out a *cache* of gold coins of which he had got wind. Some poor legionary had hid his little bit of loot there one night and the place had been rushed and sacked at dawn, the next morning. Gold coins, too! Nice, handy, portable form of loot, too! And the dirty double-crosser was only going to take one or two to look at, was he? The sacred liar! Not so *fou* as he pretended, that Cigale. Oh, very tricky. Well, other people might know a few tricks, too! What about letting the swindling silly hound sweat for the stuff, and a better man scoop it when the fool had got it?

§ 10

AN hour or so later, La Cigale straightened himself up, gazed around the moonlit ruins in a dazed manner, climbed out of the hole that he had excavated, and made his way towards the camp.

The Treasure crouched back, motionless, in the darkest shadow, until his comrade had passed, and then, rising, followed him—a large stone in his right hand.

The Treasure was a workman skilled in all branches of his trade—one of which was the throwing of knives and other weapons of offence. The heavy stone, flung at a range of six feet or so, struck the unfortunate Cigale at the base of the skull, and by the time he had recovered consciousness The Treasure had come reluctantly to the conclusion that the accursed lying swindling *crétin* had only got a single old coin of some sort, gold, and curiously shaped, about his person. One ancient gold coin, the size of a two-franc piece.

By the time La Cigale had painfully raised himself upon his hands and knees, The Treasure was working feverishly in the excavation that his comrade had recently left.

By the time La Cigale had recovered sufficiently to rise to his feet and gaze uncertainly toward the ruins whence he had come, a dull rumbling, followed by an earth-shaking crash, had startled the watchful sentries of the camp. An undermined pillar had fallen.

The Treasure was seen no more by his unsorrowing comrades.

Buried Treasure.